A

The Ballad of the Sad Café

THE NOVELS AND STORIES OF
CARSON McCULLERS

The Ballad of the Sad Café

THE NOVELS AND STORIES OF

Carson McCullers

THE RIVERSIDE PRESS CAMBRIDGE
HOUGHTON MIFFLIN COMPANY
BOSTON

1951

"*The Ballad of the Sad Café*," "*A Tree, A Rock, A Cloud*" *originally appeared in* Harper's Bazaar; "*The Jockey*," "*Madame Zilensky and the King of Finland*" *in* The New Yorker; "*Wunderkind*" *in* Story Magazine; *and* "*The Sojourner*" *in* Mademoiselle.

The Riverside Press
CAMBRIDGE · MASSACHUSETTS
PRINTED IN THE U.S.A.
BY THE HADDON CRAFTSMEN, INC., SCRANTON, PA.

CONTENTS

CONTENTS

The Ballad of the Sad Café

The Ballad of the Sad Café

THE TOWN itself is dreary; not much is there except the cotton mill, the two-room houses where the workers live, a few peach trees, a church with two colored windows, and a miserable main street only a hundred yards long. On Saturdays the tenants from the near-by farms come in for a day of talk and trade. Otherwise the town is lonesome, sad, and like a place that is far off and estranged from all other places in the world. The nearest train stop is Society City, and the Greyhound and White Bus Lines use the Forks Falls Road which is three miles away. The winters here are short and raw, the summers white with glare and fiery hot.

If you walk along the main street on an August afternoon there is nothing whatsoever to do. The largest building, in the very center of the town, is boarded up completely and leans so far to the right that it seems bound to collapse at any minute. The house is very old. There is about it a curious, cracked look that is very puzzling until you suddenly realize that at one time, and long ago, the right side of the front porch had been painted, and part of the wall—but the painting was left unfinished and one portion of the house is darker and dingier than the other. The building looks completely deserted. Nevertheless, on the second floor there is one window which is not boarded; sometimes in the late afternoon when the heat is at its worst a hand will slowly open the shutter and a face will look down on the town. It is a face like the terrible dim faces known in dreams—sexless and white, with two gray crossed eyes which are turned inward so sharply that they seem to be exchanging with each other one long and secret gaze of grief. The face lingers at the window for an hour or so, then the shutters are closed once more, and as likely as not there will not be another soul to be seen along the main street. These August afternoons — when your shift is finished there is absolutely nothing to do; you might as well walk down to the Forks Falls Road and listen to the chain gang.

However, here in this very town there was once a café, And this old boarded-up house was unlike any other place for many miles around. There were tables with cloths and paper napkins, colored streamers from the electric fans, great gatherings on Saturday nights. The owner of the place was Miss Amelia Evans. But the person most responsible for the success and gaiety of the place was a hunchback called Cousin Lymon. One other person had a part in the story of this café — he was the former husband of Miss Amelia, a terrible character who returned to the town after a long term in the penitentiary, caused ruin, and then went on his way again. The café has long since been closed, but it is still remembered.

The place was not always a café. Miss Amelia inherited the building from her father, and it was a store that carried mostly feed, guano, and staples such as meal and snuff. Miss Amelia was rich. In addition to the store she operated a still three miles back in the swamp, and ran out the best liquor in the county. She was a dark, tall woman with bones and muscles like a man. Her hair was cut short and brushed back from the forehead, and there was about her sunburned face a tense, haggard quality. She might have been a handsome woman if, even then, she was not slightly cross-eyed. There were those who would have courted her, but Miss Amelia cared nothing for the love of men and was a solitary person. Her marriage had been unlike any other marriage ever contracted in this county — it was a strange and dangerous marriage, lasting only for ten days, that left the whole town wondering and shocked. Except for this queer marriage Miss Amelia had lived her life alone. Often she spent whole nights back in her shed in the swamp, dressed in overalls and gum boots, silently guarding the low fire of the still.

With all things which could be made by the hands Miss Amelia prospered. She sold chitterlins and sausage in the town near-by. On fine autumn days she ground sorghum, and the syrup from her vats was dark golden and delicately flavored. She built the brick privy behind her store in only two weeks and was skilled in carpentering. It was only with people that Miss Amelia was not at ease. People, unless they are nilly-willy or very sick, cannot be taken into the hands and changed overnight to something more worth-while and profitable. So that the only use that Miss Amelia had for other people was to make money out of them. And in this she succeeded. Mortgages on crops and property, a sawmill, money in the bank — she was the richest woman for miles around. She would have been rich as a congressman if it were not for her one great failing, and that was her passion for lawsuits and the courts. She would involve herself in long and bitter litigation over just a trifle. It was said that if Miss Amelia so much as stumbled over a rock in the road she would glance around instinctively as though looking for something to sue about it. Aside from these lawsuits she lived a steady life and every day was very much like the day that had gone before. With the exception of her ten-day marriage, nothing happened to change this until the spring of the year that Miss Amelia was thitry years old.

It was toward midnight on a soft quiet evening in April. The sky was the color of a blue swamp iris, the moon clear and bright. The crops that spring promised well and in the past weeks the mill had run a night shift. Down by the creek the square brick factory was yellow with light, and there was the faint, steady hum of the looms. It was such a night when it is good to hear from faraway, across the dark fields, the slow song of a Negro on his way to make love. Or when it is pleasant to sit quietly and pick a guitar, or simply to rest alone and think of nothing at all. The street that evening was deserted, but Miss Amelia's store was lighted and on the porch outside there were five people. One of these was Stumpy MacPhail, a foreman with a red face and dainty, purplish hands. On the top step were two boys in overalls, the Rainey twins — both of them lanky and slow, with white hair and sleepy green eyes. The other man was Henry Macy, a shy and timid person with gentle manners and nervous ways, who sat on the edge of the bottom step. Miss Amelia herself stood leaning against the side of the open door, her feet crossed in their big swamp boots, patiently untying knots in a rope she had come across. They had not talked for a long time.

One of the twins, who had been looking down the empty road, was the first to speak. 'I see something coming,' he said.

'A calf got loose,' said his brother.

The approaching figure was still too distant to be clearly seen. The moon made dim, twisted shadows of the blossoming peach trees along the side of the road. In the air the odor of blossoms and sweet spring grass mingled with the warm, sour smell of the near-by lagoon.

'No. It's somebody's youngun,' said Stumpy MacPhail.

Miss Amelia watched the road in silence. She had put down her rope and was fingering the straps of her overalls with her brown bony hand. She scowled, and a dark lock of hair fell down on her forehead. While they were waiting there, a dog from one of the houses down the road began a wild, hoarse howl that continued until a voice called out and hushed him. It was not until the figure was quite close, within the range of the yellow light from the porch, that they saw clearly what had come.

The man was a stranger, and it is rare that a stranger enters the town on foot at that hour. Besides, the man was a hunchback. He was scarcely more than four feet tall and he wore a ragged, dusty coat that reached only to his knees. His crooked little legs seemed too thin to carry the weight of his great warped chest and the hump that sat on his shoulders. He had a very large head, with deep-set blue eyes and a sharp little mouth. His face was both soft and sassy—at the moment his pale skin was yellowed by dust and there were lavender shadows beneath his eyes. He carried a lopsided old suitcast which was tied with a rope.

'Evening,' said the hunchback, and he was out of breath.

Miss Amelia and the men on the porch neither answered his greeting nor spoke. They only looked at him.

'I am hunting for Miss Amelia Evans.'

Miss Amelia pushed back her hair from her forehead and raised her chin. 'How come?'

'Because I am kin to her,' the hunchback said.

The twins and Stumpy MacPhail looked up at Miss Amelia.

'That's me,' she said. 'How do you mean "kin"?'

'Because——' the hunchback began. He looked uneasy, almost as though he was about to cry. He rested the suitcase on the bottom step, but did not take his hand from the handle. 'My mother was Fanny Jesup and she come from Cheehaw. She left Cheehaw some thirty years ago when she married her first husband. I remember hearing her tell how she had a half-sister named Martha. And back in Cheehaw today they tell me that was your mother.'

Miss Amelia listened with her head turned slightly aside. She ate her Sunday dinners by herself; her place was never crowded with a flock of relatives, and she claimed kin with no one. She had had a great-aunt who owned the livery stable in Cheehaw, but that aunt was now dead. Aside from her there was only one double first cousin who lived in a town twenty miles away, but this cousin and Miss Amelia did not get on so well, and when they chanced to pass each other they spat on the side of the road. Other people had tried very hard, from time to time, to work out some kind of far-fetched connection with Miss Amelia, but with absolutely no success.

The hunchback went into a long rigmarole, mentioning names and places that were unknown to the listeners on the porch and seemed to have nothing to do with the subject. 'So Fanny and Martha Jesup were half-sisters. And I am the son of Fanny's third husband So that would make you and I——' He bent down and began to unfasten his suitcase. His hands were like dirty sparrow claws and they were trembling. The bag was full of all manner of junk—ragged clothes and odd rubbish that looked like parts out of a sewing machine, or something just as worthless. The hunchback scrambled among these belongings and brought out an old photograph. 'This is a picture of my mother and her half-sister.'

Miss Amelia did not speak. She was moving her jaw slowly from side to side, and you could tell from her face what she was thinking about. Stumpy MacPhail took the photograph and held it out toward the light. It was a picture of two pale, withered-up little children of about two and three years of age. The faces were tiny white blurs, and it might have been an old picture in anyone's album.

Stumpy MacPhail handed it back with no comment. 'Where you come from?' he asked.

The hunchback's voice was uncertain. 'I was traveling.'

Still Miss Amelia did not speak. She just stood leaning against the side of the door, and looked down at the hunchback. Henry Macy winked nervously and rubbed his hands together. Then quietly he left the bottom step and disappeared. He is a good soul, and the hunchback's situation had touched his heart. Therefore he did not want to wait and watch Miss Amelia chase this newcomer off her property and run him out of town. The hunchback stood with his bag open on the bottom step; he sniffled his nose, and his mouth quivered. Perhaps he began to feel his dismal predicament. Maybe he realized what a miserable thing it was to be a stranger in the town with a suitcase full of junk, and claiming kin with Miss Amelia. At any rate he sat down on the steps and suddenly began to cry.

It was not a common thing to have an unknown hunchback walk to the store at midnight and then sit down and cry. Miss Amelia rubbed back her hair from her forehead and the men looked at each other uncomfortably. All around the town was very quiet.

At last one of the twins said: 'I'll be damned if he ain't a regular Morris Finestein.'

Everyone nodded and agreed, for that is an expression having a certain special meaning. But the hunchback cried louder because he could not know what they were talking about. Morris Finestein was a person who had lived in the town years before. He was only a quick, skipping little Jew who cried if you called him Christ-killer, and ate light bread and canned salmon every day. A calamity had come over him and he had moved away to Society City. But since then if a man were prissy in any way, or if a man ever wept, he was known as a Morris Finestein.

'Well, he is afflicted,' said Stumpy MacPhail. 'There is some cause.'

Miss Amelia crossed the porch with two slow, gangling strides. She went down the steps and stood looking thoughtfully at the stranger. Gingerly, with one long brown forefinger, she touched the hump on his back. The hunchback still wept, but he was quieter now. The night was silent and the moon still shone with a soft, clear light — it was getting colder. Then Miss Amelia did a rare thing; she pulled out a bottle from her hip pocket and after polishing off the top with the palm of her hand she handed it to the hunchback to drink. Miss Ameria could seldom be persuaded to sell her liquor on credit, and for her to give so much as a drop away free was almost unknown.

'Drink,' she said. 'It will liven your gizzard.'

The hunchback stopped crying, neatly licked the tears from around his mouth, and did as he was told. When he was finished, Miss Amelia took a slow swallow, warmed and washed her mouth with it, and spat. Then she also drank. The twins and the foreman had their own bottle they had paid for.

'It is smooth liquor,' Stumpy MacPhail said. 'Miss Amelia, I have never known you to fail.'

The whisky they drank that evening (two big bottles of it) is important. Otherwise, it would be hard to account for what followed. Perhaps without it there would never have been a café. For the liquor of Miss Amelia has a special quality of its own. It is clean and sharp on the tongue, but once down a man it glows inside him for a long time afterward. And that is not all. It is known that if a message is written with lemon juice on a clean sheet of paper there will be no sign of it. But if the paper is held for a moment to the fire then the letters turn brown and the meaning becomes clear. Imagine that the whiskey is the fire and that the message is that which is known only in the soul of a man — then the worth of Miss Amelia's liquor can be understood. Things that have gone unnoticed, thoughts that have been harbored far back in the dark mind, are suddenly recognized and comprehended. A spinner who has thought only of the loom, the dinner pail, the bed, and then the loom again — this spinner might drink some on a Sunday and come across a marsh lily. And in his palm he might hold this flower, examining the golden dainty cup, and in him suddenly might come a sweetness keen as pain. A weaver might look up suddenly and see for the first time the cold, weird radiance of midnight January sky, and a deep fright at his own smallness stop his heart. Such things as these, then, happen when a man has drunk Miss Amelia's liquor. He may suffer, or he may be spent with joy — but the experience has shown the truth; he has warmed his soul and seen the message hidden there.

They drank until it was past midnight, and the moon was clouded over so that the night was cold and dark. The hunchback still sat on the bottom steps, bent over miserably with his forehead resting on his knee. Miss Amelia stood with her hands in her pockets, one foot resting on the second step of the stairs. She had been silent for a long time. Her face had the expression often seen in slightly cross-eyed persons who are thinking deeply, a look that appears to be both very wise and very crazy. At last she said: 'I don't know your name.'

'I'm Lymon Willis,' said the hunchback.

'Well, come on in,' she said. 'Some supper was left in the stove and you can eat.'

Only a few times in her life had Miss Amelia invited anyone to eat with her, unless she were planning to trick them in some way, or make money out of them. So the men on the porch felt there was something wrong. Later, they said among themselves that she must have been drinking back in the swamp the better part of the afternoon. At any rate she left the porch, and Stumpy MacPhail and the twins went on off home. She bolted the front door and looked all around to see that her goods were in order. Then she went to the kitchen, which was at the back of the store. The hunchback followed her, dragging his suitcase, sniffing and wiping his nose on the sleeve of his dirty coat.

'Sit down,' said Miss Amelia. 'I'll just warm up what's here.'

It was a good meal they had together on that night. Miss Amelia was rich and she did not grudge herself food. There was fried chicken (the breast of which the hunchback took on his own plate), mashed rootabeggars, collard greens, and hot, pale golden, sweet potatoes. Miss Amelia ate slowly and with the relish of a farm hand. She sat with both elbows on the table, bent over the plate, her knees spread wide apart and her feet braced on the rungs of the chair. As for the hunchback, he gulped down his supper as though he had not smelled food in months. During the meal one tear crept down his dingy cheek — but it was just a little leftover tear and meant nothing at all. The lamp on the table was well-trimmed, burning blue at the edges of the wick, and casting a cheerful light in the kitchen. When Miss Amelia had eaten her supper she wiped her plate carefully with a slice of light bread, and then poured her own clear, sweet syrup over the bread. The hunchback did likewise — except that he was more finicky and asked for a new plate. Having finished, Miss Amelia tilted back her chair, tightened her fist, and felt the hard, supple muscles of her right arm beneath the clean, blue cloth of her shirtsleeves — an unconscious habit with her, at the close of a meal. Then she took the lamp from the table and jerked her head toward the staircase as an invitation for the hunchback to follow after her.

Above the store there were the three rooms where Miss Amelia had lived during all her life — two bedrooms with a large parlor in between. Few people had even seen these rooms, but it was generally known that they were well-furnished and extremely clean. And now Miss Amelia was taking up with her a dirty little hunchbacked stranger, come from God knows where. Miss Amelia walked slowly, two steps at a time, holding the lamp high. The hunchback hovered so close behind her that the swinging light made on the staircase wall one great, twisted shadow of the two of them. Soon the premises above the store were dark as the rest of the town.

The next morning was serene, with a sunrise of warm purple mixed with rose. In the fields around the town the furrows were newly plowed, and very early the tenants were at work setting out the young, deep green tobacco plants. The wild crows flew down close to the fields, making swift blue shadows on the earth. In town the people set out early with their dinner pails, and the windows of the mill were blinding gold in the sun. The air was fresh and the peach trees light as March clouds with their blossoms.

Miss Amelia came down at about dawn, as usual. She washed her head at the pump and very shortly set about her business. Later in the morning she saddled her mule and went to see about her property, planted with cotton, up near the Forks Falls Road. By noon, of course, everybody had heard about the hunchback who had come to the store in the middle of the night. But no one as yet had seen him. The day soon grew hot and the sky was a rich, midday blue. Still no one had laid an eye on this strange guest. A few people remembered that Miss Amelia's mother had had a half-sister — but there was some difference of opinion as to whether she had died or had run off with a tobacco stringer. As for the hunchback's claim, everyone thought it was a trumped-up business. And the town, knowing Miss Amelia, decided that surely she had put him out of the house after feeding him. But toward evening, when the sky had whitened, and the shift was done, a woman claimed to have seen a crooked face at the window of one of the rooms up over the store. Miss Amelia herself said nothing. She clerked in the store for a while, argued for an hour with a farmer over a plow shaft, mended some chicken wire, locked up near sundown, and went to her rooms. The town was left puzzled and talkative.

The next day Miss Amelia did not open the store, but stayed locked up inside her premises and saw no one. Now this was the day that the rumor started — the rumor so terrible that the town and all the country about were stunned by it. The rumor was started by a weaver called Merlie Ryan. He is a man of not much account — sallow, shambling, and with no teeth in his head. He has the three-day malaria, which means that every third day the fever comes on him. So on two days he is dull and cross, but on the third day he livens up and sometimes has an idea or two, most of which are foolish. It was while Merlie Ryan was in his fever that he turned suddenly and said:

'I know what Miss Amelia done. She murdered that man for something in that suitcase.'

He said this in a calm voice, as a statement of fact. And within an hour the news had swept through the town. It was a fierce and sickly tale the town built up that day. In it were all the things which cause the heart to shiver — a hunchback, a midnight burial in the swamp, the dragging of Miss Amelia through the streets of the town on the way to prison, the squabbles over what would happen to her property — all told in hushed voices and repeated with some fresh and weird detail. It rained and women forgot to bring in the washing from the lines. One or two mortals, who were in debt to Miss Amelia, even put on Sunday clothes as though it were a holiday. People clustered together on the main street, talking and watching the store.

It would be untrue to say that all the town took part in this evil festival. There were a few sensible men who reasoned that Miss Amelia, being rich, would not go out of her way to murder a vagabond for a few trifles of junk. In the town there were even three good people, and they did not want this crime, not even for the sake of the interest and the great commotion it would entail; it gave them no pleasure to think of Miss Amelia holding to the bars of the penitentiary and being electrocuted in Atlanta. These good people judged Miss Amelia in a different way from what the others judged her. When a person is as contrary in every single respect as she was and when the sins of a person have amounted to such a point that they can hardly be remembered all at once — then this person plainly requires a special judgment. They remembered that Miss Amelia had been born dark and somewhat queer of face, raised motherless by her father who was a solitary man, that early in youth she had grown to be six feet two inches tall which in itself is not natural for a woman, and that her ways and habits of life were too peculiar ever to reason about. Above all, they remembered her puzzling marriage, which was the most unreasonable scandal ever to happen in this town.

So these good people felt toward her something near to pity. And when she was out on her wild business, such as rushing in a house to drag forth a sewing machine in payment for a debt, or getting herself worked up over some matter concerning the law

— they had toward her a feeling which was a mixture of exasperation, a ridiculous little inside tickle, and a deep, unnamable sadness. But enough of the good people, for there were only three of them; the rest of the town was making a holiday of this fancied crime the whole of the afternoon.

Miss Amelia herself, for some strange reason, seemed unaware of all this. She spent most of her day upstairs. When down in the store, she prowled around peacefully, her hands deep in the pockets of her overalls and head bent so low that her chin was tucked inside the collar of her shirt. There was no bloodstain on her anywhere. Often she stopped and just stood somberly looking down at the cracks in the floor, twisting a lock of her short-cropped hair, and whispering something to herself. But most of the day was spent upstairs.

Dark came on. The rain that afternoon had chilled the air, so that the evening was bleak and gloomy as in wintertime. There were no stars in the sky, and a light, icy drizzle had set in. The lamps in the houses made mournful, wavering flickers when watched from the street. A wind had come up, not from the swamp side of the town but from the cold black pinewoods to the north.

The clocks in the town struck eight. Still nothing had happened. The bleak night, after the gruesome talk of the day, put a fear in some people, and they stayed home close to the fire. Others were gathered in groups together. Some eight or ten men had convened on the porch of Miss Amelia's store. They were silent and were indeed just waiting about. They themselves did not know what they were waiting for, but it was this: in times of tension, when some great action is impending, men gather and wait in this way. And after a time there will come a moment when all together they will act in unison, not from thought or from the will of any one man, but as though their instincts had merged together so that the decision belongs to no single one of them, but to the group as a whole. A such a time no individual hesitates. And whether the matter will be settled peaceably, or whether the joint action will result in ransacking, violence, and crime, depends on destiny. So the men waited soberly on the porch of Miss Amelia's store, not one of them realizing what they would do, but knowing inwardly that they must wait, and that the time had almost come.

Now the door to the store was open. Inside it was bright and natural-looking. To the left was the counter where slabs of white meat, rock candy, and tobacco were kept. Behind this were shelves of salted white meat and meal. The right side of the store was mostly filled with farm implements and such. At the back of the store, to the left, was the door leading up the stairs, and it was open. And at the far right of the store there was another door which led to a little room that Miss Amelia called her office. This door was also open. And at eight o'clock that evening Miss Amelia could be seen there sitting before her rolltop desk, figuring with a fountain pen and some pieces of paper.

The office was cheerfully lighted, and Miss Amelia did not seem to notice the delegation on the porch. Everything around her was in great order, as usual. This office was a room well-known, in a dreadful way, throughout the country. It was there Miss Amelia transacted all business. On the desk was a carefully covered typewriter which she knew how to run, but used only for the most important documents. In the drawers were literally thousands of papers, all filed according to the alphabet. This office was also the place where Miss Amelia received sick people, for she enjoyed doctoring and did a great deal of it. Two whole shelves were crowded with bottles and various paraphernalia. Against the wall was a bench where the patients sat. She could sew up a wound with a burnt needle so that it would not turn green. For burns she had a cool, sweet syrup. For unlocated sickness there were any number of different medicines which she had brewed herself from unknown recipes. They wrenched loose the bowels very well, but they could not be given to small children, as they caused bad convulsions; for them she had an entirely separate draught, gentler and sweet-flavored. Yes, all in all, she was considered a good doctor. Her hands, though very large and bony, had a light touch about them. She possessed great imagination and used hundreds of different cures. In the face of the most dangerous and extraordinary treatment she did not hesitate, and no disease was so terrible but what she would undertake to cure it. In this there was one exception. If a patient came with a female complaint she could do nothing. Indeed at the mere mention of the words her face would slowly darken with shame, and she would stand there craning her neck against the collar of her shirt, or rubbing her swamp boots together, for all the world like a great, shamed, dumb-tongued child. But in other matters people trusted her. She charged no fees whatsoever and always had a raft of patients.

On this evening Miss Amelia wrote with her fountain pen a good deal. But even so she could not be forever unaware of the group waiting out there on the dark porch, and watching her. From time to time she looked up and regarded them steadily. But she did not holler out to them to demand why they were loafing around her property like a sorry bunch of gabbies. Her face was proud and stern, as it always was when she sat at the desk of her office. After a time their peering in like that seemed to annoy her. She wiped her cheek with a red handkerchief, got up, and closed the office door.

Now to the group on the porch this gesture acted as a signal. The time had come. They had stood for a long while with the night raw and gloomy in the street behind them. They had waited long and just at that moment the instinct to act came on them. All at once, as though moved by one will, they walked into the store. At that moment the eight men looked very much alike—all wearing blue overalls, most of them with whitish hair, all pale of face, and all with a set, dreaming look in the eye. What they would have done next no one knows. But at that instant there was a noise at the head of the staircase. The men looked up and then stood dumb with shock. It was the hunchback, whom they had already murdered in their minds. Also, the creature was not at all as had been pictured to them—not a pitiful and dirty little chatterer, alone and beggared in this world. Indeed, he was like nothing any man among them had ever beheld until that time. The room was still as death.

The hunchback came down slowly with the proudness of one

who owns every plank of the floor beneath his feet. In the past days he had greatly changed. For one thing he was clean beyond words. He still wore his little coat, but it was brushed off and neatly mended. Beneath this was a fresh red and black checkered shirt belonging to Miss Amelia. He did not wear trousers such as ordinary men are meant to wear, but a pair of tight-fitting little knee-length breeches. On his skinny legs he wore black stockings, and his shoes were of a special kind, being queerly shaped, laced up over the ankles, and newly cleaned and polished with wax. Around his neck, so that his large, pale ears were almost completely covered, he wore a shawl of lime-green wool, the fringes of which almost touched the floor.

The hunchback walked down the store with his stiff little strut and then stood in the center of the group that had come inside. They cleared a space about him and stood looking with hands loose at their sides and eyes wide open. The hunchback himself got his bearings in an odd manner. He regarded each person steadily at his own eye-level, which was about belt line for an ordinary man. Then with shrewd deliberation he examined each man's lower regions — from the waist to the sole of the shoe. When he had satisfied himself he closed his eyes for a moment and shook his head, as though in his opinion what he had seen did not amount to much. Then with assurance, only to confirm himself, he tilted back his head and took in the halo of faces around him with one long, circling stare. There was a half-filled sack of guano on the left side of the store, and when he had found his bearings in this way, the hunchback sat down upon it. Cozily settled, with his little legs crossed, he took from his coat pocket a certain object.

Now it took some moments for the men in the store to regain their ease. Merlie Ryan, he of the three-day fever who had started the rumor that day, was the first to speak. He looked at the object which the hunchback was fondling, and said in a hushed voice:

'What is it you have there?'

Each man knew well what it was the hunchback was handling. For it was the snuffbox which had belonged to Miss Amelia's father. The snuffbox was of blue enamel with a dainty embellishment of wrought gold on the lid. The group knew it well and marveled. They glanced warily at the closed office door, and heard the low sound of Miss Amelia whistling to herself.

'Yes, what is it, Peanut?'

The hunchback looked up quickly and sharpened his mouth to speak. 'Why, this is a lay-low to catch meddlers.'

The hunchback reached in the box with his scrambly little fingers and ate something, but he offered no one around him a taste. It was not even proper snuff which he was taking, but a mixture of sugar and cocoa. This he took, though, as snuff, pocketing a little wad of it beneath his lower lip and licking down neatly into this with a flick of his tongue which made a frequent grimace come over his face.

'The very teeth in my head have always tasted sour to me,' he said in explanation. 'That is the reason why I take this kind of sweet snuff.'

The group still clustered around, feeling somewhat gawky and bewildered. This sensation never quite wore off, but it was soon tempered by another feeling — an air of intimacy in the room and a vague festivity. Now the names of the men of the group there on that evening were as follows: Hasty Malone, Robert Calvert Hale, Merlie Ryan, Reverend T. M. Willin, Rosser Cline, Rip Wellborn, Henry Ford Crimp, and Horace Wells. Except for Reverend Willin, they are all alike in many ways as has been said — all having taken pleasure from something or other, all having wept and suffered in some way, most of them tractable unless exasperated. Each of them worked in the mill, and lived with others in a two- or three-room house for which the rent was ten dollars or twelve dollars a month. All had been paid that afternoon, for it was Saturday. So, for the present, think of them as a whole.

The hunchback, however, was already sorting them out in his mind. Once comfortably settled he began to chat with everyone, asking questions such as if a man was married, how old he was, how much his wages came to in an average week, et cetera —

picking his way along to inquiries which were downright intimate. Soon the group was joined by others in the town, Henry Macy, idlers who had sensed something extraordinary, women come to fetch their men who lingered on, and even one loose, towhead child who tiptoed into the store, stole a box of animal crackers, and made off very quietly. So the premises of Miss Amelia were soon crowded, and she herself had not yet opened her office door.

There is a type of person who has a quality about him that sets him apart from other and more ordinary human beings. Such a person has an instinct which is usually found only in small children, an instinct to establish immediate and vital contact between himself and all things in the world. Certainly the hunchback was of this type. He had only been in the store half an hour before an immediate contact had been established between him and each other individual. It was as though he had lived in the town for years, was a well-known character, and had been sitting and talking there on that guano sack for countless evenings. This, together with the fact that it was Saturday night, could account for the air of freedom and illicit gladness in the store. There was a tension, also, partly because of the oddity of the situation and because Miss Amelia was still closed off in her office and had not yet made her appearance.

She came out that evening at ten o'clock. And those who were expecting some drama at her entrance were disappointed. She opened the door and walked in with her slow, gangling swagger. There was a streak of ink on one side of her nose, and she had knotted the red handkerchief about her neck. She seemed to notice nothing unusual. Her gray, crossed eyes glanced over to the place where the hunchback was sitting, and for a moment lingered there. The rest of the crowd in her store she regarded with only a peaceable surprise.

'Does anyone want waiting on?' she asked quietly.

There were a number of customers, because it was Saturday night, and they all wanted liquor. Now Miss Amelia had dug up an aged barrel only three days past and had siphoned it into bottles back by the still. This night she took the money from the customers and counted it beneath the bright light. Such was the ordinary procedure. But after this what happened was not ordinary. Always before, it was necessary to go around to the dark back yard, and there she would hand out your bottle through the kitchen door. There was no feeling of joy in the transaction. After getting his liquor the customer walked off into the night. Or, if his wife would not have it in the home, he was allowed to come back around to the front porch of the store and guzzle there or in the street. Now, both the porch and the street before it were the property of Miss Amelia, and no mistake about it—but she did not regard them as her premises; the premises began at the front door and took in the entire inside of the building. There she had never allowed liquor to be opened or drunk by anyone but herself. Now for the first time she broke this rule. She went to the kitchen, with the hunchback close at her heels, and she brought back the bottles into the warm, bright store. More than that she furnished some glasses and opened two boxes of crackers so that they were there hospitably in a platter on the counter and anyone who wished could take one free.

She spoke to no one but the hunchback, and she only asked him in a somewhat harsh and husky voice: 'Cousin Lymon, will you have yours straight, or warmed in a pan with water on the stove?'

'If you please, Amelia,' the hunchback said. (And since what time had anyone presumed to address Miss Amelia by her bare name, without a title of respect?—Certainly not her bridegroom and her husband of ten days. In fact, not since the death of her father, who for some reason had always called her Little, had anyone dared to address her in such a familiar way.) 'If you please, I'll have it warmed.'

Now, this was the beginning of the café. It was as simple as that. Recall that the night was gloomy as in wintertime, and to have sat around the property outside would have made a sorry celebration. But inside there was company and a genial warmth. Someone had rattled up the stove in the rear, and those who bought bottles shared their liquor with friends. Several women were there and they had twists of licorice, a Nehi, or even a swallow of the whisky. The hunchback was still a novelty and his presence amused everyone. The bench in the office was brought in, together with several extra chairs. Other people leaned against the counter or made themselves comfortable on barrels and sacks. Nor did the opening of liquor on the premises cause any rambunctiousness, indecent giggles, or misbehavior whatsoever. On the contrary the company was polite even to the point of a certain timidness. For people in this town were then unused to gathering together for the sake of pleasure. They met to work in the mill. Or on Sunday there would be an all-day camp meeting — and though that is a pleasure, the intention of the whole affair is to sharpen your view of Hell and put into you a keen fear of the Lord Almighty. But the spirit of a café is altogether different. Even the richest, greediest old rascal will behave himself, insulting no one in a proper café. And poor people look about them gratefully and pinch up the salt in a dainty and modest manner. For the atmosphere of a proper café implies these qualities: fellowship, the satisfactions of the belly, and a certain gaiety and grace of behavior. This had never been told to the gathering in Miss Amelia's store that night. But they knew it of themselves, although never, of course, until that time had there been a café in the town.

Now, the cause of all this, Miss Amelia, stood most of the evening in the doorway leading to the kitchen. Outwardly she did not seem changed at all. But there were many who noticed her face. She watched all that went on, but most of the time her eyes were fastened lonesomely on the hunchback. He strutted about the store, eating from his snuffbox, and being at once sour and agreeable. Where Miss Amelia stood, the light from the chinks of the stove cast a glow, so that her brown, long face was somewhat brightened. She seemed to be looking inward. There was in her expression pain, perplexity, and uncertain joy. Her lips were not so firmly set as usual, and she swallowed often. Her skin had paled and her large empty hands were sweating. Her look that night, then, was the lonesome look of the lover.

This opening of the café came to an end at midnight. Everyone said good-bye to everyone else in a friendly fashion. Miss Amelia shut the front door of her premises, but forgot to bolt it. Soon everything — the main street with its three stores, the mill, the houses — all the town, in fact — was dark and silent. And so ended three days and nights in which had come an arrival of a stranger, an unholy holiday, and the start of the café.

Now time must pass. For the next four years are much alike. There are great changes, but these changes are brought about bit by bit, in simple steps which in themselves do not appear to be important. The hunchback continued to live with Miss Amelia. The café expanded in a gradual way. Miss Amelia began to sell her liquor by the drink, and some tables were brought into the store. There were customers every evening, and on Saturday a great crowd. Miss Amelia began to serve fried catfish suppers at fifteen cents a plate. The hunchback cajoled her into buying a fine mechanical piano. Within two years the place was a store no longer, but had been converted into a proper café, open every evening from six until twelve o'clock.

Each night the hunchback came down the stairs with the air of one who has a grand opinion of himself. He always smelled slightly of turnip greens, as Miss Amelia rubbed him night and morning with pot liquor to give him strength. She spoiled him to a point beyond reason, but nothing seemed to strengthen him; food only made his hump and his head grow larger while the rest of him remained weakly and deformed. Miss Amelia was the same in appearance. During the week she still wore swamp boots and overalls, but on Sunday she put on a dark red dress that hung on her in a most peculiar fashion. Her manners, however, and her way of life were greatly changed. She still loved a fierce lawsuit, but she was not so quick to cheat her fellow man and to exact cruel payments. Because the hunchback was so extremely sociable she even went about a little — to revivals, to funerals, and so forth. Her doctoring was as successful as ever, her liquor even finer than before, if that were possible. The café itself proved profitable and was the only place of pleasure for many miles around.

So for the moment regard these years from random and disjointed views. See the hunchback marching in Miss Amelia's footsteps when on a red winter morning they set out for the pinewoods to hunt. See them working on her properties — with Cousin Lymon standing by and doing absolutely nothing, but quick to point out any laziness among the hands. On autumn afternoons they sat on the back steps chopping sugar cane. The glaring summer days they spent back in the swamp where the water cypress is a deep black green, where beneath the tangled swamp trees there in a drowsy gloom. When the path leads through a bog or a stretch of blackened water see Miss Amelia bend down to let Cousin Lymon scramble on her back — and see her wading forward with the hunchback settled on her shoulders, clinging to her ears or to her broad forehead. Occasionally Miss Amelia cranked up the Ford which she had bought and treated Cousin Lymon to a picture-show in Cheehaw, or to some distant fair or cockfight; the hunchback took a passionate delight in spectacles. Of course, they were in their café every morning, they would often sit for hours together by the fireplace in the parlor upstairs. For the hunchback was sickly at night and dreaded to lie looking into the dark. He had a deep fear of death. And Miss Amelia would not leave him by himself to suffer with this fright. It may even be reasoned that the growth of the café came about mainly on this account; it was a thing that brought him company and pleasure and that helped him through the night. So compose from such flashes an image of these years as a whole. And for a moment let it rest.

Now some explanation is due for all this behavior. The time has come to speak about love. For Miss Amelia loved Cousin Lymon. So much was clear to everyone. They lived in the same house together and were never seen apart. Therefore, according to Mrs. MacPhail, a warty-nosed old busybody who is continually moving her sticks of furniture from one part of the front room to another; according to her and to certain others, these two were living in sin. If they were related, they were only a cross between first and second cousins, and even that could in no way be proved. Now, of course Miss Amelia was a powerful blunderbuss of a person, more than six feet tall—and Cousin Lymon a weakly little hunchback reaching only to her waist. But so much the better for Mrs. Stumpy MacPhail and her cronies, for they and their kind glory in conjunctions which are ill-matched and pitiful. So let them be. The good people thought that if those two had found some satisfaction of the flesh between themselves, then it was a matter concerning them and God alone. All sensible people agreed in their opinion about this conjecture—and their answer was a plain, flat *no.* What sort of thing, then, was this love?

First of all, love is a joint experience between two persons—but the fact that it is a joint experience does not mean that it is a similar experience to the two people involved. There are the lover and the beloved, but these two come from different countries. Often the beloved is only a stimulus for all the stored-up love which has lain quiet within the lover for a long time hitherto. And somehow every lover knows this. He feels in his soul that his love is a solitary thing. He comes to know a new, strange loneliness and it is this knowledge which makes him suffer. So there is only one thing for the lover to do. He must house his love within himself as best he can; he must create for himself a whole new inward world—a world intense and strange, complete in himself. Let it be added here that this lover about whom we speak need not necessarily be a young man saving for a wedding ring—this lover can be man, woman, child, or indeed any human creature on this earth.

Now, the beloved can also be of any description. The most outlandish people can be the stimulus for love. A man may be a doddering great-grandfather and still love only a strange girl he saw in the streets of Cheehaw one afternoon two decades past. The preacher may love a fallen woman. The beloved may be treacherous, greasy-headed, and given to evil habits. Yes, and the lover may see this as clearly as anyone else—but that does not affect the evolution of his love one whit. A most mediocre person can be the object of a love which is wild, extravagant, and beautiful as the poison lilies of the swamp. A good man may be the stimulus for a love both violent and debased, or a jabbering madman may bring about in the soul of someone a tender and simple idyll. Therefore, the value and quality of any love is determined solely by the lover himself.

It is for this reason that most of us would rather love than be loved. Almost everyone wants to be the lover. And the curt truth is that, in a deep secret way, the state of being beloved is intolerable to many. The beloved fears and hates the lover, and with the best of reasons. For the lover is forever trying to strip bare his beloved. The lover craves any possible relation with the beloved, even if this experience can cause him only pain.

It has been mentioned before that Miss Amelia was once married. And this curious episode might as well be accounted for at this point. Remember that it all happened long ago, and that it was Miss Amelia's only personal contact, before the hunchback came to her, with this phenomenon — love.

The town then was the same as it is now, except there were two stores instead of three and the peach trees along the street were more crooked and smaller than they are now. Miss Amelia was nineteen years old at the time, and her father had been dead many months. There was in the town at that time a loom-fixer named Marvin Macy. He was the brother of Henry Macy, although to know them you would never guess that those two could be kin. For Marvin Macy was the handsomest man in this region — being six feet one inch tall, hard-muscled, and with slow gray eyes and curly hair. He was well off, made good wages, and had a gold watch which opened in the back to a picture of a waterfall. From the outward and worldly point of view Marvin Macy was a fortunate fellow; he needed to bow and scrape to no one and always got just what he wanted. But from a more serious and thoughtful viewpoint Marvin Macy was not a person to be envied, for he was an evil character. His reputation was as bad, if not worse, than that of any young man in the county. For years, when he was a boy, he had carried about with him the dried and salted ear of a man he had killed in a razor fight. He had chopped off the tails of squirrels in the pinewoods just to please his fancy, and in his left hip pocket he carried forbidden marijuana weed to tempt those who were discouraged and drawn toward death. Yet in spite of his well-known reputation he was the beloved of many females in this region — and there were at the time several young girls who were clean-haired and soft-eyed, with tender sweet little buttocks and charming ways. These gentle young girls he degraded and shamed. Then finally, at the age of twenty-two, this Marvin Macy chose Miss Amelia. That solitary, gangling, queer-eyed girl was the one he longed for. Nor did he want her because of her money, but solely out of love.

And love changed Marvin Macy. Before the time when he loved Miss Amelia it could be questioned if such a person had within him a heart and soul. Yet there is some explanation for the ugliness of his character, for Marvin Macy had had a hard beginning in this world. He was one of seven unwanted children whose parents could hardly be called parents at all; these parents were wild younguns who liked to fish and roam around the swamp. Their own children, and there was a new one almost every year, were only a nuisance to them. At night when they came home from the mill they would look at the children as though they did not know wherever they had come from. If the children cried they were beaten, and the first thing they learned in this world was to seek the darkest corner of the room and try to hide themselves as best they could. They were as thin as little whitehaired ghosts, and they did not speak, not even to each other. Finally, they were abandoned by their parents altogether and left to the mercies of the town. It was a hard winter, with the mill closed down almost three months, and much misery everywhere. But this is not a town to let white orphans perish in the road before your eyes. So here is what came about: the eldest child, who was eight years old, walked into Cheehaw and disappeared — perhaps he took a freight train somewhere and went out into the world, nobody knows. Three other children were boarded out amongst the town, being sent around from one kitchen to another, and as they were delicate they died before Easter time. The last two children were Marvin Macy and Henry Macy, and they were taken into a home. There was a good woman in the town named Mrs. Mary Hale, and she took Marvin Macy and Henry Macy and loved them as her own. They were raised in her household and treated well.

But the hearts of small children are delicate organs. A cruel beginning in this world can twist them into curious shapes. The heart of a hurt child can shrink so that forever afterward it is hard and pitted as the seed of a peach. Or again, the heart of such a child may fester and swell until it is a misery to carry within the body, easily chafed and hurt by the most ordinary things. This last is what happened to Henry Macy, who is so opposite to his brother, is the kindest and gentlest man in town. He lends his wages to those who are unfortunate, and in the old days he used to care for the children whose parents were at the café on Saturday night. But he is a shy man, and he has the look of one who has a swollen heart and suffers. Marvin Macy, however, grew to be bold and fearless and cruel. His heart turned tough, as the horns of Satan, and until the time when he loved Miss Amelia he brought to his brother and the good woman who raised him nothing but shame and trouble.

But love reversed the character of Marvin Macy. For two years he loved Miss Amelia, but he did not declare himself. He would stand near the door of her premises, his cap in his hand, his eyes meek and longing and misty gray. He reformed himself completely. He was good to his brother and foster mother, and he saved his wages and learned thrift. Moreover, he reached out toward God. No longer did he lie around on the floor of the front porch all day Sunday, singing and playing his guitar; he attended church services and was present at all religious meetings. He learned good manners: he trained himself to rise and give his chair to a lady, and he quit swearing and fighting and using holy names in vain. So for two years he passed through this transformation and improved his character in every way. Then at the end of the two years he went one evening to Miss Amelia, carrying a bunch of swamp flowers, a sack of chitterlins, and a silver ring —that night Marvin Macy declared himself.

And Miss Amelia married him. Later everyone wondered why.

Some said it was because she wanted to get herself some wedding presents. Others believed it came about through the nagging of Miss Amelia's great-aunt in Cheehaw, who was a terrible old woman. Anyway, she strode with great steps down the aisle of the church wearing her dead mother's bridal gown, which was of yellow satin and at least twelve inches too short for her. It was a winter afternoon and the clear sun shone through the ruby windows of the church and put a curious glow on the pair before the altar. As the marriage lines were read Miss Amelia kept making an odd gesture — she would rub the palm of her right hand down the side of her satin wedding gown. She was reaching for the pocket of her overalls, and being unable to find it her face became impatient, bored, and exasperated. At last when the lines were spoken and the marriage prayer was done Miss Amelia hurried out of the church, not taking the arm of her husband, but walking at least two paces ahead of him.

The church is no distance from the store so the bride and groom walked home. It is said that on the way Miss Amelia began to talk about some deal she had worked up with a farmer over a load of kindling wood. In fact, she treated her groom in exactly the same manner she would have used with some customer who had come into the store to buy a pint from her. But so far all had gone decently enough; the town was gratified, as people had seen what this love had done to Marvin Macy and hoped that it might also reform his bride. At least, they counted on the marriage to tone down Miss Amelia's temper, to put a bit of bride-fat on her, and to change her at last into a calculable woman.

They were wrong. The young boys who watched through the window on that night said that this is what actually happened: The bride and groom ate a grand supper prepared by Jeff, the old Negro who cooked for Miss Amelia. The bride took second servings of everything, but the groom picked with his food. Then the bride went about her ordinary business — reading the newspaper, finishing an inventory of the stock in the store, and so forth. The groom hung about in the doorway with a loose, foolish, blissful face and was not noticed. At eleven o'clock the bride took a lamp and went upstairs. The groom followed close behind her. So far all had gone decently enough, but what followed after was unholy.

Within half an hour Miss Amelia had stomped down the stairs in breeches and a khaki jacket. Her face had darkened so that it looked quite black. She slammed the kitchen door and gave it an ugly kick. Then she controlled herself. She poked up the fire, sat down, and put her feet up on the kitchen stove. She read the Farmer's Almanac, drank coffee, and had a smoke with her father's pipe. Her face was hard, stern, and had now whitened to its natural color. Sometimes she paused to jot down some information from the Almanac on a piece of paper. Toward dawn she went into her office and uncovered her typewriter, which she had recently bought and was only just learning how to run. That was the way in which she spent the whole of her wedding night. At daylight she went out to her yard as though nothing whatsoever had occurred and did some carpentering on a rabbit hutch which she had begun the week before and intended to sell somewhere.

A groom is in a sorry fix when he is unable to bring his well-beloved bride to bed with him, and when the whole town knows it. Marvin Macy came down that day still in his wedding finery, and with a sick face. God knows how he had spent the night. He moped about the yard, watching Miss Amelia, but keeping some distance away from her. Then toward noon an idea came to him and he went off in the direction of Society City. He returned with presents—an opal ring, a pink enamel doreen of the sort which was then in fashion, a silver bracelet with two hearts on it, and a box of candy which had cost two dollars and a half. Miss Amelia looked over these fine gifts and opened the box of candy, for she was hungry. The rest of the presents she judged shrewdly for a moment to sum up their value—then she put them in the counter out for sale. The night was spent in much the same manner as the preceding one—except that Miss Amelia brought her feather mattress to make a pallet by the kitchen stove, and she slept fairly well.

Things went on like this for three days. Miss Amelia went about her business as usual, and took great interest in some rumor that a bridge was to be built some ten miles down the road. Marvin Macy still followed her about around the premises, and it was plain from his face how he suffered. Then on the fourth day he did an extremely simple-minded thing: he went to Cheehaw and came back with a lawyer. Then in Miss Amelia's office he signed over to her the whole of his worldly goods, which was ten acres of timberland which he had bought with the money he had saved. She studied the paper sternly to make sure there was no possibility of a trick and filed it soberly in the drawer of her desk. That afternoon Marvin Macy took a quart bottle of whisky and went with it alone out in the swamp while the sun was still shining. Toward evening he came in drunk, went up to Miss Amelia with wet wide eyes, and put his hand on her shoulder. He was trying to tell her something, but before he could open his mouth she had swung once with her fist and hit his face so hard that he was thrown back against the wall and one of his front teeth was broken.

The rest of this affair can only be mentioned in bare outline. After this first blow Miss Amelia hit him whenever he came within arm's reach of her, and whenever he was drunk. At last she turned him off the premises altogether, and he was forced to suffer publicly. During the day he hung around just outside the boundary line of Miss Amelia's property and sometimes with a drawn crazy look he would fetch his rifle and sit there cleaning it, peering at Miss Amelia steadily. If she was afraid she did not show it, but her face was sterner than ever, and often she spat on the ground. His last foolish effort was to climb in the window of her store one night and to sit there in the dark, for no purpose whatsoever, until she came down the stairs next morning. For this Miss Amelia set off immediately to the courthouse in Cheehaw with some notion that she could get him locked in the penitentiary for trespassing. Marvin Macy left the town that day, and no one saw him go, or knew just where he went. On leaving he put a long curious letter, partly written in pencil and partly with ink, beneath Miss Amelia's door. It was a wild love letter—but in it were also included threats, and he swore that in his life he would get even with her. His marriage had lasted for ten days. And the town felt the special satisfaction that people feel when someone has been thoroughly done in by some scandalous and terrible means.

Miss Amelia was left with everything that Marvin Macy had ever owned — his timberwood, his gild watch, every one of his possessions. But she seemed to attach little value to them and that spring she cut up his Klansman's robe to cover her tobacco plants. So all that he had ever done was to make her richer and to bring her love. But, strange to say, she never spoke of him but with a terrible and spiteful bitterness. She never once referred to him by name but always mentioned him scornfully as 'that loom-fixer I was married to.'

And later, when horrifying rumors concerning Marvin Macy reached the town, Miss Amelia was very pleased. For the true character of Marvin Macy finally revealed itself, once he had freed himself of his love. He became a criminal whose picture and whose name were in all the papers in the state. He robbed three filling stations and held up the A & P store of Society City with a sawed-off gun. He was suspected of the murder of Slit-Eye Sam who was a noted highjacker. All these crimes were connected with the name of Marvin Macy, so that his evil became famous through many countries. Then finally the law captured him, drunk, on the floor of a tourist cabin, his guitar by his side, and fifty-seven dollars in his right shoe. He was tried, sentenced, and sent off to the penitentiary near Atlanta. Miss Amelia was deeply gratified.

Well, all this happened a long time ago, and it is the story of Miss Amelia's marriage. The town laughed a long time over this grotesque affair. But though the outward facts of this love are indeed sad and ridiculous, it must be remembered that the real story was that which took place in the soul of the lover himself. So who but God can be the final judge of this or any other love? On the very first night of the café there were several who suddenly thought of this broken bridegroom, locked in the gloomy penitentiary, many miles away. And in the years that followed, Marvin Macy was not altogether forgotten in the town. His name was never mentioned in the presence of Miss Amelia or the hunchback. But the memory of his passion and his crimes, and the thought of him trapped in his cell in the penitentiary, was like a troubling undertone beneath the happy love of Miss Amelia and the gaiety of the café. So do not forget this Marvin Macy, as he is to act a terrible part in the story which is yet to come.

During the four years in which the store became a café the rooms upstairs were not changed. This part of the premises remained exactly as it had been all of Miss Amelia's life, as it was in the time of her father, and most likely his father before him. The three rooms, it is already known, were immaculately clean. The smallest object had its exact place, and everything was wiped and dusted by Jeff, the servant of Miss Amelia, each morning. The front room belonged to Cousin Lymon — it was the room where Marvin Macy had stayed during the few nights he was allowed on the premises, and before that it was the bedroom of Miss Amelia's father. The room was furnished with a large chiffo-robe, a bureau covered with a stiff white linen cloth crocheted at the edges, and a marble-topped table. The bed was immense, an old fourposter made of carved, dark rosewood. On it were two feather mattresses, bolsters, and a number of handmade comforts. The bed was so high that beneath it were two wooden steps — no occupant had ever used these steps before, but Cousin Lymon drew them out each night and walked up in state. Beside the steps, but pushed modestly out of view, there was a china chamberpot painted with pink roses. No rug covered the dark, polished floor and the curtains were of some white stuff, also crocheted at the edges.

On the other side of the parlor was Miss Amelia's bedroom, and it was smaller and very simple. The bed was narrow and made of pine. There was a bureau for her breeches, shirts, and Sunday dress, and she had hammered two nails in the closet wall on which to hang her swamp boots. There were no curtains, rugs, or ornaments of any kind.

The large middle room, the parlor, was elaborate. The rosewood sofa, upholstered in threadbare green silk, was before the fireplace. Marble-topped tables, two Singer sewing machines, a big vase of pampas grass — everything was rich and grand. The most important piece of furniture in the parlor was a big, glass-doored cabinet in which was kept a number of treasures and curios. Miss Amelia had added two objects to this collection — one was a large acorn from a water oak, the other a little velvet box holding two small, grayish stones. Sometimes when she had nothing much to do, Miss Amelia would take out this velvet box and stand by the window with the stones in the palm of her hand, looking down at them with a mixture of fascination, dubious respect, and fear. They were the kidney stones of Miss Amelia herself, and had been taken from her by the doctor in Cheehaw some years ago. It had been a terrible experience, from the first minute to the last, and all she had got out of it were those two little stones; she was bound to set great store by them, or else admit to a mighty sorry bargain. So she kept them and in the second year of Cousin Lymon's stay with her she had them set as ornaments in a watch chain which she gave to him. The other object she had added to the collection, the large acorn, was precious to her — but when she looked at it her face was always saddened and perplexed.

'Amelia, what does it signify?' Cousin Lyman asked her.

'Why, it's just an acorn,' she answered. 'Just an acorn I picked up on the afternoon Big Papa died.'

'How do you mean?' Cousin Lymon insisted.

'I mean it's just an acorn I spied on the ground that day. I picked it up and put it in my pocket. But I don't know why.'

'What a peculiar reason to keep it,' Cousin Lymon said.

The talks of Miss Amelia and Cousin Lymon in the rooms upstairs, usually in the first few hours of the morning when the hunchback could not sleep, were many. As a rule, Miss Amelia was a silent woman, not letting her tongue run wild on any subject that happened to pop into her head. There were certain topics of conversation, however, in which she took pleasure. All these subjects had one point in common — they were interminable. She liked to contemplate problems which could be worked over for decades and still remain insoluble. Cousin Lymon, on the other hand, enjoyed talking on any subject whatsoever, as he was a great chatterer. Their approach to any conversation was altogether different. Miss Amelia always kept to the broad, rambling generalities of the matter, going on endlessly in a low, thoughtful voice and getting nowhere — while Cousin Lymon would interrupt her suddenly to pick up, magpie fashion, some detail which, even if unimportant, was at least concrete and bearing on some practical facet close at hand. Some of the favorite subjects of Miss Amelia were: the stars, the reason why Negroes are black, the best treatment for cancer, and so forth. Her father was also an interminable subject which was dear to her.

'Why, Law,' she would say to Lymon. 'Those days I slept. I'd go to bed just as the lamp was turned on and sleep — why, I'd sleep like I was drowned in warm axle grease. Then come daybreak Big Papa would walk in and put his hand down on my shoulder. "Get stirring, Little," he would say. Then later he would holler up the stairs from the kitchen when the stove was hot. "Fried grits," he would holler. "White meat and gravy. Ham and eggs." And I'd run down the stairs and dress by the hot stove while he was out washing at the pump. Then off we'd go to the still or maybe ——'

'The grits we had this morning was poor,' Cousin Lymon said. 'Fried too quick so that the inside never heated.'

'And when Big Papa would run off the liquor in those days ——' The conversation would go on endlessly, with Miss Amelia's long legs stretched out before the hearth; for winter or summer there was always a fire in the grate, as Lymon was cold-natured. He sat in a low chair across from her, his feet not quite touching the floor and his torso usually well-wrapped in a blanket or the green wool shawl. Miss Amelia never mentioned her father to anyone else except Cousin Lymon.

That was one of the ways in which she showed her love for him. He had her confidence in the most delicate and vital matters. He alone knew where she kept the chart that showed where certain barrels of whiskey were buried on a piece of property near by. He alone had access to her bankbook and the key to the cabinet of curios. He took money from the cash register, whole handfuls of it, and appreciated the loud jingle it made inside his pockets. He owned almost everything on the premises, for when he was cross Miss Amelia would prowl about and find him some present — so that now there was hardly anything left close at hand to give him. The only part of her life that she did not want Cousin Lymon to share with her was the memory of her ten-day marriage. Marvin Macy was the one subject that was never, at any time, discussed between the two of them.

So let the slow years pass and come to a Saturday evening six years after the time when Cousin Lymon came first to the town. It was August and the sky had burned above the town like a sheet of flame all day. Now the green twilight was near and there was a feeling of repose. The street was coated an inch deep with dry golden dust and the little children ran about half-naked, sneezed often, sweated, and were fretful. The mill had closed down at noon. People in the houses along the main street sat resting on their steps and the women had palmetto fans. At Miss Amelia's there was a sign at the front of the premises saying CAFÉ. The back porch was cool with latticed shadows and there Cousin Lymon sat turning the ice-cream freezer — often he unpacked the salt and ice and removed the dasher to lick a bit and see how the work was coming on. Jeff cooked in the kitchen. Early that morning Miss Amelia had put a notice on the wall of the front porch reading: Chicken Dinner — Twenty Cents Tonite. The café was already open and Miss Amelia had just finished a period of work in her office. All the eight tables were occupied and from the mechanical piano came a jingling tune.

In a corner, near the door and sitting at a table with a child, was Henry Macy. He was drinking a glass of liquor, which was unusual for him, as liquor went easily to his head and made him cry or sing. His face was very pale and his left eye worked constantly in a nervous tic, as it was apt to do when he was agitated. He had come into the café sidewise and silent, and when he was greeted he did not speak. The child next to him belonged to Horace Wells, and he had been left at Miss Amelia's that morning to be doctored.

Miss Amelia came out from her office in good spirits. She attended to a few details in the kitchen and entered the café with the pope's nose of a hen between her fingers, as that was her favorite piece. She looked about the room, saw that in general all was well, and went over to the corner table by Henry Macy. She turned the chair around and sat straddling the back, as she only wanted to pass the time of day and was not yet ready for her supper. There was a bottle of Kroup Kure in the hip pocket of her overalls — a medicine made from whisky, rock candy, and a secret ingredient. Miss Amelia uncorked the bottle and put it to the mouth of the child. Then she turned to Henry Macy and, seeing the nervous winking of his left eye, she asked:

'What ails you?'

Henry Macy seemed on the point of saying something difficult, but, after a long look into the eyes of Miss Amelia, he swallowed and did not speak.

So Miss Amelia returned to her patient. Only the child's head showed above the table top. His face was very red, with the eyelids half-closed and the mouth partly open. He had a large, hard, swollen boil on his thigh, and had been brought to Miss Amelia so that it could be opened. But Miss Amelia used a special method with children; she did not like to see them hurt, struggling, and terrified. So she had kept the child around the premises all day, giving him licorice and frequent doses of the Kroup Kure, and toward evening she tied a napkin around his neck and let him eat his fill of the dinner. Now as he sat at the table his head wobbled slowly from side to side and sometimes as he breathed there came from him a little worn-out grunt.

There was a stir in the café and Miss Amelia looked around quickly. Cousin Lymon had come in. The hunchback strutted into the café as he did every night, and when he reached the exact center of the room he stopped short and looked shrewdly around him, summing up the people and making a quick pattern of the emotional material at hand that night. The hunchback was a great mischief-maker. He enjoyed any kind of to-do, and without saying a word he could set people at each other in a way that was miraculous. It was due to him that the Rainey twins had quarreled over a jackknife two years past, and had not spoken one word to each other since. He was present at the big fight between Rip Wellborn and Robert Calvert Hale, and every other fight for that matter since he had come into the town. He nosed around everywhere, knew the intimate business of everybody, and trespassed every waking hour. Yet, queerly enough, in spite of this it was the hunchback who was most responsible for the great popularity of the café. Things were never so gay as when he was around. When he walked into the room there was always a quick feeling of tension, because with this busybody about there was never any telling what might descent on you, or what might suddenly be brought to happen in the room. People are never so free with themselves and so recklessly glad as when there is some possibility of commotion or calamity ahead. So when the hunchback marched into the café everyone looked around at him and there was a quick outburst of talking and a drawing of corks.

Lymon waved his hand to Stumpy MacPhail who was sitting with Merlie Ryan and Henry Ford Crimp. 'I walked to Rotten Lake today to fish,' he said. 'And on the way I stepped over what appeared at first to be a big fallen tree. But then as I stepped over I felt something stir and I taken this second look and there I was straddling this here alligator long as from the front door to the kitchen and thicker than a hog.'

The hunchback chattered on. Everyone looked at him from time to time, and some kept track of his chattering and others did not. There were times when every word he said was nothing but lying and bragging. Nothing he said tonight was true. He had lain in bed with a summer quinsy all day long, and had only got up in the late afternoon in order to turn the ice-cream freezer. Everybody knew this, yet he stood there in the middle of the café and held forth with such lies and boasting that it was enough to shrivel the ears.

Miss Amelia watched him with her hands in her pockets and her head turned to one side. There was a softness about her gray, queer eyes and she was smiling gently to herself. Occasionally she glanced from the hunchback to the other people in the café

—and then her look was proud, and there was in it the hint of a threat, as though daring anyone to try to hold him to account for all his foolery. Jeff was bringing in the suppers, already served on the plates, and the new electric fans in the café made a pleasant stir of coolness in the air.

'The little youngun is asleep,' said Henry Macy finally.

Miss Amelia looked down at the patient beside her, and composed her face for the matter in hand. The child's chin was resting on the table edge and a trickle of spit or Kroup Kure had bubbled from the corner of his mouth. His eyes were quite closed, and a little family of gnats had clustered peacefully in the corners. Miss Amelia put her hand on his head and shook it roughly, but the patient did not awake. So Miss Amelia lifted the child from the table, being careful not to touch the sore part of his leg, and went into the office. Henry Macy followed after her and they closed the office door.

Cousin Lymon was bored that evening. There was not much going on, and in spite of the heat the customers in the café were good-humored. Henry Ford Crimp and Horace Wells sat at the middle table with their arms around each other, sniggering over some long joke—but when he approached them he could make nothing of it as he had missed the beginning of the story. The moonlight brightened the dusty road, and the dwarfed peach trees were black and motionless: there was no breeze. The drowsy buzz of swamp mosquitoes was like an echo of the silent night. The town seemed dark, except far down the road to the right there was the flicker of a lamp. Somewhere in the darkness a woman sang in a high wild voice and the tune had no start and no finish and was made up of only three notes which went on and on and on. The hunchback stood leaning against the banister of the porch, looking down the empty road as though hoping that someone would come along.

There were footsteps behind him, then a voice: 'Cousin Lymon, your dinner is set out upon the table.'

'My appetite is poor tonight,' said the hunchback, who had

been eating sweet snuff all the day. 'There is a sourness in my mouth.'

'Just a pick,' said Miss Amelia. 'The breast, the liver, and the heart.'

Together they went back into the bright café, and sat down with Henry Macy. Their table was the largest one in the café, and on it there was a bouquet of swamp lilies in a Coca Cola bottle. Miss Amelia had finished with her patient and was satisfied with herself. From behind the closed office door there had come only a few sleepy whimpers, and before the patient could wake up and become terrified it was all over. The child was now slung across the shoulder of his father, sleeping deeply, his little arms dangling loose along his father's back and his puffed-up face very red—they were leaving the café to go home.

Henry Macy was still silent. He ate carefully, making no noise when he swallowed, and was not a third as greedy as Cousin Lymon who had claimed to have no appetite and was now putting down helping after helping of the dinner. Occasionally Henry Macy looked across at Miss Amelia and again held his peace.

It was a typical Saturday night. An old couple who had come in from the country hesitated for a moment at the doorway, holding each other's hand, and finally decided to come inside. They had lived together so long, this old country couple, that they looked as similar as twins. They were brown, shriveled, and like two little walking peanuts. They left early, and by midnight most of the other customers were gone. Rosser Cline and Merlie Ryan still played checkers, and Stumpy MacPhail sat with a liquor bottle on his table (his wife would not allow it in the home) and carried on peaceable conversations with himself. Henry Macy had not yet gone away, and this was unusual, as he almost always went to bed soon after nightfall. Miss Amelia yawned sleepily, but Lymon was restless and she did not suggest that they close up for the night.

Finally, at one o'clock, Henry Macy looked up at the corner of the ceiling and said quietly to Miss Amelia: 'I got a letter today.'

Miss Amelia was not one to be impressed by this, because all sorts of business letters and catalogues came addressed to her.

'I got a letter from my brother,' said Henry Macy.

The hunchback, who had been goose-stepping about the café with his hands clasped behind his head, stopped suddenly. He was quick to sense any change in the atmosphere of a gathering. He glanced at each face in the room and waited.

Miss Amelia scowled and hardened her right fist. 'You are welcome to it,' she said.

'He is on parole. He is out of the penitentiary.'

The face of Miss Amelia was very dark, and she shivered although the night was warm. Stumpy MacPhail and Merlie Ryan pushed aside their checker game. The café was very quiet.

'Who?' asked Cousin Lymon. His large, pale ears seemed to grow on his head and stiffen. 'What?'

Miss Amelia slapped her hands palm down on the table. 'Because Marvin Macy is a ——' But her voice hoarsened and after a few moments she only said: 'He belongs to be in that penitentiary the balance of his life.'

'What did he do?' asked Cousin Lymon.

There was a long pause, as no one knew exactly how to answer this. 'He robbed three filling stations,' said Stumpy MacPhail. But his words did not sound complete and there was a feeling of sins left unmentioned.

The hunchback was impatient. He could not bear to be left out of anything, even a great misery. The name Marvin Macy was unknown to him, but it tantalized him as did any mention of subjects which others knew about and of which he was ignorant—such as any reference to the old sawmill that had been torn down before he came, or a chance word about poor Morris Finestein, or the recollection of any event that had occurred before his time. Aside from this inborn curiosity, the hunchback took a great interest in robbers and crimes of all varieties. As he strutted around the table he was muttering the words 'released on parole' and 'penitentiary' to himself. But although he questioned insistently, he was unable to find anything, as nobody would dare to talk about Marvin Macy before Miss Amelia in the café.

'The letter did not say very much,' said Henry Macy. 'He did not say where he was going.'

'Humph!' said Miss Amelia, and her face was still hardened and very dark. 'He will never set his split hoof on my premises.'

She pushed back her chair from the table, and made ready to close the café. Thinking about Marvin Macy may have set her to brooding, for she hauled the cash register back to the kitchen and put it in a private place. Henry Macy went off down the dark road. But Henry Ford Crimp and Merlie Ryan lingered for a time on the front porch. Later Merlie Ryan was to make certain claims, to swear that on that night he had a vision of what was to come. But the town paid no attention, for that was just the sort of thing that Merlie Ryan would claim. Miss Amelia and Cousin Lymon talked for a time in the parlor. And when at last the hunchback thought that he could sleep she arranged the mosquito netting over his bed and waited until he had finished with his prayers. Then she put on her long nightgown, smoked two pipes, and only after a long time went to sleep.

That autumn was a happy time. The crops around the countryside were good, and over at the Forks Falls market the price of tobacco held firm that year. After the long hot summer the first cool days had a clean bright sweetness. Goldenrod grew along the dusty roads, and the sugar cane was ripe and purple. The bus came each day from Cheehaw to carry off a few of the younger children to the consolidated school to get an education. Boys hunted foxes in the pinewoods, winter quilts were aired out on the wash lines, and sweet potatoes bedded in the ground with straw against the colder months to come. In the evening, delicate shreds of smoke rose from the chimneys, and the moon was round and orange in the autumn sky. There is no stillness like the quiet of the first cold nights in the fall. Sometimes, late in the night when there was no wind, there could be heard in the town the thin wild whistle of the train that goes through Society City on its way far off to the North.

For Miss Amelia Evans this was a time of great activity. She was at work from dawn until sundown. She made a new and bigger condenser for her still, and in one week ran off enough liquor to souse the whole county. Her old mule was dizzy from grinding so much sorghum, and she scalded her Mason jars and put away pear preserves. She was looking forward greatly to the first frost, because she had traded for three tremendous hogs, and intended to make much barbecue, chitterlins, and sausage.

During these weeks there was a quality about Miss Amelia that many people noticed. She laughed often, with a deep ringing laugh, and her whistling had a sassy, tuneful trickery. She was forever trying out her strength, lifting up heavy objects, or poking her tough biceps with her finger. One day she sat down to her typewriter and wrote a story—a story in which there were foreigners, trap doors, and millions of dollars. Cousin Lymon was with her always, traipsing along behind her coat-tails, and when she watched him her face had a bright, soft look, and when she spoke his name there lingered in her voice the undertone of love.

The first cold spell came at last. When Miss Amelia awoke one morning there were frost flowers on the windowpanes, and rime had silvered the patches of grass in the yard. Miss Amelia built a roaring fire in the kitchen stove, then went out of doors to judge the day. The air was cold and sharp, the sky pale green and cloudless. Very shortly people began to come in from the country to find out what Miss Amelia thought of the weather; she decided to kill the biggest hog, and word got round the countryside. The hog was slaughtered and a low oak fire started in the barbecue pit. There was the warm smell of pig blood and smoke in the back yard, the stamp of footsteps, the ring of voices in the winter air. Miss Amelia walked around giving orders and soon most of the work was done.

She had some particular business to do in Cheehaw that day, so after making sure that all was going well, she cranked up her car and got ready to leave. She asked Cousin Lymon to come with her, in fact, she asked him seven times, but he was loath to leave the commotion and wanted to remain. This seemed to trouble Miss Amelia, as she always liked to have him near to her, and was prone to be terribly homesick when she had to go any distance away. But after asking him seven times, she did not urge him any further. Before leaving she found a stick and drew a heavy line all around the barbecue pit, about two feet back from the edge, and told him not to trespass beyond that boundary. She left after dinner and intended to be back before dark.

Now, it it not so rare to have a truck or an automobile pass along the road and through the town on the way from Cheehaw to somewhere else. Every year the tax collector comes to argue with rich people such as Miss Amelia. And if somebody in the town, such as Merlie Ryan, takes a notion that he can connive to get a car on credit, or to pay down three dollars and have a fine electric icebox such as they advertise in the store windows of Cheehaw, then a city man will come out asking meddlesome questions, finding out all his troubles, and ruining his chances of buying anything on the installment plan. Sometimes, especially since they are working on the Forks Falls highway, the cars hauling the chain gang come through the town. And frequently people in automobiles get lost and stop to inquire how they can find the right road again. So, late that afternoon it was nothing unusual to have a truck pass the mill and stop in the middle of the road near the café of Miss Amelia. A man jumped down from the back of the truck, and the truck went on its way.

The man stood in the middle of the road and looked about him. He was a tall man, with brown curly hair, and slow-moving, deep-blue eyes. His lips were red and he smiled the lazy, half-mouthed smile of the braggart. The man wore a red shirt, and a wide belt of tooled leather; he carried a tin suitcase and a guitar. The first person in the town to see this newcomer was Cousin Lymon, who had heard the shifting of gears and come around to investigate. The hunchback stuck his head around the corner of the porch, but did not step out altogether into full view. He and the man stared at each other, and it was not the look of two strangers meeting for the first time and swiftly summing up each other. It was a peculiar stare they exchanged between them, like the look of two criminals who recognize each other. Then the man in the red shirt shrugged his left shoulder and turned away. The face of the hunchback was very pale as he watched the man go down the road, and after a few moments he began to follow along carefully, keeping many paces away.

It was immediately known throughout the town that Marvin Macy had come back again. First, he went to the mill, propped his elbows lazily on a window sill and looked inside. He liked to watch others hard at work, as do all born loafers. The mill was thrown into a sort of numb confusion. The dyers left the hot vats, the spinners and weavers forgot about their machines, and even Stumpy MacPhail, who was foreman, did not know exactly what to do. Marvin Macy still smiled his wet half-mouthed smiles, and when he saw his brother, his bragging expression did not change. After looking over the mill Marvin Macy went down the road to the house where he had been raised, and left his suitcase and guitar on the front porch. Then he walked around the millpond, looked over the church, the three stores, and the rest of the town. The hunchback trudged along quietly at some distance behind him, his hands in his pockets, and his little face still very pale.

It had grown late. The red winter sun was setting, and to the west the sky was deep gold and crimson. Ragged chimney swifts flew to their nests; lamps were lighted. Now and then there was the smell of smoke, and the warm rich odor of the barbecue slowly cooking in the pit behind the café. After making the rounds of the town Marvin Macy stopped before Miss Amelia's premises and read the sign above the porch. Then, not hesitating to trespass, he walked through the side yard. The mill whistle blew a thin, lonesome blast, and the day's shift was done. Soon there were others in Miss Amelia's back yard beside Marvin Macy — Henry Ford Crimp, Merlie Ryan, Stumpy MacPhail, and any number of children and people who stood around the edges of the property and looked on. Very little was said. Marvin Macy stood by himself on one side of the pit, and the rest of the people clustered together on the other side. Cousin Lymon stood somewhat apart from everyone, and he did not take his eyes from the face of Marvin Macy.

'Did you have a good time in the penitentiary?' asked Merlie Ryan, with a silly giggle.

Marvin Macy did not answer. He took from his hip pocket a large knife, opened it slowly, and honed the blade on the seat of his pants. Merlie Ryan grew suddenly very quiet and went to stand directly behind the broad back of Stumpy MacPhail.

Miss Amelia did not come home until almost dark. They heard the rattle of her automobile while she was still a long distance away, then the slam of the door and a bumping noise as though she were hauling something up the front steps of her premises. The sun had already set, and in the air there was the blue smoky glow of early winter evenings. Miss Amelia came down the back steps slowly, and the group in her yard waited very quietly. Few people in this world could stand up to Miss Amelia, and against Marvin Macy she had this special and bitter hate. Everyone waited to see her burst into a terrible holler, snatch up some dangerous object, and chase him altogether out of town. At first she did not see Marvin Macy, and her face had the relieved and dreamy expression that was natural to her when she reached home after having gone some distance away.

Miss Amelia must have seen Marvin Macy and Cousin Lymon at the same instant. She looked from one to the other, but it was not the wastrel from the penitentiary on whom she finally fixed her gaze of sick amazement. She, and everyone else, was looking at Cousin Lymon, and he was a sight to see.

The hunchback stood at the end of the pit, his pale face lighted by the soft glow from the smoldering oak fire. Cousin Lymon had a very peculiar accomplishment, which he used whenever he wished to ingratiate himself with someone. He would stand very still, and with just a little concentration, he could wiggle his large pale ears with marvelous quickness and ease. This trick he always used when he wanted to get something special out of Miss Amelia, and to her it was irresistible. Now as he stood there the hunchback's ears were wiggling furiously on his head, but it was not Miss Amelia at whom he was looking this time. The hunchback was smiling at Marvin Macy with an entreaty that was near to desperation. At first Marvin Macy paid no attention to him, and when he did finally glance at the hunchback it was without any appreciation whatsoever.

'What ails this Brokeback?' he asked with a rough jerk of his thumb.

No one answered. And Cousin Lymon, seeing that his accomplishment was getting him nowhere, added new efforts of persuasion. He fluttered his eyelids, so that they were like pale, trapped moths in his sockets. He scraped his feet around on the ground, waved his hands about, and finally began doing a little trotlike dance. In the last gloomy light of the winter afternoon he resembled the child of a swamphaunt.

Marvin Macy, alone of all the people in the yard, was unimpressed.

'Is the runt throwing a fit?' he asked, and when no one answered he stepped forward and gave Cousin Lymon a cuff on the side of his head. The hunchback staggered, then fell back on the ground. He sat where he had fallen, still looking up at Marvin Macy, and with great effort his ears managed one last forlorn little flap.

Now everyone turned to Miss Amelia to see what she would do. In all these years no one had so much as touched a hair of Cousin Lymon's head, although many had had the itch to do so. If anyone even spoke crossly to the hunchback, Miss Amelia would cut off this rash mortal's credit and find ways of making things go hard for him a long time afterward. So now if Miss Amelia had split open Marvin Macy's head with the ax on the back porch no one would have been surprised. But she did nothing of the kind.

There were times when Miss Amelia seemed to go into a sort of trance. And the cause of these trances was usually known and understood. For Miss Amelia was a fine doctor, and did not grind up swamp roots and other untried ingredients and give them to the first patient who came along; whenever she invented a new medicine she always tried it out first on herself. She would swallow an enormous dose and spend the following day walking thoughtfully back and forth from the café to the brick privy. Often, when there was a sudden keen gripe, she would stand quite still, her queer eyes staring down at the ground and her fists clenched; she was trying to decide which organ was being worked upon, and what misery the new medicine might be most likely to cure. And now as she watched the hunchback and Marvin Macy, her face wore this same expression, tense with reckoning some inward pain, although she had taken no new medicine that day.

'That will learn you, Brokeback,' said Marvin Macy.

Henry Macy pushed back his limp whitish hair from his forehead and coughed nervously. Stumpy MacPhail and Merlie Ryan shuffled their feet, and the children and black people on the outskirts of the property made not a sound. Marvin Macy folded the knife he had been honing, and after looking about him fearlessly he swaggered out of the yard. The embers in the pit were turning to gray feathery ashes and it was now quite dark.

That was the way Marvin Macy came back from the penitentiary. Not a living soul in all the town was glad to see him. Even Mrs. Mary Hale, who was a good woman and had raised him with love and care — at the first sight of him even this old foster mother dropped the skillet she was holding and burst into tears. But nothing could faze that Marvin Macy. He sat on the back steps of the Hale house, lazily picking his guitar, and when the supper was ready, he pushed the children of the household out of the way and served himself a big meal, although there had been barely enough hoecakes and white meat to go round. After eating he settled himself in the best and warmest sleeping place in the front room and was untroubled by dreams.

Miss Amelia did not open the café that night. She locked the doors and all the windows very carefully, nothing was seen of her and Cousin Lymon, and a lamp burned in her room all the night long.

Marvin Macy brought with him bad fortune, right from the first, as could be expected. The next day the weather turned suddenly, and it became hot. Even in the early morning there was a sticky sultriness in the atmosphere, the wind carried the rotten smell of the swamp, and delicate shrill mosquitoes webbed the green millpond. It was unseasonable, worse than August, and much damage was done. For nearly everyone in the county who owned a hog had copied Miss Amelia and slaughtered the day before. And what sausage could keep in such weather as this? After a few days there was everywhere the smell of slowly spoiling meat, and an atmosphere of dreary waste. Worse yet, a family reunion near the Forks Falls highway ate pork roast and died, every one of them. It was plain that their hog had been infected —and who could tell whether the rest of the meat was safe or not? People were torn between the longing for the good taste of pork, and the fear of death. It was a time of waste and confusion.

The cause of all this, Marvin Macy, had no shame in him. He was seen everywhere. During work hours he loafed about the mill, looking in at the windows, and on Sundays he dressed in his red shirt and paraded up and down the road with his guitar. He was still handsome—with his brown hair, his red lips, and his broad strong shoulders; but the evil in him was now too famous for his good looks to get him anywhere. And this evil was not measured only by the actual sins he had committed. True, he had robbed those filling stations. And before that he had ruined the tenderest girls in the county and laughed about it. Any number of wicked things could be listed against him, but quite apart from these crimes there was about him a secret meanness that clung to him almost like a smell. Another thing—he never sweated, not even in August, and that surely is a sign worth pondering over.

Now it seemed to the town that he was more dangerous than he had ever been before, as in the penitentiary in Atlanta he must have learned the method of laying charms. Otherwise how could his effect on Cousin Lymon be explained? For since first setting eyes on Marvin Macy the hunchback was possessed by an unnatural spirit. Every minute he wanted to be following along behind this jailbird, and he was full of silly schemes to attract attention to himself. Still Marvin Macy either treated him hatefully or failed to notice him at all. Sometimes the hunchback would give up, perch himself on the banister of the front porch much as a sick bird huddles on a telephone wire, and grieve publicly.

'But why?' Miss Amelia would ask, staring at him with her crossed, gray eyes, and her fists closed tight.

'Oh, Marvin Macy,' groaned the hunchback, and the sound of the name was enough to upset the rhythm of his sobs so that he hiccuped. 'He has been to Atlanta.'

Miss Amelia would shake her head and her face was dark and hardened. To begin with she had no patience with any traveling; those who had made the trip to Atlanta or traveled fifty miles from home to see the ocean — those restless people she despised. 'Going to Atlanta does no credit to him.'

'He has been to the penitentiary,' said the hunchback, miserable with longing.

How are you going to argue against such envies as these? In her perplexity Miss Amelia did not herself sound any too sure of what she was saying. 'Been to the penitentiary, Cousin Lymon? Why, a trip like that is no travel to brag about.'

During these weeks Miss Amelia was closely watched by everyone. She went about absent-mindedly, her face remote as though she had lapsed into one of her gripe trances. For some reason, after the day of Marvin Macy's arrival, she put aside her overalls and wore always the red dress she had before this time reserved for Sundays, funerals, and sessions of the court. Then as the weeks passed she began to take some steps to clear up the situation. But her efforts were hard to understand. If it hurt her to see Cousin Lymon follow Marvin Macy about the town, why did she not make the issues clear once and for all, and tell the hunchback that if he had dealings with Marvin Macy she would turn him off the premises? That would have been simple, and Cousin Lymon would have had to submit to her, or else face the sorry business of finding himself loose in the world. But Miss Amelia seemed to have lost her will; for the first time in her life she hesitated as to just what course to pursue. And, like most people in such a position of uncertainty, she did the worst thing possible — she began following several courses at once, all of them contrary to each other.

The café was opened every night as usual, and, strangely enough, when Marvin Macy came swaggering through the door, with the hunchback at his heels, she did not turn him out. She even gave him free drinks and smiled at him in a wild, crooked way. At the same time she set a terrible trap for him out in the swamp that surely would have killed him if he had got caught. She let Cousin Lymon invite him to Sunday dinner, and then tried to trip him up as he went down the steps. She began a great campaign of pleasure for Cousin Lymon — making exhausting trips to various spectacles being held in distant places, driving the automobile thirty miles to a Chautauqua, taking him to Forks Falls to watch a parade. All in all it was a distracting time for Miss Amelia. In the opinion of most people she was well on her way in the climb up fools' hill, and everyone waited to see how it would all turn out.

The weather turned cold again, the winter was upon the town, and night came before the last shift in the mill was done. Children kept on all their garments when they slept, and women raised the backs of their skirts to toast themselves dreamily at the fire. After it rained, the mud in the road made hard frozen ruts, there were faint flickers of lamplight from the windows of the houses, the peach trees were scrawny and bare. In the dark, silent nights of wintertime the café was the warm center point of the town, the lights shining so brightly that they could be seen a quarter of a mile away. The great iron stove at the back of the room roared, crackled, and turned red. Miss Amelia had made red curtains for the windows, and from a salesman who passed through the town she bought a great bunch of paper roses that looked very real.

But it was not only the warmth, the decorations, and the brightness, that made the café what it was. There is a deeper reason why the café was so precious to this town. And this deeper reason has to do with a certain pride that had not hitherto been known in these parts. To understand this new pride the cheapness of human life must be kept in mind. There were always plenty of people clustered around a mill — but it was seldom that every family had enough meal, garments, and fat back to go the rounds. Life could become one long dim scramble just to get the things needed to keep alive. And the confusing point is this: All useful things have a price, and are bought only with money, as that is the way the world is run. You know without having to reason about it the price of a bale of cotton, or a quart of molasses. But no value has been put on human life; it is given to us free and taken without being paid for. What is it worth? If you look around, at times the value may seem to be little or nothing at all. Often after you have sweated and tried and things are not better for you, there comes a feeling deep down in the soul that you are not worth much.

But the new pride that the café brought to this town had an effect on almost everyone, even the children. For in order to come to the café you did not have to buy the dinner, or a portion of liquor. There were cold bottled drinks for a nickel. And if you could not even afford that, Miss Amelia had a drink called Cherry Juice which sold for a penny a glass, and was pink-colored and very sweet. Almost everyone, with the exception of Reverent T. M. Willin, came to the café at least once during the week. Children love to sleep in houses other than their own, and to eat at a neighbor's table; on such occasions they behave themselves decently and are proud. The people in the town were likewise proud when sitting at the tables in the café. They washed before coming to Miss Amelia's, and scraped their feet very politely on the threshold as they entered the café. There, for a few hours at least, the deep bitter knowing that you are not worth much in this world could be laid low.

The café was a special benefit to bachelors, unfortunate people, and consumptives. And here it may be mentioned that there was some reason to suspect that Cousin Lymon was consumptive. The brightness of his gray eyes, his insistence, his talkativeness, and his cough — these were all signs. Besides, there is generally supposed to be some connection between a hunched spine and consumption. But whenever this subject had been mentioned to Miss Amelia she had become furious; she denied these symptoms with bitter vehemence, but on the sly she treated Cousin Lymon with hot chest plasters, Kroup Kure, and such. Now this winter the hunchback's cough was worse, and sometimes even on cold days he would break out in a heavy sweat. But this did not prevent him from following along after Marvin Macy.

Early every morning he left the premises and went to the back door of Mrs. Hale's house, and waited and waited — as Marvin Macy was a lazy sleeper. He would stand there and call out softly. His voice was just like the voices of children who squat patiently over those tiny little holes in the ground where doodlebugs are thought to live, poking the hole with a broom straw, and calling plaintively: 'Doodlebug, Doodlebug — fly away home. Mrs. Doodlebug, Mrs. Doodlebug. Come out, come out. Your house is on fire and all your children are burning up.' In just such a voice — at once sad, luring, and resigned — would the hunchback call Marvin Macy's name each morning. Then when Marvin Macy came out for the day, he would trail him about the town, and sometimes they would be gone for hours together out in the swamp.

And Miss Amelia continued to do the worst thing possible: that it, to try to follow several courses at once. When Cousin Lymon left the house she did not call him back, but only stood in the middle of the road and watched lonesomely until he was out of sight. Nearly every day Marvin Macy turned up with Cousin Lymon at dinnertime, and ate at her table. Miss Amelia opened the pear preserves, and the table was well-set with ham or chicken, great bowls of hominy grits, and winter peas. It is true that on one occasion Miss Amelia tried to poison Marvin Macy — but there was a mistake, the plates were confused, and it was she herself who got the poisoned dish. This she quickly realized by the slight bitterness of the food, and that day she ate no dinner. She sat tilted back in her chair, feeling her muscle, and looking at Marvin Macy.

Every night Marvin Macy came to the café and settled himself at the best and largest table, the one in the center of the room. Cousin Lymon brought him liquor, for which he did not pay a cent. Marvin Macy brushed the hunchback aside as if he were a swamp mosquito, and not only did he show no gratitude for these favors, but if the hunchback got in his way he would cuff him with the back of his hand, or say: 'Out of my way, Brokeback — I'll snatch you bald-headed.' When this happened Miss Amelia would come out from behind her counter and approach Marvin

Macy very slowly, her fists clenched, her peculiar red dress hanging awkwardly around her bony knees. Marvin Macy would also clench his fists and they would walk slowly and meaningfully around each other. But, although everyone watched breathlessly, nothing ever came of it. The time for the fight was not yet ready.

There is one particular reason why this winter is remembered and still talked about. A great thing happened. People woke up on the second of January and found the whole world about them altogether changed. Little ignorant children looked out of the windows, and they were so puzzled that they began to cry. Old people harked back and could remember nothing in these parts to equal the phenomenon. For in the night it had snowed. In the dark hours after midnight the dim flakes started falling softly on the town. By dawn the ground was covered, and the strange snow banked the ruby windows of the church, and whitened the roofs of the houses. The snow gave the town a drawn, bleak look. The two-room houses near the mill were dirty, crooked, and seemed about to collapse, and somehow everything was dark and shrunken. But the snow itself — there was a beauty about it few people around here had ever known before. The snow was not white, as Northerners had pictured it to be; in the snow there were soft colors of blue and silver, the sky was a gentle shining gray. And the dreamy quietness of falling snow — when had the town been so silent?

People reacted to the snowfall in various ways. Miss Amelia, on looking out of her window, thoughtfully wiggled the toes of her bare feet, gathered close to her neck the collar of her nightgown. She stood there for some time, then commenced to draw the shutters and lock every window on the premises. She closed the place completely, lighted the lamps, and sat solemnly over her bowl of grits. The reason for this was not that Miss Amelia feared the snowfall. It was simply that she was unable to form an immediate opinion of this new event, and unless she knew exactly and definitely what she thought of a matter (which was nearly always the case) she preferred to ignore it. Snow had never fallen in this county in her lifetime, and she had never thought about it one way or the other. But if she admitted this snowfall she would have to come to some decision, and in those days there was enough distraction in her life as it was already. So she poked about the gloomy, lamp-lighted house and pretended that nothing had happened. Cousin Lymon, on the contrary, chased around in the wildest excitement, and when Miss Amelia turned her back to dish him some breakfast he slipped out of the door.

Marvin Macy laid claim to the snowfall. He said that he knew snow, had seen it in Atlanta, and from the way he walked about the town that day it was as though he owned every flake. He sneered at the little children who crept timidly out of the houses and scooped up handfuls of snow to taste. Reverend Willin hurried down the road with a furious face, as he was thinking deeply and trying to weave the snow into his Sunday sermon. Most people were humble and glad about this marvel; they spoke in hushed voices and said 'thank you' and 'please' more than was necessary. A few weak characters, of course, were demoralized and got drunk — but they were not numerous. To everyone this was an occasion and many counted their money and planned to go to the café that night.

Cousin Lymon followed Marvin Macy about all day, seconding his claim to the snow. He marveled that snow did not fall as does rain, and stared up at the dreamy, gently falling flakes until he stumbled from dizziness. And the pride he took on himself, basking in the glory of Marvin Macy — it was such that many people could not resist calling out to him: '"Oho," said the fly on the chariot wheel. "What a dust we do raise."'

Miss Amelia did not intend to serve a dinner. But when, at six o'clock, there was the sound of footsteps on the porch she opened the front door cautiously. It was Henry Ford Crimp, and though there was no food, she let him sit at a table and served him a drink. Others came. The evening was blue, bitter, and though the snow fell no longer there was a wind from the pine trees that swept up delicate flurries from the ground. Cousin Lymon did not come until after dark, with him Marvin Macy, and he carried his tin suitcase and his guitar.

'So you mean to travel?' said Miss Amelia quickly.

Marvin Macy warmed himself at the stove. Then he settled down at his table and carefully sharpened a little stick. He picked his teeth, frequently taking the stick out of his mouth to look at the end and wipe it on the sleeve of his coat. He did not bother to answer.

The hunchback looked at Miss Amelia, who was behind the counter. His face was not in the least beseeching; he seemed quite sure of himself. He folded his hands behind his back and perked up his ears confidently. His cheeks were red, his eyes shining, and his clothes were soggy wet. 'Marvin Macy is going to visit a spell with us,' he said.

Miss Amelia made no protest. She only came out from behind the counter and hovered over the stove, as though the news had made her suddenly cold. She did not warm her backside modestly, lifting her skirt only an inch or so, as do most women when in public. There was not a grain of modesty about Miss Amelia, and she frequently seemed to forget altogether that there were men in the room. Now as she stood warming herself, her red dress was pulled up quite high in the back so that a piece of her strong, hairy thigh could be seen by anyone who cared to look at it. Her head was turned to one side; and she had begun talking with herself, nodding and wrinkling her forehead, and there was the tone of accusation and reproach in her voice although the words were not plain. Meanwhile, the hunchback and Marvin Macy had gone upstairs — up to the parlor with the pampas grass and the two sewing machines, to the private rooms where Miss Amelia had lived the whole of her life. Down in the café you could hear them bumping around, unpacking Marvin Macy, and getting him settled.

That is the way Marvin Macy crowded into Miss Amelia's home. At first Cousin Lymon, who had given Marvin Macy his own room, slept on the sofa in the parlor. But the snowfall had a bad effect on him; he caught a cold that turned into a winter quinsy, so Miss Amelia gave up her bed to him. The sofa in the parlor was much too short for her, her feet lapped over the edges, and often she rolled off onto the floor. Perhaps it was this lack of sleep that clouded her wits; everything she tried to do against Marvin Macy rebounded on herself. She got caught in her own tricks, and found herself in many pitiful positions. But still she did not put Marvin Macy off the premises, as she was afraid that she would be left alone. Once you have lived with another, it is a great torture to have to live alone. The silence of a firelit room when suddenly the clock stops ticking, the nervous shadows in an empty house — it is better to take in your mortal enemy than face the terror of living alone.

The snow did not last. The sun came out and within two days the town was just as it had always been before. Miss Amelia did not open her house until every flake had melted. Then she had a big house cleaning and aired everything out in the sun. But before that, the very first thing she did on going out again into her yard, was to tie a rope to the largest branch of the chinaberry tree. At the end of the rope she tied a crocus sack tightly stuffed with sand. This was the punching bag she made for herself and from that day on she would box with it out in her yard every morning. Already she was a fine fighter — a little heavy on her feet, but knowing all manner of mean holds and squeezes to make up for this.

Miss Amelia, as has been mentioned, measured six feet two inches in height. Marvin Macy was one inch shorter. In weight they were about even — both of them weighing close to a hundred and sixty pounds. Marvin Macy had the advantage in slyness of movement, and in toughness of chest. In fact from the outward point of view the odds were altogether in his favor. Yet almost everybody in the town was betting on Miss Amelia; scarcely a person would put up money on Marvin Macy. The town remembered the great fight between Miss Amelia and a Forks Fall lawyer who had tried to cheat her. He had been a huge strapping fellow, but he was left three-quarters dead when she had finished with him. And it was not only her talent as a boxer that had impressed everyone — she could demoralize her enemy by making terrifying faces and fierce noises, so that even the spectators were sometimes cowed. She was brave, she practiced faithfully with her punching bag, and in this case she was clearly in the right. So people had confidence in her, and they waited. Of course there was no set date for this fight. There were just the signs that were too plain to be overlooked.

During these times the hunchback strutted around with a pleased little pinched-up face. In many delicate and clever ways he stirred up trouble between them. He was constantly plucking at Marvin Macy's trouser leg to draw attention to himself. Sometimes he followed in Miss Amelia's footsteps — but these days it was only in order to imitate her awkward long-legged walk; he crossed his eyes and aped her gestures in a way that made her appear to be a freak. There was something so terrible about this that even the silliest customers of the café, such as Merlie Ryan, did not laugh. Only Marvin Macy drew up the left corner of his mouth and chuckled. Miss Amelia, when this happened, would be divided between two emotions. She would look at the hunchback with a lost, dismal reproach — then turn toward Marvin Macy with her teeth clamped.

'Bust a gut!' she would say bitterly.

And Marvin Macy, most likely, would pick up the guitar from the floor beside his chair. His voice was wet and slimy, as he always had too much spit in his mouth. And the tunes he sang glided slowly from his throat like eels. His strong fingers picked the strings with dainty skill, and everything he sang both lured and exasperated. This was usually more than Miss Amelia could stand.

'Bust a gut!' she would repeat, in a shout.

But always Marvin Macy had the answer ready for her. He would cover the strings to silence the quivering leftover tones, and reply with slow, sure insolence.

'Everything you holler at me bounces back on yourself. Yah! Yah!'

Miss Amelia would have to stand there helpless, as no one has ever invented a way out of this trap. She could not shout out abuse that would bounce back on herself. He had the best of her, there was nothing she could do.

So things went on like this. What happened between the three of them during the nights in the rooms upstairs nobody knows. But the café became more and more crowded every night. A new table had to be brought in. Even the Hermit, the crazy man named Rainer Smith, who took to the swamp years ago, heard something of the situation and came one night to look in at the window and brood over the gathering in the bright café. And the climax each evening was the time when Miss Amelia and Marvin Macy doubled their fists, squared up, and glared at each other. Usually this did not happen after any especial argument, but it seemed to come about mysteriously, by means of some instinct on the part of both of them. At these times the café would become so quiet that you could hear the bouquet of paper roses rustling in the draft. And each night they held this fighting stance a little longer than the night before.

The fight took place on Ground Hog Day, which is the second of February. The weather was favorable, being neither rainy nor sunny, and with a neutral temperature. There were several signs that this was the appointed day, and by ten o'clock the news spread all over the county. Early in the morning Miss Amelia went out and cut down her punching bag. Marvin Macy sat on the back step with a tin can of hog fat between his knees and carefully greased his arms and his legs. A hawk with a bloody breast flew over the town and circled twice around the property of Miss Amelia. The tables in the café were moved out to the back porch, so that the whole big room was cleared for the fight. There was every sign. Both Miss Amelia and Marvin Macy ate four helpings of half-raw roast for dinner, and then lay down in the afternoon to store up strength. Marvin Macy rested in the big room upstairs, while Miss Amelia stretched herself out on the bench in her office. It was plain from her white stiff face what a torment it was for her to be lying still and doing nothing, but she lay there quiet as a corpse with her eyes closed and her hands crossed on her chest.

Cousin Lymon had a restless day, and his little face was drawn and tightened with excitement. He put himself up a lunch, and set out to find the ground hog—within an hour he returned, the lunch eaten, and said that the ground hog had seen his shadow and there was to be bad weather ahead. Then, as Miss Amelia and

Marvin Macy were both resting to gather strength, and he was left to himself, it occurred to him that he might as well paint the front porch. The house had not been painted for years — in fact, God knows if it had ever been painted at all. Cousin Lymon scrambled around, and soon he had painted half the floor of the porch a gay bright green. It was a loblolly job, and he smeared himself all over. Typically enough he did not even finish the floor, but changed over to the walls, painting as high as he could reach and then standing on a crate to get up a foot higher. When the paint ran out, the right side of the floor was bright green and there was a jagged portion of wall that had been painted. Cousin Lymon left it at that.

There was something childish about his satisfaction with his painting. And in this respect a curious fact should be mentioned. No one in the town, not even Miss Amelia, had any idea how old the hunchback was. Some maintained that when he came to town he was about twelve years old, still a child — others were certain that he was well past forty. His eyes were blue and steady as a child's, but there were lavender crepy shadows beneath these blue eyes that hinted of age. It was impossible to guess his age by his hunched queer body. And even his teeth gave no clue — they were all still in his head (two were broken from cracking a pecan), but he had stained them with so much sweet snuff that it was impossible to decide whether they were old teeth or young teeth. When questioned directly about his age the hunchback professed to know absolutely nothing — he had no idea how long he had been on the earth, whether for ten years or a hundred! So his age remained a puzzle.

Cousin Lymon finished his painting at five-thirty o'clock in the afternoon. The day had turned colder and there was a wet taste in the air. The wind came up from the pinewoods, rattling windows, blowing an old newspaper down the road until at last it caught upon a thorn tree. People began to come in from the country; packed automobiles that bristled with the poked-out heads of children, wagons drawn by old mules who seemed to smile in a weary, sour way and plodded along with their tired eyes half-closed. Three young boys came from Society City. All three of them wore yellow rayon shirts and caps put on backward — they were as much alike as triplets, and could always be seen at cock-fights and camp meetings. At six o'clock the mill whistle sounded the end of the day's shift and the crowd was complete. Naturally, among the newcomers there were some riffraff, unknown characters, and so forth — but even so the gathering was quiet. A hush was on the town and the faces of people were strange in the fading light. Darkness hovered softly; for a moment the sky was a pale clear yellow against which the gables of the church stood out in dark and bare outline, then the sky died slowly and the darkness gathered into night.

Seven is a popular number, and especially it was a favorite with Miss Amelia. Seven swallows of water for hiccups, seven runs around the millpond for cricks in the neck, seven doses of Amelia Miracle Mover as a worm cure — her treatment nearly always hinged on this number. It is a number of mingled possibilities, and all who love mystery and charms set store by it. So the fight was to take place at seven o'clock. This was known to everyone, not by announcement or words, but understood in the unquestioning way that rain is understood, or an evil odor from the swamp. So before seven o'clock everyone gathered gravely around the property of Miss Amelia. The cleverest got into the café itself and stood lining the walls of the room. Others crowded onto the front porch, or took a stand in the yard.

Miss Amelia and Marvin Macy had not yet shown themselves. Miss Amelia, after resting all afternoon on the office bench, had gone upstairs. On the other hand Cousin Lymon was at your elbow every minute, threading his way through the crowd, snapping his fingers nervously, and batting his eyes. At one minute to seven o'clock he squirmed his way into the café and climbed up on the counter. All was very quiet.

It must have been arranged in some manner beforehand. For just at the stroke of seven Miss Amelia showed herself at the head of the stairs. At the same instant Marvin Macy appeared in front of the café and the crowd made way for him silently. They walked toward each other with no haste, their fists already gripped, and their eyes like the eyes of dreamers. Miss Amelia had changed her red dress for her old overalls, and they were rolled up to the knees. She was barefooted and she had an iron strengthband around her right wrist. Marvin Macy had also rolled his trouser legs — he was naked to the waist and heavily greased; he wore the heavy shoes that had been issued him when he left the penitentiary. Stumpy MacPhail stepped forward from the crowd and slapped their hip pockets with the palm of his right hand to make sure there would be no sudden knives. Then they were alone in the cleared center of the bright café.

There was no signal, but they both struck out simultaneously. Both blows landed on the chin, so that the heads of Miss Amelia and Marvin Macy bobbed back and they were left a little groggy. For a few seconds after the first blows they merely shuffled their feet around on the bare floor, experimenting with various positions, and making mock fists. Then, like wildcats, they were suddenly on each other. There was the sound of knocks, panting, and thumpings on the floor. They were so fast that it was hard to take in what was going on — but once Miss Amelia was hurled backward so that she staggered and almost fell, and another time Marvin Macy caught a knock on the shoulder that spun him round like a top. So the fight went on in this wild violent way with no sign of weakening on either side.

During a struggle like this, when the enemies are as quick and strong as these two, it is worth-while to turn from the confusion of the fight itself and observe the spectators. The people had flattened back as close as possible against the walls. Stumpy MacPhail was in a corner, crouched over and with his fists tight in sympathy, making strange noises. Poor Merlie Ryan had his mouth so wide open that a fly buzzed into it, and was swallowed before Merlie realized what had happened. And Cousin Lymon — he was worth watching. The hunchback still stood on the counter, so that he was raised up above everyone else in the café. He had his hands on his hips, his big head thrust forward, and his little legs bent so that the knees jutted outward. The excitement had made him break out in a rash, and his pale mouth shivered.

Perhaps it was half an hour before the course of the fight shifted. Hundreds of blows had been exchanged, and there was still a deadlock. Then suddenly Marvin Macy managed to catch hold of Miss Amelia's left arm and pinion it behind her back. She struggled and got a grasp around his waist; the real fight was now begun. Wrestling is the natural way of fighting in this county — as boxing is too quick and requires much thinking and concentration. And now that Miss Amelia and Marvin were locked in a hold together the crowd came out of its daze and pressed in closer. For a while the fighters grappled muscle to muscle, their hipbones braced against each other. Backward and forward, from side to side, they swayed in this way. Marvin Macy still had not sweated, but Miss Amelia's overalls were drenched and so much sweat had trickled down her legs that she left wet footprints on the floor. Now the test had come, and in these moments of terrible effort, it was Miss Amelia who was the stronger. Marvin Macy was greased and slippery, tricky to grasp, but she was stronger. Gradually she bent him over backward, and inch by inch she forced him to the floor. It was a terrible thing to watch and their deep hoarse breaths were the only sound in the café. At last she had him down, and straddled; her strong big hands were on his throat.

But at that instant, just as the fight was won, a cry sounded in the café that caused a shrill bright shiver to run down the spine. And what took place has been a mystery ever since. The whole town was there to testify what happened, but there were those who doubted their own eyesight. For the counter on which Cousin Lymon stood was at least twelve feet from the fighters in the center of the café. Yet at the instant Miss Amelia grasped the throat of Marvin Macy the hunchback sprang forward and sailed through the air as though he had grown hawk wings. He landed on the broad strong back of Miss Amelia and clutched at her neck with his clawed little fingers.

The rest is confusion. Miss Amelia was beaten before the crowd could come to their senses. Because of the hunchback the fight was won by Marvin Macy, and at the end Miss Amelia lay sprawled on the floor, her arms flung outward and motionless. Marvin Macy stood over her, his face somewhat popeyed, but smiling his old half-mouthed smile. And the hunchback, he had suddenly disappeared. Perhaps he was frightened about what he had done, or maybe he was so delighted that he wanted to glory with himself alone — at any rate he slipped out of the café and crawled under the back steps. Someone poured water on Miss Amelia, and after a time she got up slowly and dragged herself into her office. Through the open door the crowd could see her sitting at her desk, her head in the crook of her arm, and she was sobbing with the last of her grating, winded breath. Once she gathered her right fist together and knocked it three times on the top of her office desk, then her hand opened feebly and lay palm upward and still. Stumpy MacPhail stepped forward and closed the door.

The crowd was quiet, and one by one the people left the café. Mules were waked up and untied, automobiles cranked, and the three boys from Society City roamed off down the road on foot. This was not a fight to hash over and talk about afterward; people went home and pulled the covers up over their heads. The town was dark, except for the premises of Miss Amelia, but every room was lighted there the whole night long.

Marvin Macy and the hunchback must have left the town an hour or so before daylight. And before they went away this is what they did:

They unlocked the private cabinet of curios and took everything in it.

They broke the mechanical piano.

They carved terrible words on the café tables.

They found the watch that opened in the back to show a picture of a waterfall and took that also.

They poured a gallon of sorghum syrup all over the kitchen floor and smashed the jars of preserves.

They went out in the swamp and completely wrecked the still, ruining the big new condenser and the cooler, and setting fire to the shack itself.

They fixed a dish of Miss Amelia's favorite food, grits with sausage, seasoned it with enough poison to kill off the county, and placed this dish temptingly on the café counter.

They did everything ruinous they could think of without actually breaking into the office where Miss Amelia stayed the night. Then they went off together, the two of them.

That was how Miss Amelia was left alone in the town. The people would have helped her if they had known how, as people in this town will as often as not be kindly if they have a chance. Several housewives nosed around with brooms and offered to clear up the wreck. But Miss Amelia only looked at them with lost crossed eyes and shook her head. Stumpy MacPhail came in on the third day to buy a plug of Queenie tobacco, and Miss Amelia said the price was one dollar. Everything in the café had suddenly risen in price to be worth one dollar. And what sort of a café is that? Also, she changed very queerly as a doctor. In all the years before she had been much more popular than the Cheehaw doctor. She had never monkeyed with a patient's soul, taking away from him such real necessities as liquor, tobacco, and so forth. Once in a great while she might carefully warn a patient never to eat fried watermelon or some such dish it had never occurred to a person to want in the first place. Now all this wise doctoring was over. She told one-half of her patients that they were going to die outright, and to the remaining half she recommended cures so farfetched and agonizing that no one in his right mind would consider them for a moment.

Miss Amelia let her hair grow ragged, and it was turning gray. Her face lengthened, and the great muscles of her body shrank until she was thin as old maids are thin when they go crazy. And those gray eyes — slowly day by day they were more crossed, and it was as though they sought each other out to exchange a little glance of grief and lonely recognition. She was not pleasant to listen to; her tongue had sharpened terribly.

When anyone mentioned the hunchback she would say only this: 'Ho! If I could lay hand to him I would rip out his gizzard and throw it to the cat!' But it was not so much the words that were terrible, but the voice in which they were said. Her voice had lost its old vigor; there was none of the ring of vengeance it used to have when she would mention 'that loom-fixer I was married to,' or some other enemy. Her voice was broken, soft, and sad as the wheezy whine of the church pump-organ.

For three years she sat out on the front steps every night, alone and silent, looking down the road and waiting. But the hunchback never returned. There were rumors that Marvin Macy used him to climb into windows and steal, and other rumors that Marvin Macy had sold him into a side show. But both these reports were traced back to Merlie Ryan. Nothing true was ever heard of him. It was in the fourth year that Miss Amelia hired a Cheehaw carpenter and had him board up the premises, and there in those closed rooms she has remained ever since.

Yes, the town is dreary. On August afternoons the road is empty, white with dust, and the sky above is bright as glass. Nothing moves — there are no children's voices, only the hum of the mill. The peach trees seem to grow more crooked every summer, and the leaves are dull gray and of a sickly delicacy. The house of Miss Amelia leans so much to the right that it is now only a question of time when it will collapse completely, and people are careful not to walk around the yard. There is no good liquor to be bought in the town; the nearest still is eight miles away, and the liquor is such that those who drink it grow warts on their livers the size of goobers, and dream themselves into a dangerous inward world. There is absolutely nothing to do in the town. Walk around the millpond, stand kicking at a rotten stump, figure out what you can do with the old wagon wheel by the side of the road near the church. The soul rots with boredom. You might as well go down to the Forks Falls highway and listen to the chain gang.

THE TWELVE MORTAL MEN

The Forks Falls highway is three miles from the town, and it is here the chain gang has been working. The road is of macadam, and the county decided to patch up the rough places and widen it at a certain dangerous place. The gang is made up of twelve men, all wearing black and white striped prison suits, and chained at the ankles. There is a guard, with a gun, his eyes drawn to red slits by the glare. The gang works all the day long, arriving huddled in the prison cart soon after daybreak, and being driven off again in the gray August twilight. All day there is the sound of the picks striking into the clay earth, hard sunlight, the smell of sweat. And every day there is music. One dark voice will start a phrase, half-sung, and like a question. And after a moment another voice will join in, soon the whole gang will be singing. The voices are dark in the golden glare, the music intricately blended, both somber and joyful. The music will swell until at last it seems that the sound does not come from the twelve men on the gang, but from the earth itself, or the wide sky. It is music that causes the heart to broaden and the listener to grow cold with ecstasy and fright. Then slowly the music will sink down until at last there remains one lonely voice, then a great hoarse breath, the sun, the sound of the picks in the silence.

And what kind of gang is this that can make such music? Just twelve mortal men, seven of them black and five of them white boys from this county. Just twelve mortal men who are together.

Wunderkind

Wunderkind

She came into the living room, her music satchel plopping against her winter-stockinged legs and her other arm weighted down with school books, and stood for a moment listening to the sounds from the studio. A soft procession of piano chords and the tuning of a violin. Then Mister Bilderbach called out to her in his chunky, guttural tones:

'That you, Bienchen?'

As she jerked off her mittens she saw that her fingers were twitching to the motions of the fugue she had practiced that morning. 'Yes,' she answered. 'It's me.'

'I,' the voice corrected. 'Just a moment.'

She could hear Mister Lafkowitz talking — his words spun out in a silky, unintelligible hum. A voice almost like a woman's, she thought, compared to Mister Bilderbach's. Restlessness scattered her attention. She fumbled with her geometry book and *Le Voyage de Monsieur Perrichon* before putting them on the table. She sat down on the sofa and began to take her music from the satchel. Again she saw her hands — the quivering tendons that stretched down from her knuckles, the sore finger tip capped with curled, dingy tape. The sight sharpened the fear that had begun to torment her for the past few months.

Noiselessly she mumbled a few phrases of encouragement to herself. A good lesson — a good lesson — like it used to be — Her lips closed as she heard the stolid sound of Mister Bilderbach's footsteps across the floor of the studio and the creaking of the door as it slid open.

For a moment she had the peculiar feeling that during most of the fifteen years of her life she had been looking at the face and shoulders that jutted from behind the door, in a silence disturbed only by the muted, blank plucking of a violin string. Mister Bilderbach. Her teacher, Mister Bilderbach. The quick eyes behind the horn-rimmed glasses; the light, thin hair and the narrow face beneath; the lips full and loose shut and the lower one pink and shining from the bites of his teeth; the forked veins in his temples throbbing plainly enough to be observed across the room.

'Aren't you a little early?' he asked, glancing at the clock on the mantelpiece that had pointed to five minutes of twelve for a month. 'Josef's in here. We're running over a little sonatina by someone he knows.'

'Good,' she said, trying to smile. 'I'll listen.' She could see her fingers sinking powerless into a blur of piano keys. She felt tired — felt that if he looked at her much longer her hands might tremble.

He stood uncertain, halfway in the room. Sharply his teeth pushed down on his bright, swollen lip. 'Hungry, Bienchen?' he asked. 'There's some apple cake Anna made, and milk.'

'I'll wait till afterward,' she said. 'Thanks.'

'After you finish with a very fine lesson — eh?' His smile seemed to crumble at the corners.

There was a sound from behind him in the studio and Mister Lafkowitz pushed at the other panel of the door and stood beside him.

'Frances?' he said, smiling. 'And how is the work coming now?'

Without meaning to, Mister Lafkowitz always made her feel clumsy and overgrown. He was such a small man himself, with a weary look when he was not holding his violin. His eyebrows curved high above his sallow, Jewish face as though asking a question, but the lids of his eyes drowsed languorous and indifferent. Today he seemed distracted. She watched him come into the room for no apparent purpose, holding his pearl-tipped bow in his still fingers, slowly gliding the white horsehair through a chalky piece of rosin. His eyes were sharp bright slits today and the linen handkerchief that flowed down from his collar darkened the shadows beneath them.

'I gather you're doing a lot now,' smiled Mister Lafkowitz, although she had not yet answered the question.

She looked at Mister Bilderbach. He turned away. His heavy shoulders pushed the door open wide so that the late afternoon sun came through the window of the studio and shafted yellow over the dusty living room. Behind her teacher she could see the squat long piano, the window, and the bust of Brahms.

'No,' she said to Mister Lafkowitz, 'I'm doing terribly.' Her thin fingers flipped at the pages of her music. 'I don't know what's the matter,' she said, looking at Mister Bilderbach's stooped muscular back that stood tense and listening.

Mister Lafkowitz smiled. 'There are times, I suppose, when one ——'

A harsh chord sounded from the piano. 'Don't you think we'd better get on with this?' asked Mister Bilderbach.

'Immediately,' said Mister Lafkowitz, giving the bow one more scrape before starting toward the door. She could see him pick up his violin from the top of the piano. He caught her eye and lowered the instrument. 'You've seen the picture of Heime?'

Her fingers curled tight over the sharp corner of the satchel. 'What picture?'

'One of Heime in the *Musical Courier* there on the table. Inside the top cover.'

The sonatina began. Discordant yet somehow simple. Empty but with a sharp-cut style of its own. She reached for the magazine and opened it.

There Heime was — in the left-hand corner. Holding his violin with his fingers hooked down over the strings for a pizzicato. With his dark serge knickers strapped neatly beneath his knees, a sweater and rolled collar. It was a bad picture. Although it was snapped in profile his eyes were cut around toward the photographer and his finger looked as though it would pluck the wrong string. He seemed suffering to turn around toward the picture-taking apparatus. He was thinner — his stomach did not poke out now — but he hadn't changed much in six months.

Heime Israelsky, talented young violinist, snapped while at work in his teacher's studio on Riverside Drive. Young Master Israelsky, who will soon celebrate his fifteenth birthday, has been invited to play the Beethoven Concerta with —

That morning, after she had practiced from six until eight, her dad had made her sit down at the table with the family for breakfast. She hated breakfast; it gave her a sick feeling afterward. She would rather wait and get four chocolate bars with her twenty cents lunch money and munch them during school — bringing up little morsels from her pocket under cover of her handkerchief, stopping dead when the silver paper rattled. But this morning her dad had put a fried egg on her plate and she had known that if it burst — so that the slimy yellow oozed over the white — she would cry. And that had happened. The same feeling was upon her now. Gingerly she laid the magazine back on the table and closed her eyes.

The music in the studio seemed to be urging violently and clumsily for something that was not to be had. After a moment her thoughts drew back from Heime and the concerta and the picture — and hovered around the lesson once more. She slid over on the sofa until she could see plainly into the studio — the two of them playing, peering at the notations on the piano, lustfully drawing out all that was there.

She could not forget the memory of Mister Bilderbach's face as he had stared at her a moment ago. Her hands, still twitching unconsciously to the motions of the fugue, closed over her bony knees. Tired, she was. And with a circling, sinking away feeling like the one that often came to her just before she dropped off to sleep on the nights when she had over-practiced. Like those weary half-dreams that buzzed and carried her out into their own whirling space.

A *Wunderkind* — a *Wunderkind* — a *Wunderkind.* The syllables would come out rolling in the deep German way, roar against her ears and then fall to a murmur. Along with the faces circling, swelling out in distortion, diminishing to pale blobs — Mister Bilderbach, Mrs. Bilderbach, Heime, Mister Lafkowitz. Around and around in a circle revolving to the guttural *Wunderkind.* Mister Bilderbach looming large in the middle of the circle, his face urging — with the others around him.

Phrases of music seesawing crazily. Notes she had been practicing falling over each other like a handful of marbles dropped downstairs. Bach, Debussy, Prokofieff, Brahms — timed grotesquely to the far off throb of her tired body and the buzzing circle.

Sometimes — when she had not worked more than three hours or had stayed out from high school — the dreams were not so confused. The music soared clearly in her mind and quick, precise little memories would come back — clear as the sissy 'Age of Innocence' picture Heime had given her after their joint concert was over.

A *Wunderkind* — a *Wunderkind.* That was what Mister Bilderbach had called her when, at twelve, she first came to him. Older pupils had repeated the word.

Not that he had ever said the word to her. 'Bienchen — ' (She had a plain American name but he never used it except when her mistakes were enormous.) 'Bienchen,' he would say, 'I know it must be terrible. Carrying around all the time a head that thick. Poor Bienchen —— '

Mister Bilderbach's father had been a Dutch violinist. His mother was from Prague. He had been born in this country and had spent his youth in Germany. So many times she wished she had not been born and brought up in just Cincinnati. How do you say *cheese* in German? Mister Bilderbach, what is Dutch for *I don't understand you?*

The first day she came to the studio. After she played the whole Second Hungarian Rhapsody from memory. The room graying with twilight. His face as he leaned over the piano.

'Now we begin all over,' he said that first day. 'It — playing music — is more than cleverness. If a twelve-year-old girl's fingers cover so many keys to a second — that means nothing.'

He tapped his broad chest and his forehead with his stubby hand. 'Here and here. You are old enough to understand that.' He lighted a cigarette and gently blew the first exhalation above her head. 'And work — work — work — . We will start now with these Bach Inventions and these little Schumann pieces.' His hands moved again — this time to jerk the cord of the lamp behind her and point to the music. 'I will show you how I wish this practiced. Listen carefully now.'

She had been at the piano for almost three hours and was very tired. His deep voice sounded as though it had been straying inside her for a long time. She wanted to reach out and touch his muscle-flexed finger that pointed out the phrases, wanted to feel the gleaming gold band ring and the strong hairy back of his hand.

She had lessons Tuesday after school and on Saturday afternoons. Often she stayed, when the Saturday lesson was finished, for dinner, and then spent the night and took the streetcar home the next morning. Mrs. Bilderbach liked her in her calm, almost dumb way. She was much different from her husband. She was quiet and fat and slow. When she wasn't in the kitchen, cooking the rich dishes that both of them loved, she seemed to spend all her time in their bed upstairs, reading magazines or just looking with a half-smile at nothing. When they had married in Germany she had been a *lieder* singer. She didn't sing anymore (she said it was her throat). When he would call her in from the kitchen to listen to a pupil she would always smile and say that it was *gut,* very *gut.*

When Frances was thirteen it came to her one day that the Bilderbachs had no children. It seemed strange. Once she had been back in the kitchen with Mrs. Bilderbach when he had come striding in from the studio, tense with anger at some pupil who had annoyed him. His wife stood stirring the thick soup until his hand groped out and rested on her shoulder. Then she turned—stood placid—while he folded his arms about her and buried his sharp face in the white, nerveless flesh of her neck. They stood that way without moving. And then his face jerked back suddenly, the anger diminished to a quiet inexpressiveness, and he had returned to the studio.

After she had started with Mister Bilderbach and didn't have time to see anything of the people at high school, Hemie had been the only friend of her own age. He was Mister Lafkowitz's pupil and would come with him to Mister Bilderbach's on evenings when she would be there. They would listen to their teachers' playing. And often they themselves went over chamber music together—Mozart sonatas or Bloch.

A *Wunderkind*—a *Wunderkind.*

Heime was a *Wunderkind.* He and she, then.

Heime had been playing the violin since he was four. He didn't have to go to school; Mister Lafkowitz's brother, who was crippled, used to teach him geometry and European history and French verbs in the afternoon. When he was thirteen he had as fine a technique as any violinist in Cincinnati — everyone said so. But playing the violin must be easier than the piano. She knew it must be.

Heime always seemed to smell of corduroy pants and the food he had eaten and rosin. Half the time, too, his hands were dirty around the knuckles and the cuffs of his shirts peeped out dingily from the sleeves of his sweater. She always watched his hands when he played — thin only at the joints with the hard little blobs of flesh bulging over the short-cut nails and the babyish-looking crease that showed so plainly in his bowing wrist.

In the dreams, as when she was awake, she could remember the concert only in a blur. She had not known it was unsuccessful for her until months after. True, the papers had praised Heime more than her. But he was much shorter than she. When they stood together on the stage he came only to her shoulders. And that made a difference with people, she knew. Also, there was the matter of the sonata they played together. The Bloch.

'No, no — I don't think that would be appropriate,' Mister Bilderbach had said when the Bloch was suggested to end the programme. 'Now that John Powell thing — the Sonate Virginianesque.'

She hadn't understood then; she wanted it to be the Bloch as much as Mister Lafkowitz and Hemie.

Mister Bilderbach had given in. Later, after the reviews had said she lacked the temperament for that type of music, after they called her playing thin and lacking in feeling, she felt cheated.

'That oie oie stuff,' said Mister Bilderbach, crackling the newspapers at her. 'Not for you, Bienchen. Leave all that to the Heimes and vitses and skys.'

A *Wunderkind*. No matter what the papers said, that was what he had called her.

Why was it Heime had done so much better at the concert than she? At school sometimes, when she was supposed to be watching someone do a geometry problem on the blackboard, the question would twist knife-like inside her. She would worry about it in bed, and even sometimes when she was supposed to be concentrating at the piano. It wasn't just the Bloch and her not being Jewish — not entirely. It wasn't that Heime didn't have to go to school and had begun his training so early, either. It was —— ?

Once she thought she knew.

'Play the Fantasia and Fugue,' Mister Bilderbach had demanded one evening a year ago — after he and Mister Lafkowitz had finished reading some music together.

The Bach, as she played, seemed to her well done. From the tail of her eye she could see the calm, pleased expression on Mister Bilderbach's face, see his hands rise climactically from the chair arms and then sink down loose and satisfied when the high points of the phrases had been passed successfully. She stood up from the piano when it was over, swallowing to loosen the bands that the music seemed to have drawn around her throat and chest. But —

'Frances —' Mister Lafkowitz had said then, suddenly, looking at her with his thin mouth curved and his eyes almost covered by their delicate lids. 'Do you know how many children Bach had?'

She turned to him, puzzled. 'A good many. Twenty some odd.'

'Well then —' The corners of his smile etched themselves gently in his pale face. 'He could not have been so cold — then.'

Mister Bilderbach was not pleased; his guttural effulgence of German words had *Kind* in it somewhere. Mister Lafkowitz raised his eyebrows. She had caught the point easily enough, but she felt no deception in keeping her face blank and immature because that was the way Mister Bilderbach wanted her to look.

Yet such things had nothing to do with it. Nothing very much, at least, for she would grow older. Mister Bilderbach understood that, and even Mister Lafkowitz had not meant just what he said.

In the dreams Mister Bilderbach's face loomed out and contracted in the center of the whirling circle. The lips surging softly, the veins in his temples insisting.

But sometimes, before she slept, there were such clear memories;

as when she pulled a hole in the heel of her stocking down, so that her shoe would hide it. 'Bienchen, Bienchen!' And bringing Mrs. Bilderbach's work basket in and showing her how it should be darned and not gathered together in a lumpy heap.

And the time she graduated from Junior High.

'What you wear?' asked Mrs. Bilderbach the Sunday morning at breakfast when she told them about how they had practiced to march into the auditorium.

'An evening dress my cousin had last year.'

'Ah — Bienchen!' he said, circling his warm coffee cup with his heavy hands, looking up at her with wrinkles around his laughing eyes. 'I bet I know what Bienchen wants — '

He insisted. He would not believe her when she explained that she honestly didn't care at all.

'Like this, Anna,' he said, pushing his napkin across the table and mincing to the other side of the room, swishing his hips, rolling up his eyes behind his horn-rimmed glasses.

The next Saturday afternoon, after her lessons, he took her to the department stores downtown. His thick fingers smoothed over the filmy nets and crackling taffetas that the saleswomen unwound from their bolts. He held colors to her face, cocking his head to one side, and selected pink. Shoes, he remembered too. He liked best some white kid pumps. They seemed a little like old ladies' shoes to her and the Red Cross label in the instep had a charity look. But it really didn't matter at all. When Mrs. Bilderbach began to cut out the dress and fit it to her with pins, he interrupted his lessons to stand by and suggest ruffles around the hips and neck and a fancy rosette on the shoulder. The music was coming along nicely then. Dresses and commencement and such made no difference.

Nothing mattered much except playing the music as it must be played, bringing out the thing that must be in her, practicing, practicing, playing so that Mister Bilderbach's face lost some of its urging look. Putting the thing into her music that Myra Hess had, and Yehudi Menuhin — even Heime!

What had begun to happen to her four months ago? The notes

began springing out with a glib, dead intonation. Adolescence, she thought. Some kids played with promise — and worked and worked until, like her, the least little thing would start them crying, and worn out with trying to get the thing across — the longing thing they felt — something queer began to happen — But not she! She was like Heime. She had to be. She ——

Once it was there for sure. And you didn't lose things like that. A *Wunderkind* . . . . A *Wunderkind* . . . . Of her he said it, rolling the words in the sure, deep German way. And in the dreams even deeper, more certain than ever. With his face looming out at her, and the longing phrases of music mixed in with the zooming, circling round, round, round — A *Wunderkind.* A *Wunderkind.* . . .

This afternoon Mister Bilderbach did not show Mister Lafkowitz to the front door, as he usually did. He stayed at the piano, softly pressing a solitary note. Listening, Frances watches the violinist wind his scarf about his pale throat.

'A good picture of Heime,' she said, picking up her music. 'I got a letter from him a couple of months ago — telling about hearing Schnabel and Huberman and about Carnegie Hall and things to eat at the Russian Tea Room.'

To put off going into the studio a moment longer she waited until Mister Lafkowitz was ready to leave and then stood behind him as he opened the door. The frosty cold outside cut into the room. It was growing late and the air was seeped with the pale yellow of winter twilight. When the door swung to on its hinges, the house seemel darker and more silent than ever before she had known it to be.

As she went into the studio Mister Bilderbach got up from the piano and silently watched her settle herself at the keyboard.

'Well, Bienchen,' he said, 'this afternoon we are going to begin all over. Start from scratch. Forget the last few months.'

He looked as though he were trying to act a part in a movie. His solid body swayed from toe to heel, he rubbed his hands together, and even smiled in a satisfied, movie way. Then suddenly he thrust this manner brusquely aside. His heavy shoulders slouched and he began to run through the stack of music she had brought in. 'The Bach — no, not yet,' he murmured. 'The Beethoven? Yes. the Variation Sonata. Opus. 26.'

The keys of the piano hemmed her in — stiff and white and dead-seeming.

'Wait a minute,' he said. He stood in the curve of the piano, elbows propped, and looked at her. 'Today I expect something from you. Now this sonata — it's the first Beethoven sonata you ever worked on. Every note is under control — technically — you have nothing to cope with but the music. Only music now. That's all you think about.'

He rustled through the pages of her volume until he found the place. Then he pulled his teaching chair halfway across the room, turned it around and seated himself, straddling the back with his legs.

For some reason, she knew, this position of his usually had a good effect on her performance. But today she felt that she would notice him from the corner of her eye and be disturbed. His back was stiffly tilted, his legs looked tense. The heavy volume before him seemed to balance dangerously on the chair back. 'Now we begin,' he said with a peremptory dart of his eyes in her direction.

Her hands rounded over the keys and then sank down. The first notes were too loud, the other phrases followed dryly.

Arrestingly his hand rose up from the score. 'Wait! Think a minute what you're playing. How is this beginning marked?'

'*An-andante.*'

'All right. Don't drag it into an *adagio* then. And play deeply into the keys. Don't snatch it off shallowly that way. A graceful, deep-toned *andante* —'

She tried again. Her hands seemed separate from the music that was in her.

'Listen,' he interrupted. 'Which of these variations dominates the whole?'

'The dirge,' she answered.

'Then prepare for that. This is an *andante* — but it's not salon stuff as you just played it. Start out softly, *piano,* and make it swell out just before the arpeggio. Make it warm and dramatic. And down here—where it's marked *dolce* make the counter melody sing out. You know all that. We've gone over all that side of it before. Now play it. Feel it as Beethoven wrote it down. Feel that tragedy and restraint.'

She could not stop looking at his hands. They seemed to rest tentatively on the music, ready to fly up as a stop signal as soon as she would begin, the gleaming flash of his ring calling her to halt. 'Mister Bilderbach—maybe if I—if you let me play on through the first variation without stopping I could do better.'

'I won't interrupt,' he said.

Her pale face leaned over too close to the keys. She played through the first part, and, obeying a nod from him, began the second. There were no flaws that jarred on her, but the phrases shaped from her fingers before she had put into them the meaning that she felt.

When she had finished he looked up from the music and began to speak with dull bluntness: 'I hardly heard those harmonic fillings in the right hand. And incidentally, this part was supposed to take on intensity, develop the foreshadowings that were supposed to be inherent in the first part. Go on with the next one, though.'

She wanted to start it with subdued viciousness and progress to a feeling of deep, swollen sorrow. Her mind told her that. But her hands seemed to gum in the keys like limp macaroni and she could not imagine the music as it should be.

When the last note had stopped vibrating, he closed the book and deliberately got up from the chair. He was moving his lower jaw from side to side—and between his open lips she could glimpse the pink healthy lane to his throat and his strong, smoke-yellowed teeth. He laid the Beethoven gingerly on top of the rest of her music and propped his elbows on the smooth, black piano top once more. 'No,' he said simply, looking at her.

Her mouth began to quiver. 'I can't help it. I——'

Suddenly he strained his lips into a smile. 'Listen, Bienchen,' he began in a new, forced voice. 'You still play the Harmonious

Blacksmith, don't you? I told you not to drop it from your repertoire.'

'Yes,' she said. 'I practice it now and then.'

His voice was the one he used for children. 'It was among the first things we worked on together — remember. So strongly you used to play it — like a real blacksmith's daughter. You see, Bienchen, I know you so well — as if you were my own girl. I know what you have — I've heard you play so many things beautifully. You used to —— '

He stopped in confusion and inhaled from his pulpy stub of cigarette. The smoke drowsed out from his pink lips and clung in a gray mist around her lank hair and childish forehead.

'Make it happy and simple,' he said, switching on the lamp behind her and stepping back from the piano.

For a moment he stood just inside the bright circle the light made. Then impulsively he squatted down to the floor. 'Vigorous,' he said.

She could not stop looking at him, sitting on one heel with the other foot resting squarely before him for balance, the muscles of his strong thighs straining under the cloth of his trousers, his back straight, his elbows staunchly propped on his knees. 'Simply now,' he repeated with a gesture of his fleshy hands. 'Think of the blacksmith — working out in the sunshine all day. Working easily and undisturbed.'

She could not look down at the piano. The light brightened the hairs on the backs of his outspread hands, made the lenses of his glasses glitter.

'All of it,' he urged. 'Now!'

She felt that the marrows of her bones were hollow and there was no blood left in her. Her heart that had been springing against her chest all afternoon felt suddenly dead. She saw it gray and limp and shriveled at the edges like an oyster.

His face seemed to throb out in space before her, come closer with the lurching motion in the veins of his temples. In retreat, she looked down at the piano. Her lips shook like jelly and a surge of noiseless tears made the white keys blur in a watery line.

'I can't,' she whispered. 'I don't know why, but I just can't—can't any more.'

His tense body slackened and, holding his hand to his side, he pulled himself up. She clutched her music and hurried past him.

Her coat. The mittens and galoshes. The schoolbooks and the satchel he had given her on her birthday. All from the silent room that was hers. Quickly—before he would have to speak.

As she passed through the vestibule she could not help but see his hands—held out from his body that leaned against the studio door, relaxed and purposeless. The door shut to firmly. Dragging her books and satchel she stumbled down the stone steps, turned in the wrong direction, and hurried down the street that had become confused with noise and bicycles and the games of other children.

The Jockey

The Jockey

THE JOCKEY came to the doorway of the dining room, then after a moment stepped to one side and stood motionless, with his back to the wall. The room was crowded, as this was the third day of the season and all the hotels in the town were full. In the dining room bouquets of August roses scattered their petals on the white table linen and from the adjoining bar came a warm, drunken wash of voices. The jockey waited with his back to the wall and scrutinized the room with pinched, crêpy eyes. He examined the room until at last his eyes reached a table in a corner diagonally across from him, at which three men were sitting. As he watched, the jockey raised his chin and tilted his head back to one side, his dwarfted body grew rigid, and his hands stiffened so that the fingers curled inward like gray claws. Tense against the wall of the dining room, he watched and waited in this way.

He was wearing a suit of green Chinese silk that evening, tailored precisely and the size of a costume outfit for a child. The shirt was yellow, the tie striped with pastel colors. He had no hat with him and wore his hair brushed down in a stiff, wet bang on his forehead. His face was drawn, ageless, and gray. There were shadowed hollows at his temples and his mouth was set in a wiry smile. After a time he was aware that he had been seen by one of the three men he had been watching. But the jockey did not nod; he only raised his chin still higher and hooked the thumb of his tense hand in the pocket of his coat.

The three men at the corner table were a trainer, a bookie, and a rich man. The trainer was Sylvester — a large, loosely built fellow with a flushed nose and slow blue eyes. The bookie was Simmons. The rich man was the owner of a horse named Seltzer, which the jockey had ridden that afternoon. The three of them drank whiskey with soda, and a white-coated waiter had just brought on the main course of the dinner.

It was Sylvester who first saw the jockey. He looked away quickly, put down his whiskey glass, and nervously mashed the tip of his red nose with his thumb. 'It's Bitsy Barlow,' he said. 'Standing over there across the room. Just watching us.'

'Oh, the jockey,' said the rich man. He was facing the wall and he half turned his head to look behind him. 'Ask him over.'

'God no,' Sylvester said.

'He's crazy,' Simmons said. The bookie's voice was flat and without inflection. He had the face of a born gambler, carefully adjusted, the expression a permanent deadlock between fear and greed.

'Well, I wouldn't call him that exactly,' said Sylvester. 'I've known him a long time. He was O.K. until about six months ago. But if he goes on like this, I can't see him lasting another year. I just can't.'

'It was what happened in Miami,' said Simmons.

'What?' asked the rich man.

Sylvester glanced across the room at the jockey and wet the corner of his mouth with his red, fleshy tongue. 'A accident. A kid got hurt on the track. Broke a leg and a hip. He was a particular pal of Bitsy's. A Irish kid. Not a bad rider, either.'

'That's a pity,' said the rich man.

'Yeah. They were particular friends,' Sylvester said. 'You would always find him up in Bitsy's hotel room. They would be playing rummy or else lying on the floor reading the sports page together.'

'Well, those things happen,' said the rich man.

Simmons cut into his beefsteak. He held his fork prongs downward on the plate and carefully piled on muchrooms with the blade of his knife. 'He's crazy,' he repeated. 'He gives me the creeps.'

All the tables in the dining room were occupied. There was a party at the banquet table in the center, and green-white August moths had found their way in from the night and fluttered about the clear candle flames. Two girls wearing flannel slacks and blazers walked arm in arm across the room into the bar. From the main street outside came the echoes of holiday hysteria.

'They claim that in August Saratoga is the wealthiest town per capita in the world.' Silvester turned to the rich man. 'What do you think?'

'I wouldn't know,' said the rich man. 'It may very well be so.'

Daintily. Simmons wiped his greasy mouth with the tip of his forefinger. 'How about Hollywood? And Wall Street——'

'Wait,' said Sylvester. 'He's decided to come over here.'

The jockey had left the wall and was approaching the table in the corner. He walked with a prim strut, swinging out his legs in a half-circle with each step, his heels biting smartly into the red velvet carpet on the floor. On the way over he brushed against the elbow of a fat woman in white satin at the banquet table; he stepped back and bowed with dandified courtesy, his eyes quite closed. When he had crossed the room he drew up a chair and sat at a corner of the table, between Sylvester and the rich man, without a nod of greeting or a change in his set, gray face.

'Had dinner?' Sylvester asked.

'Some people might call it that.' The jockey's voice was high, bitter, clear.

Sylvester put his knife and fork down carefully on his plate. The rich man shifted his position, turning sidewise in his chair and crossing his legs. He was dressed in twill riding pants, unpolished boots, and a shabby brown jacket — this was his outfit day and night in the racing season, although he was never seen on a horse. Simmons went on with his dinner.

'Like a spot of seltzer water?' asked Sylvester. 'Or something like that?'

The jockey didn't answer. He drew a gold cigarette case from his pocket and snapped it open. Inside were a few cigarettes and a tiny gold penknife. He used the knife to cut a cigarette in half. When he had lighted his smoke he held up his hand to a waiter passing by the table. 'Kentucky bourbon, please.'

'Now, listen, Kid,' said Sylvester.

'Don't Kid me.'

'Be reasonable. You know you got to behave reasonable.'

The jockey drew up the left corner of his mouth in a stiff jeer.

His eyes lowered to the food spread out on the table, but instantly he looked up again. Before the rich man was a fish casserole, baked in a cream sauce and garnished with parsley. Sylvester had ordered eggs Benedict. There was asparagus, fresh buttered corn, and a side dish of wet black olives. A plate of French-fried potatoes was in the corner of the table before the jockey. He didn't look at the food again, but kept his pinched eyes on the centerpiece of full-blown lavender roses. 'I don't suppose you remember a certain person by the name of McGuire,' he said.

'Now, listen,' said Sylvester.

The waiter brought the whiskey, and the jockey sat fondling the glass with his small, strong, callused hands. On his wrist was a gold link bracelet that clinked against the table edge. After turning the glass between his palms, the jockey suddenly drank the whiskey neat in two hard swallows. He set down the glass sharply. 'No, I don't suppose your memory is that long and extensive,' he said.

'Sure enough, Bitsy,' said Sylvester. 'What makes you act like this? You hear from the kid today?'

'I received a letter,' the jockey said. 'The certain person we were speaking about was taken out from the cast on Wednesday. One leg is two inches shorter than the other one. That's all.'

Sylvester clucked his tongue and shook his head. 'I realize how you feel.'

'Do you?' The jockey was looking at the dishes on the table. His gaze passed from the fish casserole to the corn, and finally fixed on the plate of fried potatoes. His face tightened and quickly he looked up again. A rose shattered and he picked up one of the petals, bruised it between his thumb and forefinger, and put it in his mouth.

'Well, those things happen,' said the rich man.

The trainer and the bookie had finished eating, but there was food left on the serving dishes before their plates. The rich man dipped his buttery fingers in his water glass and wiped them with his napkin.

'Well,' said the jockey. 'Doesn't somebody want me to pass them something? Or maybe perhaps you desire to reorder. Another hunk of beefsteak, gentlemen, or —— '

'Please,' said Sylvester. 'Be reasonable. Why don't you go on upstairs?'

'Yes, why don't I?' the jockey said.

His prim voice had risen higher and there was about it the sharp whine of hysteria.

'Why don't I go up to my god-damn room and walk around and write some letters and go to bed like a good boy? Why don't I just —— ' He pushed his chair back and got up. 'Oh, foo,' he said. 'Foo to you. I want a drink.'

'All I can say is it's your funeral,' said Sylvester. 'You know what it does to you. You know well enough.'

The jockey crossed the dining room and went into the bar. He ordered a Manhattan, and Sylvester watched him stand with his heels pressed tight together, his body hard as a lead soldier's, holding his little finger out from the cocktail glass and sipping the drink slowly.

'He's crazy,' said Simmons. 'Like I said.'

Sylvester turned to the rich man. 'If he eats a lamb chop, you can see the shape of it in his stomach a hour afterward. He can't sweat things out of him any more. He's a hundred and twelve and a half. He's gained three pounds since we left Miami.'

'A jockey shouldn't drink,' said the rich man.

'The food don't satisfy him like it used to and he can't sweat it out. If he eats a lamb chop, you can watch it tooching out in his stomach and it don't go down.'

The jockey finished his Manhattan. He swallowed, crushed the cherry in the bottom of the glass with his thumb, then pushed the glass away from him. The two girls in blazers were standing at his left, their faces turned toward each other, and at the other end of the bar two touts had started an argument about which was the highest mountain in the world. Everyone was with somebody else; there was no other person drinking alone that night. The jockey paid with a brand-new fifty-dollar bill and didn't count the change.

He walked back to the dining room and to the table at which the three men were sitting, but he did not sit down. 'No, I wouldn't presume to think your memory is that extensive,' he said. He was so small that the edge of the table top reached almost to his belt, and when he gripped the corner with his wiry hands he didn't have to stoop. 'No, you're too busy gobbling up dinners in dining rooms. You're too——'

'Honestly,' begged Sylvester. 'You got to behave reasonable.'

'Reasonable! Reasonable!' The jockey's gray face quivered, then set in a mean, frozen grin. He shook the table so that the plates rattled, and for a moment it seemed that he would push it over. But suddenly he stopped. His hand reached out toward the plate nearest to him and deliberately he put a few of the French-fried potatoes in his mouth. He chewed slowly, his upper lip raised, then he turned and spat out the pulpy mouthful on the smooth red carpet which covered the floor. 'Libertines,' he said, and his voice was thin and broken. He rolled the word in his mouth, as though it had a flavor and a substance that gratified him. 'You libertines,' he said again, and turned and walked with his rigid swagger out of the dining room.

Sylvester shrugged one of his loose, heavy shoulders. The rich man sopped up some water that had been spilled on the tablecloth, and they didn't speak until the waiter came to clear away.

Madame Zilensky and the King of Finland

Madame Zilensky and the King of Finland

To Mr. Brook, the head of the music department at Ryder College, was due all the credit for getting Madame Zilensky on the faculty. The college considered itself fortunate; her reputation was impressive, both as a composer and as a pedagogue. Mr. Brook took on himself the responsibility of finding a house for Madame Zilensky, a comfortable place with a garden, which was convenient to the college and next to the apartment house where he himself lived.

No one in Westbridge had known Madame Zilensky before she came. Mr. Brook had seen her pictures in musical journals, and once he had written to her about the authenticity of a certain Buxtehude manuscript. Also, when it was being settled that she was to join the faculty, they had exchanged a few cables and letters on practical affairs. She wrote in a clear, square hand, and the only thing out of the ordinary in these letters was the fact that they contained an occasional reference to objects and persons altogether unknown to Mr. Brook, such as "the yellow cat in Lisbon" or "poor Heinrich." These lapses Mr. Brook put down to the confusion of getting herself and her family out of Europe.

Mr. Brook was a somewhat pastel person; years of Mozart minuets, of explanations about diminished sevenths and minor triads, had given him a watchful vocational patience. For the most part, he kept to himself. He loathed academic fiddle-faddle and committees. Years before, when the music department had decided to gang together and spend the summer in Salzburg, Mr. Brook sneaked out of the arrangement at the last moment and took a solitary trip to Peru. He had a few eccentricities himself and was tolerant of the peculiarities of others; indeed, he rather relished the ridiculous. Often, when confronted with some grave and incongruous situation, he would feel a little inside tickle, which stiffened his long, mild face and sharpened the light in his gray eyes.

Mr. Brook met Madame Zilensky at the Westbridge station a week before the beginning of the fall semester. He recognized her instantly. She was a tall, straight woman with a pale and haggard face. Her eyes were deeply shadowed and she wore her dark, ragged hair pushed back from her forehead. She had large, delicate hands, which were very grubby. About her person as a whole there was something noble and abstract that made Mr. Brook draw back for a moment and stand nervously undoing his cuff links. In spite of her clothes — a long, black skirt and a broken-down old leather jacket — she made an impression of vague elegance. With Madame Zilensky were three children, boys between the ages of ten and six, all blond, blank-eyed, and beautiful. There was one other person, an old woman who turned out later to be the Finnish servant.

This was the group he found at the station. The only luggage they had with them was two immense boxes of manuscripts, the rest of their paraphernalia having been forgotten in the station at Springfield when they changed trains. That is the sort of thing that can happen to anyone. When Mr. Brook got them all into a taxi, he thought the worst difficulties were over, but Madame Zilensky suddenly tried to scramble over his knees and get out of the door.

'My God!' she said. 'I left my — how do you say? — my tick-tick-tick ——'

'Your watch?' asked Mr. Brook.

'Oh no!' she said vehemently. 'You know, my tick-tick-tick,' and she waved her forefinger from side to side, pendulum fashion.

'Tick-tick,' said Mr. Brook, putting his hands to his forehead and closing his eyes. 'Could you possibly mean a metronome?'

'Yes! Yes! I think I must have lost it there where we changed trains.'

Mr. Brook managed to quiet her. He even said, with a kind of dazed gallantry, that he would get her another one the next day. But at the time he was bound to admit to himself that there was something curious about this panic over a metronome when there was all the rest of the lost luggage to consider.

The Zelinsky ménage moved into the house next door, and on the surface everything was all right. The boys were quiet children. Their names were Sigmund, Boris, and Sammy. They were always together and they followed each other around Indian file, Sigmund usually the first. Among themselves they spoke a desperate-sounding family Esperanto made up of Russian, French, Finnish, German, and English; when other people were around, they were strangely silent. It was not any one thing that the Zilenskys did or said that made Mr. Brook uneasy. There were just little incidents. For example, something about the Zilensky children subconsciously bothered him when they were in a house, and finally he realized that what troubled him was the fact that the Zilensky boys never walked on a rug; they skirted it single file on the bare floor, and if a room was carpeted, they stood in the doorway and did not go inside. Another thing was this: Weeks passed and Madame Zilensky seemed to make no effort to get settled or to furnish the house with anything more than a table and some beds. The front door was left open day and night, and soon the house began to take on a queer, bleak look like that of a place abandoned for years.

The college had every reason to be satisfied with Madame Zilensky. She taught with a fierce insistence. She could become deeply indignant if some Mary Owens or Bernadine Smith would not clean up her Scarlatti trills. She got hold of four pianos for her college studio and set four dazed students to playing Bach fugues together. The racket that came from her end of the department was extraordinary, but Madame Zilensky did not seem to have a nerve in her, and if pure will and effort can get over a musical idea, then Ryder College could not have done better. At night Madame Zilensky worked on her twelfth symphony. She seemed never to sleep; no matter what time of night Mr. Brook happened to look out of his sitting-room window, the light in her studio was always on. No, it was not because of any professional consideration that Mr. Brook became so dubious.

It was in late October when he felt for the first time that something was unmistakably wrong. He had lunched with Madame Zilensky and had enjoyed himself, as she had given him a very detailed account of an African safari she had made in 1928. Later in the afternoon she stopped in at his office and stood rather abstractly in the doorway.

Mr. Brook looked up from his desk and asked, 'Is there anything you want?'

'No, thank you,' said Madame Zilensky. She had a low, beautiful, sombre voice. 'I was only just wondering. You recall the metronome. Do you think perhaps that I might have left it with that French?'

'Who?' asked Mr. Brook.

'Why, that French I was married to,' she answered.

'Frenchman,' Mr. Brook said mildly. He tried to imagine the husband of Madame Zilensky, but his mind refused. He muttered half to himself, 'The father of the children.'

'But no,' said Madame Zilensky with decision. 'The father of Sammy.'

Mr. Brook had a swift prescience. His deepest instincts warned him to say nothing further. Still, his respect for order, his conscience, demanded that he ask, 'And the father of the other two?'

Madame Zilensky put her hand to the back of her head and ruffled up her short, cropped hair. Her face was dreamy, and for several moments she did not answer. Then she said gently, 'Boris is of a Pole who played the picolo.'

'And Sigmund?' he asked. Mr. Brook looked over his orderly desk, with the stack of corrected papers, the three sharpened pencils, the ivory-elephant paperweight. When he glanced up at Madame Zilensky, she was obviously thinking hard. She gazed around at the corners of the room, her brows lowered and her jaw moving from side to side. At last she said, 'We were discussing the father of Sigmund?'

'Why, no,' said Mr. Brook. 'There is no need to do that.'

Madame Zilensky answered in a voice both dignified and final. 'He was a fellow-countryman.'

Mr. Brook really did not care one way or the other. He had no prejudices; people could marry seventeen times and have Chinese children so far as he was concerned. But there was something about this conversation with Madame Zilensky that bothered him. Suddenly he understood. The children didn't look at all like Madame Zilensky, but they looked exactly like each other, and as they all had different fathers, Mr. Brook thought the resemblance astonishing.

But Madame Zilensky had finished with the subject. She zipped up her leather jacket and turned away.

'That is exactly where I left it,' she said, with a quick nod. '*Chez* that French.'

Affairs in the music department were running smoothly. Mr. Brook did not have any serious embarrassments to deal with, such as the harp teacher last year who had finally eloped with a garage mechanic. There was only this nagging apprehension about Madame Zilensky. He could not make out what was wrong in his relations with her or why his feelings were so mixed. To begin with, she was a great globe-trotter, and her conversations were incongruously seasoned with references to far-fetched places. She would go along for days without opening her mouth, prowling through the corridor with her hands in the pockets of her jacket and her face locked in meditation. Then suddenly she would buttonhole Mr. Brook and launch out on a long, volatile monologue, her eyes reckless and bright and her voice warm with eagerness. She would talk about anything or nothing at all. Yet, without exception, there was something queer, in a slanted sort of way, about every episode she ever mentioned. If she spoke of taking Sammy to the barbershop, the impression she created was just as foreign as if she were telling of an afternoon in Bagdad. Mr. Brook could not make it out.

The truth came to him very suddenly, and the truth made everything perfectly clear, or at least clarified the situation. Mr. Brook had come home early and lighted a fire in the little grate in his sitting room. He felt comfortable and at peace that evening. He sat before the fire in his stocking feet, with a volume of William Blake on the table by his side, and he had poured himself a half-glass of apricot brandy. At ten o'clock he was drowsing cozily before the fire, his mind full of cloudy phrases of Mahler and floating half-thoughts. Then all at once, out of this delicate stupor, four words came to his mind: 'The King of Finland.' The words seemed familiar, but for the first moment he could not place them. Then all at once he tracked them down. He had been walking across the campus that afternoon when Madame Zilensky stopped him and began some preposterous rigmarole, to which he had only half listened; he was thinking about the stack of canons turned in by his counterpoint class. Now the words, the inflections of her voice, came back to him with insidious exactitude. Madame Zilensky had started off with the following remark: 'One day, when I was standing in front of a *pâtisserie,* the King of Finland came by in a sled.'

Mr. Brook jerked himself up straight in his chair and put down his glass of brandy. The woman was a pathological liar. Almost every word she uttered outside of class was an untruth. If she worked all night, she would go out of her way to tell you she spent the evening at the cinema. If she ate lunch at the Old Tavern, she would be sure to mention that she had lunched with her children at home. The woman was simply a pathological liar, and that accounted for everything.

Mr. Brook cracked his knuckles and got up from his chair. His first reaction was one of exasperation. That day after day Madame Zilensky would have the gall to sit there in his office and deluge him with her outrageous falsehoods! Mr. Brook was intensely provoked. He walked up and down the room, then he went into his kitchenette and made himself a sardine sandwich.

An hour later, as he sat before the fire, his irritation had changed to a scholarly and thoughtful wonder. What he must do, he told himself, was to regard the whole situation impersonally and look on Madame Zilensky as a doctor looks on a sick patient. Her lies were of the guileless sort. She did not dissimulate with any intention to deceive, and the untruths she told were never used to any possible advantage. That was the maddening thing; there was simply no motive behind it all.

Mr. Brook finished off the rest of the brandy. And slowly, when it was almost midnight, a further understanding came to him. The reason for the lies of Madame Zilensky was painful and plain. All her life long Madame Zilensky had worked — at the piano, teaching, and writing those beautiful and immense twelve symphonies. Day and night she had drudged and struggled and thrown her soul into her work, and there was not much of her left over for anything else. Being human, she suffered from this lack and did what she could to make up for it. If she passed the evening bent over a table in the library and later declared that she had spent that time playing cards, it was as though she had managed to do both those things. Through the lies, she lived vicariously. The lies doubled the little of her existence that was left over from work and augmented the little rag end of her personal life.

Mr. Brook looked into the fire, and the face of Madame Zilensky was in his mind — a severe face, with dark, weary eyes and delicately disciplined mouth. He was conscious of a warmth in his chest, and a feeling of pity, protectiveness, and dreadful understanding. For a while he was in a state of lovely confusion.

Later on he brushed his teeth and got into his pajamas. He must be practical. What did this clear up? That French, the Pole with the piccolo, Bagdad? And the children, Sigmund, Boris, and Sammy — who were they? Were they really her children after all, or had she simply rounded them up from somewhere? Mr. Brook polished his spectacles and put them on the table by his bed. He must come to an immediate understanding with her. Otherwise, there would exist in the department a situation which could become most problematical. It was two o'clock. He glanced out of his window and saw that the light in Madame Zilensky's workroom was still on. Mr. Brook got into bed, made terrible faces in the dark, and tried to plan what he would say next day.

Mr. Brook was in his office by eight o'clock. He sat hunched up behind his desk, ready to trap Madame Zilensky as she passed down the corridor. He did not have to wait long, and as soon as he heard her footsteps he called out her name.

Madame Zilensky stood in the doorway. She looked vague and jaded. 'How are you? I had such a fine night's rest,' she said.

'Pray be seated, if you please,' said Mr. Brook. 'I would like a word with you.'

Madame Zilensky put aside her portfolio and leaned back wearily in the armchair across from him. 'Yes?' she asked.

'Yesterday you spoke to me as I was walking across the campus,' he said slowly. 'And if I am not mistaken, I believe you said something about a pastry shop and the King of Finland. Is that correct?'

Madame Zilensky turned her head to one side and stared retrospectively at a corner of the window sill.

'Something about a pastry shop,' he repeated.

Her tired face brightened. 'But of course," she said eagerly. 'I told you about the time I was standing in front of this shop and the King of Finland——'

'Madame Zilensky!' Mr. Brook cried. 'There *is* no King of Finland.'

Madame Zilensky looked absolutely blank. Then, after an instant, she started off again. 'I was standing in front of Bjarne's *pâtisserie* when I turned away from the cakes and suddenly saw the King of Finland——'

'Madame Zilensky, I just told you that there is no King of Finland.'

'In Helsingfors,' she started off again desperately, and again he let her get as far as the King, and then no further.

'Finland is a democracy,' he said. 'You could not possibly have seen the King of Finland. Therefore, what you have just said is an untruth. A pure untruth.'

Never afterward could Mr. Brook forget the face of Madame Zilensky at that moment. In her eyes there was astonishment, dismay, and a sort of cornered horror. She had the look of one who watches his whole interior world split open and disintegrate.

'It is a pity,' said Mr. Brook with real sympathy.

But Madame Zilensky pulled herself together. She raised her chin and said coldly, 'I am a Finn.'

'That I do not question,' answered Mr. Brook. On second thought, he did question it a little.

'I was born in Finland and I am a Finnish citizen.'

'That may very well be,' said Mr. Brook in a rising voice.

'In the war,' she continued passionately, 'I rode a motorcycle and was a messenger.'

'Your patriotism does not enter into it.'

'Just because I am getting out the first papers——'

'Madame Zilensky!' said Mr. Brook. His hands grasped the edge of the desk. 'That is only an irrelevant issue. The point is that you maintained and testified that you saw—that you saw——' But he could not finish. Her face stopped him. She was deadly pale and there were shadows around her mouth. Her eyes were wide open, doomed, and proud. And Mr. Brook felt suddenly like a murderer. A great commotion of feelings—understanding, remorse, and unreasonable love—made him cover his face with his hands. He could not speak until this agitation in his insides quieted down, and then he said very faintly, 'Yes. Of course. The King of Finland. And was he nice?'

An hour later, Mr. Brook sat looking out of the window of his office. The trees along the quiet Westbridge street were almost bare, and the gray buildings of the college had a calm, sad look. As he idly took in the familiar scene, he noticed the Drakes' old Airedale waddling along down the street. It was a thing he had watched a hundred times before, so what was it that struck him as strange? Then he realized with a kind of cold surprise that the old dog was running along backward. Mr. Brook watched the Airedale until he was out of sight, then resumed his work on the canons which had been turned in by the class in counterpoint.

The Sojourner

The Sojourner

THE TWILIGHT BORDER between sleep and waking was a Roman one this morning: splashing fountains and arched, narrow streets, the golden lavish city of blossoms and age-soft stone. Sometimes in this semi-consciousness he sojourned again in Paris, or war German rubble, or Swiss skiing and a snow hotel. Sometimes, also, in a fallow Georgia field at hunting dawn. Rome it was this morning in the yearless region of dreams.

John Ferris awoke in a room in a New York hotel. He had the feeling that something unpleasant was awaiting him — what it was, he did not know. The feeling, submerged by matinal necessities, lingered even after he had dressed and gone downstairs. It was a cloudless autumn day and the pale sunlight sliced between the pastel skyscrapers. Ferris went into the next-door drugstore and sat at the end booth next to the window glass that overlooked the sidewalk. He ordered an American breakfast with scrambled eggs and sausage.

Ferris had come from Paris to his father's funeral which had taken place the week before in his home town in Georgia. The shock of death had made him aware of youth already passed. His hair was receding and the veins in his now naked temples were pulsing and prominent and his body was spare except for an incipient belly bulge. Ferris had loved his father and the bond between them had once been extraordinarily close — but the years had somehow unraveled this filial devotion; the death, expected for a long time, had left him with an unforseen dismay. He had stayed as long as possible to be near his mother and brothers at home. His plane for Paris was to leave the next morning.

Ferris pulled out his address book to verify a number. He turned the pages with growing attentiveness. Names and addresses from New York, the capitals of Europe, a few faint ones from his home state in the South. Faded, printed names, sprawled drunken ones. Betty Wills: a random love, married now. Charlie Williams: wounded in the Hürtgen Forest, unheard of since. Grand old Williams — did he live or die? Don Walker: a B.T.O. in television, getting rich. Henry Green: hit the skids after the war, in a sanitarium now, they say. Cozie Hall: he had heard that she was dead. Heedless, laughing Cozie — it was strange to think that she too, silly girl, could die. As Ferris closed the address book, he suffered a sense of hazard, transience, almost of fear.

It was then that his body jerked suddenly. He was staring out of the window when there, on the sidewalk, passing by, was his ex-wife. Elizabeth passed quite close to him, walking slowly. He could not understand the wild quiver of his heart, nor the following sense of recklessness and grace that lingered after she was gone.

Quickly Ferris paid his check and rushed out to the sidewalk. Elizabeth stood on the corner waiting to cross Fifth Avenue. He hurried toward her meaning to speak, but the lights changed and she crossed the street before he reached her. Ferris followed. On the other side he could easily have overtaken her, but he found himself lagging unaccountably. Her fair brown hair was plainly rolled, and as he watched her Ferris recalled that once his father had remarked that Elizabeth had a 'beautiful carriage.' She turned at the next corner and Ferris followed, although by now his intention to overtake her had disappeared. Ferris questioned the bodily disturbance that the sight of Elizabeth aroused in him, the dampness of his hands, the hard heartstrokes.

It was eight years since Ferris had last seen his ex-wife. He knew that long ago she had married again. And there were children. During recent years he had seldom thought of her. But at first, after the divorce, the loss had almost destroyed him. Then after the anodyne of time, he had loved again, and then again. Jeannine, she was now. Certainly his love for his ex-wife was long since past. So why the unhinged body, the shaken mind? He knew only that his clouded heart was oddly dissonant with the sunny, candid autumn day. Ferris wheeled suddenly and, walking with long strides, almost running, hurried back to the hotel.

Ferris poured himself a drink, although it was not yet eleven o'clock. He sprawled out in an armchair like a man exhausted, nursing his glass of bourbon and water. He had a full day ahead of him as he was leaving by plane the next morning for Paris. He checked over his obligations: take luggage to Air France, lunch with his boss, buy shoes and an overcoat. And something— wasn't there something else? Ferris finished his drink and opened the telephone directory.

His decision to call his ex-wife was impulsive. The number was under Bailey, the husband's name, and he called before he had much time for self-debate. He and Elizabeth had exchanged cards at Christmastime, and Ferris had sent a carving set when he received the announcement of her wedding. There was no reason *not* to call. But as he waited, listening to the ring at the other end, misgiving fretted him.

Elizabeth answered; her familiar voice was a fresh shock to him. Twice he had to repeat his name, but when he was identified, she sounded glad. He explained he was only in town for that day. They had a theater engagement, she said—but she wondered if he would come by for an early dinner. Ferris said he would be delighted.

As he went from one engagement to another, he was still bothered at odd moments by the feeling that something necessary was forgotten. Ferris bathed and changed in the late afternoon, often thinking about Jeannine: he would be with her the following night. 'Jeannine,' he would say, 'I happened to run into my ex-wife when I was in New York. Had dinner with her. And her husband, of course. It was strange seeing her after all these years.'

Elizabeth lived in the East Fifties, and as Ferris taxied uptown he glimpsed at intersections the lingering sunset, but by the time he reached his destination it was already autumn dark. The place was a building with a marquee and a doorman, and the apartment was on the seventh floor.

'Come in, Mr. Ferris.'

Braced for Elizabeth or even the unimagined husband, Ferris

was astonished by the freckled red-haired child; he had known of the children, but his mind had failed somehow to acknowledge them. Surprise made him step back awkwardly.

'This is our apartment,' the child said politely. 'Aren't you Mr. Ferris? I'm Billy. Come in.'

In the living room beyond the hall, the husband provided another surprise; he too had not been acknowledged emotionally. Bailey was a lumbering red-haired man with a deliberate manner. He rose and extended a welcoming hand.

'I'm Bill Bailey. Glad to see you. Elizabeth will be in, in a minute. She's finishing dressing.'

The last words struck a gliding series of vibrations, memories of the other years. Fair Elizabeth, rosy and naked before her bath. Half-dressed before the mirror of her dressing table, brushing her fine, chestnut hair. Sweet, casual intimacy, the soft-fleshed loveliness indisputably possessed. Ferris shrank from the unbidden memories and compelled himself to meet Bill Bailey's gaze.

"Billy, will you please bring that tray of drinks from the kitchen table?'

The child obeyed promptly, and when he was gone Ferris remarked conversationally, 'Fine boy you have there.'

'We think so.'

Flat silence until the child returned with a tray of glasses and a cocktail shaker of Martinis. With the priming drinks they pumped up conversation: Russia, they spoke of, and the New York rain-making, and the apartment situation in Manhattan and Paris.

'Mr. Ferris is flying all the way across the ocean tomorrow,' Bailey said to the little boy who was perched on the arm of his chair, quiet and well behaved. 'I bet you would like to be a stowaway in his suitcase.'

Billy pushed back his limp bangs. 'I want to fly in an airplane and be a newspaperman like Mr. Ferris.' He added with sudden assurance, 'That's what I would like to do when I am big.'

Bailey said, 'I thought you wanted to be a doctor.'

'I do!' said Billy. 'I would like to be both. I want to be a atom-bomb scientist too.'

Elizabeth came in carrying in her arms a baby girl.

'Oh, John!' she said. She settled the baby in the father's lap. 'It's grand to see you. I'm awfully glad you could come.'

The little girl sat demurely on Bailey's knees. She wore a pale pink crepe de Chine frock, smocked around the yoke with rose, and a matching silk hair ribbon tying back her pale soft curls. Her skin was summer tanned and her brown eyes flecked with gold and laughing. When she reached up and fingered her father's horn-rimmed glasses, he took them off and let her look through them a moment. 'How's my old Candy?'

Elizabeth was very beautiful, more beautiful perhaps than he had ever realized. Her straight clean hair was shining. Her face was softer, glowing and serene. It was a madonna loveliness, dependent on the family ambiance.

'You've hardly changed at all,' Elizabeth said, 'but it has been a long time.'

'Eight years.' His hand touched his thinning hair self-consciously while further amenities were exchanged.

Ferris felt himself suddenly a spectator — an interloper among these Baileys. Why had he come? He suffered. His own life seemed so solitary, a fragile column supporting nothing amidst the wreckage of the years. He felt he could not bear much longer to stay in the family room.

He glanced at his watch. 'You're going to the theater?'

'It's a shame,' Elizabeth said, 'but we've had this engagement for more than a month. But surely, John, you'll be staying home one of these days before long. You're not going to be an expatriate, are you?'

'Expatriate,' Ferris repeated. 'I don't much like the word.'

'What's a better word?' she asked.

He thought for a moment. 'Sojourner might do.'

Ferris glanced again at his watch, and again Elizabeth apologized. 'If only we had known ahead of time —— '

'I just had this day in town. I came home unexpectelly. You see, Papa died last week.'

'Papa Ferris is dead?'

'Yes, at Johns-Hopkins. He had been sick there nearly a year.

The funeral was down home in Georgia.'

'Oh, I'm so sorry, John. Papa Ferris was always one of my favorite people.'

The little boy moved from behind the chair so that he could look into his mother's face. He asked, 'Who is dead?'

Ferris was oblivious to apprehension; he was thinking of his father's death. He saw again the outstretched body on the quilted silk within the coffin. The corpse flesh was bizarrely rouged and the familiar hands lay massive and joined above a spread of funeral roses. The memory closed and Ferris awakened to Elizabeth's calm voice.

'Mr. Ferris' father, Billy. A really grand person. Somebody you didn't know.'

'But why did you call him *Papa* Ferris?'

Bailey and Elizabeth exchanged a trapped look. It was Bailey who answered the questioning child. 'A long time ago,' he said, 'your mother and Mr. Ferris were once married. Before you were born — a long time ago.'

'Mr. Ferris?'

The little boy stared at Ferris, amazed and unbelieving. And Ferris' eyes, as he returned the gaze, were somehow unbelieving too. Was it indeed true that at one time he had called this stranger, Elizabeth, Little Butterduck during nights of love, that they had lived together, shared perhaps a thousand days and nights and — finally — endured in the misery of sudden solitude the fiber by fiber (jealousy, alcohol and money quarrels) destruction of the fabric of married love.

Bailey said to the children, 'It's somebody's suppertime. Come on now.'

'But Daddy! Mama and Mr. Ferris — I ——'

Billy's everlasting eyes — perplexed and with a glimmer of hostility — reminded Ferris of the gaze of another child. It was the young son of Jeannine — a boy of seven with a shadowed little face and nobby knees whom Ferris avoided and usually forgot.

'Quick march!' Bailey gently turned Billy toward the door. 'Say good night now, son.'

'Good night, Mr. Ferris.' He added resentfully, 'I thought I was staying up for the cake.'

'You can come in afterward for the cake,' Elizabeth said. 'Run along now with Daddy for your supper.'

Ferris and Elizabeth were alone. The weight of the situation descended on those first moments of silence. Ferris asked permission to pour himself another drink and Elizabeth set the cocktail shaker on the table at his side. He looked at the grand piano and noticed the music on the rack.

'Do you still play as beautifully as you used to?'

'I still enjoy it.'

'Please play, Elizabeth.'

Elizabeth arose immediately. Her readiness to perform when asked had always been one of her amiabilities; she never hung back, apologized. Now as she approached the piano there was the added readiness of relief.

She began with a Bach prelude and fugue. The prelude was as gaily iridescent as a prism in a morning room. The first voice of the fugue, an announcement pure and solitary, was repeated intermingling with a second voice, and again repeated within an elaborated frame, the multiple music, horizontal and serene, flowed with unhurried majesty. The principal melody was woven with two other voices, embellished with countless ingenuities — now dominant, again submerged, it had the sublimity of a single thing that does not fear surrender to the whole. Toward the end, the density of the material gathered for the last enriched insistence on the dominant first motif and with a chorded final statement the fugue ended. Ferris rested his head on the chair back and closed his eyes. In the following silence a clear, high voice came from the room down the hall.

'Daddy, how *could* Mama and Mr. Ferris ——' A door was closed.

The piano began again — what was this music? Unplaced, familiar, the limpid melody had lain a long while dormant in his heart. Now it spoke to him of another time, another place — it was the music Elizabeth used to play. The delicate air summoned a wilderness of memory. Ferris was lost in the riot of past longings, conflicts, ambivalent desires. Strange that the music, catalyst for this tumultuous anarchy, was so serene and clear. The singing melody was broken off by the appearance of the maid.

'Miz Bailey, dinner is out on the table now.'

Even after Ferris was seated at the table between his host and hostess, the unfinished music still overcast his mood. He was a little drunk.

'*L'improvisation de la vie humaine,*' he said. 'There's nothing that makes you so aware of the improvisation of human existence as a song unfinished. Or an old address book.'

'Address book?' repeated Bailey. Then he stopped, noncommittal and polite.

'You're still the same old boy, Johnny,' Elizabeth said with a trace of the old tenderness.

It was a Southern dinner that evening, and the dishes were his old favorites. They had fried chicken and corn pudding and rich, glozed candied sweet potatoes. During the meal Elizabeth kept alive a conversation when the silences were overlong. And it came about that Ferris was led to speak of Jeannine.

'I first knew Jeannine last autumn — about this time of the year — in Italy. She's a singer and she had an engagement in Rome. I expect we will be married soon.'

The words seemed so true, inevitable, that Ferris did not at first acknowledge to himself the lie. He and Jeannine had never in that year spoken of marriage. And indeed, she was still married — to a White Russian money-changer in Paris from whom she had been separated for five years. But it was too late to correct the lie. Already Elizabeth was saying: 'This really makes me glad to know. Congratulations, Johnny.'

He tried to make amends with truth. 'The Roman autumn is so beautiful. Balmy and blossoming.' He added. 'Jeannine has a little boy of six. A curious trilingual little fellow. We go to the Tuileries sometimes.'

A lie again. He had taken the boy once to the gardens. The sallow foreign child in shorts that bared his spindly legs had sailed his boat in the concrete pond and ridden the pony. The child had wanted to go in to the puppet show. But there was not time, for Ferris had an engagement at the Scribe Hotel. He had promised they would go to the guignol another afternoon. Only once had he taken Valentin to the Tuileries.

There was a stir. The maid brought in a white-frosted cake with pink candles. The children entered in their night clothes. Ferris still did not understand.

'Happy birthday, John,' Elizabeth said. 'Blow out the candles.'

Ferris recognized his birthday date. The candles blew out lingeringly and there was the smell of burning wax. Ferris was thirty-eight years old. The veins in his temples darkened and pulsed visibly.

'It's time you started for the theater.'

Ferris thanked Elizabeth for the birthday dinner and said the appropriate good-byes. The whole family saw him to the door.

A high, thin moon shone above the jagged, dark skyscrapers. The streets were windy, cold. Ferris hurried to Third Avenue and hailed a cab. He gazed at the nocturnal city with the deliberate attentiveness of departure and perhaps farewell. He was alone. He longed for flighttime and the coming journey.

The next day he looked down on the city from the air, burnished in sunlight, toylike, precise. Then America was left behind and there was only the Atlantic and the distant European shore. The ocean was milky pale and placid beneath the clouds. Ferris dozed most of the day. Toward dark he was thinking of Elizabeth and the visit of the previous evening. He thought of Elizabeth among her family with longing, gentle envy and inexplicable regret. He sought the melody, the unfinished air, that had so moved him. The cadence, some unrelated tones, were all that remained; the melody itself evaded him. He had found instead the first voice of the fugue that Elizabeth had played—it came to him, inverted mockingly and in a minor key. Suspended above the ocean the anxieties of transience and solitude no longer troubled him and he thought of his father's death with equanimity. During the dinner hour the plane reached the shore of France.

At midnight Ferris was in a taxi crossing Paris. It was a clouded night and mist wreathed the lights of the Place de la Concorde. The midnight bistros gleamed on the wet pavements. As always after a transocean flight the change of continents was too sudden. New York at morning, this midnight Paris. Ferris glimpsed the disorder of his life: the succession of cities, of transitory loves; and time, the sinister glissando of the years, time always.

'*Vite! Vite!*' he called in terror. '*Dépêchez-vous.*'

Valentin opened the door to him. The little boy wore pajamas and an outgrown red robe. His grey eyes were shadowed and, as Ferris passed into the flat, they flickered momentarily.

'*J'attends Maman.*'

Jeannine was singing in a night club. She would not be home before another hour. Valentin returned to a drawing, squatting with his crayons over the paper on the floor. Ferris looked down at the drawing — it was a banjo player with notes and wavy lines inside a comic-strip balloon.

'We will go again to the Tuileries.'

The child looked up and Ferris drew him closer to his knees. The melody, the unfinished music that Elizabeth had played, came to him suddenly. Unsought, the load of memory jettisoned — this time bringing only recognition and sudden joy.

'Monsieur Jean,' the child said, 'did you see him?'

Confused, Ferris thought only of another child — the freckled, family-loved boy. 'See who, Valentin?'

'Your dead papa in Georgia.' The child added, 'Was he okay?'

Ferris spoke with rapid urgency: 'We will go often to the Tuileries. Ride the pony and we will go into the guignol. We will see the puppet show and never be in a hurry any more.'

'Monsieur Jean,' Valentin said. 'The guignol is now closed.'

Again, the terror the acknowledgement of wasted years and death. Valentin, responsive and confident, still nestled in his arms. His cheek touched the soft cheek and felt the brush of the delicate eyelashes. With inner desperation he pressed the child close — as though an emotion as protean as his love could dominate the pulse of time.

A Domestic Dilemma

A Domestic Dilemma

ON THURSDAY Martin Meadows left the office early enough to make the first express bus home. It was the hour when the evening lilac glow was fading in the slushy streets, but by the time the bus had left the Mid-town terminal the bright city night had come. On Thursdays the maid had a half-day off and Martin liked to get home as soon as possible, since for the past year his wife had not been — well. This Thursday he was very tired and, hoping that no regular commuter would single him out for conversation, he fastened his attention to the newspaper until the bus had crossed the George Washington Bridge. Once on 9-W Highway Martin always felt that the trip was halfway done, he breathed deeply, even in cold weather when only ribbons of draught cut through the smoky air of the bus, confident that he was breathing country air. It used to be that at this point he would relax and begin to think with pleasure of his home. But in this last year nearness brought only a sense of tension and he did not anticipate the journey's end. This evening Martin kept his face close to the window and watched the barren fields and lonely lights of passing townships. There was a moon, pale on the dark earth and areas of late, porous snow; to Martin the countryside seemed vast and somehow desolate that evening. He took his hat from the rack and put his folded newspaper in the pocket of his overcoat a few minutes before time to pull the cord.

The cottage was a block from the bus stop, near the river but not directly on the shore; from the living-room window you could look across the street and opposite yard and see the Hudson. The cottage was modern, almost too white and new on the narrow plot of yard. In summer the grass was soft and bright and Martin carefully tended a flower border and a rose trellis. But during the cold, fallow months the yard was bleak and the cottage seemed naked. Lights were on that evening in all the rooms in the little house and Martin hurried up the front walk. Before the steps he stopped to move a wagon out of the way.

The children were in the living room, so intent on play that the opening of the front door was at first unnoticed. Martin stood looking at his safe, lovely children. They had opened the bottom drawer of the secretary and taken out the Christmas decorations. Andy had managed to plug in the Christmas tree lights and the green and red bulbs glowed with out-of-season festivity on the rug of the living room. At the moment he was trying to trail the bright cord over Marianne's rocking horse. Marianne sat on the floor pulling off an angel's wings. The children wailed a startling welcome. Martin swung the fat little baby girl up to his shoulder and Andy threw himself against his father's legs.

'Daddy, Daddy, Daddy!'

Martin set down the little girl carefully and swung Andy a few times like a pendulum. Then he picked up the Christmas tree cord.

'What's all this stuff doing out? Help me put it back in the drawer. You're not to fool with the light socket. Remember I told you that before. I mean it, Andy.'

The six-year-old child nodded and shut the secretary drawer. Martin stroked his fair soft hair and his hand lingered tenderly on the nape of the child's frail neck.

'Had supper yet, Bumpkin?'

'It hurt. The toast was hot.'

The baby girl stumbled on the rug and, after the first surprise of the fall, began to cry; Martin picked her up and carried her in his arms back to the kitchen.

'See, Daddy,' said Andy. 'The toast——'

Emily had laid the childrens' supper on the uncovered porcelain table. There were two plates with the remains of cream-of-wheat and eggs and silver mugs that had held milk. There was also a platter of cinamon toast, untouched except for one tooth-marked bite. Martin sniffed the bitten piece and nibbled gingerly. Then he put the toast into the garbage pail.

'Hoo—phui—What on earth!'

Emily had mistaken the tin of cayenne for the cinnamon.

'I like to have burnt up,' Andy said. 'Drank water and ran outdoors and opened my mouth. Marianne didn't eat none.'

'Any,' corrected Martin. He stood helpless, looking around the walls of the kitchen. 'Well, that's that, I guess,' he said finally. 'Where is your mother now?'

'She's up in you alls' room.'

Martin left the children in the kitchen and went up to his wife. Outside the door he waited for a moment to still his anger. He did not knock and once inside the room he closed the door behind him.

Emily sat in the rocking chair by the window of the pleasant room. She had been drinking something from a tumbler and as he entered she put the glass hurriedly on the floor behind the chair. In her attitude there was confusion and guilt which she tried to hide by a show of spurious vivacity.

'Oh, Marty! You home already? The time slipped up on me. I was just going down——' She lurched to him and her kiss was strong with sherry. When he stood unresponsive she stepped back a pace and giggled nervously.

'What's the matter with you? Standing there like a barber pole. Is anything wrong with you?'

'Wrong with *me?*' Martin bent over the rocking chair and picked up the tumbler from the floor. 'If you could only realize how sick I am—how bad it is for all of us.'

Emily spoke in a false, airy voice that had become too familiar to him. Often at such times she affected a slight English accent, copying perhaps some actress she admired. 'I haven't the vaguest idea what you mean. Unless you are referring to the glass I used for a spot of sherry. I had a finger of sherry—maybe two. But what is the crime in that, pray tell me? I'm quite all right. Quite all right.'

'So anyone can see.'

As she went into the bathroom Emily walked with careful gravity. She turned on the cold water and dashed some on her face with her cupped hands, then patted herself dry with the corner of a bath towel. Her face was delicately featured and young, unblemished.

'I was just going down to make dinner.' She tottered and balanced herself by holding to the door frame.

'I'll take care of dinner. You stay up here. I'll bring it up.'

'I'll do nothing of the sort. Why, whoever heard of such a thing?'

'Please,' Martin said.

'Leave me alone. I'm quite all right. I was just on the way down——'

'Mind what I say.'

'Mind your grandmother.'

She lurched toward the door, but Martin caught her by the arm. 'I don't want the children to see you in this condition. Be reasonable.'

'Condition!' Emily jerked her arm. Her voice rose angrily. 'Why, because I drink a couple of sherries in the afternoon you're trying to make me out a drunkard. Condition! Why, I don't even touch whiskey. As well you know. *I* don't swill liquor at bars. And that's more than you can say. I don't even have a cocktail at dinnertime. I only sometimes have a glass of sherry. What, I ask you, is the disgrace of that? Condition!'

Martin sought words to calm his wife. 'We'll have a quiet supper by ourselves up here. That's a good girl.' Emily sat on the side of the bed and he opened the door for a quick departure.

'I'll be back in a jiffy.'

As he busied himself with the dinner downstairs he was lost in the familiar question as to how this problem had come upon his home. He himself had always enjoyed a good drink. When they were still living in Alabama they had served long drinks or cocktails as a matter of course. For years they had drunk one or two — possible three drinks before dinner, and at bedtime a long nightcap. Evenings before holidays they might get a buzz on, might even become a little tight. But alcohol had never seemed a problem to him, only a bothersome expense that with the increase in the family they could scarcely afford. It was only after his company had transferred him to New York that Martin was aware that certainly his wife was drinking too much. She was tippling, he noticed, during the day.

The problem acknowledged, he tried to analyze the source. The change from Alabama to New York had somehow disturbed her; accustomed to the idle warmth of a small Southern town, the matrix of the family and cousinship and childhood friends, she had failed to accommodate herself to the stricter, lonelier mores of the North. The duties of motherhood and housekeeping were onerous to her. Homesick for Paris City, she had made no friends in the suburban town. She read only magazines and murder books. Her interior life was insufficient without the artifice of alcohol.

The revelations of incontinence insidiously undermined his previous conceptions of his wife. There were times of unexplainable malevolence, times when the alcoholic fuse caused an explosion of unseemly anger. He encountered a latent coarseness in Emily, inconsistent with her natural simplicity. She lied about drinking and deceived him with unsuspected stratagems.

Then there was an accident. Coming home from work one evening about a year ago, he was greeted with screams from the childrens' room. He found Emily holding the baby, wet and naked from her bath. The baby had been dropped, her frail, frail skull striking the table edge, so that a thread of blood was soaking into the gossamer hair. Emily was sobbing and intoxicated. As Martin cradled the hurt child, so infinitely precious at that moment, he had an affrighted vision of the future.

The next day Marianne was all right. Emily vowed that never again would she touch liquor, and for a few weeks she was sober, cold and downcast. Then gradually she began — not whiskey or gin — but quantities of beer, or sherry, or outlandish liqueurs; once he had come across a hatbox of empty crème de menthe bottles. Martin found a dependable maid who managed the household competently. Virgie was also from Alabama and Martin had never dared tell Emily the wage scale customary in New York. Emily's drinking was entirely secret now, done before he reached the house. Usually the affects were almost imperceptible — a looseness of movement or the heavy-lidded eyes. The times of irresponsibilities, such as the cayenne-pepper toast were rare, and Martin could dismiss his worries when Virgie was at the house. But, nevertheless, anxiety was always latent, a threat of indefined disaster that underlaid his days.

'Marianne!' Martin called, for even the recollection of that time brought the need for reassurance. The baby girl, no longer hurt, but no less precious to her father, came into the kitchen with her brother. Martin went on with the preparations for the meal. He opened a can of soup and put two chops in the frying pan. Then he sat down by the table and took his Marianne on his knees for a pony ride. Andy watched them, his fingers wobbling the tooth that had been loose all that week.

'Andy-the-candyman!' Martin said. 'Is that old critter still in your mouth? Come closer, let Daddy have a look.'

'I got a string to pull it with.' The child brought from his pocket a tangled thread. 'Virgie said to tie it to the tooth and tie the other end to the doorknob and shut the door real suddenly.'

Martin took out a clean handerchief and felt the loose tooth carefully. 'That tooth is coming out of my Andy's mouth tonight. Otherwise I'm awfully afraid we'll have a tooth tree in the family.'

'A what?'

'A tooth tree,' Martin said. 'You'll bite into something and swallow that tooth. And the tooth will take root in poor Andy's stomach and grow into a tooth tree with sharp little teeth instead of leaves.'

'Shoo, Daddy,' Andy said. But he held the tooth firmly between his grimy little thumb and forefinger. 'There ain't any tree like that. I never seen one.'

'There *isn't* any tree like that and I never *saw* one.'

Martin tensed suddenly. Emily was coming down the stairs. He listened to her fumbling footsteps, his arm embracing the little boy with dread. When Emily came into the room he saw from her movements and her sullen face that she had again been at the sherry bottle. She began to yank open drawers and set the table.

'Condition!' she said in a furry voice. 'You talk to me like that.

Don't think I'll forget. I remember every dirty lie you say to me. Don't you think for a minute that I forget.'

'Emily!' he begged. 'The children —— '

'The children — yes! Don't think I don't see through your dirty plots and schemes. Down here trying to turn my own children against me. Don't think I don't see and understand.'

'Emily! I beg you — please go upstairs.'

'So you can turn my children — my very own children ——' Two large tears coursed rapidly down her cheeks. 'Trying to turn my little boy, my Andy, against his own mother.'

With drunken impulsiveness Emily knelt on the floor before the startled child. Her hands on his shoulders balanced her. 'Listen, my Andy — you wouldn't listen to any lies your father tells you? You wouldn't believe what he says? Listen, Andy, what was your father telling you before I came downstairs?' Uncertain, the child sought his father's face. 'Tell me. Mama wants to know.'

'About the tooth tree.'

'What?'

The child repeated the words and she echoed them with unbelieving terror. 'The tooth tree!' She swayed and renewed her grasp on the child's shoulder. 'I don't know what you're talking about. But listen, Andy, Mama is all right, isn't she?' The tears were spilling down her face and Andy drew back from her, for he was afraid. Grasping the table edge, Emily stood up.

'See! You have turned my child against me.'

Marianne began to cry, and Martin took her in his arms.

'That's all right, you can take *your* child. You have always shown partiality from the very first. I don't mind, but at least you can leave me my little boy.'

Andy edged close to his father and touched his leg. 'Daddy,' he wailed.

Martin took the children to the foot of the stairs. 'Andy, you take up Marianne and Daddy will follow you in a minute.'

'But Mama?' the child asked, whispering.

'Mama will be all right. Don't worry.'

Emily was sobbing at the kitchen table, her face buried in the crook of her arm. Martin poured a cup of soup and set it before her. Her rasping sobs unnerved him; the vehemence of her emotion, irrespective of the source, touched in him a strain of tenderness. Unwillingly he laid his hand on her dark hair. 'Sit up and drink the soup.' Her face as she looked up at him was chastened and imploring. The boy's withdrawal or the touch of Martin's hand had turned the tenor of her mood.

'Ma-Martin,' she sobbed. 'I'm so ashamed.'

'Drink the soup.'

Obeying him, she drank between gasping breaths. After a second cup she allowed him to lead her up to their room. She was docile now and more restrained. He laid her nightgown on the bed and was about to leave the room when a fresh round of grief, the alcoholic tumult, came again.

'He turned away. My Andy looked at me and turned away.'

Impatience and fatigue hardened his voice, but he spoke warily. 'You forget that Andy is still a little child—he can't comprehend the meaning of such scenes.'

'Did I make a scene? Oh, Martin, did I make a scene before the children?'

Her horrified face touched and amused him against his will. 'Forget it. Put on your nightgown and go to sleep.'

'My child turned away from me. Andy looked at his mother and turned away. The children——'

She was caught in the rhythmic sorrow of alcohol. Martin withdrew from the room saying: 'For God's sake go to sleep. The children will forget by tomorrow.'

As he said this he wondered if it was true. Would the scene glide so easily from memory—or would it root in the unconscious to fester in the after-years? Martin did not know, and the last alternative sickened him. He thought of Emily, foresaw the morning-after humiliation: the shards of memory, the lucidities that glared from the obliterating darkness of shame. She would call the New York office twice—possibly three or four times. Martin anticipated his own embarrassment, wondering if the others at the office could possibly suspect. He felt that his secretary had divined the trouble long ago and that she pitied him. He suffered a moment of rebellion against his fate; he hated his wife.

Once in the childrens' room he closed the door and felt secure for the first time that evening. Marianne fell down on the floor, picked herself up and calling: 'Daddy, watch me,' fell again, got up, and continued the falling-calling routine. Andy sat in the child's low chair, wobbling the tooth. Martin ran the water in the tub, washed his own hands in the lavatory, and called the boy into the bathroom.

'Let's have another look at that tooth.' Martin sat on the toilet, holding Andy between his knees. The child's mouth gaped and Martin grasped the tooth. A wobble, a quick twist and the nacreous milk tooth was free. Andy's face was for the first moment split between terror, astonishment, and delight. He mouthed a swallow of water and spat into the lavatory.

'Look, Daddy! It's blood. Marianne!'

Martin loved to bathe his children, loved inexpressibly the tender, naked bodies as they stood in the water so exposed. It was not fair of Emily to say that he showed partiality. As Martin soaped the delicate boy-body of his son he felt that further love would be impossible. Yet he admitted the difference in the quality of his emotions for the two children. His love for his daughter was graver, touched with a strain of melancholy, a gentleness that was akin to pain. His pet names for the little boy were the absurdities of daily inspiration—he called the little girl always Marianne, and his voice as he spoke it was a caress. Martin patted dry the fat baby stomach and the sweet little genital fold. The washed child faces were radiant as flower petals, equally loved.

'I'm putting the tooth under my pillow. I'm supposed to get a quarter.'

'What for?'

'*You* know, Daddy. Johnny got a quarter for his tooth.'

'Who puts the quarter there?' asked Martin. 'I used to think the fairies left it in the night. It was a dime in my day, though.'

'That's what they say in kindergarden.'

'Who does put it there?'

'Your parents,' Andy said. 'You!'

Martin was pinning the cover on Marianne's bed. His daughter was already asleep. Scarcely breathing, Martin bent over and kissed her forehead, kissed again the tiny hand that lay palm-upward, flung in slumber beside her head.

'Good night, Andy-man.'

The answer was only a drowsy murmur. After a minute Martin took out his change and slid a quarter underneath the pillow. He left a night light in the room.

As Martin prowled about the kitchen making a late meal, it occurred to him that the children had not once mentioned their mother or the scene that must have seemed to them incomprehensible. Absorbed in the instant — the tooth, the bath, the quarter — the fluid passage of child-time had borne these weightless episodes like leaves in the swift current of a shallow stream while the adult enigma was beached and forgotten on the shore. Martin thanked the Lord for that.

But his own anger, repressed and lurking, arose again. His youth was being frittered by a drunkard's waste, his very manhood subtly undermined. And the children, once the immunity of incomprehension passed — what would it be like in a year or so? With his elbows on the table he ate his food brutishly, untasting. There was no hiding the truth — soon there would be gossip in the office and in the town; his wife was a dissolute woman. Dissolute. And he and his children were bound to a future of degradation and slow ruin.

Martin pushed away from the table and stalked into the living room. He followed the lines of a book with his eyes but his mind conjured miserable images: he saw his children drowned in the river, his wife a disgrace on the public street. By bedtime the dull, hard anger was like a weight upon his chest and his feet dragged as he climbed the stairs.

The room was dark except for the shafting light from the half-opened bathroom door. Martin undressed quietly. Little by little, mysteriously, there came in him a change. His wife was asleep, her peaceful respiration sounding gently in the room. Her high-heeled shoes with the carelessly dropped stockings made to him a mute appeal. Her underclothes were flung in disorder on the chair. Martin picked up the girdle and the soft, silk brassière and stood for a moment with them in his hands. For the first time that evening he looked at his wife. His eyes rested on the sweet forehead, the arch of the fine brow. The brow had descended to Marianne, and the tilt at the end of the delicate nose. In his son he could trace the high cheekbones and pointed chin. Her body was full-bosomed, slender and undulant. As Martin watched the tranquil slumber of his wife the ghost of the old anger vanished. All thoughts of blame or blemish were distant from him now. Martin put out the bathroom light and raised the window. Careful not to awaken Emily he slid into the bed. By moonlight he watched his wife for the last time. His hand sought the adjacent flesh and sorrow paralleled desire in the immense complexity of love.

A Tree • A Rock • A Cloud

A Tree. A Rock. A Cloud

IT WAS RAINING that morning, and still very dark. When the boy reached the streetcar café he had almost finished his route and he went in for a cup of coffee. The place was an all-night café owned by a bitter and stingy man called Leo. After the raw, empty street the café seemed friendly and bright: along the counter there were a couple of soldiers, three spinners from the cotton mill, and in a corner a man who sat hunched over with his nose and half his face down in a beer mug. The boy wore a helmet such as aviators wear. When he went into the café he unbuckled the chin strap and raised the right flap up over his pink little ear; often as he drank his coffee someone would speak to him in a friendly way. But this morning Leo did not look into his face and none of the men were talking. He paid and was leaving the café when a voice called out to him:

'Son! Hey Son!'

He turned back and the man in the corner was crooking his finger and nodding to him. He had brought his face out of the beer mug and he seemed suddenly very happy. The man was long and pale, with a big nose and faded orange hair.

'Hey Son!'

The boy went toward him. He was an undersized boy of about twelve, with one shoulder drawn higher than the other because of the weight of the paper sack. His face was shallow, freckled, and his eyes were round child eyes.

'Yeah Mister?'

The man laid one hand on the paper boy's shoulders, then grasped the boy's chin and turned his face slowly from one side to the other. The boy shrank back uneasily.

'Say! What's the big idea?'

The boy's voice was shrill; inside the café it was suddenly very quiet.

The man said slowly: 'I love you.'

All along the counter the men laughed. The boy, who had scowled and sidled away, did not know what to do. He looked over the counter at Leo, and Leo watched him with a weary, brittle jeer. The boy tried to laugh also. But the man was serious and sad.

'I did not mean to tease you, Son,' he said. 'Sit down and have a beer with me. There is something I have to explain.'

Cautiously, out of the corner of his eye, the paper boy questioned the men along the counter to see what he should do. But they had gone back to their beer or their breakfast and did not notice him. Leo put a cup of coffee on the counter and a little jug of cream.

'He is a minor,' Leo said.

The paper boy slid himself up onto the stool. His ear beneath the upturned flap of the helmet was very small and red. The man was nodding at him soberly. "It is important," he said. Then he reached in his hip pocket and brought out something which he held up in the palm of his hand for the boy to see.

'Look very carefully,' he said.

The boy stared, but there was nothing to look at very carefully. The man held in his big, grimy palm a photograph. It was the face of a woman, but blurred, so that only the hat and the dress she was wearing stood out clearly.

'See?' the man asked.

The boy nodded and the man placed another picture in his palm. The woman was standing on a beach in a bathing suit. The suit made her stomach very big, and that was the main thing you noticed.

'Got a good look?' He leaned over closer and finally asked: 'You ever seen her before?'

The boy sat motionless, staring slantwise at the man. 'Not so I know of.'

'Very well.' The man blew on the photographs and put them back into his pocket. 'That was my wife.'

'Dead?' the boy asked.

Slowly the man shook his head. He pursed his lips as though about to whistle and answered in a long-drawn way: 'Nuuu —' he said. 'I will explain.'

The beer on the counter before the man was in a large brown mug. He did not pick it up to drink. Instead he bent down and, putting his face over the rim, he rested there for a moment. Then with both hands he tilted the mug and sipped.

'Some night you'll go to sleep with your big nose in a mug and drown," said Leo. 'Prominent transient drowns in beer. That would be a cute death.'

The paper boy tried to signal to Leo. While the man was not looking he screwed up his face and worked his mouth to question soundlessly: 'Drunk?' But Leo only raised his eyebrows and turned away to put some pink strips of bacon on the grill. The man pushed the mug away from him, straightened himself, and folded his loose crooked hands on the counter. His face was sad as he looked at the paper boy. He did not blink, but from time to time the lids closed down with delicate gravity over his pale green eyes. It was nearing dawn and the boy shifted the weight of the paper sack.

'I am talking about love,' the man said. 'With me it is a science.'

The boy half slid down from the stool. But the man raised his forefinger, and there was something about him that held the boy and would not let him go away.

'Twelve years ago I married the woman in the photograph. She was my wife for one year, nine months, three days, and two nights. I loved her. Yes . . ." He tightened his blurred, rambling voice and said again: 'I loved her. I thought also that she loved me. I was a railroad engineer. She had all home comforts and luxuries. It never crept into my brain that she was not satisfied. But do you know what happened?'

'Mgneeow!' said Leo.

The man did not take his eyes from the boy's face. 'She left me. I came in one night and the house was empty and she was gone. She left me.'

'With a fellow?' the boy asked.

Gently the man placed his palm down on the counter. 'Why naturally, Son. A woman does not run off like that alone.'

The café was quiet, the soft rain black and endless in the street outside. Leo pressed down the frying bacon with the prongs of his long fork. 'So you have been chasing the floozie for eleven years. You frazzled old rascal!'

For the first time the man glanced at Leo. 'Please don't be vulgar. Besides, I was not speaking to you.' He turned back to the boy and said in a trusting and secretive undertone: 'Let's not pay any attention to him. O.K.?'

The paper boy nodded doubtfully.

'It was like this," the man continued. 'I am a person who feels many things. All my life one thing after another has impressed me. Moonlight. The leg of a pretty girl. One thing after another. But the point is that when I had enjoyed anything there was a peculiar sensation as though it was laying around loose in me. Nothing seemed to finish itself up or fit in with the other things. Women? I had my portion of them. The same. Afterwards laying around loose in me. I was a man who had never loved.'

Very slowly he closed his eyelids, and the gesture was like a curtain drawn at the end of a scene in a play. When he spoke again his voice was excited and the words came fast — the lobes of his large, loose ears seemed to tremble.

'Then I met this woman. I was fifty-one years old and she always said she was thirty. I met her at a filling station and we were married within three days. And do you know what it was like? I just can't tell you. All I had ever felt was gathered together around this woman. Nothing lay around loose in me any more but was finished up by her.'

The man stopped suddenly and stroked his long nose. His voice sank down to a steady and reproachful undertone: 'I'm not explaining this right. What happened was this. There were these beautiful feelings and loose little pleasures inside me. And this woman was something like an assembly line for my soul. I run these little pieces of myself through her and I come out complete. Now do you follow me?'

'What was her name?' the boy asked.

'Oh,' he said. 'I called her Dodo. But that is immaterial.'

'Did you try to make her come back?'

The man did not seem to hear. 'Under the circumstances you can imagine how I felt when she left me.'

Leo took the bacon from the grill and folded two strips of it between a bun. He had a gray face, with slitted eyes, and a pinched nose saddled by faint blue shadows. One of the mill workers signaled for more coffee and Leo poured it. He did not give refills on coffee free. The spinner ate breakfast there every morning, but the better Leo knew his customers the stingier he treated them. He nibbled his own bun as though he grudged it to himself.

'And you never got hold of her again?'

The boy did not know what to think of the man, and his child's face was uncertain with mingled curiosity and doubt. He was new on the paper route; it was still strange to him to be out in the town in the black, queer early morning.

'Yes,' the man said. 'I took a number of steps to get her back. I went around trying to locate her. I went to Tulsa where she had folks. And to Mobile. I went to every town she had ever mentioned to me, and I hunted down every man she had formerly been connected with. Tulsa, Atlanta, Chicago, Cheehaw, Memphis. . . . For the better part of two years I chased around the country trying to lay hold of her.'

'But the pair of them had vanished from the face of the earth!' said Leo.

'Don't listen to him,' the man said confidentially. 'And also just forget those two years. They are not important. What matters is that around the third year a curious thing begun to happen to me.'

'What?' the boy asked.

The man leaned down and tilted his mug to take a sip of beer. But as he hovered over the mug his nostrils fluttered slightly; he sniffed the staleness of the beer and did not drink. 'Love is a curious thing to begin with. At first I thought only of getting her back. It was a kind of mania. But then as time went on I tried to remember her. But do you know what happened?'

'No,' the boy said.

'When I laid myself down on a bed and tried to think about her my mind became a blank. I couldn't see her. I would take out her pictures and look. No good. Nothing doing. A blank. Can you imagine it?'

'Say Mac!' Leo called down the counter. 'Can you imagine this bozo's mind a blank!'

Slowly, as though fanning away flies, the man waved his hand. His green eyes were concentrated and fixed on the shallow little face of the paper boy.

'But a sudden piece of glass on a sidewalk. Or a nickel tune in a music box. A shadow on a wall at night. And I would remember. It might happen in a street and I would cry or bang my head against a lamppost. You follow me?'

'A piece of glass . . .' the boy said.

'Anything. I would walk around and I had no power of how and when to remember her. You think you can put up a kind of shield. But remembering don't come to a man face forward — it corners around sideways. I was at the mercy of everything I saw and heard. Suddenly instead of me combing the countryside to find her she begun to chase me around in my very soul. *She* chasing *me,* mind you! And in my soul.'

The boy asked finally: 'What part of the country were you in then?'

'Ooh,' the man groaned. 'I was a sick mortal. It was like smallpox. I confess, Son, that I boozed. I fornicated. I committed any sin that suddenly appealed to me. I am loath to confess it but I will do so. When I recall that period it is all curdled in my mind, it was so terrible.'

The man leaned his head down and tapped his forehead on the counter. For a few seconds he stayed bowed over in this position, the back of his stringy neck covered with orange furze, his hands with their long warped fingers held palm to palm in an attitude of prayer. Then the man straightened himself; he was smiling and suddenly his face was bright and tremulous and old.

'It was in the fifth year that it happened,' he said. 'And with it I started my science.'

Leo's mouth jerked with a pale, quick grin. 'Well none of we boys are getting any younger,' he said. Then with sudden anger he balled up a dishcloth he was holding and threw it down hard on the floor. 'You draggle-tailed old Romeo!'

'What happened?' the boy asked.

The old man's voice was high and clear: 'Peace,' he answered.

'Huh?'

'It is hard to explain scientifically, Son,' he said. 'I guess the logical explanation is that she and I had fleed around from each other for so long that finally we just got tangled up together and lay down and quit. Peace. A queer and beautiful blankness. It was spring in Portland and the rain came every afternoon. All evening I just stayed there on my bed in the dark. And that is how the science come to me.'

The windows in the streetcar were pale blue with light. The two soldiers paid for their beers and opened the door — one of the soldiers combed his hair and wiped off his muddy puttees before they went outside. The three mill workers bent silently over their breakfasts. Leo's clock was ticking on the wall.

'It is this. And listen carefully. I meditated on love and reasoned it out. I realized what is wrong with us. Men fall in love for the first time. And what do they fall in love with?"

The boy's soft mouth was partly open and he did not answer.

'A woman,' the old man said. 'Without science, with nothing to go by, they undertake the most dangerous and sacred experience in God's earth. They fall in love with a woman. Is that correct, Son?'

'Yeah,' the boy said faintly.

'They start at the wrong end of love. They begin at the climax. Can you wonder it is so miserable? Do you know how men should love?'

The old man reached over and grasped the boy by the collar of his leather jacket. He gave him a gentle little shake and his green eyes gazed down unblinking and grave.

'Son, do you know how love should be begun?'

The boy sat small and listening and still. Slowly he shook his head. The old man leaned closer and whispered:

'A tree. A rock. A cloud.'

It was still raining outside in the street: a mild, gray, endless rain. The mill whistle blew for the six o'clock shift and the three spinners paid and went away. There was no one in the café but Leo, the old man, and the little paper boy.

'The weather was like this in Portland,' he said. 'At the time my science was begun. I meditated and I started very cautious. I would pick up something from the street and take it home with me. I bought a goldfish and I concentrated on the goldfish and I loved it. I graduated from one thing to another. Day by day I was getting this technique. On the road from Portland to San Diego——'

'Aw shut up!' screamed Leo suddenly. 'Shut up! Shut up!'

The old man still held the collar of the boy's jacket; he was trembling and his face was earnest and bright and wild. 'For six years now I have gone around by myself and built up my science. And now I am a master. Son. I can love anything. No longer do I have to think about it even. I see a street full of people and a beautiful light comes in me. I watch a bird in the sky. Or I meet a traveler on the road. Everything, Son. And anybody. All stranger and all loved! Do you realize what a science like mine can mean?'

The boy held himself stiffly, his hands curled tight around the counter edge. Finally he asked: "Did you ever really find that lady?'

'What? What say, Son?'

'I mean,' the boy asked timidly. 'Have you fallen in love with a woman again?'

The old man loosened his grasp on the boy's collar. He turned away and for the first time his green eyes had a vague and scattered look. He lifted the mug from the counter, drank down the yellow beer. His head was shaking slowly from side to side. Then finally he answered: 'No, Son. You see that is the last step in my science. I go cautious. And I am not quite ready yet.'

'Well!' said Leo. 'Well well well!'

The old man stood in the open doorway. 'Remember,' he said.

Framed there in the gray damp light of the early morning he looked shrunken and seedy and frail. But his smile was bright. 'Remember I love you,' he said with a last nod. And the door closed quietly behind him.

The boy did not speak for a long time. He pulled down the bangs on his forehead and slid his grimy little forefinger around the rim of his empty cup. Then without looking at Leo he finally asked:

'Was he drunk?'

'No,' said Leo shortly.

The boy raised his clear voice higher. 'Then was he a dope fiend?'

'No.'

The boy looked up at Leo, and his flat little face was desperate, his voice urgent and shrill. 'Was he crazy? Do you think he was a lunatic?' The paper boy's voice dropped suddenly with doubt. 'Leo? Or not?'

But Leo would not answer him. Leo had run a night café for fourteen years, and he held himself to be a critic of craziness. There were the town characters and also the transients who roamed in from the night. He knew the manias of all of them. But he did not want to satisfy the questions of the waiting child. He tightened his pale face and was silent.

So the boy pulled down the right flap of his helmet and as he turned to leave he made the only comment that seemed safe to him, the only remark that could not be laughed down and despised:

'He sure has done a lot of traveling.'

The Heart Is a Lonely Hunter

To Reeves McCullers
and to Marguerite and Lamar Smith

PART I

1

IN THE town there were two mutes, and they were always together. Early every morning they would come out from the house where they lived and walk arm in arm down the street to work. The two friends were very different. The one who always steered the way was an obese and dreamy Greek. In the summer he would come out wearing a yellow or green polo shirt stuffed sloppily into his trousers in front and hanging loose behind. When it was colder he wore over this a shapeless gray sweater. His face was round and oily, with half-closed eyelids and lips that curved in a gentle, stupid smile. The other mute was tall. His eyes had a quick, intelligent expression. He was always immaculate and very soberly dressed.

Every morning the two friends walked silently together until they reached the main street of the town. Then when they came to a certain fruit and candy store they paused for a moment on the sidewalk outside. The Greek, Spiros Antonapoulos, worked for his cousin, who owned this fruit store. His job was to make candies and sweets, uncrate the fruits, and to keep the place clean. The thin mute, John Singer, nearly always put his hand on his friend's arm and looked for a second into his face before leaving him. Then after this good-bye Singer crossed the street and walked on alone to the jewelry store where he worked as a silverware engraver.

In the late afternoon the friends would meet again. Singer came back to the fruit store and waited until Antonapoulos was ready to go home. The Greek would be lazily unpacking a case of peaches or melons, or perhaps looking at the funny paper in the kitchen behind the store where he cooked. Before their departure Antonapoulos always opened a paper sack he kept hidden during the day on one of the kitchen shelves. Inside were stored various bits of food he had collected — a piece of fruit, samples of candy, or the butt-end of a liverwurst. Usually before leaving Antonapoulos waddled gently to the glassed case in the front of the store where some meats and cheeses were kept. He glided open the back of the case and his fat hand groped lovingly for some particular dainty inside which he had wanted. Sometimes his cousin who owned the place did not see him. But if he noticed he stared at his cousin with a warning in his tight, pale face. Sadly Antonapoulos would shuffle the morsel from one corner of the case to the other. During these times Singer stood very straight with his hands in his pockets and looked in another direction. He did not like to watch this little scene between the two Greeks. For, excepting drinking and a certain solitary secret pleasure, Antonapoulos loved to eat more than anything else in the world.

In the dusk the two mutes walked slowly home together. At home Singer was always talking to Antonapoulos. His hands shaped the words in a swift series of designs. His face was eager and his gray-green eyes sparkled brightly. With his thin, strong hands he told Antonapoulos all that had happened during the day.

Antonapoulos sat back lazily and looked at Singer. It was seldom that he ever moved his hands to speak at all — and then it was to say that he wanted to eat or to sleep or to drink. These three things he always said with the same vague, fumbling signs. At night, if he were not too drunk, he would kneel down before his bed and pray awhile. Then his plump hands shaped the words 'Holy Jesus,' or 'God,' or 'Darling Mary.' These were the only words Antonapoulos ever said. Singer never knew just how much his friend understood of all the things he told him. But it did not matter.

They shared the upstairs of a small house near the business

section of the town. There were two rooms. On the oil stove in the kitchen Antonapoulos cooked all of their meals. There were straight, plain kitchen chairs for Singer and an overstuffed sofa for Antonapoulos. The bedroom was furnished mainly with a large double bed covered with an eiderdown comfort for the big Greek and a narrow iron cot for Singer.

Dinner always took a long time, because Antonapoulos loved food and he was very slow. After they had eaten, the big Greek would lie back on his sofa and slowly lick over each one of his teeth with his tongue, either from a certain delicacy or because he did not wish to lose the savor of the meal — while Singer washed the dishes.

Sometimes in the evening the mutes would play chess. Singer had always greatly enjoyed this game, and years before he had tried to teach it to Antonapoulos. At first his friend could not be interested in the reasons for moving the various pieces about on the board. Then Singer began to keep a bottle of something good under the table to be taken out after each lesson. The Greek never got on to the erratic movements of the knights and the sweeping mobility of the queens, but he learned to make a few set, opening moves. He preferred the white pieces and would not play if the black men were given him. After the first moves Singer worked out the game by himself while his friend looked on drowsily. If Singer made brilliant attacks on his own men so that in the end the black king was killed, Antonapoulos was always very proud and pleased.

The two mutes had no other friends, and except when they worked they were alone together. Each day was very much like any other day, because they were alone so much that nothing ever disturbed them. Once a week they would go to the library for Singer to withdraw a mystery book and on Friday night they attended a movie. Then on payday they always went to the ten-cent photograph shop above the Army and Navy Store so that Antonapoulos could have his picture taken. These were the only places where they made customary visits. There were many parts in the town that they had never even seen.

The town was in the middle of the deep South. The summers were long and the months of winter cold were very few. Nearly always the sky was a glassy, brilliant azure and the sun burned down riotously bright. Then the light, chill rains of November would come, and perhaps later there would be frost and some short months of cold. The winters were changeable, but the summers always were burning hot. The town was a fairly large one. On the main street there were several blocks of two- and three-story shops and business offices. But the largest buildings in the town were the factories, which employed a large percentage of the population. These cotton mills were big and flourishing and most of the workers in the town were very poor. Often in the faces along the streets there was the desperate look of hunger and of loneliness.

But the two mutes were not lonely at all. At home they were content to eat and drink, and Singer would talk with his hands eagerly to his friend about all that was in his mind. So the years passed in this quiet way until Singer reached the age of thirty-two and had been in the town with Antonapoulos for ten years.

Then one day the Greek became ill. He sat up in bed with his hands on his fat stomach and big, oily tears rolled down his cheeks. Singer went to see his friend's cousin who owned the fruit store, and also he arranged for leave from his own work. The doctor made out a diet for Antonapoulos and said that he could drink no more wine. Singer rigidly enforced the doctor's orders. All day he sat by his friend's bed and did what he could to make the time pass quickly, but Antonapoulos only looked at him angrily from the corners of his eyes and would not be amused.

The Greek was very fretful, and kept finding fault with the

fruit drinks and food that Singer prepared for him. Constantly he made his friend help him out of bed so that he could pray. His huge buttocks would sag down over his plump little feet when he kneeled. He fumbled with his hands to say 'Darling Mary' and then held to the small brass cross tied to his neck with a dirty string. His big eyes would wall up to the ceiling with a look of fear in them, and afterward he was very sulky and would not let his friend speak to him.

Singer was patient and did all that he could. He drew little pictures, and once he made a sketch of his friend to amuse him. This picture hurt the big Greek's feelings, and he refused to be reconciled until Singer had made his face very young and handsome and colored his hair bright yellow and his eyes china blue. And then he tried not to show his pleasure.

Singer nursed his friend so carefully that after a week Antonapoulos was able to return to his work. But from that time on there was a difference in their way of life. Trouble came to the two friends.

Antonapoulos was not ill any more, but a change had come in him. He was irritable and no longer content to spend the evenings quietly in their home. When he would wish to go out Singer followed along close behind him. Antonapoulos would go into a restaurant, and while they sat at the table he slyly put lumps of sugar, or a pepper-shaker, or pieces of silverware in his pocket. Singer always paid for what he took and there was no disturbance. At home he scolded Antonapoulos, but the big Greek only looked at him with a bland smile.

The months went on and these habits of Antonapoulos grew worse. One day at noon he walked calmly out of the fruit store of his cousin and urinated in public against the wall of the First National Bank Building across the street. At times he would meet people on the sidewalk whose faces did not please him, and he would bump into these persons and push at them with his elbows and stomach. He walked into a store one day and hauled out a floor lamp without paying for it, and another time he tried to take an electric train he had seen in a showcase.

For Singer this was a time of great distress. He was continually marching Antonapoulos down to the courthouse during lunch hour to settle these infringements of the law. Singer became very familiar with the procedure of the courts and he was in a constant state of agitation. The money he had saved in the bank was spent for bail and fines. All of his efforts and money were used to keep his friend out of jail because of such charges as theft, committing public indecencies, and assault and battery.

The Greek cousin for whom Antonapoulos worked did not enter into these troubles at all. Charles Parker (for that was the name this cousin had taken) let Antonapoulos stay on at the store, but he watched him always with his pale, tight face and he made no effort to help him. Singer had a strange feeling about Charles Parker. He began to dislike him.

Singer lived in continual turmoil and worry. But Antonapoulos was always bland, and no matter what happened the gentle, flaccid smile was still on his face. In all the years before it had seemed to Singer that there was something very subtle and wise in this smile of his friend. He had never known just how much Antonapoulos understood and what he was thinking. Now in the big Greek's expression Singer thought that he could detect something sly and joking. He would shake his friend by the shoulders until he was very tired and explain things over and over with his hands. But nothing did any good.

All of Singer's money was gone and he had to borrow from the jeweler for whom he worked. On one occasion he was unable to pay bail for his friend and Antonapoulos spent the night in jail. When Singer came to get him out the next day he was very sulky. He did not want to leave. He had enjoyed his dinner of sowbelly and cornbread with syrup poured over it. And the new sleeping arrangements and his cellmates pleased him.

They had lived so much alone that Singer had no one to help him in his distress. Antonapoulos let nothing disturb him or cure him of his habits. At home he sometimes cooked the new dish he had eaten in the jail, and on the streets there was never any knowing just what he would do.

And then the final trouble came to Singer.

One afternoon he had come to meet Antonapoulos at the fruit store when Charles Parker handed him a letter. The letter explained that Charles Parker had made arrangements for his cousin to be taken to the state insane asylum two hundred miles away. Charles Parker had used his influence in the town and the details were already settled. Antonapoulos was to leave and to be admitted into the asylum the next week.

Singer read the letter several times, and for a while he could not think. Charles Parker was talking to him across the counter, but he did not even try to read his lips and understand. At last Singer wrote on the little pad he always carried in his pocket:

You cannot do this. Antonapoulos must stay with me.

Charles Parker shook his head excitedly. He did not know much American. 'None of your business,' he kept saying over and over.

Singer knew that everything was finished. The Greek was afraid that some day he might be responsible for his cousin. Charles Parker did not know much about the American language — but he understood the American dollar very well, and he had used his money and influence to admit his cousin to the asylum without delay.

There was nothing Singer could do.

The next week was full of feverish activity. He talked and talked. And although his hands never paused to rest he could not tell all that he had to say. He wanted to talk to Antonapoulos of all the thoughts that had ever been in his mind and heart, but there was not time. His gray eyes glittered and his quick, intelligent face expressed great strain. Antonapoulos watched him drowsily, and his friend did not know just what he really understood.

Then came the day when Antonapoulos must leave. Singer brought out his own suitcase and very carefully packed the best of their joint possessions. Antonapoulos made himself a lunch to eat during the journey. In the late afternoon they walked arm in arm down the street for the last time together. It was a chilly afternoon in late November, and little huffs of breath showed in the air before them.

Charles Parker was to travel with his cousin, but he stood apart from them at the station. Antonapoulos crowded into the bus and settled himself with elaborate preparations on one of the front seats. Singer watched him from the window and his hands began desperately to talk for the last time with his friend. But Antonapoulos was so busy checking over the various items in his lunch box that for a while he paid no attention. Just before the bus pulled away from the curb he turned to Singer and his smile was very bland and remote — as though already they were many miles apart.

The weeks that followed did not seem real at all. All day Singer worked over his bench in the back of the jewelry store, and then at night he returned to the house alone. More than anything he wanted to sleep. As soon as he came home from work he would lie on his cot and try to doze awhile. Dreams came to him when he lay there half-asleep. And in all of them Antonapoulos was there. His hands would jerk nervously, for in his dreams he was talking to his friend and Antonapoulos was watching him.

Singer tried to think of the time before he had ever known his friend. He tried to recount to himself certain things that had happened when he was young. But none of these things he tried to remember seemed real.

There was one particular fact that he remembered, but it was not at all important to him. Singer recalled that, although he had been deaf since he was an infant, he had not always been a real mute. He was left an orphan very young and placed in an institution for the deaf. He had learned to talk with his hands and to read. Before he was nine years old he could talk with one hand in the American way — and also could employ both of his hands after the method of Europeans. He had learned to follow the movements of people's lips and to understand what they said. Then finally he had been taught to speak.

At the school he was thought very intelligent. He learned the lessons before the rest of the pupils. But he could never become used to speaking with his lips. It was not natural to him, and his tongue felt like a whale in his mouth. From the blank expression on people's faces to whom he talked in this way he felt that his voice must be like the sound of some animal or that there was something disgusting in his speech. It was painful for him to try to talk with his mouth, but his hands were always ready to shape the words he wished to say. When he was twenty-two he had come South to this town from Chicago and he met Antonapoulos immediately. Since that time he had never spoken with his mouth again, because with his friend there was no need for this.

Nothing seemed real except the ten years with Antonapoulos. In his half-dreams he saw his friend very vividly, and when he awakened a great aching loneliness would be in him. Occasionally he would pack up a box for Antonapoulos, but he never received any reply. And so the months passed in this empty, dreaming way.

In the spring a change came over Singer. He could not sleep and his body was very restless. At evening he would walk monotonously around the room, unable to work off a new feeling of energy. If he rested at all it was only during a few hours before dawn — then he would drop bluntly into a sleep that lasted until the morning light struck suddenly beneath his opening eyelids like a scimitar.

He began spending his evenings walking around the town. He could no longer stand the rooms where Antonapoulos had lived, and he rented a place in a shambling boarding-house not far from the center of the town.

He ate his meals at a restaurant only two blocks away. This restaurant was at the very end of the long main street, and the name of the place was the New York Café. The first day he glanced over the menu quickly and wrote a short note and handed it to the proprietor.

Each morning for breakfast I want an egg, toast, and coffee — $0.15
For lunch I want soup (any kind), a meat sandwich, and milk — $0.25
Please bring me at dinner three vegetables (any kind but cabbage), fish or meat, and a glass of beer — $0.35
Thank you.

The proprietor read the note and gave him an alert, tactful glance. He was a hard man of middle height, with a beard so dark and heavy that the lower part of his face looked as though it were molded of iron. He usually stood in the corner by the cash register, his arms folded over his chest, quietly observing all that went on around him. Singer came to know this man's face very well, for he ate at one of his tables three times a day.

Each evening the mute walked alone for hours in the street. Sometimes the nights were cold with the sharp, wet winds of March and it would be raining heavily. But to him this did not matter. His gait was agitated and he always kept his hands stuffed tight into the pockets of his trousers. Then as the weeks passed the days grew warm and languorous. His agitation gave way gradually to exhaustion and there was a look about him of deep calm. In his face there came to be a brooding peace that is seen most often in the faces of the very sorrowful or the very wise. But still he wandered through the streets of the town, always silent and alone.

2

ON A black, sultry night in early summer Biff Brannon stood behind the cash register of the New York Café. It was twelve o'clock. Outside the street lights had already been turned off, so that the light from the café made a sharp, yellow rectangle on the sidewalk. The street was deserted, but inside the café there were half a dozen customers drinking beer or Santa Lucia wine or whiskey. Biff waited stolidly, his elbow resting on the counter and his thumb mashing the tip of his long nose. His eyes were intent. He watched especially a short, squat man in overalls who had become drunk and boisterous. Now and then his gaze passed on to the mute who sat by himself at one of the middle tables, or to others of the customers before the counter. But he always turned back to the drunk in overalls. The hour grew later and Biff continued to wait silently behind the counter. Then at last he gave the restaurant a final survey and went toward the door at the back which led upstairs.

Quietly he entered the room at the top of the stairs. It was dark inside and he walked with caution. After he had gone a few paces his toe struck something hard and he reached down and felt for the handle of a suitcase on the floor. He had only been in the room a few seconds and was about to leave when the light was turned on.

Alice sat up in the rumpled bed and looked at him. 'What you doing with that suitcase?' she asked. 'Can't you get rid of that lunatic without giving him back what he's already drunk up?'

'Wake up and go down yourself. Call the cop and let him get soused on the chain gang with cornbread and peas. Go to it, Misses Brannon.'

'I will all right if he's down there tomorrow. But you leave that bag alone. It don't belong to that sponger any more.'

'I know spongers, and Blount's not one,' Biff said. 'Myself — I don't know so well. But I'm not that kind of a thief.'

Calmly Biff put down the suitcase on the steps outside. The air was not so stale and sultry in the room as it was downstairs. He decided to stay for a short while and douse his face with cold water before going back.

'I told you already what I'll do if you don't get rid of that fellow for good tonight. In the daytime he takes them naps at the back, and then at night you feed him dinners and beer. For a week now he hasn't paid one cent. And all his wild talking and carrying-on will ruin any decent trade.'

'You don't know people and you don't know real business,' Biff said. 'The fellow in question first came in here twelve days ago and he was a stranger in the town. The first week he gave us twenty dollars' worth of trade. Twenty at the minimum.'

'And since then on credit,' Alice said. 'Five days on credit, and so drunk it's a disgrace to the business. And besides, he's nothing but a bum and a freak.'

'I like freaks,' Biff said.

'I reckon you do! I just reckon you certainly ought to, Mister Brannon — being as you're one yourself.'

He rubbed his bluish chin and paid her no attention. For the first fifteen years of their married life they had called each other just plain Biff and Alice. Then in one of their quarrels they had begun calling each other Mister and Misses, and since then they had never made it up enough to change it.

'I'm just warning you he'd better not be there when I come down tomorrow.'

Biff went into the bathroom, and after he had bathed his face he decided that he would have time for a shave. His beard was black and heavy as though it had grown for three days. He stood before the mirror and rubbed his cheek meditatively. He was sorry he had talked to Alice. With her, silence was better. Being around that woman always made him different from his real self. It made him tough and small and common as she was. Biff's eyes were cold and staring, half-concealed by the cynical droop of his eyelids. On the fifth finger of his calloused hand there was a woman's wedding ring. The door was open behind him, and in the mirror he could see Alice lying in the bed.

'Listen,' he said. 'The trouble with you is that you don't have any real kindness. Not but one woman I've ever known had this real kindness I'm talking about.'

'Well, I've known you to do things no man in this world would be proud of. I've known you to ——'

'Or maybe it's curiosity I mean. You don't ever see or notice anything important that goes on. You never watch and think and try to figure anything out. Maybe that's the biggest difference between you and me, after all.'

Alice was almost asleep again, and through the mirror he watched her with detachment. There was no distinctive point about her on which he could fasten his attention, and his gaze glided from her pale brown hair to the stumpy outline of her feet beneath the cover. The soft curves of her face led to the roundness of her hips and thighs. When he was away from her there was no one feature that stood out in his mind and he remembered her as a complete, unbroken figure.

'The enjoyment of a spectacle is something you have never known,' he said.

Her voice was tired. 'That fellow downstairs is a spectacle, all right, and a circus too. But I'm through putting up with him.'

'Hell, the man don't mean anything to me. He's no relative or buddy of mine. But you don't know what it is to store up a whole lot of details and then come upon something real.' He turned on the hot water and quickly began to shave.

It was the morning of May 15, yes, that Jake Blount had come in. He had noticed him immediately and watched. The man was short, with heavy shoulders like beams. He had a small, ragged mustache, and beneath this his lower lip looked as though it had been stung by a wasp. There were many things about the fellow that seemed contrary. His head was very large and well-shaped, but his neck was soft and slender as a boy's. The mustache looked false, as if it had been stuck on for a costume party and would fall off if he talked too fast. It made him seem almost middle-aged, although his face with its high, smooth forehead and wide-open eyes was young. His hands were huge, stained, and calloused, and he was dressed in a cheap white-linen suit. There was something very funny about the man, yet at the same time another feeling would not let you laugh.

He ordered a pint of liquor and drank it straight in half an hour. Then he sat at one of the booths and ate a big chicken dinner. Later he read a book and drank beer. That was the beginning. And although Biff had noticed Blount very carefully he would never have guessed about the crazy things that happened later. Never had he seen a man change so many times in twelve days. Never had he seen a fellow drink so much, stay drunk so long.

Biff pushed up the end of his nose with his thumb and shaved his upper lip. He was finished and his face seemed cooler. Alice was asleep when he went through the bedroom on the way downstairs.

The suitcase was heavy. He carried it to the front of the restaurant, behind the cash register, where he usually stood each evening. Methodically he glanced around the place. A few customers had left and the room was not so crowded, but the set-up was the same. The deaf-mute still drank coffee by himself at one of the middle tables. The drunk had not stopped talking. He was not addressing anyone around him in particular, nor was anyone listening. When he had come into the place that evening he wore those blue overalls instead of the filthy linen suit he had been wearing the twelve days. His socks were gone and his ankles were scratched and caked with mud.

Alertly Biff picked up fragments of his monologue. The fellow seemed to be talking some queer kind of politics again. Last night he had been talking about places he had been — about Texas and Oklahoma and the Carolinas. Once he had got on the subject of cat-houses, and afterward his jokes got so raw he had to be hushed up with beer. But most of the time nobody was sure just what he was saying. Talk — talk — talk. The words came out of his throat like a cataract. And the thing was that the accent he used was always changing, the kinds of words he used. Sometimes he talked like a linthead and sometimes like a professor. He would use words a foot long and then slip up on his grammar. It was hard to tell what kind of folks he had or what part of the country he was from. He was always changing. Thoughtfully Biff fondled the tip of his nose. There was no connection. Yet connection usually went with brains. This man had a good mind, all right, but he went from one thing to another without any reason behind it at all. He was like a man thrown off his track by something.

Biff leaned his weight on the counter and began to peruse the evening newspaper. The headlines told of a decision by the Board of Aldermen, after four months' deliberation, that the local budget could not afford traffic lights at certain dangerous intersections of the town. The left column reported on the war in the Orient. Biff read them both with equal attention. As his eyes followed the print the rest of his senses were on the alert to the various commotions that went on around him. When he had finished the articles he still stared down at the newspaper with his eyes half-closed. He felt nervous. The fellow was a problem, and before morning he would have to make some sort of settlement with him. Also, he felt without knowing why that something of importance would happen tonight. The fellow could not keep on forever.

Biff sensed that someone was standing in the entrance and he raised his eyes quickly. A gangling, towheaded youngster, a girl of about twelve, stood looking in the doorway. She was dressed in khaki shorts, a blue shirt, and tennis shoes — so that at first glance she was like a very young boy. Biff pushed aside the paper when he saw her, and smiled when she came up to him.

'Hello, Mick. Been to the Girl Scouts?'

'No,' she said. 'I don't belong to them.'

From the corner of his eye he noticed that the drunk slammed his fist down on a table and turned away from the men to whom he had been talking. Biff's voice roughened as he spoke to the youngster before him.

'Your folks know you're out after midnight?'

'It's O.K. There's a gang of kids playing out late on our block tonight.'

He had never seen her come into the place with anyone her own age. Several years ago she had always tagged behind her older brother. The Kellys were a good-sized family in numbers. Later she would come in pulling a couple of snotty babies in a wagon. But if she wasn't nursing or trying to keep up with the bigger ones, she was by herself. Now the kid stood there seeming not to be able to make up her mind what she wanted. She kept pushing back her damp, whitish hair with the palm of her hand.

'I'd like a pack of cigarettes, please. The cheapest kind.'

Biff started to speak, hesitated, and then reached his hand inside the counter. Mick brought out a handkerchief and began untying the knot in the corner where she kept her money. As she gave the knot a jerk the change clattered to the floor and rolled toward Blount, who stood muttering to himself. For a moment he stared in a daze at the coins, but before the kid could go after them he squatted down with concentration and picked up the money. He walked heavily to the counter and stood jiggling the two pennies, the nickel, and the dime in his palm.

'Seventeen cents for cigarettes now?'

Biff waited, and Mick looked from one of them to the other. The drunk stacked the money into a little pile on the counter, still protecting it with his big, dirty hand. Slowly he picked up one penny and flipped it down.

'Five mills for the crackers who grew the weed and five for the dupes who rolled it,' he said. 'A cent for you, Biff.' Then he tried to focus his eyes so that he could read the mottoes on the nickel and dime. He kept fingering the two coins and moving them around in a circle. At last he pushed them away. 'And that's a humble homage to liberty. To democracy and tyranny. To freedom and piracy.'

Calmly Biff picked up the money and rang it into the till. Mick looked as though she wanted to hang around awhile. She took in the drunk with one long gaze, and then she turned her eyes to the middle of the room where the mute sat at his table alone. After a moment Blount also glanced now and then in the same direction. The mute sat silently over his glass of beer, idly drawing on the table with the end of a burnt matchstick.

Jake Blount was the first to speak. 'It's funny, but I been seeing that fellow in my sleep for the past three or four nights. He won't leave me alone. If you ever noticed, he never seems to say anything.'

It was seldom that Biff ever discussed one customer with another. 'No, he don't,' he answered noncommittally.

'It's funny.'

Mick shifted her weight from one foot to the other and fitted the package of cigarettes into the pocket of her shorts. 'It's not funny if you know anything about him,' she said. 'Mister Singer lives with us. He rooms in our house.'

'Is that so?' Biff asked. 'I declare — I didn't know that.'

Mick walked toward the door and answered him without looking around. 'Sure. He's been with us three months now.'

Biff unrolled his shirt-sleeves and then folded them up carefully again. He did not take his eyes away from Mick as she left the restaurant. And even after she had been gone several minutes he still fumbled with his shirt-sleeves and stared at the empty doorway. Then he locked his arms across his chest and turned back to the drunk again.

Blount leaned heavily on the counter. His brown eyes were wet-looking and wide open with a dazed expression. He needed a bath so badly that he stank like a goat. There were dirt beads on his sweaty neck and an oil stain on his face. His lips were thick and red and his brown hair was matted on his forehead. His overalls were too short in the body and he kept pulling at the crotch of them.

'Man, you ought to know better,' Biff said finally. 'You can't go around like this. Why, I'm surprised you haven't been picked up for vagrancy. You ought to sober up. You need washing and your hair needs cutting. Motherogod! You're not fit to walk around amongst people.'

Blount scowled and bit his lower lip.

'Now, don't take offense and get your dander up. Do what I tell you. Go back in the kitchen and tell the colored boy to give you a big pan of hot water. Tell Willie to give you a towel and plenty soap and wash yourself good. Then eat you some milk toast and open up your suitcase and put you on a clean shirt and a pair of britches that fit you. Then to-morrow you can start doing whatever you're going to do and working wherever you mean to work and get straightened out.'

'You know what you can do,' Blount said drunkenly. 'You can just ——'

'All right,' Biff said very quietly. 'No, I can't. Now you just behave yourself.'

Biff went to the end of the counter and returned with two glasses of draught beer. The drunk picked up his glass so clumsily that beer slopped down on his hands and messed the counter. Biff sipped his portion with careful relish. He regarded Blount steadily with half-closed eyes. Blount was not a freak, although when you first saw him he gave you that impression. It was like something was deformed about him — but when you looked at him closely each part of him was normal and as it ought to be. Therefore if this difference was not in the body it was probably in the mind. He was like a man who had served a term in prison or had been to Harvard College or had lived for a long time with foreigners in South America. He was like a person who had been somewhere that other people are not likely to go or had done something that others are not apt to do.

Biff cocked his head to one side and said, 'Where are you from?'

'Nowhere.'

'Now, you have to be born somewhere. North Carolina — Tennessee — Alabama — some place.'

Blount's eyes were dreamy and unfocused. 'Carolina,' he said.

'I can tell you've been around,' Biff hinted delicately.

But the drunk was not listening. He had turned from the counter and was staring out at the dark, empty street. After a moment he walked to the door with loose, uncertain steps. '*Adios*,' he called back.

Biff was alone again and he gave the restaurant one of his quick, thorough surveys. It was past one in the morning, and there were only four or five customers in the room. The mute still sat by himself at the middle table. Biff stared at him idly and shook the few remaining drops of beer around in the bottom of his glass. Then he finished his drink in one slow swallow and went back to the newspaper spread out on the counter.

This time he could not keep his mind on the words before him. He remembered Mick. He wondered if he should have sold her the pack of cigarettes and if it were really harmful for kids to smoke. He thought of the way Mick narrowed her eyes and pushed back the bangs of her hair with the palm of her hand. He thought of her hoarse, boyish voice and of her habit of hitching up her khaki shorts and swaggering like a cowboy in the picture show. A feeling of tenderness came in him. He was uneasy.

Restlessly Biff turned his attention to Singer. The mute sat with his hands in his pockets and the half-finished glass of beer before him had become warm and stagnant. He would offer to treat Singer to a slug of whiskey before he left. What he had said to Alice was true — he did like freaks. He had a special friendly feeling for sick people and cripples. Whenever somebody with a harelip or T.B. came into the place he would set him up to beer. Or if the customer were a hunchback or a bad cripple, then it would be whiskey on the house. There was one fellow who had had his peter and his left leg blown off in a boiler explosion, and whenever he came to town there was a free pint waiting for him. And if Singer were a drinking kind of man he could get liquor at half price any time he wanted it. Biff nodded to himself. Then neatly he folded his newspaper and put it under the counter along with several others. At the end of the week he would take them all back to the storeroom behind the kitchen, where he kept a complete file of the evening newspaper that dated back without a break for twenty-one years.

At two o'clock Blount entered the restaurant again. He brought in with him a tall Negro man carrying a black bag. The drunk tried to bring him up to the counter for a drink, but the Negro left as soon as he realized why he had been led inside. Biff recognized him as a Negro doctor who had practiced in the town ever since he could remember. He was related in some way to young Willie back in the kitchen. Before he left Biff saw him turn on Blount with a look of quivering hatred.

The drunk just stood there.

'Don't you know you can't bring no nigger in a place where white men drink?' someone asked him.

Biff watched this happening from a distance. Blount was very angry, and now it could easily be seen how drunk he was.

'I'm part nigger myself,' he called out as a challenge.

Biff watched him alertly and the place was quiet. With his thick nostrils and the rolling whites of his eyes it looked a little as though he might be telling the truth.

'I'm part nigger and wop and bohunk and chink. All of those.'

There was laughter.

'And I'm Dutch and Turkish and Japanese and American.' He walked in zigzags around the table where the mute drank his coffee. His voice was loud and cracked. 'I'm one who knows. I'm a stranger in a strange land.'

'Quiet down,' Biff said to him.

Blount paid no attention to anyone in the place except the mute. They were both looking at each other. The mute's eyes were cold and gentle as a cat's and all his body seemed to listen. The drunk man was in a frenzy.

'You're the only one in this town who catches what I mean,' Blount said. 'For two days now I been talking to you in my mind because I know you understand the things I want to mean.'

Some people in a booth were laughing because without knowing it the drunk had picked out a deaf-mute to try to talk with. Biff watched the two men with little darting glances and listened attentively.

Blount sat down to the table and leaned over close to Singer. 'There are those who know and those who don't know. And for every ten thousand who don't know there's only one who knows. That's the miracle of all time — the fact that these millions know so much but don't know this. It's like in the fifteenth century when everybody believed the world was flat and only Columbus and a few other fellows knew the truth. But it's different in that it took talent to figure that the earth is round. While this truth is so obvious it's a miracle of all history that people don't know. You savvy.'

Biff rested his elbows on the counter and looked at Blount with curiosity. 'Know what?' he asked.

'Don't listen to him,' Blount said. 'Don't mind that flat-footed, blue-jawed, nosy bastard. For you see, when us people who know run into each other that's an event. It almost never happens. Sometimes we meet each other and neither guesses that the other is one who knows. That's a bad thing. It's happened to me a lot of times. But you see there are so few of us.'

'Masons?' Biff asked.

'Shut up, you! Else I'll snatch your arm off and beat you black with it,' Blount bawled. He hunched over close to the mute and his voice dropped to a drunken whisper. 'And how come? Why has this miracle of ignorance endured? Because of one thing. A conspiracy. A vast and insidious conspiracy. Obscurantism.'

The men in the booth were still laughing at the drunk who was trying to hold a conversation with the mute. Only Biff was serious. He wanted to ascertain if the mute really understood what was said to him. The fellow nodded frequently and his face seemed contemplative. He was only slow — that was all. Blount began to crack a few jokes along with this talk about knowing. The mute never smiled until several seconds after the funny remark had been made; then when the talk was gloomy again the smile still hung on his face a little too long. The fellow was downright uncanny. People felt themselves watching him even before they knew that there was anything different about him. His eyes made a person think that he heard things nobody else had ever heard, that he knew things no one had ever guessed before. He did not seem quite human.

Jake Blount leaned across the table and the words came out as though a dam inside him had broken. Biff could not understand him any more. Blount's tongue was so heavy with drink and he talked at such a violent pace that the sounds were all shaken up together. Biff wondered where he would go when Alice turned him out of the place. And in the morning she would do it, too — like she said.

Biff yawned wanly, patting his open mouth with his fingertips until his jaw had relaxed. It was almost three o'clock, the most stagnant hour in the day or night.

The mute was patient. He had been listening to Blount for almost an hour. Now he began to look at the clock occasionally. Blount did not notice this and went on without a pause. At last he stopped to roll a cigarette, and then the mute nodded his head in the direction of the clock, smiled in that hidden way of his, and got up from the table. His hands stayed stuffed in his pockets as always. He went out quickly.

Blount was so drunk that he did not know what had happened. He had never even caught on to the fact that the mute made no answers. He began to look around the place with his mouth open and his eyes rolling and fuddled. A red vein stood out on his forehead and he began to hit the table angrily with his fists. His bout could not last much longer now.

'Come on over,' Biff said kindly. 'Your friend has gone.'

The fellow was still hunting for Singer. He had never seemed really drunk like that before. He had an ugly look.

'I have something for you over here and I want to speak with you a minute,' Biff coaxed.

Blount pulled himself up from the table and walked with big, loose steps toward the street again.

Biff leaned against the wall. In and out — in and out. After all, it was none of his business. The room was very empty and quiet. The minutes lingered. Wearily he let his head sag forward. All motion seemed slowly to be leaving the room. The counter, faces, the booths and tables, the radio in the corner, whirring fans on the ceiling — all seemed to become very faint and still.

He must have dozed. A hand was shaking his elbow. His wits came back to him slowly and he looked up to see what was wanted. Willie, the colored boy in the kitchen, stood before him dressed in his cap and his long white apron. Willie stammered because he was excited about whatever he was trying to say.

'And so he were l-l-lamming his fist against this here brick w-w-w-all.'

'What's that?'

'Right down one of them alleys two d-d-doors away.'

Biff straightened his slumped shoulders and arranged his tie. 'What?'

'And they means to bring him in here and they liable to pile in any minute ——'

'Willie,' Biff said patiently. 'Start at the beginning and let me get this straight.'

'It this here short white man with the m-m-mustache.'

'Mr. Blount. Yes.'

'Well — I didn't see how it commenced. I were standing in the back door when I heard this here commotion. Sound like a big fight in the alley. So I r-r-run to see. And this here white man had just gone hog wild. He were butting his head against the side of this brick wall and hitting with his fists. He were cussing and fighting like I never seen a white man fight before. With just this here wall. He liable to broken his own head the way he were carrying on. Then two white mens who had heard the commotion come up and stand around and look ——'

'So what happened?'

'Well — you know this here dumb gentleman — hands in pockets — this here ——'

'Mr. Singer.'

'And he come along and just stood looking around to see what it were all about. And Mr. B-B-Blount seen him and commenced to talk and holler. And then all of a sudden he fallen down on the ground. Maybe he done really busted his head open. A p-p-p-police come up and somebody done told him Mr. Blount been staying here.'

Biff bowed his head and organized the story he had just heard into a neat pattern. He rubbed his nose and thought for a minute.

'They liable to pile in here any minute.' Willie went to the door and looked down the street. 'Here they all come now. They having to drag him.'

A dozen onlookers and a policeman all tried to crowd into the restaurant. Outside a couple of whores stood looking in through the front window. It was always funny how many people could crowd in from nowhere when anything out of the ordinary happened.

'No use creating any more disturbance than necessary,' Biff said. He looked at the policeman who supported the drunk. 'The rest of them might as well clear out.'

The policeman put the drunk in a chair and hustled the little crowd into the street again. Then he turned to Biff: 'Somebody said he was staying here with you.'

'No. But he might as well be,' Biff said.

'Want me to take him with me?'

Biff considered. 'He won't get into any more trouble to-night. Of course I can't be responsible — but I think this will calm him down.'

'O.K. I'll drop back in again before I knock off.'

Biff, Singer, and Jake Blount were left alone. For the first time since he had been brought in, Biff turned his attention to the drunk man. It seemed that Blount had hurt his jaw very badly. He was slumped down on the table with his big hand over his mouth, swaying backward and forward. There was a gash in his head and the blood ran from his temple. His knuckles were skinned raw, and he was so filthy that he looked as if he had been pulled by the scruff of the neck from a sewer. All the juice had spurted out of him and he was completely collapsed. The mute sat at the table across from him, taking it all in with his gray eyes.

Then Biff saw that Blount had not hurt his jaw, but he was

holding his hand over his mouth because his lips were trembling. The tears began to roll down his grimy face. Now and then he glanced sideways at Biff and Singer, angry that they should see him cry. It was embarrassing. Biff shrugged his shoulders at the mute and raised his eyebrows with a what-to-do? expression. Singer cocked his head on one side.

Biff was in a quandary. Musingly he wondered just how he should manage the situation. He was still trying to decide when the mute turned over the menu and began to write.

If you cannot think of any place for him to go he can go home with me. First some soup and coffee would be good for him.

With relief Biff nodded vigorously.

On the table he placed three special plates of the last evening meal, two bowls of soup, coffee, and dessert. But Blount would not eat. He would not take his hand away from his mouth, and it was as though his lips were some very secret part of himself which was being exposed. His breath came in ragged sobs and his big shoulders jerked nervously. Singer pointed to one dish after the other, but Blount just sat with his hand over his mouth and shook his head.

Biff enunciated slowly so that the mute could see. 'The jitters ——' he said conversationally.

The steam from the soup kept floating up into Blount's face, and after a little while he reached shakily for his spoon. He drank the soup and ate part of his dessert. His thick, heavy lips still trembled and he bowed his head far down over his plate.

Biff noted this. He was thinking that in nearly every person there was some special physical part kept always guarded. With the mute his hands. The kid Mick picked at the front of her blouse to keep the cloth from rubbing the new, tender nipples beginning to come out on her breast. With Alice it was her hair; she used never to let him sleep with her when he rubbed oil in his scalp. And with himself?

Lingeringly Biff turned the ring on his little finger. Anyway he knew what it was not. Not. Any more. A sharp line cut into his forehead. His hand in his pocket moved nervously toward his genitals. He began whistling a song and got up from the table. Funny to spot it in other people, though.

They helped Blount to his feet. He teetered weakly. He was not crying any more, but he seemed to be brooding on something shameful and sullen. He walked in the direction he was led. Biff brought out the suitcase from behind the counter and explained to the mute about it. Singer looked as though he could not be surprised at anything.

Biff went with them to the entrance. 'Buck up and keep your nose clean,' he said to Blount.

The black night sky was beginning to lighten and turn a deep blue with the new morning. There were but a few weak, silvery stars. The street was empty, silent, almost cool. Singer carried the suitcase with his left hand, and with his free hand he supported Blount. He nodded good-bye to Biff and they started off together down the sidewalk. Biff stood watching them. After they had gone half a block away only their black forms showed in the blue darkness — the mute straight and firm and the broad-shouldered, stumbling Blount holding on to him. When he could see them no longer, Biff waited for a moment and examined the sky. The vast depth of it fascinated and oppressed him. He rubbed his forehead and went back into the sharply lighted restaurant.

He stood behind the cash register, and his face contracted and hardened as he tried to recall the things that had happened during the night. He had the feeling that he wanted to explain something to himself. He recalled the incidents in tedious detail and was still puzzled.

The door opened and closed several times as a sudden spurt of customers began to come in. The night was over. Willie stacked some of the chairs up on the tables and mopped at the floor. He was ready to go home and was singing. Willie was lazy. In the kitchen he was always stopping to play for a while on the harmonica he carried around with him. Now he mopped the floor with sleepy strokes and hummed his lonesome Negro music steadily.

The place was still not crowded — it was the hour when men who have been up all night meet those who are freshly wakened and ready to start a new day. The sleepy waitress was serving both beer and coffee. There was no noise or conversation, for each person seemed to be alone. The mutual distrust between the men who were just awakened and those who were ending a long night gave everyone a feeling of estrangement.

The bank building across the street was very pale in the dawn. Then gradually its white brick walls grew more distinct. When at last the first shafts of the rising sun began to brighten the street, Biff gave the place one last survey and went upstairs.

Noisily he rattled the doorknob as he entered so that Alice would be disturbed. 'Motherogod!' he said. 'What a night!'

Alice awoke with caution. She lay on the rumpled bed like a sulky cat and stretched herself. The room was drab in the fresh, hot morning sun, and a pair of silk stockings hung limp and withered from the cord of the window-shade.

'Is that drunk fool still hanging around downstairs?' she demanded.

Biff took off his shirt and examined the collar to see if it were clean enough to be worn again. 'Go down and see for yourself. I told you nobody will hinder you from kicking him out.'

Sleepily Alice reached down and picked up a Bible, the blank side of a menu, and a Sunday-School book from the floor beside the bed. She rustled through the tissue pages of the Bible until she reached a certain passage and began reading, pronouncing the words aloud with painful concentration. It was Sunday, and she was preparing the weekly lesson for her class of boys in the Junior Department of her church. 'Now as he walked by the sea of Galilee, he saw Simon and Andrew his brother casting a net into the sea: for they were fishers. And Jesus said unto them, "Come ye after me, and I will make you to become fishers of men." And straightway they forsook their nets, and followed him.'

Biff went into the bathroom to wash himself. The silky murmuring continued as Alice studied aloud. He listened. '... and in the morning, rising up a great while before day, He went out, and departed into a solitary place, and there prayed. And Simon and they that were with Him followed after Him. And when they had found Him, they said unto Him, "All men seek for Thee."'

She had finished. Biff let the words revolve again gently inside him. He tried to separate the actual words from the sound of Alice's voice as she had spoken them. He wanted to remember the passage as his mother used to read it when he was a boy. With nostalgia he glanced down at the wedding ring on his fifth finger that had once been hers. He wondered again how she would have felt about his giving up church and religion.

'The lesson for today is about the gathering of the disciples,' Alice said to herself in preparation. 'And the text is, "All men seek for Thee."'

Abruptly Biff roused himself from meditation and turned on the water spigot at full force. He stripped off his undervest and began to wash himself. Always he was scrupulously clean from the belt upward. Every morning he soaped his chest and arms and neck and feet — and about twice during the season he got into the bathtub and cleaned all of his parts.

Biff stood by the bed, waiting impatiently for Alice to get up. From the window he saw that the day would be windless and burning hot. Alice had finished reading the lesson. She still lay lazily across the bed, although she knew that he was waiting. A calm, sullen anger rose in him. He chuckled ironically. Then he said with bitterness: 'If you like I can sit and read the paper awhile. But I wish you would let me sleep now.'

Alice began dressing herself and Biff made up the bed. Deftly he reversed the sheets in all possible ways, putting the top one on the bottom, and turning them over and upside down. When the bed was smoothly made he waited until Alice had left the room before he slipped off his trousers and crawled inside. His feet jutted out from beneath the cover and his wiry-haired chest was very dark against the pillow. He was glad he had not told Alice about what had happened to the drunk. He had wanted to talk to somebody about it, because maybe if he told all the facts out loud he could put his finger on the thing that puzzled him. The poor son-of-a-bitch talking and talking and not ever getting anybody to understand what he meant. Not knowing himself, most likely. And the way he gravitated around the deaf-mute and picked him out and tried to make him a free present of everything in him.

Why?

Because in some men it is in them to give up everything personal at some time, before it ferments and poisons — throw it to some human being or some human idea. They have to. In some men it is in them —— The text is 'All men seek for Thee.' Maybe that was why — maybe —— He was a Chinaman, the fellow had said. And a nigger and a wop and a Jew. And if he believed it hard enough maybe it was so. Every person and every thing he said he was ——

Biff stretched both of his arms outward and crossed his naked feet. His face was older in the morning light, with the closed, shrunken eyelids and the heavy, iron-like beard on his cheeks and jaw. Gradually his mouth softened and relaxed. The hard, yellow rays of the sun came in through the window so that the room was hot and bright. Biff turned wearily and covered his eyes with his hands. And he was nobody but

— Bartholomew — old Biff with two fists and a quick tongue — Mister Brannon — by himself.

3

THE sun woke Mick early, although she had stayed out mighty late the night before. It was too hot even to drink coffee for breakfast, so she had ice water with syrup in it and cold biscuits. She messed around the kitchen for a while and then went out on the front porch to read the funnies. She had thought maybe Mister Singer would be reading the paper on the porch like he did most Sunday mornings. But Mister Singer was not there, and later on her Dad said he came in very late the night before and had company in his room. She waited for Mister Singer a long time. All the other boarders came down except him. Finally she went back in the kitchen and took Ralph out of his high chair and put a clean dress on him and wiped off his face. Then when Bubber got home from Sunday School she was ready to take the kids out. She let Bubber ride in the wagon with Ralph because he was barefooted and the hot sidewalk burned his feet. She pulled the wagon for about eight blocks until they came to the big, new house that was being built. The ladder was still propped against the edge of the roof, and she screwed up nerve and began to climb.

'You mind Ralph,' she called back to Bubber. 'Mind the gnats don't sit on his eyelids.'

Five minutes later Mick stood up and held herself very straight. She spread out her arms like wings. This was the place where everybody wanted to stand. The very top. But not many kids could do it. Most of them were scared, for if you lost grip and rolled off the edge it would kill you. All around were the roofs of other houses and the green tops of trees. On the other side of town were the church steeples and the smokestacks from the mills. The sky was bright blue and hot as fire. The sun made everything on the ground either dizzy white or black.

She wanted to sing. All the songs she knew pushed up toward her throat, but there was no sound. One big boy who had got to the highest part of the roof last week let out a yell and then started hollering out a speech he had learned at High School — 'Friends, Romans, Countrymen, Lend me your ears!' There was something about getting to the very top that gave you a wild feeling and made you want to yell or sing or raise up your arms and fly.

She felt the soles of her tennis shoes slipping, and eased herself down so that she straddled the peak of the roof. The house was almost finished. It would be one of the largest buildings in the neighborhood — two stories, with very high ceilings and the steepest roof of any house she had ever seen. But soon the work would all be finished. The carpenters would leave and the kids would have to find another place to play.

She was by herself. No one was around and it was quiet and she could think for a while. She took from the pocket of her shorts the package of cigarettes she had bought the night before. She breathed in the smoke slowly. The cigarette gave her a drunk feeling so that her head seemed heavy and loose on her shoulders, but she had to finish it.

M. K. — That was what she would have written on everything when she was seventeen years old and very famous. She would ride back home in a red-and-white Packard automobile with her initials on the doors. She would have M. K. written in red on her handkerchiefs and underclothes. Maybe she would be a great inventor. She would invent little tiny radios the size of a green pea that people could carry around and stick in their ears. Also flying machines people could fasten on their backs like knapsacks and go zipping all over the world. After that she would be the first one to make a large tunnel through the world to China, and people could go down in big balloons. Those were the first things she would invent. They were already planned.

When Mick had finished half of the cigarette she smashed it dead and flipped the butt down the slant of the roof. Then she leaned forward so that her head rested on her arms and began to hum to herself.

It was a funny thing — but nearly all the time there was some kind of piano piece or other music going on in the back of her mind. No matter what she was doing or thinking it was nearly always there. Miss Brown, who boarded with them, had a radio in her room, and all last winter she would sit on the steps every Sunday afternoon and listen in on the programs. Those were probably classical pieces, but they were the ones she remembered best. There was one special fellow's music that made her heart shrink up every time she heard it. Sometimes this fellow's music was like little colored pieces of crystal candy, and other times it was the softest, saddest thing she had ever imagined about.

There was the sudden sound of crying. Mick sat up straight and listened. The wind ruffled the fringe of hair on her forehead and the bright sun made her face white and damp. The whimpering continued, and Mick moved slowly along the sharp-pointed roof on her hands and knees. When she reached the end she leaned forward and lay on her stomach so that her head jutted over the edge and she could see the ground below. The kids were where she had left them. Bubber was squatting over something on the ground and beside him was a little black, dwarf shadow. Ralph was still tied in the wagon. He was just old enough to sit up, and he held on to the sides of the wagon, with his cap crooked on his head, crying.

'Bubber!' Mick called down. 'Find out what that Ralph wants and give it to him.'

Bubber stood up and looked hard into the baby's face. 'He don't want nothing.'

'Well, give him a good shake, then.'

Mick climbed back to the place where she had been sitting before. She wanted to think for a long time about two or three certain people, to sing to herself, and to make plans. But that Ralph was still hollering and there wouldn't be any peace for her at all.

Boldly she began to climb down toward the ladder propped against the edge of the roof. The slant was very steep and there were only a few blocks of wood nailed down, very far apart from each other, that the workmen used for footholds. She was dizzy, and her heart beat so hard it made her tremble. Commandingly she talked out loud to herself: 'Hold on here with your hands tight and then slide down until your right toe gets a grip there and then stay close and wiggle over to the left. Nerve, Mick, you've got to keep nerve.'

Coming down was the hardest part of any climbing. It took her a long time to reach the ladder and to feel safe again. When she stood on the ground at last she seemed much shorter and smaller and her legs felt for a minute like they would crumple up with her. She hitched her shorts and jerked the belt a notch tighter. Ralph was still crying, but she paid the sound no attention and went into the new, empty house.

Last month they had put a sign out in front saying that no children were allowed on the lot. A gang of kids had been scuffling around inside the rooms one night, and a girl who couldn't see in the dark had run into a room that hadn't been floored and fallen through and broken her leg. She was still at the hospital in a plaster parish cast. Also, another time some tough boys wee-weed all over one of the walls and wrote some pretty bad words. But no matter how many Keep Out signs were put up, they couldn't run kids away until the house had been painted and finished and people had moved in.

The rooms smelled of new wood, and when she walked the soles of her tennis shoes made a flopping sound that echoed through all the house. The air was hot and quiet. She stood still in the middle of the front room for a while, and then she suddenly thought of something. She fished in her pocket and brought out two stubs of chalk — one green and the other red.

Mick drew the big block letters very slowly. At the top she wrote EDISON, and under that she drew the names of DICK TRACY and MUSSOLINI. Then in each corner with the largest letters of all, made with green and outlined in red, she wrote her initials — M. K. When that was done she crossed over to the opposite wall and wrote a very bad word — PUSSY, and beneath that she put her initials, too.

She stood in the middle of the empty room and stared at what she had done. The chalk was still in her hands and she did not feel really satisfied. She was trying to think of the name of this fellow who had written this music she heard over the radio last winter. She had asked a girl at school who owned a piano and took music lessons about him, and the girl asked her teacher. It seemed this fellow was just a kid who had lived in some country in Europe a good while ago. But even if he was just a young kid he had made up all these beautiful pieces of the piano and for the violin and for a band or orchestra too. In her mind she could remember about six different tunes from the pieces of his she had heard. A few of them were kind of quick and tinkling, and another was like that smell in the springtime after a rain. But they all made her somehow sad and excited at the same time.

She hummed one of the tunes, and after a while in the hot, empty house by herself she felt the tears come in her eyes. Her throat got tight and rough and she couldn't sing any more. Quickly she wrote the fellow's name at the very top of the list — MOTSART.

Ralph was tied in the wagon just as she had left him. He sat up quiet and still and his fat little hands held on to the sides. Ralph looked like a little Chinese baby with his square black bangs and his black eyes. The sun was in his face, and that was why he had been hollering. Bubber was nowhere around. When Ralph saw her coming he began tuning up to cry again. She pulled the wagon into the shade by the side of the new house and took from her shirt pocket a blue-colored jelly bean. She stuck the candy in the baby's warm, soft mouth.

'Put that in your pipe and smoke it,' she said to him. In a way it was a waste, because Ralph was still too little to get the real good flavor out of candy. A clean rock would be about the same to him, only the little fool would swallow it. He didn't understand any more about taste than he did about talking. When you said you were so sick and tired of dragging him around you had a good mind to throw him in the river, it was the same to him as if you had been loving him. Nothing much made any difference to him. That was why it was such an awful bore to haul him around.

Mick cupped her hands, clamped them tight together, and blew through the crack between her thumbs. Her cheeks puffed out and at first there was only the sound of air rushing through her fists. Then a high, shrill whistle sounded, and after a few seconds Bubber came out from around the corner of the house.

She rumpled the sawdust out of Bubber's hair and straightened Ralph's cap. This cap was the finest thing Ralph had. It was made out of lace and all embroidered. The ribbon under his chin was blue on one side and white on the other, and over each ear there were big rosettes. His head had got too big for the cap and the embroidery scratched, but she always put it on him when she took him out. Ralph didn't have any real baby carriage like most folks' babies did, or any summer bootees. He had to be dragged around in a tacky old wagon she had got for Christmas three years before. But the fine cap gave him face.

There was nobody on the street, for it was late Sunday morning and very hot. The wagon screeched and rattled. Bubber was barefooted and the sidewalk was so hot it burned his feet. The green oak trees made cool-looking black shadows on the ground, but that was not shade enough.

'Get up in the wagon,' she told Bubber. 'And let Ralph sit in your lap.'

'I can walk all right.'

The long summer-time always gave Bubber the colic. He didn't have on a shirt and his ribs were sharp and white. The sun made him pale instead of brown, and his little titties were like blue raisins on his chest.

'I don't mind pulling you,' Mick said. 'Get on in.'

'O.K.'

Mick dragged the wagon slowly because she was not in any hurry to get home. She began talking to the kids. But it was really more like saying things to herself than words said to them.

'This is a funny thing — the dreams I've been having lately. It's like I'm swimming. But instead of water I'm pushing out my arms and swimming through great big crowds of people. The crowd is a hundred times bigger that in Kresses store on Saturday afternoon. The biggest crowd in the world. And sometimes I'm yelling and swimming through people, knocking them all down wherever I go — and other times I'm on the ground and people are trompling all over me and my insides are oozing out on the sidewalk. I guess it's more like a nightmare than a plain dream ——'

On Sunday the house was always full of folks because the boarders had visitors. Newspapers rustled and there was cigar smoke, and footsteps always on the stairs.

'Some things you just naturally want to keep private. Not because they are bad, but because you just want them secret. There are two or three things I wouldn't want even you to know about.'

Bubber got out when they came to the corner and helped her lift the wagon down the curb and get it up on the next sidewalk.

'But there's one thing I would give anything for. And that's a piano. If we had a piano I'd practice every single night and learn every piece in the world. That's the thing I want more than anything else.'

They had come to their own home block now. Their house was only a few doors away. It was one of the biggest houses on the whole north side of town — three stories high. But then there were fourteen people in the family. There weren't that many in the real, blood Kelly family — but they ate there and slept there at five dollars a head and you might as well count them on in. Mr. Singer wasn't counted in that because he only rented a room and kept it straightened up himself.

The house was narrow and had not been painted for many years. It did not seem to be built strong enough for its three stories of height. It sagged on one side.

Mick untied Ralph and lifted him from the wagon. She darted quickly through the hall, and from the corner of her eye she saw that the living-room was full of boarders. Her Dad was in there, too. Her Mama would be in the kitchen. They were all hanging around waiting for dinner-time.

She went into the first of the three rooms that the family kept for themselves. She put Ralph down on the bed where her Dad and Mama slept and gave him a string of beads to play with. From behind the closed door of the next room she could hear the sound of voices, and she decided to go inside.

Hazel and Etta stopped talking when they saw her. Etta was sitting in the chair by the window, painting her toenails with the red polish. Her hair was done up in steel rollers and there was a white dab of face cream on a little place under her chin where a pimple had come out. Hazel was flopped out lazy on the bed as usual.

'What were you all jawing about?'

'It's none of your nosy business,' Etta said. 'Just you hush up and leave us alone.'

'It's my room just as much as it is either one of yours. I have as good a right in here as you do.' Mick strutted from one corner to the other until she had covered all the floor space. 'But then I don't care anything about picking any fight. All I want are my own rights.'

Mick brushed back her shaggy bangs with the palm of her hand. She had done this so often that there was a little row of cowlicks above her forehead. She quivered her nose and made faces at herself in the mirror. Then she began walking around the room again.

Hazel and Etta were O.K. as far as sisters went. But Etta was like she was full of worms. All she thought about was movie stars and getting in the movies. Once she had written to Jeanette MacDonald and had got a typewritten letter back saying that if ever she came out to Hollywood she could come by and swim in her swimming pool. And ever since that swimming pool had been preying on Etta's mind. All she thought about was going to Hollywood when she could scrape up the bus fare and getting a job as a secretary and being buddies with Jeanette MacDonald and getting in the movies herself.

She primped all the day long. And that was the bad part. Etta wasn't naturally pretty like Hazel. The main thing was she didn't have any chin. She would pull at her jaw and go through a lot of chin exercises she had read in a movie book. She was always looking at her side profile in the mirror and trying to keep her mouth set in a certain way. But it didn't do any good. Sometimes Etta would hold her face with her hands and cry in the night about it.

Hazel was plain lazy. She was good-looking but thick in the head. She was eighteen years old, and next to Bill she was the oldest of all the kids in the family. Maybe that was the trouble. She got the first and biggest share of everything — the first whack at the new clothes and the biggest part of any special treat. Hazel never had to grab for anything and she was soft.

'Are you just going to tramp around the room all day? It makes me sick to see you in those silly boy's clothes. Somebody ought to clamp down on you, Mick Kelly, and make you behave,' Etta said.

'Shut up,' said Mick. 'I wear shorts because I don't want to wear your old hand-me-downs. I don't want to be like either of you and I don't want to look like either of you. And I won't. That's why I wear shorts. I'd rather be a boy any day, and I wish I could move in with Bill.'

Mick scrambled under the bed and brought out a large hatbox. As she carried it to the door both of them called after her, 'Good riddance!'

Bill had the nicest room of anybody in the family. Like a den — and he had it all to himself — except for Bubber. Bill had pictures cut out from magazines tacked on the walls, mostly faces of beautiful ladies, and in another corner were some pictures Mick had painted last year herself at the free art class. There was only a bed and a desk in the room.

Bill was sitting hunched over the desk, reading *Popular Mechanics*. She went up behind him and put her arms around his shoulders. 'Hey, you old son-of-a-gun.'

He did not begin tussling with her like he used to do. 'Hey,' he said, and shook his shoulders a little.

'Will it bother you if I stay in here a little while?'

'Sure — I don't mind if you want to stay.'

Mick knelt on the floor and untied the string on the big hatbox. Her hands hovered over the edge of the lid, but for some reason she could not make up her mind to open it.

'I been thinking about what I've done on this already,' she said. 'And it may work and it may not.'

Bill went on reading. She still knelt over the box, but did not open it. Her eyes wandered over to Bill as he sat with his back to her. One of his big feet kept stepping on the other as he read. His shoes were scuffed. Once their Dad had said that all Bill's dinners went to his feet and his breakfast to one ear and his supper to the other ear. That was a sort of mean thing to say and Bill had been sour over it for a month, but it was funny. His ears flared out and were very red, and though he was just out of high school he wore a size thirteen shoe. He tried to hide his feet by scraping one foot behind the other when he stood up, but that only made it worse.

Mick opened the box a few inches and then shut it again. She felt too excited to look into it now. She got up and walked around the room until she could calm down a little. After a few minutes she stopped before the picture she had painted at the free government art class for school kids last winter. There was a picture of a storm on the ocean and a sea gull being dashed through the air by the wind. It was called 'Sea Gull with Back Broken in Storm.' The teacher had described the ocean during the first two or three lessons, and that was what nearly everybody started with. Most of the kids were like her, though, and they had never really seen the ocean with their own eyes.

That was the first picture she had done and Bill had tacked it on his wall. All the rest of her pictures were full of people. She had done some more ocean storms at first — one with an airplane crashing down and people jumping out to save themselves, and another with a trans-Atlantic liner going down and all the people trying to push and crowd into one little lifeboat.

Mick went into the closet of Bill's room and brought out some other pictures she had done in the class — some pencil drawings, some water-colors, and one canvas with oils. They were all full of people. She had imagined a big fire on Broad Street and painted how she thought it would be. The flames were bright green and orange and Mr. Brannon's restaurant and the First National Bank were about the only buildings left. People were lying dead in the streets and others were running for their lives. One man was in his nightshirt and a lady was trying to carry a bunch of bananas with her. Another picture was called 'Boiler Busts in Factory,' and men were jumping out of windows and running while a knot of kids in overalls stood scrouged together, holding the buckets of dinner they had brought to their Daddies. The oil painting was a picture of the whole town fighting on Broad Street. She never knew why she had painted this one and she couldn't think of the right name for it. There wasn't any fire or storm or reason you could see in the picture why all this battle was happening. But there were more people and more moving around than in any other picture. This was the best one, and it was too bad that she couldn't think up the real name. In the back of her mind somewhere she knew what it was.

Mick put the picture back on the closet shelf. None of them were any good much. The people didn't have any fingers and some of the arms were longer than the legs. The class had been fun, though. But she had just drawn whatever came into her head without reason — and in her heart it didn't give her near the same feeling that music did. Nothing was really as good as music.

Mick knelt down on the floor and quickly lifted the top of the big hatbox. Inside was a cracked ukulele strung with two violin strings, a guitar string and a banjo string. The crack on the back of the ukulele had been neatly mended with sticking plaster and the round hole in the middle was covered by a piece of wood. The bridge of a violin held up the strings at the end and some sound-holes had been carved on either side. Mick was making herself a violin. She held the violin in her lap. She had the feeling she had never really looked at it before. Some time ago she made Bubber a little play mandolin out of a cigar box with rubber bands, and that put the idea into her head. Since that she had hunted all over everywhere for the different parts and added a little to the job every day. It seemed to her she had done everything except use her head.

'Bill, this don't look like any real violin I ever saw.'

He was still reading — 'Yeah — ?'

'It just don't look right. It just don't ——'

She had planned to tune the fiddle that day by screwing the pegs. But since she had suddenly realized how all the work had turned out she didn't want to look at it. Slowly she plucked one string after another. They all made the same little hollow-sounding ping.

'How anyway will I ever get a bow? Are you sure they have to be made out of just horses' hair?'

'Yeah,' said Bill impatiently.

'Nothing like thin wire or human hair strung on a limber stick would do?'

Bill rubbed his feet against each other and didn't answer.

Anger made beads of sweat come out on her forehead. Her voice was hoarse. 'It's not even a bad violin. It's only a cross between a mandolin and a ukulele. And I hate them. I hate them ——'

Bill turned around.

'It's all turned out wrong. It won't do. It's no good.'

'Pipe down,' said Bill. 'Are you just carrying on about that old broken ukulele you've been fooling with? I could have told you at first it was crazy to think you could make any violin. That's one thing you don't sit down and make — you got to buy them. I thought anybody would know a thing like that. But I figured it wouldn't hurt you if you found out for yourself.'

Sometimes she hated Bill more than anyone else in the world. He was different entirely from what he used to be. She started to slam the violin down on the floor and stomp on it, but instead she put it back roughly into the hatbox. The tears were hot in her eyes as fire. She gave the box a kick and ran from the room without looking at Bill.

As she was dodging through the hall to get to the back yard she ran into her Mama.

'What's the matter with you? What have you been into now?'

Mick tried to jerk loose, but her Mama held on to her arm. Sullenly she wiped the tears from her face with the back of her hand. Her Mama had been in the kitchen and she wore her apron and house-shoes. As usual she looked as though she had a lot on her mind and didn't have time to ask her any more questions.

'Mr. Jackson has brought his two sisters to dinner and there won't be but just enough chairs, so today you're to eat in the kitchen with Bubber.'

'That's hunky-dory with me,' Mick said.

Her Mama let her go and went to take off her apron. From the dining-room there came the sound of the dinner bell and a sudden glad outbreak of talking. She could hear her Dad saying how much he had lost by not keeping up his accident insurance until the time he broke his hip. That was one thing her Dad could never get off his mind — ways he could have made money and didn't. There was a clatter of dishes, and after a while the talking stopped.

Mick leaned on the banisters of the stairs. The sudden crying had started her with the hiccups. It seemed to her as she thought back over the last month that she had never really believed in her mind that the violin would work. But in her heart she had kept making herself believe. And even now it was hard not to believe a little. She was tired out. Bill wasn't ever a help with anything now. She used to think Bill was the grandest person in the world. She used to follow after him every place he went — out fishing in the woods, to the clubhouses he built with other boys, to the slot machine in the back of Mr. Brannon's restaurant — everywhere. Maybe he hadn't meant to let her down like this. But anyway they could never be good buddies again.

In the hall there was the smell of cigarettes and Sunday dinner. Mick took a deep breath and walked back toward the kitchen. The dinner began to smell good and she was hungry. She could hear Portia's voice as she talked to Bubber, and it was like she was half-singing something or telling him a story.

'And that is the various reason why I'm a whole lot more fortunate than most colored girls,' Portia said as she opened the door.

'Why?' asked Mick.

Portia and Bubber were sitting at the kitchen table eating their dinner. Portia's green print dress was cool-looking against her dark brown skin. She had on green earrings and her hair was combed very tight and neat.

'You all time pounce in on the very tail of what somebody say and then want to know all about it,' Portia said. She got up and stood over the hot stove, putting dinner on Mick's plate. 'Bubber and me was just talking about my Grandpapa's home out on the Old Sardis Road. I was telling Bubber how he and my uncles owns the whole place themself. Fifteen and a half acre. They always plants four of them in cotton, some years swapping back to peas to keep the dirt rich, and one acre on a hill is just for peaches. They haves a mule and a breed sow and all the time from twenty to twenty-five laying hens and fryers. They haves a vegetable patch and two pecan trees and plenty figs and plums and berries. This here is the truth. Not many white farms has done with their land good as my Grandpapa.'

Mick put her elbows on the table and leaned over her plate. Portia had always rather talk about the farm than anything else, except about her husband and brother. To hear her tell it you would think that colored farm was the very White House itself.

'The home started with just one little room. And through the years they done built on until there's space for my Grandpapa, his four sons and their wives and childrens, and my brother Hamilton. In the parlor they haves a real organ and a gramophone. And on the wall they haves a large picture of my Grandpapa taken in his lodge uniform. They cans all the fruit and vegetables and no matter how cold and rainy the winter turns they pretty near always haves plenty to eat.'

'How come you don't go live with them, then?' Mick asked.

Portia stopped peeling her potatoes and her long, brown fingers tapped on the table in time to her words. 'This here the way it is. See — each person done built on his room for his fambly. They all done worked hard during all these years. And of course times is hard for everbody now. But see — I lived with my Grandpapa when I were a little girl. But I haven't never done any work out there since. Any time, though, if me and Willie and Highboy gets in bad trouble us can always go back.'

'Didn't your Father build on a room?'

Portia stopped chewing. 'Whose Father? You mean *my* Father?'

'Sure,' said Mick.

'You know good and well my Father is a colored doctor right here in town.'

Mick had heard Portia say that before, but she had thought it was a tale. How could a colored man be a doctor?

'This here the way it is. Before the time my Mama married my Father she had never known anything but real kindness. My Grandpapa is Mister Kind hisself. But my Father is different from him as day is from night.'

'Mean?' asked Mick.

'No, he not a mean man,' Portia said slowly. 'It just that something is the matter. My Father not like other colored mens. This here is hard to explain. My Father all the time studying by hisself. And a long time ago he taken up all these notions about how a fambly ought to be. He bossed over ever little thing in the house and at night he tried to teach us children lessons.'

'That don't sound so bad to me,' said Mick.

'Listen here. You see most of the time he were very quiet.

But then some nights he would break out in a kind of fit. He could get madder than any man I ever seen. Everbody who know my Father say that he was a sure enough crazy man. He done wild, crazy things and our Mama quit him. I were ten years old at the time. Our Mama taken us children with her to Grandpapa's farm and us were raised out there. Our Father all the time wanted us to come back. But even when our Mama died us children never did go home to live. And now my Father stay all by hisself.'

Mick went to the stove and filled her plate a second time. Portia's voice was going up and down like a song, and nothing could stop her now.

'I doesn't see my Father much — maybe once a week — but I done a lot of thinking about him. I feels sorrier for him than anybody I knows. I expect he done read more books than any white man in this town. He done read more books and he done worried about more things. He full of books and worrying. He done lost God and turned his back to religion. All his troubles come down just to that.'

Portia was excited. Whenever she got to talking about God — or Willie, her brother, or Highboy, her husband — she got excited.

'Now, I not a big shouter. I belongs to the Presbyterian Church and us don't hold with all this rolling on the floor and talking in tongues. Us don't get sanctified ever week and wallow around together. In our church we sings and lets the preacher do the preaching. And tell you the truth I don't think a little singing and a little preaching would hurt you, Mick. You ought to take your little brother to the Sunday School and also you plenty big enough to sit in church. From the biggity way you been acting lately it seem to me like you already got one toe in the pit.'

'Nuts,' Mick said.

'Now Highboy he were a Holiness boy before us were married. He loved to get the spirit ever Sunday and shout and sanctify hisself. But after us were married I got him to join with me, and although it kind of hard to keep him quiet sometime I think he doing right well.'

'I don't believe in God any more than I do Santa Claus,' Mick said.

'You wait a minute! That's why it sometime seem to me you favor my Father more than any person I ever knowed.'

'*Me?* You say *I* favor him?'

'I don't mean in the face or in any kind of looks. I was speaking about the shape and color of your souls.'

Bubber sat looking from one to the other. His napkin was tied around his neck and in his hand he still held his empty spoon. 'What all does God eat?' he asked.

Mick got up from the table and stood in the doorway, ready to leave. Sometimes it was fun to devil Portia. She started on the same tune and said the same thing over and over — like that was all she knew.

'Folks like you and my Father who don't attend the church can't never have nair peace at all. Now take me here — I believe and I haves peace. And Bubber, he haves his peace too. And my Highboy and my Willie likewise. And it seem to me just from looking at him this here Mr. Singer haves peace too. I done felt that the first time I seen him.'

'Have it your own way,' Mick said. 'You're crazier than any father of yours could ever be.'

'But you haven't never loved God nor even nair person. You hard and tough as cowhide. But just the same I knows you. This afternoon you going to roam all over the place without never being satisfied. You going to traipse all around like you haves to find something lost. You going to work yourself up with excitement. Your heart going to beat hard enough to kill you because you don't love and don't have peace. And then some day you going to bust loose and be ruined. Won't nothing help you then.'

'What, Portia?' Bubber asked. 'What kind of things does He eat?'

Mick laughed and stamped out of the room.

She did roam around the house during the afternoon because she could not get settled. Some days were just like that. For one thing the thought of the violin kept worrying her. She could never have made it like a real one — and after all those weeks of planning the very thought of it made her sick. But how could she have been so sure the idea would work? So dumb? Maybe when people longed for a thing that bad the longing made them trust in anything that might give it to them.

Mick did not want to go back into the rooms where the family stayed. And she did not want to have to talk to any of the boarders. No place was left but the street — and there the sun was too burning hot. She wandered aimlessly up and down the hall and kept pushing back her rumpled hair with the palm of her hand. 'Hell,' she said aloud to herself. 'Next to a real piano I sure would rather have some place to myself than anything I know.'

That Portia had a certain kind of niggery craziness, but she was O.K. She never would do anything mean to Bubber or Ralph on the sly like some colored girls. But Portia had said that she never loved anybody. Mick stopped walking and stood very still, rubbing her fist on the top of her head. What would Portia think if she really knew? Just what would she think?

She had always kept things to herself. That was one sure truth.

Mick went slowly up the stairs. She passed the first landing and went on to the second. Some of the doors were open to make a draught and there were many sounds in the house. Mick stopped on the last flight of stairs and sat down. If Miss Brown turned on her radio she could hear the music. Maybe some good program would come on.

She put her head on her knees and tied knots in the strings of her tennis shoes. What would Portia say if she knew that always there had been one person after another? And every time it was like some part of her would bust in a hundred pieces.

But she had always kept it to herself and no person had ever known.

Mick sat on the steps a long time. Miss Brown did not turn on her radio and there was nothing but the noises that people made. She thought a long time and kept hitting her thighs with her fists. Her face felt like it was scattered in pieces and she could not keep it straight. The feeling was a whole lot worse than being hungry for any dinner, yet it was like that. I want — I want — I want — was all that she could think about — but just what this real want was she did not know.

After about an hour there was the sound of a doorknob being turned on the landing above. Mick looked up quickly and it was Mister Singer. He stood in the hall for a few minutes and his face was sad and calm. Then he went across to the bathroom. His company did not come out with him. From where she was sitting she could see part of the room, and the company was asleep on the bed with a sheet pulled over him. She waited for Mister Singer to come out of the bathroom. Her cheeks were very hot and she felt them with her hands. Maybe it was true that she came up on these top steps sometimes so she could see Mister Singer while she was listening to Miss Brown's radio on the floor below. She wondered what kind of music he heard in his mind that his ears couldn't hear. Nobody knew. And what kind of things he would say if he could talk. Nobody knew that either.

Mick waited, and after a while he came out into the hall again. She hoped he would look down and smile at her. And then when he got to his door he did glance down and nod his head. Mick's grin was wide and trembling. He went into his room and shut the door. It might have been he meant to invite her in to see him. Mick wanted suddenly to go into his room. Sometime soon when he didn't have company she would really go in and see Mister Singer. She really would do that.

The hot afternoon passed slowly and Mick still sat on the steps by herself. This fellow Motsart's music was in her mind again. It was funny, but Mister Singer reminded her of this music. She wished there was some place where she could go to hum it out loud. Some kind of music was too private to sing in a house cram full of people. It was funny, too, how lonesome a person could be in a crowded house. Mick tried to think of some good private place where she could go and be by herself and study about this music. But though she thought about this a long time she knew in the beginning that there was no good place.

4

LATE in the afternoon Jake Blount awoke with the feeling that he had slept enough. The room in which he lay was small and neat, furnished with a bureau, a table, a bed, and a few chairs. On the bureau an electric fan turned its face slowly from one wall to another, and as the breeze from it passed Jake's face he thought of cool water. By the window a man sat before the table and stared down at a chess game laid out before him. In the daylight the room was not familiar to Jake, but he recognized the man's face instantly and it was as though he had known him a very long time.

Many memories were confused in Jake's mind. He lay motionless with his eyes open and his hands turned palm upward. His hands were huge and very brown against the white sheet. When he held them up to his face he saw that they were scratched and bruised — and the veins were swollen as though he had been grasping hard at something for a long time. His face looked tired and unkempt. His brown hair fell down over his forehead and his mustache was awry. Even his wing-shaped eyebrows were rough and tousled. As he lay there his lips moved once or twice and his mustache jerked with a nervous quiver.

After a while he sat up and gave himself a thump on the side of his head with one of his big fists to straighten himself out. When he moved, the man playing chess looked up quickly and smiled at him.

'God, I'm thirsty,' Jake said. 'I feel like the whole Russian army marched through my mouth in its stocking feet.'

The man looked at him, still smiling, and then suddenly he reached down on the other side of the table and brought up a frosted pitcher of ice water and a glass. Jake drank in great panting gulps — standing half-naked in the middle of the room, his head thrown back and one of his hands closed in a tense fist. He finished four glasses before he took a deep breath and relaxed a little.

Instantly certain recollections came to him. He couldn't remember coming home with this man, but things that had happened later were clearer now. He had waked up soaking in a tub of cold water, and afterward they drank coffee and talked. He had got a lot of things off his chest and the man had listened. He had talked himself hoarse, but he could remember the expressions on the man's face better than anything that was said. They had gone to bed in the morning with the shade pulled down so no light could come in. At first he would keep waking up with nightmares and have to turn the light on to get himself clear again. The light would wake this fellow also, but he hadn't complained at all.

'How come you didn't kick me out last night?'

The man only smiled again. Jake wondered why he was so quiet. He looked around for his clothes and saw that his suitcase was on the floor by the bed. He couldn't remember how he had got it back from the restaurant where he owed for the drinks. His books, a white suit, and some shirts were all there as he had packed them. Quickly he began to dress himself.

An electric coffee-pot was perking on the table by the time he had his clothes on. The man reached into the pocket of the vest that hung over the back of a chair. He brought out a card and Jake took it questioningly. The man's name — John Singer — was engraved in the center, and beneath this, written in ink with the same elaborate precision as the engraving, there was a brief message.

> *I am a deaf-mute, but I read the lips and understand what is said to me. Please do not shout.*

The shock made Jake feel light and vacant. He and John Singer just looked at each other.

'I wonder how long it would have taken me to find that out,' he said.

Singer looked very carefully at his lips when he spoke — he had noticed that before. But a dummy!

They sat at the table and drank hot coffee out of blue cups. The room was cool and the half-drawn shades softened the hard glare from the windows. Singer brought from his closet a tin box that contained a loaf of bread, some oranges, and cheese. He did not eat much, but sat leaning back in his chair with one hand in his pocket. Jake ate hungrily. He would have to leave the place immediately and think things over. As long as he was stranded he ought to scout around for some sort of job in a hurry. The quiet room was too peaceful and comfortable to worry in — he would get out and walk by himself for a while.

'Are there any other deaf-mute people here?' he asked. 'You have many friends?'

Singer was still smiling. He did not catch on to the words at first, and Jake had to repeat them. Singer raised his sharp, dark eyebrows and shook his head.

'Find it lonesome?'

The man shook his head in a way that might have meant

either yes or no. They sat silently for a little while and then Jake got up to leave. He thanked Singer several times for the night's lodging, moving his lips carefully so that he was sure to be understood. The mute only smiled again and shrugged his shoulders. When Jake asked if he could leave his suitcase under the bed for a few days the mute nodded that he could.

Then Singer took his hands from his pocket and wrote carefully on a pad of paper with a silver pencil. He shoved the pad over toward Jake.

> *I can put a mattress on the floor and you can stay here until you find a place. I am out most of the day. It will not be any trouble.*

Jake felt his lips tremble with a sudden feeling of gratefulness. But he couldn't accept. 'Thanks,' he said. 'I already got a place.'

As he was leaving the mute handed him a pair of blue overalls, rolled into a tight bundle, and seventy-five cents. The overalls were filthy and as Jake recognized them they aroused in him a whirl of sudden memories from the past week. The money, Singer made him understand, had been in his pockets.

'*Adios*,' Jake said. 'I'll be back sometime soon.'

He left the mute standing in the doorway with his hands still in his pockets and the half-smile on his face. When he had gone down several steps of the stairs he turned and waved. The mute waved back to him and closed his door.

Outside the glare was sudden and sharp against his eyes. He stood on the sidewalk before the house, too dazzled at first by the sunlight to see very clearly. A youngun was sitting on the banisters of the house. He had seen her somewhere before. He remembered the boy's shorts she was wearing and the way she squinted her eyes.

He held up the dirty roll of overalls. 'I want to throw these away. Know where I can find a garbage can?'

The kid jumped down from the banisters. 'It's in the back yard. I'll show you.'

He followed her through the narrow, dampish alley at the side of the house. When they came to the back yard Jake saw that two Negro men were sitting on the back steps. They were both dressed in white suits and white shoes. One of the Negroes was very tall and his tie and socks were brilliant green. The other was a light mulatto of average height. He rubbed a tin harmonica across his knee. In contrast with his tall companion his socks and tie were a hot red.

The kid pointed to the garbage can by the back fence and then turned to the kitchen window. 'Portia!' she called. 'Highboy and Willie here waiting for you.'

A soft voice answered from the kitchen. 'You neen holler so loud. I know they is. I putting on my hat right now.'

Jake unrolled the overalls before throwing them away. They were stiff with mud. One leg was torn and a few drops of blood stained the front. He dropped them in the can. A Negro girl came out of the house and joined the white-suited boys on the steps. Jake saw that the youngun in shorts was looking at him very closely. She changed her weight from one foot to the other and seemed excited.

'Are you kin to Mister Singer?' she asked.

'Not a bit.'

'Good friend?'

'Good enough to spend the night with him.'

'I just wondered ——'

'Which direction is Main Street?'

She pointed to the right. 'Two blocks down this way '

Jake combed his mustache with his fingers and started off. He jingled the seventy-five cents in his hand and bit his lower lip until it was mottled and scarlet. The three Negroes were walking slowly ahead of him, talking among themselves. Because he felt lonely in the unfamiliar town he kept close behind them and listened. The girl held both of them by the arm. She wore a green dress with a red hat and shoes. The boys walked very close to her.

'What we got planned for this evening?' she asked.

'It depend entirely upon you, Honey,' the tall boy said. 'Willie and me don't have no special plans.'

She looked from one to the other. 'You all got to decide.'

'Well ——' said the shorter boy in the red socks. 'Highboy and me thought m-maybe us three go to church.'

The girl sang her answer in three different tones. 'O — K — And after church I got a notion I ought to go and set with Father for a while — just a short while.' They turned at the first corner, and Jake stood watching them a moment before walking on.

The main street was quiet and hot, almost deserted. He had not realized until now that it was Sunday — and the thought of this depressed him. The awnings over the closed stores were raised and the buildings had a bare look in the bright sun. He passed the New York Café. The door was open, but the place looked empty and dark. He had not found any socks to wear that morning, and the hot pavement burned through the thin soles of his shoes. The sun felt like a hot piece of iron pressing down on his head. The town seemed more lonesome than any place he had ever known. The stillness of the street gave him a strange feeling. When he had been drunk the place had seemed violent and riotous. And now it was as though everything had come to a sudden, static halt.

He went into a fruit and candy store to buy a paper. The Help-Wanted column was very short. There were several calls for young men between twenty-five and forty with automobiles to sell various products on commission. These he skipped over quickly. An advertisement for a truck-driver held his attention for a few minutes. But the notice at the bottom interested him most. It read:

> *Wanted — Experienced Mechanic. Sunny Dixie Show. Apply Corner Weavers Lane & 15th Street.*

Without knowing it he had walked back to the door of the

restaurant where he had spent his time during the past two weeks. This was the only place on the block besides the fruit store which was not closed. Jake decided suddenly to drop in and see Biff Brannon.

The café was very dark after the brightness outside. Everything looked dingier and quieter than he had remembered it. Brannon stood behind the cash register as usual, his arms folded over his chest. His good-looking plump wife sat filing her fingernails at the other end of the counter. Jake noticed that they glanced at each other as he came in.

'Afternoon,' said Brannon.

Jake felt something in the air. Maybe the fellow was laughing because he remembered things that had happened when he was drunk. Jake stood wooden and resentful. 'Package of Target, please.' As Brannon reached beneath the counter for the tobacco Jake decided that he was not laughing. In the daytime the fellow's face was not as hard-looking as it was at night. He was pale as though he had not slept, and his eyes had the look of a weary buzzard's.

'Speak up,' Jake said. 'How much do I owe you?'

Brannon opened a drawer and put on the counter a public-school tablet. Slowly he turned over the pages and Jake watched him. The tablet looked more like a private notebook than the place where he kept his regular accounts. There were long lines of figures, added, divided, and subtracted, and little drawings. He stopped at a certain page and Jake saw his last name written at the corner. On the page there were no figures — only small checks and crosses. At random across the page were drawn little round, seated cats with long curved lines for tails. Jake stared. The faces of the little cats were human and female. The faces of the little cats were Mrs. Brannon.

'I have checks here for the beers,' Brannon said. 'And crosses for dinners and straight lines for the whiskey. Let me see ——' Brannon rubbed his nose and his eyelids drooped down. Then he shut the tablet. 'Approximately twenty dollars.'

'It'll take me a long time,' Jake said. 'But maybe you'll get it.'

'There's no big hurry.'

Jake leaned against the counter. 'Say, what kind of a place is this town?'

'Ordinary,' Brannon said. 'About like any other place the same size.'

'What population?'

'Around thirty thousand.'

Jake opened the package of tobacco and rolled himself a cigarette. His hands were shaking. 'Mostly mills?'

'That's right. Four big cotton mills — those are the main ones. A hosiery factory. Some gins and sawmills.'

'What kind of wages?'

'I'd say around ten or eleven a week on the average — but then of course they get laid off now and then. What makes you ask all this? You mean to try to get a job in a mill?'

Jake dug his fist into his eye and rubbed it sleepily. 'Don't know. I might and I might not.' He laid the newspaper on the counter and pointed out the advertisement he had just read. 'I think I'll go around and look into this.'

Brannon read and considered. 'Yeah,' he said finally. 'I've seen that show. It's not much — just a couple of contraptions such as a flying-jinny and swings. It corrals the colored people and mill hands and kids. They move around to different vacant lots in town.'

'Show me how to get there.'

Brannon went with him to the door and pointed out the direction. 'Did you go on home with Singer this morning?'

Jake nodded.

'What do you think of him?'

Jake bit his lips. The mute's face was in his mind very clearly. It was like the face of a friend he had known for a long time. He had been thinking of the man ever since he had left his room. 'I didn't even know he was a dummy,' he said finally.

He began walking again down the hot, deserted street. He did not walk as a stranger in a strange town. He seemed to be looking for someone. Soon he entered one of the mill districts bordering the river. The streets became narrow and unpaved and they were not empty any longer. Groups of dingy, hungry-looking children called to each other and played games. The two-room shacks, each one like the other, were rotten and unpainted. The stink of food and sewage mingled with the dust in the air. The falls up the river made a faint rushing sound. People stood silently in doorways or lounged on steps. They looked at Jake with yellow, expressionless faces. He stared back at them with wide, brown eyes. He walked jerkily, and now and then he wiped his mouth with the hairy back of his hand.

At the end of Weavers Lane there was a vacant block. It had once been used as a junk yard for old automobiles. Rusted pieces of machinery and torn inner tubes still littered the ground. A trailer was parked in one corner of the lot, and near-by was a flying-jinny partly covered with canvas.

Jake approached slowly. Two little younguns in overalls stood before the flying-jinny. Near them, seated on a box, a Negro man drowsed in the late sunshine, his knees collapsed against each other. In one hand he held a sack of melted chocolate. Jake watched him stick his fingers in the miry candy and then lick them slowly.

'Who's the manager of this outfit?'

The Negro thrust his two sweet fingers between his lips and rolled over them with his tongue. 'He a red-headed man,' he said when he had finished. 'That all I know, Cap'n.'

'Where's he now?'

'He over there behind that largest wagon.'

Jake slipped off his tie as he walked across the grass and stuffed it into his pocket. The sun was beginning to set in the west. Above the black line of housetops the sky was warm crimson. The owner of the show stood smoking a cigarette by himself. His red hair sprang up like a sponge on the top of his head and he stared at Jake with gray, flabby eyes.

'You the manager?'

'Uh-huh. Patterson's my name.'

'I come about the job in this morning's paper.'

'Yeah. I don't want no greenhorn. I need a experienced mechanic.'

'I got plenty of experience,' Jake said.

'What you ever done?'

'I've worked as a weaver and loom-fixer. I've worked in garages and an automobile assembly shop. All sorts of different things.'

Patterson guided him toward the partly covered flying-jinny. The motionless wooden horses were fantastic in the late afternoon sun. They pranced up statically, pierced by their dull gilt bars. The horse nearest Jake had a splintery wooden crack in its dingy rump and the eyes walled blind and frantic, shreds of paint peeled from the sockets. The motionless merry-go-round seemed to Jake like something in a liquor dream.

'I want a experienced mechanic to run this and keep the works in good shape,' Patterson said.

'I can do that all right.'

'It's a two-handed job,' Patterson explained. 'You're in charge of the whole attraction. Besides looking after the machinery you got to keep the crowd in order. You got to be sure that everybody gets on has a ticket. You got to be sure that the tickets are O.K. and not some old dance-hall ticket. Everybody wants to ride them horses, and you'd be surprised what niggers will try to put over on you when they don't have no money. You got to keep three eyes open all the time.'

Patterson led him to the machinery inside the circle of horses and pointed out the various parts. He adjusted a lever and the thin jangle of mechanical music began. The wooden cavalcade around them seemed to cut them off from the rest of the world. When the horses stopped, Jake asked a few questions and operated the mechanism himself.

'The fellow I had quit on me,' Patterson said when they had come out again into the lot. 'I always hate to break in a new man.'

'When do I start?'

'Tomorrow afternoon. We run six days and nights a week — beginning at four and shutting up at twelve. You're to come about three and help get things going. And it takes about a hour after the show to fold up for the night.'

'What about pay?'

'Twelve dollars.'

Jake nodded, and Patterson held out a dead-white, boneless hand with dirty fingernails.

It was late when he left the vacant lot. The hard, blue sky had blanched and in the east there was a white moon. Dusk softened the outline of the houses along the street. Jake did not return immediately through Weavers Lane, but wandered in the neighborhoods near-by. Certain smells, certain voices heard from a distance, made him stop short now and then by the side of the dusty street. He walked erratically, jerking from one direction to another for no purpose. His head felt very light, as though it were made of thin glass. A chemical change was taking place in him. The beers and whiskey he had stored so continuously in his system set in a reaction. He was sideswiped by drunkenness. The streets which had seemed so dead before were quick with life. There was a ragged strip of grass bordering the street, and as Jake walked along the ground seemed to rise nearer to his face. He sat down on the border of grass and leaned against a telephone pole. He settled himself comfortably, crossing his legs Turkish fashion and smoothing down the ends of his mustache. Words came to him and dreamily he spoke them aloud to himself.

'Resentment is the most precious flower of poverty. Yeah.'

It was good to talk. The sound of his voice gave him

pleasure. The tones seemed to echo and hang on the air so that each word sounded twice. He swallowed and moistened his mouth to speak again. He wanted suddenly to return to the mute's quiet room and tell him of the thoughts that were in his mind. It was a queer thing to want to talk with a deaf-mute. But he was lonesome.

The street before him dimmed with the coming evening. Occasionally men passed along the narrow street very close to him, talking in monotones to each other, a cloud of dust rising around their feet with each step. Or girls passed by together, or a mother with a child across her shoulder. Jake sat numbly for some time, and at last he got to his feet and walked on.

Weavers Lane was dark. Oil lamps made yellow, trembling patches of light in the doorways and windows. Some of the houses were entirely dark and the families sat on their front steps with only the reflections from a neighboring house to see by. A woman leaned out of a window and splashed a pail of dirty water into the street. A few drops of it splashed on Jake's face. High, angry voices could be heard from the backs of some of the houses. From others there was the peaceful sound of a chair slowly rocking.

Jake stopped before a house where three men sat together on the front steps. A pale yellow light from inside the house shone on them. Two of the men wore overalls but no shirts and were barefooted. One of these was tall and loose-jointed. The other was small and he had a running sore on the corner of his mouth. The third man was dressed in shirt and trousers. He held a straw hat on his knee.

'Hey,' Jake said.

The three men stared at him with mill-sallow, dead-pan faces. They murmured but did not change their positions. Jake pulled the package of Target from his pocket and passed it around. He sat down on the bottom step and took off his shoes. The cool, damp ground felt good to his feet.

'Working now?'

'Yeah,' said the man with the straw hat. 'Most of the time.'

Jake picked between his toes. 'I got the Gospel in me,' he said. 'I want to tell it to somebody.'

The men smiled. From across the narrow street there was the sound of a woman singing. The smoke from their cigarettes hung close around them in the still air. A little youngun passing along the street stopped and opened his fly to make water.

'There's a tent around the corner and it's Sunday,' the small man said finally. 'You can go there and tell all the Gospel you want.'

'It's not that kind. It's better. It's the truth.'

'What kind?'

Jake sucked his mustache and did not answer. After a while he said, 'You ever have any strikes here?'

'Once,' said the tall man. 'They had one of these here strikes around six years ago.'

'What happened?'

The man with the sore on his mouth shuffled his feet and dropped the stub of his cigarette to the ground. 'Well — they just quit work because they wanted twenty cents a hour. There was about three hundred did it. They just hung around the streets all day. So the mill sent out trucks, and in a week the whole town was swarming with folks come here to get a job.'

Jake turned so that he was facing them. The men sat two steps above him so that he had to raise his head to look into their eyes. 'Don't it make you mad?' he asked.

'How you mean — mad?'

The vein in Jake's forehead was swollen and scarlet. 'Christamighty, man! I mean mad — m-a-d — *mad*.' He scowled up into their puzzled, sallow faces. Behind them, through the open front door he could see the inside of the house. In the front room there were three beds and a washstand. In the back room a barefooted woman sat sleeping in a chair. From one of the dark porches near-by there was the sound of a guitar.

'I was one of them come in on the trucks,' the tall man said.

'That makes no difference. What I'm trying to tell you is plain and simple. The bastards who own these mills are millionaires. While the doffers and carders and all the people behind the machines who spin and weave the cloth can't hardly make enough to keep their guts quiet. See? So when you walk around the streets and think about it and see hungry, worn-out people and ricket-legged younguns, don't it make you mad? Don't it?'

Jake's face was flushed and dark and his lips trembled. The three men looked at him warily. Then the man in the straw hat began to laugh.

'Go on and snicker. Sit there and bust your sides open.'

The men laughed in the slow and easy way that three men laugh at one. Jake brushed the dirt from the soles of his feet and put on his shoes. His fists were closed tight and his mouth was contorted with an angry sneer. 'Laugh — that's all you're good for. I hope you sit there and snicker 'til you rot!' As he walked stiffly down the street the sound of their laughter and catcalls still followed him.

The main street was brightly lighted. Jake loitered on a corner, fondling the change in his pocket. His head throbbed, and although the night was hot a chill passed through his body. He thought of the mute and he wanted urgently to go back and sit with him awhile. In the fruit and candy store where he had bought the newspaper that afternoon he selected a basket of fruit wrapped in cellophane. The Greek behind the counter said the price was sixty cents, so that when he had paid he was left with only a nickel. As soon as he had come out of the store the present seemed a funny one to take a healthy man. A few grapes hung down below the cellophane, and he picked them off hungrily.

Singer was at home when he arrived. He sat by the window with the chess game laid out before him on the table. The room was just as Jake had left it, with the fan turned on and the pitcher of ice water beside the table. There was a panama hat on the bed and a paper parcel, so it seemed that the mute had just come in. He jerked his head toward the chair across from him at the table and pushed the chessboard to one side. He leaned back with his hands in his pockets, and his face seemed to question Jake about what had happened since he had left.

Jake put the fruit on the table. 'For this afternoon,' he said. 'The motto has been: Go out and find an octopus and put socks on it.'

The mute smiled, but Jake could not tell if he had caught what he had said. The mute looked at the fruit with surprise and then undid the cellophane wrappings. As he handled the fruits there was something very peculiar in the fellow's face. Jake tried to understand this look and was stumped. Then Singer smiled brightly.

'I got a job this afternoon with a sort of show. I'm to run the flying-jinny.'

The mute seemed not at all surprised. He went into the closet and brought out a bottle of wine and two glasses. They drank in silence. Jake felt that he had never been in such a quiet room. The light above his head made a queer reflection of himself in the glowing wineglass he held before him — the same caricature of himself he had noticed many times before on the curved surfaces of pitchers or tin mugs — with his face egg-shaped and dumpy and his mustache straggling almost up to his ears. Across from him the mute held his glass in both hands. The wine began to hum through Jake's veins and he felt himself entering again the kaleidoscope of drunkenness. Excitement made his mustache tremble jerkily. He leaned forward with his elbows on his knees and fastened a wide, searching gaze on Singer.

'I bet I'm the only man in this town that's been mad — I'm talking about really mean mad — for ten solid long years. I damn near got in a fight just a little while ago. Sometimes it seems to me like I might even be crazy. I just don't know.'

Singer pushed the wine toward his guest. Jake drank from the bottle and rubbed the top of his head.

'You see, it's like I'm two people. One of me is an educated man. I been in some of the biggest libraries in the country. I read. I read all the time. I read books that tell the pure honest truth. Over there in my suitcase I have books by Karl Marx and Thorstein Veblen and such writers as them. I read them over and over, and the more I study the madder I get. I know every word printed on every page. To begin with I like words. Dialectic materialism — Jesuitical prevarication' — Jake rolled the syllables in his mouth with loving solemnity — 'teleological propensity.'

The mute wiped his forehead with a neatly folded handkerchief.

'But what I'm getting at is this. When a person *knows* and can't make the others understand, what does he do?'

Singer reached for a wineglass, filled it to the brim, and put it firmly into Jake's bruised hand. 'Get drunk, huh?' Jake said with a jerk of his arm that spilled drops of wine on his white trousers. 'But listen! Wherever you look there's meanness and corruption. This room, this bottle of grape wine, these fruits in the basket, are all products of profit and loss. A fellow can't live without giving his passive acceptance to meanness. Somebody wears his tail to a frazzle for every mouthful we eat and every stitch we wear — and nobody seems to know. Everybody is blind, dumb, and blunt-headed — stupid and mean.'

Jake pressed his fists to his temples. His thoughts had careened in several directions and he could not get control of them. He wanted to go berserk. He wanted to get out and fight violently with someone in a crowded street.

Still looking at him with patient interest, the mute took out his silver pencil. He wrote very carefully on a slip of paper, *Are you Democrat or Republican?* and passed the paper across the table. Jake crumpled it in his hand. The room had begun to turn around him again and he could not even read.

He kept his eyes on the mute's face to steady himself. Singer's eyes were the only things in the room that did not seem to move. They were varied in color, flecked with amber, gray, and a soft brown. He stared at them so long that he almost hypnotized himself. He lost the urge to be riotous and felt calm again. The eyes seemed to understand all that he had meant to say and to hold some message for him. After a while the room was steady again.

'You get it,' he said in a blurred voice. 'You know what I mean.'

From afar off there was the soft, silver ring of church bells. The moonlight was white on the roof next door and the sky was a gentle summer blue. It was agreed without words that Jake would stay with Singer a few days until he found a room. When the wine was finished the mute put a mattress on the floor beside the bed. Without removing any of his clothes Jake lay down and was instantly asleep.

5

FAR from the main street, in one of the Negro sections of the town, Doctor Benedict Mady Copeland sat in his dark kitchen alone. It was past nine o'clock and the Sunday bells were silent now. Although the night was very hot, there was a small fire in the round-bellied wood stove. Doctor Copeland sat close to it, leaning forward in a straight-backed kitchen chair with his head cupped in his long, slender hands. The red glow from the chinks of the stove shone on his face — in this light his heavy lips looked almost purple against his black skin, and his gray hair, tight against his skull like a cap of lamb's wool, took on a bluish color also. He sat motionless in this position for a long time. Even his eyes, which stared from behind the silver rims of his spectacles, did not change their fixed, somber gaze. Then he cleared his throat harshly and picked up a book from the floor beside his chair. All around him the room was very dark, and he had to hold the book close to the stove to make out the print. Tonight he read Spinoza. He did not wholly understand the intricate play of ideas and the complex phrases, but as he read he sensed a strong, true purpose behind the words and he felt that he almost understood.

Often at night the sharp jangle of the doorbell would rouse him from his silence, and in the front room he would find a patient with a broken bone or with a razor wound. But this evening he was not disturbed. And after the solitary hours spent sitting in the dark kitchen it happened that he began swaying slowly from side to side and from his throat there came a sound like a kind of singing moan. He was making this sound when Portia came.

Doctor Copeland knew of her arrival in advance. From the street outside he caught the sound of an harmonica playing a blues song and he knew that the music was played by William, his son. Without turning on the light he went through the hall and opened the front door. He did not step out on the porch, but stood in the dark behind the screen. The moonlight was bright and the shadows of Portia and William and Highboy lay black and solid on the dusty street. The houses in the neighborhood had a miserable look. Doctor Copeland's house was different from any other building near-by. It was built solidly of brick and stucco. Around the small front yard there was a picket fence. Portia said good-bye to her husband and brother at the gate and knocked on the screen door.

'How come you sit here in the dark like this?'

They went together through the dark hall back to the kitchen.

'You haves grand electric lights. It don't seem natural why you all the time sitting in the dark like this.'

Doctor Copeland twisted the bulb suspended over the table and the room was suddenly very bright. 'The dark suits me,' he said.

The room was clean and bare. On one side of the kitchen table there were books and an inkstand — on the other side a fork, spoon, and plate. Doctor Copeland held himself bolt upright with his long legs crossed and at first Portia sat stiffly, too. The father and daughter had a strong resemblance to each other — both of them had the same broad, flat noses, the same mouths and foreheads. But Portia's skin was very light when compared to her Father's.

'It sure is roasting in here,' she said. 'Seem to me you would let this here fire die down except when you cooking.'

'If you prefer we can go up to my office,' Doctor Copeland said.

'I be all right, I guess. I don't prefer.'

Doctor Copeland adjusted his silver-rimmed glasses and then folded his hands in his lap. 'How have you been since we were last together? You and your husband — and your brother?'

Portia relaxed and slipped her feet out of her pumps. 'Highboy and Willie and me gets along just fine.'

'William still boards with you?'

'Sure he do,' Portia said. 'You see — us haves our own way of living and our own plan. Highboy — he pay the rent. I buys all the food out of my money. And Willie — he tends to all of our church dues, insurance, lodge dues, and Saturday Night. Us three haves our own plan and each one of us does our parts.'

Doctor Copeland sat with his head bowed, pulling at his long fingers until he had cracked all of his joints. The clean cuffs of his sleeves hung down past his wrists — below them his thin hands seemed lighter in color than the rest of his body and the palms were soft yellow. His hands had always an immaculate, shrunken look, as though they had been scrubbed with a brush and soaked for a long time in a pan of water.

'Here, I almost forgot what I brought,' Portia said. 'Haves you had your supper yet?'

Doctor Copeland always spoke so carefully that each syllable seemed to be filtered through his sullen, heavy lips. 'No, I have not eaten.'

Portia opened a paper sack she had placed on the kitchen table. 'I done brought a nice mess of collard greens and I thought maybe we have supper together. I done brought a piece of side meat, too. These here greens needs to be seasoned with that. You don't care if the collards is just cooked in meat, do you?'

'It does not matter.'

'You still don't eat nair meat?'

'No. For purely private reasons I am a vegetarian, but it does not matter if you wish to cook the collards with a piece of meat.'

Without putting on her shoes Portia stood at the table and carefully began to pick over the greens. 'This here floor sure do feel good to my feets. You mind if I just walk around like this without putting back on them tight, hurting pumps?'

'No,' said Doctor Copeland. 'That will be all right.'

'Then — us'll have these nice collards and some hoecake and coffee. And I going to cut me off a few slices of this here white meat and fry it for myself.'

Doctor Copeland followed Portia with his eyes. She moved slowly around the room in her stockinged feet, taking down the scrubbed pans from the wall, building up the fire, washing the grit from the collards. He opened his mouth to speak once and then composed his lips again.

'So you and your husband and your brother have your own co-operative plan,' he said finally.

'That's right.'

Doctor Copeland jerked at his fingers and tried to pop the joints again. 'Do you intend to plan for children?'

Portia did not look at her father. Angrily she sloshed the water from the pan of collards. 'There be some things,' she said, 'that seem to me to depend entirely upon God.'

They did not say anything else. Portia left the supper to cook on the stove and sat silently with her long hands dropping down limp between her knees. Doctor Copeland's head rested on his chest as though he slept. But he was not sleeping; now and then a nervous tremor would pass over his face. Then he would breathe deeply and compose his face again. Smells of the supper began to fill the stifling room. In the quietness the clock on top of the cupboard sounded very loud, and because of what they had just said to each other the monotonous ticking was like the word 'chil-dren, chil-dren,' said over and over.

He was always meeting one of them — crawling naked on a floor or engaged in a game of marbles or even on a dark street with his arms around a girl. Benedict Copeland, the boys were all called. But for the girls there were such names as Benny Mae or Madyben or Benedine Madine. He had counted one day, and there were more than a dozen named for him.

But all his life he had told and explained and exhorted. You cannot do this, he would say. There are all reasons why this sixth or fifth or ninth child cannot be, he would tell them. It is not more children we need but more chances for the ones already on the earth. Eugenic Parenthood for the Negro Race was what he would exhort them to. He would tell them in simple words, always the same way, and with the years it came to be a sort of angry poem which he had always known by heart.

He studied and knew the development of any new theory. And from his own pocket he would distribute the devices to his patients himself. He was by far the first doctor in the town to even think of such. And he would give and explain and give and tell them. And then deliver maybe two score times a week. Madyben and Benny Mae.

That was only one point. Only one.

All of his life he knew that there was a reason for his working. He always knew that he was meant to teach his people. All day he would go with his bag from house to house and on all things he would talk to them.

After the long day a heavy tiredness would come in him. But in the evening when he opened the front gate the tiredness would go away. There were Hamilton and Karl Marx and Portia and little William. There was Daisy, too.

Portia took the lid from the pan on the stove and stirred the collards with a fork. 'Father ——' she said after a while.

Doctor Copeland cleared his throat and spat into a handkerchief. His voice was bitter and rough. 'Yes?'

'Less us quit this here quarreling with each other.'

'We were not quarreling,' said Doctor Copeland.

'It don't take words to make a quarrel,' Portia said. 'It look to me like us is always arguing even when we sitting perfectly quiet like this. It just this here feeling I haves. I tell you the truth — ever time I come to see you it mighty near wears me out. So less us try not to quarrel in any way no more.'

'It is certainly not my wish to quarrel. I am sorry if you have that feeling, Daughter.'

She poured out coffee and handed one cup unsweetened to her father. In her own portion she put several spoons of sugar. 'I getting hungry and this will taste good to us. Drink your coffee while I tell you something which happened to us a piece back. Now that it all over it seem a little bit funny, but we got plenty reason not to laugh too hard.'

'Go ahead,' said Doctor Copeland.

'Well — sometime back a real fine-looking, dressed-up colored man come in town here. He called hisself Mr. B. F. Mason and said he come from Washington, D.C. Ever day he would walk up and down the street with a walking-cane and a pretty colored shirt on. Then at night he would go to the Society Café. He eaten finer than any man in this town. Ever night he would order hisself a bottle of gin and two pork chops for his supper. He always had a smile for everbody and was always bowing around to the girls and holding a door open for you to come in or go out. For about a week he made hisself mighty pleasant wherever he were. Peoples begun to ask questions and wonder about this rich Mr. B. F. Mason. Then pretty soon, after he acquaints hisself, he begun to settle down to business.'

Portia spread out her lips and blew into her saucer of coffee. 'I suppose you done read in the paper about this Goverment Pincher business for old folks?'

Doctor Copeland nodded. 'Pension,' he said.

'Well — he were connected with that. He were from the goverment. He had come down from the President in Washington, D.C., to join everbody up for the Goverment Pinchers. He went around from one door to the next explaining how you pay one dollar down to join and after that twenty-five cents a week — and how when you were forty-five year old the goverment would pay you fifty dollars ever month of your life. All the peoples I know were very excited about this. He give everbody that joined a free picture of the President with his name signed under it. He told how at the end of six months there were going to be free uniforms for ever member. The club was called the Grand League of Pincheners for Colored Peoples — and at the end of two months everbody was going to get a orange ribbon with a G.L.P.C.P. on it to stand for the name. You know, like all these other letter things in the goverment. He come around from house to house with this little book and everbody commenced to join. He wrote their names down and took the money. Ever Saturday he would collect. In three weeks this Mr. B. F. Mason had joined up so many peoples he couldn't get all the way around on Saturday. He have to pay somebody to take up the collections in each three four blocks. I collected early ever Saturday for near where we live and got that quarter. Course Willie had joined at the beginning for him and Highboy and me.'

'I have come across many pictures of the President in various houses near where you live and I remember hearing the name Mason mentioned,' said Doctor Copeland. 'He was a thief?'

'He were,' said Portia. 'Somebody begun to find out about this Mr. B. F. Mason and he were arrested. They find out he were from just plain Atlanta and hadn't never smelled no Washington, D.C., or no President. All the money were hid or spent. Willie had just throwed away seven dollars and fifty cents.'

Doctor Copeland was excited. 'That is what I mean by ——'

'In the hereafter,' Portia said, 'that man sure going to wake up with a hot pitchfork in his gut. But now that it all over it do seem a little bit funny, but of course we got plenty reason not to laugh too hard.'

'The Negro race of its own accord climbs up on the cross on every Friday,' said Doctor Copeland.

Portia's hands shook and coffee trickled down from the saucer she was holding. She licked it from her arm. 'What you mean?'

'I mean that I am always looking. I mean that if I could just find ten Negroes — ten of my own people — with spine and brains and courage who are willing to give all that they have ——'

Portia put down the coffee. 'Us was not talking about anything like that.'

'Only four Negroes,' said Doctor Copeland. 'Only the sum of Hamilton and Karl Marx and William and you. Only four Negroes with these real true qualities and backbone ——'

'Willie and Highboy and me have backbone,' said Portia

angrily. 'This here is a hard world and it seem to me us three struggles along pretty well.'

For a minute they were silent. Doctor Copeland laid his spectacles on the table and pressed his shrunken fingers to his eyeballs.

'You all the time using that word — Negro,' said Portia. 'And that word haves a way of hurting peoples' feelings. Even old plain nigger is better than that word. But polite peoples — no matter what shade they is — always says colored.'

Doctor Copeland did not answer.

'Take Willie and me. Us aren't all the way colored. Our Mama was real light and both of us haves a good deal of white folks' blood in us. And Highboy — he Indian. He got a good part Indian in him. None of us is pure colored and the word you all the time using haves a way of hurting peoples' feelings.'

'I am not interested in subterfuges,' said Doctor Copeland. 'I am interested only in real truths.'

'Well, this here is a truth. Everbody is scared of you. It sure would take a whole lot of gin to get Hamilton or Buddy or Willie or my Highboy to come in this house and sit with you like I does. Willie say he remember you when he were only a little boy and he were afraid of his own father then.'

Doctor Copeland coughed harshly and cleared his throat.

'Everbody haves feelings — no matter who they is — and nobody is going to walk in no house where they certain their feelings will be hurt. You the same way. I seen your feelings injured too many times by white peoples not to know that.'

'No,' said Doctor Copeland. 'You have not seen my feelings injured.'

'Course I realize that Willie or my Highboy or me — that none of us is scholars. But Highboy and Willie is both good as gold. There just is a difference between them and you.'

'Yes,' said Doctor Copeland.

'Hamilton or Buddy or Willie or me — none of us ever cares

to talk like you. Us talk like our own Mama and her peoples and their peoples before them. You think out everthing in your brain. While us rather talk from something in our hearts that has been there for a long time. That's one of them differences.'

'Yes,' said Doctor Copeland.

'A person can't pick up they children and just squeeze them to which-a-way they wants them to be. Whether it hurt them or not. Whether it right or wrong. You done tried that hard as any man could try. And now I the only one of us that would come in this here house and sit with you like this.'

The light was very bright in Doctor Copeland's eyes and her voice was loud and hard. He coughed and his whole face trembled. He tried to pick up the cup of cold coffee, but his hand would not hold it steadily. The tears came up to his eyes and he reached for his glasses to try to hide them.

Portia saw and went up to him quickly. She put her arms around his head and pressed her cheek to his forehead. 'I done hurt my Father's feelings,' she said softly.

His voice was hard. 'No. It is foolish and primitive to keep repeating this about hurt feelings.'

The tears went slowly down his cheek and the fire made them take on the colors of blue and green and red. 'I be really and truly sorry,' said Portia.

Doctor Copeland wiped his face with his cotton handkerchief. 'It is all right.'

'Less us not ever quarrel no more. I can't stand this here fighting between us. It seem to me that something real bad come up in us ever time we be together. Less us never quarrel like this no more.'

'No,' said Doctor Copeland. 'Let us not quarrel.'

Portia sniffled and wiped her nose with the back of her hand. For a few minutes she stood with her arms around her father's head. Then after a while she wiped her face for a final time and went over to the pot of greens on the stove.

'It mighty nigh time for these to be tender,' she said cheerfully. 'Now I think I'll start making some of them good little hoecakes to go along with them.'

Portia moved slowly around the kitchen in her stockinged feet and her father followed her with his eyes. For a while again they were silent.

With his eyes wet, so that the edges of things were blurred, Portia was truly like her mother. Years ago Daisy had walked like that around the kitchen, silent and occupied. Daisy was not black as he was — her skin had been like the beautiful color of dark honey. She was always very quiet and gentle. But beneath that soft gentleness there was something stubborn in her, and no matter how conscientiously he studied it all out, he could not understand the gentle stubbornness in his wife.

He would exhort her and he would tell her all that was in his heart and still she was gentle. And still she would not listen to him but would go on her own way.

Then later there were Hamilton and Karl Marx and William and Portia. And this feeling of real true purpose for them was so strong that he knew exactly how each thing should be with them. Hamilton would be a great scientist and Karl Marx a teacher of the Negro race and William a lawyer to fight against injustice and Portia a doctor for women and children.

And when they were even babies he would tell them of the yoke they must thrust from their shoulders — the yoke of submission and slothfulness. And when they were a little older he would impress upon them that there was no God, but that their lives were holy and for each one of them there was this real true purpose. He would tell it to them over and over, and they would sit together far away from him and look with their big Negro-children eyes at their mother. And Daisy would sit without listening, gentle and stubborn.

Because of the true purpose for Hamilton, Karl Marx, William, and Portia, he knew how every detail should be. In the autumn of each year he took them all into town and bought for them good black shoes and black stockings. For Portia he bought black woolen material for dresses and white linen for collars and cuffs. For the boys there was black wool for trousers and fine white linen for shirts. He did not want them to wear bright-colored, flimsy clothes. But when they went to school those were the ones they wished to wear, and Daisy said that they were embarrassed and that he was a hard father. He knew how the house should be. There could be no fanciness — no gaudy calendars or lace pillows or knickknacks — but everything in the house must be plain and dark and indicative of work and the real true purpose.

Then one night he found that Daisy had pierced holes in little Portia's ears for earrings. And another time a kewpie doll with feather skirts was on the mantelpiece when he came home, and Daisy was gentle and hard and would not put it away. He knew, too, that Daisy was teaching the children the cult of meekness. She told them about hell and heaven. Also she convinced them of ghosts and of haunted places. Daisy went to church every Sunday and she talked sorrowfully to the preacher of her own husband. And with her stubbornness she always took the children to the church, too, and they listened.

The whole Negro race was sick, and he was busy all the day and sometimes half the night. After the long day a great weariness would come in him, but when he opened the front gate of his home the weariness would go away. Yet when he went into the house William would be playing music on a comb wrapped in toilet paper, Hamilton and Karl Marx would be shooting craps for their lunch money, Portia would be laughing with her mother.

He would start all over with them, but in a different way. He would bring out their lessons and talk with them. They would sit close together and look at their mother. He would talk and talk, but none of them wanted to understand.

The feeling that would come on him was a black, terrible, Negro feeling. He would try to sit in his office and read and meditate until he could be calm and start again. He would pull down the shades of the room so that there would be only the bright light and the books and the feeling of meditation. But sometimes this calmness would not come. He was young, and the terrible feeling would not go away with study.

Hamilton, Karl Marx, William, and Portia would be afraid of him and look at their mother — and sometimes when he realized this the black feeling would conquer him and he knew not what he did.

He could not stop those terrible things, and afterward he could never understand.

'This here supper sure smells good to me,' said Portia. 'I expect us better eat now because Highboy and Willie liable to come trooping in any minute.'

Doctor Copeland settled his spectacles and pulled his chair up to the table. 'Where have your husband and William been spending the evening?'

'They been throwing horseshoes. This here Raymond Jones haves a horseshoe place in his back yard. This Raymond and his sister, Love Jones, plays ever night. Love is such a ugly girl I don't mind about Highboy or Willie going around to their house any time they wishes. But they said they would come back for me at quarter to ten and I expecting them now any minute.'

'Before I forget,' said Doctor Copeland. 'I suppose you hear frequently from Hamilton and Karl Marx.'

'I does from Hamilton. He practically taken over all the work on our Grandpapa's place. But Buddy, he in Mobile — and you know he were never a big hand at writing letters. However, Buddy always haves such a sweet way with peoples that I don't ever worry concerning him. He the kind to always get along right well.'

They sat silently at the table before the supper. Portia kept looking up at the clock on the cupboard because it was time for Highboy and Willie to come. Doctor Copeland bent his head over his plate. He held the fork in his hand as though it were heavy, and his fingers trembled. He only tasted the food and with each mouthful he swallowed hard. There was a feeling of strain, and it seemed as though both of them wanted to keep up some conversation.

Doctor Copeland did not know how to begin. Sometimes he thought that he had talked so much in the years before to his children and they had understood so little that now there was nothing at all to say. After a while he wiped his mouth with his handkerchief and spoke in an uncertain voice.

'You have hardly mentioned yourself. Tell me about your job and what you have been doing lately.'

'Course I still with the Kellys,' said Portia. 'But I tells you, Father, I don't know how long I going to be able to keep on with them. The work is hard and it always take me a long time to get through. However, that don't bother me none. It about the pay I worries about. I suppose to get three dollars a week — but sometimes Mrs. Kelly likes a dollar or fifty cents of paying me the full amount. Course she always catches up on it soon as she able. But it haves a way of leaving me in a pinch.'

'That is not right,' said Doctor Copeland. 'Why do you stand for it?'

'It ain't her fault. She can't help it,' said Portia. 'Half the folks in that house don't pay the rent, and it a big expense to keep everthing up. I tell you the truth — the Kellys is just barely keeping one jump ahead of the sheriff. They having a mighty hard time.'

'There ought to be some other job you can get.'

'I know. But the Kellys is really grand white peoples to work for. I really fond of them as I can be. Them three little children is just like some of my own kinfolks. I feel like I done really raised Bubber and the baby. And although Mick and me is always getting into some kind of quarrel together, I haves a real close fondness for her, too.'

'But you must think of yourself,' said Doctor Copeland.

'Mick, now ——' said Portia. 'She a real case. Not a soul know how to manage that child. She just as biggity and headstrong as she can be. Something going on in her all the time. I haves a funny feeling about that child. It seem to me that one of these days she going to really surprise somebody. But whether that going to be a good surprise or a bad surprise I just don't know. Mick puzzle me sometimes. But still I really fond of her.'

'You must look out for your own livelihood first.'

'As I say, it ain't Mrs. Kelly's fault. It cost so much to run that big old house and the rent just don't be paid. Ain't but one person in the house who pay a decent amount for his room and pay it on the dot without fail. And that man only been living there a short while. He one of these here deaf-and-dumb folks. He the first one of them I ever seen close up — but he a mighty fine white man.'

'Tall, thin, with gray and green eyes?' asked Doctor Copeland suddenly. 'And always polite to everyone and very well dressed? Not like someone from this town — more like a Northerner or maybe a Jew?'

'That him,' said Portia.

Eagerness came into Doctor Copeland's face. He crumbled his hoecake into the collard juice in his plate and began to eat with a new appetite. 'I have a deaf-mute patient,' he said.

'How come you acquainted with Mr. Singer?' asked Portia.

Doctor Copeland coughed and covered his mouth with his handkerchief. 'I have just seen him several times.'

'I better clean up now,' said Portia. 'It sure enough time for Willie and my Highboy. But with this here real sink and grand running water these little dishes won't take me two winks.'

The quiet insolence of the white race was one thing he had tried to keep out of his mind for years. When the resentment would come to him he would cogitate and study. In the streets and around white people he would keep the dignity on his face and always be silent. When he was younger it was 'Boy' — but now it was 'Uncle.' 'Uncle, run down to that filling station on the corner and send me a mechanic.' A white man in a car had called out those words to him not long ago. 'Boy, give me a hand with this.' — 'Uncle, do that.' And he would not listen, but would walk on with the dignity in him and be silent.

A few nights ago a drunken white man had come up to him and begun pulling him along the street. He had his bag with him and he was sure someone was hurt. But the drunkard had pulled him into a white man's restaurant and the white men at the counter had begun hollering out with their insolence. He knew that the drunkard was making fun of him. Even then he had kept the dignity in him.

But with this tall, thin white man with the gray-green eyes something had happened that had never happened to him with any white man before.

It came about on a dark, rainy night several weeks ago. He had just come from a maternity case and was standing in the rain on a corner. He had tried to light a cigarette and one by one the matches in his box fizzled out. He had been standing with the unlighted cigarette in his mouth when the white man stepped up and held for him a lighted match. In the dark with the flame between them they could see each other's faces. The white man smiled at him and lighted for him his cigarette. He did not know what to say, for nothing like that had ever happened to him before.

They had stood for a few minutes on the street corner together, and then the white man had handed him his card. He wanted to talk to the white man and ask him some questions, but he did not know for sure if he could really understand.

Because of the insolence of all the white race he was afraid to lose his dignity in friendliness.

But the white man had lighted his cigarette and smiled and seemed to want to be with him. Since then he had thought this over many times.

'I have a deaf-mute patient,' said Doctor Copeland to Portia. 'The patient is a boy five years of age. And somehow I cannot get over the feeling that I am to blame for his handicap. I delivered him, and after two post-delivery visits of course I forgot about him. He developed ear trouble, but the mother paid no attention to the discharges from his ears and did not bring him to me. When it was finally brought to my attention it was too late. Of course he hears nothing and of course he therefore cannot speak. But I have watched him carefully, and it seems to me that if he were normal he would be a very intelligent child.'

'You always had a great interest in little children,' said Portia. 'You care a heap more about them than about grown peoples, don't you?'

'There is more hope in the young child,' said Doctor Copeland. 'But this deaf boy — I have been meaning to make inquiries and find if there is some institution that would take him.'

'Mr. Singer would tell you. He a truly kind white man and he not a bit biggity.'

'I do not know ——' said Doctor Copeland. 'I have thought once or twice about writing him a note and seeing if he could give me information.'

'Sure I would if I was you. You a grand letter-writer and I would give it to Mr. Singer for you,' said Portia. 'He come down in the kitchen two-three weeks ago with a few shirts he wanted me to rinch out for him. Them shirts were no more dirty than if Saint John the Baptist hisself had been wearing them. All I had to do were dip them in warm water and give the collars a small rub and press them. But that night when

I taken them five clean shirts up to his room you know how much he give me?'

'No.'

'He smile like he always do and hand over to me a dollar. A whole dollar just for them little shirts. He one really kind and pleasant white man and I wouldn't be afraid to ask him any question. I wouldn't even mind writing that nice white man a letter myself. You go right ahead and do it, Father, if you wants to.'

'Perhaps I will,' said Doctor Copeland.

Portia sat up suddenly and began arranging her tight, oily hair. There was the faint sound of a harmonica and then gradually the music grew louder. 'Here come Willie and Highboy,' Portia said. 'I got to go out now and meet them. You take care of yourself now, and send me a word if you needs me for anything. I did enjoy the supper with you and the talking very much.'

The music from the harmonica was very clear now, and they could tell that Willie was playing while he waited at the front gate.

'Wait a minute,' said Doctor Copeland. 'I have only seen your husband with you about two times and I believe we have never really met each other. And it has been three years since William has visited his father. Why not tell them to drop in for a little while?'

Portia stood in the doorway, fingering her hair and her earrings.

'Last time Willie come in here you hurted his feelings. You see you don't understand just how ——'

'Very well,' said Doctor Copeland. 'It was only a suggestion.'

'Wait,' said Portia. 'I going to call them. I going to invite them in right now.'

Doctor Copeland lighted a cigarette and walked up and down the room. He could not straighten his glasses to just the right position and his fingers kept trembling. From the front yard there was the sound of low voices. Then heavy footsteps were in the hall and Portia, William, and Highboy entered the kitchen.

'Here we is,' said Portia. 'Highboy, I don't believe you and my Father has ever truly been introduced to each other. But you knows who each other is.'

Doctor Copeland shook hands with both of them. Willie hung back shyly against the wall, but Highboy stepped forward and bowed formally. 'I has always heard so much about you,' he said. 'I be very pleased to make your acquaintance.'

Portia and Doctor Copeland brought in chairs from the hall and the four of them sat around the stove. They were silent and uneasy. Willie gazed nervously around the room — at the books on the kitchen table, the sink, the cot against the wall, and at his father. Highboy grinned and picked at his tie. Doctor Copeland seemed about to speak, and then he wet his lips and was still silent.

'Willie, you were going pretty good with your harp,' said Portia finally. 'Look to me like you and Highboy must of got into somebody's gin bottle.'

'No, ma'am,' said Highboy very politely. 'Us haven't had anything since Saturday. Us have just been enjoying our horseshoe game.'

Doctor Copeland still did not speak, and they all kept glancing at him and waiting. The room was close and the quietness made everyone nervous.

'I do haves the hardest time with them boys' clothes,' Portia said. 'I washes both of them white suits ever Saturday and I presses them twice a week. And look at them now. Course they don't wear them except when they gets home from work. But after two days they seems to be potty black. I ironed them pants just last night and now there not a crease left.'

Still Doctor Copeland was silent. He kept his eyes on his

son's face, but when Willie noticed this he bit his rough, blunt fingers and stared at his feet. Doctor Copeland felt his pulse hammering at his wrists and temples. He coughed and held his fist to his chest. He wanted to speak to his son, but he could think of nothing to say. The old bitterness came up in him and he did not have time to cogitate and push it down. His pulse hammered in him and he was confused. But they all looked at him, and the silence was so strong that he had to speak.

His voice was high and it did not sound as though it came from himself. 'William, I wonder how much of all the things I have said to you when you were a child have stayed in your mind.'

'I don't know what you m-m-means,' Willie said.

The words came before Doctor Copeland knew what he would say. 'I mean that to you and Hamilton and Karl Marx I gave all that was in me. And I put all of my trust and hope in you. And all I get is blank misunderstanding and idleness and indifference. Of all I have put in nothing has remained. All has been taken away from me. All that I have tried to do ——'

'Hush,' said Portia. 'Father, you promised me that us would not quarrel. This here is crazy. Us can't afford to quarrel.'

Portia got up and started toward the front door. Willie and Highboy followed quickly. Doctor Copeland was the last to come.

They stood in the dark before the front door. Doctor Copeland tried to speak, but his voice seemed lost somewhere deep inside him. Willie and Portia and Highboy stood in a group together.

With one arm Portia held to her husband and brother and with the other she reached out to Doctor Copeland. 'Less us all make up now before us goes. I can't stand this here fighting between us. Less us not ever quarrel no more.'

In silence Doctor Copeland shook hands again with each of them. 'I am sorry,' he said.

'It quite all right with me,' said Highboy politely.

'It quite all right with me too,' Willie mumbled.

Portia held all of their hands together. 'Us just can't afford to quarrel.'

They said good-bye, and Doctor Copeland watched them from the dark front porch as they went together up the street. Their footsteps as they walked away had a lonesome sound and he felt weak and tired. When they were a block away William began playing his harmonica again. The music was sad and empty. He stayed on the front porch until he could neither see nor hear them any longer.

Doctor Copeland turned off the lights in his house and sat in the dark before the stove. But peace would not come to him. He wanted to remove Hamilton and Karl Marx and William from his mind. Each word that Portia had said to him came back in a loud, hard way to his memory. He got up suddenly and turned on the light. He settled himself at the table with his books by Spinoza and William Shakespeare and Karl Marx. When he read the Spinoza aloud to himself the words had a rich, dark sound.

He thought of the white man of whom they had spoken. It would be good if the white man could help him with Augustus Benedict Mady Lewis, the deaf patient. It would be good to write to the white man even if he did not have this reason and these questions to ask. Doctor Copeland held his head in his hands and from his throat there came the strange sound like a kind of singing moan. He remembered the white man's face when he smiled behind the yellow match flame on that rainy night — and peace was in him.

6

BY MIDSUMMER Singer had visitors more often than any other person in the house. From his room in the evening there was nearly always the sound of a voice. After dinner at the New York Café he bathed and dressed himself in one of his cool wash suits and as a rule did not go out again. The room was cool and pleasant. He had an icebox in the closet where he kept bottles of cold beer and fruit drinks. He was never busy or in a hurry. And always he met his guests at the door with a welcome smile.

Mick loved to go up to Mister Singer's room. Even if he was a deaf-and-dumb mute he understood every word she said to him. Talking with him was like a game. Only there was a whole lot more to it than any game. It was like finding out new things about music. She would tell him some of her plans that she would not tell anybody else. He let her meddle with his cute little chess men. Once when she was excited and caught her shirt-tail in the electric fan he acted in such a kindly way that she was not embarrassed at all. Except for her Dad, Mister Singer was the nicest man she knew.

When Doctor Copeland wrote the note to John Singer about Augustus Benedict Mady Lewis there was a polite reply and an invitation for him to make a call when he found the opportunity. Doctor Copeland went to the back of the house and sat with Portia awhile in the kitchen. Then he climbed the stairs to the white man's room. There was truly none of the quiet insolence about this man. They had a lemonade together and the mute wrote down the answer to the questions he wished to know. This man was different from any person of the white race whom Doctor Copeland had ever encountered. Afterward he pondered about this white man a long time. Then later, inasmuch as he had been invited in a cordial manner to return, he made another visit.

Jake Blount came every week. When he walked up to Singer's room the whole stairway shook. Usually he carried a paper sack of beers. Often his voice would come out loud and angry from the room. But before he left his voice gradually quieted. When he descended the stairs he did not carry the sack of beers any longer, and he walked away thoughtfully without seeming to notice where he was going.

Even Biff Brannon came to the mute's room one night. But as he could never stay away from the restaurant for long, he left in a half-hour.

Singer was always the same to everyone. He sat in a straight chair by the window with his hands stuffed tight into his pockets, and nodded or smiled to show his guests that he understood.

If he did not have a visitor in the evening, Singer went to a late movie. He liked to sit back and watch the actors talking and walking about on the screen. He never looked at the title of a picture before going into a movie, and no matter what was showing he watched each scene with equal interest.

Then, one day in July, Singer suddenly went away without warning. He left the door of his room open, and on the table in an envelope addressed to Mrs. Kelly there were four dollars for the past week's rent. His few simple possessions were gone and the room was very clean and bare. When his visitors came and saw this empty room they went away with hurt surprise. No one could imagine why he had left like this.

Singer spent all of his summer vacation in the town where Antonapoulos was being kept in the asylum. For months he had planned this trip and imagined about each moment they would have together. Two weeks beforehand his hotel reservation had been made and for a long time he had carried his railroad ticket in an envelope in his pocket.

Antonapoulos was not changed at all. When Singer came into his room he ambled placidly to meet his friend. He was even fatter than before, but the dreamy smile on his face was just the same. Singer had some packages in his arms and the big Greek gave them his first attention. His presents were a scarlet dressing-gown, soft bedroom slippers, and two monogrammed nightshirts. Antonapoulos looked beneath all the tissue papers in the boxes very carefully. When he saw that nothing good to eat had been concealed there, he dumped the gifts disdainfully on his bed and did not bother with them any more.

The room was large and sunny. Several beds were spaced in a row together. Three old men played a game of slapjack in a corner. They did not notice Singer or Antonapoulos, and the two friends sat alone on the other side of the room.

It seemed to Singer that years had passed since they had been together. There was so much to say that his hands could not shape the signs with speed enough. His green eyes burned and sweat glittered on his forehead. The old feeling of gaiety and bliss was so quick in him again that he could not control himself.

Antonapoulos kept his dark, oily eyes on his friend and did not move. His hands fumbled languidly with the crotch of his trousers. Singer told him, among other things, about the visitors who had been coming to see him. He told his friend that they helped take his mind away from his lonesomeness. He told Antonapoulos that they were strange people and always talking — but that he liked to have them come. He drew quick sketches of Jake Blount and Mick and Doctor Copeland. Then as soon as he saw that Antonapoulos was not interested Singer crumpled the sketches and forgot about them. When the attendant came in to say that their time was up, Singer had not finished half of the things he wanted to say. But he left the room very tired and happy.

The patients could receive their friends only on Thursday and Sunday. On the days when he could not be with Antonapoulos, Singer walked up and down in his room at the hotel.

His second visit to his friend was like the first, except that the old men in the room watched them listlessly and did not play slapjack.

After much trouble Singer obtained permission to take Antonapoulos out with him for a few hours. He planned each detail of the little excursion in advance. They drove out into the country in a taxi, and then at four-thirty they went to the dining-room at the hotel. Antonapoulos greatly enjoyed this extra meal. He ordered half the dishes on the menu and ate very greedily. But when he had finished he would not leave. He held to the table. Singer coaxed him and the cab driver wanted to use force. Antonapoulos sat stolidly and made obscene gestures when they came too close to him. At last Singer bought a bottle of whiskey from the hotel manager and lured him into the taxi again. When Singer threw the unopened bottle out of the window Antonapoulos wept with disappointment and offense. The end of their little excursion made Singer very sad.

His next visit was the last one, for his two weeks' vacation was almost over. Antonapoulos had forgotten what had happened before. They sat in their same corner of the room. The minutes slipped by quickly. Singer's hands talked desperately and his narrow face was very pale. At last it was time for him to go. He held his friend by the arm and looked into his face in the way that he used to do when they parted each day before work. Antonapoulos stared at him drowsily and did not move. Singer left the room with his hands stuffed hard into his pockets.

Soon after Singer returned to his room at the boardinghouse, Mick and Jake Blount and Doctor Copeland began to come again. Each one of them wanted to know where he had been and why he had not let them know about his plans. But Singer pretended that he did not understand their questions, and his smile was inscrutable.

One by one they would come to Singer's room to spend the evening with him. The mute was always thoughtful and composed. His many-tinted gentle eyes were grave as a sorcerer's. Mick Kelly and Jake Blount and Doctor Copeland would come and talk in the silent room — for they felt that the mute would always understand whatever they wanted to say to him. And maybe even more than that.

PART II

1

THIS summer was different from any other time Mick could remember. Nothing much happened that she could describe to herself in thoughts or words — but there was a feeling of change. All the time she was excited. In the morning she couldn't wait to get out of bed and start going for the day. And at night she hated like hell to have to sleep again.

Right after breakfast she took the kids out, and except for meals they were gone most of the day. A good deal of the time they just roamed around the streets — with her pulling Ralph's wagon and Bubber following along behind. Always she was busy with thoughts and plans. Sometimes she would look up suddenly and they would be way off in some part of town she didn't even recognize. And once or twice they ran into Bill on the streets and she was so busy thinking he had to grab her by the arm to make her see him.

Early in the mornings it was a little cool and their shadows stretched out tall on the sidewalk in front of them. But in the middle of the day the sky was always blazing hot. The glare was so bright it hurt to keep your eyes open. A lot of times the plans about the things that were going to happen to her were mixed up with ice and snow. Sometimes it was like she was out in Switzerland and all the mountains were covered with snow and she was skating on cold, greenish-colored ice. Mister Singer would be skating with her. And maybe Carole Lombard or Arturo Toscanini who played on the radio. They would be skating together and then Mister Singer would fall through the ice and she would dive in without regard for peril and swim under the ice and save his life. That was one of the plans always going on in her mind.

Usually after they had walked awhile she would park Bubber and Ralph in some shady place. Bubber was a swell kid and she had trained him pretty good. If she told him not to go out of hollering distance from Ralph she wouldn't ever find him shooting marbles with kids two or three blocks away. He played by himself near the wagon, and when she left them she didn't have to worry much. She either went to the library and looked at the *National Geographic* or else just roamed around and thought some more. If she had any money she bought a dope or a Milky Way at Mister Brannon's. He gave kids a reduction. He sold them nickel things for three cents.

But all the time — no matter what she was doing — there was music. Sometimes she hummed to herself as she walked, and other times she listened quietly to the songs inside her. There were all kinds of music in her thoughts. Some she heard over radios, and some was in her mind already without her ever having heard it anywhere.

In the night-time, as soon as the kids were in bed, she was free. That was the most important time of all. A lot of things happened when she was by herself and it was dark. Right after supper she ran out of the house again. She couldn't tell anybody about the things she did at night, and when her Mama asked her questions she would answer with any little tale that sounded reasonable. But most of the time if anybody called her she just ran away like she hadn't heard. That went for everybody except her Dad. There was something about her Dad's voice she couldn't run away from. He was one of the biggest, tallest men in the whole town. But his voice was so quiet and kindly that people were surprised when he spoke. No matter how much of a hurry she was in, she always had to stop when her Dad called.

This summer she realized something about her Dad she had never known before. Up until then she had never thought about him as being a real separate person. A lot of times he would call her. She would go in the front room where he worked and stand by him a couple of minutes — but when she listened to him her mind was never on the things he said to her. Then one night she suddenly realized about her Dad. Nothing unusual happened that night and she didn't know what it was that made her understand. Afterward she felt older and as though she knew him as good as she could know any person.

It was a night in late August and she was in a big rush. She had to be at this house by nine o'clock, and no maybe either. Her Dad called and she went into the front room. He was sitting slumped over his workbench. For some reason it never did seem natural to see him there. Until the time of his accident last year he had been a painter and carpenter. Before daylight every morning he would leave the house in his overalls, to be gone all day. Then at night sometimes he fiddled around with clocks as an extra work. A lot of times he had tried to get a job in a jewelry store where he could sit by himself at a desk all day with a clean white shirt on and a tie. Now when he couldn't carpenter any more he had put a sign at the front of the house reading 'Clocks and Watches Repaired Cheap.' But he didn't look like most jewelers — the ones downtown were quick, dark little Jew men. Her Dad was too tall for his workbench, and his big bones seemed joined together in a loose way.

Her Dad just stared at her. She could tell he didn't have any reason for calling. He only wanted real bad to talk to her. He tried to think of some way to begin. His brown eyes were too big for his long, thin face, and since he had lost every single hair the pale, bald top of his head gave him a naked look. He still looked at her without speaking and she was in a hurry. She had to be at that house by nine sharp and there was no time to waste. Her Dad saw she was in a hurry and he cleared his throat.

'I got something for you,' he said. 'Nothing much, but maybe you can treat yourself with it.'

He didn't have to give her any nickel or dime just because he was lonesome and wanted to talk. Out of what he made he only kept enough to have beer about twice a week. Two bottles were on the floor by his chair now, one empty and one just opened. And whenever he drank beer he liked to talk to somebody. Her Dad fumbled with his belt and she looked away. This summer he had gotten like a kid about hiding those nickels and dimes he kept for himself. Sometimes he hid them in his shoes, and other times in a little slit he had cut in his belt. She only halfway wanted to take the dime, but when he held it out her hand was just naturally open and ready.

'I got so much work to do I don't know where to begin,' he said.

That was just the opposite to the truth, and he knew it good as she did. He never had many watches to fix, and when he finished he would fool around the house doing any little job that was needed. Then at night he sat at his bench, cleaning old springs and wheels and trying to make the work last out until bedtime. Ever since he broke his hip and couldn't work steady he had to be doing something every minute.

'I been thinking a lot tonight,' her Dad said. He poured out his beer and sprinkled a few grains of salt on the back of his hand. Then he licked up the salt and took a swallow out of the glass.

She was in such a hurry that it was hard to stand still. Her Dad noticed this. He tried to say something — but he had not called to tell her anything special. He only wanted to talk with her for a little while. He started to speak and swallowed. They just looked at each other. The quietness grew out longer and neither of them could say a word.

That was when she realized about her Dad. It wasn't like she was learning a new fact — she had understood it all along in every way except with her brain. Now she just suddenly *knew* that she knew about her Dad. He was lonesome and he was an old man. Because none of the kids went to him for anything and because he didn't earn much money he felt like he was cut off from the family. And in his lonesomeness he wanted to be close to one of his kids — and they were all so busy that they didn't know it. He felt like he wasn't much real use to anybody.

She understood this while they were looking at each other. It gave her a queer feeling. Her Dad picked up a watch spring and cleaned it with a brush dipped in gasoline.

'I know you're in a hurry. I just hollered to say hello.'

'No, I'm not in any rush,' she said. 'Honest.'

That night she sat down in a chair by his bench and they talked awhile. He talked about accounts and expenses and how things would have been if he had just managed in a different way. He drank beer, and once the tears came to his eyes and he snuffled his nose against his shirt-sleeve. She stayed with him a good while that night. Even if she was in an awful hurry. Yet for some reason she couldn't tell him about the things in her mind — about the hot, dark nights.

These nights were secret, and of the whole summer they were the most important time. In the dark she walked by herself and it was like she was the only person in the town. Almost every street came to be as plain to her in the nighttime as her own home block. Some kids were afraid to walk through strange places in the dark, but she wasn't. Girls were scared a man would come out from somewhere and put his teapot in them like they was married. Most girls were nuts. If a person the size of Joe Louis or Mountain Man Dean would jump out at her and want to fight she would run. But if it was somebody within twenty pounds her weight she would give him a good sock and go right on.

The nights were wonderful, and she didn't have time to think about such things as being scared. Whenever she was in the dark she thought about music. While she walked along the streets she would sing to herself. And she felt like the whole town listened without knowing it was Mick Kelly.

She learned a lot about music during these free nights in the summer-time. When she walked out in the rich parts of town every house had a radio. All the windows were open and she could hear the music very marvelous. After a while she knew which houses tuned in for the programs she wanted to hear. There was one special house that got all the good orchestras. And at night she would go to this house and sneak into the dark yard to listen. There was beautiful shrubbery around this house, and she would sit under a bush near the window. And after it was all over she would stand in the dark yard with her hands in her pockets and think for a long time. That was the realest part of all the summer — her listening to this music on the radio and studying about it.

'*Cerra la puerta, señor*,' Mick said.

Bubber was sharp as a briar. '*Haga me usted el favor, señorita*,' he answered as a comeback.

It was grand to take Spanish at Vocational. There was something about speaking in a foreign language that made her feel like she'd been around a lot. Every afternoon since school had started she had fun speaking the new Spanish words and sentences. At first Bubber was stumped, and it was funny to watch his face while she talked the foreign language. Then he caught on in a hurry, and before long he could copy everything she said. He remembered the words he learned, too. Of course he didn't know what all the sentences meant, but she didn't say them for the sense they made, anyway. After a while the kid learned so fast she gave out of Spanish and just gabbled along with made-up sounds. But it wasn't long before he caught her out at that — nobody could put a thing over on old Bubber Kelly.

'I'm going to pretend like I'm walking into this house for the first time,' Mick said. 'Then I can tell better if all the decoration looks good or not.'

She walked out on the front porch and then came back and

stood in the hall. All day she and Bubber and Portia and her Dad had been fixing the hall and the dining-room for the party. The decoration was autumn leaves and vines and red crêpe paper. On the mantelpiece in the dining-room and sticking up behind the hatrack there were bright yellow leaves. They had trailed vines along the walls and on the table where the punch bowl would be. The red crêpe paper hung down in long fringes from the mantel and also was looped around the backs of the chairs. There was plenty decoration. It was O.K.

She rubbed her hand on her forehead and squinted her eyes. Bubber stood beside her and copied every move she made. 'I sure do want this party to turn out all right. I sure do.'

This would be the first party she had ever given. She had never even been to more than four or five. Last summer she had gone to a prom party. But none of the boys asked her to prom or dance, so she just stood by the punch bowl until all the refreshments were gone and then went home. This party was not going to be a bit like that one. In a few hours now the people she had invited would start coming and the to-do would begin.

It was hard to remember just how she got the idea of this party. The notion came to her soon after she started at Vocational. High School was swell. Everything about it was different from Grammar School. She wouldn't have liked it so much if she had had to take a stenographic course like Hazel and Etta had done — but she got special permission and took mechanical shop like a boy. Shop and Algebra and Spanish were grand. English was mighty hard. Her English teacher was Miss Minner. Everybody said Miss Minner had sold her brains to a famous doctor for ten thousand dollars, so that after she was dead he could cut them up and see why she was so smart. On written lessons she cracked such questions as 'Name eight famous contemporaries of Doctor Johnson,' and 'Quote ten lines from "The Vicar of Wakefield."' She called on people by the alphabet and kept her grade book open during the lessons. And even if she was brainy she was an old sourpuss. The Spanish teacher had traveled once in Europe. She said that in France the people carried home loaves of bread without having them wrapped up. They would stand talking on the streets and hit the bread on a lamp post. And there wasn't any water in France — only wine.

In nearly all ways Vocational was wonderful. They walked back and forth in the hall between classes, and at lunch period students hung around the gym. Here was the thing that soon began to bother her. In the halls the people would walk up and down together and everybody seemed to belong to some special bunch. Within a week or two she knew people in the halls and in classes to speak to them — but that was all. She wasn't a member of any bunch. In Grammar School she would have just gone up to any crowd she wanted to belong with and that would have been the end of the matter. Here it was different.

During the first week she walked up and down the halls by herself and thought about this. She planned about being with some bunch almost as much as she thought of music. Those two things were in her head all the time. And finally she got the idea of the party.

She was strict with the invitations. No Grammar School kids and nobody under twelve years old. She just asked people between thirteen and fifteen. She knew everybody she invited good enough to speak to them in the halls — and when she didn't know their names she asked to find out. She called up those who had a telephone, and the rest she invited at school.

On the telephone she always said the same thing. She let Bubber stick in his ear to listen. 'This is Mick Kelly,' she said. If they didn't understand the name she kept on until they got it. 'I'm having a prom party at eight o'clock Saturday night and I'm inviting you now. I live at 103 Fourth Street, Apartment A.' That Apartment A sounded swell on the telephone. Nearly everybody said they would be delighted. A couple of tough boys tried to be smarty and kept on asking her name over and over. One of them tried to act cute and said, 'I don't know you.' She squelched him in a hurry: 'You go eat grass!' Outside of that wise guy there were ten boys and ten girls and she knew that they were all coming. This was a real party, and it would be better than and different from any party she had ever gone to or heard about before.

Mick looked over the hall and dining-room one last time. By the hatrack she stopped before the picture of Old Dirty-Face. This was a photo of her Mama's grandfather. He was a major way back in the Civil War and had been killed in a battle. Some kid once drew eyeglasses and a beard on his picture, and when the pencil marks were erased it left his face all dirty. That was why she called him Old Dirty-Face. The picture was in the middle of a three-part frame. On both sides were pictures of his sons. They looked about Bubber's age. They had on uniforms and their faces were surprised. They had been killed in a battle also. A long time ago.

'I'm going to take this down for the party. I think it looks common. Don't you?'

'I don't know,' Bubber said. 'Are we common, Mick?'

'*I'm* not.'

She put the picture underneath the hatrack. The decoration was O.K. Mister Singer would be pleased when he came home. The rooms seemed very empty and quiet. The table was set for supper. And then after supper it would be time for the party. She went into the kitchen to see about the refreshments.

'You think everything will be all right?' she asked Portia.

Portia was making biscuits. The refreshments were on top of the stove. There were peanut butter and jelly sandwiches and chocolate snaps and punch. The sandwiches were covered with a damp dishcloth. She peeped at them but didn't take one.

'I done told you forty times that everthing going to be all right,' Portia said. 'Just soon as I come back from fixing supper at home I going to put on that white apron and serve the food real nice. Then I going to push off from here by nine-thirty. This here is Saturday night and Highboy and Willie and me haves our plans, too.'

'Sure,' Mick said. 'I just want you to help out till things sort of get started — you know.'

She gave in and took one of the sandwiches. Then she made Bubber stay with Portia and went into the middle room. The dress she would wear was laying out on the bed. Hazel and Etta had both been good about lending her their best clothes — considering that they weren't supposed to come to the party. There was Etta's long blue crêpe de chine evening dress and some white pumps and a rhinestone tiara for her hair. These clothes were really gorgeous. It was hard to imagine how she would look in them.

The late afternoon had come and the sun made long, yellow slants through the window. If she took two hours over dressing for the party it was time to begin now. When she thought about putting on the fine clothes she couldn't just sit around and wait. Very slowly she went into the bathroom and shucked off her old shorts and shirt and turned on the water. She scrubbed the rough parts of her heels and her knees and especially her elbows. She made the bath take a long time.

She ran naked into the middle room and began to dress. Silk teddies she put on, and silk stockings. She even wore one of Etta's brassières just for the heck of it. Then very carefully she put on the dress and stepped into the pumps. This was the first time she had ever worn an evening dress. She stood for a long time before the mirror. She was so tall that the dress came up two or three inches above her ankles — and the shoes were so short they hurt her. She stood in front of the mirror a long time, and finally decided she either looked like a sap or else she looked very beautiful. One or the other.

Six different ways she tried out her hair. The cowlicks were a little trouble, so she wet her bangs and made three spit curls. Last of all she stuck the rhinestones in her hair and put on plenty of lipstick and paint. When she finished she lifted up her chin and half-closed her eyes like a movie star. Slowly she turned her face from one side to the other. It was beautiful she looked — just beautiful.

She didn't feel like herself at all. She was somebody different from Mick Kelly entirely. Two hours had to pass before the party would begin, and she was ashamed for any of the family to see her dressed so far ahead of time. She went into the bathroom again and locked the door. She couldn't mess up her dress by sitting down, so she stood in the middle of the floor. The close walls around her seemed to press in all the excitement. She felt so different from the old Mick Kelly that she knew this would be better than anything else in all her whole life — this party.

'Yippee! The punch!'

'The cutest dress ——'

'Say! You solve that one about the triangle forty-six by twen ——'

'Lemme by! Move out my way!'

The front door slammed every second as the people swarmed into the house. Sharp voices and soft voices sounded together until there was just one roaring noise. Girls stood in bunches in their long, fine evening dresses, and the boys roamed around in clean duck pants or R.O.T.C. uniforms or new dark fall suits. There was so much commotion that Mick couldn't notice any separate face or person. She stood by the hatrack and stared around at the party as a whole.

'Everybody get a prom card and start signing up.'

At first the room was too loud for anyone to hear and pay attention. The boys were so thick around the punch bowl that the table and the vines didn't show at all. Only her

Dad's face rose up above the boys' heads as he smiled and dished up the punch into the little paper cups. On the seat of the hatrack beside her were a jar of candy and two handkerchiefs. A couple of girls thought it was her birthday, and she had thanked them and unwrapped the presents without telling them she wouldn't be fourteen for eight more months. Every person was as clean and fresh and dressed up as she was. They smelled good. The boys had their hair plastered down wet and slick. The girls with their different-colored long dresses stood together, and they were like a bright hunk of flowers. The start was marvelous. The beginning of this party was O.K.

'I'm part Scotch-Irish and French and ——'

'I got German blood ——'

She hollered about the prom cards one more time before she went into the dining-room. Soon they began to pile in from the hall. Every person took a prom card and they lined up in bunches against the walls of the room. This was the real start now.

It came all of a sudden in a very queer way — this quietness. The boys stood together on one side of the room and the girls were across from them. For some reason every person quit making noise at once. The boys held their cards and looked at the girls and the room was very still. None of the boys started asking for proms like they were supposed to do. The awful quietness got worse and she had not been to enough parties to know what she should do. Then the boys started punching each other and talking. The girls giggled — but even if they didn't look at the boys you could tell they only had their minds on whether they were going to be popular or not. The awful quietness was gone now, but there was something jittery about the room.

After a while a boy went up to a girl named Delores Brown. As soon as he had signed her up the other boys all began to rush Delores at once. When her whole card was full they started on another girl, named Mary. After that everything suddenly stopped again. One or two extra girls got a couple of proms — and because she was giving the party three boys came up to her. That was all.

The people just hung around in the dining-room and the hall. The boys mostly flocked around the punch bowl and tried to show off with each other. The girls bunched together and did a lot of laughing to pretend like they were having a good time. The boys thought about the girls and the girls thought about the boys. But all that came of it was a queer feeling in the room.

It was then she began to notice Harry Minowitz. He lived in the house next door and she had known him all her life. Although he was two years older she had grown faster than him, and in the summer-time they used to wrestle and fight out on the plot of grass by the street. Harry was a Jew boy, but he did not look so much like one. His hair was light brown and straight. Tonight he was dressed very neat, and when he came in the door he had hung a grown man's panama hat with a feather in it on the hatrack.

It wasn't his clothes that made her notice him. There was something changed about his face because he was without the horn-rimmed specs he usually wore. A red, droopy sty had come out on one of his eyes and he had to cock his head sideways like a bird in order to see. His long, thin hands kept touching around his sty as though it hurt him. When he asked for punch he stuck the paper cup right into her Dad's face. She could tell he needed his glasses very bad. He was nervous and kept bumping into people. He didn't ask any girl to prom except her — and that was because it was her party.

All the punch had been drunk. Her Dad was afraid she would be embarrassed, so he and her Mama had gone back to the kitchen to make lemonade. Some of the people were on the front porch and the sidewalk. She was glad to get out in the cool night air. After the hot, bright house she could smell the new autumn in the darkness.

Then she saw something she hadn't expected. Along the edge of the sidewalk and in the dark street there was a bunch of neighborhood kids. Pete and Sucker Wells and Baby and Spareribs — the whole gang that started at below Bubber's age and went on up to over twelve. There were even kids she didn't know at all who had somehow smelled a party and come to hang around. And there were kids her age and older that she hadn't invited either because they had done something mean to her or she had done something mean to them. They were all dirty and in plain shorts or draggle-tailed knickers or old everyday dresses. They were just hanging around in the dark to watch the party. She thought of two feelings when she saw those kids — one was sad and the other was a kind of warning.

'I got this prom with you.' Harry Minowitz made out like he was reading on his card, but she could see nothing was written on it. Her Dad had come onto the porch and blown the whistle that meant the beginning of the first prom.

'Yeah,' she said. 'Let's get going.'

They started out to walk around the block. In the long dress she still felt very ritzy. 'Look yonder at Mick Kelly!' one of the kids in the dark hollered. 'Look at her!' She just walked on like she hadn't heard, but it was that Spareribs, and some day soon she would catch him. She and Harry walked fast along the dark sidewalk, and when they came to the end of the street they turned down another block.

'How old are you now, Mick — thirteen?'

'Going on fourteen.'

She knew what he was thinking. It used to worry her all the time. Five feet six inches tall and a hundred and three pounds, and she was only thirteen. Every kid at the party was a runt beside her, except Harry, who was only a couple of inches shorter. No boy wanted to prom with a girl so much taller than him. But maybe cigarettes would help stunt the rest of her growth.

'I grew three and a fourth inches just in last year,' she said. 'Once I saw a lady at the fair who was eight and a half feet tall. But you probably won't grow that big.'

Harry stopped beside a dark crêpe myrtle bush. Nobody was in sight. He took something out of his pocket and started fooling with whatever it was. She leaned over to see — it was his pair of specs and he was wiping them with his handkerchief.

'Pardon me,' he said. Then he put on his glasses and she could hear him breathe deep.

'You ought to wear your specs all the time.'

'Yeah.'

'How come you go around without them?'

'Oh, I don't know ——'

The night was very quiet and dark. Harry held her elbow when they crossed the street.

'There's a certain young lady back at the party that thinks it's sissy for a fellow to wear glasses. This certain person — oh well, maybe I am a ——'

He didn't finish. Suddenly he tightened up and ran a few steps and sprang for a leaf about four feet above his head. She just could see that high leaf in the dark. He had a good spring to his jumping and he got it the first time. Then he put the leaf in his mouth and shadowboxed for a few punches in the dark. She caught up with him.

As usual a song was in her mind. She was humming to herself.

'What's that you're singing?'

'It's a piece by a fellow named Mozart.'

Harry felt pretty good. He was sidestepping with his feet like a fast boxer. 'That sounds like a sort of German name.'

'I reckon so.'

'Fascist?' he asked.

'What?'

'I say is that Mozart a Fascist or a Nazi?'

Mick thought a minute. 'No. They're new, and this fellow's been dead some time.'

'It's a good thing.' He began punching in the dark again. He wanted her to ask why.

'I say it's a good thing,' he said again.

'Why?'

'Because I hate Fascists. If I met one walking on the street I'd kill him.'

She looked at Harry. The leaves against the street light made quick, freckly shadows on his face. He was excited.

'How come?' she asked.

'Gosh! Don't you ever read the paper? You see, it's this way ——'

They had come back around the block. A commotion was going on at her house. People were yelling and running on the sidewalk. A heavy sickness came in her belly.

'There's not time to explain unless we prom around the block again. I don't mind telling you why I hate Fascists. I'd like to tell about it.'

This was probably the first chance he had got to spiel these ideas out to somebody. But she didn't have time to listen. She was busy looking at what she saw in the front of her house. 'O.K. I'll see you later.' The prom was over now, so she could look and put her mind on the mess she saw.

What had happened while she was gone? When she left the people were standing around in the fine clothes and it was a real party. Now — after just five minutes — the place looked more like a crazy house. While she was gone those kids had come out of the dark and right into the party itself. The nerve they had! There was old Pete Wells banging out of the front door with a cup of punch in his hand. They bellowed and ran and mixed with the invited people — in their old loose-legged knickers and everyday clothes.

Baby Wilson messed around on the front porch — and Baby wasn't more than four years old. Anybody could see she ought to be home in bed by now, same as Bubber. She walked down the steps one at a time, holding the punch high up over her head. There was no reason for her to be here at all. Mister Brannon was her uncle and she could get free candy and drinks at his place any time she wanted to. As soon as she was on the sidewalk Mick caught her by the arm. 'You go right home, Baby Wilson. Go on, now.' Mick looked around to see what else she could do to straighten things out again like they ought to be. She went up to Sucker Wells. He stood farther down the sidewalk, where it was dark, holding his paper cup and looking at everybody in a dreamy way. Sucker was seven years old and he had on shorts. His chest and feet were naked. He wasn't causing any of the commotion, but she was mad as hell at what had happened.

She grabbed Sucker by the shoulders and began to shake him. At first he held his jaws tight, but after a minute his teeth began to rattle. 'You go home, Sucker Wells. You quit hanging around where you're not invited.' When she let him go, Sucker tucked his tail and walked slowly down the street. But he didn't go all the way home. After he got to the corner she saw him sit down on the curb and watch the party where he thought she couldn't see him.

For a minute she felt good about shaking the spit out of Sucker. And then right afterward she had a bad worry feeling in her and she started to let him come back. The big kids were the ones who messed up everything. Real brats they were, and with the worst nerve she had ever seen. Drinking up the refreshments and ruining the real party into all this commotion. They slammed through the front door and hollered and bumped into each other. She went up to Pete Wells because he was the worst of all. He wore his football helmet and butted into people. Pete was every bit of fourteen, yet he was still stuck in the seventh grade. She went up to him, but he was too big to shake like Sucker. When she told him to go home he shimmied and made a nose dive at her.

'I been in six different states. Florida, Alabama ——'

'Made out of silver cloth with a sash ——'

The party was all messed up. Everybody was talking at once. The invited people from Vocational were mixed with the neighborhood gang. The boys and the girls still stood in separate bunches, though — and nobody prommed. In the house the lemonade was just about gone. There was only a little puddle of water with floating lemon peels at the bottom of the bowl. Her Dad always acted too nice with kids. He had served out the punch to anybody who stuck a cup at him. Portia was serving the sandwiches when she went into the dining-room. In five minutes they were all gone. She only got one — a jelly kind with pink sops come through the bread.

Portia stayed in the dining-room to watch the party. 'I having too good a time to leave,' she said. 'I done sent word to Highboy and Willie to go on with the Saturday Night without me. Everbody so excited here I going to wait and see the end of this party.'

Excitement — that was the word. She could feel it all through the room and on the porch and the sidewalk. She felt excited, too. It wasn't just her dress and the beautiful way her face looked when she passed by the hatrack mirror and saw the red paint on her cheeks and the rhinestone tiara in her hair. Maybe it was the decoration and all these Vocational people and kids being jammed together.

'Watch her run!'

'Ouch! Cut it out ——'

'Act your age!'

A bunch of girls were running down the street, holding up their dresses and with their hair flying out behind them. Some boys had cut off the long, sharp spears of a Spanish bayonet bush and they were chasing the girls with them. Freshmen in Vocational all dressed up for a real prom party and acting just like kids. It was half playlike and half not playlike at all. A boy came up to her with a sticker and she started running too.

The idea of the party was over entirely now. This was just a regular playing-out. But it was the wildest night she had ever seen. The kids had caused it. They were like a catching sickness, and their coming to the party made all the other people forget about High School and being almost grown. It was like just before you take a bath in the afternoon when you might wallow around in the back yard and get plenty dirty just for the good feel of it before getting into the tub. Everybody was a wild kid playing out on Saturday night — and she felt like the very wildest of all.

She hollered and pushed and was the first to try any new stunt. She made so much noise and moved around so fast she couldn't notice what anybody else was doing. Her breath wouldn't come fast enough to let her do all the wild things she wanted to do.

'The ditch down the street! The ditch! The ditch!'

She started for it first. Down a block they had put in new pipes under the street and dug a swell deep ditch. The flambeaux around the edge were bright and red in the dark. She wouldn't wait to climb down. She ran until she reached the little wavy flames and then she jumped.

With her tennis shoes she would have landed like a cat — but the high pumps made her slip and her stomach hit this pipe. Her breath was stopped. She lay quiet with her eyes closed.

The party —— For a long time she remembered how she thought it would be, how she imagined the new people at Vocational. And about the bunch she wanted to be with every day. She would feel different in the halls now, knowing that they were not something special but like any other kids. It was O.K. about the ruined party. But it was all over. It was the end.

Mick climbed out of the ditch. Some kids were playing around the little pots of flames. The fire made a red glow and there were long, quick shadows. One boy had gone home and put on a dough-face bought in advance for Hallowe'en. Nothing was changed about the party except her.

She walked home slowly. When she passed kids she didn't speak or look at them. The decoration in the hall was torn down and the house seemed very empty because everyone had gone outside. In the bathroom she took off the blue evening dress. The hem was torn and she folded it so the raggedy place wouldn't show. The rhinestone tiara was lost somewhere. Her old shorts and shirt were lying on the floor just where she had left them. She put them on. She was too big to wear shorts any more after this. No more after this night. Not any more.

Mick stood out on the front porch. Her face was very white without the paint. She cupped her hands before her mouth and took a deep breath. 'Everybody go home! The door is shut! The party is over!'

In the quiet, secret night she was by herself again. It was not late — yellow squares of light showed in the windows of the houses along the streets. She walked slow, with her hands in her pockets and her head to one side. For a long time she walked without noticing the direction.

Then the houses were far apart from each other and there were yards with big trees in them and black shrubbery. She looked around and saw she was near this house where she had gone so many times in the summer. Her feet had just taken her here without her knowing. When she came to the house she waited to be sure no person could see. Then she went through the side yard.

The radio was on as usual. For a second she stood by the window and watched the people inside. The bald-headed man and the gray-haired lady were playing cards at a table. Mick sat on the ground. This was a very fine and secret place. Close around were thick cedars so that she was completely hidden by herself. The radio was no good tonight — somebody sang popular songs that all ended in the same way. It was like she was empty. She reached in her pockets and felt around with her fingers. There were raisins and a buckeye and a string of beads — one cigarette with matches. She lighted the cigarette and put her arms around her knees. It was like she was so empty there wasn't even a feeling or thought in her.

One program came on after another, and all of them were punk. She didn't especially care. She smoked and picked a little bunch of grass blades. After a while a new announcer started talking. He mentioned Beethoven. She had read in the library about that musician — his name was pronounced with an *a* and spelled with double *e*. He was a German fellow like Mozart. When he was living he spoke in a foreign language and lived in a foreign place — like she wanted to do. The announcer said they were going to play his third symphony. She only halfway listened because she wanted to walk some more and she didn't care much what they played. Then the music started. Mick raised her head and her fist went up to her throat.

How did it come? For a minute the opening balanced from one side to the other. Like a walk or march. Like God strutting in the night. The outside of her was suddenly froze and only that first part of the music was hot inside her heart. She could not even hear what sounded after, but she sat there waiting and froze, with her fists tight. After a while the music came again, harder and loud. It didn't have anything to do with God. This was her, Mick Kelly, walking in the daytime and by herself at night. In the hot sun and in the dark with all the plans and feelings. This music was her — the real plain her.

She could not listen good enough to hear it all. The music boiled inside her. Which? To hang on to certain wonderful parts and think them over so that later she would not forget — or should she let go and listen to each part that came without thinking or trying to remember? Golly! The whole world was this music and she could not listen hard enough. Then at last the opening music came again, with all the different instruments bunched together for each note like a hard, tight fist that socked at her heart. And the first part was over.

This music did not take a long time or a short time. It did not have anything to do with time going by at all. She sat with her arms held tight around her legs, biting her salty knee very hard. It might have been five minutes she listened or half the night. The second part was black-colored — a slow march. Not sad, but like the whole world was dead and black and there was no use thinking back how it was before. One of those horn kind of instruments played a sad and silver tune. Then the music rose up angry and with excitement underneath. And finally the black march again.

But maybe the last part of the symphony was the music she loved the best — glad and like the greatest people in the world running and springing up in a hard, free way. Wonderful music like this was the worst hurt there could be. The whole world was this symphony, and there was not enough of her to listen.

It was over, and she sat very stiff with her arms around her knees. Another program came on the radio and she put her fingers in her ears. The music left only this bad hurt in her, and a blankness. She could not remember any of the symphony, not even the last few notes. She tried to remember, but no sound at all came to her. Now that it was over there was only her heart like a rabbit and this terrible hurt.

The radio and the lights in the house were turned off. The night was very dark. Suddenly Mick began hitting her thigh with her fists. She pounded the same muscle with all her strength until the tears came down her face. But she could not feel this hard enough. The rocks under the bush were sharp. She grabbed a handful of them and began scraping them up and down on the same spot until her hand was bloody. Then she fell back to the ground and lay looking up at the night. With the fiery hurt in her leg she felt better. She was limp on the wet grass, and after a while her breath came slow and easy again.

Why hadn't the explorers known by looking at the sky that the world was round? The sky was curved, like the inside of a huge glass ball, very dark blue with the sprinkles of bright stars. The night was quiet. There was the smell of warm cedars. She was not trying to think of the music at all when it came back to her. The first part happened in her mind just as it had been played. She listened in a quiet, slow way and thought the notes out like a problem in geometry so she would remember. She could see the shape of the sounds very clear and she would not forget them.

Now she felt good. She whispered some words out loud: 'Lord forgiveth me, for I knoweth not what I do.' Why did she think of that? Everybody in the past few years knew there wasn't any real God. When she thought of what she used to imagine was God she could only see Mister Singer with a long, white sheet around him. God was silent — maybe that was why she was reminded. She said the words again, just as she would speak them to Mister Singer: 'Lord forgiveth me, for I knoweth not what I do.'

This part of the music was beautiful and clear. She could sing it now whenever she wanted to. Maybe later on, when she had just waked up some morning, more of the music would come back to her. If ever she heard the symphony again there would be other parts to add to what was already in her mind. And maybe if she could hear it four more times, just four more times, she would know it all. Maybe.

Once again she listened to this opening part of the music. Then the notes grew slower and soft and it was like she was sinking down slowly into the dark ground.

Mick awoke with a jerk. The air had turned chilly, and as she was coming up out of the sleep she dreamed old Etta Kelly was taking all the cover. 'Gimme some blanket ——' she tried to say. Then she opened her eyes. The sky was very black and all the stars were gone. The grass was wet. She got up in a hurry because her Dad would be worried. Then she remembered the music. She couldn't tell whether the time was midnight or three in the morning, so she started beating it for home in a rush. The air had a smell in it like autumn. The music was loud and quick in her mind, and she ran faster and faster on the sidewalks leading to the home block.

2

BY OCTOBER the days were blue and cool. Biff Brannon changed his light seersucker trousers for dark-blue serge ones. Behind the counter of the café he installed a machine that made hot chocolate. Mick was very partial to hot chocolate, and she came in three or four times a week to drink a cup. He served it to her for a nickel instead of a dime and he wanted to give it to her free. He watched her as she stood behind the counter and he was troubled and sad. He wanted to reach out his hand and touch her sunburned, tousled hair — but not as he had ever touched a woman. In him there was an uneasiness, and when he spoke to her his voice had a rough, strange sound.

There were many worries on his mind. For one thing, Alice was not well. She worked downstairs as usual from seven in the morning until ten at night, but she walked very slowly and brown circles were beneath her eyes. It was in the business that she showed this illness most plainly. One Sunday, when she wrote out the day's menu on the typewriter, she marked the special dinner with chicken à la king at twenty cents instead of fifty, and did not discover the mistake until several customers had already ordered and were ready to pay. Another time she gave back two fives and three ones as change for ten dollars. Biff would stand looking at her for a long time, rubbing his nose thoughtfully and with his eyes half-closed.

They did not speak of this together. At night he worked downstairs while she slept, and during the morning she managed the restaurant alone. When they worked together he stayed behind the cash register and looked after the kitchen and the tables, as was their custom. They did not talk except on matters of business, but Biff would stand watching her with his face puzzled.

Then in the afternoon of the eighth of October there was a sudden cry of pain from the room where they slept. Biff hurried upstairs. Within an hour they had taken Alice to the hospital and the doctor had removed from her a tumor almost the size of a newborn child. And then within another hour Alice was dead.

Biff sat by her bed at the hospital in stunned reflection. He had been present when she died. Her eyes had been drugged and misty from the ether and then they hardened like glass. The nurse and the doctor withdrew from the room. He continued to look into her face. Except for the bluish pallor there was little difference. He noted each detail about her as though he had not watched her every day for twenty-one years. Then gradually as he sat there his thoughts turned to a picture that had long been stored inside him.

The cold green ocean and a hot gold strip of sand. The little children playing on the edge of the silky line of foam. The sturdy brown baby girl, the thin little naked boys, the half-grown children running and calling out to each other with sweet, shrill voices. Children were here whom he knew, Mick and his niece, Baby, and there were also strange young faces no one had ever seen before. Biff bowed his head.

After a long while he got up from his chair and stood in the middle of the room. He could hear his sister-in-law, Lucile, walking up and down the hall outside. A fat bee crawled across the top of the dresser, and adroitly Biff caught it in his hand and put it out the open window. He glanced at the dead face one more time, and then with widowed sedateness he opened the door that led out into the hospital corridor.

Late the next morning he sat sewing in the room upstairs. Why? Why was it that in cases of real love the one who is left does not more often follow the beloved by suicide? Only because the living must bury the dead? Because of the measured rites that must be fulfilled after a death? Because it is as though the one who is left steps for a time upon a stage and each second swells to an unlimited amount of time and he is watched by many eyes? Because there is a function he must carry out? Or perhaps, when there is love, the widowed must stay for the resurrection of the beloved — so that the one who has gone is not really dead, but grows and is created for a second time in the soul of the living? Why?

Biff bent close over his sewing and meditated on many things. He sewed skillfully, and the calluses on the tips of his fingers were so hard that he pushed the needle through the cloth without a thimble. Already the mourning bands had been sewn around the arms of two gray suits, and now he was on the last.

The day was bright and hot, and the first dead leaves of the new autumn scraped on the sidewalks. He had gone out early. Each minute was very long. Before him there was infinite leisure. He had locked the door of the restaurant and hung on the outside a white wreath of lilies. To the funeral home he went first and looked carefully at the selection of caskets. He touched the materials of the linings and tested the strength of the frames.

'What is the name of the crêpe of this one — Georgette?'

The undertaker answered his questions in an oily, unctuous voice.

'And what is the percentage of cremations in your business?'

Out on the street again Biff walked with measured formality. From the west there was a warm wind and the sun was very bright. His watch had stopped, so he turned down toward the street where Wilbur Kelly had recently put out his sign as watchmaker. Kelly was sitting at his bench in a patched bathrobe. His shop was also a bedroom, and the baby Mick pulled around with her in a wagon sat quietly on a pallet on the floor. Each minute was so long that in it there was ample time for contemplation and enquiry. He asked Kelly to explain the exact use of jewels in a watch. He noted the distorted look of Kelly's right eye as it appeared through his watchmaker's loupe. They talked for a while about Chamberlain and Munich. Then as the time was still early he decided to go up to the mute's room.

Singer was dressing for work. Last night there had come from him a letter of condolence. He was to be a pallbearer at the funeral. Biff sat on the bed and they smoked a cigarette together. Singer looked at him now and then with his green observant eyes. He offered him a drink of coffee. Biff did not talk, and once the mute stopped to pat him on the shoulder and look for a second into his face. When Singer was dressed they went out together.

Biff bought the black ribbon at the store and saw the preacher of Alice's church. When all was arranged he came back home. To put things in order — that was the thought in his mind. He bundled up Alice's clothes and personal possessions to give to Lucile. He thoroughly cleaned and straightened the bureau drawers. He even rearranged the shelves of the kitchen downstairs and removed the gaily colored crêpe streamers from the electric fans. Then when this was done he sat in the tub and bathed himself all over. And the morning was done.

Biff bit the thread and smoothed the black band on the sleeve of his coat. By now Lucile would be waiting for him.

He and she and Baby would ride in the funeral car together. He put away the work basket and fitted the coat with the mourning band very carefully on his shoulders. He glanced swiftly around the room to see that all was well before going out again.

An hour later he was in Lucile's kitchenette. He sat with his legs crossed, a napkin over his thigh, drinking a cup of tea. Lucile and Alice had been so different in all ways that it was easy to realize they were sisters. Lucile was thin and dark, and today she had dressed completely in black. She was fixing Baby's hair. The little kid waited patiently on the kitchen table with her hands folded in her lap while her mother worked on her. The sunlight was quiet and mellow in the room.

'Bartholomew ——' said Lucile.

'What?'

'Don't you ever start thinking backward?'

'I don't,' said Biff.

'You know it's like I got to wear blinders all the time so I won't think sideways or in the past. All I can let myself think about is going to work every day and fixing meals and Baby's future.'

'That's the right attitude.'

'I been giving Baby finger waves down at the shop. But they come out so quick I been thinking about letting her have a permanent. I don't want to give it to her myself — I think maybe I'll take her up to Atlanta when I go to the cosmetologist convention and let her get it there.'

'Motherogod! She's not but four. It's liable to scare her. And besides, permanents tend to coarsen the hair.'

Lucile dipped the comb in a glass of water and mashed the curls over Baby's ears. 'No, they don't. And she wants one. Young as Baby is, she already has as much ambition as I got. And that's saying plenty.'

Biff polished his nails on the palm of his hand and shook his head.

'Every time Baby and I go to the movies and see these kids in all the good rôles she feels the same way I do. I swear she does, Bartholomew. I can't even get her to eat her supper afterward.'

'For goodness' sake,' Biff said.

'She's getting along so fine with her dancing and expression lessons. Next year I want her to start with the piano because I think it'll be a help for her to play some. Her dancing teacher is going to give her a solo in the soirée. I feel like I got to push Baby all I can. Because the sooner she gets started on her career the better it'll be for both of us.'

'Motherogod!'

'You don't understand. A child with talent can't be treated like ordinary kids. That's one reason I want to get Baby out of this common neighborhood. I can't let her start to talk vulgar like these brats around here or run wild like they do.'

'I know the kids on this block,' Biff said. 'They're all right. Those Kelly kids across the street — the Crane boy ——'

'You know good and well that none of them are up to Baby's level.'

Lucile set the last wave in Baby's hair. She pinched the kid's little cheeks to put more color in them. Then she lifted her down from the table. For the funeral Baby had on a little white dress with white shoes and white socks and even small white gloves. There was a certain way Baby always held her head when people looked at her, and it was turned that way now.

They sat for a while in the small, hot kitchenette without saying anything. Then Lucile began to cry. 'It's not like we was ever very close as sisters. We had our differences and we didn't see much of each other. Maybe it was because I was so much younger. But there's something about your own blood kin, and when anything like this happens ——'

Biff clucked soothingly.

'I know how you two were,' she said. 'It wasn't all just roses with you and she. But maybe that sort of makes it worse for you now.'

Biff caught Baby under the arms and swung her up to his shoulder. The kid was getting heavier. He held her carefully as he stepped into the living-room. Baby felt warm and close on his shoulder, and her little silk skirt was white against the dark cloth of his coat. She grasped one of his ears very tight with her little hand.

'Unca Biff! Watch me do the split.'

Gently he set Baby on her feet again. She curved both arms above her head and her feet slid slowly in opposite directions on the yellow waxed floor. In a moment she was seated with one leg stretched straight in front of her and one behind. She posed with her arms held at a fancy angle, looking sideways at the wall with a sad expression.

She scrambled up again. 'Watch me do a handspring. Watch me do a ——'

'Honey, be a little quieter,' Lucile said. She sat down beside Biff on the plush sofa. 'Don't she remind you a little of him — something about her eyes and face?'

'Hell, no. I can't see the slightest resemblance between Baby and Leroy Wilson.'

Lucile looked too thin and worn out for her age. Maybe it was the black dress and because she had been crying. 'After all, we got to admit he's Baby's father,' she said.

'Can't you ever forget about that man?'

'I don't know. I guess I always been a fool about two things. And that's Leroy and Baby.'

Biff's new growth of beard was blue against the pale skin of his face and his voice sounded tired. 'Don't you ever just think a thing through and find out what's happened and what ought to come from that? Don't you ever use logic — if these are the given facts this ought to be the result?'

'Not about him, I guess.'

Biff spoke in a weary manner and his eyes were almost closed. 'You married this certain party when you were seventeen, and afterward there was just one racket between you after another. You divorced him. Then two years later you married him a second time. And now he's gone off again and you don't know where he is. It seems like those facts would show you one thing — you two are not suited to each other. And that's aside from the more personal side — the sort of man this certain party happens to be anyway.'

'God knows I been realizing all along he's a heel. I just hope he won't ever knock on that door again.'

'Look, Baby,' Biff said quickly. He laced his fingers and held up his hands. 'This is the church and this is the steeple. Open the door and here are God's people.'

Lucile shook her head. 'You don't have to bother about Baby. I tell her everything. She knows about the whole mess from A to Z.'

'Then if he comes back you'll let him stay here and sponge on you just as long as he pleases — like it was before?'

'Yeah. I guess I would. Every time the doorbell or the phone rings, every time anybody steps up on the porch, something in the back of my mind thinks about that man.'

Biff spread out the palms of his hands. 'There you are.'

The clock struck two. The room was very close and hot. Baby turned another handspring and made a split again on the waxed floor. Then Biff took her up into his lap. Her little legs dangled against his shin. She unbuttoned his vest and burrowed her face into him.

'Listen,' Lucile said. 'If I ask you a question will you promise to answer me the truth?'

'Sure.'

'No matter what it is?'

Biff touched Baby's soft gold hair and laid his hand gently on the side of her little head. 'Of course.'

'It was about seven years ago. Soon after we was married

the first time. And he came in one night from your place with big knots all over his head and told me you caught him by the neck and banged his head against the side of the wall. He made up some tale about why you did it, but I want to know the real reason.'

Biff turned the wedding ring on his finger. 'I just never did like Leroy, and we had a fight. In those days I was different from now.'

'No. There was some definite thing you did that for. We been knowing each other a pretty long time, and I understand by now that you got a real reason for every single thing you ever do. Your mind runs by reasons instead of just wants. Now, you promised you'd tell me what it was, and I want to know.'

'It wouldn't mean anything now.'

'I tell you I got to know.'

'All right,' Biff said. 'He came in that night and started drinking, and when he was drunk he shot off his mouth about you. He said he would come home about once a month and beat hell out of you and you would take it. But then afterward you would step outside in the hall and laugh aloud a few times so that the neighbors in the other rooms would think you both had just been playing around and it had all been a joke. That's what happened, so just forget about it.'

Lucile sat up straight and there was a red spot on each of her cheeks. 'You see, Bartholomew, that's why I got to be like I have blinders on all the time so as not to think backward or sideways. All I can let my mind stay on is going to work every day and fixing three meals here at home and Baby's career.'

'Yes.'

'I hope you'll do that too, and not start thinking backward.'

Biff leaned his head down on his chest and closed his eyes. During the whole long day he had not been able to think of

Alice. When he tried to remember her face there was a queer blankness in him. The only thing about her that was clear in his mind was her feet — stumpy, very soft and white and with puffy little toes. The bottoms were pink and near the left heel there was a tiny brown mole. The night they were married he had taken off her shoes and stockings and kissed her feet. And, come to think of it, that was worth considering, because the Japanese believe that the choicest part of a woman ——

Biff stirred and glanced at his watch. In a little while they would leave for the church where the funeral would be held. In his mind he went through the motions of the ceremony. The church — riding dirge-paced behind the hearse with Lucile and Baby — the group of people standing with bowed heads in the September sunshine. Sun on the white tombstones, on the fading flowers and the canvas tent covering the newly dug grave. Then home again — and what?

'No matter how much you quarrel there's something about your own blood sister,' Lucile said.

Biff raised his head. 'Why don't you marry again? Some nice young man who's never had a wife before, who would take care of you and Baby? If you'd just forget about Leroy you would make a good man a fine wife.'

Lucile was slow to answer. Then finally she said: 'You know how we always been — we nearly all the time understand each other pretty well without any kind of throbs either way. Well, that's the closest I ever want to be to any man again.'

'I feel the same way,' Biff said.

Half an hour later there was a knock on the door. The car for the funeral was parked before the house. Biff and Lucile got up slowly. The three of them, with Baby in her white silk dress a little ahead, walked in solemn quietness outside.

Biff kept the restaurant closed during the next day. Then in the early evening he removed the faded wreath of lilies from the front door and opened the place for business again. Old customers came in with sad faces and talked with him a few minutes by the cash register before giving their orders. The usual crowd was present — Singer, Blount, various men who worked in stores along the block and in the mills down on the river. After supper Mick Kelly showed up with her little brother and put a nickel into the slot machine. When she lost the first coin she banged on the machine with her fists and kept opening the receiver to be sure that nothing had come down. Then she put in another nickel and almost won the jackpot. Coins came clattering out and rolled along the floor. The kid and her little brother both kept looking around pretty sharp as they picked them up, so that no customer would put his foot on one before they could get to it. The mute was at the table in the middle of the room with his dinner before him. Across from him Jake Blount sat drinking beer, dressed in his Sunday clothes, and talking. Everything was the same as it had always been before. After a while the air became gray with cigarette smoke and the noise increased. Biff was alert, and no sound or movement escaped him.

'I go around,' Blount said. He leaned earnestly across the table and kept his eyes on the mute's face. 'I go all around and try to tell them. And they laugh. I can't make them understand anything. No matter what I say I can't seem to make them see the truth.'

Singer nodded and wiped his mouth with his napkin. His dinner had got cold because he couldn't look down to eat, but he was so polite that he let Blount go on talking.

The words of the two children at the slot machine were high and clear against the coarser voices of the men. Mick was putting her nickels back into the slot. Often she looked around at the middie table, but the mute had his back turned to her and did not see.

'Mister Singer's got fried chicken for his supper and he hasn't eat one piece yet,' the little boy said.

Mick pulled down the lever of the machine very slowly. 'Mind your own business.'

'You're always going up to his room or some place where you know he'll be.'

'I told you to hush, Bubber Kelly.'

'You do.'

Mick shook him until his teeth rattled and turned him around toward the door. 'You go on home to bed. I already told you I get a bellyful of you and Ralph in the daytime, and I don't want you hanging around me at night when I'm supposed to be free.'

Bubber held out his grimy little hand. 'Well, give me a nickel, then.' When he had put the money in his shirt pocket he left for home.

Biff straightened his coat and smoothed back his hair. His tie was solid black, and on the sleeve of his gray coat there was the mourning band that he had sewn there. He wanted to go up to the slot machine and talk with Mick, but something would not let him. He sucked in his breath sharply and drank a glass of water. A dance orchestra came in on the radio, but he did not want to listen. All the tunes in the last ten years were so alike he couldn't tell one from the other. Since 1928 he had not enjoyed music. Yet when he was young he used to play the mandolin, and he knew the words and the melody of every current song.

He laid his finger on the side of his nose and cocked his head to one side. Mick had grown so much in the past year that soon she would be taller than he was. She was dressed in the red sweater and blue pleated skirt she had worn every day since school started. Now the pleats had come out and the hem dragged loose around her sharp, jutting knees. She was at the age when she looked as much like an overgrown boy as a girl. And on that subject why was it that the smartest people mostly missed that point? By nature all people are of both sexes. So that marriage and the bed is not all by any means. The proof? Real youth and old age. Because often old men's voices grow high and reedy and they take on a mincing walk. And old women sometimes grow fat and their voices get rough and deep and they grow dark little mustaches. And he even proved it himself — the part of him that sometimes almost wished he was a mother and that Mick and Baby were his kids. Abruptly Biff turned from the cash register.

The newspapers were in a mess. For two weeks he hadn't filed a single one. He lifted a stack of them from under the counter. With a practiced eye he glanced from the masthead to the bottom of the sheet. Tomorrow he would look over the stacks of them in the back room and see about changing the system of files. Build shelves and use those solid boxes canned goods were shipped in for drawers. Chronologically from October 27, 1918, on up to the present date. With folders and top markings outlining historical events. Three sets of outlines — one international beginning with the Armistice and leading through the Munich aftermath, the second national, the third all the local dope from the time Mayor Lester shot his wife at the country club up to the Hudson Mill fire. Everything for the past twenty years docketed and outlined and complete. Biff beamed quietly behind his hand as he rubbed his jaw. And yet Alice had wanted him to haul out the papers so she could turn the room into a ladies' toilet. That was just what she had nagged him to do, but for once he had battered her down. For that one time.

With peaceful absorption Biff settled down to the details of the newspaper before him. He read steadily and with concentration, but from habit some secondary part of him was alert to everything around him. Jake Blount was still talking, and often he would hit his fist on the table. The mute sipped beer. Mick walked restlessly around the radio and stared at the customers. Biff read every word in the first paper and made a few notes on the margins.

Then suddenly he looked up with a surprised expression.

His mouth had been open for a yawn and he snapped it shut. The radio swung into an old song that dated back to the time when he and Alice were engaged. 'Just a Baby's Prayer at Twilight.' They had taken the streetcar one Sunday to Old Sardis Lake and had rented a rowboat. At sunset he played on the mandolin while she sang. She had on a sailor hat, and when he put his arm around her waist she — Alice ——

A dragnet for lost feelings. Biff folded the newspapers and put them back under the counter. He stood on one foot and then the other. Finally he called across the room to Mick. 'You're not listening, are you?'

Mick turned off the radio. 'No. Nothing on tonight.'

All of that he would keep out of his mind, and concentrate on something else. He leaned over the counter and watched one customer after another. Then at last his attention rested on the mute at the middle table. He saw Mick edge gradually up to him and at his invitation sit down. Singer pointed to something on the menu and the waitress brought a Coca-Cola for her. Nobody but a freak like a deaf-mute, cut off from other people, would ask a right young girl to sit down to the table where he was drinking with another man. Blount and Mick both kept their eyes on Singer. They talked, and the mute's expression changed as he watched them. It was a funny thing. The reason — was it in them or in him? He sat very still with his hands in his pockets, and because he did not speak it made him seem superior. What did that fellow think and realize? What did he know?

Twice during the evening Biff started to go over to the middle table, but each time he checked himself. After they were gone he still wondered what it was about this mute — and in the early dawn when he lay in bed he turned over questions and solutions in his mind without satisfaction. The puzzle had taken root in him. It worried him in the back of his mind and left him uneasy. There was something wrong.

3

MANY times Doctor Copeland talked to Mr. Singer. Truly he was not like other white men. He was a wise man, and he understood the strong, true purpose in a way that other white men could not. He listened, and in his face there was something gentle and Jewish, the knowledge of one who belongs to a race that is oppressed. On one occasion he took Mr. Singer with him on his rounds. He led him through cold, narrow passages smelling of dirt and sickness and fried fat-back. He showed him a successful skin graft made on the face of a woman patient who had been severely burned. He treated a syphilitic child and pointed out to Mr. Singer the scaling eruption on the palms of the hand, the dull, opaque surface of the eye, the sloping upper front incisors. They visited two-room shacks that housed as many as twelve or fourteen persons. In a room where the fire burned low and orange on the hearth they were helpless while an old man strangled with pneumonia. Mr. Singer walked behind him and watched and understood. He gave nickels to the children, and because of his quietness and decorum he did not disturb the patients as would have another visitor.

The days were chilly and treacherous. In the town there was an outbreak of influenza so that Doctor Copeland was busy most of the hours of the day and night. He drove through the Negro sections of the town in the high Dodge automobile he had used for the past nine years. He kept the isinglass curtains snapped to the windows to cut off the draughts, and tight around his neck he wore his gray wool shawl. During this time he did not see Portia or William or Highboy, but often he thought of them. Once when he was away Portia came to see him and left a note and borrowed half a sack of meal.

There came a night when he was so exhausted that, although there were other calls to make, he drank hot milk and went to bed. He was cold and feverish so that at first he could not rest. Then it seemed that he had only begun to sleep when a voice called him. He got up wearily and, still in his long flannel nightshirt, he opened the front door. It was Portia.

'The Lord Jesus help us, Father,' she said.

Doctor Copeland stood shivering with his nightshirt drawn close around his waist. He held his hand to his throat and looked at her and waited.

'It about our Willie. He been a bad boy and done got hisself in mighty bad trouble. And us got to do something.'

Doctor Copeland walked from the hall with rigid steps. He stopped in the bedroom for his bathrobe, shawl, and slippers and went back to the kitchen. Portia was waiting for him there. The kitchen was lifeless and cold.

'All right. What has he done? What is it?'

'Just wait a minute. Just let me find brain room so I can study it all out and tell it to you plain.'

He crushed some sheets of newspaper lying on the hearth and picked up a few sticks of kindling.

'Let me make the fire,' Portia said. 'You just sit down at the table, and soon as this here stove is hot us going to have a cup of coffee. Then maybe it all won't seem so bad.'

'There is not any coffee. I used the last of it yesterday.'

When he said this Portia began to cry. Savagely she stuffed paper and wood into the stove and lighted it with a trembling hand. 'This here the way it is,' she said. 'Willie and Highboy were messing around tonight at a place where they got no business being. You know how I feels like I always got to keep my Willie and my Highboy close to me? Well, if I'd been there none of this trouble would of come about. But I were at the Ladies' Meeting at the church and them boys got restless. They went down to Madame Reba's Palace of Sweet Pleasure. And Father, that is sure one bad, wicked place.

They got a man sells tickets on the bug — but they also got these strutting, bad-blood, tail-shaking nigger gals and these here red satin curtains and ——'

'Daughter,' said Doctor Copeland irritably. He pressed his hands to the sides of his head. 'I know the place. Get to the point.'

'Love Jones were there — and she is one bad colored gal. Willie he drunk liquor and shimmied around with her until first thing you know he were in a fight. He were in a fight with this boy named Junebug — over Love. And for a while they fights there with their hands and then this Junebug got out his knife. Our Willie didn't have no knife, so he commenced to bellow and run around the parlor. Then finally Highboy found Willie a razor and he backed up and nearbout cut this Junebug's head off.'

Doctor Copeland drew his shawl closer around him. 'Is he dead?'

'That boy too mean to die. He in the hospital, but he going to be out and making trouble again before long.'

'And William?'

'The police come in and taken him to the jail in the Black Maria. He still locked up.'

'And he did not get hurt?'

'Oh, he got a busted eye and a little chunk cut out his behind. But it won't bother him none. What I can't understand is how come he would be messing around with that Love. She at least ten shades blacker than I is and she the ugliest nigger I ever seen. She walk like she have a egg between her legs and don't want to break it. She ain't even clean. And here Willie done cut the buck like this over her.'

Doctor Copeland leaned close to the stove and groaned. He coughed and his face stiffened. He held his paper handkerchief to his mouth and it became spotted with blood. The dark skin of his face took on a greenish pallor.

'Course Highboy come and tell me soon as it all happened.

Understand, my Highboy didn't have nothing to do with these here bad gals. He were just keeping Willie company. He so grieved about Willie he been sitting out on the street curb front of the jail ever since.' The fire-colored tears rolled down Portia's face. 'You know how us three has always been. Us haves our own plan and nothing ever went wrong with it before. Even money hasn't bothered us none. Highboy he pay the rent and I buys the food — and Willie he takes care Saturday Night. Us has always been like three-piece twinses.'

At last it was morning. The mill whistles blew for the first shift. The sun came out and brightened the clean saucepans hanging on the wall above the stove. They sat for a long time. Portia pulled at the rings on her ears until her lobes were irritated and purplish red. Doctor Copeland still held his head in his hands.

'Seem to me,' Portia said finally, 'if us can just get a lot of white peoples to write letters about Willie it might help out some. I already been to see Mr. Brannon. He written exactly what I told him to. He were at his café after it all happened like he is ever night. So I just went in there and explained how it was. I taken the letter home with me. I done put it in the Bible so I won't lose it or dirty it.'

'What did the letter say?'

'Mr. Brannon he wrote just like I asked him to. The letter tell about how Willie has been working for Mr. Brannon going on three year. It tell how Willie is one fine upstanding colored boy and how he hasn't ever been in no trouble before now. It tell how he always had plenty chances to take things in the café if he were like some other type of colored boy and how ——'

'Pshaw!' said Doctor Copeland. 'All that is no good.'

'Us just can't sit around and wait. With Willie locked up in the jail. My Willie, who is such a sweet boy even if he did do wrong tonight. Us just can't sit around and wait.'

'We will have to. That is the only thing we can do.'

'Well, I know I ain't.'

Portia got up from the chair. Her eyes roved distractedly around the room as though searching for something. Then abruptly she went toward the front door.

'Wait a minute,' said Doctor Copeland. 'Where do you intend to go now?'

'I got to work. I sure got to keep my job. I sure have to stay on with Mrs. Kelly and get my pay ever week.'

'I want to go to the jail,' said Doctor Copeland. 'Maybe I can see William.'

'I going to drop by the jail on my way to work. I got to send Highboy off to his work, too — else he liable to sit there grieving about Willie all the morning.'

Doctor Copeland dressed hurriedly and joined Portia in the hall. They went out into the cool, blue autumn morning. The men at the jail were rude to them and they were able to find out very little. Doctor Copeland then went to consult a lawyer with whom he had had dealings before. The following days were long and full of worried thoughts. At the end of three weeks the trial for William was held and he was convicted of assault with a deadly weapon. He was sentenced to nine months of hard labor and sent immediately to a prison in the northern part of the state.

Even now the strong true purpose was always in him, but he had no time in which to think on it. He went from one house to another and the work was unending. Very early in the morning he drove off in the automobile, and then at eleven o'clock the patients came to the office. After the sharp autumn air outside there would be a hot, stale odor in the house that made him cough. The benches in the hall were always full of sick and patient Negroes who waited for him, and sometimes even the front porch and his bedroom would be crowded. All the day and frequently half the night there was work. Because of the tiredness in him he wanted sometimes to lie down on the floor and beat with his fists and cry. If he could rest he might get well. He had tuberculosis of the lungs, and he measured his temperature four times a day and had an X-ray once a month. But he could not rest. For there was another thing bigger than the tiredness — and this was the strong true purpose.

He would think of this purpose until sometimes, after a long day and night of work, he would become blank so that he would forget for a minute just what the purpose was. And then it would come to him again and he would be restless and eager to take on a new task. But the words often stuck in his mouth, and his voice now was hoarse and not loud as it had been before. He pushed the words into the sick and patient faces of the Negroes who were his people.

Often he talked to Mr. Singer. With him he spoke of chemistry and the enigma of the universe. Of the infinitesimal sperm and the cleavage of the ripened egg. Of the complex million-fold division of the cells. Of the mystery of living matter and the simplicity of death. And also he spoke with him of race.

'My people were brought from the great plains, and the dark, green jungles,' he said once to Mr. Singer. 'On the long chained journeys to the coast they died by the thousands. Only the strong survived. Chained in the foul ships that brought them here they died again. Only the hardy Negroes with will could live. Beaten and chained and sold on the block, the least of these strong ones perished again. And finally through the bitter years the strongest of my people are still here. Their sons and daughters, their grandsons and great grandsons.'

'I come to borrow and I come to ask a favor,' Portia said.

Doctor Copeland was alone in his kitchen when she walked through the hall and stood in the doorway to tell him this. Two weeks had passed since William had been sent away.

Portia was changed. Her hair was not oiled and combed as usual, her eyes were bloodshot as though she had partaken of strong drink. Her cheeks were hollow, and with her sorrowful, honey-colored face she truly resembled her mother now.

'You know them nice white plates and cups you haves?'

'You may have them and keep them.'

'No, I only wants to borrow. And also I come here to ask a favor of you.'

'Anything you wish,' said Doctor Copeland.

Portia sat down across the table from her father. 'First I suppose I better explain. Yesdiddy I got this here message from Grandpapa saying they all are coming in tomorrow and spend the night and part of Sunday with us. Course they been mighty worried about Willie, and Grandpapa feel like us all ought to get together again. He right, too. I sure do want to see our kinfolks again. I been mighty homesick since Willie been gone.'

'You may have the plates and anything else you can find around here,' Doctor Copeland said. 'But hold up your shoulders, Daughter. Your carriage is bad.'

'It going to be a real reunion. You know this the first time Grandpapa have spent the night in town for twenty years. He haven't ever slept outside of his own home except two times in his whole life. And anyway he kind of nervous at night. All during the dark he have to get up and drink water and be sure the childrens is covered up and all right. I a little worried about if Grandpapa will be comfortable here.'

'Anything of mine you think you will need ——'

'Course Lee Jackson bringing them in,' said Portia. 'And with Lee Jackson it going to take them all day to get here. I not expecting them till around supper-time. Course Grandpapa always so patient with Lee Jackson he wouldn't make him hurry none.'

'My soul! Is that old mule still alive? He must be fully eighteen years old.'

'He even older than that. Grandpapa been working him now for twenty years. He done had that mule so long he always say it just like Lee Jackson is one of his blood kin. He understand and love Lee Jackson like he do his own grandchildrens. I never seen a human who know so good what a animal is thinking as Grandpapa. He haves a close feeling for everthing that walks and eats.'

'Twenty years is a long time to work a mule.'

'It sure is. Now Lee Jackson is right feeble. But Grandpapa sure do take good care of him. When they plows out in the hot sun Lee Jackson haves a great big straw hat on his head just like Grandpapa — with holes cut for his ears. That mule's straw hat is a real joke, and Lee Jackson won't budge a step when he going to plow without that hat is on his head.'

Doctor Copeland took down the white china dishes from the shelf and began to wrap them in newspaper. 'Have you enough pots and pans to cook all the food you will need?'

'Plenty,' Portia said. 'I not going to any special trouble. Grandpapa, he Mr. Thoughtful hisself — and he always bring in something to help out when the fambly come to dinner. I only going to have plenty meal and cabbage and two pounds of nice mullet.'

'Sounds good.'

Portia laced her nervous yellow fingers together. 'There one thing I haven't told you yet. A surprise. Buddy going to be here as well as Hamilton. Buddy just come back from Mobile. He helping out on the farm now.'

'It has been five years since I last saw Karl Marx.'

'And that just what I come to ask you about,' said Portia. 'You remember when I walked in the door I told you I come to borrow and to ask a favor.'

Doctor Copeland cracked the joints of his fingers. 'Yes.'

'Well, I come to see if I can't get you to be there tomorrow at the reunion. All your childrens but Willie going to be there. Seem to me like you ought to join us. I sure will be glad if you come.'

Hamilton and Karl Marx and Portia — and William. Doctor Copeland removed his spectacles and pressed his fingers against his eyelids. For a minute he saw the four of them very plainly as they were a long time ago. Then he looked up and straightened his glasses on his nose. 'Thank you,' he said. 'I will come.'

That night he sat alone by the stove in the dark room and remembered. He thought back to the time of his childhood. His mother had been born a slave, and after freedom she was a washerwoman. His father was a preacher who had once known John Brown. They had taught him, and out of the two or three dollars they had earned each week they saved. When he was seventeen years old they had sent him North with eighty dollars hidden in his shoe. He had worked in a blacksmith's shop and as a waiter and as a bellboy in a hotel. And all the while he studied and read and went to school. His father died and his mother did not live long without him. And after ten years of struggle he was a doctor and he knew his mission and he came South again.

He married and made a home. He went endlessly from house to house and spoke the mission and the truth. The hopeless suffering of his people made in him a madness, a wild and evil feeling of destruction. At times he drank strong liquor and beat his head against the floor. In his heart there was a savage violence, and once he grasped the poker from the hearth and struck down his wife. She took Hamilton, Karl Marx, William, and Portia with her to her father's home. He wrestled in his spirit and fought down the evil blackness. But Daisy did not come back to him. And eight years later when she died his sons were not children any more and they did not return to him. He was left an old man in an empty house.

Promptly at five o'clock the next afternoon he arrived at the house where Portia and Highboy lived. They resided in the part of town called Sugar Hill, and the house was a narrow cottage with a porch and two rooms. From inside there was a babble of mixed voices. Doctor Copeland approached stiffly and stood in the doorway holding his shabby felt hat in his hand.

The room was crowded and at first he was not noticed. He sought the faces of Karl Marx and Hamilton. Besides them there was Grandpapa and two children who sat together on the floor. He was still looking into the faces of his sons when Portia perceived him standing in the door.

'Here Father,' she said.

The voices stopped. Grandpapa turned around in his chair. He was thin and bent and very wrinkled. He was wearing the same greenish-black suit that he had worn thirty years before at his daughter's wedding. Across his vest there was a tarnished brass watch chain. Karl Marx and Hamilton looked at each other, then down at the floor, and finally at their father.

'Benedict Mady ——' said the old man. 'Been a long time. A real long time.'

'Ain't it, though!' Portia said. 'This here the first reunion us is all had in many a year. Highboy, you get a chair from the kitchen. Father, here Buddy and Hamilton.'

Doctor Copeland shook hands with his sons. They were both tall and strong and awkward. Against their blue shirts and overalls their skin had the same rich brown color as did Portia's. They did not look him in the eye, and in their faces there was neither love nor hate.

'It sure is a pity everbody couldn't come — Aunt Sara and Jim and all the rest,' said Highboy. 'But this here is a real pleasure to us.'

'Wagon too full,' said one of the children. 'Us had to walk a long piece 'cause the wagon too full anyways.'

Grandpapa scratched his ear with a matchstick. 'Somebody got to stay home.'

Nervously Portia licked her dark, thin lips. 'It our Willie I thinking about. He were always a big one for any kind of party or to-do. My mind just won't stay off our Willie.'

Through the room there was a quiet murmur of agreement. The old man leaned back in his chair and waggled his head up and down. 'Portia, Hon, supposing you reads to us a little while. The word of God sure do mean a lot in a time of trouble.'

Portia took up the Bible from the table in the center of the room. 'What part you want to hear now, Grandpapa?'

'It all the book of the Holy Lord. Just any place your eye fall on will do.'

Portia read from the Book of Luke. She read slowly, tracing the words with her long, limp finger. The room was still. Doctor Copeland sat on the edge of the group, cracking his knuckles, his eyes wandering from one point to another. The room was very small, the air close and stuffy. The four walls were cluttered with calendars and crudely painted advertisements from magazines. On the mantel there was a vase of red paper roses. The fire on the hearth burned slowly and the wavering light from the oil lamp made shadows on the wall. Portia read with such slow rhythm that the words slept in Doctor Copeland's ears and he was drowsy. Karl Marx lay sprawled upon the floor beside the children. Hamilton and Highboy dozed. Only the old man seemed to study the meaning of the words.

Portia finished the chapter and closed the book.

'I done pondered over this thing a many a time,' said Grandpapa.

The people in the room came out of their drowsiness. 'What?' asked Portia.

'It this way. You recall them parts about Jesus raising the dead and curing the sick?'

'Course we does, sir,' said Highboy deferentially.

'Many a day when I be plowing or working,' Grandpapa

said slowly, 'I done thought and reasoned about the time when Jesus going to descend again to this earth. 'Cause I done always wanted it so much it seem to me like it will be while I am living. I done studied about it many a time. And this here the way I done planned it. I reason I will get to stand before Jesus with all my childrens and grandchildrens and great grandchildrens and kinfolks and friends and I say to Him, "Jesus Christ, us is all sad colored peoples." And then he will place His holy hand upon our heads and straightway us will be white as cotton. That the plan and reasoning that been in my heart a many and a many a time.'

A hush fell on the room. Doctor Copeland jerked the cuffs of his sleeves and cleared his throat. His pulse beat too fast and his throat was tight. Sitting in the corner of the room he felt isolated and angry and alone.

'Has any of you ever had a sign from Heaven?' asked Grandpapa.

'I has, sir,' said Highboy. 'Once when I were sick with the pneumonia I seen God's face looking out the fireplace at me. It were a large white man's face with a white beard and blue eyes.'

'I seen a ghost,' said one of the children — the girl.

'Once I seen ——' began the little boy.

Grandpapa held up his hand. 'You childrens hush. You, Celia — and you, Whitman — it now the time for you to listen but not be heard,' he said. 'Only one time has I had a real sign. And this here the way it come about. It were in the summer of last year, and hot. I were trying to dig up the roots of that big oak stump near the hogpen and when I leaned down a kind of catch, a misery, come suddenly in the small of my back. I straightened up and then all around went dark. I were holding my hand to my back and looking up at the sky when suddenly I seen this little angel. It were a little white girl angel — look to me about the size of a field pea — with yellow hair and a white robe. Just flying around near the sun. After that I come in the house and prayed. I studied the Bible for three days before I went out in the field again.'

Doctor Copeland felt the old evil anger in him. The words rose inchoately to his throat and he could not speak them. They would listen to the old man. Yet to words of reason they would not attend. These are my people, he tried to tell himself — but because he was dumb this thought did not help him now. He sat tense and sullen.

'It a queer thing,' said Grandpapa suddenly. 'Benedict Mady, you a fine doctor. How come I get them miseries sometime in the small of my back after I been digging and planting for a good while? How come that misery bother me?'

'How old are you now?'

'I somewhere between seventy and eighty year old.'

The old man loved medicine and treatment. Always when he used to come in with his family to see Daisy he would have himself examined and take home medicine and salves for the whole group of them. But when Daisy left him the old man did not come anymore and he had to content himself with purges and kidney pills advertised in the newspapers. Now the old man was looking at him with timid eagerness.

'Drink plenty of water,' said Doctor Copeland. 'And rest as much as you can.'

Portia went into the kitchen to prepare the supper. Warm smells began to fill the room. There was quiet, idle talking, but Doctor Copeland did not listen or speak. Now and then he looked at Karl Marx or Hamilton. Karl Marx talked about Joe Louis. Hamilton spoke mostly of the hail that had ruined some of the crops. When they caught their father's eye they grinned and shuffled their feet on the floor. He kept staring at them with angry misery.

Doctor Copeland clamped his teeth down hard. He had thought so much about Hamilton and Karl Marx and William and Portia, about the real true purpose he had had for them, that the sight of their faces made a black swollen feeling in him. If once he could tell it all to them, from the far away beginning until this very night, the telling would ease the sharp ache in his heart. But they would not listen or understand.

He hardened himself so that each muscle in his body was rigid and strained. He did not listen or look at anything around him. He sat in a corner like a man who is blind and dumb. Soon they went into the supper table and the old man said grace. But Doctor Copeland did not eat. When Highboy brought out a pint bottle of gin, and they laughed and passed the bottle from mouth to mouth, he refused that also. He sat in rigid silence, and at last he picked up his hat and left the house without a farewell. If he could not speak the whole long truth no other word would come to him.

He lay tense and wakeful throughout the night. Then the next day was Sunday. He made half a dozen calls, and in the middle of the morning he went to Mr. Singer's room. The visit blunted the feeling of loneliness in him so that when he said good-bye he was at peace with himself once more.

However, before he was out of the house this peace had left him. An accident occurred. As he started down the stairs he saw a white man carrying a large paper sack and he drew close to the banisters so that they could pass each other. But the white man was running up the steps two at a time, without looking, and they collided with such force that Doctor Copeland was left sick and breathless.

'Christ! I didn't see you.'

Doctor Copeland looked at him closely but made no answer. He had seen this white man once before. He remembered the stunted, brutal-looking body and the huge, awkward hands. Then with sudden clinical interest he observed the white man's face, for in his eyes he saw a strange, fixed, and withdrawn look of madness.

'Sorry,' said the white man.

Doctor Copeland put his hand on the banister and passed on.

4

'WHO was that?' Jake Blount asked. 'Who was the tall, thin colored man that just come out of here?'

The small room was very neat. The sun lighted a bowl of purple grapes on the table. Singer sat with his chair tilted back and his hands in his pockets, looking out of the window.

'I bumped into him on the steps and he gave me this look — why, I never had anybody to look at me so dirty.'

Jake put the sack of ales down on the table. He realized with a shock that Singer did not know he was in the room. He walked over to the window and touched Singer on the shoulder.

'I didn't mean to bump into him. He had no cause to act like that.'

Jake shivered. Although the sun was bright there was a chill in the room. Singer held up his forefinger and went into the hall. When he returned he brought with him a scuttle of coal and some kindling. Jake watched him kneel before the hearth. Neatly he broke the sticks of kindling over his knee and arranged them on the foundation of paper. He put the coal on according to a system. At first the fire would not draw. The flames quivered weakly and were smothered by a black roll of smoke. Singer covered the grate with a double sheet of newspaper. The draught gave the fire new life. In the room there was a roaring sound. The paper glowed and was sucked inward. A crackling orange sheet of flame filled the grate.

The first morning ale had a fine mellow taste. Jake gulped

his share down quickly and wiped his mouth with the back of his hand.

'There was this lady I knew a long time ago,' he said. 'You sort of remind me of her. Miss Clara. She had a little farm in Texas. And made pralines to sell in the cities. She was a tall, big, fine-looking lady. Wore those long, baggy sweaters and clodhopper shoes and a man's hat. Her husband was dead when I knew her. But what I'm getting at is this: If it hadn't been for her I might never have known. I might have gone on through life like the millions of others who don't know. I would have just been a preacher or a lint-head or a salesman. My whole life might have been wasted.'

Jake shook his head wonderingly.

'To understand you got to know what went before. You see, I lived in Gastonia when I was a youngun. I was a knock-kneed little runt, too small to put in the mill. I worked as pin boy in a bowling joint and got meals for pay. Then I heard a smart, quick boy could make thirty cents a day stringing tobacco not very far from there. So I went and made that thirty cents a day. That was when I was ten years old. I just left my folks. I didn't write. They were glad I was gone. You understand how those things are. And besides, nobody could read a letter but my sister.'

He waved his hand in the air as though brushing something from his face. 'But I mean this. My first belief was Jesus. There was this fellow working in the same shed with me. He had a tabernacle and preached every night. I went and listened and I got this faith. My mind was on Jesus all day long. In my spare time I studied the Bible and prayed. Then one night I took a hammer and laid my hand on the table. I was angry and I drove the nail all the way through. My hand was nailed to the table and I looked at it and the fingers fluttered and turned blue.'

Jake held out his palm and pointed to the ragged, dead-white scar in the center.

'I wanted to be an evangelist. I meant to travel around the country preaching and holding revivals. In the meantime I moved around from one place to another, and when I was nearly twenty I got to Texas. I worked in a pecan grove near where Miss Clara lived. I got to know her and at night sometimes I would go to her house. She talked to me. Understand, I didn't begin to know all at once. That's not the way it happens to any of us. It was gradual. I began to read. I would work just so I could put aside enough money to knock off for a while and study. It was like being born a second time. Just us who know can understand what it means. We have opened our eyes and have seen. We're like people from way off yonder somewhere.'

Singer agreed with him. The room was comfortable in a homey way. Singer brought out from the closet the tin box in which he kept crackers and fruit and cheese. He selected an orange and peeled it slowly. He pulled off shreds of pith until the fruit was transparent in the sun. He sectioned the orange and divided the plugs between them. Jake ate two sections at a time and with a loud whoosh spat the seeds into the fire. Singer ate his share slowly and deposited his seeds neatly in the palm of one hand. They opened two more ales.

'And how many of us are there in this country? Maybe ten thousand. Maybe twenty thousand. Maybe a lot more. I been to a lot of places but I never met but a few of us. But say a man does *know*. He sees the world as it is and he looks back thousands of years to see how it all come about. He watches the slow agglutination of capital and power and he sees its pinnacle today. He sees America as a crazy house. He sees how men have to rob their brothers in order to live. He sees children starving and women working sixty hours a week to get to eat. He sees a whole damn army of unemployed and billions of dollars and thousands of miles of land wasted. He sees war coming. He sees how when people suffer just so much they get mean and ugly and something dies in them.

But the main thing he sees is that the whole system of the world is built on a lie. And although it's as plain as the shining sun — the don't-knows have lived with that lie so long they just can't see it.'

The red corded vein in Jake's forehead swelled angrily. He grasped the scuttle on the hearth and rattled an avalanche of coal on the fire. His foot had gone to sleep, and he stamped it so hard that the floor shook.

'I been all over this place. I walk around. I talk. I try to explain to them. But what good does it do? Lord God!'

He gazed into the fire, and a flush from the ale and heat deepened the color of his face. The sleepy tingling in his foot spread up his leg. He drowsed and saw the colors of the fire, the tints of green and blue and burning yellow. 'You're the only one,' he said dreamily. 'The only one.'

He was a stranger no longer. By now he knew every street, every alley, every fence in all the sprawling slums of the town. He still worked at the Sunny Dixie. During the fall the show moved from one vacant lot to another, staying always within the fringes of the city limit, until at last it had encircled the town. The locations were changed but the settings were alike — a strip of wasteland bordered by rows of rotted shacks, and somewhere near a mill, a cotton gin, or a bottling plant. The crowd was the same, for the most part factory workers and Negroes. The show was gaudy with colored lights in the evening. The wooden horses of the flying-jinny revolved in the circle to the mechanical music. The swings whirled, the rail around the penny throwing game was always crowded. From the two booths were sold drinks and bloody brown hamburgers and cotton candy.

He had been hired as a machinist, but gradually the range of his duties widened. His coarse, bawling voice called out through the noise, and continually he was lounging from one place on the show grounds to another. Sweat stood out on his forehead and often his mustache was soaked with beer. On

Saturday his job was to keep the people in order. His squat, hard body pushed through the crowd with savage energy. Only his eyes did not share the violence of the rest of him. Wide gazing beneath his massive scowling forehead, they had a withdrawn and distracted appearance.

He reached home between twelve and one in the morning. The house where he lived was squared into four rooms and the rent was a dollar fifty per person. There was a privy in the back and a hydrant on the stoop. In his room the walls and floor had a wet, sour smell. Sooty, cheap lace curtains hung at the window. He kept his good suit in his bag and hung his overalls on a nail. The room had no heat and no electricity. However, a street light shone outside the window and made a pale greenish reflection inside. He never lighted the oil lamp by his bed unless he wanted to read. The acrid smell of burning oil in the cold room nauseated him.

If he stayed at home he restlessly walked the floor. He sat on the edge of the unmade bed and gnawed savagely at the broken, dirty ends of his fingernails. The sharp taste of grime lingered in his mouth. The loneliness in him was so keen that he was filled with terror. Usually he had a pint of bootleg white lightning. He drank the raw liquor and by daylight he was warm and relaxed. At five o'clock the whistles from the mills blew for the first shift. The whistles made lost, eerie echoes, and he could never sleep until after they had sounded.

But usually he did not stay at home. He went out into the narrow, empty streets. In the first dark hours of the morning the sky was black and the stars hard and bright. Sometimes the mills were running. From the yellow-lighted buildings came the racket of the machines. He waited at the gates for the early shift. Young girls in sweaters and print dresses came out into the dark street. The men came out carrying their dinner pails. Some of them always went to a streetcar café for Coca-Cola or coffee before going home, and Jake went with them. Inside the noisy mill the men could hear plainly every word that was spoken, but for the first hour outside they were deaf.

In the streetcar Jake drank Coca-Cola with whiskey added. He talked. The winter dawn was white and smoky and cold. He looked with drunken urgency into the drawn, yellow faces of the men. Often he was laughed at, and when this happened he held his stunted body very straight and spoke scornfully in words of many syllables. He stuck his little finger out from his glass and haughtily twisted his mustache. And if he was still laughed at he sometimes fought. He swung his big brown fists with crazed violence and sobbed aloud.

After such mornings he returned to the show with relief. It eased him to push through the crowds of people. The noise, the rank stinks, the shouldering contact of human flesh soothed his jangled nerves.

Because of the blue laws in the town the show closed for the Sabbath. On Sunday he got up early in the morning and took from the suitcase his serge suit. He went to the main street. First he dropped into the New York Café and bought a sack of ales. Then he went to Singer's room. Although he knew many people in the town by name or face, the mute was his only friend. They would idle in the quiet room and drink the ales. He would talk, and the words created themselves from the dark mornings spent in the streets or in his room alone. The words were formed and spoken with relief.

The fire had died down. Singer was playing a game of fools with himself at the table. Jake had been asleep. He awoke with a nervous quiver. He raised his head and turned to Singer. 'Yeah,' he said as though in answer to a sudden question. 'Some of us are Communists. But not all of us ——. Myself, I'm not a member of the Communist Party. Because in the first place I never knew but one of them. You can bum around for years and not meet Communists. Around here there's no office where you can go up and say you want to join — and if there is I never heard of it. And you just don't take off for New York and join. As I say I never knew but one — and he was a seedy little teetotaler whose breath stunk. We had a fight. Not that I hold that against the Communists. The main fact is I don't think so much of Stalin and Russia. I hate every damn country and government there is. But even so maybe I ought to joined up with the Communists first place. I'm not certain one way or the other. What do you think?'

Singer wrinkled his forehead and considered. He reached for his silver pencil and wrote on his pad of paper that he didn't know.

'But there's this. You see, we just can't settle down after knowing, but we got to act. And some of us go nuts. There's too much to do and you don't know where to start. It makes you crazy. Even me — I've done things that when I look back at them they don't seem rational. Once I started an organization myself. I picked out twenty lintheads and talked to them until I thought they *knew*. Our motto was one word: Action. Huh! We meant to start riots — stir up all the big trouble we could. Our ultimate goal was freedom — but a real freedom, a great freedom made possible only by the sense of justice of the human soul. Our motto, "Action," signified the razing of capitalism. In the constitution (drawn up by myself) certain statutes dealt with the swapping of our motto from "Action" to "Freedom" as soon as our work was through.'

Jake sharpened the end of a match and picked a troublesome cavity in a tooth. After a moment he continued:

'Then when the constitution was all written down and the first followers well organized — then I went out on a hitch-hiking tour to organize component units of the society. Within three months I came back, and what do you reckon I found? What was the first heroic action? Had their righteous fury overcome planned action so that they had gone ahead without me? Was it destruction, murder, revolution?'

Jake leaned forward in his chair. After a pause he said somberly:

'My friend, they had stole the fifty-seven dollars and thirty cents from the treasury to buy uniform caps and free Saturday suppers. I caught them sitting around the conference table, rolling the bones, their caps on their heads, and a ham and a gallon of gin in easy reach.'

A timid smile from Singer followed Jake's outburst of laughter. After a while the smile on Singer's face grew strained and faded. Jake still laughed. The vein in his forehead swelled, his face was dusky red. He laughed too long.

Singer looked up at the clock and indicated the time — half-past twelve. He took his watch, his silver pencil and pad, his cigarettes and matches from the mantel and distributed them among his pockets. It was dinner-time.

But Jake still laughed. There was something maniacal in the sound of his laughter. He walked about the room, jingling the change in his pockets. His long, powerful arms swung tense and awkward. He began to name over parts of his coming meal. When he spoke of food his face was fierce with gusto. With each word he raised his upper lip like a ravenous animal.

'Roast beef with gravy. Rice. And cabbage and light bread. And a big hunk of apple pie. I'm famished. Oh, Johnny, I can hear the Yankees coming. And speaking of meals, my friend, did I ever tell you about Mr. Clark Patterson, the gentleman who owns the Sunny Dixie Show? He's so fat he hasn't seen his privates for twenty years, and all day he sits in his trailer playing solitaire and smoking reefers. He orders his meals from a short-order joint near-by and every day he breaks his fast with ——'

Jake stepped back so that Singer could leave the room. He always hung back at doorways when he was with the mute. He always followed and expected Singer to lead. As they descended the stairs he continued to talk with nervous volubility. He kept his brown, wide eyes on Singer's face.

The afternoon was soft and mild. They stayed indoors. Jake had brought back with them a quart of whiskey. He sat brooding and silent on the foot of the bed, leaning now and then to fill his glass from the bottle on the floor. Singer was at his table by the window playing a game of chess. Jake had relaxed somewhat. He watched the game of his friend and felt the mild, quiet afternoon merge with the darkness of evening. The firelight made dark, silent waves on the walls of the room.

But at night the tension came in him again. Singer had put away his chess men and they sat facing each other. Nervousness made Jake's lips twitch raggedly and he drank to soothe himself. A backwash of restlessness and desire overcame him. He drank down the whiskey and began to talk again to Singer. The words swelled within him and gushed from his mouth. He walked from the window to the bed and back again — again and again. And at last the deluge of swollen words took shape and he delivered them to the mute with drunken emphasis:

'The things they have done to us! The truths they have turned into lies. The ideals they have fouled and made vile. Take Jesus. He was one of us. He knew. When he said that it is harder for a camel to pass through the eye of a needle than for a rich man to enter the kingdom of God — he damn well meant just what he said. But look what the Church has done to Jesus during the last two thousand years. What they have made of him. How they have turned every word he spoke for their own vile ends. Jesus would be framed and in jail if he was living today. Jesus would be one who really knows. Me and Jesus would sit across the table and I would look at him and he would look at me and we would both know that the other knew. Me and Jesus and Karl Marx could all sit at a table and ——

'And look what has happened to our freedom. The men who fought the American Revolution were no more like these

D.A.R. dames than I'm a pot-bellied, perfumed Pekingese dog. They meant what they said about freedom. They fought a real revolution. They fought so that this could be a country where every man would be free and equal. Huh! And that meant every man was equal in the sight of Nature — with an equal chance. This didn't mean that twenty per cent of the people were free to rob the other eighty per cent of the means to live. This didn't mean for one rich man to sweat the piss out of ten thousand poor men so that he can get richer. This didn't mean the tyrants were free to get this country in such a fix that millions of people are ready to do anything — cheat, lie, or whack off their right arm — just to work for three squares and a flop. They have made the word freedom a blasphemy. You hear me? They have made the word freedom stink like a skunk to all who know.'

The vein in Jake's forehead throbbed wildly. His mouth worked convulsively. Singer sat up, alarmed. Jake tried to speak again and the words choked in his mouth. A shudder passed through his body. He sat down in the chair and pressed his trembling lips with his fingers. Then he said huskily:

'It's this way, Singer. Being mad is no good. Nothing we can do is any good. That's the way it seems to me. All we can do is go around telling the truth. And as soon as enough of the don't knows have learned this truth then there won't be any use for fighting. The only thing for us to do is let them know. All that's needed. But how? Huh?'

The fire shadows lapped against the walls. The dark, shadowy waves rose higher and the room took on motion. The room rose and fell and all balance was gone. Alone Jake felt himself sink downward, slowly in wavelike motions downward into a shadowed ocean. In helplessness and terror he strained his eyes, but he could see nothing except the dark and scarlet waves that roared hungrily over him. Then at last he made out the thing which he sought. The mute's face was faint and verv far away. Jake closed his eyes.

The next morning he awoke very late. Singer had been gone for hours. There was bread, cheese, an orange, and a pot of coffee on the table. When he had finished his breakfast it was time for work. He walked somberly, his head bent, across the town toward his room. When he reached the neighborhood where he lived he passed through a certain narrow street that was flanked on one side by a smoke-blackened brick warehouse. On the wall of this building there was something that vaguely distracted him. He started to walk on, and then his attention was suddenly held. On the wall a message was written in bright red chalk, the letters drawn thickly and curiously formed:

Ye shall eat the flesh of the mighty, and drink the blood of the princes of the earth.

He read the message twice and looked anxiously up and down the street. No one was in sight. After a few minutes of puzzled deliberation he took from his pocket a thick red pencil and wrote carefully beneath the inscription:

Whoever wrote the above meet me here tomorrow at noon. Wednesday, November 29. Or the next day.

At twelve o'clock the next day he waited before the wall. Now and then he walked impatiently to the corner to look up and down the streets. No one came. After an hour he had to leave for the show.

The next day he waited, also.

Then on Friday there was a long, slow winter rain. The wall was sodden and the messages streaked so that no word could be read. The rain continued, gray and bitter and cold.

5

'MICK,' Bubber said. 'I come to believe we all gonna drown.'

It was true that it like to never quit raining. Mrs. Wells rode them back and forth to school in her car, and every afternoon they had to stay on the front porch or in the house. She and Bubber played Parcheesi and Old Maid and shot marbles on the living-room rug. It was nearing along toward Christmas time and Bubber began to talk about the Little Lord Jesus and the red bicycle he wanted Santa Claus to bring him. The rain was silver on the windowpanes and the sky was wet and cold and gray. The river rose so high that some of the factory people had to move out of their houses. Then when it looked like the rain would keep on and on forever it suddenly stopped. They woke up one morning and the bright sun was shining. By afternoon the weather was almost warm as summer. Mick came home late from school and Bubber and Ralph and Spareribs were on the front sidewalk. The kids looked hot and sticky and their winter clothes had a sour smell. Bubber had his slingshot and a pocketful of rocks. Ralph sat up in his wagon, his hat crooked on his head, and he was fretful. Spareribs had his new rifle with him. The sky was a wonderful blue.

'We waited for you a long time, Mick,' Bubber said. 'Where you been?'

She jumped up the front steps three at a time and threw her sweater toward the hat rack. 'Practicing on the piano in the gym.'

Every afternoon she stayed after school for an hour to play. The gym was crowded and noisy because the girls' team had basketball games. Twice today she was hit on the head with the ball. But getting a chance to sit at a piano was worth any amount of knocks and trouble. She would arrange bunches of notes together until the sound came that she wanted. It was easier than she had thought. After the first two or three hours she figured out some sets of chords in the bass that would fit in with the main tune her right hand was playing. She could pick out almost any piece now. And she made up new music too. That was better than just copying tunes. When her hands hunted out these beautiful new sounds it was the best feeling she had ever known.

She wanted to learn how to read music already written down. Delores Brown had taken music lessons for five years. She paid Delores the fifty cents a week she got for lunch money to give her lessons. This made her very hungry all through the day. Delores played a good many fast, runny pieces — but Delores did not know how to answer all the questions she wanted to know. Delores only taught her about the different scales, the major and minor chords, the values of the notes, and such beginning rules as those.

Mick slammed the door of the kitchen stove. 'This all we got to eat?'

'Honey, it the best I can do for you,' Portia said.

Just cornpones and margarine. As she ate she drank a glass of water to help wash down the swallows.

'Quit acting so greedy. Nobody going to snatch it out your hand.'

The kids still hung around in front of the house. Bubber had put his slingshot in his pocket and now he played with the rifle. Spareribs was ten years old and his father had died the month before and this had been his father's gun. All the smaller kids loved to handle that rifle. Every few minutes Bubber would haul the gun up to his shoulder. He took aim and made a loud *pow* sound.

'Don't monkey with the trigger,' said Spareribs. 'I got the gun loaded.'

Mick finished the cornbread and looked around for something to do. Harry Minowitz was sitting on his front porch banisters with the newspaper. She was glad to see him. For a joke she threw up her arm and hollered to him, 'Heil!'

But Harry didn't take it as a joke. He went into his front hall and shut the door. It was easy to hurt his feelings. She was sorry, because lately she and Harry had been right good friends. They had always played in the same gang when they were kids, but in the last three years he had been at Vocational while she was still in grammar school. Also he worked at part-time jobs. He grew up very suddenly and quit hanging around the back and front yards with kids. Sometimes she could see him reading the paper in his bedroom or undressing late at night. In mathematics and history he was the smartest boy at Vocational. Often, now that she was in high school too, they would meet each other on the way home and walk together. They were in the same shop class, and once the teacher made them partners to assemble a motor. He read books and kept up with the newspapers every day. World politics were all the time on his mind. He talked slow, and sweat stood out on his forehead when he was very serious about something. And now she had made him mad with her.

'I wonder has Harry still got his gold piece,' Spareribs said.

'What gold piece?'

'When a Jew boy is born they put a gold piece in the bank for him. That's what Jews do.'

'Shucks. You got it mixed up,' she said. 'It's Catholics you're thinking about. Catholics buy a pistol for a baby soon as it's born. Some day the Catholics mean to start a war and kill everybody else.'

'Nuns give me a funny feeling,' Spareribs said. 'It scares me when I see one on the street.'

She sat down on the steps and laid her head on her knees. She went into the inside room. With her it was like there was two places — the inside room and the outside room. School and the family and the things that happened every day were in the outside room. Mister Singer was in both rooms. Foreign countries and plans and music were in the inside room. The songs she thought about were there. And the symphony. When she was by herself in this inside room the music she had heard that night after the party would come back to her. This symphony grew slow like a big flower in her mind. During the day sometimes, or when she had just waked up in the morning, a new part of the symphony would suddenly come to her. Then she would have to go into the inside room and listen to it many times and try to join it into the parts of the symphony she remembered. The inside room was a very private place. She could be in the middle of a house full of people and still feel like she was locked up by herself.

Spareribs stuck his dirty hand up to her eyes because she had been staring off at space. She slapped him.

'What is a nun?' Bubber asked.

'A Catholic lady,' Spareribs said. 'A Catholic lady with a big black dress that comes up over her head.'

She was tired of hanging around with the kids. She would go to the library and look at pictures in the *National Geographic*. Photographs of all the foreign places in the world. Paris, France. And big ice glaciers. And the wild jungles in Africa.

'You kids see that Ralph don't get out in the street,' she said.

Bubber rested the big rifle on his shoulder. 'Bring me a story back with you.'

It was like that kid had been born knowing how to read. He was only in the second grade but he loved to read stories by himself — and he never asked anybody else to read to him. 'What kind you want this time?'

'Pick out some stories with something to eat in them. I like that one a whole lot about them German kids going out in the forest and coming to this house made out of all different kinds of candy and the witch. I like a story with something to eat in it.'

'I'll look for one,' said Mick.

'But I'm getting kinda tired of candy,' Bubber said. 'See if you can't bring me a story with something like a barbecue sandwich in it. But if you can't find none of them I'd like a cowboy story.'

She was ready to leave when suddenly she stopped and stared. The kids stared too. They all stood still and looked at Baby Wilson coming down the steps of her house across the street.

'Ain't Baby cute!' said Bubber softly.

Maybe it was the sudden hot, sunny day after all those rainy weeks. Maybe it was because their dark winter clothes were ugly to them on an afternoon like this one. Anyway Baby looked like a fairy or something in the picture show. She had on her last year's soirée costume — with a little pink-gauze skirt that stuck out short and stiff, a pink body waist, pink dancing shoes, and even a little pink pocketbook. With her yellow hair she was all pink and white and gold — and so small and clean that it almost hurt to watch her. She prissed across the street in a cute way, but would not turn her face toward them.

'Come over here,' said Bubber. 'Lemme look at your little pink pocketbook ——'

Baby passed them along the edge of the street with her head held to one side. She had made up her mind not to speak to them.

There was a strip of grass between the sidewalk and the street, and when Baby reached it she stood still for a second and then turned a handspring.

'Don't pay no mind to her,' said Spareribs. 'She always tries to show off. She's going down to Mister Brannon's café to get candy. He's her uncle and she gets it free.'

Bubber rested the end of the rifle on the ground. The big gun was too heavy for him. As he watched Baby walk off down the street he kept pulling the straggly bangs of his hair. 'That sure is a cute little pink pocketbook,' he said.

'Her Mama always talks about how talented she is,' said Spareribs. 'She thinks she's gonna get Baby in the movies.'

It was too late to go look at the *National Geographic*. Supper was almost ready. Ralph tuned up to cry and she took him off the wagon and put him on the ground. Now it was December, and to a kid Bubber's age that was a long time from summer. All last summer Baby had come out in that pink soirée costume and danced in the middle of the street. At first the kids would flock around and watch her, but soon they got tired of it. Bubber was the only one who would watch her as she came out to dance. He would sit on the curb and yell to her when he saw a car coming. He had watched Baby do her soirée dance a hundred times — but summer had been gone for three months and now it seemed new to him again.

'I sure do wish I had a costume,' Bubber said.

'What kind do you want?'

'A real cool costume. A real pretty one made out of all different colors. Like a butterfly. That's what I want for Christmas. That and a bicycle!'

'Sissy,' said Spareribs.

Bubber hauled the big rifle up to his shoulder again and took aim at a house across the street. 'I'd dance around in my costume if I had one. I'd wear it every day to school.'

Mick sat on the front steps and kept her eyes on Ralph. Bubber wasn't a sissy like Spareribs said. He just loved pretty things. She'd better not let old Spareribs get away with that.

'A person's got to fight for every single thing they get,' she said slowly. 'And I've noticed a lot of times that the farther down a kid comes in the family the better the kid really is. Youngest kids are always the toughest. I'm pretty hard 'cause I've a lot of them on top of me. Bubber — he looks sick, and likes pretty things, but he's got guts underneath that. If all this is true Ralph sure ought to be a real strong one when he's old enough to get around. Even though he's just seventeen months old I can read something hard and tough in that Ralph's face already.'

Ralph looked around because he knew he was being talked about. Spareribs sat down on the ground and grabbed Ralph's hat off his head and shook it in his face to tease him.

'All right!' Mick said. 'You know what I'll do to you if you start him to cry. You just better watch out.'

Everything was quiet. The sun was behind the roofs of the houses and the sky in the west was purple and pink. On the next block there was the sound of kids skating. Bubber leaned up against a tree and he seemed to be dreaming about something. The smell of supper came out of the house and it would be time to eat soon.

'Lookit,' Bubber said suddenly. 'Here comes Baby again. She sure is pretty in the pink costume.'

Baby walked toward them slowly. She had been given a prize box of popcorn candy and was reaching in the box for the prize. She walked in that same prissy, dainty way. You could tell that she knew they were all looking at her.

'Please, Baby ——' Bubber said when she started to pass them. 'Lemme see your little pink pocketbook and touch your pink costume.'

Baby started humming a song to herself and did not listen. She passed by without letting Bubber play with her. She only ducked her head and grinned at him a little.

Bubber still had the big rifle up to his shoulder. He made a loud *pow* sound and pretended like he had shot. Then he called to Baby again — in a soft, sad voice like he was calling a little kitty. 'Please Baby — Come here, Baby ——'

He was too quick for Mick to stop him. She had just seen his hand on the trigger when there was the terrible *ping* of the gun. Baby crumpled down to the sidewalk. It was like she was nailed to the steps and couldn't move or scream. Spareribs had his arm up over his head.

Bubber was the only one that didn't realize. 'Get up, Baby,' he hollered. 'I ain't mad with you.'

It all happened in a second. The three of them reached Baby at the same time. She lay crumpled down on the dirty sidewalk. Her skirt was over her head, showing her pink panties and her little white legs. Her hands were open — in one there was the prize from the candy and in the other the pocketbook. There was blood all over her hair ribbon and the top of her yellow curls. She was shot in the head and her face was turned down toward the ground.

So much happened in a second. Bubber screamed and dropped the gun and ran. She stood with her hands up to her face and screamed too. Then there were many people. Her Dad was the first to get there. He carried Baby into the house.

'She's dead,' said Spareribs. 'She's shot through the eyes. I seen her face.'

Mick walked up and down the sidewalk, and her tongue stuck in her mouth when she tried to ask was Baby killed. Mrs. Wilson came running down the block from the beauty parlor where she worked. She went into the house and came back out again. She walked up and down in the street, crying and pulling a ring on and off her finger. Then the ambulance came and the doctor went in to Baby. Mick followed him. Baby was lying on the bed in the front room. The house was quiet as a church.

Baby looked like a pretty little doll on the bed. Except for the blood she did not seem hurt. The doctor bent over and looked at her head. After he finished they took Baby out on a stretcher. Mrs. Wilson and her Dad got into the ambulance with her.

The house was still quiet. Everybody had forgotten about Bubber. He was nowhere around. An hour passed. Her Mama and Hazel and Etta and all the boarders waited in the front room. Mister Singer stood in the doorway. After a long time her Dad came home. He said Baby wouldn't die but that her skull was fractured. He asked for Bubber. Nobody knew where he was. It was dark outside. They called Bubber in the back yard and in the street. They sent Spareribs and some other boys out to hunt for him. It looked like Bubber had gone clear out of the neighborhood. Harry went around to a house where they thought he might be.

Her Dad walked up and down the front porch. 'I never have whipped any of my kids yet,' he kept saying. 'I never believed in it. But I'm sure going to lay it onto that kid as soon as I get my hands on him.'

Mick sat on the banisters and watched down the dark street. 'I can manage Bubber. Once he comes back I can take care of him all right.'

'You go out and hunt for him. You can find him better than anybody else.'

As soon as her Dad said that she suddenly knew where Bubber was. In the back yard there was a big oak and in the summer they had built a tree house. They had hauled a big box up in this oak, and Bubber used to love to sit up in the tree house by himself. Mick left the family and the boarders on the front porch and walked back through the alley to the dark yard.

She stood for a minute by the trunk of the tree. 'Bubber —,' she said quietly. 'It's Mick.'

He didn't answer, but she knew he was there. It was like she could smell him. She swung up on the lowest branch and climbed slowly. She was really mad with that kid and would have to teach him a lesson. When she reached the tree house she spoke to him again — and still there wasn't any answer. She climbed into the big box and felt around the edges. At last she touched him. He was scrouged up in a corner and his legs were trembling. He had been holding his breath, and when she touched him the sobs and the breath came out all at once.

'I — I didn't mean Baby to fall. She was just so little and cute — seemed to me like I just had to take a pop at her.'

Mick sat down on the floor of the tree house. 'Baby's dead,' she said. 'They got a lot of people hunting for you.'

Bubber quit crying. He was very quiet.

'You know what Dad's doing in the house?'

It was like she could hear Bubber listening.

'You know Warden Lawes — you heard him over the radio. And you know Sing Sing. Well, our Dad's writing a letter to Warden Lawes for him to be a little bit kind to you when they catch you and send you to Sing Sing.'

The words were so awful-sounding in the dark that a shiver came over her. She could feel Bubber trembling.

'They got little electric chairs there — just your size. And when they turn on the juice you just fry up like a piece of burnt bacon. Then you go to Hell.'

Bubber was squeezed up in the corner and there was not a sound from him. She climbed over the edge of the box to get down. 'You better stay up here because they got policemen guarding the yard. Maybe in a few days I can bring you something to eat.'

Mick leaned against the trunk of the oak tree. That would teach Bubber all right. She had always managed him and she knew more about that kid than anybody else. Once, about a year or two ago, he was always wanting to stop off behind bushes and pee and play with himself awhile. She had caught on to that pretty quick. She gave him a good slap every time it happened and in three days he was cured. Afterwards he never even peed normal like other kids — he held his hands behind him. She always had to nurse that Bubber and she could always manage him. In a little while she would go back up to the tree house and bring him in. After this he would never want to pick up a gun again in all his life.

There was still this dead feeling in the house. The boarders all sat on the front porch without talking or rocking in the chairs. Her Dad and her Mama were in the front room. Her Dad drank beer out of a bottle and walked up and down the floor. Baby was going to get well all right, so this worry was not about her. And nobody seemed to be anxious about Bubber. It was something else.

'That Bubber!' said Etta.

'I'm shamed to go out of the house after this,' Hazel said.

Etta and Hazel went into the middle room and closed the door. Bill was in his room at the back. She didn't want to talk with them. She stood around in the front hall and thought it over by herself.

Her Dad's footsteps stopped. 'It was deliberate,' he said. 'It's not like the kid was just fooling with the gun and it went off by accident. Everybody who saw it said he took deliberate aim.'

'I wonder when we'll hear from Mrs. Wilson,' her Mama said.

'We'll hear plenty, all right!'

'I reckon we will.'

Now that the sun was down the night was cold again like November. The people came in from the front porch and sat in the living-room — but nobody lighted a fire. Mick's sweater was hanging on the hat rack, so she put it on and stood with her shoulders bent over to keep warm. She thought about Bubber sitting out in the cold, dark tree house. He had really believed every word she said. But he sure deserved to worry some. He had nearly killed that Baby.

'Mick, can't you think of some place where Bubber might be?' her Dad asked.

'He's in the neighborhood, I reckon.'

Her Dad walked up and down with the empty beer bottle in his hand. He walked like a blind man and there was sweat on his face. 'The poor kid's scared to come home. If we could find him I'd feel better. I've never laid a hand on Bubber. He oughtn't be scared of me.'

She would wait until an hour and a half was gone. By that time he would be plenty sorry for what he did. She always could manage that Bubber and make him learn.

After a while there was a big excitement in the house. Her Dad telephoned again to the hospital to see how Baby was, and in a few minutes Mrs. Wilson called back. She said she wanted to have a talk with them and would come to the house.

Her Dad still walked up and down the front room like a blind man. He drank three more bottles of beer. 'The way it all happened she can sue my britches off. All she could get would be the house outside of the mortgage. But the way it happened we don't have any comeback at all.'

Suddenly Mick thought about something. Maybe they would really try Bubber in court and put him in a children's jail. Maybe Mrs. Wilson would send him to reform school. Maybe they would really do something terrible to Bubber. She wanted to go out to the tree house right away and sit with him and tell him not to worry. Bubber was always so thin and little and smart. She would kill anybody that tried to send that kid out of the family. She wanted to kiss him and bite him because she loved him so much.

But she couldn't miss anything. Mrs. Wilson would be there in a few minutes and she had to know what was going on. Then she would run out and tell Bubber that all the things she said were lies. And he would really have learned the lesson he had coming to him.

A ten-cent taxicab drove up to the sidewalk. Everybody waited on the front porch, very quiet and scared. Mrs. Wilson got out of the taxi with Mister Brannon. She could hear her Dad grinding his teeth together in a nervous way as they came up the steps. They went into the front room and she followed along after them and stood in the doorway. Etta and Hazel and Bill and the boarders kept out of it.

'I've come to talk over all this with you,' Mrs. Wilson said.

The front room looked tacky and dirty and she saw Mister Brannon notice everything. The mashed celluloid doll and the beads and junk Ralph played with were scattered on the floor. There was beer on her Dad's workbench, and the pillows on the bed where her Dad and Mama slept were right gray.

Mrs. Wilson kept pulling the wedding ring on and off her finger. By the side of her Mister Brannon was very calm. He sat with his legs crossed. His jaws were blue-black and he looked like a gangster in the movies. He had always had this grudge against her. He always spoke to her in this rough voice different from the way he talked to other people. Was it because he knew about the time she and Bubber swiped a pack of chewing gum off his counter? She hated him.

'It all boils down to this,' said Mrs. Wilson. 'Your kid shot my Baby in the head on purpose.'

Mick stepped into the middle of the room. 'No, he didn't,' she said. 'I was right there. Bubber had been aiming that gun at me and Ralph and everything around there. He just happened to aim it at Baby and his finger slipped. I was right there.'

Mister Brannon rubbed his nose and looked at her in a sad way. She sure did hate him.

'I know how you all feel — so I want to come to the point right now.'

Mick's Mama rattled a bunch of keys and her Dad sat very still with his big hands hanging over his knees.

'Bubber didn't have it in his mind beforehand,' Mick said. 'He just ——'

Mrs. Wilson jabbed the ring on and off her finger. 'Wait a minute. I know how everything is. I could bring it to court and sue you for every cent you own.'

Her Dad didn't have any expression on his face. 'I tell you one thing,' he said. 'We don't have much to sue for. All we got is ——'

'Just listen to me,' said Mrs. Wilson. 'I haven't come here with any lawyer to sue you. Bartholomew — Mister Brannon — and I talked it over when we came and we just about agree on the main points. In the first place, I want to do the fair, honest thing — and in the second place, I don't want Baby's name mixed up in no common lawsuit at her age.'

There was not a sound and everybody in the room sat stiff in their chairs. Only Mister Brannon halfway smiled at Mick, but she squinted her eyes back at him in a tough way.

Mrs. Wilson was very nervous and her hand shook when she lighted a cigarette. 'I don't want to have to sue you or anything like that. All I want is for you to be fair. I'm not asking you to pay for all the suffering and crying Baby went through with until they gave her something to sleep. There's not any pay that would make up for that. And I'm not asking you to pay for the damage this will do to her career and the plans we had made. She's going to have to wear a bandage for several months. She won't get to dance in the soirée — maybe there'll even be a little bald place on her head.'

Mrs. Wilson and her Dad looked at each other like they was hypnotized. Then Mrs. Wilson reached around to her pocketbook and took out a slip of paper.

'The things you got to pay are just the actual price of what it will cost us in money. There's Baby's private room in the hospital and a private nurse until she can come home. There's the operating room and the doctor's bill — and for once I intend the doctor to be paid right away. Also, they shaved all Baby's hair off and you got to pay me for the permanent wave I took her to Atlanta to get — so when her hair grows back natural she can have another one. And there's the price of her costume and other little extra bills like that. I'll write all the items down just as soon as I know what they'll be. I'm trying to be just as fair and honest as I can, and you'll have to pay the total when I bring it to you.'

Her Mama smoothed her dress over her knees and took a quick, short breath. 'Seems to me like the children's ward would be a lot better than a private room. When Mick had pneumonia ——'

'I said a private room.'

Mister Brannon held out his white, stumpy hands and balanced them like they was on scales. 'Maybe in a day or two Baby can move into a double room with some other kid.'

Mrs. Wilson spoke hard-boiled. 'You heard what I said. Long as your kid shot my Baby she certainly ought to have every advantage until she gets well.'

'You're in your rights,' her Dad said. 'God knows we don't have anything now — but maybe I can scrape it up. I realize you're not trying to take advantage of us and I appreciate it. We'll do what we can.'

She wanted to stay and hear everything that they said, but Bubber was on her mind. When she thought of him sitting up in the dark, cold tree house thinking about Sing Sing she felt uneasy. She went out of the room and down the hall toward the back door. The wind was blowing and the yard was very dark except for the yellow square that came from the light in the kitchen. When she looked back she saw Portia sitting at the table with her long, thin hands up to her face, very still. The yard was lonesome and the wind made quick, scary shadows and a mourning kind of sound in the darkness.

She stood under the oak tree. Then just as she started to reach for the first limb a terrible notion came over her. It came to her all of a sudden that Bubber was gone. She called him and he did not answer. She climbed quick and quiet as a cat.

'Say! Bubber!'

Without feeling in the box she knew he wasn't there. To make sure she got into the box and felt in all the corners. The kid was gone. He must have started down the minute she left. He was running away for sure now, and with a smart kid like Bubber it was no telling where they'd catch him.

She scrambled down the tree and ran to the front porch. Mrs. Wilson was leaving and they had all come out to the front steps with her.

'Dad!' she said. 'We got to do something about Bubber

He's run away. I'm sure he left our block. We all got to get out and hunt him.'

Nobody knew where to go or how to begin. Her Dad walked up and down the street, looking in all the alleys. Mister Brannon telephoned for a ten-cent taxi for Mrs. Wilson and then stayed to help with the hunt. Mister Singer sat on the banisters of the porch and he was the only person who kept calm. They all waited for Mick to plan out the best places to look for Bubber. But the town was so big and the little kid was so smart that she couldn't think what to do.

Maybe he had gone to Portia's house over in Sugar Hill. She went back into the kitchen where Portia was sitting at the table with her hands up to her face.

'I got this sudden notion he went down to your house. Help us hunt him.'

'How come I didn't think of that! I bet a nickel my little scared Bubber been staying in my home all the time.'

Mister Brannon had borrowed an automobile. He and Mister Singer and Mick's Dad got into the car with her and Portia. Nobody knew what Bubber was feeling except her. Nobody knew he had really run away like he was escaping to save his life.

Portia's house was dark except for the checkered moonlight on the floor. As soon as they stepped inside they could tell there was nobody in the two rooms. Portia lighted the front lamp. The rooms had a colored smell, and they were crowded with cut-out pictures on the walls and the lace table covers and lace pillows on the bed. Bubber was not there.

'He been here,' Portia suddenly said. 'I can tell somebody been in here.'

Mister Singer found the pencil and piece of paper on the kitchen table. He read it quickly and then they all looked at it. The writing was round and scraggly and the smart little kid hadn't misspelled but one word. The note said:

Dear Portia,

I gone to Florada. Tell every body.

Yours truly,

Bubber Kelly

They stood around surprised and stumped. Her Dad looked out the doorway and picked his nose with his thumb in a worried way. They were all ready to pile in the car and ride toward the highway leading south.

'Wait a minute,' Mick said. 'Even if Bubber is seven years old he's got brains enough not to tell us where he's going if he wants to run away. That about Florida is just a trick.'

'A trick?' her Dad said.

'Yeah. There only two places Bubber knows very much about. One is Florida and the other is Atlanta. Me and Bubber and Ralph have been on the Atlanta road many a time. He knows how to start there and that's where he's headed. He always talks about what he's going to do when he gets a chance to go to Atlanta.'

They went out to the automobile again. She was ready to climb into the back seat when Portia pinched her on the elbow. 'You know what Bubber done?' she said in a quiet voice. 'Don't you tell nobody else, but my Bubber done also taken my gold earrings off my dresser. I never thought my Bubber would have done such a thing to me.'

Mister Brannon started the automobile. They rode slow, looking up and down the streets for Bubber, headed toward the Atlanta road.

It was true that in Bubber there was a tough, mean streak. He was acting different today than he had ever acted before. Up until now he was always a quiet little kid who never really done anything mean. When anybody's feelings were hurt it always made him ashamed and nervous. Then how come he could do all the things he had done today?

They drove very slow out the Atlanta road. They passed the

last line of houses and came to the dark fields and woods. All along they had stopped to ask if anyone had seen Bubber. 'Has a little barefooted kid in corduroy knickers been by this way?' But even after they had gone about ten miles nobody had seen or noticed him. The wind came in cold and strong from the open windows and it was late at night.

They rode a little farther and then went back toward town. Her Dad and Mister Brannon wanted to look up all the children in the second grade, but she made them turn around and go back on the Atlanta road again. All the while she remembered the words she had said to Bubber. About Baby being dead and Sing Sing and Warden Lawes. About the small electric chairs that were just his size, and Hell. In the dark the words had sounded terrible.

They rode very slow for about half a mile out of town, and then suddenly she saw Bubber. The lights of the car showed him up in front of them very plain. It was funny. He was walking along the edge of the road and he had his thumb out trying to get a ride. Portia's butcher knife was stuck in his belt, and on the wide, dark road he looked so small that it was like he was five years old instead of seven.

They stopped the automobile and he ran to get in. He couldn't see who they were, and his face had the squint-eyed look it always had when he took aim with a marble. Her Dad held him by the collar. He hit with his fists and kicked. Then he had the butcher knife in his hand. Their Dad yanked it away from him just in time. He fought like a little tiger in a trap, but finally they got him into the car. Their Dad held him in his lap on the way home and Bubber sat very stiff, not leaning against anything.

They had to drag him into the house, and all the neighbors and the boarders were out to see the commotion. They dragged him into the front room and when he was there he backed off into a corner, holding his fists very tight and with his squinted eyes looking from one person to the other like he was ready to fight the whole crowd.

He hadn't said one word since they came into the house until he began to scream: 'Mick done it! I didn't do it. Mick done it!'

There were never any kind of yells like the ones Bubber made. The veins in his neck stood out and his fists were hard as little rocks.

'You can't get me! Nobody can get me!' he kept yelling.

Mick shook him by the shoulder. She told him the things she had said were stories. He finally knew what she was saying but he wouldn't hush. It looked like nothing could stop that screaming.

'I hate everybody! I hate everybody!'

They all just stood around. Mister Brannon rubbed his nose and looked down at the floor. Then finally he went out very quietly. Mister Singer was the only one who seemed to know what it was all about. Maybe this was because he didn't hear that awful noise. His face was still calm, and whenever Bubber looked at him he seemed to get quieter. Mister Singer was different from any other man, and at times like this it would be better if other people would let him manage. He had more sense and he knew things that ordinary people couldn't know. He just looked at Bubber, and after a while the kid quieted down enough so that their Dad could get him to bed.

In the bed he lay on his face and cried. He cried with long, big sobs that made him tremble all over. He cried for an hour and nobody in the three rooms could sleep. Bill moved to the living-room sofa and Mick got into bed with Bubber. He wouldn't let her touch him or snug up to him. Then after another hour of crying and hiccoughing he went to sleep.

She was awake a long time. In the dark she put her arms around him and held him very close. She touched him all over and kissed him everywhere. He was so soft and little and there was this salty, boy smell about him. The love she felt was so hard that she had to squeeze him to her until her arms were tired. In her mind she thought about Bubber and music together. It was like she could never do anything good enough for him. She would never hit him or even tease him again. She slept all night with her arms around his head. Then in the morning when she woke up he was gone.

But after that night there was not much of a chance for her to tease him any more — her or anybody else. After he shot Baby the kid was not ever like little Bubber again. He always kept his mouth shut and he didn't fool around with anybody. Most of the time he just sat in the back yard or in the coal house by himself. It got closer and closer toward Christmas time. She really wanted a piano, but naturally she didn't say anything about that. She told everybody she wanted a Mickey Mouse watch. When they asked Bubber what he wanted from Santa Claus he said he didn't want anything. He hid his marbles and jack-knife and wouldn't let anyone touch his story books.

After that night nobody called him Bubber any more. The big kids in the neighborhood started calling him Baby-Killer Kelly. But he didn't speak much to any person and nothing seemed to bother him. The family called him by his real name — George. At first Mick couldn't stop calling him Bubber and she didn't want to stop. But it was funny how after about a week she just naturally called him George like the others did. But he was a different kid — George — going around by himself always like a person much older and with nobody, not even her, knowing what was really in his mind.

She slept with him on Christmas Eve night. He lay in the dark without talking. 'Quit acting so peculiar,' she said to him. 'Less talk about the wise men and the way the children in Holland put out their wooden shoes instead of hanging up their stockings.'

George wouldn't answer. He went to sleep.

She got up at four o'clock in the morning and waked everybody in the family. Their Dad built a fire in the front room and then let them go in to the Christmas tree and see what they got. George had an Indian suit and Ralph a rubber doll. The rest of the family just got clothes. She looked all through her stocking for the Mickey Mouse watch but it wasn't there. Her presents were a pair of brown Oxford shoes and a box of cherry candy. While it was still dark she and George went out on the sidewalk and cracked nigger-toes and shot firecrackers and ate up the whole two-layer box of cherry candy. And by the time it was daylight they were sick to the stomach and tired out. She lay down on the sofa. She shut her eyes and went into the inside room.

6

AT EIGHT o'clock Doctor Copeland sat at his desk, studying a sheaf of papers by the bleak morning light from the window. Beside him the tree, a thick-fringed cedar, rose up dark and green to the ceiling. Since the first year he began to practice he had given an annual party on Christmas Day, and now all was in readiness. Rows of benches and chairs lined the walls of the front rooms. Throughout the house there was the sweet spiced odor of newly baked cake and steaming coffee. In the office with him Portia sat on a bench against the wall, her hands cupped beneath her chin, her body bent almost double.

'Father, you been scrouched over that desk since five o'clock. You got no business to be up. You ought to stayed in bed until time for the to-do.'

Doctor Copeland moistened his thick lips with his tongue So much was on his mind that he had no attention to give to Portia. Her presence fretted him.

At last he turned to her irritably. 'Why do you sit there moping?'

'I just got worries,' she said. 'For one thing, I worried about our Willie.'

'William?'

'You see he been writing me regular ever Sunday. The letter will get here on Monday or Tuesday. But last week he didn't write. Course I not really anxious. Willie — he always so good-natured and sweet I know he going to be all right. He been transferred from the prison to the chain gang and they going to work up somewhere north of Atlanta. Two weeks ago he wrote this here letter to say they going to attend a church service today, and he done asked me to send him his suit of clothes and his red tie.'

'Is that all William said?'

'He written that this Mr. B. F. Mason is at the prison, too. And that he run into Buster Johnston — he a boy Willie used to know. And also he done asked me to please send him his harp because he can't be happy without he got his harp to play on. I done sent everthing. Also a checker set and a white-iced cake. But I sure hope I hears from him in the next few days.'

Doctor Copeland's eyes glowed with fever and he could not rest his hands. 'Daughter, we shall have to discuss this later. It is getting late and I must finish here. You go back to the kitchen and see that all is ready.'

Portia stood up and tried to make her face bright and happy. 'What you done decided about that five-dollar prize?'

'As yet I have been unable to decide just what is the wisest course,' he said carefully.

A certain friend of his, a Negro pharmacist, gave an award of five dollars every year to the high-school student who wrote the best essay on a given subject. The pharmacist always made Doctor Copeland sole judge of the papers and the winner was announced at the Christmas party. The subject of the composition this year was 'My Ambition: How I Can Better the Position of the Negro Race in Society.'

There was only one essay worthy of real consideration. Yet this paper was so childish and ill-advised that it would hardly be prudent to confer upon it the award. Doctor Copeland put on his glasses and re-read the essay with deep concentration.

> This is my ambition. First I wish to attend Tuskegee College but I do not wish to be a man like Booker Washington or Doctor Carver. Then when I deem that my education is complete I wish to start off being a fine lawyer like the one who defended the Scottsboro Boys. I would only take cases for colored people against white people. Every day our people are made in every way and by every means to feel that they are inferior. This is not so. We are a Rising Race. And we cannot sweat beneath the white man's burdens for long. We cannot always sow where others reap.
>
> I want to be like Moses, who led the children of Israel from the land of the oppressors. I want to get up a Secret Organization of Colored Leaders and Scholars. All colored people will organize under the direction of these picked leaders and prepare for revolt. Other nations in the world who are interested in the plight of our race and who would like to see the United States divided would come to our aid. All colored people will organize and there will be a revolution, and at the close colored people will take all the territory east of the Mississippi and south of the Potomac. I shall set up a mighty country under the control of the Organization of Colored Leaders and Scholars. No white person will be allowed a passport — and if they get into the country they will have no legal rights.
>
> I hate the whole white race and will work always so that the colored race can achieve revenge for all their sufferings. That is my ambition.

Doctor Copeland felt the fever warm in his veins. The ticking of the clock on his desk was loud and the sound jarred his nerves. How could he give the award to a boy with such wild notions as this? What should he decide?

The other essays were without any firm content at all. The young people would not think. They wrote only about their ambitions and omitted the last part of the title altogether. Only one point was of some significance. Nine out of the lot of twenty-five began with the sentence, 'I do not want to be a servant.' After that they wished to fly airplanes, or be prizefighters, or preachers or dancers. One girl's sole ambition was to be kind to the poor.

The writer of the essay that troubled him was Lancy Davis. He had known the identity of the author before he turned the last sheet over and saw the signature. Already he had had some trouble with Lancy. His older sister had gone out to work as a servant when she was eleven years old and she had been raped by her employer, a white man past middle age. Then a year or so later he had received an emergency call to attend Lancy.

Doctor Copeland went to the filing case in his bedroom where he kept notes on all of his patients. He took out the card marked 'Mrs. Dan Davis and Family' and glanced through the notations until he reached Lancy's name. The date was four years ago. The entries on him were written with more care than the others and in ink: 'thirteen years old — past puberty. Unsuccessful attempt self-emasculation. Oversexed and hyperthyroid. Wept boisterously during two visits, though little pain. Voluble — very glad to talk though paranoiac. Environment fair with one exception. See Lucy Davis — mother washerwoman. Intelligent and well worth watching and all possible help. Keep contact. Fee: $1 (?)'

'It is a difficult decision to make this year,' he said to Portia. 'But I suppose I will have to confer the award on Lancy Davis.'

'If you done decide', then — come tell me about some of these here presents.'

The gifts to be distributed at the party were in the kitchen. There were paper sacks of groceries and clothing, all marked with a red Christmas card. Anyone who cared to come was invited to the party, but those who meant to attend had stopped by the house and written (or had asked a friend to write) their names in a guest book kept on the table in the hall for that purpose. The sacks were piled on the floor. There were about forty of them, each one depending in size on the need of the receiver. Some gifts were only small packages of nuts or raisins and others were boxes almost too heavy for a man to lift. The kitchen was crowded with good things. Doctor Copeland stood in the doorway and his nostrils quivered with pride.

'I think you done right well this year. Folks certainly have been kindly.'

'Pshaw!' he said. 'This is not a hundredth part of what is needed.'

'Now, there you go, Father! I know good and well you just as pleased as you can be. But you don't want to show it. You got to find something to grumble about. Here we haves about four pecks of peas, twenty sacks of meal, about fifteen pounds of side meat, mullet, six dozen eggs, plenty grits, jars of tomatoes and peaches. Apples and two dozen oranges. Also garments. And two mattresses and four blankets. I call this something!'

'A drop in the bucket.'

Portia pointed to a large box in the corner. 'These here — what you intend to do with them?'

The box contained nothing but junk — a headless doll, some dirty lace, a rabbitskin. Doctor Copeland scrutinized each article. 'Do not throw them away. There is use for everything. These are the gifts from our guests who have nothing better to contribute. I will find some purpose for them later.'

'Then suppose you look over these here boxes and sacks so I can commence to tie them up. There ain't going to be room here in the kitchen. Time they all pile in for the refreshments. I just going to put these here presents out on the back steps and in the yard.'

The morning sun had risen. The day would be bright and cold. In the kitchen there were rich, sweet odors. A dishpan of coffee was on the stove and iced cakes filled a shelf in the cupboard.

'And none of this comes from white people. All from Colored.'

'No,' said Doctor Copeland. 'That is not wholly true. Mr. Singer contributed a check for twelve dollars to be used for coal. And I have invited him to be present today.'

'Holy Jesus!' Portia said. 'Twelve dollars!'

'I felt that it was proper to ask him. He is not like other people of the Caucasian race.'

'You right,' Portia said. 'But I keep thinking about my Willie. I sure do wish he could enjoy this here party today. And I sure do wish I could get a letter from him. It just prey on my mind. But here! Us got to quit this here talking and get ready. It mighty near time for the party to come.'

Time enough remained. Doctor Copeland washed and clothed himself carefully. For a while he tried to rehearse what he would say when the people had all come. But expectation and restlessness would not let him concentrate. Then at ten o'clock the first guests arrived and within half an hour they were all assembled.

'Joyful Christmas gift to you!' said John Roberts, the postman. He moved happily about the crowded room, one shoulder held higher than the other, mopping his face with a white silk handkerchief.

'Many happy returns of the day!'

The front of the house was thronged. Guests were blocked at the door and they formed groups on the front porch and in the yard. There was no pushing or rudeness; the turmoil was orderly. Friends called out to each other and strangers were introduced and clasped hands. Children and young people clotted together and moved back toward the kitchen.

'Christmas gift!'

Doctor Copeland stood in the center of the front room by the tree. He was dizzy. He shook hands and answered salutations with confusion. Personal gifts, some tied elaborately with ribbons and others wrapped in newspaper, were thrust into his hands. He could find no place to put them. The air thickened and voices grew louder. Faces whirled about him so that he could recognize no one. His composure returned to him gradually. He found space to lay aside the presents in his arms. The dizziness lessened, the room cleared. He settled his spectacles and began to look around him.

'Merry Christmas! Merry Christmas!'

There was Marshall Nicolls, the pharmacist, in a long-tailed coat, conversing with his son-in-law who worked on a garbage truck. The preacher from the Most Holy Ascension Church had come. And two deacons from other churches. Highboy, wearing a loud checked suit, moved sociably through the crowd. Husky young dandies bowed to young women in long, bright-colored dresses. There were mothers with children and deliberate old men who spat into gaudy handkerchiefs. The room was warm and noisy.

Mr. Singer stood in the doorway. Many people stared at him. Doctor Copeland could not remember if he had welcomed him or not. The mute stood by himself. His face resembled somewhat a picture of Spinoza. A Jewish face. It was good to see him.

The doors and the windows were open. Draughts blew through the room so that the fire roared. The noises quieted. The seats were all filled and the young people sat in rows on the floor. The hall, the porch, even the yard were crowded with silent guests. The time had come for him to speak —

and what was he to say? Panic tightened his throat. The room waited. At a sign from John Roberts all sounds were hushed.

'My People,' began Doctor Copeland blankly. There was a pause. Then suddenly the words came to him.

'This is the nineteenth year that we have gathered together in this room to celebrate Christmas Day. When our people first heard of the birth of Jesus Christ it was a dark time. Our people were sold as slaves in this town on the courthouse square. Since then we have heard and told the story of His life more times than we could number. So today our story will be a different one.

'One hundred and twenty years ago another man was born in the country that is known as Germany — a country far across the Atlantic Ocean. This man understood as did Jesus. But his thoughts were not concerned with Heaven or the future of the dead. His mission was for the living. For the great masses of human beings who work and suffer and work until they die. For people who take in washing and work as cooks, who pick cotton and work at the hot dye vats of factories. His mission was for us, and the name of this man is Karl Marx.

'Karl Marx was a wise man. He studied and worked and understood the world around him. He said that the world was divided into two classes, the poor and the rich. For every rich man there were a thousand poor people who worked for this rich man to make him richer. He did not divide the world into Negroes or white people or Chinese — to Karl Marx it seemed that being one of the millions of poor people or one of the few rich was more important to a man than the color of his skin. The life mission of Karl Marx was to make all human beings equal and to divide the great wealth of the world so that there would be no poor or rich and each person would have his share. This is one of the commandments Karl Marx left to us: "From each according to his ability, to each according to his needs."'

A wrinkled, yellow palm waved timidly from the hall. 'Were he the Mark in the Bible?'

Doctor Copeland explained. He spelled the two names and cited dates. 'Are there any more questions? I wish each one of you to feel free to start or enter into any discussion.'

'I presume Mr. Marx was a Christian church man?' asked the preacher.

'He believed in the holiness of the human spirit.'

'Were he a white man?'

'Yes. But he did not think of himself as a white man. He said, "I consider nothing human as alien to myself." He thought of himself as a brother to all people.'

Doctor Copeland paused a moment longer. The faces around him were waiting.

'What is the value of any piece of property, of any merchandise we buy in a store? The value depends only on one thing — and that is the work it took to make or to raise this article. Why does a brick house cost more than a cabbage? Because the work of many men goes into the making of one brick house. There are the people who made the bricks and mortar and the people who cut down the trees to make the planks used for the floor. There are the men who made the building of the brick house possible. There are the men who carried the materials to the ground where the house was to be built. There are the men who made the wheelbarrows and trucks that carried the materials to this place. Then finally there are the workmen who built the house. A brick house involves the labor of many, many people — while any of us can raise a cabbage in his back yard. A brick house costs more than a cabbage because it takes more work to make. So when a man buys this brick house he is paying for the labor that went to make it. But who gets the money — the profit? Not the many men who did the work — but the bosses who control them. And if you study this further you will find that these bosses have bosses above them and those bosses have bosses higher up — so that the real people who control all this work, which makes any article worth money, are very few. Is this clear so far?'

'Us understand!'

But did they? He started all over and retold what he had said. This time there were questions.

'But don't clay for these here bricks cost money? And don't it take money to rent land and raise crops on?'

'That is a good point,' said Doctor Copeland. 'Land, clay, timber — those things are called natural resources. Man does not make these natural resources — man only develops them, only uses them for work. Therefore should any one person or group of persons own these things? How can a man own ground and space and sunlight and rain for crops? How can a man say "this is mine" about those things and refuse to let others share them? Therefore Marx says that these natural resources should belong to everyone, not divided into little pieces but used by all the people according to their ability to work. It is like this. Say a man died and left his mule to his four sons. The sons would not wish to cut up the mule into four parts and each take his share. They would own and work the mule together. That is the way Marx says all of the natural resources should be owned — not by one group of rich people but by all the workers of the world as a whole.

'We in this room have no private properties. Perhaps one or two of us may own the homes we live in, or have a dollar or two set aside — but we own nothing that does not contribute directly toward keeping us alive. All that we own is our bodies. And we sell our bodies every day we live. We sell them when we go out in the morning to our jobs and when we labor all the day. We are forced to sell at any price, at any time, for any purpose. We are forced to sell our bodies so that we can eat and live. And the price which is given us for this is only enough so that we will have the strength to labor longer for the profits of others. Today we are not put up on the platforms and sold at the courthouse square. But we are forced to sell our strength, our time, our souls during almost every hour that we live. We have been freed from one kind of slavery only to be delivered into another. Is this freedom? Are we yet free men?'

A deep voice called out from the front yard. 'That the real truth!'

'That how things is!'

'And we are not alone in this slavery. There are millions of others throughout the world, of all colors and races and creeds. This we must remember. There are many of our people who hate the poor of the white race, and they hate us. The people in this town living by the river who work in the mills. People who are almost as much in need as we are ourselves. This hatred is a great evil, and no good can ever come from it. We must remember the words of Karl Marx and see the truth according to his teachings. The injustice of need must bring us all together and not separate us. We must remember that we all make the things on this earth of value because of our labor. These main truths from Karl Marx we must keep in our hearts always and not forget.

'But my people! We in this room — we Negroes — have another mission that is for ourselves alone. Within us there is a strong, true purpose, and if we fail in this purpose we will be forever lost. Let us see, then, what is the nature of this special mission.'

Doctor Copeland loosened the collar of his shirt, for in his throat there was a choked feeling. The grievous love he felt within him was too much. He looked around him at the hushed guests. They waited. The groups of people in the yard and on the porch stood with the same quiet attention as did those in the room. A deaf old man leaned forward with his hand to his ear. A woman hushed a fretful baby with a pacifier. Mr. Singer stood attentively in the doorway. Most of the young people sat on the floor. Among them was Lancy

Davis. The boy's lips were nervous and pale. He clasped his knees very tightly with his arms, and his young face was sullen. All the eyes in the room watched, and in them there was hunger for truth.

'Today we are to confer the five-dollar award upon the high-school student who wrote the best essay on the topic, "My Ambition: How I Can Better the Position of the Negro Race in Society." This year the award goes to Lancy Davis.' Doctor Copeland took an envelope from his pocket. 'There is no need for me to tell you that the value of this award is not wholly in the sum of money it represents — but the sacred trust and faith that goes with it.'

Lancy rose awkwardly to his feet. His sullen lips trembled. He bowed and accepted the award. 'Do you wish me to read the essay I have written?'

'No,' said Doctor Copeland. 'But I wish you to come and talk with me sometime this week.'

'Yes, sir.' The room was quiet again.

'"I do not wish to be a servant!" That is the desire I have read over and over in these essays. Servant? Only one in a thousand of us is allowed to be a servant. We do not work! We do not serve!'

The laughter in the room was uneasy.

'Listen! One out of five of us labors to build roads, or to take care of the sanitation of this city, or works in a sawmill or on a farm. Another one out of the five is unable to get any work at all. But the other three out of this five — the greatest number of our people? Many of us cook for those who are incompetent to prepare the food that they themselves eat. Many work a lifetime tending flower gardens for the pleasure of one or two people. Many of us polish slick waxed floors of fine houses. Or we drive automobiles for rich people who are too lazy to drive themselves. We spend our lives doing thousands of jobs that are of no real use to anybody. We labor and all of our labor is wasted. Is that service? No, that is slavery.

'We labor, but our labor is wasted. We are not allowed to serve. You students here this morning represent the fortunate few of our race. Most of our people are not allowed to go to school at all. For each one of you there are dozens of young people who can hardly write their names. We are denied the dignity of study and wisdom.

'"From each according to his ability, to each according to his needs." All of us here know what it is to suffer for real need. That is a great injustice. But there is one injustice bitterer even than that — to be denied the right to work according to one's ability. To labor a lifetime uselessly. To be denied the chance to serve. It is far better for the profits of our purse to be taken from us than to be robbed of the riches of our minds and souls.

'Some of you young people here this morning may feel the need to be teachers or nurses or leaders of your race. But most of you will be denied. You will have to sell yourselves for a useless purpose in order to keep alive. You will be thrust back and defeated. The young chemist picks cotton. The young writer is unable to learn to read. The teacher is held in useless slavery at some ironing-board. We have no representatives in government. We have no vote. In all of this great country we are the most oppressed of all people. We cannot lift up our voice. Our tongues rot in our mouths from lack of use. Our hearts grow empty and lose strength for our purpose.

'People of the Negro race! We bring with us all the riches of the human mind and soul. We offer the most precious of all gifts. And our offerings are held in scorn and contempt. Our gifts are trampled in the mud and made useless. We are put to labor more useless than the work of beasts. Negroes! We must arise and be whole again! We must be free!'

In the room there was a murmur. Hysteria mounted. Doctor Copeland choked and clenched his fists. He felt as though he had swelled up to the size of a giant. The love in him made his chest a dynamo, and he wanted to shout so that his voice could be heard throughout the town. He wanted to fall upon the floor and call out in a giant voice. The room was full of moans and shouts.

'Save us!'

'Mighty Lord! Lead us from this wilderness of death!'

'Hallelujah! Save us, Lord!'

He struggled for the control in him. He struggled and at last the discipline returned. He pushed down the shout in him and sought for the strong, true voice.

'Attention!' he called. 'We will save ourselves. But not by prayers of mourning. Not by indolence or strong drink. Not by the pleasures of the body or by ignorance. Not by submission and humbleness. But by pride. By dignity. By becoming hard and strong. We must build strength for our real true purpose.'

He stopped abruptly and held himself very straight. 'Each year at this time we illustrate in our small way the first commandment from Karl Marx. Every one of you at this gathering has brought in advance some gift. Many of you have denied yourselves comfort that the needs of others may be lessened. Each of you has given according to his best ability, without thought to the value of the gift he will receive in return. It is natural for us to share with each other. We have long realized that it is more blessed to give than to receive. The words of Karl Marx have always been known in our hearts: "From each according to his ability, to each according to his needs."'

Doctor Copeland was silent a long time as though his words were complete. Then he spoke again:

'Our mission is to walk with strength and dignity through the days of our humiliation. Our pride must be strong, for we know the value of the human mind and soul. We must teach our children. We must sacrifice so that they may earn the dignity of study and wisdom. For the time will come.

The time will come when the riches in us will not be held in scorn and contempt. The time will come when we will be allowed to serve. When we will labor and our labor will not be wasted. And our mission is to await this time with strength and faith.'

It was finished. Hands were clapped, feet were stamped upon the floor and on the hard winter ground outside. The odor of hot, strong coffee floated from the kitchen. John Roberts took charge of the presents, calling out the names written on the cards. Portia ladled the coffee from the dishpan on the stove while Marshall Nicolls passed slices of cake. Doctor Copeland moved about among the guests, a little crowd always surrounding him.

Someone nagged at his elbow: 'He the one your Buddy named for?' He answered yes. Lancy Davis followed him with questions; he answered yes to everything. The joy made him feel like a drunken man. To teach and exhort and explain to his people — and to have them understand. That was the best of all. To speak the truth and be attended.

'Us certainly have had one fine time at this party.'

He stood in the vestibule saying good-bye. Over and over he shook hands. He leaned heavily against the wall and only his eyes moved, for he was tired.

'I certainly do appreciate.'

Mr. Singer was the last to leave. He was a truly good man. He was a white man of intellect and true knowledge. In him there was none of the mean insolence. When all had departed he was the last to remain. He waited and seemed to expect some final word.

Doctor Copeland held his hand to his throat because his larynx was sore. 'Teachers,' he said huskily. 'That is our greatest need. Leaders. Someone to unite and guide us.'

After the festivity the rooms had a bare, ruined look. The house was cold. Portia was washing the cups in the kitchen. The silver snow on the Christmas tree had been tracked over the floors and two of the ornaments were broken.

He was tired, but the joy and the fever would not let him rest. Beginning with the bedroom, he set to work to put the house in order. On top of the filing case there was a loose card — the note on Lancy Davis. The words that he would say to him began to form in his mind, and he was restless because he could not speak them now. The boy's sullen face was full of heart and he could not thrust it from his thoughts. He opened the top drawer of the file to replace the card. A, B, C — he thumbed through the letters nervously. Then his eye was fixed on his own name: Copeland, Benedict Mady.

In the folder were several lung X-rays and a short case history. He held an X-ray up to the light. On the upper left lung there was a bright place like a calcified star. And lower down a large clouded spot that duplicated itself in the right lung farther up. Doctor Copeland quickly replaced the X-rays in the folder. Only the brief notes he had written on himself were still in his hand. The words stretched out large and scrawling so that he could hardly read them. '1920 — calcif. of lymph glands — very pronounced thickening of hili. Lesions arrested — duties resumed. 1937 — lesion reopened — X-ray shows ——' He could not read the notes. At first he could not make out the words, and then when he read them clearly they made no reason. At the finish there were three words: 'Prognosis: Don't know.'

The old black, violent feeling came in him again. He leaned down and wrenched open a drawer at the bottom of the case. A jumbled pile of letters. Notes from the Association for the Advancement of Colored People. A yellowed letter from Daisy. A note from Hamilton asking for a dollar and a half. What was he looking for? His hands rummaged in the drawer and then at last he arose stiffly.

Time wasted. The past hour gone.

Portia peeled potatoes at the kitchen table. She was slumped over and her face was dolorous.

'Hold up your shoulders,' he said angrily. 'And cease moping. You mope and drool around until I cannot bear to look on you.'

'I were just thinking about Willie,' she said. 'Course the letter is only three days due. But he got no business to worry me like this. He not that kind of a boy. And I got this queer feeling.'

'Have patience, Daughter.'

'I reckon I have to.'

'There are a few calls I must make, but I will be back shortly.'

'O.K.'

'All will be well,' he said.

Most of his joy was gone in the bright, cool noonday sun. The diseases of his patients lay scattered in his mind. An abscessed kidney. Spinal meningitis. Pott's disease. He lifted the crank of the automobile from the back seat. Usually he hailed some passing Negro from the street to crank the car for him. His people were always glad to help and serve. But today he fitted the crank and turned it vigorously himself. He wiped the perspiration from his face with the sleeve of his overcoat and hurried to get beneath the wheel and on his way.

How much that he had said today was understood? How much would be of any value? He recalled the words he had used, and they seemed to fade and lose their strength. The words left unsaid were heavier on his heart. They rolled up to his lips and fretted them. The faces of his suffering people moved in a swelling mass before his eyes. And as he steered the automobile slowly down the street his heart turned with this angry, restless love.

7

THE town had not known a winter as cold as this one for years. Frost formed on the windowpanes and whitened the roofs of houses. The winter afternoons glowed with a hazy lemon light and shadows were a delicate blue. A thin coat of ice crusted the puddles in the streets, and it was said on the day after Christmas that only ten miles to the north there was a light fall of snow.

A change came over Singer. Often he went out for the long walks that had occupied him during the months when Antonapoulos was first gone. These walks extended for miles in every direction and covered the whole of the town. He rambled through the dense neighborhoods along the river that were more squalid than ever since the mills had been slack this winter. In many eyes there was a look of somber loneliness. Now that people were forced to be idle, a certain restlessness could be felt. There was a fervid outbreak of new beliefs. A young man who had worked at the dye vats in a mill claimed suddenly that a great holy power had come in him. He said it was his duty to deliver a new set of commandments from the Lord. The young man set up a tabernacle and hundreds of people came each night to roll on the ground and shake each other, for they believed that they were in the presence of something more than human. There was murder, too. A woman who could not make enough to eat believed that a foreman had cheated on her work tokens and she stabbed him in the throat. A family of Negroes moved into the end house on one of the most dismal streets, and this caused so much indignation that the house was burned and the black man beaten by his neighbors. But these were incidents. Nothing had really changed. The strike that was talked about never came off because they could not get together. All was the same as before. Even on the coldest nights the Sunny Dixie Show was open. The people dreamed and fought and slept as much as ever. And by habit they shortened their thoughts so that they would not wander out into the darkness beyond tomorrow.

Singer walked through the scattered odorous parts of town where the Negroes crowded together. There was more gaiety and violence here. Often the fine, sharp smell of gin lingered in the alleys. Warm, sleepy firelight colored the windows. Meetings were held in the churches almost every night. Comfortable little houses set off in plots of brown grass — Singer walked in these parts also. Here the children were huskier and more friendly to strangers. He roamed through the neighborhoods of the rich. There were houses, very grand and old, with white columns and intricate fences of wrought iron. He walked past the big brick houses where automobiles honked in driveways and where the plumes of smoke rolled lavishly from chimneys. And out to the very edges of the roads that led from the town to general stores where farmers came on Saturday nights and sat around the stove. He wandered often about the four main business blocks that were brightly lighted and then through the black, deserted alleys behind. There was no part of the town that Singer did not know. He watched the yellow squares of light reflect from a thousand windows. The winter nights were beautiful. The sky was a cold azure and the stars were very bright.

Often it happened now that he would be spoken to and stopped during these walks. All kinds of people became acquainted with him. If the person who spoke to him was a stranger, Singer presented his card so that his silence would be understood. He came to be known through all the town. He walked with his shoulders very straight and kept his hands always stuffed down into his pockets. His gray eyes seemed to take in everything around him, and in his face there was still the look of peace that is seen most often in those who are very wise or very sorrowful. He was always glad to stop with anyone who wished his company. For after all he was only walking and going nowhere.

Now it came about that various rumors started in the town concerning the mute. In the years before with Antonapoulos they had walked back and forth to work, but except for this they were always alone together in their rooms. No one had bothered about them then — and if they were observed it was the big Greek on whom attention was focused. The Singer of those years was forgotten.

So the rumors about the mute were rich and varied. The Jews said that he was a Jew. The merchants along the main street claimed he had received a large legacy and was a very rich man. It was whispered in one browbeaten textile union that the mute was an organizer for the C.I.O. A lone Turk who had roamed into the town years ago and who languished with his family behind the little store where they sold linens claimed passionately to his wife that the mute was Turkish. He said that when he spoke his language the mute understood. And as he claimed this his voice grew warm and he forgot to squabble with his children and he was full of plans and activity. One old man from the country said that the mute had come from somewhere near his home and that the mute's father had the finest tobacco crop in all the county. All these things were said about him.

Antonapoulos! Within Singer there was always the memory of his friend. At night when he closed his eyes the Greek's face was there in the darkness — round and oily, with a wise and gentle smile. In his dreams they were always together.

It was more than a year now since his friend had gone away. This year seemed neither long nor short. Rather is was removed from the ordinary sense of time — as when one is drunk or half-asleep. Behind each hour there was always his friend. And this buried life with Antonapoulos changed and developed as did the happenings around him. During the first few months he had thought most of the terrible weeks before Antonapoulos was taken away — of the trouble that followed his illness, of the summons for arrest, and the misery in trying to control the whims of his friend. He thought of times in the past when he and Antonapoulos had been unhappy. There was one recollection, far in the past, that came back to him several times.

They had no friends. Sometimes they would meet other mutes — there were three of them with whom they became acquainted during the ten years. But something always happened. One moved to another state the week after they met him. Another was married and had six children and did not talk with his hands. But it was their relation with the third of these acquaintances that Singer remembered when his friend was gone.

The mute's name was Carl. He was a sallow young man who worked in one of the mills. His eyes were pale yellow and his teeth so brittle and transparent that they seemed pale yellow also. In his blue overalls that hung limp over his skinny little body he was like a blue-and-yellow rag doll.

They invited him to dinner and arranged to meet him beforehand at the store where Antonapoulos worked. The Greek was still busy when they arrived. He was finishing a batch of caramel fudge in the cooking room at the back of the store. The fudge lay golden and glossy over the long marble-topped table. The air was warm and rich with sweet smells. Antonapoulos seemed pleased to have Carl watch him as he glided the knife down the warm candy and cut it into squares. He offered their new friend a corner of the fudge on the edge of his greased knife, and showed him the trick that he always performed for anyone when he wished to be liked. He pointed to a vat of syrup boiling on the stove and fanned his face and squinted his eyes to show how hot it was. Then he wet his hand in a pot of cold water, plunged it into the boiling syrup, and swiftly put it back into the water again. His eyes bulged and he rolled out his tongue as though he were in great agony. He even wrung his hand and hopped on one foot so that the building shook. Then he smiled suddenly and held out his hand to show that it was a joke and hit Carl on the shoulder.

It was a pale winter evening, and their breath clouded in the cold air as they walked with their arms interlocked down the street. Singer was in the middle and he left them on the sidewalk twice while he went into stores to shop. Carl and Antonapoulos carried the sacks of groceries, and Singer held to their arms tightly and smiled all the way home. Their rooms were cozy and he moved happily about, making conversation with Carl. After the meal the two of them talked while Antonapoulos watched with a slow smile. Often the big Greek would lumber to the closet and pour out drinks of gin. Carl sat by the window, only drinking when Antonapoulos pushed the glass into his face, and then taking solemn little sips. Singer could not ever remember his friend so cordial to a stranger before, and he thought ahead with pleasure to the time when Carl would visit them often.

Midnight had passed when the thing happened that ruined the festive party. Antonapoulos returned from one of his trips to the closet and his face had a glowering look. He sat on his bed and began to stare repeatedly at their new friend with expressions of offense and great disgust. Singer tried to make eager conversation to hide this strange behavior, but the Greek was persistent. Carl huddled in a chair, nursing his bony knees, fascinated and bewildered by the grimaces of the big Greek. His face was flushed and he swallowed timidly. Singer could ignore the situation no longer, so at last he asked Antonapoulos if his stomach pained him or if he perhaps felt bad and wished to go to sleep. Antonapoulos shook his head. He pointed to Carl and began to make all the gestures of obscenity which he knew. The disgust on his face was terrible to see. Carl was small with fear. At last the big

Greek ground his teeth and rose from his chair. Hurriedly Carl picked up his cap and left the room. Singer followed him down the stairs. He did not know how to explain his friend to this stranger. Carl stood hunched in the doorway downstairs, limp, with his peaked cap pulled down over his face. At last they shook hands and Carl went away.

Antonapoulos let him know that while they were not noticing, their guest had gone into the closet and drunk up all the gin. No amount of persuasion could convince Antonapoulos that it was he himself who had finished the bottle. The big Greek sat up in bed and his round face was dismal and reproachful. Large tears trickled slowly down to the neck of his undershirt and he could not be comforted. At last he went to sleep, but Singer was awake in the dark a long time. They never saw Carl again.

Then years later there was the time Antonapoulos took the rent money from the vase on the mantelpiece and spent it all on the slot machines. And the summer afternoon Antonapoulos went downstairs naked to get the paper. He suffered so from the summer heat. They bought an electric refrigerator on the installment plan, and Antonapoulos would suck the cubes of ice constantly and even let a few of them melt in the bed with him as he slept. And the time Antonapoulos got drunk and threw a bowl of macaroni in his face.

Those ugly memories wove through his thoughts during the first months like bad threads through a carpet. And then they were gone. All the times that they had been unhappy were forgotten. For as the year went on his thoughts of his friend spiraled deeper until he dwelt only with the Antonapoulos whom he alone could know.

This was the friend to whom he told all that was in his heart. This was the Antonapoulos who no one knew was wise but him. As the year passed his friend seemed to grow larger in his mind, and his face looked out in a very grave and subtle way from the darkness at night. The memories of his friend changed in his mind so that he remembered nothing that was wrong or foolish — only the wise and good.

He saw Antonapoulos sitting in a large chair before him. He sat tranquil and unmoving. His round face was inscrutable. His mouth was wise and smiling. And his eyes were profound. He watched the things that were said to him. And in his wisdom he understood.

This was the Antonapoulos who now was always in his thoughts. This was the friend to whom he wanted to tell things that had come about. For something had happened in this year. He had been left in an alien land. Alone. He had opened his eyes and around him there was much he could not understand. He was bewildered.

He watched the words shape on their lips.

We Negroes want a chance to be free at last. And freedom is only the right to contribute. We want to serve and to share, to labor and in turn consume that which is due to us. But you are the only white man I have ever encountered who realizes this terrible need of my people.

You see, Mister Singer? I got this music in me all the time. I got to be a real musician. Maybe I don't know anything now, but I will when I'm twenty. See, Mister Singer? And then I mean to travel in a foreign country where there's snow.

Let's finish up the bottle. I want a small one. For we were thinking of freedom. That's the word like a worm in my brain. Yes? No? How much? How little? The word is a signal for piracy and theft and cunning. We'll be free and the smartest will then be able to enslave the others. But! But there is another meaning to the word. Of all words this one is the most dangerous. We who know must be wary. The word makes us feel good — in fact the word is a great ideal. But it's with this ideal that the spiders spin their ugliest webs for us.

The last one rubbed his nose. He did not come often and he did not say much. He asked questions.

The four people had been coming to his rooms now for more than seven months. They never came together — always alone. And invariably he met them at the door with a cordial smile. The want for Antonapoulos was always with him — just as it had been the first months after his friend had gone — and it was better to be with any person than to be too long alone. It was like the time years ago when he had made a pledge to Antonapoulos (and even written it on a paper and tacked it on the wall above his bed) — a pledge that he would give up cigarettes, beer, and meat for one month. The first days had been very bad. He could not rest or be still. He visited Antonapoulos so much at the fruit store that Charles Parker was unpleasant to him. When he had finished all the engraving on hand he would dawdle around the front of the store with the watchmaker and the salesgirl or wander out to some soda fountain to drink a Coca-Cola. In those days being near any stranger was better than thinking alone about the cigarettes and beer and meat that he wanted.

At first he had not understood the four people at all. They talked and they talked — and as the months went on they talked more and more. He became so used to their lips that he understood each word they said. And then after a while he knew what each one of them would say before he began, because the meaning was always the same.

His hands were a torment to him. They would not rest. They twitched in his sleep, and sometimes he awoke to find them shaping the words in his dreams before his face. He did not like to look at his hands or to think about them. They were slender and brown and very strong. In the years before he had always tended them with care. In the winter he used oil to prevent chapping, and he kept the cuticles pushed down and his nails always filed to the shape of his finger-tips. He had loved to wash and tend his hands. But now he only scrubbed them roughly with a brush two times a day and stuffed them back into his pockets.

When he walked up and down the floor of his room he would crack the joints of his fingers and jerk at them until they ached. Or he would strike the palm of one hand with the fist of the other. And then sometimes when he was alone and his thoughts were with his friend his hands would begin to shape the words before he knew about it. Then when he realized he was like a man caught talking aloud to himself. It was almost as though he had done some moral wrong. The shame and the sorrow mixed together and he doubled his hands and put them behind him. But they would not let him rest.

Singer stood in the street before the house where he and Antonapoulos had lived. The late afternoon was smoky and gray. In the west there were streaks of cold yellow and rose. A ragged winter sparrow flew in patterns against the smoky sky and at last came to light on a gable of the house. The street was deserted.

His eyes were fixed on a window on the right side of the second story. This was their front room, and behind was the big kitchen where Antonapoulos had cooked all of their meals. Through the lighted window he watched a woman move back and forth across the room. She was large and vague against the light and she wore an apron. A man sat with the evening newspaper in his hand. A child with a slice of bread came to the window and pressed his nose against the pane. Singer saw the room just as he had left it — with the large bed for Antonapoulos and the iron cot for himself, the big overstuffed sofa and the camp chair. The broken sugar bowl used for an ash tray, the damp spot on the ceiling where the roof leaked, the laundry box in the corner. On late afternoons like this there would be no light in the kitchen except the glow from the oil-burners of the big stove. Antonapoulos always turned the wicks so that only a ragged fringe of gold and blue could be seen inside each burner. The room was warm and full of the good smells from the supper. Antonapoulos tasted the dishes with his wooden spoon and they drank glasses of red wine. On the linoleum rug before the stove the flames from the burners made luminous reflections — five little golden lanterns. As the milky twilight grew darker these little lanterns were more intense, so that when at last the night had come they burned with vivid purity. Supper was always ready by that time and they would turn on the light and draw their chairs to the table.

Singer looked down at the dark front door. He thought of them going out together in the morning and coming home at night. There was the broken place in the pavement where Antonapoulos had stumbled once and hurt his elbow. There was the mailbox where their bill from the light company came each month. He could feel the warm touch of his friend's arm against his fingers.

The street was dark now. He looked up at the window once more and he saw the strange woman and the man and the child in a group together. The emptiness spread in him. All was gone. Antonapoulos was away; he was not here to remember. The thoughts of his friend were somewhere else. Singer shut his eyes and tried to think of the asylum and the room that Antonapoulos was in tonight. He remembered the narrow white beds and the old men playing slapjack in the corner. He held his eyes shut tight, but that room would not become clear in his mind. The emptiness was very deep inside him, and after a while he glanced up at the window once more and started down the dark sidewalk where they had walked together so many times.

It was Saturday night. The main street was thick with people. Shivering Negroes in overalls loitered before the windows of the ten-cent store. Families stood in line before the ticket box of the movie and young boys and girls stared at the posters on display outside. The traffic from the automobiles was so dangerous that he had to wait a long time before crossing the street.

He passed the fruit store. The fruits were beautiful inside the windows — bananas, oranges, alligator pears, bright little cumquats, and even a few pineapples. But Charles Parker waited on a customer inside. The face of Charles Parker was very ugly to him. Several times when Charles Parker was away he had entered the store and stood around a long while. He had even gone to the kitchen in the back where Antonapoulos made the candies. But he never went into the store while Charles Parker was inside. They had both taken care to avoid each other since that day when Antonapoulos left on the bus. When they met in the street they always turned away without nodding. Once when he had wanted to send his friend a jar of his favorite tupelo honey he had ordered it from Charles Parker by mail so as not to be obliged to meet him.

Singer stood before the window and watched the cousin of his friend wait on a group of customers. Business was always good on Saturday night. Antonapoulos sometimes had to work as late as ten o'clock. The big automatic popcorn popper was near the door. A clerk shoved in a measure of kernels and the corn whirled inside the case like giant flakes of snow. The smell from the store was warm and familiar. Peanut hulls were trampled on the floor.

Singer passed on down the street. He had to weave his way carefully in the crowds to keep from being jostled. The streets were strung with red and green electric lights because of the holidays. People stood in laughing groups with their arms about each other. Young fathers nursed cold and crying babies on their shoulders. A Salvation Army girl in her red-and-blue bonnet tinkled a bell on the corner, and when she looked at Singer he felt obliged to drop a coin into the pot beside her. There were beggars, both Negro and white, who held out caps or crusty hands. The neon advertisements cast an orange glow on the faces of the crowd.

He reached the corner where he and Antonapoulos had once

seen a mad dog on an August afternoon. Then he passed the room above the Army and Navy Store where Antonapoulos had had his picture taken every pay-day. He carried many of the photographs in his pocket now. He turned west toward the river. Once they had taken a picnic lunch and crossed the bridge and eaten in a field on the other side.

Singer walked along the main street for about an hour. In all the crowd he seemed the only one alone. At last he took out his watch and turned toward the house where he lived. Perhaps one of the people would come this evening to his room. He hoped so.

He mailed Antonapoulos a large box of presents for Christmas. Also he presented gifts to each four of the people and to Mrs. Kelly. For all of them together he had bought a radio and put it on the table by the window. Doctor Copeland did not notice the radio. Biff Brannon noticed it immediately and raised his eyebrows. Jake Blount kept it turned on all the time he was there, at the same station, and as he talked he seemed to be shouting above the music, for the veins stood out on his forehead. Mick Kelly did not understand when she saw the radio. Her face was very red and she asked him over and over if it was really his and whether she could listen. She worked with a dial for several minutes before she got it to the place that suited her. She sat leaning forward in her chair with her hands on her knees, her mouth open and a pulse beating very fast in her temple. She seemed to listen all over to whatever it was she heard. She sat there the whole afternoon, and when she grinned at him once her eyes were wet and she rubbed them with her fists. She asked him if she could come in and listen sometimes when he was at work and he nodded yes. So for the next few days whenever he opened the door he found her by the radio. Her hand raked through her short rumpled hair and there was a look in her face he had never seen before.

One night soon after Christmas all four of the people chanced to visit him at the same time. This had never happened before. Singer moved about the room with smiles and refreshments and did his best in the way of politeness to make his guests comfortable. But something was wrong.

Doctor Copeland would not sit down. He stood in the doorway, hat in hand, and only bowed coldly to the others. They looked at him as though they wondered why he was there. Jake Blount opened the beers he had brought with him and the foam spilled down on his shirtfront. Mick Kelly listened to the music from the radio. Biff Brannon sat on the bed, his knees crossed, his eyes scanning the group before him and then becoming narrow and fixed.

Singer was bewildered. Always each of them had so much to say. Yet now that they were together they were silent. When they came in he had expected an outburst of some kind. In a vague way he had expected this to be the end of something. But in the room there was only a feeling of strain. His hands worked nervously as though they were pulling things unseen from the air and binding them together.

Jake Blount stood beside Doctor Copeland. 'I know your face. We run into each other once before — on the steps outside.'

Doctor Copeland moved his tongue precisely as though he clipped out his words with scissors. 'I was not aware that we were acquainted,' he said. Then his stiff body seemed to shrink. He stepped back until he was just outside the threshold of the room.

Biff Brannon smoked his cigarette composedly. The smoke lay in thin blue layers across the room. He turned to Mick and when he looked at her a blush reddened his face. He half-closed his eyes and in a moment his face was bloodless once more. 'And how are you getting on with your business now?'

'What business?' Mick asked suspiciously.

'Just the business of living,' he said. 'School — and so forth.'

'O.K., I reckon,' she said.

Each one of them looked at Singer as though in expectation. He was puzzled. He offered refreshments and smiled.

Jake rubbed his lips with the palm of his hand. He left off trying to make conversation with Doctor Copeland and sat down on the bed beside Biff. 'You know who it is that used to write those bloody warnings in red chalk on the fences and walls around the mills?'

'No,' Biff said. 'What bloody warnings?'

'Mostly from the Old Testament. I been wondering about that for a long time.'

Each person addressed his words mainly to the mute. Their thoughts seemed to converge in him as the spokes of a wheel lead to the center hub.

'The cold has been very unusual,' Biff said finally. 'The other day I was looking through some old records and I found that in the year 1919 the thermometer got down to ten degrees Fahrenheit. It was only sixteen degrees this morning, and that's the coldest since the big freeze that year.'

'There were icicles hanging off the roof of the coal house this morning,' Mick said.

'We didn't take in enough money last week to meet the payroll,' Jake said.

They discussed the weather some more. Each one seemed to be waiting for the others to go. Then on an impulse they all rose to leave at the same time. Doctor Copeland went first and the others followed him immediately. When they were gone Singer stood alone in the room, and as he did not understand the situation he wanted to forget it. He decided to write to Antonapoulos that night.

The fact that Antonapoulos could not read did not prevent Singer from writing to him. He had always known that his friend was unable to make out the meaning of words on paper, but as the months went by he began to imagine that perhaps he had been mistaken, that perhaps Antonapoulos only kept his knowledge of letters a secret from everyone. Also, it was possible there might be a deaf-mute at the asylum who could read his letters and then explain them to his friend. He thought of several justifications for his letters, for he always felt a great need to write to his friend when he was bewildered or sad. Once written, however, these letters were never mailed. He cut out the comic strips from the morning and evening papers and sent them to his friend each Sunday. And every month he mailed a postal money order. But the long letters he wrote to Antonapoulos accumulated in his pockets until he would destroy them.

When the four people had gone, Singer slipped on his warm gray overcoat and his gray felt hat and left his room. He always wrote his letters at the store. Also, he had promised to deliver a certain piece of work the next morning, and he wanted to finish it now so that there would be no question of delay. The night was sharp and frosty. The moon was full and rimmed with a golden light. The rooftops were black against the starlit sky. As he walked he thought of ways to begin his letter, but he had already reached the store before the first sentence was clear in his mind. He let himself into the dark store with his key and switched on the front lights.

He worked at the very end of the store. A cloth curtain separated his place from the rest of the shop so that it was like a small private room. Besides his workbench and chair there was a heavy safe in the corner, a lavatory with a greenish mirror, and shelves full of boxes and worn-out clocks. Singer rolled up the top of his bench and removed from its felt case the silver platter he had promised to have ready. Although the store was cold he took off his coat and turned up the blue-striped cuffs of his shirt so that they would not get in his way.

For a long time he worked at the monogram in the center of the platter. With delicate, concentrated strokes he guided the scriver on the silver. As he worked his eyes had a curiously penetrating look of hunger. He was thinking of his letter to his friend Antonapoulos. Midnight had passed before the work was finished. When he put the platter away his forehead was damp with excitement. He cleared his bench and began to write. He loved to shape words with a pen on paper and he formed the letters with as much care as if the paper had been a plate of silver.

My Only Friend:

I see from our magazine that the Society meets this year at a convention in Macon. They will have speakers and a four-course banquet. I imagine it. Remember we always planned to attend one of the conventions but we never did. I wish now that we had. I wish we were going to this one and I have imagined how it would be. But of course I could never go without you. They will come from many states and they will all be full of words and long dreams from the heart. There is also to be a special service at one of the churches and some kind of a contest with a gold medal for the prize. I write that I imagine all of this. I both do and do not. My hands have been still so long that it is difficult to remember how it is. And when I imagine the convention I think of all the guests being like you, my Friend.

I stood before our home the other day. Other people live in it now. Do you remember the big oak tree in front? The branches were cut back so as not to interfere with the telephone wires and the tree died. The limbs are rotten and there is a hollow place in the trunk. Also, the cat here at the store (the one you used to stroke and fondle) ate something poisonous and died. It was very sad.

Singer held the pen poised above the paper. He sat for a long while, erect and tense, without continuing the letter. Then he stood up and lighted himself a cigarette. The room was cold and the air had a sour stale odor — the mixed smells of kerosene and silver polish and tobacco. He put on his overcoat and muffler and began writing again with slow determination.

> You remember the four people I told you about when I was there. I drew their pictures for you, the black man, the young girl, the one with the mustache, and the man who owns the New York Café. There are some things I should like to tell you about them but how to put them in words I am not sure.
>
> They are all very busy people. In fact they are so busy that it will be hard for you to picture them. I do not mean that they work at their jobs all day and night but that they have much business in their minds always that does not let them rest. They come up to my room and talk to me until I do not understand how a person can open and shut his or her mouth so much without being weary. (However, the New York Café owner is different — he is not just like the others. He has a very black beard so that he has to shave twice daily, and he owns one of these electric razors. He watches. The others all have something they hate. And they all have something they love more than eating or sleeping or wine or friendly company. That is why they are always so busy.)
>
> The one with the mustache I think is crazy. Sometimes he speaks his words very clear like my teacher long ago at the school. Other times he speaks such a language that I cannot follow. Sometimes he is dressed in a plain suit, and the next time he will be black with dirt and smelling bad and in the overalls he wears to work. He will shake

his fist and say ugly drunken words that I would not wish you to know about. He thinks he and I have a secret together but I do not know what it is. And let me write you something hard to believe. He can drink three pints of Happy Days whiskey and still talk and walk on his feet and not wish for the bed. You will not believe this but it is true.

I rent my room from the girl's mother for $16 per month. The girl used to dress in short trousers like a boy but now she wears a blue skirt and a blouse. She is not yet a young lady. I like her to come and see me. She comes all the time now that I have a radio for them. She likes music. I wish I knew what it is she hears. She knows I am deaf but she thinks I know about music.

The black man is sick with consumption but there is not a good hospital for him to go to here because he is black. He is a doctor and he works more than anyone I have ever seen. He does not talk like a black man at all. Other Negroes I find it hard to understand because their tongues do not move enough for the words. This black man frightens me sometimes. His eyes are hot and bright. He asked me to a party and I went. He has many books. However, he does not own any mystery books. He does not drink or eat meat or attend the movies.

Yah Freedom and pirates. Yah Capital and Democrats, says the ugly one with the mustache. Then he contradicts himself and says, Freedom is the greatest of all ideals. I just got to get a chance to write this music in me and be a musician. I got to have a chance, says the girl. We are not allowed to serve, says the black Doctor. That is the Godlike need of my people. Aha, says the owner of the New York Café. He is a thoughtful one.

That is the way they talk when they come to my room. Those words in their heart do not let them rest, so they are always very busy. Then you would think when they are together they would be like those of the Society who meet at the convention in Macon this week. But that is not so. They all came to my room at the same time today. They sat like they were from different cities. They were even rude, and you know how I have always said that to be rude and not attend to the feelings of others is wrong. So it was like that. I do not understand, so I write it to you because I think you will understand. I have queer feelings. But I have written of this matter enough and I know you are weary of it. I am also.

It has been five months and twenty-one days now. All of that time I have been alone without you. The only thing I can imagine is when I will be with you again. If I cannot come to you soon I do not know what.

Singer put his head down on the bench and rested. The smell and the feel of the slick wood against his cheek reminded him of his schooldays. His eyes closed and he felt sick. There was only the face of Antonapoulos in his mind, and his longing for his friend was so sharp that he held his breath. After some time Singer sat up and reached for his pen.

The gift I ordered for you did not come in time for the Christmas box. I expect it shortly. I believe you will like it and be amused. I think of us always and remember everything. I long for the food you used to make. At the New York Café it is much worse than it used to be. I found a cooked fly in my soup not long ago. It was mixed with the vegetables and the noodles like letters. But that is nothing. The way I need you is a loneliness I cannot bear. Soon I will come again. My vacation is not due for six months more but I think I can arrange it before then. I think I will have to. I am not meant to be alone and without you who understand.

Always,
JOHN SINGER

It was two o'clock in the morning before he was home again. The big, crowded house was in darkness, but he felt his way carefully up three flights of stairs and did not stumble. He took from his pockets the cards he carried about with him, his watch, and his fountain pen. Then he folded his clothes neatly over the back of his chair. His gray-flannel pajamas were warm and soft. Almost as soon as he pulled the blankets to his chin he was asleep.

Out of the blackness of sleep a dream formed. There were dull yellow lanterns lighting up a dark flight of stone steps. Antonapoulos kneeled at the top of these steps. He was naked and he fumbled with something that he held above his head and gazed at it as though in prayer. He himself knelt halfway down the steps. He was naked and cold and he could not take his eyes from Antonapoulos and the thing he held above him. Behind him on the ground he felt the one with the mustache and the girl and the black man and the last one. They knelt naked and he felt their eyes on him. And behind them there were uncounted crowds of kneeling people in the darkness. His own hands were huge windmills and he stared fascinated at the unknown thing that Antonapoulos held. The yellow lanterns swayed to and fro in the darkness and all else was motionless. Then suddenly there was a ferment. In the upheaval the steps collapsed and he felt himself falling downward. He awoke with a jerk. The early light whitened the window. He felt afraid.

Such a long time had passed that something might have happened to his friend. Because Antonapoulos did not write to him he would not know. Perhaps his friend had fallen and hurt himself. He felt such an urge to be with him once more that he would arrange it at any cost — and immediately.

In the post-office that morning he found a notice in his box that a package had come for him. It was the gift he had ordered for Christmas that did not arrive in time. The gift was a very fine one. He had bought it on the installment plan to be paid for over a period of two years. The gift was a moving-picture machine for private use, with a half-dozen of the Mickey Mouse and Popeye comedies that Antonapoulos enjoyed.

Singer was the last to reach the store that morning. He handed the jeweler for whom he worked a formal written request for leave on Friday and Saturday. And although there were four weddings on hand that week, the jeweler nodded that he could go.

He did not let anyone know of the trip beforehand, but on leaving he tacked a note to his door saying that he would be absent for several days because of business. He traveled at night, and the train reached the place of his destination just as the red winter dawn was breaking.

In the afternoon, a little before time for the visiting hour, he went out to the asylum. His arms were loaded with the parts of the moving-picture machine and the basket of fruit he carried his friend. He went immediately to the ward where he had visited Antonapoulos before.

The corridor, the door, the rows of beds were just as he remembered them. He stood at the threshold and looked eagerly for his friend. But he saw at once that though all the chairs were occupied, Antonapoulos was not there.

Singer put down his packages and wrote at the bottom of one of his cards, 'Where is Spiros Antonapoulos?' A nurse came into the room and he handed her the card. She did not understand. She shook her head and raised her shoulders. He went out into the corridor and handed the card to everyone he met. Nobody knew. There was such a panic in him that he began motioning with his hands. At last he met an interne in a white coat. He plucked at the interne's elbow and gave him the card. The interne read it carefully and then guided him through several halls. They came to a small room where a young woman sat at a desk before some papers. She read the card and then looked through some files in a drawer.

Tears of nervousness and fear swam in Singer's eyes. The young woman began deliberately to write on a pad of paper, and he could not restrain himself from twisting around to see immediately what was being written about his friend.

Mr. Antonapoulos has been transferred to the infirmary. He is ill with nephritis. I will have someone show you the way.

On the way through the corridors he stopped to pick up the packages he had left at the door of the ward. The basket of fruit had been stolen, but the other boxes were intact. He followed the interne out of the building and across a plot of grass to the infirmary.

Antonapoulos! When they reached the proper ward he saw him at the first glance. His bed was placed in the middle of the room and he was sitting propped with pillows. He wore a scarlet dressing-gown and green silk pajamas and a turquoise ring. His skin was a pale yellow color, his eyes very dreamy and dark. His black hair was touched at the temples with silver. He was knitting. His fat fingers worked with the long ivory needles very slowly. At first he did not see his friend. Then when Singer stood before him he smiled serenely, without surprise, and held out his jeweled hand.

A feeling of shyness and restraint such as he had never known before came over Singer. He sat down by the bed and folded his hands on the edge of the counterpane. His eyes did not leave the face of his friend and he was deathly pale. The splendor of his friend's raiment startled him. On various occasions he had sent him each article of the outfit, but he had not imagined how they would look when all combined. Antonapoulos was more enormous than he had remembered. The great pulpy folds of his abdomen showed beneath his silk pajamas. His head was immense against the white pillow. The placid composure of his face was so profound that he seemed hardly to be aware that Singer was with him.

Singer raised his hands timidly and began to speak. His strong, skilled fingers shaped the signs with loving precision. He spoke of the cold and of the long months alone. He mentioned old memories, the cat that had died, the store, the place where he lived. At each pause Antonapoulos nodded graciously. He spoke of the four people and the long visits to his room. The eyes of his friend were moist and dark, and in them he saw the little rectangled pictures of himself that he had watched a thousand times. The warm blood flowed back to his face and his hands quickened. He spoke at length of the black man and the one with the jerking mustache and the girl. The designs of his hands shaped faster and faster. Antonapoulos nodded with slow gravity. Eagerly Singer leaned closer and he breathed with long, deep breaths and in his eyes there were bright tears.

Then suddenly Antonapoulos made a slow circle in the air with his plump forefinger. His finger circled toward Singer and at last he poked his friend in the stomach. The big Greek's smile grew very broad and he stuck out his fat, pink tongue. Singer laughed and his hands shaped the words with wild speed. His shoulders shook with laughter and his head hung backward. Why he laughed he did not know. Antonapoulos rolled his eyes. Singer continued to laugh riotously until his breath was gone and his fingers trembled. He grasped the arm of his friend and tried to steady himself. His laughs came slow and painfully like hiccoughs.

Antonapoulos was the first to compose himself. His fat little feet had untucked the cover at the bottom of the bed.

His smile faded and he kicked contemptuously at the blanket. Singer hastened to put things right, but Antonapoulos frowned and held up his finger regally to a nurse who was passing through the ward. When she had straightened the bed to his liking the big Greek inclined his head so deliberately that the gesture seemed one of benediction rather than a simple nod of thanks. Then he turned gravely to his friend again.

As Singer talked he did not realize how the time had passed. Only when a nurse brought Antonapoulos his supper on a tray did he realize that it was late. The lights in the ward were turned on and outside the windows it was almost dark. The other patients had trays of supper before them also. They had put down their work (some of them wove baskets, others did leatherwork or knitted) and they were eating listlessly. Beside Antonapoulos they all seemed very sick and colorless. Most of them needed a haircut and they wore seedy gray nightshirts slit down the back. They stared at the two mutes with wonder.

Antonapoulos lifted the cover from his dish and inspected the food carefully. There was fish and some vegetables. He picked up the fish and held it to the light in the palm of his hand for a thorough examination. Then he ate with relish. During supper he began to point out the various people in the room. He pointed to one man in the corner and made faces of disgust. The man snarled at him. He pointed to a young boy and smiled and nodded and waved his plump hand. Singer was too happy to feel embarrassment. He picked up the packages from the floor and laid them on the bed to distract his friend. Antonapoulos took off the wrappings, but the machine did not interest him at all. He turned back to his supper.

Singer handed the nurse a note explaining about the movie. She called an interne and then they brought in a doctor. As the three of them consulted they looked curiously at Singer. The news reached the patients and they propped up on their elbows excitedly. Only Antonapoulos was not disturbed.

Singer had practiced with the movie beforehand. He set up the screen so that it could be watched by all the patients. Then he worked with the projector and the film. The nurse took out the supper trays and the lights in the ward were turned off. A Mickey Mouse comedy flashed on the screen.

Singer watched his friend. At first Antonapoulos was startled. He heaved himself up for a better view and would have risen from the bed if the nurse had not restrained him. Then he watched with a beaming smile. Singer could see the other patients calling out to each other and laughing. Nurses and orderlies came in from the hall and the whole ward was in commotion. When the Mickey Mouse was finished Singer put on a Popeye film. Then at the conclusion of this film he felt that the entertainment had lasted long enough for the first time. He switched on the light and the ward settled down again. As the interne put the machine under his friend's bed he saw Antonapoulos slyly cut his eyes across the ward to be certain that each person realized that the machine was his.

Singer began to talk with his hands again. He knew that he would soon be asked to leave, but the thoughts he had stored in his mind were too big to be said in a short time. He talked with frantic haste. In the ward there was an old man whose head shook with palsy and who picked feebly at his eyebrows. He envied the old man because he lived with Antonapoulos day after day. Singer would have exchanged places with him joyfully.

His friend fumbled for something in his bosom. It was the little brass cross that he had always worn. The dirty string had been replaced by a red ribbon. Singer thought of the dream and he told that, also, to his friend. In his haste the signs sometimes became blurred and he had to shake his hands and begin all over. Antonapoulos watched him with his dark, drowsy eyes. Sitting motionless in his bright, rich garments he seemed like some wise king from a legend.

The interne in charge of the ward allowed Singer to stay for an hour past the visiting time. Then at last he held out his thin, hairy wrist and showed him his watch. The patients were settled for sleep. Singer's hand faltered. He grasped his friend by the arm and looked intently into his eyes as he used to do each morning when they parted for work. Finally Singer backed himself out of the room. At the doorway his hands signed a broken farewell and then clenched into fists.

During the moonlit January nights Singer continued to walk about the streets of the town each evening when he was not engaged. The rumors about him grew bolder. An old Negro woman told hundreds of people that he knew the ways of spirits come back from the dead. A certain piece-worker claimed that he had worked with the mute at another mill somewhere else in the state — and the tales he told were unique. The rich thought that he was rich and the poor considered him a poor man like themselves. And as there was no way to disprove these rumors they grew marvelous and very real. Each man described the mute as he wished him to be.

8

WHY?

The question flowed through Biff always, unnoticed, like the blood in his veins. He thought of people and of objects and of ideas and the question was in him. Midnight, the dark morning, noon. Hitler and the rumors of war. The price of loin of pork and the tax on beer. Especially he meditated on the puzzle of the mute. Why, for instance, did Singer go away on the train and, when he was asked where he had been, pretend that he did not understand the question? And why did everyone persist in thinking the mute was exactly as they wanted him to be — when most likely it was all a very queer mistake? Singer sat at the middle table three times a day. He ate what was put before him — except cabbage and oysters. In the battling tumult of voices he alone was silent. He liked best little green soft butter beans and he stacked them in a neat pile on the prongs of his fork. And sopped their gravy with his biscuits.

Biff thought also of death. A curious incident occurred. One day while rummaging through the bathroom closet he found a bottle of Agua Florida that he had overlooked when taking Lucile the rest of Alice's cosmetics. Meditatively he held the bottle of perfume in his hands. It was four months now since her death — and each month seemed as long and full of leisure as a year. He seldom thought of her.

Biff uncorked the bottle. He stood shirtless before the mirror and dabbed some of the perfume on his dark, hairy armpits. The scent made him stiffen. He exchanged a deadly secret glance with himself in the mirror and stood motionless. He was stunned by the memories brought to him with the perfume, not because of their clarity, but because they gathered together the whole long span of years and were complete. Biff rubbed his nose and looked sideways at himself. The boundary of death. He felt in him each minute that he had lived with her. And now their life together was whole as only the past can be whole. Abruptly Biff turned away.

The bedroom was done over. His entirely now. Before it had been tacky and flossy and drab. There were always stockings and pink rayon knickers with holes in them hung on a string across the room to dry. The iron bed had been flaked and rusty, decked with soiled lace boudoir pillows. A bony mouser from downstairs would arch its back and rub mournfully against the slop jar.

All of this he had changed. He traded the iron bed for a studio couch. There was a thick red rug on the floor, and he had bought a beautiful cloth of Chinese blue to hang on the side of the wall where the cracks were worst. He had unsealed the fireplace and kept it laid with pine logs. Over the mantel was a small photograph of Baby and a colored picture of a little boy in velvet holding a ball in his hands. A glassed case in the corner held the curios he had collected — specimens of butterflies, a rare arrowhead, a curious rock shaped like a human profile. Blue-silk cushions were on the studio couch, and he had borrowed Lucile's sewing-machine to make deep red curtains for the windows. He loved the room. It was both luxurious and sedate. On the table there was a little Japanese pagoda with glass pendants that tinkled with strange musical tones in a draught.

In this room nothing reminded him of her. But often he would uncork the bottle of Agua Florida and touch the stopper to the lobes of his ears or to his wrists. The smell mingled with his slow ruminations. The sense of the past grew in him. Memories built themselves with almost architectural order. In a box where he stored souvenirs he came across old pictures taken before their marriage. Alice sitting in a field of daisies. Alice with him in a canoe on the river. Also among the souvenirs there was a large bone hairpin that had belonged to his mother. As a little boy he had loved to watch her comb and knot her long black hair. He had thought that hairpins were curved as they were to copy the shape of a lady and he would sometimes play with them like dolls. At that time he had a cigar box full of scraps. He loved the feel and colors of beautiful cloth and he would sit with his scraps for hours under the kitchen table. But when he was six his mother took the scraps away from him. She was a tall, strong woman with a sense of duty like a man. She had loved him best. Even now he sometimes dreamed of her. And her worn gold wedding ring stayed on his finger always.

Along with the Agua Florida he found in the closet a bottle of lemon rinse Alice had always used for her hair. One day he tried it on himself. The lemon made his dark, white-streaked hair seem fluffy and thick. He liked it. He discarded the oil he had used to guard against baldness and rinsed with the lemon preparation regularly. Certain whims that he had ridiculed in Alice were now his own. Why?

Every morning Louis, the colored boy downstairs, brought him a cup of coffee to drink in bed. Often he sat propped on the pillows for an hour before he got up and dressed. He smoked a cigar and watched the patterns the sunlight made on the wall. Deep in meditation he ran his forefinger between his long, crooked toes. He remembered.

Then from noon until five in the morning he worked downstairs. And all day Sunday. The business was losing money. There were many slack hours. Still at meal-times the place was usually full and he saw hundreds of acquaintances every day as he stood guard behind the cash register.

'What do you stand and think about all the time?' Jake Blount asked him. 'You look like a Jew in Germany.'

'I am an eighth part Jew,' Biff said. 'My Mother's grandfather was a Jew from Amsterdam. But all the rest of my folks that I know about were Scotch-Irish.'

It was Sunday morning. Customers lolled at the tables and there were the smell of tobacco and the rustle of newspaper. Some men in a corner booth shot dice, but the game was a quiet one.

'Where's Singer?' Biff asked. 'Won't you be going up to his place this morning?'

Blount's face turned dark and sullen. He jerked his head forward. Had they quarreled — but how could a dummy quarrel? No, for this had happened before. Blount hung around sometimes and acted as though he were having an argument with himself. But pretty soon he would go — he always did — and the two of them would come in together, Blount talking.

'You live a fine life. Just standing behind a cash register. Just standing with your hand open.'

Biff did not take offense. He leaned his weight on his elbows and narrowed his eyes. 'Let's me and you have a serious talk. What is it you want anyway?'

Blount smacked his hands down on the counter. They were warm and meaty and rough. 'Beer. And one of them little packages of cheese crackers with peanut butter in the inside.'

'That's not what I meant,' Biff said. 'But we'll come around to it later.'

The man was a puzzle. He was always changing. He still drank like a crazy fish, but liquor did not drag him down as it did some men. The rims of his eyes were often red, and he had a nervous trick of looking back startled over his shoulder. His head was heavy and huge on his thin neck. He was the sort of fellow that kids laughed at and dogs wanted to bite. Yet when he was laughed at it cut him to the quick — he got rough and loud like a sort of clown. And he was always suspecting that somebody was laughing.

Biff shook his head thoughtfully. 'Come,' he said. 'What makes you stick with that show? You can find something better than that. I could even give you a part-time job here.'

'Christamighty! I wouldn't park myself behind that cash box if you was to give me the whole damn place, lock, stock, and barrel.'

There he was. It was irritating. He could never have friends or even get along with people.

'Talk sense,' Biff said. 'Be serious.'

A customer had come up with his check and he made change. The place was still quiet. Blount was restless. Biff felt him drawing away. He wanted to hold him. He reached for two A-1 cigars on the shelf behind the counter and offered Blount a smoke. Warily his mind dismissed one question after another, and then finally he asked:

'If you could choose the time in history you could have lived, what era would you choose?'

Blount licked his mustache with his broad, wet tongue.

'If you had to choose between being a stiff and never asking another question, which would you take?'

'Sure enough,' Biff insisted. 'Think it over.'

He cocked his head to one side and peered down over his long nose. This was a matter he liked to hear others talk about. Ancient Greece was his. Walking in sandals on the edge of the blue Aegean. The loose robes girdled at the waist. Children. The marble baths and the contemplations in the temples.

'Maybe with the Incas. In Peru.'

Biff's eyes scanned over him, stripping him naked. He saw Blount burned a rich, red brown by the sun, his face smooth and hairless, with a bracelet of gold and precious stones on his forearm. When he closed his eyes the man was a good Inca. But when he looked at him again the picture fell away. It was the nervous mustache that did not belong to his face, the way he jerked his shoulder, the Adam's apple on his thin neck, the bagginess of his trousers. And it was more than that.

'Or maybe around 1775.'

'That was a good time to be living,' Biff agreed.

Blount shuffled his feet self-consciously. His face was rough and unhappy. He was ready to leave. Biff was alert to detain him. 'Tell me — why did you ever come to this town anyway?' He knew immediately that the question had not been a politic one and he was disappointed with himself. Yet it was queer how the man could land up in a place like this.

'It's the God's truth I don't know.'

They stood quietly for a moment, both leaning on the counter. The game of dice in the corner was finished. The first dinner order, a Long Island duck special, had been served to the fellow who managed the A. and P. store. The radio was turned halfway between a church sermon and a swing band.

Blount leaned over suddenly and smelled in Biff's face.

'Perfume?'

'Shaving lotion,' Biff said composedly.

He could not keep Blount longer. The fellow was ready to go. He would come in with Singer later. It was always like this. He wanted to draw Blount out completely so that he could understand certain questions concerning him. But Blount would never really talk — only to the mute. It was a most peculiar thing.

'Thanks for the cigar,' Blount said. 'See you later.'

'So long.'

Biff watched Blount walk to the door with his rolling, sailor-like gait. Then he took up the duties before him. He looked over the display in the window. The day's menu had been pasted on the glass and a special dinner with all the trimmings was laid out to attract customers. It looked bad. Right nasty. The gravy from the duck had run into the cranberry sauce and a fly was stuck in the dessert.

'Hey, Louis!' he called. 'Take this stuff out the window. And bring me that red pottery bowl and some fruit.'

He arranged the fruits with an eye for color and design. At last the decoration pleased him. He visited the kitchen and had a talk with the cook. He lifted the lids of the pots and sniffed the food inside, but without heart for the matter. Alice always had done this part. He disliked it. His nose sharpened when he saw the greasy sink with its scum of food bits at the bottom. He wrote down the menus and the orders for the next day. He was glad to leave the kitchen and take his stand by the cash register again.

Lucile and Baby came for Sunday dinner. The little kid was not so good now. The bandage was still on her head and the doctor said it could not come off until next month. The binding of gauze in place of the yellow curls made her head look naked.

'Say hello to Uncle Biff, Hon,' Lucile prompted.

Baby bridled fretfully. 'Hello to Unca Biff Hon,' she sassed.

She put up a struggle when Lucile tried to take off her Sunday coat. 'Now you just behave yourself,' Lucile kept saying. 'You got to take it off or you'll catch pneumonia when we go out again. Now you just behave yourself.'

Biff took the situation in charge. He soothed Baby with a ball of candy gum and eased the coat from her shoulders. Her dress had lost its set in the struggle with Lucile. He straightened it so that the yoke was in line across her chest. He retied her sash and crushed the bow to just the right shape with his fingers. Then he patted Baby on her little behind. 'We got some strawberry ice cream today,' he said.

'Bartholomew, you'd make a mighty good mother.'

'Thanks,' Biff said. 'That's a compliment.'

'We just been to Sunday School and church. Baby, say the verse from the Bible you learned for your Uncle Biff.'

The kid hung back and pouted. 'Jesus wept,' she said finally. The scorn that she put in the two words made it sound like a terrible thing.

'Want to see Louis?' Biff asked. 'He's back in the kitchen.'

'I wanna see Willie. I wanna hear Willie play the harp.'

'Now, Baby, you're just trying yourself,' Lucile said impatiently. 'You know good and well that Willie's not here. Willie was sent off to the penitentiary.'

'But Louis,' Biff said. 'He can play the harp, too. Go tell him to get the ice cream ready and play you a tune.'

Baby went toward the kitchen, dragging one heel on the floor. Lucile laid her hat on the counter. There were tears in her eyes. 'You know I always said this: If a child is kept clean and well cared for and pretty then that child will usually be sweet and smart. But if a child's dirty and ugly then you can't expect anything much. What I'm trying to get at is that Baby is so shamed over losing her hair and that bandage on her head that it just seems like it makes her cut the buck all the time. She won't practice her elocution — she won't do a thing. She feels so bad I just can't manage her.'

'If you'd quit picking with her so much she'd be all right.'

At last he settled them in a booth by the window. Lucile had a special and there was a breast of chicken cut up fine, cream of wheat, and carrots for Baby. She played with her food and spilled milk on her little frock. He sat with them until the rush started. Then he had to be on his feet to keep things going smoothly.

People eating. The wide-open mouths with the food pushed in. What was it? The line he had read not long ago. Life was only a matter of intake and alimentation and reproduction. The place was crowded. There was a swing band on the radio.

Then the two he was waiting for came in. Singer entered the door first, very straight and swank in his tailored Sunday suit. Blount followed along just behind his elbow. There was something about the way they walked that struck him. They sat at their table, and Blount talked and ate with gusto while Singer watched politely. When the meal was finished they stopped by the cash register for a few minutes. Then as they went out he noticed again there was something about their walking together that made him pause and question himself. What could it be? The suddenness with which the memory opened up deep down in his mind was a shock. The big deaf-mute moron whom Singer used to walk with sometimes on the way to work. The sloppy Greek who made candy for Charles Parker. The Greek always walked ahead and Singer followed. He had never noticed them much because they never came into the place. But why had he not remembered this? Of all times he had wondered about the mute to neglect such an angle. See everything in the landscape except the three waltzing elephants. But did it matter after all?

Biff narrowed his eyes. How Singer had been before was not important. The thing that mattered was the way Blount and Mick made of him a sort of home-made God. Owing to the fact he was a mute they were able to give him all the qualities they wanted him to have. Yes. But how could such a strange thing come about? And why?

A one-armed man came in and Biff treated him to a whiskey on the house. But he did not feel like talking to anyone. Sunday dinner was a family meal. Men who drank beer by themselves on weeknights brought their wives and little kids with them on Sunday. The highchair they kept in the back was often needed. It was two-thirty and though many tables were occupied the meal was almost over. Biff had been on his feet for the past four hours and was tired. He used to stand for fourteen or sixteen hours and not notice any effects at all. But now he had aged. Considerably. There was no doubt about it. Or maybe matured was the word. Not aged—certainly not — yet. The waves of sound in the room swelled and subsided against his ears. Matured. His eyes smarted and it was as though some fever in him made everything too bright and sharp.

He called to one of the waitresses: 'Take over for me will you, please? I'm going out.'

The street was empty because of Sunday. The sun shone bright and clear, without warmth. Biff held the collar of his coat close to his neck. Alone in the street he felt out of pocket. The wind blew cold from the river. He should turn back and stay in the restaurant where he belonged. He had no business going to the place where he was headed. For the past four Sundays he had done this. He had walked in the neighborhood where he might see Mick. And there was something about it that was — not quite right. Yes. Wrong.

He walked slowly down the sidewalk opposite the house where she lived. Last Sunday she had been reading the funny papers on the front steps. But this time as he glanced swiftly toward the house he saw she was not there. Biff tilted the brim of his felt hat down over his eyes. Perhaps she would come into the place later. Often on Sunday after supper she came for a hot cocoa and stopped for a while at the table where Singer was sitting. On Sunday she wore a different outfit from the blue skirt and sweater she wore on other days. Her Sunday dress was wine-colored silk with a dingy lace collar. Once she had had on stockings — with runs in them. Always he wanted to set her up to something, to give to her. And not only a sundae or some sweet to eat — but something real. That was all he wanted for himself — to give to her. Biff's mouth hardened. He had done nothing wrong but in him he felt a strange guilt. Why? The dark guilt in all men, unreckoned and without a name.

On the way home Biff found a penny lying half concealed by rubbish in the gutter. Thriftily he picked it up, cleaned the coin with his handkerchief, and dropped it into the black pocket purse he carried. It was four o'clock when he reached the restaurant. Business was stagnant. There was not a single customer in the place.

Business picked up around five. The boy he had recently hired to work part time showed up early. The boy's name was Harry Minowitz. He lived in the same neighborhood with Mick and Baby. Eleven applicants had answered the ad in the paper, but Harry seemed to be best bet. He was well developed for his age, and neat. Biff had noticed the boy's teeth while talking to him during the interview. Teeth were always a good indication. His were large and very clean and white. Harry wore glasses, but that would not matter in the work. His mother made ten dollars a week sewing for a tailor down the street, and Harry was an only child.

'Well,' Biff said. 'You've been with me a week, Harry Think you're going to like it?'

'Sure, sir. Sure I like it.'

Biff turned the ring on his finger. 'Let's see. What time do you get off from school?'

'Three o'clock, sir.'

'Well, that gives you a couple of hours for study and recreation. Then here from six to ten. Does that leave you enough time for plenty of sleep.'

'Plenty. I don't need near that much.'

'You need about nine and a half hours at your age, son. Pure, wholesome sleep.'

He felt suddenly embarrassed. Maybe Harry would think it was none of his business. Which it wasn't anyway. He started to turn aside and then thought of something.

'You go to Vocational?'

Harry nodded and rubbed his glasses on his shirtsleeve.

'Let's see. I know a lot of girls and boys there. Alva Richards — I know his father. And Maggie Henry. And a kid named Mick Kelly ——' He felt as though his ears had caught afire. He knew himself to be a fool. He wanted to turn and walk away and yet he only stood there, smiling and mashing his nose with his thumb. 'You know her?' he asked faintly.

'Sure, I live right next door to her. But in school I'm a senior while she's a freshman.'

Biff stored this meager information neatly in his mind to be thought over later when he was alone. 'Business will be quiet here for a while,' he said hurriedly. 'I'll leave it with you. By now you know how to handle things. Just watch any customers drinking beer and remember how many they've drunk so you won't have to ask them and depend on what they say. Take your time making change and keep track of what goes on.'

Biff shut himself in his room downstairs. This was the place where he kept his files. The room had only one small window that looked out on the side alley, and the air was musty and cold. Huge stacks of newspapers rose up to the ceiling. A home-made filing case covered one wall. Near the door there was an old-fashioned rocking-chair and a small table laid with a pair of shears, a dictionary, and a mandolin. Because of the piles of newspaper it was impossible to take more than two steps in any direction. Biff rocked himself in the chair and languidly plucked the strings of the mandolin. His eyes closed and he began to sing in a doleful voice:

I went to the animal fair.
The birds and the beasts were there,
And the old baboon by the light of the moon
Was combing his auburn hair.

He finished with a chord from the strings and the last sounds shivered to silence in the cold air.

To adopt a couple of little children. A boy and a girl. About three or four years old so they would always feel like he was their own father. Their Dad. Our Father. The little girl like Mick (or Baby?) at that age. Round cheeks and gray eyes and flaxen hair. And the clothes he would make for her — pink crêpe de Chine frocks with dainty smocking at the yoke and sleeves. Silk socks and white buckskin shoes. And a little red-velvet coat and cap and muff for winter. The boy was dark and black-haired. The little boy walked behind him and copied the things he did. In the summer the three of them would go to a cottage on the Gulf and he would dress the children in their sun suits and guide them carefully into the green, shallow waves. And then they would bloom as he grew old. Our Father. And they would come to him with questions and he would answer them.

Why not?

Biff took up his mandolin again. '*Tum*-ti-*tim*-ti-*tee*, ti-*tee*, the *wedd*-ing of the painted *doll*.' The mandolin mocked the refrain. He sang through all the verses and wagged his foot to the time. Then he played 'K-K-K-Katie,' and 'Love's Old Sweet Song.' These pieces were like the Agua Florida in the way they made him remember. Everything. Through the first year when he was happy and when she seemed happy even too. And when the bed came down with them twice in three months. And he didn't know that all the time her brain was busy with how she could save a nickel or squeeze out an extra dime. And then him with Rio and the girls at her place. Gyp and Madeline and Lou. And then later when suddenly he lost it. When he could lie with a woman no longer. Motherogod! So that at first it seemed everything was gone.

Lucile always understood the whole set-up. She knew the kind of woman Alice was. Maybe she knew about him, too. Lucile would urge them to get a divorce. And she did all a person could to try to straighten out their messes.

Biff winced suddenly. He jerked his hands from the strings of the mandolin so that a phrase of music was chopped off. He sat tense in his chair. Then suddenly he laughed quietly to himself. What had made him come across this? Ah, Lordy Lordy Lord! It was the day of his twenty-ninth birthday, and Lucile had asked him to drop by her apartment when he finished with an appointment at the dentist's. He expected from this some little remembrance — a plate of cherry tarts or a good shirt. She met him at the door and blindfolded his eyes before he entered. Then she said she would be back in a second. In the silent room he listened to her footsteps and when she had reached the kitchen he broke wind. He stood in the room with his eyes blindfolded and pooted. Then all at once he knew with horror he was not alone. There was a titter and soon great rolling whoops of laughter deafened him. At that minute Lucile came back and undid his eyes. She held a caramel cake on a platter. The room was full of people. Leroy and that bunch and Alice, of course. He wanted to crawl up the wall. He stood there with his bare face hanging out, burning hot all over. They kidded him and the next hour was almost as bad as the death of his mother — the way he took it. Later that night he drank a quart of whiskey. And for weeks after —— Motherogod!

Biff chuckled coldly. He plucked a few chords on his mandolin and started a rollicking cowboy song. His voice was a mellow tenor and he closed his eyes as he sang. The room was almost dark. The damp chill penetrated to his bones so that his legs ached with rheumatism.

At last he put away his mandolin and rocked slowly in the darkness. Death. Sometimes he could almost feel it in the room with him. He rocked to and fro in the chair. What did he understand? Nothing. Where was he headed? Nowhere. What did he want? To know. What? A meaning. Why? A riddle.

Broken pictures lay like a scattered jigsaw puzzle in his head. Alice soaping in the bathtub. Mussolini's mug. Mick pulling the baby in a wagon. A roast turkey on display. Blount's mouth. The face of Singer. He felt himself waiting. The room was completely dark. From the kitchen he could hear Louis singing.

Biff stood up and touched the arm of the chair to still its rocking. When he opened the door the hall outside was very warm and bright. He remembered that perhaps Mick would come. He straightened his clothes and smoothed back his hair. A warmth and liveliness returned to him. The restaurant was in a hubbub. Beer rounds and Sunday supper had begun. He smiled genially to young Harry and settled himself behind the cash register. He took in the room with a glance like a lasso. The place was crowded and humming with noise. The bowl of fruit in the window was a genteel, artistic display. He watched the door and continued to examine the room with a practiced eye. He was alert and intently waiting. Singer came finally and wrote with his silver pencil that he wanted only soup and whiskey as he had a cold. But Mick did not come.

9

SHE never even had a nickel to herself any more. They were that poor. Money was the main thing. All the time it was money, money, money. They had to pay through the nose for Baby Wilson's private room and private nurse. But even that was just one bill. By the time one thing was paid for something else always would crop up. They owed around two hundred dollars that had to be paid right away. They lost the house. Their Dad got a hundred dollars out of the deal and let the bank take over the mortgage. Then he borrowed another fifty dollars and Mister Singer went on the note with him. Afterward they had to worry about rent every month instead of taxes. They were mighty near as poor as factory folks. Only nobody could look down on them.

Bill had a job in a bottling plant and made ten dollars a week. Hazel worked as a helper in a beauty parlor for eight dollars. Etta sold tickets at a movie for five dollars. Each of them paid half of what they earned for their keep. Then the house had six boarders at five dollars a head. And Mister Singer, who paid his rent very prompt. With what their Dad picked up it all came to about two hundred dollars a month — and out of that they had to feed the six boarders pretty good and feed the family and pay rent for the whole house and keep up the payments on the furniture.

George and her didn't get any lunch money now. She had to stop the music lessons. Portia saved the leftovers from the dinner for her and George to eat after school. All the time they had their meals in the kitchen. Whether Bill and Hazel and Etta sat with the boarders or ate in the kitchen depended on how much food there was. In the kitchen they had grits and grease and side meat and coffee for breakfast. For supper they had the same thing along with whatever could be spared from the dining-room. The big kids griped whenever they had to eat in the kitchen. And sometimes she and George were downright hungry for two or three days.

But this was in the outside room. It had nothing to do with music and foreign countries and the plans she made. The winter was cold. Frost was on the windowpanes. At night the fire in the living-room crackled very warm. All the family sat by the fire with the boarders, so she had the middle bedroom to herself. She wore two sweaters and a pair of Bill's outgrown corduroy pants. Excitement kept her warm. She would bring out her private box from under the bed and sit on the floor to work.

In the big box there were the pictures she had painted at the government free art class. She had taken them out of Bill's room. Also in the box she kept three mystery books her Dad had given her, a compact, a box of watch parts, a rhinestone necklace, a hammer, and some notebooks. One notebook was marked on the top with red crayon — PRIVATE. KEEP OUT. PRIVATE — and tied with a string.

She had worked on music in this notebook all the winter. She quit studying school lessons at night so she could have more time to spend on music. Mostly she had written just little tunes — songs without any words and without even any bass notes to them. They were very short. But even if the tunes were only half a page long she gave them names and drew her initials underneath them. Nothing in this book was a real piece or a composition. They were just songs in her mind she wanted to remember. She named them how they reminded her — 'Africa' and 'A Big Fight' and 'The Snowstorm.'

She couldn't write the music just like it sounded in her mind. She had to thin it down to only a few notes; otherwise she got too mixed up to go further. There was so much she didn't know about how to write music. But maybe after she learned how to write these simple tunes fairly quick she could begin to put down the whole music in her mind.

In January she began a certain very wonderful piece called 'This Thing I Want, I Know Not What.' It was a beautiful and marvelous song — very slow and soft. At first she had started to write a poem along with it, but she couldn't think of ideas to fit the music. Also it was hard to get a word for the third line to rhyme with *what*. This new song made her feel sad and excited and happy all at once. Music beautiful as this was hard to work on. Any song was hard to write. Something she could hum in two minutes meant a whole week's work before it was down in the notebook — after she had figured up the scale and the time and every note.

She had to concentrate hard and sing it many times. Her voice was always hoarse. Her Dad said this was because she had bawled so much when she was a baby. Her Dad would have to get up and walk with her every night when she was Ralph's age. The only thing would hush her, he always said, was for him to beat the coal scuttle with a poker and sing 'Dixie.'

She lay on her stomach on the cold floor and thought. Later on — when she was twenty — she would be a great world-famous composer. She would have a whole symphony orchestra and conduct all of her music herself. She would stand up on the platform in front of the big crowds of people. To conduct the orchestra she would wear either a real man's evening suit or else a red dress spangled with rhinestones. The curtains of the stage would be red velvet and M. K. would be printed on them in gold. Mister Singer would be there, and afterward they would go out and eat fried chicken. He would admire her and count her as his very best friend. George would bring up big wreaths of flowers to the stage. It would be in New York City or else in a foreign country. Famous people would point at her — Carole Lombard and Arturo Toscanini and Admiral Byrd.

And she could play the Beethoven symphony any time she wanted to. It was a queer thing about this music she had heard last autumn. The symphony stayed inside her always and grew little by little. The reason was this: the whole symphony was in her mind. It had to be. She had heard every note, and somewhere in the back of her mind the whole of the music was still there just as it had been played. But she could do nothing to bring it all out again. Except wait and be ready for the times when suddenly a new part came to her. Wait for it to grow like leaves grow slowly on the branches of a spring oak tree.

In the inside room, along with music, there was Mister Singer. Every afternoon as soon as she finished playing on the piano in the gym she walked down the main street past the store where he worked. From the front window she couldn't see Mister Singer. He worked in the back, behind a curtain. But she looked at the store where he stayed every day and saw the people he knew. Then every night she waited on the front porch for him to come home. Sometimes she followed him upstairs. She sat on the bed and watched him put away his hat and undo the button on his collar and brush his hair. For some reason it was like they had a secret together. Or like they waited to tell each other things that had never been said before.

He was the only person in the inside room. A long time ago there had been others. She thought back and remembered how it was before he came. She remembered a girl way back in the sixth grade named Celeste. This girl had straight blonde hair and a turned-up nose and freckles. She wore a red-wool jumper with a white blouse. She walked pigeon-toed. Every day she brought an orange for little recess and a blue tin box of lunch for big recess. Other kids would gobble the food they had brought at little recess and then were hungry later — but not Celeste. She pulled off the crusts of her sandwiches and ate only the soft middle part. Always she had a stuffed hard-boiled egg and she would hold it in her hand, mashing the yellow with her thumb so that the print of her finger was left there.

Celeste never talked to her and she never talked to Celeste. Although that was what she wanted more than anything else. At night she would lie awake and think about Celeste. She would plan that they were best friends and think about the time when Celeste could come home with her to eat supper and spend the night. But that never happened. The way she felt about Celeste would never let her go up and make friends with her like she would any other person. After a year Celeste moved to another part of town and went to another school.

Then there was a boy called Buck. He was big and had pimples on his face. When she stood by him in line to march in at eight-thirty he smelled bad — like his britches needed airing. Buck did a nose dive at the principal once and was suspended. When he laughed he lifted his upper lip and shook all over. She thought about him like she had thought about Celeste. Then there was the lady who sold lottery tickets for a turkey raffle. And Miss Anglin, who taught the seventh grade. And Carole Lombard in the movies. All of them.

But with Mister Singer there was a difference. The way she felt about him came on her slowly, and she could not think back and realize just how it happened. The other people had been ordinary, but Mister Singer was not. The first day he rang the doorbell to ask about a room she had looked a long time into his face. She had opened the door and read over the card he handed her. Then she called her Mama and went back in the kitchen to tell Portia and Bubber about him. She followed him and her Mama up the stairs and watched him poke the mattress on the bed and roll up the shades to see if they worked. The day he moved she sat on the front porch banisters and watched him get out of the ten-cent taxi with his suitcase and his chessboard. Then later she listened to him thump around in his room and imagined about him. The rest came in a gradual way. So that now there was this secret feeling between them. She talked to him more than she had ever talked to a person before. And if he could have talked he would have told her many things. It was like he was some kind of a great teacher, only because he was a mute he did not teach. In the bed at night she planned about how she was an orphan and lived with Mister Singer — just the two of them in a foreign house where in the winter it would snow. Maybe in a little Switzerland town with the high glaciers and the mountains all around. Where rocks were on top of all the houses and the roofs were steep and pointed. Or in France where the people carried home bread from the store without its being wrapped. Or in the foreign country of Norway by the gray winter ocean.

In the morning the first thing she would think of him. Along with music. When she put on her dress she wondered where she would see him that day. She used some of Etta's perfume or a drop of vanilla so that if she met him in the hall she would smell good. She went to school late so she could see him come down the stairs on his way to work. And in the afternoon and night she never left the house if he was there.

Each new thing she learned about him was important. He kept his toothbrush and toothpaste in a glass on his table. So instead of leaving her toothbrush on the bathroom shelf she kept it in a glass, also. He didn't like cabbage. Harry, who worked for Mister Brannon, mentioned that to her. Now she couldn't eat cabbage either. When she learned new facts about him, or when she said something to him and he wrote a few words with his silver pencil, she had to be off by herself for a long time to think it over. When she was with him the main thought in her mind was to store up everything so that later she could live it over and remember.

But in the inside room with music and Mister Singer was not all. Many things happened in the outside room. She fell down the stairs and broke off one of her front teeth. Miss

Minner gave her two bad cards in English. She lost a quarter in a vacant lot, and although she and George hunted for three days they never found it.

This happened:

One afternoon she was studying for an English test out on the back steps. Harry began to chop wood over on his side of the fence and she hollered to him. He came and diagrammed a few sentences for her. His eyes were quick behind his horn-rimmed glasses. After he explained the English to her he stood up and jerked his hands in and out the pockets of his lumberjack. Harry was always full of energy, nervous, and he had to be talking or doing something every minute.

'You see, there's just two things nowadays,' he said.

He liked to surprise people and sometimes she didn't know how to answer him.

'It's the truth, there's just two things ahead nowadays.'

'What?'

'Militant Democracy or Fascism.'

'Don't you like Republicans?'

'Shucks,' Harry said. 'That's not what I mean.'

He had explained all about the Fascists one afternoon. He told how the Nazis made little Jew children get down on their hands and knees and eat grass from the ground. He told about how he planned to assassinate Hitler. He had it all worked out thoroughly. He told about how there wasn't any justice or freedom in Fascism. He said the newspapers wrote deliberate lies and people didn't know what was going on in the world. The Nazis were terrible—everybody knew that. She plotted with him to kill Hitler. It would be better to have four or five people in the conspiracy so that if one missed him the others could bump him off just the same. And even if they died they would all be heroes. To be a hero was almost like being a great musician.

'Either one or the other. And although I don't believe in war I'm ready to fight for what I know is right.'

'Me too,' she said. 'I'd like to fight the Fascists. I could dress up like a boy and nobody could ever tell. Cut my hair off and all.'

It was a bright winter afternoon. The sky was blue-green and the branches of the oak trees in the back yard were black and bare against this color. The sun was warm. The day made her feel full of energy. Music was in her mind. Just to be doing something she picked up a tenpenny nail and drove it into the steps with a few good wallops. Their Dad heard the sound of the hammer and came out in his bathrobe to stand around awhile. Under the tree there were two carpenter's horses, and little Ralph was busy putting a rock on top of one and then carrying it over to the other one. Back and forth. He walked with his hands out to balance himself. He was bowlegged and his diapers dragged down to his knees. George was shooting marbles. Because he needed a haircut his face looked thin. Some of his permanent teeth had already come — but they were small and blue like he had been eating blackberries. He drew a line for taw and lay on his stomach to take aim for the first hole. When their Dad went back to his watch work he carried Ralph with him. And after a while George went off into the alley by himself. Since he shot Baby he wouldn't buddy with a single person.

'I got to go,' Harry said. 'I got to be at work before six.'

'You like it at the café? Do you get good things to eat free?'

'Sure. And all kinds of folks come in the place. I like it better than any job I ever had. It pays more.'

'I hate Mister Brannon,' Mick said. It was true that even though he never said anything mean to her he always spoke in a rough, funny way. He must have known all along about the pack of chewing-gum she and George swiped that time. And then why would he ask her how her business was coming along — like he did up in Mister Singer's room? Maybe he thought they took things regular. And they didn't. They certainly did not. Only once a little water-color set from the ten-cent store. And a nickel pencil-sharpener.

'I can't stand Mister Brannon.'

'He's all right,' Harry said. 'Sometimes he seems a right queer kind of person, but he's not crabby. When you get to know him.'

'One thing I've thought about,' Mick said. 'A boy has a better advantage like that than a girl. I mean a boy can usually get some part-time job that don't take him out of school and leaves him time for other things. But the're not jobs like that for girls. When a girl wants a job she has to quit school and work full time. I'd sure like to earn a couple of bucks a week like you do, but there's just not any way.'

Harry sat on the steps and untied his shoestrings. He pulled at them until one broke. 'A man comes to the café named Mr. Blount. Mr. Jake Blount. I like to listen to him. I learn a lot from the things he says when he drinks beer. He's given me some new ideas.'

'I know him good. He comes here every Sunday.'

Harry unlaced his shoe and pulled the broken string to even lengths so he could tie it in a bow again. 'Listen' — he rubbed his glasses on his lumberjack in a nervous way — 'You needn't mention to him what I said. I mean I doubt if he would remember me. He don't talk to me. He just talks to Mr. Singer. He might think it was funny if you — you know what I mean.'

'O.K.' She read between the words that he had a crush on Mister Blount and she knew how he felt. 'I wouldn't mention it.'

Dark came on. The moon, white like milk, showed in the blue sky and the air was cold. She could hear Ralph and George and Portia in the kitchen. The fire in the stove made the kitchen window a warm orange. There was the smell of smoke and supper.

'You know this is something I never have told anybody,' he said. 'I hate to realize about it myself.'

'What?'

'You remember when you first began to read the newspapers and think about the things you read?'

'Sure.'

'I used to be a Fascist. I used to think I was. It was this way. You know all the pictures of the people our age in Europe marching and singing songs and keeping step together I used to think that was wonderful. All of them pledged to each other and with one leader. All of them with the same ideals and marching in step together. I didn't worry much about what was happening to the Jewish minorities because I didn't want to think about it. And because at the time I didn't want to think like I was Jewish. You see, I didn't know. I just looked at the pictures and read what it said underneath and didn't understand. I never knew what an awful thing it was. I thought I was a Fascist. Of course later on I found out different.'

His voice was bitter against himself and kept changing from a man's voice to a young boy's.

'Well, you didn't realize then ——' she said.

'It was a terrible transgression. A moral wrong.'

That was the way he was. Everything was either very right or very wrong — with no middle way. It was wrong for anyone under twenty to touch beer or wine or smoke a cigarette. It was a terrible sin for a person to cheat on a test, but not a sin to copy homework. It was a moral wrong for girls to wear lipstick or sun-backed dresses. It was a terrible sin to buy anything with a German or Japanese label, no matter if it cost only a nickel.

She remembered Harry back to the time when they were kids. Once his eyes got crossed and stayed crossed for a year. He would sit out on his front steps with his hands between his knees and watch everything. Very quiet and cross-eyed. He skipped two grades in grammar school and when he was eleven he was ready for Vocational. But at Vocational when they read about the Jew in 'Ivanhoe' the other kids would look around at Harry and he would come home and cry. So his mother took him out of school. He stayed out for a whole year. He grew taller and very fat. Every time she climbed the fence she would see him making himself something to eat in his kitchen. They both played around on the block, and sometimes they would wrestle. When she was a kid she liked to fight with boys — not real fights but just in play. She used a combination jujitsu and boxing. Sometimes he got her down and sometimes she got him. Harry never was very rough with anybody. When little kids ever broke any toy they would come to him and he always took the time to fix it. He could fix anything. The ladies on the block got him to fix their electric lights or sewing-machines when something went wrong. Then when he was thirteen he started back at Vocational and began to study hard. He threw papers and worked on Saturdays and read. For a long time she didn't see much of him — until after that party she gave. He was very changed.

'Like this,' Harry said. 'It used to be I had some big ambition for myself all the time. A great engineer or a great doctor or lawyer. But now I don't have it that way. All I can think about is what happens in the world now. About Fascism and the terrible things in Europe — and on the other hand Democracy. I mean I can't think and work on what I mean to be in life because I think too much about this other. I dream about killing Hitler every night. And I wake up in the dark very thirsty and scared of something — I don't know what.'

She looked at Harry's face and a deep, serious feeling made her sad. His hair hung over his forehead. His upper lip was thin and tight, but the lower one was thick and it trembled. Harry didn't look old enough to be fifteen. With the darkness a cold wind came. The wind sang up in the oak trees on the block and banged the blinds against the side of the house. Down the street Mrs. Wells was calling Sucker home. The dark late afternoon made the sadness heavy inside her. I want a piano — I want to take music lessons, she said to herself. She looked at Harry and he was lacing his thin fingers together in different shapes. There was a warm boy smell about him.

What was it made her act like she suddenly did? Maybe it was remembering the times when they were younger. Maybe it was because the sadness made her feel queer. But anyway all of a sudden she gave Harry a push that nearly knocked him off the steps. 'S.O.B. to your Grandmother,' she hollered to him. Then she ran. That was what kids used to say in the neighborhood when they picked a fight. Harry stood up and looked surprised. He settled his glasses on his nose and watched her for a second. Then he ran back to the alley.

The cold air made her strong as Samson. When she laughed there was a short, quick echo. She butted Harry with her shoulder and he got a holt on her. They wrestled hard and laughed. She was the tallest but his hands were strong. He didn't fight good enough and she got him on the ground. Then suddenly he stopped moving and she stopped too. His breathing was warm on her neck and he was very still. She felt his ribs against her knees and his hard breathing as she sat on him. They got up together. They did not laugh any more and the alley was very quiet. As they walked across the dark back yard for some reason she felt funny. There was nothing to feel queer about, but suddenly it had just happened. She gave him a little push and he pushed her back. Then she laughed again and felt all right.

'So long,' Harry said. He was too old to climb the fence, so he ran through the side alley to the front of his house.

'Gosh, it's hot!' she said. 'I could smother in here.'

Portia was warming her supper in the stove. Ralph banged his spoon on his high-chair tray. George's dirty little hand pushed up his grits with a piece of bread and his eyes were squinted in a faraway look. She helped herself to white meat and gravy and grits and a few raisins and mixed them up together on her plate. She ate three baits of them. She ate until all the grits were gone but still she wasn't full.

She had thought about Mister Singer all the day, and as soon as supper was over she went upstairs. But when she reached the third floor she saw that his door was open and his room dark. This gave her an empty feeling.

Downstairs she couldn't sit still and study for the English test. It was like she was so strong she couldn't sit on a chair in a room the same as other people. It was like she could knock down all the walls of the house and then march through the streets big as a giant.

Finally she got out her private box from under the bed. She lay on her stomach and looked over the notebook. There were about twenty songs now, but she didn't feel satisfied with them. If she could write a symphony! For a whole orchestra — how did you write that? Sometimes several instruments played one note, so the staff would have to be very large. She drew five lines across a big sheet of test paper — the lines about an inch apart. When a note was for violin or 'cello or flute she would write the name of the instrument to show. And when they all played the same note together she would draw a circle around them. At the top of the page she wrote SYMPHONY in large letters. And under that MICK KELLY. Then she couldn't go any further.

If she could only have music lessons!

If only she could have a real piano!

A long time passed before she could get started. The tunes were in her mind but she couldn't figure how to write them. It looked like this was the hardest play in the world. But she kept on figuring until Etta and Hazel came into the room and got into bed and said she had to turn the light off because it was eleven o'clock.

10

FOR six weeks Portia had waited to hear from William. Every evening she would come to the house and ask Doctor Copeland the same question: 'You seen anybody who gotten a letter from Willie yet?' And every night he was obliged to tell her that he had heard nothing.

At last she asked the question no more. She would come into the hall and look at him without a word. She drank. Her blouse was often half unbuttoned and her shoestrings loose.

February came. The weather turned milder, then hot. The sun glared down with hard brilliance. Birds sang in the bare trees and children played out of doors barefoot and naked to the waist. The nights were torrid as in midsummer. Then after a few days winter was upon the town again. The mild skies darkened. A chill rain fell and the air turned dank and bitterly cold. In the town the Negroes suffered badly. Supplies of fuel had been exhausted and there was a struggle everywhere for warmth. An epidemic of pneumonia raged through the wet, narrow streets, and for a week Doctor Copeland slept at odd hours, fully clothed. Still no word came from William. Portia had written four times and Doctor Copeland twice.

During most of the day and night he had no time to think. But occasionally he found a chance to rest for a moment at home. He would drink a pot of coffee by the kitchen stove and a deep uneasiness would come in him. Five of his patients had died. And one of these was Augustus Benedict Mady Lewis, the little deaf-mute. He had been asked to speak at the burial service, but as it was his rule not to attend funerals he was unable to accept this invitation. The five patients had not been lost because of any negligence on his part. The blame was in the long years of want which lay behind. The diets of cornbread and sowbelly and syrup, the crowding of four and five persons to a single room. The death of poverty. He brooded on this and drank coffee to stay awake. Often he held his hand to his chin, for recently a slight tremor in the nerves of his neck made his head nod unsteadily when he was tired.

Then during the fourth week of February Portia came to the house. It was only six o'clock in the morning and he was sitting by the fire in the kitchen, warming a pan of milk for breakfast. She was badly intoxicated. He smelled the keen, sweetish odor of gin and his nostrils widened with disgust. He did not look at her but busied himself with his breakfast. He crumbled some bread in a bowl and poured over it hot milk. He prepared coffee and laid the table.

Then when he was seated before his breakfast he looked at Portia sternly. 'Have you had your morning meal?'

'I not going to eat breakfast,' she said.

'You will need it. If you intend to get to work today.'

'I not going to work.'

A dread came in him. He did not wish to question her further. He kept his eyes on his bowl of milk and drank from a spoon that was unsteady in his hand. When he had finished he looked up at the wall above her head. 'Are you tongue-tied?'

'I going to tell you. You going to hear about it. Just as soon as I able to say it I going to tell you.'

Portia sat motionless in the chair, her eyes moving slowly from one corner of the wall to the other. Her arms hung down limp and her legs were twisted loosely about each other. When he turned from her he had for a moment a perilous sense of ease and freedom, which was more acute because he knew that soon it was to be shattered. He mended the fire and warmed his hands. Then he rolled a cigarette. The kitchen was in a state of spotless order and cleanliness. The saucepans on the wall glowed with the light of the stove and behind each one there was a round, black shadow.

'It about Willie.'

'I know.' He rolled the cigarette gingerly between his palms. His eyes glanced recklessly about him, greedy for the last sweet pleasures.

'Once I mentioned to you this here Buster Johnston were at the prison with Willie. Us knowed him before. He were sent home yesdiddy.'

'So?'

'Buster been crippled for life.'

His head quavered. He pressed his hand to his chin to steady himself, but the obstinate trembling was difficult to control.

'Last night these here friends come round to my house and say that Buster were home and had something to tell me about Willie. I run all the way and this here is what he said.'

'Yes.'

'There were three of them. Willie and Buster and this other boy. They were friends. Then this here trouble come up.' Portia halted. She wet her finger with her tongue and then moistened her dry lips with her finger. 'It were something to do with the way this here white guard picked on them all the time. They were out on roadwork one day and Buster he sassed back and then the other boy he try to run off in the woods. They taken all three of them. They taken all three of them to the camp and put them in this here ice-cold room.'

He said yes again. But his head quavered and the word sounded like a rattle in his throat.

'It were about six weeks ago,' Portia said. 'You remember that cold spell then. They put Willie and them boys in this room like ice.'

Portia spoke in a low voice, and she neither paused between words nor did the grief in her face soften. It was like a low song. She spoke and he could not understand. The sounds were distinct in his ear but they had no shape or meaning.

It was as though his head were the prow of a boat and the sounds were water that broke on him and then flowed past. He felt he had to look behind to find the words already said.

'... and their feets swolled up and they lay there and struggle on the floor and holler out. And nobody come. They hollered there for three days and three nights and nobody come.'

'I am deaf,' said Doctor Copeland. 'I cannot understand.'

'They put our Willie and them boys in this here ice-cold room. There were a rope hanging down from the ceiling. They taken their shoes off and tied their bare feets to this rope. Willie and them boys lay there with their backs on the floor and their feets in the air. And their feets swolled up and they struggle on the floor and holler out. It were ice-cold in the room and their feets froze. Their feets swolled up and they hollered for three nights and three days. And nobody come.'

Doctor Copeland pressed his head with his hands, but still the steady trembling would not stop. 'I cannot hear what you say.'

'Then at last they come to get them. They quickly taken Willie and them boys to the sick ward and their legs were all swolled and froze. Gangrene. They sawed off both our Willie's feets. Buster Johnson lost one foot and the other boy got well. But our Willie — he crippled for life now. Both his feet sawed off.'

The words were finished and Portia leaned over and struck her head upon the table. She did not cry or moan, but she struck her head again and again on the hard-scrubbed top of the table. The bowl and spoon rattled and he removed them to the sink. The words were scattered in his mind, but he did not try to assemble them. He scalded the bowl and spoon and washed out the dishtowel. He picked up something from the floor and put it somewhere.

'Crippled?' he asked. 'William?'

Portia knocked her head on the table and the blows had a rhythm like the slow beat of a drum and his heart took up this rhythm also. Quietly the words came alive and fitted to the meaning and he understood.

'When will they send him home?'

Portia leaned her drooping head on her arm. 'Buster don't know that. Soon afterward they separate all three of them in different places. They sent Buster to another camp. Since Willie only haves a few more months he think he liable to be home soon now.'

They drank coffee and sat for a long time, looking into each other's eyes. His cup rattled against his teeth. She poured her coffee into a saucer and some of it dripped down on her lap.

'William ——' Doctor Copeland said. As he pronounced the name his teeth bit deeply into his tongue and he moved his jaw with pain. They sat for a long while. Portia held his hand. The bleak morning light made the windows gray. Outside it was still raining.

'If I means to get to work I better go on now,' Portia said.

He followed her through the hall and stopped at the hat-rack to put on his coat and shawl. The open door let in a gust of wet, cold air. Highboy sat out on the street curb with a wet newspaper over his head for protection. Along the sidewalk there was a fence. Portia leaned against this as she walked. Doctor Copeland followed a few paces after her and his hands, also, touched the boards of the fence to steady himself. Highboy trailed behind them.

He waited for the black, terrible anger as though for some beast out of the night. But it did not come to him. His bowels seemed weighted with lead, and he walked slowly and lingered against fences and the cold, wet walls of buildings by the way. Descent into the depths until at last there was no further chasm below. He touched the solid bottom of despair and there took ease.

In this he knew a certain strong and holy gladness. The persecuted laugh, and the black slave sings to his outraged soul beneath the whip. A song was in him now — although it was not music but only the feeling of a song. And the sodden heaviness of peace weighted down his limbs so that it was only with the strong, true purpose that he moved Why did he go onward? Why did he not rest here upon this bottom of utmost humiliation and for a while take his content? But he went onward.

'Uncle,' said Mick. 'You think some hot coffee would make you feel better?'

Doctor Copeland looked into her face but gave no sign that he heard. They had crossed the town and come at last to the alley behind the Kellys' house. Portia had entered first and then he followed. Highboy remained on the steps outside. Mick and her two little brothers were already in the kitchen. Portia told of William. Doctor Copeland did not listen to the words but her voice had a rhythm — a start, a middle, and an end. Then when she was finished she began all over. Others came into the room to hear.

Doctor Copeland sat on a stool in the corner. His coat and shawl steamed over the back of a chair by the stove. He held his hat on his knees and his long, dark hands moved nervously around the worn brim. The yellow insides of his hands were so moist that occasionally he wiped them with a handkerchief. His head trembled, and all of his muscles were stiff with the effort to make it be still.

Mr. Singer came into the room. Doctor Copeland raised up his face to him. 'Have you heard of this?' he asked. Mr. Singer nodded. In his eyes there was no horror or pity or hate. Of all those who knew, his eyes alone did not express these reactions. For he alone understood this thing.

Mick whispered to Portia, 'What's your father's name?'

'He named Benedict Mady Copeland.'

Mick leaned over close to Doctor Copeland and shouted in his face as though he were deaf. 'Benedict, don't you think some hot coffee would make you feel a little better?'

Doctor Copeland started.

'Quit that hollering,' Portia said. 'He can hear well as you can.'

'Oh,' said Mick. She emptied the grounds from the pot and put the coffee on the stove to boil again.

The mute still lingered in the doorway. Doctor Copeland still looked into his face. 'You heard?'

'What'll they do to those prison guards?' Mick asked.

'Honey, I just don't know,' Portia said. 'I just don't know.'

'I'd do something. I'd sure do something about it.'

'Nothing us could do would make no difference. Best thing us can do is keep our mouth shut.'

'They ought to be treated just like they did Willie and them. Worse. I wish I could round up some people and kill those men myself.'

'That ain't no Christian way to talk,' Portia said. 'Us can just rest back and know they going to be chopped up with pitchforks and fried everlasting by Satan.'

'Anyway Willie can still play his harp.'

'With both feets sawed off that about all he can do.'

The house was full of noise and unrest. In the room above the kitchen someone was moving furniture about. The dining-room was crowded with boarders. Mrs. Kelly hurried back and forth from the breakfast table to the kitchen. Mr. Kelly wandered about in a baggy pair of trousers and a bathrobe. The young Kelly children ate greedily in the kitchen. Doors banged and voices could be heard in all parts of the house.

Mick handed Doctor Copeland a cup of coffee mixed with watery milk. The milk gave the drink a gray-blue sheen. Some of the coffee had sloshed over into the saucer, so first he dried the saucer and the rim of the cup with his handkerchief. He had not wanted coffee at all.

'I wish I could kill them,' Mick said.

The house quieted. The people in the dining-room went out to work. Mick and George left for school and the baby was shut into one of the front rooms. Mrs. Kelly wrapped a towel around her head and took a broom with her upstairs.

The mute still stood in the doorway. Doctor Copeland gazed up into his face. 'You know of this?' he asked again. The words did not sound — they choked in his throat — but his eyes asked the question all the same. Then the mute was gone. Doctor Copeland and Portia were alone. He sat for some time on the stool in the corner. At last he rose to go.

'You sit back down, Father. Us going to stay together this morning. I going to fry some fish and have egg-bread and potatoes for the dinner. You stay on here, and then I means to serve you a good hot meal.'

'You know I have calls.'

'Less us just this one day. Please, Father. I feels like I going to really bust loose. Besides, I don't want you messing around in the streets by yourself.'

He hesitated and felt the collar of his overcoat. It was very damp. 'Daughter, I am sorry. You know I have visits.'

Portia held his shawl over the stove until the wool was hot. She buttoned his coat and turned up the collar about his neck. He cleared his throat and spat into one of the squares of paper that he carried with him in his pocket. Then he burned the paper in the stove. On the way out he stopped and spoke to Highboy on the steps. He suggested that Highboy stay with Portia if he could arrange to get leave from work.

The air was piercing and cold. From the low, dark skies the drizzling rain fell steadily. The rain had seeped into the garbage cans and in the alley there was the rank odor of wet refuse. As he walked he balanced himself with the help of a fence and kept his dark eyes on the ground.

He made all of the strictly necessary visits. Then he attended to office patients from noon until two o'clock. Afterward he sat at his desk with his fists clenched tight. But it was useless to try to cogitate on this thing.

He wished never again to see a human face. Yet at the same time he could not sit alone in the empty room. He put on his overcoat and went out again into the wet, cold street. In his pocket were several prescriptions to be left at the pharmacy. But he did not wish to speak with Marshall Nicolls. He went into the store and laid the prescriptions upon the counter. The pharmacist turned from the powders he was measuring and held out both his hands. His thick lips worked soundlessly for a moment before he gained his poise.

'Doctor,' he said formally. 'You must be aware that I and all our colleagues and the members of my lodge and church — we have your sorrow uppermost in our minds and wish to extend to you our deepest sympathy.'

Doctor Copeland turned shortly and left without a word. That was too little. Something more was needed. The strong, true purpose, the will to justice. He walked stiffly, his arms held close to his sides, toward the main street. He cogitated without success. He could think of no white person of power in all the town who was both brave and just. He thought of every lawyer, every judge, every public official with whose name he was familiar — but the thought of each one of these white men was bitter in his heart. At last he decided on the judge of the Superior Court. When he reached the courthouse he did not hesitate but entered quickly, determined to see the judge that afternoon.

The wide front hall was empty except for a few idlers who lounged in the doorways leading to the offices on either side. He did not know where he could find the judge's office, so he wandered uncertainly through the building, looking at the placards on the doors. At last he came to a narrow passage. Halfway through this corridor three white men stood talking together and blocked the way. He drew close to the wall to pass, but one of them turned to stop him.

'What you want?'

'Will you please tell me where the judge's office is located?'

The white man jerked his thumb toward the end of the passage. Doctor Copeland recognized him as a deputy sheriff. They had seen each other dozens of times but the deputy did not remember him. All white people looked similar to Negroes but Negroes took care to differentiate between them. On the other hand, all Negroes looked similar to white men but white men did not usually bother to fix the face of a Negro in their minds. So the white man said, 'What you want, Reverend?'

The familiar joking title nettled him. 'I am not a minister,' he said. 'I am a physician, a medical doctor. My name is Benedict Mady Copeland and I wish to see the judge immediately on urgent business.'

The deputy was like other white men in that a clearly enunciated speech maddened him. 'Is that so?' he mocked. He winked at his friends. 'Then I am the deputy sheriff and my name is Mister Wilson and I tell you the judge is busy. Come back some other day.'

'It is imperative that I see the judge,' Doctor Copeland said. 'I will wait.'

There was a bench at the entrance of the passage and he sat down. The three white men continued to talk, but he knew that the sheriff watched him. He was determined not to leave. More than half an hour passed. Several white men went freely back and forth through the corridor. He knew that the deputy was watching him and he sat rigid, his hands pressed between his knees. His sense of prudence told him to go away and return later in the afternoon when the sheriff was not there. All of his life he had been circumspect in his dealings with such people. But now something in him would not let him withdraw.

'Come here, you!' the deputy said finally.

His head trembled, and when he arose he was not steady on his feet. 'Yes?'

'What you say you wanted to see the judge about?'

'I did not say,' said Doctor Copeland. 'I merely said that my business with him was urgent.'

'You can't stand up straight. You been drinking liquor, haven't you? I smell it on your breath.'

'That is a lie,' said Doctor Copeland slowly. 'I have not ——'

The sheriff struck him on the face. He fell against the wall. Two white men grasped him by the arms and dragged him down the steps to the main floor. He did not resist.

'That's the trouble with this country,' the sheriff said. 'These damn biggity niggers like him.'

He spoke no word and let them do with him as they would. He waited for the terrible anger and felt it arise in him. Rage made him weak, so that he stumbled. They put him into the wagon with two men as guards. They took him to the station and then to the jail. It was only when they had entered the jail that the strength of his rage came to him. He broke loose suddenly from their grasp. In a corner he was surrounded. They struck him on the head and shoulders with their clubs. A glorious strength was in him and he heard himself laughing aloud as he fought. He sobbed and laughed at the same time. He kicked wildly with his feet. He fought with his fists and even struck at them with his head. Then he was clutched fast so that he could not move. They dragged him foot by foot through the hall of the jail. The door to a cell was opened. Someone behind kicked him in the groin and he fell to his knees on the floor.

In the cramped cubicle there were five other prisoners — three Negroes and two white men. One of the white men was very old and drunk. He sat on the floor and scratched himself. The other white prisoner was a boy not more than fifteen years of age. The three Negroes were young. As Doctor Copeland lay on the bunk looking up into their faces he recognized one of them.

'How come you here?' the young man asked. 'Ain't you Doctor Copeland?'

He said yes.

'My name Dary White. You taken out my sister's tonsils last year.'

The icy cell was permeated with a rotten odor. A pail brimming with urine was in a corner. Cockroaches crawled upon the walls. He closed his eyes and immediately he must have slept, for when he looked up again the small barred window was black and a bright light burned in the hall. Four empty tin plates were on the floor. His dinner of cabbage and cornbread was beside him.

He sat on the bunk and sneezed violently several times. When he breathed the phlegm rattled in his chest. After a while the young white boy began to sneeze also. Doctor Copeland gave out of squares of paper and had to use sheets from a notebook in his pocket. The white boy leaned over the pail in the corner or simply let the water run from his nose onto the front of his shirt. His eyes were dilated, his clear cheeks flushed. He huddled on the edge of a bunk and groaned.

Soon they were led out to the lavatory, and on their return they prepared for sleep. There were six men to occupy four bunks. The old man lay snoring on the floor. Dary and another boy squeezed into a bunk together.

The hours were long. The light in the hall burned his eyes and the odor in the cell made every breath a discomfort. He could not keep warm. His teeth chattered and he shook with a hard chill. He sat up with the dirty blanket wrapped around him and swayed to and fro. Twice he reached over to cover the white boy, who muttered and threw out his arms in sleep. He swayed, his head in his hands, and from his throat there came a singing moan. He could not think of William. Nor could he even cogitate upon the strong, true purpose and draw strength from that. He could only feel the misery in him.

Then the tide of his fever turned. A warmth spread through him. He lay back, and it seemed he sank down into a place warm and red and full of comfort.

The next morning the sun came out. The strange Southern winter was at its end. Doctor Copeland was released. A little group waited outside the jail for him. Mr. Singer was there. Portia and Highboy and Marshall Nicolls were present also. Their faces were confused and he could not see them clearly. The sun was very bright.

'Father, don't you know that ain't no way to help our Willie? Messing around at a white folks' courthouse? Best thing us can do is keep our mouth shut and wait.'

Her loud voice echoed wearily in his ears. They climbed into a ten-cent taxicab, and then he was home and his face pressed into the fresh white pillow.

11

MICK could not sleep all night. Etta was sick, so she had to sleep in the living-room. The sofa was too narrow and short. She had nightmares about Willie. Nearly a month had gone by since Portia had told about what they had done to him — but still she couldn't forget it. Twice in the night she had these bad dreams and woke up on the floor. A bump came out on her forehead. Then at six o'clock she heard Bill go to the kitchen and fix his breakfast. It was daylight, but the shades were down so that the room was half-dark.

She felt queer waking up in the living-room. She didn't like it. The sheet was twisted around her, half on the sofa and half on the floor. The pillow was in the middle of the room. She got up and opened the door to the hall. Nobody was on the stairs. She ran in her nightgown to the back room.

'Move over, George.'

The kid lay in the very center of the bed. The night had been warm and he was naked as a jay bird. His fists were shut tight, and even in sleep his eyes were squinted like he was thinking about something very hard to figure out. His mouth was open and there was a little wet spot on the pillow. She pushed him.

'Wait ——' he said in his sleep.

'Move over on your side.'

'Wait —— Lemme just finish this here dream — this here —— '

She hauled him over where he belonged and lay down close to him. When she opened her eyes again it was late, because the sun shone in through the back window. George was gone. From the yard she heard kids' voices and the sound of water running. Etta and Hazel were talking in the middle room. As she dressed a sudden notion came to her. She listened at the door but it was hard to hear what they said. She jerked the door open quick to surprise them.

They were reading a movie magazine. Etta was still in bed. She had her hand halfway over the picture of an actor. 'From here up don't you think he favors that boy who used to date with ——'

'How you feel this morning, Etta?' Mick asked. She looked down under the bed and her private box was still in the exact place where she had left it.

'A lot you care,' Etta said.

'You needn't try to pick a fight.'

Etta's face was peaked. There was a terrible pain in her stomach and her ovary was diseased. It had something to do with being unwell. The doctor said they would have to cut out her ovary right away. But their Dad said they would have to wait. There wasn't any money.

'How you expect me to act, anyway?' Mick said. 'I ask you a polite question and then you start to nag at me. I feel like I ought to be sorry for you because you're sick, but you won't let me be decent. Therefore I naturally get mad.' She pushed back the bangs of her hair and looked close into the mirror. 'Boy! See this bump I got! I bet my head's broke. Twice I fell out last night and it seemed to me like I hit that table by the sofa. I can't sleep in the living-room. That sofa cramps me so much I can't stay in it.'

'Hush that talking so loud,' Hazel said.

Mick knelt down on the floor and pulled out the big box. She looked carefully at the string that was tied around it. 'Say, have either of you fooled with this?'

'Shoot!' Etta said. 'What would we want to mess with your junk for?'

'You just better not. I'd kill anybody that tried to mess with my private things.'

'Listen to that,' Hazel said. 'Mick Kelly, I think you're the most selfish person I've ever known. You don't care a thing in the world about anybody but ——'

'Aw, poot!' She slammed the door. She hated both of them. That was a terrible thing to think, but it was true.

Her Dad was in the kitchen with Portia. He had on his bathrobe and was drinking a cup of coffee. The whites of his eyes were red and his cup rattled against his saucer. He walked round and round the kitchen table.

'What time is it? Has Mister Singer gone yet?'

'He been gone, Hon,' Portia said. 'It near about ten o'clock.'

'Ten o'clock! Golly! I never have slept that late before.'

'What you keep in that big hatbox you tote around with you?'

Mick reached into the stove and brought out half a dozen biscuits. 'Ask me no questions and I'll tell you no lies. A bad end comes to a person who pries.'

'If there's a little extra milk I think I'll just have it poured over some crumbled bread,' her Dad said. 'Graveyard soup. Maybe that will help settle my stomach.'

Mick split open the biscuits and put slices of fried white meat inside them. She sat down on the back steps to eat her breakfast. The morning was warm and bright. Spareribs and Sucker were playing with George in the back yard. Sucker wore his sun suit and the other two kids had taken off all their clothes except their shorts. They were scooting each other with the hose. The stream of water sparkled bright in the sun. The wind blew out sprays of it like mist and in this mist there were the colors of the rainbow. A line of clothes flapped in the wind — white sheets, Ralph's blue dress, a red blouse and nightgowns — wet and fresh and blowing out in different shapes. The day was almost like summer-time. Fuzzy little yellow jackets buzzed around the honeysuckle on the alley fence.

'Watch me hold it up over my head!' George hollered. 'Watch how the water runs down.'

She was too full of energy to sit still. George had filled a meal sack with dirt and hung it to a limb of the tree for a punching bag. She began to hit this. Puck! Pock! She hit it in time to the song that had been in her mind when she woke up. George had mixed a sharp rock in the dirt and it bruised her knuckles.

'Aoow! You skeeted the water right in my ear. It's busted my eardrum. I can't even hear.'

'Gimme here. Let me skeet some.'

Sprays of the water blew into her face, and once the kids turned the hose on her legs. She was afraid her box would get wet, so she carried it with her through the alley to the front porch. Harry was sitting on his steps reading the newspaper. She opened her box and got out the notebook. But it was hard to settle her mind on the song she wanted to write down. Harry was looking over in her direction and she could not think.

She and Harry had talked about so many things lately. Nearly every day they walked home from school together. They talked about God. Sometimes she would wake up in the night and shiver over what they had said. Harry was a Pantheist. That was a religion, the same as Baptist or Catholic or Jew. Harry believed that after you were dead and buried you changed to plants and fire and dirt and clouds and water. It took thousands of years and then finally you were a part of all the world. He said he thought that was better than being one single angel. Anyhow it was better than nothing.

Harry threw the newspaper into his hall and then came over. 'It's like hot summer,' he said. 'And only March.'

'Yeah. I wish we could go swimming.'

'We would if there was any place.'

'There's not any place. Except that country club pool.'

'I sure would like to do something — to get out and go somewhere.'

'Me too,' she said. 'Wait! I know one place. It's out in the country about fifteen miles. It's a deep, wide creek in the woods. The Girl Scouts have a camp there in the summertime. Mrs. Wells took me and George and Pete and Sucker swimming there one time last year.'

'If you want to I can get bicycles and we can go tomorrow. I have a holiday one Sunday a month.'

'We'll ride out and take a picnic dinner,' Mick said.

'O.K. I'll borrow the bikes.'

It was time for him to go to work. She watched him walk down the street. He swung his arms. Halfway down the block there was a bay tree with low branches. Harry took a running jump, caught a limb, and chinned himself. A happy feeling came in her because it was true they were real good friends. Also he was handsome. Tomorrow she would borrow Hazel's blue necklace and wear the silk dress. And for dinner they would take jelly sandwiches and Nehi. Maybe Harry would bring something queer, because they ate orthodox Jew. She watched him until he turned the corner. It was true that he had grown to be a very good-looking fellow.

Harry in the country was different from Harry sitting on the back steps reading the newspapers and thinking about Hitler. They left early in the morning. The wheels he borrowed were the kind for boys — with a bar between the legs. They strapped the lunches and bathing-suits to the fenders and were gone before nine o'clock. The morning was hot and sunny. Within an hour they were far out of town on a red clay road. The fields were bright green and the sharp smell of pine trees was in the air. Harry talked in a very excited way. The warm wind blew into their faces. Her mouth was very dry and she was hungry.

'See that house up on the hill there? Less us stop and get some water.'

'No, we better wait. Well water gives you typhoid.'

'I already had typhoid. I had pneumonia and a broken leg and a infected foot.'

'I remember.'

'Yeah,' Mick said. 'Me and Bill stayed in the front room when we had typhoid fever and Pete Wells would run past on the sidewalk holding his nose and looking up at the window. Bill was very embarrassed. All my hair came out so I was bald-headed.'

'I bet we're at least ten miles from town. We've been riding an hour and a half — fast riding, too.'

'I sure am thirsty,' Mick said. 'And hungry. What you got in that sack for lunch?'

'Cold liver pudding and chicken salad sandwiches and pie.'

'That's a good picnic dinner.' She was ashamed of what she had brought. 'I got two hard-boiled eggs — already stuffed — with separate little packages of salt and pepper. And sandwiches — blackberry jelly with butter. Everything wrapped in oil paper. And paper napkins.'

'I didn't intend for you to bring anything,' Harry said. 'My Mother fixed lunch for both of us. I asked you out here and all. We'll come to a store soon and get cold drinks.'

They rode half an hour longer before they finally came to the filling-station store. Harry propped up the bicycles and she went in ahead of him. After the bright glare the store seemed dark. The shelves were stacked with slabs of white meat, cans of oil, and sacks of meal. Flies buzzed over a big, sticky jar of loose candy on the counter.

'What kind of drinks you got?' Harry asked.

The storeman started to name them over. Mick opened the ice box and looked inside. Her hands felt good in the cold water. 'I want a chocolate Nehi. You got any of them?'

'Ditto,' Harry said. 'Make it two.'

'No, wait a minute. Here's some ice-cold beer. I want a bottle of beer if you can treat as high as that.'

Harry ordered one for himself, also. He thought it was a sin for anybody under twenty to drink beer — but maybe he just suddenly wanted to be a sport. After the first swallow he made a bitter face. They sat on the steps in front of the store. Mick's legs were so tired that the muscles in them jumped. She wiped the neck of the bottle with her hand and took a long, cold pull. Across the road there was a big empty field of grass, and beyond that a fringe of pine woods. The trees were every color of green — from a bright yellow-green to a dark color that was almost black. The sky was hot blue.

'I like beer,' she said. 'I used to sop bread down in the drops our Dad left. I like to lick salt out my hand while I drink. This is the second bottle to myself I've ever had.'

'The first swallow was sour. But the rest tastes good.'

The storeman said it was twelve miles from town. They had four more miles to go. Harry paid him and they were out in the hot sun again. Harry was talking loud and he kept laughing without any reason.

'Gosh, the beer along with this hot sun makes me dizzy. But I sure do feel good,' he said.

'I can't wait to get in swimming.'

There was sand in the road and they had to throw all their weight on the pedals to keep from bogging. Harry's shirt was stuck to his back with sweat. He still kept talking. The road changed to red clay and the sand was behind them. There was a slow colored song in her mind — one Portia's brother used to play on his harp. She pedaled in time to it.

Then finally they reached the place she had been looking for. 'This is it! See that sign that says PRIVATE? We got to climb the bob-wire fence and then take that path there — see!'

The woods were very quiet. Slick pine needles covered the ground. Within a few minutes they had reached the creek. The water was brown and swift. Cool. There was no sound except from the water and a breeze singing high up in the pine trees. It was like the deep, quiet woods made them timid, and they walked softly along the bank beside the creek.

'Don't it look pretty.'

Harry laughed. 'What makes you whisper? Listen here!' He clapped his hand over his mouth and gave a long Indian whoop that echoed back at them. 'Come on. Let's jump in the water and cool off.'

'Aren't you hungry?'

'O.K. Then we'll eat first. We'll eat half the lunch now and half later on when we come out.'

She unwrapped the jelly sandwiches. When they were finished Harry balled the papers neatly and stuffed them into a hollow tree stump. Then he took his shorts and went down the path. She shucked off her clothes behind a bush and struggled into Hazel's bathing-suit. The suit was too small and cut her between the legs.

'You ready?' Harry hollered.

She heard a splash in the water and when she reached the bank Harry was already swimming. 'Don't dive yet until I find out if there are any stumps or shallow places,' he said. She just looked at his head bobbing in the water. She had never intended to dive, anyway. She couldn't even swim. She had been in swimming only a few times in her life — and then she always wore water-wings or stayed out of parts that were over her head. But it would be sissy to tell Harry. She was embarrassed. All of a sudden she told a tale:

'I don't dive any more. I used to dive, high dive, all the time. But once I busted my head open, so I can't dive any more.' She thought a minute. 'It was a double jack-knife dive I was doing. And when I came up there was blood all in the water. But I didn't think anything about it and just began to do swimming tricks. These people were hollering at me. Then I found out where all this blood in the water was coming from. And I never have swam good since.'

Harry scrambled up the bank. 'Gosh! I never heard about that.'

She meant to add on to the tale to make it sound more reasonable, but instead she just looked at Harry. His skin was light brown and the water made it shining. There were hairs on his chest and legs. In the tight trunks he seemed very naked. Without his glasses his face was wider and more handsome. His eyes were wet and blue. He was looking at her and it was like suddenly they got embarrassed.

'The water's about ten feet deep except over on the other bank, and there it's shallow.'

'Less us get going. I bet that cold water feels good.'

She wasn't scared. She felt the same as if she had got caught at the top of a very high tree and there was nothing to do but just climb down the best way she could — a dead-calm feeling. She edged off the bank and was in the ice-cold water. She held to a root until it broke in her hands and then she began to swim. Once she choked and went under, but she kept going and didn't lose any face. She swam and reached the other side of the bank where she could touch bottom. Then she felt good. She smacked the water with her fists and called out crazy words to make echoes.

'Watch here!'

Harry shimmied up a tall, thin little tree. The trunk was limber and when he reached the top it swayed down with him. He dropped into the water.

'Me too! Watch me do it!'

'That's a sapling.'

She was as good a climber as anybody on the block. She copied exactly what he had done and hit the water with a hard smack. She could swim, too. Now she could swim O.K.

They played follow the leader and ran up and down the bank and jumped in the cold brown water. They hollered and jumped and climbed. They played around for maybe two hours. Then they were standing on the bank and they both looked at each other and there didn't seem to be anything new to do. Suddenly she said:

'Have you ever swam naked?'

The woods was very quiet and for a minute he did not answer. He was cold. His titties had turned hard and purple. His lips were purple and his teeth chattered. 'I — I don't think so.'

This excitement was in her, and she said something she didn't mean to say. 'I would if you would. I dare you to.'

Harry slicked back the dark, wet bangs of his hair. 'O.K.'

They both took off their bathing-suits. Harry had his back to her. He stumbled and his ears were red. Then they turned toward each other. Maybe it was half an hour they stood there — maybe not more than a minute.

Harry pulled a leaf from a tree and tore it to pieces. 'We better get dressed.'

All through the picnic dinner neither of them spoke. They spread the dinner on the ground. Harry divided everything in half. There was the hot, sleepy feeling of a summer afternoon. In the deep woods they could hear no sound except the slow flowing of the water and the songbirds. Harry held his stuffed egg and mashed the yellow with his thumb. What did that make her remember? She heard herself breathe.

Then he looked up over her shoulder. 'Listen here. I think you're so pretty, Mick. I never did think so before. I don't mean I thought you were very ugly — I just mean that ——'

She threw a pine cone in the water. 'Maybe we better start back if we want to be home before dark.'

'No,' he said. 'Let's lie down. Just for a minute.'

He brought handfuls of pine needles and leaves and gray moss. She sucked her knee and watched him. Her fists were tight and it was like she was tense all over.

'Now we can sleep and be fresh for the trip home.'

They lay on the soft bed and looked up at the dark-green pine clumps against the sky. A bird sang a sad, clear song she had never heard before. One high note like an oboe — and then it sank down five tones and called again. The song was sad as a question without words.

'I love that bird,' Harry said. 'I think it's a vireo.'

'I wish we was at the ocean. On the beach and watching the ships far out on the water. You went to the beach one summer — exactly what is it like?'

His voice was rough and low. 'Well — there are the waves. Sometimes blue and sometimes green, and in the bright sun they look glassy. And on the sand you can pick up these little shells. Like the kind we brought back in a cigar box. And over the water are these white gulls. We were at the Gulf of Mexico — these cool bay breezes blew all the time and there it's never baking hot like it is here. Always ——'

'Snow,' Mick said. 'That's what I want to see. Cold, white drifts of snow like in pictures. Blizzards. White, cold snow that keeps falling soft and falls on and on and on through all the winter. Snow like in Alaska.'

They both turned at the same time. They were close against each other. She felt him trembling and her fists were tight enough to crack. 'Oh, God,' he kept saying over and over. It was like her head was broke off from her body and thrown away. And her eyes looked up straight into the blinding sun while she counted something in her mind. And then this was the way.

This was how it was.

They pushed the wheels slowly along the road. Harry's head hung down and his shoulders were bent. Their shadows were long and black on the dusty road, for it was late afternoon.

'Listen here,' he said.

'Yeah.'

'We got to understand this. We got to. Do you — any?'

'I don't know. I reckon not.'

'Listen here. We got to do something. Let's sit down.'

They dropped the bicycles and sat by a ditch beside the road. They sat far apart from each other. The late sun burned down on their heads and there were brown, crumbly ant beds all around them.

'We got to understand this,' Harry said.

He cried. He sat very still and the tears rolled down his white face. She could not think about the thing that made him cry. An ant stung her on the ankle and she picked it up in her fingers and looked at it very close.

'It's this way,' he said. 'I never had even kissed a girl before.'

'Me neither. I never kissed any boy. Out of the family.'

'That's all I used to think about — was to kiss this certain girl. I used to plan about it during school and dream about it at night. And then once she gave me a date. And I could tell she meant for me to kiss her. And I just looked at her in the dark and I couldn't. That was all I had thought about — to kiss her — and when the time came I couldn't.'

She dug a hole in the ground with her finger and buried the dead ant.

'It was all my fault. Adultery is a terrible sin any way you look at it. And you were two years younger than me and just a kid.'

'No, I wasn't. I wasn't any kid. But now I wish I was, though.'

'Listen here. If you think we ought to we can get married — secretly or any other way.'

Mick shook her head. 'I didn't like that. I never will marry with any boy.'

'I never will marry either. I know that. And I'm not just saying so — it's true.'

His face scared her. His nose quivered and his bottom lip was mottled and bloody where he had bitten it. His eyes were bright and wet and scowling. His face was whiter than any face she could remember. She turned her head from him. Things would be better if only he would just quit talking. Her eyes looked slowly around her — at the streaked red-and-white clay of the ditch, at a broken whiskey bottle, at a pine tree across from them with a sign advertising for a man for county sheriff. She wanted to sit quietly for a long time and not think and not say a word.

'I'm leaving town. I'm a good mechanic and I can get a job some other place. If I stayed home Mother could read this in my eyes.'

'Tell me. Can you look at me and see the difference?'

Harry watched her face a long time and nodded that he could. Then he said:

'There's just one more thing. In a month or two I'll send you my address and you write and tell me for sure whether you're all right.'

'How you mean?' she asked slowly.

He explained to her. 'All you need to write is "O.K." and then I'll know.'

They were walking home again, pushing the wheels. Their shadows stretched out giant-sized on the road. Harry was bent over like an old beggar and kept wiping his nose on his sleeve. For a minute there was a bright, golden glow over everything before the sun sank down behind the trees and their shadows were gone on the road before them. She felt very old, and it was like something was heavy inside her. She was a grown person now, whether she wanted to be or not.

They had walked the sixteen miles and were in the dark alley at home. She could see the yellow light from their kitchen. Harry's house was dark — his mother had not come home. She worked for a tailor in a shop on a side street. Sometimes even on Sunday. When you looked through the window you could see her bending over the machine in the back or pushing a long needle through the heavy pieces of goods. She never looked up while you watched her. And at night she cooked these orthodox dishes for Harry and her.

'Listen here ——' he said.

She waited in the dark, but he did not finish. They shook hands with each other and Harry walked up the dark alley between the houses. When he reached the sidewalk he turned and looked back over his shoulder. A light shone on his face and it was white and hard. Then he was gone.

'This here is a riddle,' George said.

'I listening.'

'Two Indians was walking on a trail. The one in front was the son of the one behind but the one behind was not his father. What kin was they?'

'Less see. His stepfather.'

George grinned at Portia with his little square, blue teeth.

'His uncle, then.'

'You can't guess. It was his mother. The trick is that you don't think about a Indian being a lady.'

She stood outside the room and watched them. The doorway framed the kitchen like a picture. Inside it was homey and clean. Only the light by the sink was turned on and there were shadows in the room. Bill and Hazel played blackjack at the table with matches for money. Hazel felt the braids of her hair with her plump, pink fingers while Bill sucked in his cheeks and dealt the cards in a very serious way. At the sink Portia was drying the dishes with a clean checked towel. She looked thin and her skin was golden yellow, her greased black hair slicked neat. Ralph sat quietly on the floor and George was tying a little harness on him made out of old Christmas tinsel.

'This here is another riddle, Portia. If the hand of a clock points to half-past two ——'

She went into the room. It was like she had expected them to move back when they saw her and stand around in a circle and look. But they just glanced at her. She sat down at the table and waited.

'Here you come traipsing in after ever body done finished supper. Seem to me like I never will get off from work.'

Nobody noticed her. She ate a big plateful of cabbage and salmon and finished off with junket. It was her Mama she was thinking about. The door opened and her Mama came in and told Portia that Miss Brown had said she found a bedbug in her room. To get out the gasoline.

'Quit frowning like that, Mick. You're coming to the age where you ought to fix up and try to look the best you can. And hold on — don't barge out like that when I speak with you — I mean you to give Ralph a good sponge bath before he goes to bed. Clean his nose and ears good.'

Ralph's soft hair was sticky with oatmeal. She wiped it with a dishrag and rinched his face and hands at the sink. Bill and Hazel finished their game. Bill's long fingernails scraped on the table as he took up the matches. George carried Ralph off to bed. She and Portia were alone in the kitchen.

'Listen! Look at me. Do you notice anything different?'

'Sure I notice, Hon.'

Portia put on her red hat and changed her shoes.

'Well —?'

'Just you take a little grease and rub it on your face. Your nose already done peeled very bad. They say grease is the best thing for bad sunburn.'

She stood by herself in the dark back yard, breaking off pieces of bark from the oak tree with her fingernails. It was almost worse this way. Maybe she would feel better if they could look at her and tell. If they knew.

Her Dad called her from the back steps. 'Mick! Oh, Mick!'

'Yes, sir.'

'The telephone.'

George crowded up close and tried to listen in, but she pushed him away. Mrs. Minowitz talked very loud and excited.

'My Harry should be home by now. You know where he is?'

'No, ma'am.'

'He said you two would ride out on bicycles. Where should he be now? You know where he is?'

'No, ma'am,' Mick said again.

12

NOW that the days were hot again the Sunny Dixie Show was always crowded. The March wind quieted. Trees were thick with their foliage of ocherous green. The sky was a cloudless blue and the rays of the sun grew stronger. The air was sultry. Jake Blount hated this weather. He thought dizzily of the long, burning summer months ahead. He did not feel well. Recently a headache had begun to trouble him constantly. He had gained weight so that his stomach developed a little pouch. He had to leave the top button of his trousers undone. He knew that this was alcoholic fat, but he kept on drinking. Liquor helped the ache in his head. He had only to take one small glass to make it better. Nowadays one glass was the same to him as a quart. It was not the liquor of the moment that gave him the kick — but the reaction of the first swallow to all the alcohol which had saturated his blood during these last months. A spoonful of beer would help the throbbing in his head, but a quart of whiskey could not make him drunk.

He cut out liquor entirely. For several days he drank only water and Orange Crush. The pain was like a crawling worm in his head. He worked wearily during the long afternoons and evenings. He could not sleep and it was agony to try to read. The damp, sour stink in his room infuriated him. He lay restless in the bed and when at last he fell asleep daylight had come.

A dream haunted him. It had first come to him four months ago. He would awake with terror — but the strange point was that never could he remember the contents of this dream. Only the feeling remained when his eyes were opened. Each time his fears at awakening were so identical that he did not doubt but what these dreams were the same. He was used to dreams, the grotesque nightmares of drink that led him down into a madman's region of disorder, but always the morning light scattered the effects of these wild dreams and he forgot them.

This blank, stealthy dream was of a different nature. He awoke and could remember nothing. But there was a sense of menace that lingered in him long after. Then he awoke one morning with the old fear but with a faint remembrance of the darkness behind him. He had been walking among a crowd of people and in his arms he carried something. That was all he could be sure about. Had he stolen? Had he been trying to save some possession? Was he being hunted by all these people around him? He did not think so. The more he studied this simple dream the less he could understand. Then for some time afterward the dream did not return.

He met the writer of signs whose chalked message he had seen the past November. From the first day of their meeting the old man clung to him like an evil genius. His name was Simms and he preached on the sidewalks. The winter cold had kept him indoors, but in the spring he was out on the streets all day. His white hair was soft and ragged on his neck and he carried around with him a woman's big silk pocketbook full of chalk and Jesus ads. His eyes were bright and crazy. Simms tried to convert him.

'Child of adversity, I smell the sinful stink of beer on thy breath. And you smoke cigarettes. If the Lord had wanted us to smoke cigarettes He would have said so in His Book. The mark of Satan is on thy brow. I see it. Repent. Let me show you the light.'

Jake rolled up his eyes and made a slow pious sign in the air. Then he opened his oil-stained hand. 'I reveal this only to you,' he said in a low stage voice. Simms looked down at the scar in his palm. Jake leaned close and whispered: 'And there's the other sign. The sign you know. For I was born with them.'

Simms backed against the fence. With a womanish gesture

he lifted a lock of silver hair from his forehead and smoothed it back on his head. Nervously his tongue licked the corners of his mouth. Jake laughed.

'Blasphemer!' Simms screamed. 'God will get you. You and all your crew. God remembers the scoffers. He watches after me. God watches everybody but He watches me the most. Like He did Moses. God tells me things in the night. God will get you.'

He took Simms down to a corner store for Coca-Colas and peanut-butter crackers. Simms began to work on him again. When he left for the show Simms ran along behind him.

'Come to this corner tonight at seven o'clock. Jesus has a message just for you.'

The first days of April were windy and warm. White clouds trailed across the blue sky. In the wind there was the smell of the river and also the fresher smell of fields beyond the town. The show was crowded every day from four in the afternoon until midnight. The crowd was a tough one. With the new spring he felt an undertone of trouble.

One night he was working on the machinery of the swings when suddenly he was roused from thought by the sounds of angry voices. Quickly he pushed through the crowd until he saw a white girl fighting with a colored girl by the ticket booth of the flying-jinny. He wrenched them apart, but still they struggled to get at each other. The crowd took sides and there was a bedlam of noise. The white girl was a hunchback. She held something tight in her hand.

'I seen you,' the colored girl yelled. I ghy beat that hunch off your back, too.'

'Hush your mouth, you black nigger!'

'Low-down factory tag. I done paid my money and I ghy ride. White man, you make her give me back my ticket.'

'Black nigger slut!'

Jake looked from one to the other. The crowd pressed close. There were mumbled opinions on every side.

'I seen Lurie drop her ticket and I watched this here white lady pick it up. That the truth,' a colored boy said.

'No nigger going to put her hands on no white girl while ——'

'You quit that pushing me. I ready to hit back even if your skin do be white.'

Roughly Jake pushed into the thick of the crowd. 'All right!' he yelled. 'Move on — break it up. Every damn one of you.' There was something about the size of his fists that made the people drift sullenly away. Jake turned back to the two girls.

'This here the way it is,' said the colored girl. 'I bet I one of the few peoples here who done saved over fifty cents till Friday night. I done ironed double this week. I done paid a good nickel for that ticket she holding. And now I means to ride.'

Jake settled the trouble quickly. He let the hunchback keep the disputed ticket and issued another one to the colored girl. For the rest of that evening there were no more quarrels. But Jake moved alertly through the crowd. He was troubled and uneasy.

In addition to himself there were five other employees at the show — two men to operate the swings and take tickets and three girls to manage the booths. This did not count Patterson. The show-owner spent most of his time playing cards with himself in his trailer. His eyes were dull, with the pupils shrunken, and the skin of his neck hung in yellow, pulpy folds. During the past few months Jake had had two raises in pay. At midnight it was his job to report to Patterson and hand over the takings of the evening. Sometimes Patterson did not notice him until he had been in the trailer for several minutes; he would be staring at the cards, sunk in a stupor. The air of the trailer was heavy with the stinks of food and reefers. Patterson held his hand over his stomach as though protecting it from something. He always checked over the accounts very thoroughly.

Jake and the two operators had a squabble. These men were both former doffers at one of the mills. At first he had tried to talk to them and help them to see the truth. Once he invited them to a pool room for a drink. But they were so dumb he couldn't help them. Soon after this he overheard the conversation between them that caused the trouble. It was an early Sunday morning, almost two o'clock, and he had been checking the accounts with Patterson. When he stepped out of the trailer the grounds seemed empty. The moon was bright. He was thinking of Singer and the free day ahead. Then as he passed by the swings he heard someone speak his name. The two operators had finished work and were smoking together. Jake listened.

'If there's anything I hate worse than a nigger it's a Red.'

'He tickles me. I don't pay him no mind. The way he struts around. I never seen such a sawed-off runt. How tall is he, you reckon?'

'Around five foot. But he thinks he got to tell everybody so much. He oughta be in jail. That's where. The Red Bolshivik.'

'He just tickles me. I can't look at him without laughing.'

'He needn't act biggity with me.'

Jake watched them follow the path toward Weavers Lane. His first thought was to rush out and confront them, but a certain shrinking held him back. For several days he fumed in silence. Then one night after work he followed the two men for several blocks and as they turned a corner he cut in front of them.

'I heard you,' he said breathlessly. 'It so happened I heard every word you said last Saturday night. Sure I'm a Red. At least I reckon I am. But what are you?' They stood beneath a street light. The two men stepped back from him. The neighborhood was deserted. 'You pasty-faced, shrunk-gutted, ricket-ridden little rats! I could reach out and choke your stringy necks — one to each hand. Runt or no, I could lay you on this sidewalk where they'd have to scrape you up with shovels.'

The two men looked at each other, cowed, and tried to walk on. But Jake would not let them pass. He kept step with them, walking backward, a furious sneer on his face.

'All I got to say is this: In the future I suggest you come to me whenever you feel the need to make remarks about my height, weight, accent, demeanor, or ideology. And that last is not what I take a leak with either — case you don't know. We will discuss it together.'

Afterward Jake treated the two men with angry contempt. Behind his back they jeered at him. One afternoon he found that the engine of the swings had been deliberately damaged and he had to work three hours overtime to fix it. Always he felt someone was laughing at him. Each time he heard the girls talking together he drew himself up straight and laughed carelessly aloud to himself as though thinking of some private joke.

The warm southwest winds from the Gulf of Mexico were heavy with the smells of spring. The days grew longer and the sun was bright. The lazy warmth depressed him. He began to drink again. As soon as work was done he went home and lay down on his bed. Sometimes he stayed there, fully clothed and inert, for twelve or thirteen hours. The restlessness that had caused him to sob and bite his nails only a few months before seemed to have gone. And yet beneath his inertia Jake felt the old tension. Of all the places he had been this was the loneliest town of all. Or it would be without Singer. Only he and Singer understood the truth. He knew and could not get the don't-knows to see. It was like trying to fight darkness or heat or a stink in the air. He stared morosely out of his window. A stunted, smoke-blackened tree at the corner had put out new leaves of a bilious green. The sky was always a deep, hard blue. The mosquitoes from a fetid stream that ran through this part of the town buzzed in the room.

He caught the itch. He mixed some sulphur and hog fat and greased his body every morning. He clawed himself raw and it seemed that the itching would never be soothed. One night he broke loose. He had been sitting alone for many hours. He had mixed gin and whiskey and was very drunk. It was almost morning. He leaned out of the window and looked at the dark silent street. He thought of all the people around him. Sleeping. The don't-knows. Suddenly he bawled out in a loud voice: 'This is the truth! You bastards don't know anything. You don't know. You don't know!'

The street awoke angrily. Lamps were lighted and sleepy curses were called to him. The men who lived in the house rattled furiously on his door. The girls from a cat-house across the street stuck their heads out of the windows.

'You dumb dumb dumb dumb bastards. You dumb dumb dumb dumb ——'

'Shuddup! Shuddup!'

The fellows in the hall were pushing against the door: 'You drunk bull! You'll be a sight dumber when we get thu with you.'

'How many out there?' Jake roared. He banged an empty bottle on the windowsill. 'Come on, everybody. Come one, come all. I'll settle you three at a time.'

'That's right, Honey,' a whore called.

The door was giving way. Jake jumped from the window and ran through a side alley. 'Hee-haw! Hee-haw!' he yelled drunkenly. He was barefooted and shirtless. An hour later he stumbled into Singer's room. He sprawled on the floor and laughed himself to sleep.

On an April morning he found the body of a man who had been murdered. A young Negro. Jake found him in a ditch about thirty yards from the showgrounds. The Negro's throat had been slashed so that the head was rolled back at a crazy angle. The sun shone hot on his open, glassy eyes and flies hovered over the dried blood that covered his chest. The dead man held a red-and-yellow cane with a tassel like the ones sold at the hamburger booth at the show. Jake stared gloomily down at the body for some time. Then he called the police. No clues were found. Two days later the family of the dead man claimed his body at the morgue.

At the Sunny Dixie there were frequent fights and quarrels. Sometimes two friends would come to the show arm in arm, laughing and drinking — and before they left they would be struggling together in a panting rage. Jake was always alert. Beneath the gaudy gaiety of the show, the bright lights, and the lazy laughter, he felt something sullen and dangerous.

Through these dazed, disjointed weeks Simms nagged his footsteps constantly. The old man liked to come with a soap-box and a Bible and take a stand in the middle of the crowd to preach. He talked of the second coming of Christ. He said that the Day of Judgment would be October 2, 1951. He would point out certain drunks and scream at them in his raw, worn voice. Excitement made his mouth fill with water so that his words had a wet, gurgling sound. Once he had slipped in and set up his stand no arguments could make him budge. He made Jake a present of a Gideon Bible, and told him to pray on his knees for one hour each night and to hurl away every glass of beer or cigarette that was offered him.

They quarreled over walls and fences. Jake had begun to carry chalk in his pockets, also. He wrote brief sentences. He tried to word them so that a passerby would stop and ponder over the meaning. So that a man would wonder. So that a man would think. Also, he wrote short pamphlets and distributed them in the streets.

If it had not been for Singer, Jake knew that he would have left the town. Only on Sunday, when he was with his friend, did he feel at peace. Sometimes they would go for a walk together or play chess — but more often they spent the day quietly in Singer's room. If he wished to talk Singer was always attentive. If he sat morosely through the day the mute understood his feelings and was not surprised. It seemed to him that only Singer could help him now.

Then one Sunday when he climbed the stairs he saw that Singer's door was open. The room was empty. He sat alone for more than two hours. At last he heard Singer's footsteps on the stairs.

'I was wondering about you. Where you been?'

Singer smiled. He brushed off his hat with a handkerchief and put it away. Then deliberately he took his silver pencil from his pocket and leaned over the mantelpiece to write a note.

'What you mean?' Jake asked when he read what the mute had written. 'Whose legs are cut off?'

Singer took back the note and wrote a few additional sentences.

'Huh!' Jake said. 'That don't surprise me.'

He brooded over the piece of paper and then crumpled it in his hand. The listlessness of the past month was gone and he was tense and uneasy. 'Huh!' he said again.

Singer put on a pot of coffee and got out his chessboard. Jake tore the note to pieces and rolled the fragments between his sweating palms.

'But something can be done about this,' he said after a while. 'You know it?'

Singer nodded uncertainly.

'I want to see the boy and hear the whole story. When can you take me around there?'

Singer deliberated. Then he wrote on a pad of paper, 'To-night.'

Jake held his hand to his mouth and began to walk restlessly around the room. 'We can do something.'

13

JAKE and Singer waited on the front porch. When they pushed the doorbell there was no sound of a ring in the darkened house. Jake knocked impatiently and pressed his nose against the screen door. Beside him Singer stood wooden and smiling, with two spots of color on his cheeks, for they had drunk a bottle of gin together. The evening was quiet and dark. Jake watched a yellow light shaft softly through the hall. And Portia opened the door for them.

'I certainly trust you not been waiting long. So many folks been coming that us thought it wise to untach the bell. You gentlemens just let me take you hats — Father been mighty sick.'

Jake tiptoed heavily behind Singer down the bare, narrow hall. At the threshold of the kitchen he stopped short. The room was crowded and hot. A fire burned in the small wood stove and the windows were closed tight. Smoke mingled with a certain Negro smell. The glow from the stove was the only light in the room. The dark voices he had heard back in the hall were silent.

'These here are two white gentlemens come to inquire about Father,' Portia said. 'I think maybe he be able to see you but I better go on in first and prepare him.'

Jake fingered his thick lower lip. On the end of his nose there was a latticed impression from the front screen door. 'That's not it,' he said. 'I come to talk with your brother.'

The Negroes in the room were standing. Singer motioned to them to be seated again. Two grizzled old men sat down on a bench by the stove. A loose-limbed mulatto lounged against the window. On a camp cot in a corner was a boy without legs whose trousers were folded and pinned beneath his stumpy thighs.

'Good evening,' Jake said awkwardly. 'Your name Copeland?'

The boy put his hands over the stumps of his legs and shrank back close to the wall. 'My name Willie.'

'Honey, don't you worry none,' said Portia. 'This here is Mr. Singer that you heard Father speak about. And this other white gentleman is Mr. Blount and he a very close friend of Mr. Singer. They just kindly come to inquire about us in our trouble.' She turned to Jake and motioned to the three other people in the room. 'This other boy leaning on the window is my brother too. Named Buddy. And these here over by the stove is two dear friends of my Father. Named Mr. Marshall Nicolls and Mr. John Roberts. I think it a good idea to understand who all is in a room with you.'

'Thanks,' Jake said. He turned to Willie again. 'I just want you to tell me about it so I can get it straight in my mind.'

'This the way it is,' Willie said. 'I feel like my feets is still hurting. I got this here terrible misery down in my toes. Yet the hurt in my feets is down where my feets should be if they were on my l-l-legs. And not where my feets is now. It a hard thing to understand. My feets hurt me so bad all the time and I don't know where they is. They never given them back to me. They s-somewhere more than a hundred m-miles from here.'

'I mean about how it all happened,' Jake said.

Uneasily Willie looked up at his sister. 'I don't remember — very good.'

'Course you remember, Honey. You done already told us over and over.'

'Well ——' The boy's voice was timid and sullen. 'Us were all out on the road and this here Buster say something to the guard. The w-white man taken a stick to him. Then this other boy he tries to run off. And I follow him. It all come about so quick I don't remember good just how it were. Then they taken us back to the camp and ——'

'I know the rest,' Jake said. 'But give me the names and

addresses of the other two boys. And tell me the names of the guards.'

'Listen here, white man. It seem to me like you meaning to get me into trouble.'

'Trouble!' Jake said rudely. 'What in the name of Christ do you think you're in now?'

'Less us quiet down,' Portia said nervously. 'This here the way it is, Mr. Blount. They done let Willie off at the camp before his time were served. But they done also impressed it on him not to — I believe you understand what us means. Naturally Willie he scared. Naturally us means to be careful — 'cause that the best thing us can do. We already got enough trouble as is.'

'What happened to the guards?'

'Them w-white men were fired. That what they told me.'

'And where are your friends now?'

'What friends?'

'Why, the other two boys.'

'They n-not my friends,' Willie said. 'Us all has had a big falling out.'

'How you mean?'

Portia pulled her earrings so that the lobes of her ears stretched out like rubber. 'This here what Willie means. You see, during them three days when they hurt so bad they commenced to quarrel. Willie don't ever want to see any of them again. That one thing Father and Willie done argued about already. This here Buster ——'

'Buster got a wooden leg,' said the boy by the window. 'I seen him on the street today.'

'This here Buster don't have no folks and it were Father's idea to have him move on in with us. Father want to round up all the boys together. How he reckons us can feed them I sure don't know.'

'That ain't a good idea. And besides us was never very good friends anyway.' Willie felt the stumps of his legs with his dark, strong hands. 'I just wish I knowed where my f-f-feets are. That the main thing worries me. The doctor never given them back to me. I sure do wish I knowed where they are.'

Jake looked around him with dazed, gin-clouded eyes. Everything seemed unclear and strange. The heat in the kitchen dizzied him so that voices echoed in his ears. The smoke choked him. The light hanging from the ceiling was turned on but, as the bulb was wrapped in newspaper to dim its strength, most of the light came from between the chinks of the hot stove. There was a red glow on all the dark faces around him. He felt uneasy and alone. Singer had left the room to visit Portia's father. Jake wanted him to come back so that they could leave. He walked awkwardly across the floor and sat down on the bench between Marshall Nicolls and John Roberts.

'Where is Portia's father?' he asked.

'Doctor Copeland is in the front room, sir,' said Roberts.

'Is he a doctor?'

'Yes, sir. He is a medical doctor.'

There was a scuffle on the steps outside and the back door opened. A warm, fresh breeze lightened the heavy air. First a tall boy dressed in a linen suit and gilded shoes entered the room with a sack in his arms. Behind him came a young boy of about seventeen.

'Hey, Highboy. Hey there, Lancy,' Willie said. 'What you all brought me?'

Highboy bowed elaborately to Jake and placed on the table two fruit jars of wine. Lancy put beside them a plate covered with a fresh white napkin.

'This here wine is a present from the Society,' Highboy said. 'And Lancy's mother sent some peach puffs.'

'How is the Doctor, Miss Portia?' Lancy asked.

'Honey, he been mighty sick these days. What worries me is he so strong. It a bad sign when a person sick as he is suddenly come to be so strong.' Portia turned to Jake. Don't you think it a bad sign, Mr. Blount?'

Jake stared at her dazedly. 'I don't know.'

Lancy glanced sullenly at Jake and pulled down the cuffs of his outgrown shirt. 'Give the Doctor my family's regards.'

'Us certainly do appreciate this,' Portia said. 'Father was speaking of you just the other day. He haves a book he wants to give you. Wait just one minute while I get it and rinch out this plate to return to your Mother. This were certainly a kindly thing for her to do.'

Marshall Nicolls leaned toward Jake and seemed about to speak to him. The old man wore a pair of pin-striped trousers and a morning coat with a flower in the buttonhole. He cleared his throat and said: 'Pardon me, sir — but unavoidably we overheard a part of your conversation with William regarding the trouble he is now in. *Inevitably* we have considered what is the best course to take.'

'You one of his relatives or the preacher in his church?'

'No, I am a pharmacist. And John Roberts on your left is employed in the postal department of the government.'

'A postman,' repeated John Roberts.

'With your permission ——' Marshall Nicolls took a yellow silk handkerchief from his pocket and gingerly blew his nose. 'Naturally we have discussed this matter *extensively*. And without doubt as members of the colored race here in this free country of America we are anxious to do our part toward extending *amicable* relationships.'

'We wish always to do the right thing,' said John Roberts.

'And it behooves us to strive with care and not endanger this amicable relationship already established. Then by gradual means a better *condition* will come about.'

Jake turned from one to the other. 'I don't seem to follow you.' The heat was suffocating him. He wanted to get out. A film seemed to have settled over his eyeballs so that all the faces around him were blurred.

Across the room Willie was playing his harp. Buddy and Highboy were listening. The music was dark and sad. When the song was finished Willie polished his harp on the front of his shirt. 'I so hungry and thirsty the slobber in my mouth done wet out the tune. I certainly will be glad to taste some of that boogie-woogie. To have something good to drink is the only thing m-made me forget this misery. If I just knowed where my f-feets are now and could drink a glass of gin ever night I wouldn't mind so much.'

'Don't fret, Hon. You going to have something,' Portia said. 'Mr. Blount, would you care to take a peach puff and a glass of wine?'

'Thanks,' Jake said. 'That would be good.'

Quickly Portia laid a cloth on the table and set down one plate and a fork. She poured a large tumblerful of the wine. 'You just make yourself comfortable here. And if you don't mind I going to serve the others.'

The fruit jars were passed from mouth to mouth. Before Highboy passed a jar to Willie he borrowed Portia's lipstick and drew a red line to set the boundary of the drink. There were gurgling noises and laughter. Jake finished his puff and carried his glass back with him to his place between the two old men. The home-made wine was rich and strong as brandy. Willie started a low dolorous tune on his harp. Portia snapped her fingers and shuffled around the room.

Jake turned to Marshall Nicolls. 'You say Portia's father is a doctor?'

'Yes, sir. Yes, indeed. A skilled doctor.'

'What's the matter with him?'

The two Negroes glanced warily at each other.

'He were in an accident,' said John Roberts.

'What kind of an accident?'

'A bad one. A deplorable one.'

Marshall Nicolls folded and unfolded his silk handkerchief. 'As we were remarking a while ago, it is important not to *impair* these amicable relations but to promote them in all ways earnestly possible. We members of the colored race must strive in all ways to uplift our citizens. The Doctor in yonder has strived in every way. But sometimes it has seemed to me like he had not recognized fully enough certain *elements* of the different races and the situation.'

Impatiently Jake gulped down the last swallows of his wine. 'Christ' sake, man, speak out plain, because I can't understand a thing you say.'

Marshall Nicolls and John Roberts exchanged a hurt look. Across the room Willie still sat playing music. His lips crawled over the square holes of the harmonica like fat, puckered caterpillars. His shoulders were broad and strong. The stumps of his thighs jerked in time to the music. Highboy danced while Buddy and Portia clapped out the rhythm.

Jake stood up, and once on his feet he realized that he was drunk. He staggered and then glanced vindictively around him, but no one seemed to have noticed. 'Where's Singer?' he asked Portia thickly.

The music stopped. 'Why, Mr. Blount, I thought you knowed he was gone. While you were sitting at the table with your peach puff he come to the doorway and held out his watch to show it were time for him to go. You looked straight at him and shaken your head. I thought you knowed that.'

'Maybe I was thinking about something else.' He turned to Willie and said angrily to him: 'I never did even get to tell you what I come here for. I didn't come to ask you to *do* anything. All I wanted — all I wanted was this. You and the other boys were to testify what happened and I was to explain why. *Why* is the only important thing — not *what*. I would have pushed you all around in a wagon and you would have told your story and afterward I would have explained *why*. And maybe it might have meant something. Maybe it ——'

He felt they were laughing at him. Confusion caused him to forget what he had meant to say. The room was full of dark, strange faces and the air was too thick to breath. He saw a door and staggered across to it. He was in a dark closet smelling of medicine. Then his hand was turning another doorknob.

He stood on the threshold of a small white room furnished only with an iron bed, a cabinet, and two chairs. On the bed lay the terrible Negro he had met on the stairs at Singer's house. His face was very black against the white, stiff pillows. The dark eyes were hot with hatred but the heavy, bluish lips were composed. His face was motionless as a black mask except for the slow, wide flutters of his nostrils with each breath.

'Get out,' the Negro said.

'Wait ——' Jake said helplessly. 'Why do you say that?'

'This is my house.'

Jake could not draw his eyes away from the Negro's terrible face. 'But why?'

'You are a white man and a stranger.'

Jake did not leave. He walked with cumbersome caution to one of the straight white chairs and seated himself. The Negro moved his hands on the counterpane. His black eyes glittered with fever. Jake watched him. They waited. In the room there was a feeling tense as conspiracy or as the deadly quiet before an explosion.

It was long past midnight. The warm, dark air of the spring morning swirled the blue layers of smoke in the room On the floor were crumpled balls of paper and a half-empty bottle of gin. Scattered ashes were gray on the counterpane. Doctor Copeland pressed his head tensely into the pillow. He had removed his dressing-gown and the sleeves of his white cotton nightshirt were rolled to the elbow. Jake leaned forward in his chair. His tie was loosened and the collar of his shirt had wilted with sweat. Through the hours there had grown between them a long, exhausting dialogue. And now a pause had come.

'So the time is ready for ——' Jake began.

But Doctor Copeland interrupted him. 'Now it is perhaps necessary that we ——' he murmured huskily. They halted. Each looked into the eyes of the other and waited. 'I beg your pardon,' Doctor Copeland said.

'Sorry,' said Jake. 'Go on.'

'No, you continue.'

'Well ——' Jake said. 'I won't say what I started to say. Instead we'll have one last word about the South. The strangled South. The wasted South. The slavish South.'

'And the Negro people.'

To steady himself Jake swallowed a long, burning draught from the bottle on the floor beside him. Then deliberately he walked to the cabinet and picked up a small, cheap globe of the world that served as a paperweight. Slowly he turned the sphere in his hands. 'All I can say is this: The world is full of meanness and evil. Huh! Three fourths of this globe is in a state of war or oppression. The liars and fiends are united and the men who *know* are isolated and without defense. But! But if you was to ask me to point out the most uncivilized area on the face of this globe I would point here ——'

'Watch sharp,' said Doctor Copeland. 'You're out in the ocean.'

Jake turned the globe again and pressed his blunt, grimy thumb on a carefully selected spot. 'Here. These thirteen states. I know what I'm talking about. I read books and I go around. I been in every damn one of these thirteen states. I've worked in every one. And the reason I think like I do is this: We live in the richest country in the world. There's plenty and to spare for no man, woman, or child to be in want. And in addition to this our country was founded on what should have been a great, true principle — the freedom, equality, and rights of each individual. Huh! And what has come of that start? There are corporations worth billions of dollars — and hundreds of thousands of people who don't get to eat. And here in these thirteen states the exploitation of human beings is so that — that it's a thing you got to take in with your own eyes. In my life I seen things that would make a man go crazy. At least one third of all Southerners live and die no better off than the lowest peasant in any European Fascist state. The average wage of a worker on a tenant farm is only seventy-three dollars per year. And mind you, that's the average! The wages of sharecroppers run from thirty-five to ninety dollars per person. And thirty-five dollars a year means just about ten cents for a full day's work. Everywhere there's pellagra and hookworm and anaemia. And just plain, pure starvation. But!' Jake rubbed his lips with the knuckles of his dirty fist. Sweat stood out on his forehead. 'But!' he repeated. 'Those are only the evils you can see and touch. The other things are worse. I'm talking about the way that the truth has been hidden from the people. The things they have been told so they can't see the truth. The poisonous lies. So they aren't allowed to know.'

'And the Negro,' said Doctor Copeland. 'To understand what is happening to us you have to ——'

Jake interrupted him savagely. 'Who owns the South? Corporations in the North own three fourths of all the South. They say the old cow grazes all over — in the south, the west, the north, and the east. But she's milked in just one place. Her old teats swing over just one spot when she's full. She grazes everywhere and is milked in New York. Take our cotton mills, our pulp mills, our harness factories, our mattress factories. The North owns them. And what happens?' Jake's mustache quivered angrily. 'Here's an example. Locale, a mill village according to the great paternal system of American industry. Absentee ownership. In the village is one huge brick mill and maybe four or five hundred shanties. The houses aren't fit for human beings to live in. Moreover, the houses were built to be nothing but slums in the first place. These shanties are nothing but two or maybe three rooms and a privy — built with far less forethought than barns to house cattle. Built with far less attention to needs than sties for pigs. For under this system pigs are valuable and men are not. You can't make pork chops and sausage out of skinny little mill kids. You can't sell but half the people these days. But a pig ——'

'Hold on!' said Doctor Copeland. 'You are getting off on a tangent. And besides, you are giving no attention to the very separate question of the Negro. I cannot get a word in edgeways. We have been over all this before, but it is impossible to see the full situation without including us Negroes.'

'Back to our mill village,' Jake said. 'A young linthead begins working at the fine wage of eight or ten dollars a week at such times as he can get himself employed. He marries. After the first child the woman must work in the mill also. Their combined wages come to say eighteen dollars a week when they both got work. Huh! They pay a fourth of this for the shack the mill provides them. They buy food and clothes at a company-owned or dominated store. The store overcharges on every item. With three or four younguns they are held down the same as if they had on chains. That is the whole principle of serfdom. Yet here in America we call ourselves free. And the funny thing is that this has been drilled into the heads of sharecroppers and lintheads and all the rest so hard that they really believe it. But it's taken a hell of a lot of lies to keep them from knowing.'

'There is only one way out ——' said Doctor Copeland.

'Two ways. And only two ways. Once there was a time when this country was expanding. Every man thought he had a chance. Huh! But that period has gone — and gone for good. Less than a hundred corporations have swallowed all but a few leavings. These industries have already sucked the blood and softened the bones of the people. The old days of expansion are gone. The whole system of capitalistic democracy is — rotten and corrupt. There remain only two roads ahead. One: Fascism. Two: reform of the most revolutionary and permanent kind.'

'And the Negro. Do not forget the Negro. So far as I and my people are concerned the South is Fascist now and always has been.'

'Yeah.'

'The Nazis rob the Jews of their legal, economic, and cultural life. Here the Negro has always been deprived of these. And if wholesale and dramatic robbery of money and goods has not taken place here as in Germany, it is simply because the Negro has never been allowed to accrue wealth in the first place.'

'That's the system,' Jake said.

'The Jew and the Negro,' said Doctor Copeland bitterly. 'The history of my people will be commensurate with the interminable history of the Jew — only bloodier and more violent. Like a certain species of sea gull. If you capture one of the birds and tie a red string of twine around his leg the rest of the flock will peck him to death.'

Doctor Copeland took off his spectacles and rebound a wire around a broken hinge. Then he polished the lenses on his nightshirt. His hand shook with agitation. 'Mr. Singer is a Jew.'

'No, you're wrong there.'

'But I am positive that he is. The name, Singer. I recognized his race the first time I saw him. From his eyes. Besides, he told me so.'

'Why, he couldn't have,' Jake insisted. 'He's pure Anglo-Saxon if I ever saw it. Irish and Anglo-Saxon.'

'But ——'

'I'm certain. Absolutely.'

'Very well,' said Doctor Copeland. 'We will not quarrel.'

Outside the dark air had cooled so that there was a chill in the room. It was almost dawn. The early morning sky was deep, silky blue and the moon had turned from silver to white. All was still. The only sound was the clear, lonely song of a spring bird in the darkness outside. Though a faint breeze blew in from the window the air in the room was sour and close. There was a feeling both of tenseness and exhaustion. Doctor Copeland leaned forward from the pillow. His eyes were bloodshot and his hands clutched the counterpane. The neck of his nightshirt had slipped down over his bony shoulder. Jake's heels were balanced on the rungs of his chair and his giant hands folded between his knees in a waiting and childlike attitude. Deep black circles were beneath his eyes, his hair was unkempt. They looked at each other and waited. As the silence grew longer the tenseness between them became more strained.

At last Doctor Copeland cleared his throat and said: 'I am certain you did not come here for nothing. I am sure we have not discussed these subjects all through the night to no purpose. We have talked of everything now except the most vital subject of all — the way out. What must be done.'

They still watched each other and waited. In the face of each there was expectation. Doctor Copeland sat bolt upright against the pillows. Jake rested his chin in his hand and leaned forward. The pause continued. And then hesitantly they began to speak at the same time.

'Excuse me,' Jake said. 'Go ahead.'

'No, you. You started first.'

'Go on.'

'Pshaw!' said Doctor Copeland. 'Continue.'

Jake stared at him with clouded, mystical eyes. 'It's this way. This is how I see it. The only solution is for the people to *know*. Once they know the truth they can be oppressed no longer. Once just half of them know the whole fight is won.'

'Yes, once they understand the workings of this society. But how do you propose to tell them?'

'Listen,' Jake said. 'Think about chain letters. If one person sends a letter to ten people and then each of the ten people send letters to ten more — you get it?' He faltered. 'Not that I write letters, but the idea is the same. I just go around telling. And if in one town I can show the truth to just ten of the don't-knows, then I feel like some good has been done. See?'

Doctor Copeland looked at Jake in surprise. Then he snorted. 'Do not be childish. You cannot just go about talking. Chain letters indeed! Knows and don't-knows!'

Jake's lips trembled and his brow lowered with quick anger. 'O.K. What have you got to offer?'

'I will say first that I used to feel somewhat as you do on this question. But I have learned what a mistake that attitude is. For half a century I thought it wise to be patient.'

'I didn't say be patient.'

'In the face of brutality I was prudent. Before injustice I held my peace. I sacrificed the things in hand for the good of the hypothetical whole. I believed in the tongue instead of the fist. As an armor against oppression I taught patience and faith in the human soul. I know now how wrong I was. I have been a traitor to myself and to my people. All that is rot. Now is the time to act and to act quickly. Fight cunning with cunning and might with might.'

'But how?' Jake asked. 'How?'

'Why, by getting out and doing things. By calling crowds of people together and getting them to demonstrate.'

'Huh! That last phrase gives you away — "getting them to demonstrate." What good will it do if you get them to demonstrate against a thing if they don't *know?* You're trying to stuff the hog by way of his ass.'

'Such vulgar expressions annoy me,' Doctor Copeland said prudishly.

'For Christ' sake! I don't care if they annoy you or not.'

Doctor Copeland held up his hand. 'Let us not get so overheated,' he said. 'Let us attempt to see eye to eye with each other.'

'Suits me. I don't want to fight with you.'

They were silent. Doctor Copeland moved his eyes from one corner of the ceiling to the other. Several times he wet his lips to speak and each time the word remained half-formed and silent in his mouth. Then at last he said: 'My advice to you is this. Do not attempt to stand alone.'

'But ——'

'*But*, nothing,' said Doctor Copeland didactically. 'The most fatal thing a man can do is try to stand alone.'

'I see what you're getting at.'

Doctor Copeland pulled the neck of his nightshirt up over his bony shoulder and held it gathered tight to his throat. 'You believe in the struggle of my people for their human rights?'

The Doctor's agitation and his mild and husky question made Jake's eyes brim suddenly with tears. A quick, swollen rush of love caused him to grasp the black, bony hand on the counterpane and hold it fast. 'Sure,' he said.

'The extremity of our need?'

'Yes.'

'The lack of justice? The bitter inequality?'

Doctor Copeland coughed and spat into one of the squares of paper which he kept beneath his pillow. 'I have a program. It is a very simple, concentrated plan. I mean to focus on only one objective. In August of this year I plan to lead more than one thousand Negroes in this county on a march. A march to Washington. All of us together in one solid body. If you will look in the cabinet yonder you will see a stack of letters which I have written this week and will deliver personally.' Doctor Copeland slid his nervous hands up and down the sides of the narrow bed. 'You remember what

I said to you a short while ago? You will recall that my only advice to you was: Do not attempt to stand alone.'

'I get it,' Jake said.

'But once you enter this it must be all. First and foremost. Your work now and forever. You must give of your whole self without stint, without hope of personal return, without rest or hope of rest.'

'For the rights of the Negro in the South.'

'In the South and here in this very county. And it must be either all or nothing. Either yes or no.'

Doctor Copeland leaned back on the pillow. Only his eyes seemed alive. They burned in his face like red coals. The fever made his cheekbones a ghastly purple. Jake scowled and pressed his knuckles to his soft, wide, trembling mouth. Color rushed to his face. Outside the first pale light of morning had come. The electric bulb suspended from the ceiling burned with ugly sharpness in the dawn.

Jake rose to his feet and stood stiffly at the foot of the bed. He said flatly: 'No. That's not the right angle at all. I'm dead sure it's not. In the first place, you'd never get out of town. They'd break it up by saying it's a menace to public health — or some such trumped-up reason. They'd arrest you and nothing would come of it. But even if by some miracle you got to Washington it wouldn't do any good. Why, the whole notion is crazy.'

The sharp rattle of phlegm sounded in Doctor Copeland's throat. His voice was harsh. 'As you are so quick to sneer and condemn, what do you have to offer instead?'

'I didn't sneer,' Jake said. 'I only remarked that your plan is crazy. I come here tonight with an idea much better than that. I wanted your son, Willie, and the other two boys to let me push them around in a wagon. They were to tell what happened to them and afterward I was to tell why. In other words, I was to give a talk on the dialectics of capitalism — and show up all of its lies. I would explain so that everyone would understand *why* those boys' legs were cut off. And make everyone who saw them *know*.'

'Pshaw! Double pshaw!' said Doctor Copeland furiously 'I do not believe you have good sense. If I were a man who felt it worth my while to laugh I would surely laugh at that. Never have I had the opportunity to hear of such nonsense first hand.'

They stared at each other in bitter disappointment and anger. There was the rattle of a wagon in the street outside. Jake swallowed and bit his lips. 'Huh!' he said finally. 'You're the only one who's crazy. You got everything exactly backward. The only way to solve the Negro problem under capitalism is to geld every one of the fifteen million black men in these states.'

'So that is the kind of idea you harbor beneath your ranting about justice.'

'I didn't say it should be done. I only said you couldn't see the forest for the trees.' Jake spoke with slow and painful care. 'The work has to start at the bottom. The old traditions smashed and the new ones created. To forge a whole new pattern for the world. To make man a social creature for the first time, living in an orderly and controlled society where he is not forced to be unjust in order to survive. A social tradition in which ——'

Doctor Copeland clapped ironically. 'Very good,' he said. 'But the cotton must be picked before the cloth is made. You and your crackpot do-nothing theories can ——'

'Hush! Who cares whether you and your thousand Negroes straggle up to that stinking cesspool of a place called Washington? What difference does it make? What do a few people matter — a few thousand people, black, white, good or bad? When the whole of our society is built on a foundation of black lies.'

'Everything!' Doctor Copeland panted. 'Everything! Everything!'

'Nothing!'

'The soul of the meanest and most evil of us on this earth is worth more in the sight of justice than ——'

'Oh, the Hell with it!' Jake said. 'Balls!'

'Blasphemer!' screamed Doctor Copeland. 'Foul blasphemer!'

Jake shook the iron bars of the bed. The vein in his forehead swelled to the point of bursting and his face was dark with rage. 'Short-sighted bigot!'

'White ——' Doctor Copeland's voice failed him. He struggled and no sound would come. At last he was able to bring forth a choked whisper: 'Fiend.'

The bright yellow morning was at the window. Doctor Copeland's head fell back on the pillow. His neck twisted at a broken angle, a fleck of bloody foam on his lips. Jake looked at him once before, sobbing with violence, he rushed headlong from the room.

14

NOW she could not stay in the inside room. She had to be around somebody all the time. Doing something every minute. And if she was by herself she counted or figured with numbers. She counted all the roses on the living-room wallpaper. She figured out the cubic area of the whole house. She counted every blade of grass in the back yard and every leaf on a certain bush. Because if she did not have her mind on numbers this terrible afraidness came in her. She would be walking home from school on these May afternoons and suddenly she would have to think of something quick. A good thing — very good. Maybe she would think about a phrase of hurrying jazz music. Or that a bowl of jello would be in the refrigerator when she got home. Or plan to smoke a cigarette behind the coal house. Maybe she would try to think a long way ahead to the time when she would go north and see snow, or even travel somewhere in a foreign land. But these thoughts about good things wouldn't last. The jello was gone in five minutes and the cigarette smoked. Then what was there after that? And the numbers mixed themselves up in her brain. And the snow and the foreign land were a long, long time away. Then what was there?

Just Mister Singer. She wanted to follow him everywhere. In the morning she would watch him go down the front steps to work and then follow along a half a block behind him. Every afternoon as soon as school was over she hung around at the corner near the store where he worked. At four o'clock he went out to drink a Coca-Cola. She watched him cross the street and go into the drugstore and finally come out again. She followed him home from work and sometimes even when he took walks. She always followed a long way behind him. And he did not know.

She would go up to see him in his room. First she scrubbed her face and hands and put some vanilla on the front of her dress. She only went to visit him twice a week now, because she didn't want him to get tired of her. Most always he would be sitting over the queer, pretty chess game when she opened the door. And then she was with him.

'Mister Singer, have you ever lived in a place where it snowed in the winter-time?'

He tilted his chair back against the wall and nodded.

'In some different country than this one — in a foreign place?'

He nodded yes again and wrote on his pad with his silver pencil. Once he had traveled to Ontario, Canada — across the river from Detroit. Canada was so far in the north that the white snow drifted up to the roofs of the houses. That was where the Quints were and the St. Lawrence River. The people ran up and down the streets speaking French to each other.

And far up in the north there were deep forests and white ice igloos. The arctic region with the beautiful northern lights.

'When you was in Canada did you go out and get any fresh snow and eat it with cream and sugar? Once I read where it was mighty good to eat that way.'

He turned his head to one side because he didn't understand. She couldn't ask the question again because suddenly it sounded silly. She only looked at him and waited. A big, black shadow of his head was on the wall behind him. The electric fan cooled the thick, hot air. All was quiet. It was like they waited to tell each other things that had never been told before. What she had to say was terrible and afraid. But what he would tell her was so true that it would make everything all right. Maybe it was a thing that could not be spoken with words or writing. Maybe he would have to let her understand this in a different way. That was the feeling she had with him.

'I was just asking you about Canada — but it didn't amount to anything, Mister Singer.'

Downstairs in the home rooms there was plenty of trouble. Etta was still so sick that she couldn't sleep crowded three in a bed. The shades were kept drawn and the dark room smelled bad with a sick smell. Etta's job was gone, and that meant eight dollars less a week besides the doctor's bill. Then one day when Ralph was walking around in the kitchen he burned himself on the hot kitchen stove. The bandages made his hands itch and somebody had to watch him all the time else he would bust the blisters. On George's birthday they had bought him a little red bike with a bell and a basket on the handlebars. Everybody had chipped in to give it to him. But when Etta lost her job they couldn't pay, and after two installments were past due the store sent a man out to take the wheel away. George just watched the man roll the bike off the porch, and when he passed George kicked the back fender and then went into the coal house and shut the door.

It was money, money, money all the time. They owed to the grocery and they owed the last payment on some furniture. And now since they had lost the house they owed money there too. The six rooms in the house were always taken, but nobody ever paid the rent on time.

For a while their Dad went out every day to hunt another job. He couldn't do carpenter work any more because it made him jittery to be more than ten feet off the ground. He applied for many jobs but nobody would hire him. Then at last he got this notion.

'It's advertising, Mick,' he said. 'I've come to the conclusion that's all in the world the matter with my watch-repairing business right now. I got to sell myself. I got to get out and let people know I can fix watches, and fix them good and cheap. You just mark my words. I'm going to build up this business so I'll be able to make a good living for this family the rest of my life. Just by advertising.'

He brought home a dozen sheets of tin and some red paint. For the next week he was very busy. It seemed to him like this was a hell of a good idea. The signs were all over the floor of the front room. He got down on his hands and knees and took great care over the printing of each letter. As he worked he whistled and wagged his head. He hadn't been so cheerful and glad in months. Every now and then he would have to dress in his good suit and go around the corner for a glass of beer to calm himself. On the signs at first he had:

Wilbur Kelly

Watch Repairing

Very Cheap and Expert

'Mick, I want them to hit you right bang in the eye. To stand out wherever you see them.'

She helped him and he gave her three nickels. The signs were O.K. at first. Then he worked on them so much that they were ruined. He wanted to add more and more things — in the corners and at the top and bottom. Before he had finished the signs were plastered all over with 'Very Cheap' and 'Come At Once' and 'You Give Me Any Watch And I Make It Run.'

'You tried to write so much in the signs that nobody will read anything,' she told him.

He brought home some more tin and left the designing up to her. She painted them very plain, with great big block letters and a picture of a clock. Soon he had a whole stack of them. A fellow he knew rode him out in the country where he could nail them to trees and fenceposts. At both ends of the block he put up a sign with a black hand pointing toward the house. And over the front door there was another sign.

The day after this advertising was finished he waited in the front room dressed in a clean shirt and a tie. Nothing happened. The jeweler who gave him overflow work to do at half price sent in a couple of clocks. That was all. He took it hard. He didn't go out to look for other jobs any more, but every minute he had to be busy around the house. He took down the doors and oiled the hinges — whether they needed it or not. He mixed the margarine for Portia and scrubbed the floors upstairs. He worked out a contraption where the water from the ice box could be drained through the kitchen window. He carved some beautiful alphabet blocks for Ralph and invented a little needle-threader. Over the few watches that he had to work on he took great pains.

Mick still followed Mister Singer. But she didn't want to. It was like there was something wrong about her following after him without his knowing. Two or three days she played hooky from school. She walked behind him when he went to work and hung around on the corner near his store all day. When he ate his dinner at Mister Brannon's she went into the café and spent a nickel for a sack of peanuts. Then at night she followed him on these dark, long walks. She stayed on the opposite side of the street from him and about a block behind. When he stopped, she stopped also — and when he walked fast she ran to keep up with him. So long as she could see him and be near him she was right happy. But sometimes this queer feeling would come to her and she knew that she was doing wrong. So she tried hard to keep busy at home.

She and her Dad were alike in the way that now they always had to be fooling with something. She kept up with all that went on in the house and the neighborhood. Sparerib's big sister won fifty dollars at a movie bank night. Baby Wilson had the bandage off her head now, but her hair was cut short like a boy's. She couldn't dance in the soirée this year, and when her mother took her to see it Baby began to yell and cut up during one of the dances. They had to drag her out of the Opera House. And on the sidewalk Mrs. Wilson had to whip her to make her behave. And Mrs. Wilson cried, too. George hated Baby. He would hold his nose and stop up his ears when she passed by the house. Pete Wells ran away from home and was gone three weeks. He came back barefooted and very hungry. He bragged about how he had gone all the way to New Orleans.

Because of Etta, Mick still slept in the living-room. The short sofa cramped her so much that she had to make up sleep in study hall at school. Every other night Bill swapped with her and she slept with George. Then a lucky break came for them. A fellow who had a room upstairs moved away. When after a week had gone by and nobody answered the ad in the paper, their Mama told Bill he could move up to the vacant room. Bill was very pleased to have a place entirely by himself away from the family. She moved in with George. He slept like a little warm kitty and breathed very quiet.

She knew the night-time again. But not the same as in the last summer when she walked in the dark by herself and listened to the music and made plans. She knew the night a different way now. In bed she lay awake. A queer afraidness came to her. It was like the ceiling was slowly pressing down toward her face. How would it be if the house fell apart? Once their Dad had said the whole place ought to be condemned. Did he mean that maybe some night when they were asleep the walls would crack and the house collapse? Bury them under all the plaster and broken glass and smashed furniture? So that they could not move or breathe? She lay awake and her muscles were stiff. In the night there was a creaking. Was that somebody walking — somebody else awake besides her — Mister Singer?

She never thought about Harry. She had made up her mind to forget him and she did forget him. He wrote that he had a job with a garage in Birmingham. She answered with a card saying 'O.K.' as they had planned. He sent his mother three dollars every week. It seemed like a very long time had passed since they went to the woods together.

During the day she was busy in the outside room. But at night she was by herself in the dark and figuring was not enough. She wanted somebody. She tried to keep George awake. 'It sure is fun to stay awake and talk in the dark. Less us talk awhile together.'

He made a sleepy answer.

'See the stars out the window. It's a hard thing to realize that every single one of those little stars is a planet as large as the earth.'

'How do they know that?'

'They just do. They got ways of measuring. That's science.'

'I don't believe in it.'

She tried to egg him on to an argument so that he would get mad and stay awake. He just let her talk and didn't seem to pay attention. After a while he said:

'Look, Mick! You see that branch of the tree? Don't it look like a pilgrim forefather lying down with a gun in his hand?'

'It sure does. That's exactly what it's like. And see over there on the bureau. Don't that bottle look like a funny man with a hat on?'

'Naw,' George said. 'It don't look a bit like one to me.'

She took a drink from a glass of water on the floor. 'Less me and you play a game — the name game. You can be It if you want to. Whichever you like. You can choose.'

He put his little fists up to his face and breathed in a quiet, even way because he was falling asleep.

'Wait, George!' she said. 'This'll be fun. I'm somebody beginning with an M. Guess who I am.'

George sighed and his voice was tired. 'Are you Harpo Marx?'

'No. I'm not even in the movies.'

'I don't know.'

'Sure you do. My name begins with the letter M and I live in Italy. You ought to guess this.'

George turned over on his side and curled up in a ball. He did not answer.

'My name begins with an M but sometimes I'm called a name beginning with D. In Italy. You can guess.'

The room was quiet and dark and George was asleep. She pinched him and twisted his ear. He groaned but did not awake. She fitted in close to him and pressed her face against his hot little naked shoulder. He would sleep all through the night while she was figuring with decimals.

Was Mister Singer awake in his room upstairs? Did the ceiling creak because he was walking quietly up and down, drinking a cold orange crush and studying the chess men laid out on the table? Had ever he felt a terrible afraidness like this one? No. He had never done anything wrong. He had never done wrong and his heart was quiet in the night-time. Yet at the same time he would understand.

If only she could tell him about this, then it would be better. She thought of how she would begin to tell him. Mister

Singer — I know this girl not any older than I am — Mister Singer, I don't know whether you understand a thing like this or not — Mister Singer. Mister Singer. She said his name over and over. She loved him better than anyone in the family, better even than George or her Dad. It was a different love. It was not like anything she had ever felt in her life before.

In the mornings she and George would dress together and talk. Sometimes she wanted very much to be close to George. He had grown taller and was pale and peaked. His soft, reddish hair lay raggedy over the tops of his little ears. His sharp eyes were always squinted so that his face had a strained look. His permanent teeth were coming in, but they were blue and far apart like his baby teeth had been. Often his jaw was crooked because he had a habit of feeling out the sore new teeth with his tongue.

'Listen here, George,' she said. 'Do you love me?'

'Sure. I love you O.K.'

It was a hot, sunny morning during the last week of school. George was dressed and he lay on the floor doing his number work. His dirty little fingers squeezed the pencil tight and he kept breaking the lead point. When he was finished she held him by the shoulders and looked hard into his face. 'I mean a lot. A whole lot.'

'Lemme go. Sure I love you. Ain't you my sister?'

'I know. But suppose I wasn't your sister. Would you love me then?'

George backed away. He had run out of shirts and wore a dirty pullover sweater. His wrists were thin and blue-veined. The sleeves of the sweater had stretched so that they hung loose and made his hands look very small.

'If you wasn't my sister then I might not know you. So I couldn't love you.'

'But if you did know me and I wasn't your sister.'

'But how do you know I would? You can't prove it.'

'Well, just take it for granted and pretend.'

'I reckon I would like you all right. But I still say you can't prove ——'

'*Prove!* You got that word on the brain. *Prove* and *trick*. Everything is either a trick or it's got to be proved. I can't stand you, George Kelly. I hate you.'

'O.K. Then I don't like you none either.'

He crawled down under the bed for something.

'What you want under there? You better leave my things alone. If ever I caught you meddling in my private box I'd bust your head against the side of the wall. I would. I'd stomp on your brains.'

George came out from under the bed with his spelling book. His dirty little paw reached in a hole in the mattress where he hid his marbles. Nothing could faze that kid. He took his time about choosing three brown agates to take with him. 'Aw, shucks, Mick,' he answered her. George was too little and too tough. There wasn't any sense in loving him. He knew even less about things than she did.

School was out and she had passed every subject — some with A plus and some by the skin of her teeth. The days were long and hot. Finally she was able to work hard at music again. She began to write down pieces for the violin and piano. She wrote songs. Always music was in her mind. She listened to Mister Singer's radio and wandered around the house thinking about the programs she had heard.

'What ails Mick?' Portia asked. 'What kind of cat is it got her tongue? She walk around and don't say a word. She not even greedy like she used to be. She getting to be a regular lady these days.'

It was as though in some way she was waiting — but what she waited for she did not know. The sun burned down glaring and white-hot in the streets. During the day she either worked hard at music or messed with kids. And waited. Sometimes she would look all around her quick and this panic would come in her. Then in late June there was a sudden happening so important that it changed everything.

That night they were all out on the porch. The twilight was blurred and soft. Supper was almost ready and the smell of cabbage floated to them from the open hall. All of them were together except Hazel, who had not come home from work, and Etta, who still lay sick in bed. Their Dad leaned back in a chair with his sock-feet on the banisters. Bill was on the steps with the kids. Their Mama sat on the swing fanning herself with the newspaper. Across the street a girl new in the neighborhood skated up and down the sidewalk on one roller skate. The lights on the block were just beginning to be turned on, and far away a man was calling someone.

Then Hazel came home. Her high heels clopped up the steps and she leaned back lazily on the banisters. In the half-dark her fat, soft hands were very white as she felt the back of her braided hair. 'I sure do wish Etta was able to work,' she said. 'I found out about this job today.'

'What kind of a job?' asked their Dad. 'Anything I could do, or just for girls?'

'Just for a girl. A clerk down at Woolworth's is going to get married next week.'

'The ten-cent store ——' Mick said.

'You interested?'

The question took her by surprise. She had just been thinking about a sack of wintergreen candy she had bought there the day before. She felt hot and tense. She rubbed her bangs up from her forehead and counted the first few stars.

Their Dad flipped his cigarette down to the sidewalk. 'No,' he said. 'We don't want Mick to take on too much responsibility at her age. Let her get her growth out. Her growth through with, anyway.'

'I agree with you,' Hazel said. 'I really do think it would be a mistake for Mick to have to work regular. I don't think it would be right.'

Bill put Ralph down from his lap and shuffled his feet on the steps. 'Nobody ought to work until they're around sixteen. Mick should have two more years and finish at Vocational — if we can make it.'

'Even if we have to give up the house and move down in mill town,' their Mama said. 'I rather keep Mick at home for a while.'

For a minute she had been scared they would try to corner her into taking the job. She would have said she would run away from home. But the way they took the attitude they did touched her. She felt excited. They were all talking about her — and in a kindly way. She was ashamed for the first scared feeling that had come to her. Of a sudden she loved all of the family and a tightness came in her throat.

'About how much money is in it?' she asked.

'Ten dollars.'

'Ten dollars a week?'

'Sure,' Hazel said. 'Did you think it would be only ten a month?'

'Portia don't make but about that much.'

'Oh, colored people ——' Hazel said.

Mick rubbed the top of her head with her fist. 'That's a whole lot of money. A good deal.'

'It's not to be grinned at,' Bill said. 'That's what I make.'

Mick's tongue was dry. She moved it around in her mouth to gather up spit enough to talk. 'Ten dollars a week would buy about fifteen fried chickens. Or five pairs of shoes or five dresses. Or installments on a radio.' She thought about a piano, but she did not mention that aloud.

'It would tide us over,' their Mama said. 'But at the same time I rather keep Mick at home for a while. Now, when Etta ——'

'Wait!' She felt hot and reckless. 'I want to take the job. I can hold it down. I know I can.'

'Listen to little Mick,' Bill said.

Their Dad picked his teeth with a matchstick and took his feet down from the banisters. 'Now, let's not rush into anything. I rather Mick take her time and think this out. We can get along somehow without her working. I mean to increase my watch work by sixty per cent soon as ——'

'I forgot,' Hazel said. 'I think there's a Christmas bonus every year.'

Mick frowned. 'But I wouldn't be working then. I'd be in school. I just want to work during vacation and then go back to school.'

'Sure,' Hazel said quickly.

'But tomorrow I'll go down with you and take the job if I can get it.'

It was as though a great worry and tightness left the family. In the dark they began to laugh and talk. Their Dad did a trick for George with a matchstick and a handkerchief. Then he gave the kid fifty cents to go down to the corner store for Coca-Colas to be drunk after supper. The smell of cabbage was stronger in the hall and pork chops were frying. Portia called. The boarders already waited at the table. Mick had supper in the dining-room. The cabbage leaves were limp and yellow on her plate and she couldn't eat. When she reached for the bread she knocked a pitcher of iced tea over the table.

Then later she waited on the front porch by herself for Mister Singer to come home. In a desperate way she wanted to see him. The excitement of the hour before had died down and she was sick to the stomach. She was going to work in the ten-cent store and she did not want to work there. It was like she had been trapped into something. The job wouldn't be just for the summer — but for a long time, as long a time as she could see ahead. Once they were used to the money coming in it would be impossible to do without again. That was the way things were. She stood in the dark and held tight to the banisters. A long time passed and Mister Singer still did not come. At eleven o'clock she went out to see if she could find him.

But suddenly she got frightened in the dark and ran back home.

Then in the morning she bathed and dressed very careful. Hazel and Etta loaned her the clothes to wear and primped her to look nice. She wore Hazel's green silk dress and a green hat and high-heeled pumps with silk stockings. They fixed her face with rouge and lipstick and plucked her eyebrows. She looked at least sixteen years old when they were finished.

It was too late to back down now. She was really grown and ready to earn her keep. Yet if she would go to her Dad and tell him how she felt he would tell her to wait a year. And Hazel and Etta and Bill and their Mama, even now, would say that she didn't have to go. But she couldn't do it. She couldn't lose face like that. She went up to see Mister Singer. The words came all in a rush:

'Listen — I believe I got this job. What do you think? Do you think it's a good idea? Do you think it's O.K. to drop out of school and work now? You think it's good?'

At first he did not understand. His gray eyes half-closed and he stood with his hands deep down in his pockets. There was the old feeling that they waited to tell each other things that had never been told before. The thing she had to say now was not much. But what he had to tell her would be right — and if he said the job sounded O.K. then she would feel better about it. She repeated the words slowly and waited.

'You think it's good?'

Mister Singer considered. Then he nodded yes.

She got the job. The manager took her and Hazel back to a little office and talked with them. Afterward she couldn't remember how the manager looked or anything that had been said. But she was hired, and on the way out of the place she bought ten cents' worth of chocolate and a little modeling-clay set for George. On June the fifth she was to start work. She stood for a long while before the window of Mister Singer's jewelry store. Then she hung around on the corner.

15

THE time had come for Singer to go to Antonapoulos again. The journey was a long one. For, although the distance between them was something less than two hundred miles, the train meandered to points far out of the way and stopped for long hours at certain stations during the night. Singer would leave the town in the afternoon and travel all through the night and until the early morning of the next day. As usual, he was ready far in advance. He planned to have a full week with his friend this visit. His clothes had been sent to the cleaner's, his hat blocked, and his bags were in readiness. The gifts he would carry were wrapped in colored tissue paper — and in addition there was a de luxe basket of fruits done up in cellophane and a crate of late-shipped strawberries. On the morning before his departure Singer cleaned his room. In his ice box he found a bit of left-over goose liver and took it out to the alley for the neighborhood cat. On his door he tacked the same sign he had posted there before, stating that he would be absent for several days on business. During all these preparations he moved about leisurely with two vivid spots of color on his cheekbones. His face was very solemn.

Then at last the hour for departure was at hand. He stood on the platform, burdened with his suitcases and gifts, and watched the train roll in on the station tracks. He found himself a seat in the day coach and hoisted his luggage on the rack above his head. The car was crowded, for the most part with mothers and children. The green plush seats had a grimy smell. The windows of the car were dirty and rice thrown at some recent bridal pair lay scattered on the floor. Singer smiled cordially to his fellow-travelers and leaned back in his seat. He closed his eyes. The lashes made a dark, curved fringe above the hollows of his cheeks. His right hand moved nervously inside his pocket.

For a while his thoughts lingered in the town he was leaving behind him. He saw Mick and Doctor Copeland and Jake Blount and Biff Brannon. The faces crowded in on him out of the darkness so that he felt smothered. He thought of the quarrel between Blount and the Negro. The nature of this quarrel was hopelessly confused in his mind — but each of them had on several occasions broken out into a bitter tirade against the other, the absent one. He had agreed with each of them in turn, though what it was they wanted him to sanction he did not know. And Mick — her face was urgent and she said a good deal that he did not understand in the least. And then Biff Brannon at the New York Café. Brannon with his dark, iron-like jaw and his watchful eyes. And strangers who followed him about the streets and buttonholed him for unexplainable reasons. The Turk at the linen shop who flung his hands up in his face and babbled with his tongue to make words the shape of which Singer had never imagined before. A certain mill foreman and an old black woman. A businessman on the main street and an urchin who solicited soldiers for a whorehouse near the river. Singer wriggled his shoulders uneasily. The train rocked with a smooth, easy motion. His head nodded to rest on his shoulder and for a short while he slept.

When he opened his eyes again the town was far behind him. The town was forgotten. Outside the dirty window there was the brilliant midsummer countryside. The sun slanted in strong, bronze-colored rays over the green fields of the new cotton. There were acres of tobacco, the plants heavy and green like some monstrous jungle weed. The orchards of peaches with the lush fruit weighting down the dwarfed trees. There were miles of pastures and tens of miles of wasted, washed-out land abandoned to the hardier weeds. The train cut through deep green pine forests where the ground was covered with the slick brown needles and the tops of the trees stretched up virgin and tall into the sky. And farther, a long way south of the town, the cypress swamps — with the gnarled roots of the trees writhing down into the brackish waters, where the gray, tattered moss trailed from the branches, where tropical water flowers blossomed in dankness and gloom. Then out again into the open beneath the sun and the indigo-blue sky.

Singer sat solemn and timid, his face turned fully toward the window. The great sweeps of space and the hard, elemental coloring almost blinded him. This kaleidoscopic variety of scene, this abundance of growth and color, seemed somehow connected with his friend. His thoughts were with Antonapoulos. The bliss of their reunion almost stifled him. His nose was pinched and he breathed with quick, short breaths through his slightly open mouth.

Antonapoulos would be glad to see him. He would enjoy the fresh fruits and the presents. By now he would be out of the sick ward and able to go on an excursion to the movies, and afterward to the hotel where they had eaten dinner on the first visit. Singer had written many letters to Antonapoulos, but he had not posted them. He surrendered himself wholly to thoughts of his friend.

The half-year since he had last been with him seemed neither a long nor a short span of time. Behind each waking moment there had always been his friend. And this submerged communion with Antonapoulos had grown and changed as though they were together in the flesh. Sometimes he thought of Antonapoulos with awe and self-abasement, sometimes with pride — always with love unchecked by criticism, freed of will. When he dreamed at night the face of his friend was always before him, massive and wise and gentle. And in his waking thoughts they were eternally united.

The summer evening came slowly. The sun sank down behind a ragged line of trees in the distance and the sky paled. The twilight was languid and soft. There was a white full moon, and low purple clouds lay over the horizon. The earth, the trees, the unpainted rural dwellings darkened slowly. At intervals mild summer lightning quivered in the air. Singer watched all of this intently until at last the night had come, and his own face was reflected in the glass before him.

Children staggered up and down the aisle of the car with dripping paper cups of water. An old man in overalls who had the seat before Singer drank whiskey from time to time from a Coca-Cola bottle. Between swallows he plugged the bottle carefully with a wad of paper. A little girl on the right combed her hair with a sticky red lollipop. Shoeboxes were opened and trays of supper were brought in from the dining-car. Singer did not eat. He leaned back in his seat and kept desultory account of all that went on around him. At last the car settled down. Children lay on the broad plush seats and slept, while men and women doubled up with their pillows and rested as best they could.

Singer did not sleep. He pressed his face close against the glass and strained to see into the night. The darkness was heavy and velvety. Sometimes there was a patch of moonlight or the flicker of a lantern from the window of some house along the way. From the moon he saw that the train had turned from its southward course and was headed toward the east. The eagerness he felt was so keen that his nose was too pinched to breathe through and his cheeks were scarlet. He sat there, his face pressed close against the cold, sooty glass of the window, through most of the long night journey.

The train was more than an hour late, and the fresh, bright summer morning was well under way when they arrived. Singer went immediately to the hotel, a very good hotel where he had made reservations in advance. He unpacked his bags and arranged the presents he would take Antonapoulos on the bed. From the menu the bellboy brought him he selected a luxurious breakfast — broiled bluefish, hominy, French toast, and hot black coffee. After breakfast he rested before the electric fan in his underwear. At noon he began to dress. He bathed and shaved and laid out fresh linen and his best seersucker suit. At three o'clock the hospital was open for visiting hours. It was Tuesday and the eighteenth of July.

At the asylum he sought Antonapoulos first in the sick ward where he had been confined before. But at the doorway of the room he saw immediately that his friend was not there. Next he found his way through the corridors to the office where he had been taken the time before. He had his question already written on one of the cards he carried about with him. The person behind the desk was not the same as the one who had been there before. He was a young man, almost a boy, with a half-formed, immature face and a lank mop of hair. Singer handed him the card and stood quietly, his arms heaped with packages, his weight resting on his heels.

The young man shook his head. He leaned over the desk and scribbled loosely on a pad of paper. Singer read what he had written and the spots of color drained from his cheekbones instantly. He looked at the note a long time, his eyes cut sideways and his head bowed. For it was written there that Antonapoulos was dead.

On the way back to the hotel he was careful not to crush the fruit he had brought with him. He took the packages up to his room and then wandered down to the lobby. Behind a potted palm tree there was a slot machine. He inserted a nickel but when he tried to pull the lever he found that the machine was jammed. Over this incident he made a great to-do. He cornered the clerk and furiously demonstrated what had happened. His face was deathly pale and he was so beside himself that tears rolled down the ridges of his nose. He flailed his hands and even stamped once with his long, narrow, elegantly shoed foot on the plush carpet. Nor was he satisfied when his coin was refunded, but insisted on checking out immediately. He packed his bag and was obliged to work energetically to make it close again. For in addition to the articles he had brought with him he carried away three towels, two cakes of soap, a pen and a bottle of ink, a roll of toilet paper, and a Holy Bible. He paid his bill and walked to the railway station to put his belongings in custody. The train did not leave until nine in the evening and he had the empty afternoon before him.

This town was smaller than the one in which he lived. The business streets intersected to form the shape of a cross. The stores had a countrified look; there were harnesses and sacks of feed in half of the display windows. Singer walked listlessly along the sidewalks. His throat felt swollen and he wanted to swallow but was unable to do so. To relieve this strangled feeling he bought a drink in one of the drugstores. He idled in the barber shop and purchased a few trifles at the ten-cent store. He looked no one full in the face and his head drooped down to one side like a sick animal's.

The afternoon was almost ended when a strange thing happened to Singer. He had been walking slowly and irregularly along the curb of the street. The sky was overcast and the air humid. Singer did not raise his head, but as he passed the town pool room he caught a sidewise glance of something that disturbed him. He passed the pool room and then stopped in the middle of the street. Listlessly he retraced his steps and stood before the open door of the place. There were three mutes inside and they were talking with their hands together. All three of them were coatless. They wore bowler hats and bright ties. Each of them held a glass of beer in his left hand. There was a certain brotherly resemblance between them.

Singer went inside. For a moment he had trouble taking his hand from his pocket. Then clumsily he formed a word of greeting. He was clapped on the shoulder. A cold drink was ordered. They surrounded him and the fingers of their hands shot out like pistons as they questioned him.

He told his own name and the name of the town where he lived. After that he could think of nothing else to tell about himself. He asked if they knew Spiros Antonapoulos. They did not know him. Singer stood with his hands dangling loose. His head was still inclined to one side and his glance was oblique. He was so listless and cold that the three mutes in the bowler hats looked at him queerly. After a while they left him out of their conversation. And when they had paid for the rounds of beers and were ready to depart they did not suggest that he join them.

Although Singer had been adrift on the streets for half a day he almost missed his train. It was not clear to him how this happened or how he had spent the hours before. He reached the station two minutes before the train pulled out, and barely had time to drag his luggage aboard and find a seat. The car he chose was almost empty. When he was settled he opened the crate of strawberries and picked them over with finicky care. The berries were of a giant size, large as walnuts and in full-blown ripeness. The green leaves at the top of the rich-colored fruit were like tiny bouquets. Singer put a berry in his mouth and though the juice had a lush, wild sweetness there was already a subtle flavor of decay. He ate until his palate was dulled by the taste and then rewrapped the crate and placed it on the rack above him. At midnight he drew the window-shade and lay down on the seat. He was curled in a ball, his coat pulled over his face and head. In this position he lay in a stupor of half-sleep for about twelve hours. The conductor had to shake him when they arrived.

Singer left his luggage in the middle of the station floor. Then he walked to the shop. He greeted the jeweler for whom he worked with a listless turn of his hand. When he went out again there was something heavy in his pocket. For a while he rambled with bent head along the streets. But the unrefracted brilliance of the sun, the humid heat, oppressed him. He returned to his room with swollen eyes and an aching head. After resting he drank a glass of iced coffee and smoked a cigarette. Then when he had washed the ash tray and the glass he brought out a pistol from his pocket and put a bullet in his chest.

PART III

1

August 21, 1939
Morning

I WILL not be hurried,' Doctor Copeland said. 'Just let me be. Kindly allow me to sit here in peace a moment.'

'Father, us not trying to rush you. But it time now to get gone from here.'

Doctor Copeland rocked stubbornly, his gray shawl drawn close around his shoulders. Although the morning was warm and fresh, a small wood fire burned in the stove. The kitchen was bare of all furniture except the chair in which he sat. The other rooms were empty, too. Most of the furniture had been moved to Portia's house, and the rest was tied to the automobile outside. All was in readiness except his own mind. But how could he leave when there was neither beginning nor end, neither truth nor purpose in his thoughts? He put up his hand to steady his trembling head and continued to rock himself slowly in the creaking chair.

Behind the closed door he heard their voices:

'I done all I can. He determined to sit there till he good and ready to leave.'

'Buddy and me done wrapped the china plates and ——'

'Us should have left before the dew dried,' said the old man. 'As is, night liable to catch us on the road.'

Their voices quieted. Footsteps echoed in the empty hallway and he could hear them no more. On the floor beside him was a cup and saucer. He filled it with coffee from the pot on the top of the stove. As he rocked he drank the coffee and warmed his fingers in the steam. This could not truly be the end. Other voices called wordless in his heart. The voice of Jesus and of John Brown. The voice of the great Spinoza and of Karl Marx. The calling voices of all those who had fought and to whom it had been vouchsafed to complete their missions. The grief-bound voices of his people. And also the voice of the dead. Of the mute Singer, who was a righteous white man of understanding. The voices of the weak and of the mighty. The rolling voice of his people growing always in strength and in power. The voice of the strong, true purpose. And in answer the words trembled on his lips — the words which are surely the root of all human grief — so that he almost said aloud: 'Almighty Host! Utmost power of the universe! I have done those things which I ought not to have done and left undone those things which I ought to have done. So this cannot truly be the end.'

He had first come into the house with her whom he loved. And Daisy was dressed in her bridal gown and wore a white lace veil. Her skin was the beautiful color of dark honey and her laughter was sweet. At night he had shut himself in the bright room to study alone. He had tried to cogitate and to discipline himself to study. But with Daisy near him there was a strong desire in him that would not go away with study. So sometimes he surrendered to these feelings, and again he bit his lips and meditated with the books throughout the night. And then there were Hamilton and Karl Marx and William and Portia. All lost. No one remained.

And Madyben and Benny Mae. And Benedine Madine and Mady Copeland. Those who carried his name. And those whom he had exhorted. But out of the thousands of them where was there one to whom he could entrust the mission and then take ease?

All of his life he had known it strongly. He had known the reason for his working and was sure in his heart because he knew each day what lay ahead of him. He would go with his bag from house to house, and on all things he would talk to them and patiently explain. And then in the night he would be happy in the knowledge that the day had been a day of purpose. And even without Daisy and Hamilton and

Karl Marx and William and Portia he could sit by the stove alone and take joy from this knowledge. He would drink a pot of turnip-green liquor and eat a pone of cornbread. A deep feeling of satisfaction would be in him because the day was good.

There were thousands of such times of satisfaction. But what had been their meaning? Out of all the years he could think of no work of lasting value.

After a while the door to the hall was opened and Portia came in. 'I reckon I going to have to dress you like a baby,' she said. 'Here your shoes and socks. Let me take off your bedroom shoes and put them on. We got to get gone from here pretty soon.'

'Why have you done this to me?' he asked bitterly.

'What I done to you now?'

'You know full well that I do not want to leave. You pressed me into saying yes when I was in no fit condition to make a decision. I wish to remain where I have always been, and you know it.'

'Listen to you carry on!' Portia said angrily. 'You done grumbled so much that I nearly worn out. You done fumed and fussed so that I right shamed for you.'

'Pshaw! Say what you will. You only come before me like a gnat. I know what I wish and will not be pestered into doing that which is wrong.'

Portia took off his bedroom shoes and unrolled a pair of clean black cotton socks. 'Father, less us quit this here argument. Us have all done the best we knew how. It entirely the best plan for you to go on out with Grandpapa and Hamilton and Buddy. They going to take good care of you and you going to get well.'

'No, I will not,' said Doctor Copeland. 'But I would have recovered here. I know it.'

'Who you think could pay the note on this here house? How you think us could feed you? Who you think could take care you here?'

'I have always managed, and I can manage yet '

'You just trying to be contrary.'

'Pshaw! You come before me like a gnat. And I ignore you.'

'That certainly is a nice way to talk to me while I trying to put on your shoes and socks.'

'I am sorry. Forgive me, Daughter.'

'Course you sorry,' she said. 'Course we both sorry. Us can't afford to quarrel. And besides, once we get you settled on the farm you going to like it. They got the prettiest vegetable garden I ever seen. Make my mouth slobber to think about it. And chickens and two breed sows and eighteen peach trees. You just going to be crazy about it there. I sure do wish it was me could get a chance to go.'

'I wish so, too.'

'How come you so determined to grieve?'

'I just feel that I have failed,' he said.

'How you mean you done failed?'

'I do not know. Just leave me be, Daughter. Just let me sit here in peace a moment.'

'O.K. But us got to get gone from here pretty soon.'

He would be silent. He would sit quietly and rock in the chair until the sense of order was in him once more. His head trembled and his backbone ached.

'I certainly hope this,' Portia said. 'I certainly hope that when I dead and gone as many peoples grieves for me as grieves for Mr. Singer. I sure would like to know I were going to have as sad a funeral as he had and as many peoples ——'

'Hush!' said Doctor Copeland roughly. 'You talk too much.'

But truly with the death of that white man a dark sorrow had lain down in his heart. He had talked to him as to no other white man and had trusted him. And the mystery of his suicide had left him baffled and without support. There was neither beginning nor end to this sorrow. Nor understanding. Always he would return in his thoughts to this white man who was not insolent or scornful but who was just. And how can the dead be truly dead when they still live in the souls of those who are left behind? But of all this he must not think. He must thrust it from him now.

For it was discipline he needed. During the past month the black, terrible feelings had arisen again to wrestle with his spirit. There was the hatred that for days had truly let him down into the regions of death. After the quarrel with Mr. Blount, the midnight visitor, there had been in him a murderous darkness. Yet now he could not clearly recall those issues which were the cause of their dispute. And then the different anger that came in him when he looked on the stumps of Willie's legs. The warring love and hatred — love for his people and hatred for the oppressors of his people — that left him exhausted and sick in spirit.

'Daughter,' he said. 'Get me my watch and coat. I am going.'

He pushed himself up with the arms of the chair. The floor seemed a far way from his face and after the long time in bed his legs were very weak. For a moment he felt he would fall. He walked dizzily across the bare room and stood leaning against the side of the doorway. He coughed and took from his pocket one of the squares of paper to hold over his mouth.

'Here your coat,' Portia said. 'But it so hot outside you not going to need it.'

He walked for the last time through the empty house. The blinds were closed and in the darkened rooms there was the smell of dust. He rested against the wall of the vestibule and then went outside. The morning was bright and warm. Many friends had come to say good-bye the night before and in the very early morning — but now only the family was congregated on the porch. The wagon and the automobile were parked out in the street.

'Well, Benedict Mady,' the old man said. 'I reckon you

ghy be a little bit homesick these first few days. But won't be long.'

'I do not have any home. So why should I be homesick?'

Portia wet her lips nervously and said: 'He coming back whenever he get good and ready. Buddy will be glad to ride him to town in the car. Buddy just love to drive.'

The automobile was loaded. Boxes of books were tied to the running-board. The back seat was crowded with two chairs and the filing case. His office desk, legs in the air, had been fastened to the top. But although the car was weighted down the wagon was almost empty. The mule stood patiently, a brick tied to his reins.

'Karl Marx,' Doctor Copeland said. 'Look sharp. Go over the house and make sure that nothing is left. Bring the cup I left on the floor and my rocking-chair.'

'Less us get started. I anxious to be home by dinner-time,' Hamilton said.

At last they were ready. Highboy cranked the automobile. Karl Marx sat at the wheel and Portia, Highboy, and William were crowded together on the back seat.

'Father, suppose you set on Highboy's lap. I believe you be more comfortable than scrouged up here with us and all this furniture.'

'No, it is too crowded. I would rather ride in the wagon.'

'But you not used to the wagon,' Karl Marx said. 'It going to be very bumpy and the trip liable to take all day.'

'That does not matter. I have ridden in many a wagon before this.'

'Tell Hamilton to come with us. I sure he rather ride in the automobile.'

Grandpapa had driven the wagon into town the day before. They brought with them a load of produce, peaches and cabbages and turnips, for Hamilton to sell in town. All except a sack of peaches had been marketed.

'Well, Benedict Mady, I see you riding home with me,' the old man said.

Doctor Copeland climbed into the back of the wagon. He was weary as though his bones were made of lead. His head trembled and a sudden spasm of nausea made him lie down flat on the rough boards.

'I right glad you coming,' Grandpapa said. 'You understand I always had deep respect for scholars. Deep respect. I able to overlook and forget a good many things if a man be a scholar. I very glad to have a scholar like you in the fambly again.'

The wheels of the wagon creaked. They were on the way. 'I will return soon,' Doctor Copeland said. 'After only a month or two I will return.'

'Hamilton he a right good scholar. I think he favors you some. He do all my figuring on paper for me and he read the newspapers. And Whitman I think he ghy be a scholar. Right now he able to read the Bible to me. And do number work. Small a child as he is. I always had a deep respect for scholars.'

The motion of the wagon jolted his back. He looked up at the branches overhead, and then when there was no shade he covered his face with a handkerchief to shield his eyes from the sun. It was not possible that this could be the end. Always he had felt in him the strong, true purpose. For forty years his mission was his life and his life was his mission. And yet all remained to be done and nothing was completed.

'Yes, Benedict Mady, I right glad to have you with us again. I been waiting to ask you about this peculiar feeling in my right foot. A queer feeling like my foot gone to sleep. I taken 666 and rubbed it with liniment. I hoping you will find me a good treatment.'

'I will do what I can.'

'Yes, I glad to have you. I believe in all kinfolks sticking together — blood kin and marriage kin. I believe in all us struggling along and helping each other out, and some day us will have a reward in the Beyond.'

'Pshaw!' Doctor Copeland said bitterly. 'I believe in justice now.'

'What that you say you believe in? You speak so hoarse I ain't able to hear you.'

'In justice for us. Justice for us Negroes.'

'That right.'

He felt the fire in him and he could not be still. He wanted to sit up and speak in a loud voice — yet when he tried to raise himself he could not find the strength. The words in his heart grew big and they would not be silent. But the old man had ceased to listen and there was no one to hear him.

'Git, Lee Jackson. Git, Honey. Pick up your feets and quit this here poking. Us got a long way to go.'

2

Afternoon

JAKE ran at a violent, clumsy pace. He went through Weavers Lane and then cut into a side alley, climbed a fence, and hastened onward. Nausea rose in his belly so that there was the taste of vomit in his throat. A barking dog chased beside him until he stopped long enough to threaten it with a rock. His eyes were wide with horror and he held his hand clapped to his open mouth.

Christ! So this was the finish. A brawl. A riot. A fight with every man for himself. Bloody heads and eyes cut with broken bottles. Christ! And the wheezy music of the flying-jinny above the noise. The dropped hamburgers and cotton candy and the screaming younguns. And him in it all. Fighting blind with the dust and sun. The sharp cut of teeth against his knuckles. And laughing. Christ! And the feeling that he had let loose a wild, hard rhythm in him that wouldn't stop. And then looking close into the dead black face and not knowing. Not even knowing if he had killed or not. But wait. Christ! Nobody could have stopped it.

Jake slowed and jerked his head nervously to look behind him. The alley was empty. He vomited and wiped his mouth and forehead with the sleeve of his shirt. Afterward he rested for a minute and felt better. He had run for about eight blocks and with short cuts there was about half a mile to go. The dizziness cleared in his head so that from all the wild feelings he could remember facts. He started off again, this time at a steady jog.

Nobody could have stopped it. All through the summer he had stamped them out like sudden fires. All but this one. And this fight nobody could have stopped. It seemed to blaze up out of nothing. He had been working on the machinery of the swings and had stopped to get a glass of water. As he passed across the grounds he saw a white boy and a Negro walking around each other. They were both drunk. Half the crowd was drunk that afternoon, for it was Saturday and the mills had run full time that week. The heat and the sun were sickening and there was a heavy stink in the air.

He saw the two fighters close in on each other. But he knew that this was not the beginning. He had felt a big fight coming for a long time. And the funny thing was he found time to think of all this. He stood watching for about five seconds before he pushed into the crowd. In that short time he thought of many things. He thought of Singer. He thought of the sullen summer afternoons and the black, hot nights, of all the fights he had broken up and the quarrels he had hushed.

Then he saw the flash of a pocketknife in the sun. He shouldered through a knot of people and jumped on the back of the Negro who held the knife. The man went down with him and they were on the ground together. The smell of the Negro was mixed with the heavy dust in his lungs. Someone trampled on his legs and his head was kicked. By the time he got to his feet again the fight had become general. The Negroes were fighting the white men and the white men were fighting the Negroes. He saw clearly, second by second. The white boy who had picked the fight seemed a kind of leader. He was the head of a gang that came often to the show. They were about sixteen years old and they wore white duck trousers and fancy rayon polo shirts. The Negroes fought back as best they could. Some had razors.

He began to yell out words: Order! Help! Police! But it was like yelling at a breaking dam. There was a terrible sound in his ear — terrible because it was human and yet without words. The sound rose to a roar that deafened him. He was hit on the head. He could not see what went on around him. He saw only eyes and mouths and fists — wild eyes and half-closed eyes, wet, loose mouths and clenched ones, black fists and white. He grabbed a knife from a hand and caught an upraised fist. Then the dust and the sun blinded him and the one thought in his mind was to get out and find a telephone to call for help.

But he was caught. And without knowing when it happened he piled into the fight himself. He hit out with his fists and felt the soft sqush of wet mouths. He fought with his eyes shut and his head lowered. A crazy sound came out of his throat. He hit with all his strength and charged with his head like a bull. Senseless words were in his mind and he was laughing. He did not see who he hit and did not know who hit him. But he knew that the line-up of the fight had changed and now each man was for himself.

Then suddenly it was finished. He tripped and fell over backward. He was knocked out so that it may have been a minute or it may have been much longer before he opened his eyes. A few drunks were still fighting but two dicks were breaking it up fast. He saw what he had tripped over. He lay half on and half beside the body of a young Negro boy. With only one look he knew that he was dead. There was a cut on the side of his neck but it was hard to see how he had died in such a hurry. He knew the face but could not place it.

The boy's mouth was open and his eyes were open in surprise. The ground was littered with papers and broken bottles and trampled hamburgers. The head was broken off one of the jinny horses and a booth was destroyed. He was sitting up. He saw the dicks and in a panic he started to run. By now they must have lost his track.

There were only four more blocks ahead, and then he would be safe for sure. Fear had shortened his breath so that he was winded. He clenched his fists and lowered his head. Then suddenly he slowed and halted. He was alone in an alley near the main street. On one side was the wall of a building and he slumped against it, panting, the corded vein in his forehead inflamed. In his confusion he had run all the way across the town to reach the room of his friend. And Singer was dead. He began to cry. He sobbed aloud, and water dripped down from his nose and wet his mustache.

A wall, a flight of stairs, a road ahead. The burning sun was like a heavy weight on him. He started back the way he had come. This time he walked slowly, wiping his wet face with the greasy sleeve of his shirt. He could not stop the trembling of his lips and he bit them until he tasted blood.

At the corner of the next block he ran into Simms. The old codger was sitting on a box with his Bible on his knees. There was a tall board fence behind him, and on it a message was written with purple chalk.

He Died to Save You

Hear the Story of His Love and Grace

Every Nite 7.15 P.M.

The street was empty. Jake tried to cross over to the other sidewalk, but Simms caught him by the arm.

'Come, all ye disconsolate and sore of heart. Lay down your sins and troubles before the blessed feet of Him who died to save you. Wherefore goest thou, Brother Blount?'

'Home to hockey,' Jake said. 'I got to hockey. Does the Saviour have anything against that?'

'Sinner! The Lord remembers all your transgressions. The Lord has a message for you this very night.'

'Does the Lord remember that dollar I gave you last week?'

'Jesus has a message for you at seven-fifteen tonight. You be here on time to hear His Word.'

Jake licked his mustache. 'You have such a crowd every night I can't get up close enough to hear.'

'There is a place for scoffers. Besides, I have had a sign that soon the Saviour wants me to build a house for Him. On that lot at the corner of Eighteenth Avenue and Sixth Street. A tabernacle large enough to hold five hundred people. Then you scoffers will see. The Lord prepareth a table before me in the presence of mine enemies; he anointeth my head with oil. My cup runneth ——'

'I can round you up a crowd tonight,' Jake said.

'How?'

'Give me your pretty colored chalk. I promise a big crowd.'

'I've seen your signs,' Simms said. '"Workers! America Is the Richest Country in the World Yet a Third of Us Are Starving. When Will We Unite and Demand Our Share?" — all that. Your signs are radical. I wouldn't let you use my chalk.'

'But I don't plan to write signs.'

Simms fingered the pages of his Bible and waited suspiciously.

'I'll get you a fine crowd. On the pavements at each end of the block I'll draw you some good-looking naked floozies. All in color with arrows to point the way. Sweet, plump, bare-tailed ——'

'Babylonian!' the old man screamed. 'Child of Sodom! God will remember this.'

Jake crossed over to the other sidewalk and started toward the house where he lived. 'So long, Brother.'

'Sinner,' the old man called. 'You come back here at seven-fifteen sharp. And hear the message from Jesus that will give you faith. Be saved.'

Singer was dead. And the way he had felt when he first heard that he had killed himself was not sad — it was angry. He was before a wall. He remembered all the innermost thoughts that he had told to Singer, and with his death it seemed to him that they were lost. And why had Singer wanted to end his life? Maybe he had gone insane. But anyway he was dead, dead, dead. He could not be seen or touched or spoken to, and the room where they had spent so many hours had been rented to a girl who worked as a typist. He could go there no longer. He was alone. A wall, a flight of stairs, an open road.

Jake locked the door of his room behind him. He was hungry and there was nothing to eat. He was thirsty and only a few drops of warm water were left in the pitcher by the table. The bed was unmade and dusty fluff had accumulated on the floor. Papers were scattered all about the room, because recently he had written many short notices and distributed them through the town. Moodily he glanced at one of the papers labeled 'The T.W.O.C. Is Your Best Friend.' Some of the notices consisted of only one sentence, others were longer. There was one full-page manifesto entitled 'The Affinity Between Our Democracy and Fascism.'

For a month he had worked on these papers, scribbling them during working hours, typing and making carbons on the typewriter at the New York Café, distributing them by hand. He had worked day and night. But who read them? What good had any of it done? A town this size was too big for any one man. And now he was leaving.

But where would it be this time? The names of cities called to him — Memphis, Wilmington, Gastonia, New Orleans. He would go somewhere. But not out of the South. The old restlessness and hunger were in him again. It was different this time. He did not long for open space and freedom — just the reverse. He remembered what the Negro, Copeland, had said to him, 'Do not attempt to stand alone.' There were times when that was best.

Jake moved the bed across the room. On the part of the floor the bed had hidden there were a suitcase and a pile of books and dirty clothes. Impatiently he began to pack. The old Negro's face was in his mind and some of the words they had said came back to him. Copeland was crazy. He was a fanatic, so that it was maddening to try to reason with him. Still the terrible anger that they had felt that night had later been hard to understand. Copeland *knew*. And those who knew were like a handful of naked soldiers before an armed battalion. And what had they done? They had turned to quarrel with each other. Copeland was wrong — yes — he was crazy. But on some points they might be able to work together after all. If they didn't talk too much. He would go and see him. A sudden urge to hurry came in him. Maybe that would be the best thing after all. Maybe that was the sign, the hand he had so long awaited.

Without pausing to wash the grime from his face and hands he strapped his suitcase and left the room. Outside the air was sultry and there was a foul odor in the street. Clouds had formed in the sky. The atmosphere was so still that the smoke from a mill in the district went up in a straight, unbroken line. As Jake walked the suitcase bumped awkwardly against his knees, and often he jerked his head to look behind him. Copeland lived all the way across the town, so there was need to hurry. The clouds in the sky grew steadily denser, and foretold a heavy summer rain before nightfall.

When he reached the house where Copeland lived he saw that the shutters were drawn. He walked to the back and peered through the window at the abandoned kitchen. A hollow, desperate disappointment made his hands feel sweaty and his heart lose the rhythm of its beat. He went to the house on the left but no one was at home. There was nothing to do except to go to the Kelly house and question Portia.

He hated to be near that house again. He couldn't stand to see the hatrack in the front hall and the long flight of stairs he had climbed so many times. He walked slowly back across the town and approached by way of the alley. He went in the rear door. Portia was in the kitchen and the little boy was with her.

'No, sir, Mr. Blount,' Portia said. 'I know you were a mighty good friend of Mr. Singer and you understand what Father thought of him. But we taken Father out in the country this morning and I know in my soul I got no business telling you exactly where he is. If you don't mind I rather speak out and not minch the matter.'

'You don't have to minch anything,' Jake said. 'But why?'

'After the time you come to see us Father were so sick us expected him to die. It taken us a long time to get him able to sit up. He doing right well now. He going to get a lot stronger where he is now. But whether you understand this or not he right bitter against white peoples just now and he very easy to upset. And besides, if you don't mind speaking out, what you want with Father, anyway?'

'Nothing,' Jake said. 'Nothing you would understand.'

'Us colored peoples have feelings just like anybody else. And I stand by what I said, Mr. Blount. Father just a sick old colored man and he had enough trouble already. Us got to look after him. And he not anxious to see you — I know that.'

Out in the street again he saw that the clouds had turned a deep, angry purple. In the stagnant air there was a storm smell. The vivid green of the trees along the sidewalk seemed to steal into the atmosphere so that there was a strange greenish glow over the street. All was so hushed and still that Jake paused for a moment to sniff the air and look around him. Then he grasped his suitcase under his arm and began to run toward the awnings of the main street. But he was not quick enough. There was one metallic crash of thunder and the air chilled suddenly. Large silver drops of rain hissed on the pavement. An avalanche of water blinded him. When he reached the New York Café his clothes clung wet and shriveled to his body and his shoes squeaked with water.

Brannon pushed aside his newspaper and leaned his elbows on the counter. 'Now, this is really curious. I had this intuition you would come here just after the rain broke. I knew in my bones you were coming and that you would make it just too late.' He mashed his nose with his thumb until it was white and flat. 'And a suitcase?'

'It looks like a suitcase,' Jake said. 'And it feels like a suitcase. So if you believe in the actuality of suitcases I reckon this is one, all right.'

'You ought not to stand around like this. Go on upstairs and throw me down your clothes. Louis will run over them with a hot iron.'

Jake sat at one of the back booth tables and rested his head in his hands. 'No, thanks. I just want to rest here and get my wind again.'

'But your lips are turning blue. You look all knocked up.'

'I'm all right. What I want is some supper.'

'Supper won't be ready for half an hour,' Brannon said patiently.

'Any old leftovers will do. Just put them on a plate. You don't even have to bother to heat them.'

The emptiness in him hurt. He wanted to look neither backward nor forward. He walked two of his short, chunky fingers across the top of the table. It was more than a year now since he had sat at this table for the first time. And how much further was he now than then? No further. Nothing had happened except that he had made a friend and lost him. He had given Singer everything and then the man had killed himself. So he was left out on a limb. And now it was up to him to get out of it by himself and make a new start again. At the thought of it panic came in him. He was tired. He leaned his head against the wall and put his feet on the seat beside him.

'Here you are,' Brannon said. 'This ought to help out.'

He put down a glass of some hot drink and a plate of chicken pie. The drink had a sweet, heavy smell. Jake inhaled the steam and closed his eyes. 'What's in it?'

'Lemon rind rubbed on a lump of sugar and boiling water with rum. It's a good drink.'

'How much do I owe you?'

'I don't know offhand, but I'll figure it out before you leave.'

Jake took a deep draught of the toddy and washed it around in his mouth before swallowing. 'You'll never get the money,' he said. 'I don't have it to pay you — and if I did I probably wouldn't, anyway.'

'Well, have I been pressing you? Have I ever made you out a bill and asked you to pay up?'

'No,' Jake said. 'You been very reasonable. And since I think about it you're a right decent guy — from the personal perspective, that is.'

Brannon sat across from him at the table. Something was on his mind. He slid the salt-shaker back and forth and kept smoothing his hair. He smelled like perfume and his striped blue shirt was very fresh and clean. The sleeves were rolled and held in place by old-fashioned blue sleeve garters.

At last he cleared his throat in a hesitating way and said: 'I was glancing through the afternoon paper just before you came. It seems you had a lot of trouble at your place today.'

'That's right. What did it say?'

'Wait. I'll get it.' Brannon fetched the paper from the counter and leaned against the partition of the booth. 'It says on the front page that at the Sunny Dixie Show, located so and so, there was a general disturbance. Two Negroes were fatally injured with wounds inflicted by knives. Three others suffered minor wounds and were taken for treatment to the city hospital. The dead were Jimmy Macy and Lancy Davis. The wounded were John Hamlin, white, of Central Mill City, Various Wilson, Negro, and so forth and so on. Quote: "A number of arrests were made. It is alleged that the disturbance was caused by labor agitation, as papers of a subversive nature were found on and about the site of disturbance. Other arrests are expected shortly."' Brannon clicked his teeth together. 'The set-up of this paper gets worse every day. Subversive spelled with a *u* in the second syllable and arrests with only one *r*.'

'They're smart, all right,' Jake said sneeringly. '"Caused by labor agitation." That's remarkable.'

'Anyway, the whole thing is very unfortunate.'

Jake held his hand to his mouth and looked down at his empty plate.

'What do you mean to do now?'

'I'm leaving. I'm getting out of here this afternoon.'

Brannon polished his nails on the palm of his hand. 'Well, of course it's not necessary — but it might be a good thing. Why so headlong? No sense in starting out this time of day.'

'I just rather.'

'I do think it behooves you to make a new start. At the same time why don't you take my advice on this? Myself — I'm a conservative and of course I think your opinions are radical. But at the same time I like to know all sides of a matter. Anyway, I want to see you straighten out. So why don't you go some place where you can meet a few people more or less like yourself? And then settle down?'

Jake pushed his plate irritably away from him. 'I don't know where I'm going. Leave me alone. I'm tired.'

Brannon shrugged his shoulders and went back to the counter.

He was tired enough. The hot rum and the heavy sound

of the rain made him drowsy. It felt good to be sitting safe in a booth and to have just eaten a good meal. If he wanted to he could lean over and take a nap — a short one. Already his head felt swollen and heavy and he was more comfortable with his eyes closed. But it would have to be a short sleep because soon he must get out of here.

'How long will this rain keep on?'

Brannon's voice had drowsy overtones. 'You can't tell — a tropical cloudburst. Might clear up suddenly — or — might thin a little and set in for the night.'

Jake laid his head down on his arms. The sound of the rain was like the swelling sound of the sea. He heard a clock tick and the far-off rattle of dishes. Gradually his hands relaxed. They lay open, palm upward, on the table.

Then Brannon was shaking him by the shoulders and looking into his face. A terrible dream was in his mind. 'Wake up,' Brannon was saying. 'You've had a nightmare. I looked over here and your mouth was open and you were groaning and shuffling your feet on the floor. I never saw anything to equal it.'

The dream was still heavy in his mind. He felt the old terror that always came as he awakened. He pushed Brannon away and stood up. 'You don't have to tell me I had a nightmare. I remember just how it was. And I've had the same dream for about fifteen times before.'

He did remember now. Every other time he had been unable to get the dream straight in his waking mind. He had been walking among a great crowd of people — like at the show. But there was also something Eastern about the people around him. There was a terrible bright sun and the people were half-naked. They were silent and slow and their faces had a look in them of starvation. There was no sound, only the sun, and the silent crowd of people. He walked among them and he carried a huge covered basket. He was taking the basket somewhere but he could not find the place to leave it. And in the dream there was a peculiar horror in wandering on and on through the crowd and not knowing where to lay down the burden he had carried in his arms so long.

'What was it?' Brannon asked. 'Was the devil chasing you?'

Jake stood up and went to the mirror behind the counter. His face was dirty and sweaty. There were dark circles beneath his eyes. He wet his handkerchief under the fountain faucet and wiped off his face. Then he took out a pocket comb and neatly combed his mustache.

'The dream was nothing. You got to be asleep to understand why it was such a nightmare.'

The clock pointed to five-thirty. The rain had almost stopped. Jake picked up his suitcase and went to the front door. 'So long. I'll send you a postcard maybe.'

'Wait,' Brannon said. 'You can't go now. It's still raining a little.'

'Just dripping off the awning. I rather get out of town before dark.'

'But hold on. Do you have any money? Enough to keep going for a week?'

'I don't need money. I been broke before.'

Brannon had an envelope ready and in it were two twenty-dollar bills. Jake looked at them on both sides and put them in his pocket. 'God knows why you do it. You'll never smell them again. But thanks. I won't forget.'

'Good luck. And let me hear from you.'

'*Adios*.'

'Good-bye.'

The door closed behind him. When he looked back at the end of the block, Brannon was watching from the sidewalk. He walked until he reached the railroad tracks. On either side there were rows of dilapidated two-room houses. In the cramped back yards were rotted privies and lines of torn, smoky rags hung out to dry. For two miles there was not one sight of comfort or space or cleanliness. Even the earth itself seemed filthy and abandoned. Now and then there were signs that a vegetable row had been attempted, but only a few withered collards had survived. And a few fruitless, smutty fig trees. Little younguns swarmed in this filth, the smaller of them stark naked. The sight of this poverty was so cruel and hopeless that Jake snarled and clenched his fists.

He reached the edge of the town and turned off on a highway. Cars passed him by. His shoulders were too wide and his arms too long. He was so strong and ugly that no one wanted to take him in. But maybe a truck would stop before long. The late afternoon sun was out again. Heat made the steam rise from the wet pavement. Jake walked steadily. As soon as the town was behind a new surge of energy came to him. But was this flight or was it onslaught? Anyway, he was going. All was to begin another time. The road ahead lay to the north and slightly to the west. But he would not go too far away. He would not leave the South. That was one clear thing. There was hope in him, and soon perhaps the outline of his journey would take form.

3

Evening

WHAT good was it? That was the question she would like to know. What the hell good it was. All the plans she had made, and the music. When all that came of it was this trap — the store, then home to sleep, and back at the store again. The clock in front of the place where Mister Singer used to work pointed to seven. And she was just getting off. Whenever there was overtime the manager always told her to stay. Because she could stand longer on her feet and work harder before giving out than any other girl.

The heavy rain had left the sky a pale, quiet blue. Dark

was coming. Already the lights were turned on. Automobile horns honked in the street and the newsboys hollered out the headlines in the papers. She didn't want to go home. If she went home now she would lie down on the bed and bawl. That was how tired she was. But if she went into the New York Café and ate some ice cream she might feel O.K. And smoke and be by herself a little while.

The front part of the café was crowded, so she went to the very last booth. It was the small of her back and her face that got so tired. Their motto was supposed to be 'Keep on your toes and smile.' Once she was out of the store she had to frown a long time to get her face natural again. Even her ears were tired. She took off the dangling green earrings that pinched the lobes of her ears. She had bought the earrings the week before — and also a silver bangle bracelet. At first she had worked in Pots and Pans, but now they had changed her to Costume Jewelry.

'Good evening, Mick,' Mister Brannon said. He wiped the bottom of a glass of water with a napkin and set it on the table.

'I want me a chocolate sundae and a nickel glass of draw beer.'

'Together?' He put down a menu and pointed with his little finger that wore a lady's gold ring. 'See — here's some nice roast chicken or some veal stew. Why don't you have a little supper with me?'

'No, thanks. All I want is the sundae and the beer. Both plenty cold.'

Mick raked her hair from her forehead. Her mouth was open so that her cheeks seemed hollow. There were these two things she could never believe. That Mister Singer had killed himself and was dead. And that she was grown and had to work at Woolworth's.

She was the one found him. They had thought the noise was a backfire from a car, and it was not until the next day that they knew. She went in to play the radio. The blood was all over his neck and when her Dad came he pushed her out the room. She had run from the house. The shock wouldn't let her be still. She had run into the dark and hit herself with her fists. And then the next night he was in a coffin in the living-room. The undertaker had put rouge and lipstick on his face to make him look natural. But he didn't look natural. He was very dead. And mixed with the smell of flowers there was this other smell so that she couldn't stay in the room. But through all those days she held down the job. She wrapped packages and handed them across the counter and rung the money in the till. She walked when she was supposed to walk and ate when she sat down to the table. Only at first when she went to bed at night she couldn't sleep. But now she slept like she was supposed to, also.

Mick turned sideways in the seat so that she could cross her legs. There was a run in her stocking. It had started while she was walking to work and she had spit on it. Then later the run had gone farther and she had stuck a little piece of chewing-gum on the end. But even that didn't help. Now she would have to go home and sew. It was hard to know what she could do about stockings. She wore them out so fast. Unless she was the kind of common girl that would wear cotton stockings.

She oughtn't to have come in here. The bottoms of her shoes were clean worn out. She ought to have saved the twenty cents toward a new half-sole. Because if she kept on standing on a shoe with a hole in it what would happen? A blister would come on her foot. And she would have to pick it with a burnt needle. She would have to stay home from work and be fired. And then what would happen?

'Here you are,' said Mister Brannon. 'But I never heard of such a combination before.'

He put the sundae and the beer on the table. She pretended to clean her fingernails because if she noticed him he would start talking. He didn't have this grudge against her any more, so he must have forgotten about the pack of gum. Now he always wanted to talk to her. But she wanted to be quiet and by herself. The sundae was O.K., covered all over with chocolate and nuts and cherries. And the beer was relaxing. The beer had a nice bitter taste after the ice cream and it made her drunk. Next to music beer was best.

But now no music was in her mind. That was a funny thing. It was like she was shut out from the inside room. Sometimes a quick little tune would come and go — but she never went into the inside room with music like she used to do. It was like she was too tense. Or maybe because it was like the store took all her energy and time. Woolworth's wasn't the same as school. When she used to come home from school she felt good and was ready to start working on the music. But now she was always too tired. At home she just ate supper and slept and then ate breakfast and went off to the store again. A song she had started in her private notebook two months before was still not finished. And she wanted to stay in the inside room but she didn't know how. It was like the inside room was locked somewhere away from her. A very hard thing to understand.

Mick pushed her broken front tooth with her thumb. But she did have Mister Singer's radio. All the installments hadn't been paid and she took on the responsibility. It was good to have something that had belonged to him. And maybe one of these days she might be able to set aside a little for a second-hand piano. Say two bucks a week. And she wouldn't let anybody touch this private piano but her — only she might teach George little pieces. She would keep it in the back room and play on it every night. And all day Sunday. But then suppose some week she couldn't make a payment. So then would they come to take it away like the little red bicycle? And suppose like she wouldn't let them. Suppose she hid the piano under the house. Or else she would meet them at the front door. And fight. She would knock down both the two men so they would have shiners and broke noses and would be passed out on the hall floor.

Mick frowned and rubbed her fist hard across her forehead. That was the way things were. It was like she was mad all the time. Not how a kid gets mad quick so that soon it is all over — but in another way. Only there was nothing to be mad at. Unless the store. But the store hadn't asked her to take the job. So there was nothing to be mad at. It was like she was cheated. Only nobody had cheated her. So there was nobody to take it out on. However, just the same she had that feeling. Cheated.

But maybe it would be true about the piano and turn out O.K. Maybe she would get a chance soon. Else what the hell good had it all been — the way she felt about music and the plans she had made in the inside room? It had to be some good if anything made sense. And it was too and it was too and it was too and it was too. It was some good.

All right!

O.K.!

Some good.

4

Night

ALL was serene. As Biff dried his face and hands a breeze tinkled the glass pendants of the little Japanese pagoda on the table. He had just awaked from a nap and had smoked his night cigar. He thought of Blount and wondered if by now he had traveled far. A bottle of Agua Florida was on the bathroom shelf and he touched the stopper to his temples. He whistled an old song, and as he descended the narrow stairs the tune left a broken echo behind him.

Louis was supposed to be on duty behind the counter. But

he had soldiered on the job and the place was deserted. The front door stood open to the empty street. The clock on the wall pointed to seventeen minutes before midnight. The radio was on and there was talk about the crisis Hitler had cooked up over Danzig. He went back to the kitchen and found Louis asleep in a chair. The boy had taken off his shoes and unbuttoned his trousers. His head drooped on his chest. A long wet spot on his shirt showed that he had been sleeping a good while. His arms hung straight down at his sides and the wonder was he did not fall forward on his face. He slept soundly and there was no use to wake him. The night would be a quiet one.

Biff tiptoed across the kitchen to a shelf which held a basket of tea olive and two water pitchers full of zinnias. He carried the flowers up to the front of the restaurant and removed the cellophane-wrapped platters of the last special from the display window. He was sick of food. A window of fresh summer flowers — that would be good. His eyes were closed as he imagined how it could be arranged. A foundation of the tea olive strewn over the bottom, cool and green. The red pottery tub filled with the brilliant zinnias. Nothing more. He began to arrange the window carefully. Among the flowers there was a freak plant, a zinnia with six bronze petals and two red. He examined this curio and laid it aside to save. Then the window was finished and he stood in the street to regard his handiwork. The awkward stems of the flowers had been bent to just the right degree of restful looseness. The electric lights detracted, but when the sun rose the display would show at its best advantage. Downright artistic.

The black, starlit sky seemed close to the earth. He strolled along the sidewalk, pausing once to knock an orange peel into the gutter with the side of his foot. At the far end of the next block two men, small from the distance and motionless, stood arm in arm together. No one else could be seen. His place was the only store on all the street with an open door and lights inside.

And why? What was the reason for keeping the place open all through the night when every other café in the town was closed? He was often asked that question and could never speak the answer out in words. Not money. Sometimes a party would come for beer and scrambled eggs and spend five or ten dollars. But that was rare. Mostly they came one at a time and ordered little and stayed long. And on some nights, between the hours of twelve and five o'clock, not a customer would enter. There was no profit in it — that was plain.

But he would never close up for the night — not as long as he stayed in the business. Night was the time. There were those he would never have seen otherwise. A few came regularly several times a week. Others had come into the place only once, had drunk a Coca-Cola, and never returned.

Biff folded his arms across his chest and walked more slowly. Inside the arc of the street light his shadow showed angular and black. The peaceful silence of the night settled in him. These were the hours for rest and meditation. Maybe that was why he stayed downstairs and did not sleep. With a last quick glance he scanned the empty street and went inside.

The crisis voice still talked on the radio. The fans on the ceiling made a soothing whir. From the kitchen came the sound of Louis snoring. He thought suddenly of poor Willie and decided to send him a quart of whiskey sometime soon. He turned to the crossword puzzle in the newspaper. There was a picture of a woman to identify in the center. He recognized her and wrote the name — Mona Lisa — across the first spaces. Number one down was a word for beggar, beginning with *m* and nine letters long. Mendicant. Two horizontal was some word meaning to remove afar off. A six-letter word beginning with *e*. Elapse? He sounded trial combinations of letters aloud. Eloign. But he had lost interest. There were puzzles enough without this kind. He folded and put away the paper. He would come back to it later.

He examined the zinnia he had intended to save. As he held it in the palm of his hand to the light the flower was not such a curious specimen after all. Not worth saving. He plucked the soft, bright petals and the last one came out on love. But who? Who would he be loving now? No one person. Anybody decent who came in out of the street to sit for an hour and have a drink. But no one person. He had known his loves and they were over. Alice. Madeline and Gyp. Finished. Leaving him either better or worse. Which? However you looked at it.

And Mick. The one who in the last months had lived so strangely in his heart. Was that love done with too? Yes. It was finished. Early in the evenings Mick came in for a cold drink or a sundae. She had grown older. Her rough and childish ways were almost gone. And instead there was something ladylike and delicate about her that was hard to point out. The earrings, the dangle of her bracelets, and the new way she crossed her legs and pulled the hem of her skirt down past her knees. He watched her and felt only a sort of gentleness. In him the old feeling was gone. For a year this love had blossomed strangely. He had questioned it a hundred times and found no answer. And now, as a summer flower shatters in September, it was finished. There was no one.

Biff tapped his nose with his forefinger. A foreign voice was now speaking on the radio. He could not decide for certain whether the voice was German, French, or Spanish. But it sounded like doom. It gave him the jitters to listen to it. When he turned it off the silence was deep and unbroken. He felt the night outside. Loneliness gripped him so that his breath quickened. It was far too late to call Lucile on the telephone and speak to Baby. Nor could he expect a customer to enter at this hour. He went to the door and looked up and down the street. All was empty and dark.

'Louis!' he called. 'Are you awake, Louis?'

No answer. He put his elbows on the counter and held his

head in his hands. He moved his dark bearded jaw from side to side and slowly his forehead lowered in a frown.

The riddle. The question that had taken root in him and would not let him rest. The puzzle of Singer and the rest of them. More than a year had gone by since it had started. More than a year since Blount had hung around the place on his first long drunk and seen the mute for the first time. Since Mick had begun to follow him in and out. And now for a month Singer had been dead and buried. And the riddle was still in him, so that he could not be tranquil. There was something not natural about it all — something like an ugly joke. When he thought of it he felt uneasy and in some unknown way afraid.

He had managed about the funeral. They had left all that to him. Singer's affairs were in a mess. There were installments due on everything he owed and the beneficiary of his life insurance was deceased. There was just enough to bury him. The funeral was at noon. The sun burned down on them with savage heat as they stood around the open dank grave. The flowers curled and turned brown in the sun. Mick cried so hard that she choked herself and her father had to beat her on the back. Blount scowled down at the grave with his fist to his mouth. The town's colored doctor, who was somehow related to poor Willie, stood on the edge of the crowd and moaned to himself. And there were strangers nobody had ever seen or heard of before. God knows where they came from or why they were there.

The silence in the room was deep as the night itself. Biff stood transfixed, lost in his meditations. Then suddenly he felt a quickening in him. His heart turned and he leaned his back against the counter for support. For in a swift radiance of illumination he saw a glimpse of human struggle and of valor. Of the endless fluid passage of humanity through endless time. And of those who labor and of those who —one word — love. His soul expanded. But for a moment only.

For in him he felt a warning, a shaft of terror. Between the two worlds he was suspended. He saw that he was looking at his own face in the counter glass before him. Sweat glistened on his temples and his face was contorted. One eye was opened wider than the other. The left eye delved narrowly into the past while the right gazed wide and affrighted into a future of blackness, error, and ruin. And he was suspended between radiance and darkness. Between bitter irony and faith. Sharply he turned away.

'Louis!' he called. 'Louis! Louis!'

Again there was no answer. But, motherogod, was he a sensible man or was he not? And how could this terror throttle him like this when he didn't even know what caused it? And would he just stand here like a jittery ninny or would he pull himself together and be reasonable? For after all *was* he a sensible man or was he not? Biff wet his handkerchief beneath the water tap and patted his drawn, tense face. Somehow he remembered that the awning had not yet been raised. As he went to the door his walk gained steadiness. And when at last he was inside again he composed himself soberly to await the morning sun.

THE END

Reflections in a Golden Eye

For Annemarie Clarac-Schwarzenbach

I

I

AN ARMY POST in peacetime is a dull place. Things happen, but then they happen over and over again. The general plan of a fort in itself adds to the monotony — the huge concrete barracks, the neat rows of officers' homes built one precisely like the other, the gym, the chapel, the golf course and the swimming pools — all is designed according to a certain rigid pattern. But perhaps the dullness of a post is caused most of all by insularity and by a surfeit of leisure and safety, for once a man enters the army he is expected only to follow the heels ahead of him. At the same time things do occasionally happen on an army post that are not likely to re-occur. There is a fort in the South where a few years ago a murder was committed. The participants of this tragedy were: two officers, a soldier, two women, a Filipino, and a horse.

The soldier in this affair was Private Ellgee Williams. Often in the late afternoon he could be seen sitting alone on one of the benches that lined the sidewalk before the barracks. This was a pleasant place, as here there was a long double row of young maple trees that patterned the lawn and the walk with cool, delicate, windblown shadows. In the spring the leaves of the trees were a lucent green that as the hot months came took on a darker, restful hue. In late autumn they were flaming gold. Here Private Williams would sit and wait for the call to evening mess. He was a silent young soldier and in the barracks he had neither an enemy nor a friend. His round sunburned face was marked by a certain watchful innocence. His full lips were red and the bangs of his hair lay brown and matted on his forehead. In his eyes, which were of a curious blend of amber and brown, there was a mute expression that is found usually in the eyes of animals. At first glance Private Williams seemed a bit heavy and awkward in his bearing.

But this was a deceptive impression; he moved with the silence and agility of a wild creature or a thief. Often soldiers who had thought themselves alone were startled to see him appear as from nowhere by their sides. His hands were small, delicately boned, and very strong.

Private Williams did not smoke, drink, fornicate, or gamble. In the barracks he kept to himself and was something of a mystery to the other men. Most of his leisure time Private Williams spent out in the woods surrounding the post. The reservation, fifteen miles square, was wild unspoiled country. Here were to be found giant virgin pines, many varieties of flowers, and even such shy animals as deer, wild pig, and foxes. Except for riding, Private Williams cared for none of the sports available to enlisted men. No one had ever seen him in the gym or at the swimming pool. Nor had he ever been known to laugh, to become angry, or to suffer in any way. He ate three wholesome, bounteous meals a day and never grumbled about the food as did the other soldiers. He slept in a room accommodating a long double row of about three dozen cots. This was not a peaceful room. At night when the lights were out there was often the sound of snores, of curses, and of strangled nightmare groans. But Private Williams rested tranquilly. Only sometimes from his cot there would be a stealthy rustle from the wrapper of a candy bar.

When Private Williams had been in the army for two years he was sent one day to the quarters of a certain Captain Penderton. This came about in the following manner. For the past six months Private Williams had been detailed to permanent stable fatigue, as he was quite a hand with horses. Captain Penderton had telephoned the post Sergeant Major and by chance, as many of the horses were out on maneuvers and work around the stables was slack, Private Williams was chosen for this particular duty. The nature of the assignment was simple. Captain Penderton wished a small part of the woods behind his quarters cleared so that later when a steak grill was put up he could give alfresco parties. This job would require about one full day's work.

Private Williams set out for this assignment at about seven-thirty in the morning. It was a mild and sunny day in October. He knew already where the Captain lived, as he had passed his house often when starting out for his walks in the woods. Also, he knew the Captain well by sight. In fact he had once done the Captain an accidental injury. A year and a half ago Private Williams had for a few weeks served as striker to the Lieutenant in command of the company to which he was then attached. One afternoon the Lieutenant received a visit from Captain Penderton and while serving them refreshments Private Williams had spilled a cup of coffee on the Captain's trousers. In addition to this he now saw the Captain frequently at the stables and he had in his charge the horse of the Captain's wife — a chestnut stallion which was easily the handsomest mount on the post.

The Captain lived on the outskirts of the fort. His house, an eight-room two-story building of stucco, was identical with all the other houses on the street except for the distinction of being an end house. On two sides the lawn adjoined the forest of the reservation. On the right the Captain had as his only near neighbor Major Morris Langdon. The houses on this street faced a large, flat expanse of brown sward which had until recently served as the polo field.

When Private Williams arrived, the Captain came out to explain in detail what he wanted done. The scrub oaks, the low briary bushes were to be cleared, the limbs of the large trees growing at a level less than six feet would be cut away. The Captain pointed out a large old oak about twenty yards from the lawn as the boundary for the space to be worked on. The Captain wore a gold ring on one of his white, fattish hands. He was dressed this morning in knee-length khaki shorts, high wool socks, and a suede jacket. His face was sharp and strained. He had black hair and eyes of a glassy blue. The Captain did not seem to recognize Private Williams and he gave his directions in a nervous. finicky manner. He told Private Williams he wanted the work completed that day and said he would be back sometime in the late afternoon.

The soldier worked steadily all morning. At noon he went to

the mess hall for his lunch. By four o'clock the job was finished. He had done even more than the Captain specifically requested. The large oak marking the boundary had an unusual shape — the branches on the side toward the lawn were high enough to walk beneath, but the branches on the opposite side swept down gracefully to the ground. The soldier had with a great deal of trouble cut off these down-sweeping limbs. Then, when all was done, he leaned against the trunk of a pine tree to wait. He seemed at peace with himself and quite content to stand there waiting forever.

'Why, what are *you* doing here?' a voice asked him suddenly.

The soldier had seen the Captain's wife come out of the rear entrance of the house next door and walk toward him across the lawn. He saw her, but she did not enter the dark sphere of his consciousness until she spoke to him.

'I was just down at the stables,' Mrs. Penderton said. 'My Firebird has been kicked.'

'Yes, ma'am,' the soldier answered vaguely. He waited for a moment to digest the meaning of her words. 'How?'

'That I don't know. Maybe some damn mule or maybe they let him in with the mares. I was mad about it and I asked for you.'

The Captain's wife lay down in a hammock that was slung between two trees on the edge of the lawn. Even in the clothes she was now wearing — boots, soiled whipcord breeches very worn at the knees, and a gray jersey — she was a handsome woman. Her face had the bemused placidity of a Madonna's and she wore her straight bronze hair brought back in a knot at the nape of her neck. As she was resting there the servant, a young Negress, came out with a tray holding a pint bottle of rye, a whiskey jigger, and some water. Mrs. Penderton was not pernickety about her liquor. She drank down two jiggers straight and chased them with a swallow of cold water. She did not speak to the soldier again and he did not question her further about the horse. Neither seemed aware of the presence of the other in any way. The soldier leaned back against his pine tree and stared unblinking into space.

The late autumn sun laid a radiant haze over the new sodded

winter grass of the lawn, and even in the woods the sun shone through in places where the leave were not so dense, to make fiery golden patterns on the ground. Then suddenly the sun was gone. There was a chill in the air and a light, pure wind. It was time for retreat. From far away came the sound of the bugle, clarified by distance and echoing in the woods with a lost hollow tone. The night was near at hand.

At this point Captain Penderton returned. He parked his car before the house and crossed the yard immediately to see how the work had been done. He greeted his wife and curtly saluted the soldier who now stood at rather lax attention before him. The Captain glanced over the cleared space. All at once he snapped his fingers and his lips sharpened with a thin, stiff sneer. He turned his light blue eyes to the soldier. Then he said very quietly: 'Private, the whole idea was in the big oak tree.'

The soldier received his comment in silence. His round serious face did not change.

'The instructions were for the ground to be cleared only so far as the oak tree,' the officer continued in a higher voice. Stiffly he walked back to the tree in question and pointed to the cut stark limbs. 'The way the boughs swept down and made a background shutting off the rest of the woods was the whole point. Now it is all ruined.' The Captain's agitation seemed more than such a mishap warranted. Standing alone in the woods he was a small man.

'What does the Captain want me to do?' Private Williams asked after a long pause.

Mrs. Penderton laughed suddenly and put down one booted foot to rock the hammock. 'The Captain wants you to pick up the branches and sew them back on again.'

Her husband was not amused. 'Here!' he said to the soldier. 'Bring some leaves and spread them on the ground to cover the bare spaces where the bushes have been cleared. Then you may go.' He tipped the soldier and went into the house.

Private Williams walked slowly back into the darkened woods to gather fallen leaves. The Captain's wife rocked herself and seemed about to go to sleep. The sky filled with a pale, cold yellow light and all was still.

Captain Penderton was in no comfortable state of mind this evening. On coming into the house he went straight to his study. This was a small room planned originally as a sun porch and leading from the dining-room. The Captain settled himself at his desk and opened a thick notebook. He spread out a map before him and took his slide rule from a drawer. In spite of these preparations he was unable to put his mind to his work. He leaned over the desk with his head in his hands and his eyes closed.

In part his restlessness was caused by his annoyance with Private Williams. He had been irritated when he saw that it was this particular soldier who had been sent him. There were perhaps only half a dozen enlisted men on all the post whose faces were familiar to the Captain. He looked on all soldiers with bored contempt. To him officers and men might belong to the same biological genus, but they were of an altogether different species. The Captain well remembered the accident of the spilled coffee, as it had ruined for him a brand-new and costly outfit. The suit was of heavy Chinese silk and the stain had never been entirely removed. (The Captain always wore uniform when away from the post, but on all social occasions among other officers he affected mufti and was a great swell.) Aside from this grievance Private Williams was associated in the Captain's mind with the stables and his wife's horse, Firebird — an unpleasant association. And now the blunder about the oak tree was the last straw. Sitting at his desk the Captain indulged in a brief, peevish day-dream — he imagined a fantastic situation in which he caught the soldier transgressing in some way and was instrumental in having him court-martialed. This consoled him a little. He poured himself a cup of tea from the thermos bottle on his desk and became absorbed in other and more pertinent worries.

The Captain's restlessness this evening had many causes. His personality differed in some respects from the ordinary. He stood in a somewhat curious relation to the three fundaments of existence — life itself, sex, and death. Sexually the Captain obtained within himself a delicate balance between the male and female elements, with the susceptibilities of both the sexes and the active powers of neither. For a person content to withdraw a bit from life, and able to collect his scattered passions and throw himself wholeheartedly into some impersonl work, some art or even some crack-brained fixed idea such as an attempt to square the circle — for such a person this state of being is bearable enough. The Captain had his work and he did not spare himself; it was said that he had a brilliant career ahead of him. Perhaps he would not have felt this basic lack, or superfluity, if it had not been for his wife. But with her he suffered. He had a sad penchant for becoming enamoured of his wife's lovers.

As to his relations with the other two fundaments, his position was simple enough. In his balance between the two great instincts, toward life and toward death, the scale was heavily weighted to one side — to death. Because of this the Captain was a coward.

Captain Penderton was also something of a savant. During the years when he was a young Lieutenant and a bachelor he had had much opportunity to read, as his fellow officers tended to avoid his room in the bachelors' quarters or else to visit him in pairs or groups. His head was filled with statistics and information of scholarly exactitude. For instance, he could describe in detail the curious digestive apparatus of a lobster or the life history of a Trilobite. He spoke and wrote three languages gracefully. He knew something of astronomy and had read much poetry. But in spite of his knowledge of many separate facts, the Captain never in his life had had an idea in his head. For the formation of an idea involves the fusion of two or more known facts. And this the Captain had not the courage to do.

As he sat alone at his desk this evening, unable to work, he did not question himself as to his feelings. He thought again of the face of Private Williams. Then he recollected that the Langdons next door were dining with them that evening. Major Morris Langdon was his wife's lover, but the Captain did not dwell on this.

Instead he suddenly remembered an evening long ago, soon after he had married. On that evening he had felt this same unhappy restlessness and had seen fit to relieve himself in a curious manner. He had driven into a town near the post where he was then stationed, had parked his car, and had walked for a long time in the streets. It was a late winter night. In the course of this walk the Captain came upon a tiny kitten hovered in a doorway. The kitten had found shelter and made itself warm; when the Captain leaned down he found that it was purring. He picked up the kitten and felt it vibrate in his palm. For a long time he looked into the soft, gentle little face and stroked the warm fur. The kitten was at the age when it was first able to open wide its clear green eyes. At last the Captain had taken the kitten with him down the street. On the corner there was a mailbox and after one quick glance around him he had opened the freezing letter slot and squeezed the kitten inside. Then he had continued on his way.

The Captain heard the back door slam and he left his desk. In the kitchen his wife sat on a table while Susie, the colored servant, pulled off her boots. Mrs. Penderton was not a pure-bred Southerner. She had been born and brought up in the army, and her father, who a year before his retirement had reached the rank of Brigadier General, was originally from the West coast. Her mother, however, had been a South Carolinian. And in her ways the Captain's wife was Southern enough. Their gas stove was not crusted with generations of dirt as her grandmother's had been, but then it was by no means clean. Mrs. Penderton also held to many other old Southern notions, such as the belief that pastry or bread is not fit to eat unless it is rolled on a marble-topped table. For this reason they had once, when the Captain was detailed to Schofield Barracks, hauled the table on which she was now sitting all the way to Hawaii and back. If the Captain's wife ever chanced to find a black, crooked hair in her food, she wiped it calmly on her napkin and went right on with the enjoyment of her dinner without the bat of an eye.

'Susie,' said Mrs. Penderton, 'do people have gizzards like chickens do?'

The Captain stood in the doorway and was noticed neither by his wife nor his servant. When she had been relieved of her boots, Mrs. Penderton moved about the kitchen barefooted. She took a ham from the oven and sprinkled the top with brown sugar and bread crumbs. She poured herself another drink, only half a jigger this time, and in a sudden excess of vigor she performed a little shag dance. The Captain was intensely irritated with his wife, and she knew it.

'For God's sake, Leonora, go up and put on some shoes.'

For an answer Mrs. Penderton hummed a queer little tune to herself and went past the Captain and into the living-room.

Her husband followed close behind her. 'You look like a slattern going around the house like this.'

A fire was laid in the grate and Mrs. Penderton bent down to light it. Her smooth sweet face was very rosy and there were little glistening sweat beads on her upper lip.

'The Langdons are coming any minute now and you will sit down to dinner like this, I suppose?'

'Sure,' she said. 'And why not, you old prissy?'

The Captain said in a cold, taut voice: 'You disgust me.'

Mrs. Penderton's answer was a sudden laugh, a laugh both soft and savage, as though she had received some long expected piece of scandalous news or had thought of some sly joke. She pulled off her jersey, crushed it into a ball, and threw it into the corner of the room. Then deliberately she unbuttoned her breeches and stepped out of them. In a moment she was standing naked by the hearth. Before the bright gold and orange light of the fire her body was magnificent. The shoulders were straight so that the collar bone made a sharp pure line. Between her round breasts there were delicate blue veins. In a few years her body would be fullblown like a rose with loosened petals, but now the soft roundness was controlled and disciplined by sport. Although she stood quite still and placid, there was about her body a subtle quality of vibration, as though on touching her fair flesh one would feel the slow live coursing of the bright blood beneath. While the Captain looked at her with the stunned indignation of a man who has suffered a slap in the face, she walked serenely to the vestibule on her way to the stairs. The front door was open and from the dark night outside a breeze blew in and lifted a loose strand of her bronze hair.

She was halfway up the steps before the Captain recovered from his shock. Then he ran trembling after her. 'I will kill you!' he said in a strangled voice. 'I will do it! I will do it!' He crouched with his hand to the banister and one foot on the second step of the stairway as though ready to spring up after her.

She turned slowly and looked down at him with unconcern for a moment before she spoke. 'Son, have you ever been collared and dragged out in the street and thrashed by a naked woman?'

The Captain stood as she had left him. Then he put his head down on his outstretched arm and rested his weight against the banister. From his throat came a rasping sound like a sob, but there were no tears on his face. After a time he stood up and wiped his neck with his handkerchief. Only then did he notice that the front door was open, the house brightly lighted, and all the shades raised. He felt himself sicken strangely. Anyone might have passed along the dark street before the house. He thought of the soldier whom he had left a short while ago on the edge of the woods. Even he might have seen what had occurred. The Captain looked all about him with frightened eyes. Then he went into his study where he kept a decanter of old, strong brandy.

Leonora Penderton feared neither man, beast, nor the devil; God she had never known. At the very mention of the Lord's name she thought only of her old father who had sometimes read the Bible on a Sunday afternoon. Of that book she remembered two things clearly: one, that Jesus had been crucified at a place called Cavalry Hill — the other, that once He had ridden somewhere on a jackass, and what sort of person would want to ride a jackass?

Within five minutes Leonora Penderton had forgotten the scene with her husband. She ran the water for her bath and laid out her clothes for the evening. Leonora Penderton was the subject of much lively gossip among the ladies of the post. According to them her past and present affairs were a rich medley of amorous exploits. But most if what these ladies told was hearsay and conjecture — for Leonora Penderton was a person who liked to settle herself and was adverse to complications. When she married the Captain she had been a virgin. Four nights after her wedding she was still a virgin, and on the fifth night her status was changed only enough to leave her somewhat puzzled. As for the rest it would be hard to say. She herself would probably have reckoned her affairs according to a system of her own — giving the old Colonel at Leavenworth only half a count and the young Lieutenant in Hawaii several units in her calculations. But now for the past two years there had been only Major Morris Langdon and no one else. With him she was content.

On the post Leonora Penderton enjoyed a reputation as a good hostess, an excellent sportswoman, and even as a great lady. However, there was something about her that puzzled her friends and acquaintances. They sensed an element in her personality that they could not quite put their fingers on. The truth of the matter was that she was a little feebleminded.

This sad fact did not reveal itself at parties, or in the stables, or at her dinner table. There were only three persons who understood this: her old father, the General, who had worried no little about it until she was safely married; her husband, who looked on it as a condition natural to all women under forty; and Major Morris Langdon, who loved her for it all the more. She could not have multiplied twelve by thirteen under threat of the rack. If ever it was strictly necessary that she write a letter, such as a note to thank her uncle for a birthday check or a letter ordering a new bridle, it was a weighty enterprise for her. She and Susie shut themselves in the kitchen with scholarly seclusion. They sat down to a table furnished with an abundance of paper and several nicely sharpened pencils. Then, when the final draft was finished and copied, they were both exhausted and in great need of a quiet, restoring drink.

Leonora Penderton enjoyed her warm bath that evening. She dressed herself slowly in the clothes she had already laid out on the bed. She wore a simple gray skirt, a blue Angora sweater, and pearl earrings. She was downstairs again at seven o'clock and their guests were waiting.

She and the Major found the dinner first-rate. To begin with there was a clear soup. Then with the ham they had rich oily turnip greens, and candied sweet potatoes that were a transparent amber beneath the light and richly glazed with sweet sauce. There were rolls and hot spoon-bread. Susie passed the vegetables only once and left the serving dishes on the table between the Major and Leonora, for those two were great eaters. The Major sat with one elbow on the table and was altogether very much at home. His red-brown face had a blunt, jovial, and friendly expression; among both officers and men he was very popular. Except for the mention of Firebird's accident there was almost no table-talk. Mrs. Langdon hardly touched her dinner. She was a small, dark, fragile woman with a large nose and a sensitive mouth. She was very ill and she looked it. Not only was this illness physical, but she had been tortured to the bone by grief and anxiety so that now she was on the verge of actual lunacy. Captain Penderton sat very straight with his elbows held close to his sides. Once he cordially congratulated the Major on a medal he had received. Several times during the course of the meal he flicked the rim of his water goblet and listened to the clear, resonant ring. The dinner ended with a dessert of hot mince pie. Then the four of them went into the sitting-room to finish out the evening with cards and conversation.

'My dear, you are a damn fine cook,' the Major said comfortably.

The four people at the table had not been alone. In the autumn darkness outside the window there stood a man who watched them in silence. The night was cold and the clean scent of pine trees sharpened the air. A wind sang in the forest near-by. The sky glittered with icy stars. The man who watched them stood so close to the window that his breath showed on the cold glass pane.

Private Williams had indeed seen Mrs. Penderton as she left the hearth and walked upstairs to her bath. And never before in his life had this young soldier seen a naked woman. He had been brought up in a household exclusively male. From his father, who ran a one-mule farm and preached on Sunday at a Holiness church, he had learned that women carried in them a deadly and catching disease which made men blind, crippled, and doomed to hell. In the army he also heard much talk of this bad sickness and was even himself examined once a month by the doctor to see if he had touched a woman. Private Williams had never willingly touched, or looked at, or spoken to a female since he was eight years old.

He had been late in gathering the armfuls of damp, rank autumn leaves back in the woods. When at last his duty was done, he had crossed the Captain's lawn on his way to evening mess. By chance he glanced into the sharply lighted vestibule. And since then he had not found it in him to go away. He stood motionless in the silent night with his arms hanging loose at his sides. When at dinner the ham was carved, he had swallowed painfully. But he kept his grave, deep gaze on the Captain's wife. The expression of his mute face had not been changed by his experience, but now and then he narrowed his gold-brown eyes as though he were forming within himself some subtle scheme. When the Captain's wife had left the dining-room, he still stood there for a time. Then very slowly he turned away. The light behind him laid a great dim shadow of himself on the smooth grass of the lawn. The soldier walked like a man weighted by a dark dream and his footsteps were soundless.

II

II

VERY EARLY the next morning Private Williams went to the stables. The sun had not yet risen and the air was colorless and cold. Milky ribbons of mist clung to the damp earth and the sky was silver-gray. The path leading to the stables passed a bluff which commanded a sweeping view of the reservation. The woods were in full autumn color, and scattered among the blackish green of the pine trees there were blunt splashes of crimson and yellow. Private Williams walked slowly along the leafy path. Now and then he stopped altogether and stood perfectly still, in the attitude of one who listens to a call from a long distance. His sun-browned skin was flushed in the morning air and on his lips there were still the white traces of the milk he had drunk for breakfast. Loitering and stopping in this way he reached the stables just as the sun came up in the sky.

Inside the stable it was still almost dark and no one was about. The air was close, warm, and sour-sweet. As the soldier passed between the stalls he heard the placid breath of the horses, a sleepy snuffle and a whinny. Dumb, luminous eyes turned toward him. The young soldier took from his pocket an envelope of sugar and soon his hands were warm and sticky with slaver. He went into the stall of a little mare who was almost ready to drop her foal. He stroked her swollen belly and stood for a time with his arms around her neck. Then he let the mules out into their pen. The soldier was not long alone with the beasts — soon the other men reported for their duty. It was Saturday, a busy day at the stables, as in the morning there were riding classes for the children and women of the post. The stable was soon noisy with talk and heavy footsteps; the horses grew restive in their stalls.

Mrs. Penderton was one of the first riders to come this morning.

With her, as often, was Major Langdon. Captain Penderton accompanied them today, which was unusual, as he customarily took his ride alone and in the late afternoon. The three of them sat on the paddock fence while their mounts were being saddled. Private Williams led out Firebird first. The injury of which the Captain's wife complained the day before had been greatly exaggerated. On the horse's left foreleg there was a slight abrasion that had been painted with iodine. On being led out into the bright sunlight, the horse rounded his nostrils nervously and turned his long neck to look about him. His coat was curried smooth as satin and his mane was thick and glossy in the sun.

At first glance the horse seemed overgrown and too heavy-set for a thoroughbred. His great haunches were broad and fleshy, and his legs were somewhat thick. But he moved with marvelous, fiery grace, and once at Camden he had outraced his own great sire who was a champion. When Mrs. Penderton was mounted, he reared up twice and tried to break away toward the bridle path. Then, straining against the bit, with arched neck and tail raised high, he sidestepped furiously and a light froth of foam showed on his muzzle. During this struggle between horse and rider, Mrs. Penderton laughed aloud and spoke to Firebird in a voice that was vibrant with passion and excitement: 'You sweet old bastard, you!' The struggle ended as abruptly as it had begun. Indeed, as this volatile fracas took place every morning, it could hardly be called a real struggle any longer. When the horse, as an ill-trained two-year-old, had first come to the stables, it had been earnest enough. Twice Mrs. Penderton was badly thrown, and once when she returned from her ride the soldiers saw that she had bitten her lower lip quite through so that there was blood on her sweater and shirt.

But now this brief daily struggle had a theatrical, affected air — it was a jocular pantomime performed for their own amusement and the benefit of spectators. Even when the froth showed on his mouth, the horse moved with a certain fractious grace as though aware of being watched. And after it was over he stood quite still and sighed once, in much the same manner as a young husband would sigh laughingly and shrug his shoulders when giving in to the will of a beloved and termagant wife. Except for these mock rebellions the horse was now perfectly trained.

To all the regular riders the soldiers at the stables had given nicknames that they used when speaking among themselves. Major Langdon was called The Buffalo. This was because when in the saddle he slumped his great heavy shoulders and lowered his head. The Major was a fine horseman and, when a young Lieutenant, he had made a rare name for himself on the polo field. On the other hand, Captain Penderton was no rider at all, although he himself was not aware of this. He sat rigid as a ramrod in the exact position taught by the riding master. Perhaps he would not have ridden at all if he could have seen himself from the rear. His buttocks spread and jounced flabbily in the saddle. For this reason he was known to the soldiers as Captain Flap-Fanny. Mrs. Penderton was called simply The Lady, so great was the esteem in which she was held at the stables.

This morning the three riders started at a sedate walk, Mrs. Penderton leading. Private Williams stood watching them until they were out of sight. Soon he heard from the ring of the horses' hoofs on the hard path that they had broken into a canter. The sun was brighter now and the sky had darkened to a warm, brilliant blue. In the fresh air there was the odor of dung and burning leaves. The soldier stood so long that at last the Sergeant came up to him and roared good-naturedly: 'Hey, Unconscious, you mean to gawk there forever?' The sound of the horses' hoofs could be heard no longer. The young soldier pushed back his bangs from his forehead and slowly set about his work. He did not speak all day.

Then late in the evening Private Williams dressed in fresh clothes and went out to the woods. He walked along the edge of the reservation until he reached the stretch of woods he had cleared for Captain Penderton. The house was not brightly lighted as it had been before. Lights showed only in one room to the right upstairs, and in the small porch leading from the dinning-room. When the soldier approached, he found the Captain in his study alone; the Captain's wife, then, was in the lighted room upstairs where the shades were drawn. The house, like all the houses on the block, was new, so that there had been no time for shrubs to grow in the yard. But the Captain had had twelve ligustrum trees transplanted and put in rows along the sides so that the place would not seem so raw and bare. Shielded by these thick-leaved evergreens, the soldier could not easily be seen from the street or the house next door. He stood so close to the Captain that if the window had been open he could have reached out and touched him with his hand.

Captain Penderton sat at his desk with his back turned to Private Williams. He was in a constant fidget as he studied. Besides the books and papers on his desk there was a purple glass decanter, a thermos bottle of tea, and a box of cigarettes. He drank hot tea and red wine. Every ten or fifteen minutes he put a new cigarette in his amber cigarette holder. He worked until two o'clock and the soldier watched him.

From this night there began a strange time. The soldier returned each evening, approaching by way of the forest. and looked at all that went on within the Captain's house. At the windows of the dining- and sitting-rooms there were lace curtains through which he could see, but not easily be seen himself. He stood to the side of the window, looking in obliquely, and the light did not fall on his face. Nothing of much consequence happened inside. Often they spent the evening away from home and did not return until after midnight. Once they entertained six guests at dinner. Most evenings, however, they spent with Major Langdon, who came either alone or with his wife. They would drink, play cards, and talk in the sitting-room. The soldier kept his eyes on the Captain's wife.

During this time a change was noticed in Private Williams. His new habit of suddenly stopping and looking for a long time into space was still with him. He would be cleaning out a stall or saddling a mule when all at once he seemed to withdraw into a trance. He would stand immovable and sometimes he did not even realize when his name was called. The Sergeant at the stables noticed this and was uneasy. He had occasionally seen this same queer habit in young soldiers who have grown homesick for the farm and womenfolk, and who plan to 'go over the hill.' But when the Sergeant questioned Private Williams, he answered that he was thinking about nothing at all.

The young soldier spoke the truth. Although his face wore an expression of still concentration, there were in his mind no plans or thoughts of which he was aware. In him was a deep reflection of the sight he had seen that night when passing before the Captain's lighted vestibule. But he did not think actively of The Lady or of anything else. However, it was necessary for him to pause and wait in this trancelike attitude, for far down in his mind there had begun a dark, slow germination.

Four times in his twenty years of life the soldier had acted of his own accord and without the pressure of immediate circumstance. Each of these four actions had been preceded by these same odd trances. The first of these actions was the sudden, inexplicable purchase of a cow. By the time he was a boy of seventeen, he had accumulated a hundred dollars by plowing and picking cotton. With this money he had bought this cow, and he named her Ruby Jewel. There was no need on his father's one-mule farm for a cow. It was unlawful for them to sell the milk, for their makeshift stable would not pass government inspection, and the milk that she yielded was far more than their small household could use. On winter mornings the boy would get up before daylight and go out with a lantern to his cow's stall. He would press his forehead against her warm flank as he milked and talk to her in soft, urgent whispers. He put his cupped hands down into the pail of frothy milk and drank with lingering swallows.

The second of these actions was a sudden, violent declaration of his faith in the Lord. He always had sat quietly on one of the back benches of the church where his father preached on Sunday. But one night during a revival he suddenly leaped up onto the platform. He called to God with strange wild sounds and rolled in convulsions on the floor. Afterward he had been very languid for a week and he never again found the spirit in this way.

The third of these actions was a crime which he committed and successfully concealed. And the fourth was his enlistment in the army.

Each of these happenings had come about very suddenly and without any conscious planning on his part. Still, in a curious way, he had prepared for them. For instance, just before the purchase of his cow he had stood gazing into space for a long while and then he cleaned out a lean-to by the barn that had been used for storing junk; when he brought home the cow there was a place ready for her. In the same manner he had got his small affairs in order before his enlistment. But he did not actually know that he was going to buy a cow until he counted out his money and put his hand on the halter. And it was only as he stepped over the threshold of the enlistment office that the vaporish impressions within him condensed to a thought, so that he realized he would be a soldier.

For almost two weeks Private Williams reconnoitered in this secret manner around the Captain's quarters. He learned the habits of the household. The servant was usually in bed at ten o'clock. When Mrs. Penderton spent the evening at home, she went upstairs at about eleven and the light in her room was turned off. As a rule the Captain worked from about ten-thirty until two o'clock.

Then on the twelfth night the soldier walked through the woods even more slowly than usual. From a far distance he saw that the house was lighted. In the sky there was a white brilliant moon and the night was cold and silvery. The soldier could be plainly seen as he left the woods to cross the lawn. In his right hand there was a pocket-knife and he had changed his clumsy boots for tennis shoes. From the sitting-room there was the sound of voices. The soldier went up to the window.

'Hit me, Morris,' said Leonora Penderton. 'Give me a big number this time.'

Major Langdon and the Captain's wife were playing a game of blackjack. The stakes were worth while and their system of reckoning very simple. If the Major won all the chips on the table, he was to have Firebird for a week — if Leonora won them, she would get a bottle of her favorite rye. During the last hour the Major had raked in most of the chips. The firelight reddened his handsome face and he was drumming a military tattoo with the heel of his boot on the floor. His black hair was turning white at the temples; already his clipped mustache was a becoming gray. Tonight he was in uniform. His heavy shoulders were slouched and he seemed warmly contented except when he glanced over at his wife — then his light eyes were uneasy and beseeching. Across from him Leonora had a studious, serious air, as she was trying to add fourteen and seven on her fingers underneath the table. At last she put the cards down.

'Am I busted?'

'No, my dear,' said the Major. 'Twenty-one exactly. Blackjack.'

Captain Penderton and Mrs. Langdon sat before the hearth. Neither of them was comfortable at all. They were both nervous this evening and had been talking with grim vivacity about gardening. There were good reasons for their nervousness. These days the Major was not altogether the same easy-go-lucky man he used to be. And even Leonora vaguely felt the general depression. For one reason, a strange and tragic thing had happened among these four people a few months ago. They had been sitting like this late one night when suddenly Mrs. Langdon, who had a high temperature, left the room and ran over to her own house. The Major did not follow her immediately, as he was comfortably stupefied with whiskey. Then later Anacleto, the Langdons' Filipino servant, rushed wailing into the room with such a wild-eyed face that they followed him without a word. They found Mrs. Langdon unconscious and she had cut off the tender nipples of her breasts with the garden shears.

'Does anybody want a drink?' the Captain asked.

They were all thirsty, and the Captain went back to the kitchen for another bottle of soda water. His deep uneasiness of mind was caused by the fact that he knew things could not go on much longer as they were. And although the affair between his wife and Major Langdon had been a torment to him, he could not think of any likely change without dread. Indeed his torment had been a rather special one, as he was just as jealous of his wife as he was of her love. In the last year he had come to feel an emotional regard for the Major that was the nearest thing to love that he had ever known. More than anything else he longed to distinguish himself in the eyes of this man. He carried his cuckoldry with a cynical good grace that was respected on the post. Now as he poured out the Major's drink his hand was shaking.

'You work too hard, Weldon,' Major Langdon said. 'And let me tell you one thing — it's not worth it. Your health comes first because where would you be if you lost it? Leonora, do you want another card?'

As Captain Penderton poured Mrs. Langdon's drink, he avoided her eyes. He loathed her so much that he could scarcely bear to look at her. She sat very quiet and stiff before the fire and she was knitting. Her face was deadly pale and her lips were rather swollen and chapped. She had soft, black eyes of feverish brilliance. She was twenty-nine years old, two years younger than Leonora. It was said that she once had had a beautiful voice, but no one on this post had ever heard her sing. As the Captain looked at her hands, he felt a quiver of nausea. Her hands were slender to the point of emaciation, with long fragile fingers and delicate branchings of greenish veins from the knuckles to the wrist. They were sickly pale against the crimson wool of the sweater she was knitting. Frequently, in many mean and subtle ways, the Captain tried to hurt this woman. He disliked her first of all because of her total indifference to himself. The Captain despised her also for the fact that she had done him a service — she knew, and kept secret, a matter which if gossiped about could cause him the most distressing embarrassment.

'Another sweater for your husband?'

'No,' she said quietly. 'I haven't decided just what I mean to do with this.'

Alison Langdon wanted terribly to cry. She had been thinking of her baby, Catherine, who had died three years before. She knew that she should go home and let her houseboy, Anacleto, help her get to bed. She was in pain and nervous. Even the fact that she did not know for whom she was knitting this sweater was a source of irritation to her. She had taken to knitting only when she had learned about her husband. At first she had done a number of sweaters for him. Then she had knitted a suit for Leonora. During the first months she could not quite believe that he could be so faithless to her. When at last she had scornfully given up her husband, she had turned desperately to Leonora. There began one of those peculiar friendships between the wife who had been betrayed and the object of her husband's love. This morbid, emotional attachment, bastard of shock and jealousy, she knew was unworthy of her. Of its own accord it had soon ended. Now she felt the tears come to her eyes and she drank a little whiskey to brace herself, although liquor was forbidden her because of her heart. She herself did not even like the taste of it. She much preferred a tiny glass of some syrupy liqueur, or a little sherry, or even a cup of coffee if it came to that. But now she drank the whiskey because it was there, and the others were drinking, and there was nothing else to do.

'Weldon!' called out the Major suddenly, 'your wife is cheating! She peeked under the card to find if she wanted it.'

'No, I didn't. You caught me before I had a chance to see it. What have you got there?'

'I'm surprised at you, Morris,' said Captain Penderton. 'Don't you know you can never trust a woman at cards?'

Mrs. Langdon watched this friendly badinage with an on-the-defensive expression that is often seen in the eyes of persons who have been ill for a long time and dependent upon the thoughtfulness, or negligence, of others. Since the night she had rushed home and hurt herself, she had felt in her a constant, nauseous shame. She was sure that everyone who looked at her must be thinking of what she had done. But as a matter of fact the scandal had been kept secret; besides those in the room only the doctor and the nurse knew what had happened — and the young Filipino servant who had been with Mrs. Langdon since he was seventeen years old and who adored her. Now she stopped knitting and put the tips of her fingers to her cheekbones. She knew that she should get up and leave the room, and break with her husband altogether. But lately she had been overcome by a terrible helplessness. And where on earth would she go? When she tried to think ahead, weird fancies crept into her mind and she was beset by a number of nervous compulsions. It had come to the point where she feared her own self as much as she feared others. And all the time, unable to break away, she had the feeling that some great disaster was in wait for her.

'What's the matter, Alison?' Leonora asked. 'Are you hungry? There's some sliced chicken in the icebox.' For the past few months Leonora often addressed Mrs. Langdon in a curious manner. She worked her mouth exaggeratedly to form the words and spoke in the careful and reasonable voice that one would use when addressing an abject idiot. 'Both white meat and dark. *Very* good. Mmmmmh?'

'No, thank you.'

'Are you sure, darling?' the Major asked. 'You don't want anything?'

'I'm quite all right. But would you mind—? Don't tap your heel like that on the floor. It bothers me.'

'I beg your pardon.'

The Major took his legs from under the table and crossed them sideways in his chair. On the surface the Major naïvely believed that his wife knew nothing about his affair. However, this soothing thought had become increasingly more difficult for him to hold on to; the strain of not realizing the truth had given him hemorrhoids and had almost upset his good digestion. He tried, and succeeded, in looking on her obvious unhappiness as something morbid and female, altogether outside his control. He remembered an incident that had happened soon after they were married. He had taken Alison out quail shooting and, although she had done target practice, she had never been hunting before. They had flushed a covey and he remembered still the pattern of the flying birds against the winter sunset. As he was watching Alison, he had only brought down one quail, and that one he insisted gallantly was hers. But when she took the bird from the dog's mouth, her face had changed. The bird was still living, so he brained it carelessly and then gave it back to her. She held the little warm, ruffled body that had somehow become degraded in its fall, and looked into the dead little glassy black eyes. Then she had burst into tears. That was the sort of thing the Major meant by 'female' and 'morbid'; and it did a man no good to try to figure it all out. Also, when the Major was troubled about his wife these days he thought instinctively, as a means of self-defense, of a certain Lieutenant Weincheck, who was a company commander in the Major's own battalion and a close friend of Alison's. So now as her face troubled his conscience he said, to soothe himself:

'Did you say you spent the afternoon with Weincheck?'

'Yes. I was there,' she said.

'That's good. How did you find him?'

'Fairly well.' She decided suddenly to give the sweater to Lieutenant Weincheck, as he could put it to good use, and she hoped it was not too broad across the shoulders.

'That man!' said Leonora. 'I can't understand what in the world you see in him, Alison. Of course I know you all get together and talk about highbrow things. He calls me "Madam." He can't stand me and he says "Yes, Madam," and "No Madam." Think of it!'

Mrs. Langdon smiled somewhat wryly, but made no comment.

Here a few words might be due this Lieutenant Weincheck, although with the exception of Mrs. Langdon he was of no consequence to anyone on the post. In the service he cut a sorry figure, as he was nearing fifty and had never yet earned his Captain's bars. His eyes gave him so much trouble that soon he was to be retired. He lived in one of the apartment houses set aside for bachelor lieutenants, most of whom were just out of West Point. In his two small rooms was crowded an accumulation of a lifetime, including a grand piano, a shelf of phonograph albums, many hundreds of books, a big Angora cat, and about a dozen potted plants. He grew some sort of green creeper on the walls of his sitting-room and often one was likely to stumble over an empty beer bottle or a coffee cup that had been set down on the floor.

Finally, this old Lieutenant played the violin. From his rooms there would come the lost sound of some naked melody from a string trio or quartet, a sound that made the young officers passing along the corridor scratch their heads and wink at each other. Here Mrs. Langdon often came to visit in the late afternoon. She and Lieutenant Weincheck would play Mozart sonatas, or drink coffee and eat crystallized ginger before the fire. In addition to his other handicaps the Lieutenant was very poor, as he was trying to send two nephews through school. He had to practice any number of mean little economies to make ends meet, and his one dress uniform was so seedy that he only attended the most obligatory social affairs. When Mrs. Langdon learned that he did his own mending, she got in the habit of bringing over her own sewing and taking care of the Lieutenant's underwear and linen along with her husband's. Sometimes the two of them went in the Major's car on trips together — to concerts in a city about a hundred and fifty miles away. On these occasions they took Anacleto with them.

'I'm putting up everything on this one hand and if I win I'll have every chip,' Mrs. Penderton said. 'It's about time we finished this.'

As Mrs. Penderton dealt, she managed to pick up an ace and king from her lap and give herself a blackjack. Everyone in the room saw this and the Major chuckled. Also it was observed that the Major patted Leonora on her thigh underneath the table before he pushed back his chair. Mrs. Langdon got up at the same time and put her knitting in her bag.

'I must be getting along,' she said. 'But you stay, Morris, and don't break up the party. Good night everybody.'

Mrs. Langdon walked rather slowly and stiffly, and when she was gone Leonora said, 'I wonder what ails her now.'

'There's no telling,' said the Major miserably. 'But I guess I'll have to go. Here, let's make it one last round.'

Major Langdon hated to leave the cheerful room, but after he had told the Pendertons good-bye he stood for a time on the walk before the house. He was looking up at the stars and thinking that life sometimes was a bad business. He remembered suddenly the baby who had died. What bedlam all the way through! In her labor Alison had clung to Anacleto (for he, the Major, could not stand it) and she had screamed for thirty-three solid hours. And when the doctor said, 'You're not trying hard enough, bear down' — why, the little Filipino would bear down also, with bent knees and the sweat pouring down his face, giving out wail for wail with Alison. Then, when it was over, they found the baby's index and third fingers were grown together, and the Major's only thought was that if he had to touch that baby he would shudder all over.

It had drawn out for eleven months. They had been stationed in the Middle West and he would come in out of the snow to find something such as a cold plate of tuna fish salad in the icebox and the doctors and trained nurses all over the place. Anacleto would be upstairs bringing a diaper up to the light to judge the stool, or perhaps holding the baby for Alison while she walked up and down, up and down the room with her jaws clamped. When the whole business was over, he could feel nothing except relief. But not Alison! How bitter and cold it had left her! And how damned, damned finicky! Yes, life could be sad.

The Major opened the front door and saw Anacleto coming down the stairs. The little Filipino walked with grace and composure. He was dressed in sandals, soft gray trousers, and a blouse of aquamarine linen. His flat little face was creamy white and his black eyes glowed. He did not appear to notice the Major — but when he reached the bottom of the stairs he slowly raised his right leg, with the toes flexed like a ballet dancer's, and gave an airy little skip.

'Idiot!' the Major said. 'How is she?'

Anacleto lifted his eyebrows and closed his delicate white eyelids very slowly. '*Très fatiguée.*'

'Ah!' said the Major furiously, for he did not speak a word of French. 'Vooley voo rooney mooney moo! I say, how is she?'

'*C'est les* —— ' But Anacleto himself had only recently taken up his study of French and he did not know of the word for 'sinuses.' However, he completed his reply with the most impressive dignity, '*Maître Corbeau sur un arbre perché,* Major.' He paused, snapped his fingers, and then added pensively, as though speaking aloud to himself, 'Some hot broth very attractively arranged.'

'You can fix me an Old Fashioned,' the Major said.

'I will suddenly,' said Anacleto. He knew very well that 'suddenly' could not be used in the place of 'immediately,' as he spoke choice and beautifully enunciated English in a voice that was exactly like Mrs. Langdon's; he made this mistake only in order further to addle the Major. 'I shall do so as soon as I have arranged the tray and made Madame Alison comfortable.'

By the Major's watch the preparations for this tray took thirty-eight minutes. The little Filipino aired about the kitchen in the liveliest manner and brought in a bowl of flowers from the dining-room. The Major watched him with his hairy fists on his hips. All the while Anacleto kept up a soft and vivacious chattering to himself. The Major caught something about Mr. Rudolph Serkin and about a cat which was walking around in a candy counter with bits of peanut-brittle stuck to its fur. In the meantime the Major mixed his own drink and fried himself two eggs. When this thirty-eight-minute tray was finished, Anacleto stood with his feet crossed, hands clasped behind his head, and rocked himself slowly.

'God! You're a rare bird,' the Major said. 'What I wouldn't do if I could get you in my battalion!'

The little Filipino shrugged. It was common knowledge that he thought the Lord had blundered grossly in the making of everyone except himself and Madame Alison — the sole exceptions to this were people behind footlights, midgets, great artists, and such-like fabulous folk. He looked down with satisfaction at the tray. On it were a cloth of yellow linen, a brown pottery jug of hot water, the broth cup, and two bouillon cubes. In the right corner there was a little blue Chinese rice bowl holding a bouquet of feathery Michaelmas daisies. Very deliberately Anacleto reached down, plucked off three of the blue petals, and placed them on the yellow napkin. He was not really as frisky as he appeared to be this evening. At times his eyes were anxious, and often he shot the Major a glance that was subtle, swift, and accusing.

'I'll take the tray up,' said the Major, for he saw that, although there was nothing to eat involved, it was the sort of thing that would please his wife and he might get the credit for it.

Alison sat propped in her bed with a book. In her reading glasses her face seemed all nose and eyes, and there were sickly blue shadows about the corners of her mouth. She wore a white linen nightgown and a bed-jacket of warm rose velvet. The room was very still and a fire burned on the hearth. There was little furniture, and the room, with its soft gray rug and cerise curtains, had a bare and very simple look. While Alison drank the broth, the Major, bored, sat in a chair by the bed and tried to think up something to say. Anacleto meddled lightly about the bed. He was whistling a melody that was sprightly, sad and clear.

'Look, Madame Alison!' he said suddenly. 'Do you feel well enough to discuss a certain matter with me?'

She put down her cup and took off her glasses. 'Why, what it is?'

'This!' Anacleto brought a footstool to the side of the bed and eagerly drew from his pocket some little scraps of cloth. 'These samples I ordered for us to look over. And now think back to the time two years ago when we passed by the window of Peck and Peck in New York City and I pointed out a certain little suit to you.' He selected one of the samples and handed it to her. 'This material made exactly in that way.'

'But I don't need a suit, Anacleto,' she said.

'Oh, but you do! You have not bought a garment in more than a year. And the green frock is *bien usée* at the elbows and ready for the Salvation Army.'

When Anacleto brought out his French phrase he gave the Major a glance of the merriest malice. It always made the Major feel rather eerie to listen to them talking together in the quiet room. Their voices and enunciation were so precisely alike that they seemed to be softly echoing each other. The only difference was that Anacleto spoke in a chattering, breathless manner, while Alison's voice was measured and composed.

'How much is it?' she asked.

'It is costly. But one could not expect to get such a quality for anything less. And think of the years of service.'

Alison turned back to her book again. 'We'll see about it.'

'For God's sake, go ahead and buy the dress,' the Major said. It bothered him to hear Alison haggle.

'And while we're about it we might order an extra yard or so that I can have a jacket.' Anacelto said.

'All right. If I decide to get it.'

Anacleto poured Alison's medicine and made a face for her as she drank it. Then he put an electric pad behind her back and brushed her hair. But as he started out of the room, he could not quite get past the full-length mirror on the closet door. He stopped and looked at himself, pointed his toe and cocked his head.

Then he turned back to Alison and began to whistle again. 'What is that? You and Lieutenant Weincheck were playing it last Thursday afternoon.'

'The opening bar of the Franck A Major Sonata.'

'Look!' said Anacleto excitedly. 'It has just this minute made me compose a ballet. Black velvet curtains and a glow like winter twilight. Very slowly, with the whole cast. Then a spotlight for the solo like a flame — very dashing, and with the waltz Mr. Sergei Rachmaninoff played. Then the finish goes back to the Franck, only this time ——' He looked at Alison and with his strange, bright eyes, 'Drunk!'

And with that he began to dance. He had been taken to the Russian ballet a year before and he had never got over it. Not a trick, not a gesture had escaped him. On the gray rug he moved about in a languid pantomime that slowed down until he stood quite still with his feet in their sandals crossed and his fingertips touched together in a meditative attitude. Then without warning he whirled lightly and began a furious little solo. It was apparent from his bright face that in his own mind he was out on an immense stage, the cynosure in a dazzling spectacle. Alison, also, was plainly enjoying herself. The Major looked from one to the other in disgusted disbelief. The last of the dance was a drunken satire of the first. Anacleto finished with an odd little pose, his elbow held in one hand and his fist to his chin with an expression of wry puzzlement.

Alison burst out laughing. 'Bravo! Bravo! Anacleto!'

They laughed together and the little Filipino leaned against the door, happy and a bit dazed. At last he caught his breath and exclaimed in a marveling voice, 'Have you ever noticed how well "Bravo" and "Anacleto" go together?'

Alison stopped laughing and nodded thoughtfully. 'Indeed, Anacleto, I have noticed it many times.'

The little Filipino hesitated in the doorway. He glanced around the room to make sure that nothing was wanting. Then he looked into her face and his eyes were suddenly shrewd and very sad. 'Call me if you need me,' he said shortly.

They heard him start down the stairs slowly, then quicken to a skip. On the last steps he must have tried something altogether too ambitious, for there was a sudden thud. When the Major reached the head of the stairs, Anacleto was picking himself up with brave dignity.

'Did he hurt himself?' Alison asked tensely.

Anacleto looked up at the Major with angry tears in his eyes. 'I'm all right, Madame Alison,' he called.

The Major leaned forward and said slowly and soundlessly, working his mouth so that Anacleto could read the words, 'I — wish — you — had — bro — ken — your — neck.'

Anacleto smiled, shrugged his shoulders, and limped into the dining-room. When the Major went back to his wife, he found her reading. She did not look up at him, so he crossed the hall to his own room and slammed the door. His room was small, rather untidy, and the only ornaments in it were the cups he had won at horse shows. On the Major's bedside table there was an open book — a very recondite and literary book. The place was marked with a matchstick. The Major turned over forty pages or so, a reasonable evening's reading, and marked the new place with the match again. Then from under a pile of shirts in his bureau drawer he took a pulp magazine called *Scientification.* He settled himself comfortably in the bed and began reading of a wild, interplanetary superwar.

Across the hall from him, his wife had put down her book and was lying in a half-sitting position. Her face was stiff with pain and her dark, glittering eyes looked restlessly around the walls of the room. She was trying to make plans. She would divorce Morris, certainly. But how could she go about it? And above all how could she and Anacleto manage to make a living? She always had been contemptuous of women without children who accepted alimony, and her last shred of pride depended on the fact that she would not, could not, live on his money after she had left him. But what would they do — she and Anacleto? She had taught Latin in a girls' school the year before she married, but with her health as it was that would now be out of the question. A bookshop somewhere? It would have to be something that Anacleto could keep going when she was ill. Could the two of them possibly manage a prawn boat? Once she had talked to some shrimp fishermen on the coast. It had been a blue-and-gold seaside day and they had told her many things. She and Anacleto would stay out at sea all day with their nets lowered and there would be only the cold salt air, the ocean and the sun — Alison turned her head restlessly on the pillow. But what frippery!

It had been a shock, eight months ago, when she had learned about her husband. She and Lieutenant Weincheck and Anacleto had made a trip to the city with the intention of staying two days and nights for a concert and a play. But on the second day she was feverish and they decided to go back home. Late in the afternoon Anacleto had let her out at the front door and driven the car back to the garage. She had stopped on the front walk to look at some bulbs. It was almost dark and there was a light in her husband's room. The front door was locked and as she was standing there she saw Leonora's coat on the chest in the hall. And she had thought to herself how strange it was that if the Pendertons were there the front door should be locked. Then it occurred to her that they were mixing drinks in the kitchen while Morris had his bath. And she went around to the back. But then before she entered the house Anacleto rushed down the steps with such a horrified little face! He had whispered that they must go into town ten miles away as they had forgotten something. And when, rather dazed, she started up the steps he had caught her by the arm and said in a flat, frightened voice: 'You must not go in there now, Madame Alison.'

With what a shock it had come to her. She and Anacleto had got back into the car and driven off again. The insult of it happening in her own house — that was what she could not swallow. And then, of all times in the world, when they slowed down at the outpost there was a new soldier on duty who did not know them, and he had stopped the car. He looked into the little coupé as though they might be concealing a machine gun and then stood staring at Anacleto who, dressed in his jaunty burnt-orange jacket, was ready to burst into tears. He asked for the name in a tone of voice which suggested that he did not believe they could possibly screw up one between them.

Never would she forget that soldier's face. At the moment she did not have it in her to speak her husband's name. The young soldier waited, stared, and said not a word. Later she had seen this same soldier at the stables when she went to fetch Morris in the car. He had the strange, rapt face of a Gauguin primitive. They looked at each other for perhaps a minute and at last an officer came up.

She and Anacleto had driven for three hours in the cold without speaking. And after that the plans she had made at night when she was sick and restless, schemes that as soon as the sun came up would seem so foolish. And the evening she had run home from the Pendertons' and done that ghastly thing. She had seen the garden shears on the wall and, beside herself with anger and despair, she had tried to stab and kill herself. But the shears were too blunt. And then for a few moments she must have been quite out of her head, for she herself did not know just how it had happened. Alison shuddered and hid her face in her hands. She heard her husband open his door and put his boots out in the hall. Quickly she turned off her light.

The Major had finished his magazine and hidden it again in the drawer. He took a last drink and then lay comfortably in the bed, looking up into the dark. What was it that meeting Leonora for the first time reminded him of? It had happened the year after the baby died, when for twelve solid months Alison had either been in the hospital or prowling around the house like a ghost. Then he had met Leonora down at the stables the first week he had come to this post, and she had offered to show him around. They left the bridle path and had a dandy gallop. When they had tied the horses for a rest, Leonora had seen some blackberry bushes near-by and said she might as well pick enough to make a cobbler for dinner. And Lord! when they were scrambling around those bushes together filling his hat with berries, it had first happened. At nine in the morning and two hours after they met! Even now he could hardly believe it. But what had it seemed like to him at the time? Oh, yes — it was like being out on maneuvers, shivering all through a cold rainy night in a tent that leaked. And then to get up at dawn and see that the rain was over and the sun was out again. And to watch the fine-looking soldiers making coffee over campfires and see the sparks rise up into a clear white sky. A wonderful feeling — the best in the world!

The Major giggled guiltily, hid his head underneath the sheet, and began to snore immediately.

At twelve-thirty Captain Penderton fretted alone in his study. He was working on a monograph and had made little progress that night. He had drunk a good deal of wine and tea and had smoked dozens of cigarettes. At last he had given up work altogether and now he was walking restlessly up and down the room. There are times when a man's greatest need is to have someone to love, some focal point for his diffused emotions. Also there are times when the irritations, disappointments, and fears of life, restless as spermatozoids, must be released in hate. The unhappy Captain had no one to hate and for the past months he had been miserable.

Alison Langdon, that big-nosed female Job, together with her loathsome Filipino — those two he abhorred. But he could not hate Alison, as she did not give him the opportunity. It chafed him no end to be under obligation to her. She was the only person in the world who knew of a certain woeful shortcoming in his nature; Captain Penderton was inclined to be a thief. He was continually resisting an urge to take things he saw in other people's houses. However, only twice had this weakness got the best of him. When he was a child of seven he had become so infatuated with the school-yard bully who had once beaten him that he stole from his aunt's dressing-table an old-fashioned hair-receiver as a love offering. And here on the post, twenty-seven years later, the Captain had once again succumbed.

At a dinner party given by a young bride he had been so fascinated by a certain piece of silver that he had carried it home in his pocket. It was an unusual and beautiful little dessert spoon, delicately chased and very old. The Captain had been miserably enchanted with it (the rest of the silver at his place was quite ordinary) and in the end he could not resist. When after some skillful manipulation he had his booty safe in his pocket, he realized that Alison, who was next to him, had seen the theft. She looked him full in the face with the most amazed expression. Even now he could not think of it without a shudder. And after a horribly long stare Alison had burst out laughing — yes, laughing. She laughed so hard that she choked herself and someone had to beat her on the back. Finally she excused herself from the table. And all through that tormenting evening whenever he looked at her she gave him such a mocking smile. Since then she was careful to keep a sharp watch on him when he was a guest at her table. The spoon was now hidden in his closet, wrapped carefully in a silk handkerchief and concealed in the box that his truss had come in.

But in spite of this he could not hate Alison. Nor could he truly hate his wife. Leonora maddened him to insanity, but even in the wildest fits of jealousy he could not hate her any more than he could hate a cat, or a horse, or a tiger cub. The Captain walked around in his study and once gave the closed door a fretful kick. If that Alison finally made up her mind to divorce Morris, then how would it go? He could not bear to contemplate this possibility, so distressed was he at the thought of being left alone.

It seemed to the Captain that he heard a sound and he stopped short. The house was still. It has been mentioned before that the Captain was a coward. Sometimes when he was by himself he was overcome by a rootless terror. And now, as he stood in the silent room, it seemed that his nervousness and distress were not caused by forces within himself and others, things that in some measure he could control—but by some menacing outward circumstance which he could only sense from a distance. Fearfully the Captain looked all about the room. Then he straightened his desk and opened the door.

Leonora had fallen asleep on the rug before the fire in the sitting-room. The Captain looked down at her and laughed to himself. She was turned over on her side and he gave her a sharp little kick on the buttocks. She grumbled something about the stuffing for a turkey, but did not awake. The Captain bent down, shook her, talked into her face, and finally got her on her feet. But like a child who has to be aroused and taken to the toilet the last thing at night, Leonora had the gift of being able to remain asleep even while standing up. As the Captain let her ponderously to the stairs, her eyes were closed and she still grumbled about the turkey.

'I'll be damned if I'll undress you,' the Captain said.

But Leonora sat where he had left her on the bed, and after watching her for several minutes he laughed again and took off her clothes. He did not put a nightgown on her, for the bureau drawers were in such a mess he could not find one. Besides, Leonora always liked sleeping 'in the raw,' as she called it. When she was in bed, the Captain went up to a picture on the wall that had amused him for years. It was a photograph of a girl of about seventeen, and at the bottom there was written the touching inscription: 'To Leonora with Oodles of Love from Bootsie.' This masterpiece had adorned the walls of Leonora's bedrooms for more than a decade, and had been carried halfway around the globe. But when questioned about Bootsie, who for a time had been her roommate in a boarding-school, Leonora said vaguely that it seemed to her that she had once heard Bootsie had drowned some years ago. Indeed, after pressing her about this matter, he found she did not even remember this Bootsie's lawful name. And yet, simply because of habit, the picture had hung on her wall for eleven years. The Captain looked once again at his wife as she lay sleeping. She was hot-natured and already the cover had been pushed down below her naked breasts. She smiled in her sleep, and it occurred to the Captain that she was now eating the turkey she had prepared in her dream.

The Captain used Seconal, and his habit was of such long standing that one capsule had no effect on him. He considered that with his hard work at the Infantry School it was a great imposition for him to have to lie awake at night and get up jaded the next morning. Without sufficient Seconal his slumber was light and wrought with dreams. Tonight he decided to treat himself to a triple dose, and he knew that then he would drop immediately into a blunt, sodden sleep that would last six or seven hours. The Captain swallowed his capsules and lay down in the dark with pleasant anticipation. This quantity of the drug gave him a unique and voluptuous sensation; it was as though a great dark bird alighted on his chest, looked at him once with fierce, golden eyes, and stealthily enfolded him in his dark wings.

Private Williams waited outside the house until the lights had been out for almost two hours. The stars were faded a little and the blackness of the night sky had changed to deep violet. Still, however, Orion was brilliant and the Big Dipper shone with a wonderful radiance. The soldier walked around to the back of the house and quietly tried the screen door. It was fastened from the inside, as he knew it would be. However, the door was slightly loose and when the soldier inserted the blade of his knife in the crack he was able to raise the hook latch. The back door itself was not locked.

Once inside the house the soldier waited for a moment. All was dark and there was not a sound. He stared about him with his wide, vague eyes until he was accustomed to the darkness. The plan of the house was already familiar to him. The long front hall and the stairs divided the house, leaving on one side the large sitting-room and, farther back, the servant's room. On the other side were the dining-room, the Captain's study, and the kitchen. Upstairs to the right there was a double bedroom and a small cubicle. To the left were two bedrooms of medium size. The Captain used the large room and his wife slept across the hall from him. The soldier walked carefully up the stairs, which were carpeted. He moved with delibrate composure. The door of The Lady's room was open, and when he reached it the soldier did not hesitate. With the lithe silence of a cat he stepped inside.

Green shadowy moonlight filled the room. The Captain's wife slept as her husband had left her. Her soft hair lay loosened upon the pillow and her gently breathing chest was half-uncovered. A yellow silk spread was on the bed and an open flask of perfume sweetened the air with a drowsy scent. Very slowly the soldier tiptoed to the side of the bed and bent over the Captain's wife. The moon softly lighted their faces and he was so close that he could feel her warm, even breath. In the soldier's grave eyes there was at first an expression of intent curiosity, but as the moments passed a look of bliss awakened in his heavy face. The young soldier felt in him a keen, strange sweetness that never before in his life had he known.

He stood in this way, bent close over the Capatin's wife, for some time. Then he touched his hand to the window-sill to steady himself and very slowly squatted down beside the bed. He balanced himself on the broad balls of his feet, his back held straight, and his strong delicate hands resting on his knees. His eyes were round as amber buttons and his bangs lay in a tangled mat on his forehead.

On a few occasions before this Private Williams had had this look of suddenly awakened happiness in his face, but no one on the spot had seen him then. If he had been seen at such a time he would have been court-martialed. The truth was that in his long ramblings through the forest of the reservation the soldier was sometimes not alone. When he could get leave from work in the afternoon, he took a certain horse from the stables with him. He rode about five miles from the post to a secluded spot far from any paths, that was difficult to reach. Here in the woods there was a flat, clear space, covered with a grassy weed of the color of burnished bronze. In this lonely place the soldier always unsaddled his horse and let him go free. Then he took off his clothes and lay down on a large flat rock in the middle of the field. For there was one thing that this soldier could not do without — the sun. Even on the coldest days he would lie still and naked and let the sunlight soak into his flesh. Sometimes, still naked, he stood in the rock and slipped upon the horse's bare back. His horse was an ordinary army plug which, with anyone but Private Williams, could sustain only two gaits — a clumsy trot and a rocking-horse gallop. But with the soldier a marvelous change came over the animal; he cantered or single-footed with proud, stiff elegance. The soldier's body was of a pale golden brown and he held himself erect. Without his clothes he was so slim that the pure, curved lines of his ribs could be seen. As he cantered about in the sunlight, there was a sensual, savage smile on his lips that would have surprised his barrack mates. After such outings he came back weary to the stables and spoke to no one.

Private Williams squatted by the bed in The Lady's room until almost dawn. He did not move, or make a sound, or take his eyes from the body of the Captain's wife. Then, as the day was breaking, he balanced himself again with his hand on the window-sill and got up carefully. He went down the stairs and closed the back door cautiously behind him. Already the sky was a pale blue and Venus was fading.

III

III

ALISON LANGDON had lived through a night of torment. She did not sleep until the sun came up and the bugle sounded reveille. During those long hours many eerie thoughts had troubled her. Once just at dawn she even fancied, she was almost sure, that she saw someone come out of the Pendertons' house and walk off into the woods. Then, soon after she finally got to sleep, a great racket awakened her. Hurriedly she put on her bathrobe, went downstairs, and found herself confronting a shocking and ridiculous spectacle. Her husband was chasing Anacleto round and round the dining-room table with a boot in his hand. He was in his sock feet, but otherwise completely uniformed for Saturday morning inspection. His sword banged against his thigh as he ran. They both stopped short when they saw her. Then Anacleto hastened to take refuge behind her back.

'He did it on purpose!' the Major said in an outraged voice. 'I'm already late. Six hundred men are waiting for me. And look, just please take a glance, at what he brings me!'

The boots indeed were a sorry sight. It looked as though they had been rubbed over with flour and water. She scolded Anacleto and stood over him as he cleaned them properly. He wept piteously, but she found the strength of mind not to console him. When he had finished, Anacleto mentioned something about running away from home and opening a linen shop in Quebec. She carried the polished boots up to her husband and handed them to him without a word, but with a look that took care of him also. Then, as her heart bothered her, she went back to bed with a book.

Anacleto brought her up coffee and then drove over to the Post Exchange to do the marketing for Sunday. Later in the morning, when she had finished her book and was looking out the window at the sunny autumn day, he came to her room again. He was blithe, and had quite forgotten the scolding about the boots. He built up a roaring fire and then quietly opened the top bureau drawer to do a bit of meddling. He took out a little crystal cigarette lighter which she had had made from an old-fashioned vinaigrette. This trinket so fascinated him that she had given it to him years ago. He still kept it with her things, however, so that he would have a legitimate reason for opening the drawer whenever he wished. He asked for the loan of her glasses and peered for a long time at the linen scarf on the chest of drawers. Then with his thumb and forefinger he picked up something invisible and carefully carried this speck over to the wastebasket. He was talking away to himself, but she paid no attention to his chatter.

What would become of Anacleto when she was dead? That was a question that worried her constantly. Morris, of course, had promised her never to let him be in want — but what would such a promise be worth when Morris married again, as he would be sure to do? She remembered the time seven years ago in the Philippines when Anacleto first came to her household. What a sad, strange little creature he had been! He was so tormented by the other houseboys that he dogged her footsteps all day long. If anyone so much as looked at him he would burst into tears and wring his hands. He was seventeen years old, but his sickly, clever, frightened face had the innocent expression of a child of ten. When they were making preparations to return to the States, he had begged her to take him with her, and she had done so. The two of them, she and Anacleto, could perhaps find a way to get along in the world together — but what would he do when she was gone?

'Anacleto, are you happy?' she asked him suddenly.

The litle Filipino was not one to be disturbed by any unexpected, intimate question. 'Why, certainly,' he said, without a moment's consideration. 'When you are well.'

The sun and firelight were bright in the room. There was a dancing spectrum on one of the walls and she watched this, half-listening to Anacleto's soft conversation. 'What I find it so difficult to realize is that they *know*,' he was saying. Often he would begin a discussion with such a vague and mysterious remark, and she waited to catch the drift of it later. 'It was not until after I had been in your service for a long time that I really believed that you knew. Now I can believe it about everybody else except Mr. Sergei Rachmaninoff.

She turned her face toward him. 'What are you talking about?'

'Madame Alison,' he said, 'do you yourself really believe that Mr. Sergei Rachmaninoff knows that a chair is something to be sat on and that a clock shows one the time? And if I should take off my shoe and hold it up to his face and say, "What is this, Mr. Sergei Rachmaninoff?" then he would answer, like anyone else, "Why, Anacleto, that is a shoe." I myself find it hard to realize.'

The Rachmaninoff recital had been the last concert they had heard, and consequently from Anacleto's point of view it was the best. She herself did not care for crowded concert halls and would have preferred to spend the money on phonograph records — but it was good to get away from the post occasionally, and these trips were the joy of Anacleto's life. For one thing they stayed the night in a hotel, which was an enormous delight to him.

'Do you think if I beat your pillows you would be more comfortable?' Anacleto asked.

And the dinner the night of that last concert! Anacleto sailed proudly after her into the hotel dining-room wearing his orange velvet jacket. When it was his turn to order he held the menu up to his face and then completely closed his eyes. To the astonishment of the colored waiter he ordered in French. And although she had wanted to burst out laughing, she controlled herself and translated after him with the best gravity she could assume — as though she were a sort of duenna or lady-in-waiting to him. Because of his limited French this dinner of his was rather peculiar. He had got it out of the lesson in his book called 'Le Jardin Potager.' and his order consisted only of cabbage, string beans, and carrots. So when on her own she had added an order of chicken for him, Anacleto had opened his eyes just long enough to give her a deep, grateful little look. The white-coated waiters clustered about this phenomenon like flies, and Anacleto was much too exalted to touch a crumb.

'Suppose we have some music,' she said. 'Let's hear the Brahms G. Minor Quartet.'

'Fameux,' said Anacleto.

He put on the first record and settled down to listen on his footstool by the fire. But the opening passage, the lovely dialogue between the piano and the strings, was hardly completed when there was a knock on the door. Anacleto spoke to someone in the hall, closed the door again, and turned off the phonograph.

'Mrs. Penderton,' he whispered, lifting his eyebrows.

'I knew I could knock on the door downstairs till doomsday and you all would never hear me with this music going on,' Leonora said when she came into the room. She sat down on the foot of the bed so hard that it felt as though she had broken a spring. Then, remembering that Alison was not well, Leonora tried to look sickly also, as that was her notion of the proper behavior in a sickroom. 'Do you think you can make it tonight?'

'Make what?'

'Why, my God, Alison! My party! I've been working like a nigger for the past three days getting everything ready. I don't give a party like this but twice a year.'

'Of course,' said Alison. 'It just slipped my mind for a moment.'

'Listen!' said Leonora, and her fresh rosy face flamed suddenly with anticipation. 'I just wish you could see my kitchen now. Here's the way it will go. I'm putting in all the leaves in the dining-room table and everybody will just mill around and help themselves. I'm having a couple of Virginia hams, a huge turkey, fried chicken, sliced cold pork, plenty of barbecued spareribs, and all sorts of little knicknacks like pickled onions and olives and radishes. And hot rolls and little cheese biscuits passed around. The punch-bowl is in the corner, and for people who like their liquor straight I'm having on the sideboard eight quarts of Kentucky Bourbon, five of rye, and five of Scotch. And an entertainer from town is coming out to play the accordion——'

'But who on earth is going to eat all that food?' Alison asked, with a little swallow of nausea.

'The whole shebang,' said Leonora enthusiastically. 'I've telephoned everybody from Old Sugar's wife on down.'

'Old Sugar' was Leonora's name for the Commanding General of the post, and she called him by it to his face. With the General, as with all men, she had a flip and affectionate manner, and the General, like most of the officers on the post, fairly ate out of her hand. The General's wife was very fat, slow, gushed over, and completely out of things.

'One thing I came over about this morning,' said Leonora, 'is to find out if Anacleto will serve the punch for me.'

'He will be glad to help you out,' Alison answered for him.

Anacleto, who was standing in the doorway, did not look so glad about it. He glanced reproachfully at Alison and went downstairs to see about luncheon.

'Susie's two brothers are helping in the kitchen and, my God, how that crowd can eat! I never saw anything to equal it. We—'

'By the way,' said Alison, 'is Susie married?'

'Heavens, no! She won't have anything to do with men. She got caught when she was fourteen years old and has never forgotten it. But why?'

'I just wondered because I was almost sure that I saw someone go into your house by the back way late last night and come out again before dawn.'

'You just imagined it,' said Leonora soothingly. She considered Alison to be quite off her head, and did not believe even the simplest remark that she made.

'Perhaps so.'

Leonora was bored and ready to go home. Still, she thought that a neighborly visit should last at least an hour, so she stuck it out dutifully. She sighed and tried again to look somewhat ill. It was her idea, when she was not too carried away with thoughts of food and sport, that the tactful topic of conversation in a sickroom was an account of other illnesses. Like all very stupid people she had a predilection for the gruesome, which she could indulge in or throw off at will. Her repertoire of tragedies was limited for the most part to violent sporting accidents.

'Did I tell you about the thirteen-year-old girl who came along with us on a fox hunt as a whipper-in and broke her neck?'

'Yes, Leonora,' said Alison in a voice of controlled exasperation. 'You have told me of every terrible detail five times.'

'Does it make you nervous?'

'Extremely.'

'Hmmm——' said Leonora. She was not at all troubled by this rebuff. Calmly she lighted a cigarette. 'Don't ever let anybody tell you that's the way to fox-hunt. I know. I've hunted both ways. Listen, Alison!' She worked her mouth exaggeratedly and spoke in a deliberately encouraging voice as though addressing a small child. 'Do you know how to hunt 'possums?'

Alison nodded shortly and straightened the counterpane. 'You tree them.'

'On foot,' said Leonora. 'That's the way to hunt a fox. Now this uncle of mine has a cabin in the mountains and my brothers and I used to visit him. About six of us would start out with our dogs on a cold evening when the sun had set. A colored boy would run along behind with a jug of good mellow corn on his back. Sometimes we'd be after a fox all night long in the mountains. Gosh, I can't tell you about it. Somehow——' The feeling was in Leonora, but she had not the words to express it.

'Then to have one last drink at six o'clock and sit down to breakfast. And God! everybody said this uncle of mine was peculiar, but he sure set a good table. After a hunt we'd come in to a table just loaded with fish roe, broiled ham, fried chicken, biscuits the size of your hand——'

When Leonora was gone at last, Alison did not know whether to laugh or cry; she did a little of both, rather hysterically. Anacleto came up to her and carefully beat out the big dent at the foot of the bed where Leonora had been sitting.

'I am going to divorce the Major, Anacleto,' she said suddenly when she had stopped laughing. 'I will inform him of it tonight.'

From Anacleto's expression she could not tell whether or not this was a surprise to him. He waited for a time and then asked: 'Then where shall we go after that, Madame Alison?'

Through her mind passed a long panorama of plans which she had made during sleepless nights — tutoring Latin in some college town, shrimp fishing, hiring Anacleto out to drudge while she sat in a boarding-house and took in sewing —— But she only said: 'That I have not yet decided.'

'I wonder,' Anacleto said meditatively, 'what the Pendertons will do about it.'

'You needn't wonder because that is not our affair.'

Anacleto's little face was dark and thoughtful. He stood with his hand resting on the footpiece of the bed. She felt that he had some further question to put to her, and she looked up at him and waited. Finally he asked hopefully, 'Do you think we might live in a hotel?'

In the afternoon Captain Penderton went down to the stables for his usual ride. Private Williams was still on duty, although he was to be free that day at four o'clock. When the Captain spoke, he did not look at the young soldier and his voice was high-pitched and arrogant.

'Saddle Mrs. Penderton's horse, Firebird.'

Private Williams stood motionless, staring into the Captain's white strained face. 'The Captain said?'

'Firebird,' the Captain repeated. 'Mrs. Penderton's horse.'

This order was unusual. Captain Penderton had ridden Firebird only three times before, and on each of these occasions his wife had been with him. The Captain himself did not own a horse, and used the mounts belonging to the stable. As he waited out in the open court, the Captain nervously jerked the fingertips of his glove. Then, when Firebird was led out, he was not satisfied; Private Williams had put on Mrs. Penderton's flat, English type saddle, while the Captain preferred an army McClellan. As this change was being made, the Captain looked into the horse's round, purple eyes and saw there a liquid image of his own frightened face. Private Williams held the bridle as he mounted. The Captain sat tense, his jaws hard, and his knees gripping the saddle desperately. The soldier still stood impassive with his hand on the bridle.

After a moment the Captain said:

'Well, Private, you can see that I am seated. Let go!'

Private Williams stepped back a few paces. The Captain held tight to the reins and hardened his thighs. Nothing happened. The horse did not plunge and strain at the bit as he did each morning with Mrs. Penderton, but waited quietly for the signal to start. When the Captain realized this, he quickened with a sudden vicious joy. 'Ah,' he thought. 'She has broken his spirit as I knew she would.' The Captain dug in his heels and struck the horse with his short, plaited crop. They started on the bridle path at a gallop.

The afternoon was fine and sunny. The air was bracing, bitter sweet with the odor of pines and rotting leaves. Not a cloud could be seen in all the wide blue sky. The horse, which had not been exercised that day, seemed to go a little mad from the pleasure of galloping with unchecked freedom. Firebird, like most horses, was apt to be hard to manage if given free rein immediately after being led out from the pasture. The Captain knew this; therefore his next action was a very curious one. They had galloped rhythmically for perhaps three quarters of a mile when suddenly, with no preliminary tightening of the reins, the Captain jerked the horse up short. He pulled the reins with such unexpected sharpness that Firebird lost his balance, sidestepped awkwardly and reared. Then he stood quite still, surprised but tractable. The Captain was exceedingly satisfied.

This procedure was repeated twice. The Captain gave Firebird his head just long enough for the joy of freedom to be aroused and then checked him without warning. This sort of behavior was not new to the Captain. Often in his life he had exacted many strange and secret little penances on himself which he would have found difficult to explain to others.

The third time the horse stopped as usual, but at this point something happened which disturbed the Captain so that all of his satisfaction instantly vanished. As they were standing still, alone on the path, the horse slowly turned his head and looked into the

Captain's face. Then deliberately he lowered his head to the ground with his ears flattened back.

The Captain felt suddenly that he was to be thrown, and not only thrown but killed. The Captain always had been afraid of horses: he only rode because it was the thing to do, and because this was another one of his ways of tormenting himself. He had had his wife's comfortable saddle exchanged for the clumsy McClellan for the reason that the raised saddlebow gave him something to grasp in case of an emergency. Now he sat rigid, trying to hold to the saddle and the reins at the same time. Then, so great was his sudden apprehension, he gave up completely in advance, slipped his feet from the stirrups, lifted his hands to his face, and looked about him to see where he would fall. This weakness lasted only a few moments, however. When the Captain realized that he was not to be thrown after all, a great feeling of triumph came in him. They started at a gallop once more.

The path had been leading steadily upward with the woods on either side. Now they approached the bluff from which could be seen miles of the reservation. Far in the distance the green pine forest made a dark line against the bright autumn sky. Struck by the wonder of the view, the Captain had it in his mind to pause for a moment and he drew in his reins. But here a totally unexpected happening occurred, an incident that might have cost the Captain his life. They were still riding hard when they reached the top of the ridge. At this point, without warning and with the speed of a demon, the horse swerved to the left and plunged down the side of the embankment.

The Captain was so stunned that he lost his seat. He was hurled forward on the horse's neck and his feet dangled stirrupless. Somehow he managed to hold on. With one hand grasping the mane and the other feebly holding to the reins, he was able to slide himself back into the saddle. But that was all he could do. They were riding with such dizzying speed that his head swam when he opened his eyes. He could not find his seat firmly enough to control the reins. And he knew in one fateful instant that even so it would be of no use; there was not the power in him to stop this horse. Every muscle, every nerve in his body was intent on only one purpose — to hold on. With the speed of Firebird's great racing sire they were flying over the wide open space of sward that separated the bluff from the woods. The grass was glinted with bronze and red beneath the sun. Then suddenly the Captain felt a green dimness fall over them and he knew that they had entered the forest by way of some narrow footpath. Even when the horse had left the open space, he seemed hardly to slacken his speed. The dazed Captain was in a half-crouching position. A thorn from a tree ripped open his left cheek. The Captain felt no pain, but he saw vividly the hot scarlet blood that dripped on his arm. He crouched down so that the right side of his face rubbed against the short stiff hair of Firebird's neck. Clinging desperately to the mane, the reins, and the saddlebow, he dared not raise his head for fear it would be broken by the branch of a tree.

Three words were in the Captain's heart. He shaped them soundlessly with his trembling lips, as he had not breath to spare for a whisper: 'I am lost.'

And having given up life, the Captain suddenly began to live. A great mad joy surged through him. This emotion, coming as unexpectedly as the plunge of the horse when he had broken away, was one that the Captain had never experienced. His eyes were glassly and half-open, as in delirium, but he saw suddenly as he had never seen before. The world was a kaleidoscope, and each of the multiple visions which he saw impressed itself on his mind with burning vividness. On the ground half-buried in the leaves there was a little flower, dazzling white and beautifully wrought. A thorny pine cone, the flight of a bird in the blue windy sky, a fiery shaft of sunshine in the green gloom — these the Captain saw as though for the first time in his life. He was conscious of the pure keen air and he felt the marvel of his own tense body, his laboring heart, and the miracle of blood, muscle, nerves, and bone. The Captain knew no terror now; he had soared to the rare level of consciousness where the mystic feels that the earth is he and that he is the earth. Clinging crabwise to the runaway horse, there was a grin of rapture on his bloody mouth.

How long this mad ride lasted the Captain would never know. Toward the end he knew that they had come out from the woods and were galloping through an open plain. It seemed to him that from the corner of his eye he saw a man lying on a rock in the sun and a horse grazing. This did not surprise him and in an instant was forgotten. The only thing which concerned the Captain now was the fact that when they entered the forest again the horse was giving out. In an agony of dread the Captain thought: 'When this ends, all will be over for me.'

The horse slowed to an exhausted trot and at last stopped altogether. The Captain raised himself in the saddle and looked about him. When he struck the horse in the face with the reins, they stumbled on a few paces farther. Then the Captain could make him go no farther. Trembling, he dismounted. Slowly and methodically he tied the horse to a tree. He broke off a long switch, and with the last of his spent strength he began to beat the horse savagely. Breathing in great gasps, his coat dark and curled with sweat, the horse at first moved restively about the tree. The Captain kept on beating him. Then at last the horse stood motionless and gave a broken sigh. A pool of sweat darkened the pine straw beneath him and his head hung down. The Captain threw the whip away. He was smeared with blood, and a rash caused by rubbing against the horse's bristly hair had come out on his face and neck. His anger was unappeased and he could hardly stand from exhaustion. He sank down on the ground and lay in a curious position with his head in his arms. Out in the forest there, the Captain looked like a broken doll that has been thrown away. He was sobbing aloud.

For a brief time the Captain lost consciousness. Then, as he came out of his faint, he had a vision of the past. He looked back at the years behind him as one stares at a shaking image at the bottom of a well. He remembered his boyhood. He had been brought up by five old-maid aunts. His aunts were not bitter except when alone; they laughed a great deal and were constantly arranging picnics, fussy excursions, and Sunday dinners to which they invited other old maids. Nevertheless, they had used the little boy as a sort of fulcrum to lift the weight of their own heavy crosses. The Captain had never known real love. His aunts gushed over him with sentimental effulgence and knowing no better he repaid them with the same counterfeit coin. In addition, the Captain was a Southerner and was never allowed by his aunts to forget it. On his mother's side he was descended from Huguenots who left France in the seventeenth century, lived in Haiti until the great uprising, and then were planters in Georgia before the Civil War. Behind him was a history of barbarous splendor, ruined poverty, and family hauteur. But the present generation had not come to much; the Captain's only male first cousin was a policeman in the city of Nashville. Being a great snob, and with no real pride in him, the Captain set exaggerated store by the lost past.

The Captain kicked his feet on the pine straw and sobbed with a high wail that echoed thinly in the woods. Then abruptly he lay still and quiet. A strange feeling that had lingered in him for some time took sudden shape. He was sure that there was someone near him. Painfully he turned himself over on his back.

At first the Captain did not believe what he saw. Two yards from him, leaning against an oak tree, the young soldier whose face the Captain hated looked down at him. He was completely naked. His slim body glistened in the late sun. He stared at the Captain with vague, impersonal eyes as though looking at some insect he had never seen before. The Captain was too paralyzed by surprise to move. He tried to speak, but only a dry rattle came from his throat. As he watched him, the soldier turned his gaze to the horse. Firebird was still soaked with sweat and there were welts on his rump. In one afternoon the horse seemed to have changed from a thoroughbred to a plug fit for the plow.

The Captain lay between the soldier and the horse. The naked man did not bother to walk around his outstretched body. He left his place by the tree and lightly stepped over the officer. The Captain had a close swift view of the young soldier's bare foot; it was slim and delicately built, with a high instep marked by blue veins. The soldier untied the horse and put his hand to his muzzle in a caressing gesture. Then, without a glance at the Captain, he led the horse off into the dense woods.

It had happened so quickly that the Captain had not found a chance to sit up or to utter a word. At first he could feel only astonishment. He dwelt on the pure-cut lines of the young man's body. He called out something inarticulate and received no reply. A rage came in him. He felt a rush of hatred for the soldier that was as exorbitant as the joy he had experienced on runaway Firebird. All the humiliations, the envies, and the fears of his life found vent in this great anger. The Captain stumbled to his feet and started blindly through the darkening woods.

He did not know where he was, or how far he had come from the post. His mind swarmed with a dozen cunning schemes by which he could make the soldier suffer. In his heart the Captain knew that this hatred, passionate as love, would be with him all the remaining days of his life.

After walking for a long time, when it was almost night, he found himself on a path familiar to him.

The Pendertons' party began at seven, and half an hour later the front rooms were crowded. Leonora, stately in a gown of cream-colored velvet, received her guests alone. When replying to inquiries about the absence of the host, she said that, devil take him, she didn't know — he might have run away from home. Everyone laughed and repeated this — they pictured the Captain trudging off with a stick over his shoulder and his notebooks wrapped in a red bandanna. He had planned to drive into town after his ride and perhaps he was having car trouble.

The long table in the dining-room was more than lavishly laid and replenished. The air was so thick with the odor of ham, spare-ribs, and whiskey that it seemed one might almost eat it with a spoon. From the sitting-room came the sound of the accordion, augmented from time to time by bits of spurious part singing. The sideboard was perhaps the gayest spot. Anacleto, with an imposed-on-expression, ladled stingy half-cups of punch and took his time about it. After he spotted Lieutenant Weincheck, standing alone near the front door, he was engaged for fifteen minutes in fishing out every cherry and piece of pineapple, then he left a dozen officers waiting in order to present this choice cup to the old Lieutenant. There was so much lively conversation that it was impossible to follow any one line of thought. There was talk of the new army appropriation by the Government and gossip about a recent suicide. Below the general hubbub, and with cautious glances to ascertain the whereabouts of Major Langdon, a joke sneaked its way through the party — a story to the effect that the little Filipino thoughtfully scented Alison Langdon's specimen of wee-wee with perfume before taking it to the hospital for a urinalysis. The congestion was beginning to be disastrous. Already a tart had fallen from a plate and, unnoticed, had been tracked halfway up the stairs.

Leonora was in the highest spirits. She had a gay cliché for everyone, and she patted the Quartermaster Colonel, an old favorite of hers, on the top of his bald head. Once she left the hall personally to carry a drink to the young entertainer from town who played the accordion. 'My God! the talent this boy has!' she said. 'Why, he can play anything at all you hum to him! "Oh Pretty Red Wing" — anything!'

'Really wonderful,' Major Langdon agreed, and looked at the group clustered around. 'Now my wife goes in for classical stuff — Bach, you know — all that. But to me it's like swallowing a bunch of angleworms. Now take "The Merry Widow's Waltz" — that's the sort of thing I love. Tuneful music!'

The gliding waltz, together with the arrival of the General, quieted some of the racket. Leonora was enjoying her party so much that it was not until after eight o'clock that she began to be concerned about her husband. Already most of the guests were bewildered by the protracted absence of their host. There was even the lively feeling that some accident might have occurred, or that an unexpected scandal was afoot. Consequently, even the earliest arrivals tended to stay on long past the customary time for such a coming-and-going affair; the house was so crowded that it took a keen sense of strategy to get from one room to the next.

Meanwhile, Captain Penderton waited at the entrance of the bridle path with a hurricane lamp and the Sergeant in charge of the stables. He had reached the post well after dark and his story was that the horse had thrown him and run away. They were hoping that Firebird would find his way back. The Captain had bathed his wounded, rash-red face, and then had driven to the hospital and had three stitches put in his cheek. But he could not go home. Not only did he lack the daring to face Leonora until the horse was in his stall — the real reason was that he was in wait for the man he hated. The night was mild, bright, and the moon was in its third quarter.

At nine o'clock they heard in the distance the sound of horses' hoofs, coming in very slowly. Soon the weary, shadowy figures of Private Williams and the two horses could be seen. The soldier led them both by the bridle. Blinking a little, he came up to the hurricane lamp. He looked into the Captain's face with such a long strange stare that the Sergeant felt a sudden shock. He did not know what to make of this, and he left it with the Captain to deal with the situation. The Captain was silent, but his eyelids twitched and his hard mouth trembled.

The Captain followed Private Williams into the stable. The young soldier fed the horses mash and gave them a rubdown. He did not speak, and the Captain stood outside the stall and watched him. He looked at the fine, skillful hands and the tender roundness of the soldier's neck. The Captain was overcome by a feeling that both repelled and fascinated him — it was as though he and the young soldier were wrestling together naked, body to body, in a fight to death. The Captain's strained loin muscles were so weak that he could hardly stand. His eyes, beneath his twitching eyelids, were like blue burning flames. The soldier quietly finished his work and left the stable. The Captain followed and stood watching as he walked off into the night. They had not spoken a word.

It was only when he got into his automobile that the Captain remembered the party at his house.

Anacleto did not come home until late in the evening. He stood in the doorway of Alison's room looking rather green and jaded, as crowds exhausted him. 'Ah,' he said philosophically, 'the world is choked up with too many people.'

Alison saw, however, from a swift little snap of his eyes, that something had happened. He went into her bathroom and rolled up the sleeves of his yellow linen shirt to wash his hands. 'Did Lieutenant Weincheck come over to see you?'

'Yes, he visited with me quite a while.'

The Lieutenant had been depressed. She sent him downstairs for a bottle of sherry. Then after they had drunk the wine he sat by the bed with the chessboard on his knees and they played a game of Russian bank. She had not realized until too late that it was very tactless of her to suggest the game, as the Lieutenant could hardly make out the cards and tried to hide this failing from her.

'He has just heard that the medical board did not pass him,' she said. 'He will get his retirement papers shortly.'

'Tssk! What a pity!' Then Anacleto added, 'At the same time I should be glad about it if I were he.'

The doctor had left her a new prescription that afternoon and from the bathroom mirror she saw Anacleto examine the bottle carefully and then take a taste of it before measuring it out for her. Judging by the look on his face, he did not much like the flavor. But he smiled brightly when he came back into the room.

'You have never been to such a party,' he said. 'What a great constellation!'

'Con*stern*ation, Anacleto.'

'At any rate, havoc. Captain Penderton was two hours late to his own party. Then, when he came in, I thought he had been half-eaten by a lion. The horse threw him in a blackberry bush and ran away. You have never seen such a face.'

'Did he break any bones?'

'He looked to me as though he had broken his back,' said Anacleto, with some satisfaction. 'But he carried it off fairly well — went upstairs and put on his evening clothes and tried to pretend that he wasn't upset. Now everybody has left except the Major and the Colonel with the red hair whose wife looks like a woery woman.'

'Anacleto,' she warned him softly. Anacleto had used the term 'woery woman' several times before she caught on to the meaning. At first she had thought it might be a native term, and then it had come to her finally that he meant 'whore.'

Anacleto shrugged his shoulders and then turned suddenly to her, his face flushed. 'I hate people!' he said vehemently. 'At the party someone told this joke, not knowing that I was near. And it was vulgar and insulting and not true!'

'What do you mean?'

'I wouldn't repeat it to you.'

'Well, forget it,' she said. 'Go on to bed and have a good night's sleep.'

Alison was troubled over Anacleto's outburst. It seemed to her that she also loathed people. Everyone she had known in the past five years was somehow wrong—that is, everyone except Weincheck and of course Anacleto and little Catherine. Morris Langdon in his blunt way was as stupid and heartless as a man could be. Leonora was nothing but an animal. And thieving Weldon Penderton was at bottom hopelessly corrupt. What a gang! Even she herself she loathed. If it were not for sordid procrastination and if she had a rag of pride, she and Anacleto would not be in this house tonight.

She turned her face to the window and looked into the night. A wind had come up, and downstairs a loose shutter was banging against the side of the house. She turned off the light so that she could see out of the window. Orion was wonderfully clear and bright tonight. In the forest the tops of the trees moved in the wind like dark waves. It was then that she glanced down toward the Pendertons' house and saw a man standing again by the edge of the woods. The man himself was hidden by the trees, but his shadow defined itself clearly on the grass of the lawn. She could not distinguish the features of this person, but she was certain now that a man was lurking there. She watched him ten minutes, twenty minutes, half an hour. He did not move. It gave her such an eerie shock that it occurred to her that perhaps she was really going out of her mind. She closed her eyes and counted by sevens to two hundred and eighty. Then when she looked out again the shadow was gone.

Her husband knocked on the door. Receiving no answer, he turned the knob cautiously and peered inside. 'My dear, are you asleep?' he asked in a voice loud enough to wake anyone.

'Yes,' she said bitterly. 'Dead asleep.'

The Major, puzzled, did not know whether to shut the door or to come inside. All the way across the room she could sense the fact that he had made frequent visits to Leonora's sideboard.

'Tomorrow I am going to tell you something,' she said. 'You ought to have an inkling of what it's about. So prepare yourself.'

'I haven't any idea,' the Major said helplessly. 'Have I done something wrong?' He bethought himself for a few moments. 'But if it's money for anything peculiar, I don't have it, Alison. Lost a bet on a football game and board for my horse——' The door closed warily.

It was past midnight and she was alone again. These hours, from twelve o'clock until dawn, were always dreadful. If ever she told Morris that she had not slept at all, he, of course, did not believe her. Neither did he believe that she was ill. Four years ago, when her health first broke down, he had been alarmed by her condition. But when one calamity followed another — empyema, kidney trouble, and now this heart disease — he became exasperated and ended finally by not believing her. He thought it all a hypochondriacal fake that she used in order to shirk her duties — that is, the routine of sports and parties which he thought suitable. In the same way it is wise to give an insistent hostess a single, firm excuse, for if one declines with a number of reasons, no matter how sound they may be, the hostess will not believe you. She heard her husband walking about in his room across the hall and carrying on a long didactic conversation with himself. She switched on her bed light and began reading.

At two o'clock in the morning it came to her suddenly, without warning, that she was going to die that night. She sat propped up with pillows in the bed, a young woman with a face already sharp and aged, looking restlessly from one corner of the wall to another. She moved her head in a curious little gesture, lifting her chin upward and sideways, as though something were choking her. The silent room seemed to her full of jarring sounds. Water dripped into the bowl of the lavatory in the bathroom. The clock on the mantelpiece, an old pendulum clock with white and gilt swans painted on the glass of the case, ticked with a rusty sound. But the third of these sounds, the loudest and the one which bothered her most, was the beating of her own heart. A great turmoil was going on inside her. Her heart seemed to be vaulting — it would beat rapidly like the footsteps of someone running, leap up, and then thud with a violence that shocked her all over. With slow, cautious movements she opened the drawer of the bedside table and took out her knitting. 'I must think of something pleasant,' she told herself reasonably.

She thought back to the happiest time of her life. She was twenty-one and for nine months had been trying to work a little Cicero and Virgil into the heads of boarding-school girls. Then when vacation came she was in New York with two hundred dollars in her pocketbook. She had got on a bus and headed north with no idea where she was going. And somewhere in Vermont she came to a village she liked the looks of, got off, and within a few days found and rented a little shack out in the woods. She had brought her cat, Petronius, with her — and before the summer was over she was obliged to put a feminine ending onto his name because he suddenly had a litter of kittens. Several stray hounds took up with them and once a week she would go into the village to buy cans of groceries for the cats, the dogs, and herself. Morning and night, every day of that fine summer, she had her favorite foods — chili con carne, zwieback, and tea. In the afternoons she chopped firewood and at night she sat in the kitchen with her feet on the stove and read or sang aloud to herself.

Alison's pale, flaky lips shaped whispering words and she stared with concentration at the footboard of the bed. Then all at once she dropped the knitting and held her breath. Her heart had stopped beating. The room was silent as a sepulcher and she waited with her mouth open and her head twisted sideways on the pillow. She was terrified, but when she tried to call out and break this silence, no sound would come.

There was a light tapping on the door, but she did not hear this. Neither for a few moments did she realize that Anacleto had come into the room and was holding her hand in his. After the long, terrible silence (and surely it had lasted more than a minute), her heart was beating again; the folds of her nightgown fluttered lightly over her chest.

'A bad time?' Anacleto asked in a cheerful, encouraging little voice. But his face, as he looked down at her, wore the same sickly grimace as her own—with the upper lip drawn back sharply over the teeth.

'I was so frightened,' she said. 'Has something happened?'

'Nothing has happened. But don't look like that.' He took his handkerchief from the pocket of his blouse and dipped it in a glass of water to bathe her forehead. 'I'll go down and get my paraphernalia and stay with you until you can sleep.'

Along with his water-colors he brought a tray of hot Ovaltine. He built a fire and put up a card table before the hearth. His presence was such a comfort that she wanted to sob with relief. After he had given her the tray, he settled himself cozily at the table and drank his cup of Ovaltine with slow, appreciative little sips. This was one of the things she loved the very most about Anacleto; he had a genius for making some sort of festival out of almost any occasion. He acted, not as though out of kindness he had left his bed in the dead of the night to sit up with a sick woman, but as though of their own free will they had chosen this particular hour for a very special party. Whenever they had anything disagreeable to go through with, he always managed to follow it up with some little treat. And now he sat with a white napkin over his crossed knees drinking the Ovaltine with as much ceremony as if the cup had been filled with choice wine—although he disliked the taste of the stuff quite as much as she did, and only bought it because he was so taken in by the glowing promises on the label of the can.

'Are you sleepy?' she asked.

'Not at all.' But at the very mention of sleep he was so tired that he could not keep from yawning. Loyally he turned away and tried to pretend that he had opened his mouth in order to feel one of his new wisdom teeth with his forefinger. 'I had a nap this afternoon and then I slept awhile tonight. I dreamed about Catherine.'

Alison could never think about her baby without experiencing an emotion so loaded with love and grief that it was like an insupportable weight on her chest. It was not true that time could muffle the keenness of this loss. Now she had more control over herself, but that was all. For a while, after those eleven months of joy, suspense, and suffering, she was quite unchanged. Catherine had been buried in the cemetery on the post where they were stationed. And for a long time she had been obsessed by the sharp, morbid image of the little body in the grave. Her horrified broodings on decay and on that tiny lonely skeleton had brought her to such a state that at last, after considerable red tape, she had had the coffin disinterred. She had taken what was left of the body to the crematorium in Chicago and had scattered the ashes in the snow. And now all that was left of Catherine were the memories that she and Anacleto shared together.

Alison waited until her voice should be steady and then she asked: 'What was it you dreamed?'

'It was troubling,' he said quietly. 'Rather like holding a butterfly in my hands. I was nursing her on my lap — then sudden convulsions — and you were trying to get the hot water to run.' Anacleto opened his paint box and arranged his paper, brushes, and watercolors before him. The fire brightened his pale face and put a glow in his dark eyes. 'Then the dream changed, and instead of Catherine I had on my knees one of the Major's boots that I had to clean twice today. The boot was full of squirming slithery newborn mice and I was trying to hold them in and keep them from crawling up all over me. Whoo! It was like ——'

'Hush, Anacleto!' she said, with a shiver. 'Please!'

He began to paint and she watched him. He dipped his brush into the glass and a lavender cloud showed in the water. His face was thoughtful as he bent over the paper and once he paused to make a few rapid measurements with a ruler on the table. As a painter Anacleto had great talent—of that she was sure. In his other accomplishments he had a certain knack, but at bottom he was imitative—almost, as Morris said, a little monkey. In his little water-colors, and drawings, however, he was quite himself. When they were stationed near New York, he had gone into the city in the afternoons to the Art Students' League, and she had been very proud, but not at all surprised, to observe how many people at the school exhibition came back to look at his pictures more than once.

His work was at once primitive and over-sophisticated, and it laid a queer spell on the beholder. But she could not get him to take his gift with proper seriousness and to work hard enough.

'The quality of dreams,' he was saying softly. 'That is a strange thing to think about. On afternoons in the Philippines, when the pillow is damp and the sun shines in the room, the dream is of one sort. And then in the North at night when it is snowing——'

But already Alison had got back into her rut of worry, and she was not listening to him. 'Tell me,' she interrupted suddenly. 'When you had the sulks this morning and said you were going to open a linen shop in Quebec, did you have anything particular in mind?'

'Why, certainly,' he said. 'You know I have always wanted to see the city of Quebec. And I think there is nothing quite so pleasant as handling beautiful linen.'

'And that's all you had in mind——' she said. Her voice lacked the inflections of a question and he did not reply to this. 'How much money do you have in the bank?'

He thought a moment with his brush poised above the water glass. 'Four hundred dollars and six cents. Do you want me to draw it out?'

'Not now. But we might need it later.'

'For Heaven's sake,' he said, 'don't worry. It does not a particle of good.'

The room was filled with the rose glow of the fire and gray

flickering shadows. The clock made a little whirring sound and then struck three.

'Look!' Anacleto said suddenly. He crumpled up the paper he had been painting on and threw it aside. Then he sat in a meditative gesture with his chin in his hands, staring at the embers of the fire. 'A peacock of a sort of ghastly green. With one immense golden eye. And in it these reflections of something tiny and——'

In his effort to find just the right word he held up his hand with the thumb and forefinger touched together. His hand made a great shadow on the wall behind him. 'Tiny and——'

'Grotesque,' she finished for him.

He nodded shortly. 'Exactly.'

But after he had already begun working, some sound in the silent room, or perhaps the memory of the last tone of her voice, made him turn suddenly around. 'Oh, don't!' he said. And as he rushed from the table he overturned the water glass so that it shattered on the hearth.

Private Williams had been in the room where the Captain's wife lay sleeping for only an hour that night. He waited near the outskirts of the woods during the party. Then, when most of the guests were gone, he watched through the sitting-room window until the Captain's wife went upstairs to bed. Later he came into the house as he had done before. Again that night the moonlight was clear and silver in the room. The Lady lay on her side with her oval face cupped between her rather grubby hands. She wore a satin nightgown and the cover was pushed down to her waist. The young soldier crouched silent by the bedside. Once he reached out warily and felt the slippery cloth of her nightgown with his thumb and forefinger. He had looked about him on coming into the room. For a time he stood before the bureau and contemplated the bottles, powder-puffs, and toilet articles. One object, an atomizer, had aroused his interest, and he had taken it to the window and examined it with a puzzled face. On the table there was a saucer holding a half-eaten chicken leg. The soldier touched it, smelled, and took a bite.

Now he squatted in the moonlight, his eyes half-closed and a wet smile on his lips. Once the Captain's wife turned in her sleep, sighed, and stretched herself. With curious fingers the soldier touched a brown strand of hair which lay loose on the pillow.

It was past three o'clock when Private Williams stiffened suddenly. He looked about him and seemed to listen to some sound. He did not realize all at once what caused this change, this uneasiness to come in him. Then he saw that the lights in the house next door had been turned on. In the still night he could hear the voice of a woman crying. Later he heard an automobile stop before the lighted house. Private Williams walked noiselessly into the dark hall. The door of the Captain's room was closed. Within a few moments he was walking slowly along the outskirts of the woods.

The soldier had slept very little during the past two days and nights and his eyes were swollen with fatigue. He made a half-circle around the post until he reached the shortest cut to the barracks. In this way he did not meet the sentry. But at dawn, for the first time in years, he had a dream and called out in his sleep. A soldier across the room awakened and threw a shoe at him.

As Private Williams had no friends among his barrack mates, his absence on these nights was of little interest to anyone. It was guessed that the soldier had found himself a woman. Many of the enlisted men were secretly married and sometimes stayed the night in town with their wives. Lights were out in the long crowded sleeping room at ten o'clock, but not all of the men were in bed at this hour. Sometimes, especially around the first of the month, there were poker games in the latrine that lasted the whole night through. Once at three o'clock Private Williams had encountered the sentry on his way to the barracks, but as the soldier had been in the army for two years and was familiar to the guard on duty, he was not questioned.

During the next few nights Private Williams rested and slept normally. In the late afternoons he sat alone on a bench before the barracks and at night he sometimes frequented the places of amusement on the post. He went to the movie and to the gymnasium. In the evening the gymnasium was converted into a roller-skating rink. There was music and a corner set aside where the men could rest at tables and drink cool, frothy beer. Private Williams ordered a glass and for the first time tasted alcohol. With a great rolling clatter the men skated around in a circle and the air smelled sharply of sweat and floor-wax. Three men, all old-timers, were surprised when Private Williams left his table to sit with them for a while. The young soldier looked into their faces and seemed to be on the point of asking some question of them. But in the end he did not speak, and after a time he went away.

Private Williams always had been so unsociable that hardly half of his sleeping mates even knew his name. Actually the name he used in the army was not his own. On his enlistment a tough old Sergeant had glared down at his signature — L. G. Williams — and then bawled out at him: 'Write your name, you snotty little hayseed, your full name!' The soldier had waited a long time before revealing the fact that those initials were his name, and the only name he had. 'Well, you can't go into the U.S. Army with a goddamn name like that,' the Sergeant said. 'I'll change it to E-l-l-g-e-e. O.K.?' Private Williams nodded and in the face of such indifference the Sergeant burst into a loud raw laugh. 'The half-wits they do sent us now,' he had said as he turned back to his papers.

It was now November and for two days a high wind had blown. Overnight the young maples along the sidewalks were stripped of their leaves. The leaves lay in a bright gold blanket beneath the trees and the sky was filled with white changing clouds. The next day there was a cold rain. The leaves were left sodden and dun-colored, trampled on the wet streets, and finally raked away. The weather had cleared again and the bare branches of the trees made a sharp filigree against the winter sky. In the early morning there was frost on the dead grass.

After four nights of rest Private Williams returned to the Captain's house. This time, as he knew the habits of the house, he did not wait until the Captain had gone to bed. At midnight while the officer worked in his study he went up to The Lady's room and stayed an hour there. Then he stood by the study window and watched curiously until at two o'clock the Captain went upstairs. For something was happening at this time that the soldier did not understand.

In these reconnoiterings, and during the dark vigils in The Lady's room, the soldier had no fear. He felt, but did not think; he experienced without making any mental résumé of his present or past actions. Five years before L. G. Williams had killed a man. In an argument over a wheelbarrow of manure he had stabbed a negro to death and hidden the body in an abandoned quarry. He had struck out in a fit of fury, and he could remember the violent color of blood and the weight of the limp body as he dragged it through the woods. He could remember the hot sun of that July afternoon, the smell of dust and death. He had felt a certain wondering, numb distress, but there was no fear in him, and not once since that time had the thought shaped definitely in his mind that he was a murderer. The mind is like a richly woven tapestry in which the colors are distilled from the experiences of the senses, and the design drawn from the convolutions of the intellect. The mind of Private Williams was imbued with various colors of strange tones, but it was without delineation, void of form.

Through these first winter days only one realization came to Private Williams, and it was this: he began to perceive that the Captain was following him. Twice a day, his face bandaged and still raw with rash, the Captain went out for short rides. And then when he had checked in the horse he lingered for a while before the stables. Three times on his way to mess Private Williams had looked behind him to see the Captain only about ten yards away. Far more often than chance could account for the officer passed him on the sidewalk. Once after one of these encounters the soldier stopped and looked behind him. After a short distance the Captain paused also and turned halfway around. It was late afternoon and the winter dusk had in it a pale violet tint. The Captain's eyes were steady, cruel, and bright. Almost a minute passed before, with one accord, they turned to continue on their ways.

stared at her there. Then he stood by the study window and watched uneasily until at two o'clock the Captain went upstairs. For something was happening at the time that the soldier did not understand.

In all these wanderings and during the dark vigils in The Lady's room the soldier had no fear. He felt, but did not think. He experienced without making any mental résumé of his present or past actions. Five years before Private Williams had killed a man. In an argument over a wheelbarrow of manure he had stabbed a negro to death and hidden the body in an abandoned quarry. He had struck out in a fit of fury, and he could remember the violent color of blood and the weight of the limp body as he dragged it through the woods. He could remember the hot sun of that July afternoon, the smell of dust and death. He had felt a certain wondering, numb distress, but there was no fear in him; and not once since that time had the thought shaped definitely in his mind that he was a murderer. The mind is like a richly woven tapestry in which the colors are distilled from the experiences of the senses, and the design drawn from the convolutions of the intellect. The mind of Private Williams was imbued with various colors of strange tones, but it was without delineation, void of form.

Through these first weeks only one realization came to Private Williams, and this was that he began to perceive that the Captain was following him. Twice a day, his face bandaged and still raw with rash, the Captain went out for short rides. And then when he had checked in the horse he lingered for a while beside the stables. Three times on his way to these Private Williams had looked behind him to see the Captain only about fifty yards away. Far more often than chance could account for the officer passed him on the sidewalk. Once after one of these encounters the soldier looked behind him; after a short distance the Captain paused also and turned halfway around. It was late afternoon and the winter dusk had lent a pale wavering. The Captain's eyes were steady, cruel, and anxious. Almost a minute passed before, with one accord, they turned to continue on their ways.

IV

IV

It is not easy on an army post for an officer to bring himself into personal contact with an enlisted man. Captain Penderton was now aware of this. Had he been serving as an ordinary line officer such as Major Morris Langdon, heading a company, a battalion, or a regiment, a certain amount of intercourse with the men in his command would have been open to him. Thus Major Langdon knew the name and face of almost every soldier in his charge. But Captain Penderton with his work at the School was in no such position. Except through his riding (and no feat of horsemanship was reckless enough for the Captain these days) there was no way at all for him to establish relations with the soldier whom he had come to hate.

Yet the Captain felt an aching want for contact between them of some sort. The thought of the soldier tantalized him continually. He went down to the stables as often as he could reasonably do so. Private Williams saddled his horse for him and held the bridle as he mounted. When the Captain knew in advance that he would meet the soldier, he felt himself grow dizzy. During their brief, impersonal meetings he suffered a curious lapse of sensory impressions; when he was near the soldier he found himself unable to see or to hear properly, and it was only after he had ridden away and was alone again that the scene developed itself for the first time in his mind. The thought of the young man's face — the dumb eyes, the heavy sensual lips that were often wet, the childish page-boy bangs — this image was intolerable to him. He rarely heard the soldier speak, but the sound of his slurring Southern voice meandered constantly in the back of his mind like a troubling song.

Late in the afternoons the Captain walked on the streets between the stables and the barracks in the hope of meeting Private Williams. When from a distance he saw him, walking with sluggish grace, the Captain felt his throat contract so that he could scarcely swallow. Then, when they were face to face, Private Williams always stared vaguely over the Captain's shoulder and saluted very slowly with his hand quite relaxed. Once as they were nearing each other the Captain saw him unwrap a bar of candy and drop the paper carelessly on the neat strip of grass bordering the sidewalk. This had infuriated the Captain and, after walking for some distance, he turned back, picked up the wrapper (it was from a bar of Baby Ruth), and put it in his pocket.

Captain Penderton, who on the whole had lived a most rigid and unemotional life, did not question this strange hate of his. Once or twice, when he awoke late after taking too much Seconal, he made himself uncomfortable by thinking back over his recent behavior. But he made no real effort to force himself to an inward reckoning.

One afternoon he drove before the barracks and saw the soldier resting alone on one of the benches. The Captain parked his car farther down the street and sat watching him. The soldier sprawled in the abandoned position of one who is on the point of napping. The sky was a pale green and the last of the wintry sun made sharp, long shadows. The Captain watched the soldier until the call for supper. Then, when Private Williams had gone inside, the Captain still sat in his car, looking at the outside of the barracks.

Dark came on and the building was brightly lighted. In a recreation room downstairs he could see the men playing billiards or lounging with magazines. The Captain thought of the mess hall with the long tables laden with hot food and the hungry soldiers eating and laughing together with lusty camaraderie. The Captain was not familiar with enlisted men and his picture of the life inside the barracks was greatly enriched by his imagination. The Captain was drawn toward the Middle Ages and had made a careful study of European history during feudal times. His imaginings of the barracks were flavored by this predilection. As he thought of the two thousand men living together in this great quadrangle, he felt suddenly alone. He sat in the dark car and as he stared at the lighted, crowded rooms inside, as he heard the sounds of shouts and ringing voices, the tears came to his glassy eyes. A bitter loneliness gnawed in him. He drove quickly home.

Leonora Penderton was resting in the hammock by the edge of the woods when her husband arrived. She went into the house and helped Susie finish in the kitchen, as they were to dine at home that evening and then go out to a party. A friend had sent them half a dozen quail and she planned to take over a tray to Alison, who had had a bad heart attack on the night of their party more than two weeks ago, and was now kept permanently in bed. Leonora and Susie arranged the food on a huge silver waiter. On a service plate they put two quail and generous helpings of several vegetables, the juices of which ran together to form a little pool in the middle of the plate. There were a good many other dainties besides, and when Leonora staggered out carrying the big waiter, Susie had to follow after her with a tray holding the overflow.

'Why didn't you bring Morris home with you?' the Captain asked when she returned.

'Poor fellow!' said Leonora. 'He was already gone. Eating his meals at the Officers' Club. Think of it!'

They had dressed for the evening and were standing before the fire in the sitting-room with a bottle of whiskey and their glasses on the mantelpiece. Leonora wore her red crêpe frock and the Captain his tuxedo. The Captain was nervous and kept tinkling the ice in his glass.

'Hah! Listen!' he said suddenly. 'Here is a pretty good one I heard today.' He put his forefinger along the side of his nose and drew his lips back over his teeth. He was going to tell a story, and was sketching out the skeleton in advance. The Captain had a nice feeling for wit and was a sharp gossip.

'Not long ago there was a telephone call for the General, and the Adjutant, recognizing Alison's voice, put it through immediately. "General, here is a request," said the voice in a very poised and cultivated manner. "I want you to do me the great service of seeing to it that that soldier does not get up and blow his bugle at six o'clock in the morning. It disturbs Mrs. Langdon's rest." There was a long pause and at last the General said: "I beg your pardon, but I don't believe I quite understand you." The request was repeated, and there was a still longer pause. "And pray tell me," the General said finally, "whom do I have the honor of addressing?" The voice answered: "This is the *garçon de maison* to Mrs. Langdon, Anacleto. I thank you."'

The Captain waited soberly, for he was not one to laugh at his own jokes. Neither did Leonora laugh — she seemed puzzled.

'What did he say he was?' she asked.

'He was trying to say "houseboy" in French.'

'And you mean Anacleto called up like that about reveille. Well, if that doesn't beat anything I ever heard. I can hardly believe it!'

'Nit-wit!' said the Captain. 'It didn't really happen. It's just a story, a joke.'

Leonora did not get the point. She was no gossip. First, she always found it a little difficult to picture a situation that did not actually take place in the room with her. Also, she was not in the least malicious.

'Why, how mean!' she said. 'If it didn't happen, why should anyone go to the trouble to make it up? It makes Anacleto sound like a fool. Who do you suppose started it?'

The Captain shrugged and finished his drink. He had fabricated any number of ridiculous anecdotes about Alison and Anacleto, and they had all gone the rounds of the post with great success. The composition and sharpening of these scandalous vignettes afforded the Captain much pleasure. He launched them discreetly, making it understood that he was not the originator but was passing them on from some other source. He did this less out of modesty than from the fear that they might sometime come to the ears of Morris Langdon.

Tonight the Captain's new story did not please him. In the house alone with his wife he felt again the melancholy that had come to him while sitting out in the car before the lighted barracks. He saw in his mind the deft, brown hands of the soldier and felt himself shiver inwardly.

'What in the hell are you thinking about?' Leonora asked.

'Nothing.'

'Well, you look awfully peculiar to me.'

They had arranged to pick up Morris Langdon, and just as they were ready to leave he called for them to come over for a drink. Alison was resting, so they did not go upstairs. They had their drinks hurriedly at the dining-room table, as they were already late. When they were finished, Anacleto brought to the Major, who was in uniform, his military evening cape. The little Filipino followed them to the door and said very sweetly: 'I hope you have a pleasant evening.'

'Thank you,' said Leonora. 'Same to you.'

The Major, however, was not so guileless. He looked at Anacleto with suspicion.

When Anacleto had closed the door, he hurried into the sitting-room and drew back the curtain an inch to peek outside. The three of them, each of whom Anacleto hated with all his heart, had paused on the steps to light cigarettes. Anacleto watched with great impatience. While they had been in the kitchen a fine scheme had come to him. He had moved three bricks from the rose garden and placed them at the end of the dark front sidewalk. In his mind he saw all three of them tumbling like ninepins. When at last they strolled across the lawn toward the car parked before the Penderton's house, Anacleto was so vexed that he gave his thumb a mean little bite. Then he hurried out to remove the obstruction, as he did not wish to catch anyone else in his snare.

The evening of that night was like any other evening. The Pendertons and Major Langdon went to a dance at the Polo Club and enjoyed themselves. Leonora had her usual rush from the young Lieutenants and Captain Penderton found the opportunity, over a quiet highball out on the veranda, to entrust his new story to a certain artillery officer who had a reputation as a wit. The Major stuck in the lounge with a cluster of his cronies, talking of fishing, politics, and ponies. There was to be a drag hunt the next morning and the Pendertons left with Major Langdon at about eleven o'clock. By that hour Anacleto, who had stayed with his mistress for a time and given her an injection, was in bed. He always lay propped up with pillows, just as did Madame Alison, although this position was so uncomfortable that he could hardly ever get a good night's rest. Alison, herself, was dozing. The Major and Leonora were in their rooms and sleeping soundly by midnight. Captain Penderton had settled down for a quiet period of work in his study. It was a warm night for the month of November and the scent of the pines was balmy in the air. There was no wind and the shadows lay still and dark on the lawns.

At about this time Alison Langdon felt herself awaking from a half-sleep. She had had a series of curious and vivid dreams that went back to the time of her childhood, and she struggled against returning consciousness. But such a struggle was useless, and soon she was lying wide awake with her eyes open to the dark. She began to cry, and the sound of her soft nervous sobbing seemed not to come from herself, but from some mysterious sufferer out somewhere in the night. She had had a very bad two weeks and she cried often. To begin with, she was supposed to keep strictly to the bed, as the doctor had told her that the next attack would finish her. However, she had no high opinion of her doctor and privately she thought of him as an old army sawbones — and a first-class jackass to boot. He drank, although he was a surgeon, and once in an argument with her he had insisted that Mozambique was on the west instead of the east coast of Africa and would not admit his error until she got out an atlas; altogether she set little store by his opinions, and advice. She was restless, and two days before she had suddenly felt such a longing to play the piano that she had got up, dressed, and gone downstairs when Anacleto and her husband were away. She played for a while and enjoyed herself. On the way back to her room she took the stairs very slowly and although she was very tired there were no ill effects.

The feeling of being trapped — because now she would certainly have to wait until she was better before going on with her plans — made her difficult to care for. At first they had had a hospital nurse, but the nurse and Anacleto did not get on well together and after a week she had left. Alison was continually imagining things.

That afternoon a child somewhere in the neighborhood had screamed, as children often scream in play, and she had had the unreasonable fear that the child was hit by an automobile. She sent Anacleto rushing out into the street, and even after he had assured her the children were only playing I-spy, she could not get over her anxiety. Then the day before she had smelled smoke and was certain the house was on fire. Anacleto went over every inch of the premises and still she was not reassured. Any sudden noise or trivial mishap would make her cry. Anacleto had bitten his fingernails to the quick and the Major stayed away from home as much as possible.

Now at midnight as she lay crying in the dark room another delusion came to her. She looked out of the window and saw again the shadow of a man on the Pendertons' back lawn. He was standing quite still, leaning against a pine tree. Then, as she watched him, he crossed the grass and went in by the back door. It came to her then with a fearful shock that this man, this skulker, was her own husband. He was sneaking in to Weldon Penderton's wife, even though Weldon himself was at home and working in his study. So great was her feeling of outrage that she did not stop to reason. Sick with anger she got out of bed and vomited in the bathroom. Then she put on a coat over her nightgown and stepped into a pair of shoes.

She did not hesitate on her way over to the Pendertons'. Nor did she once ask herself what she, who hated scenes above all things, would do in the situation which she was about to precipitate. She went in by the front way and closed the door behind her noisily. The hall was half-dark, as only a lamp was lighted in the sitting-room. Breathing painfully she climbed the stairs. Leonora's door was open and she saw the silhouette of a man squatting by the bedside. She stepped inside the room and switched on the lamp in the corner.

The soldier blinked in the light. He put his hand to the window-sill and half-rose from his crouching position. Leonora stirred in her sleep, murmured, and turned over toward the wall. Alison stood in the doorway, her face white and twisted with amazement.

Then without a word she backed out of the room.

In the meantime Captain Penderton had heard the front door open and close. He felt that something was amiss, but an instinct cautioned him to remain at his desk. He nibbled the eraser of his pencil and waited tensely. He had not known what to expect, but he was surprised when there was a knock on the door, and before he could reply Alison had come into the study.

'Why, whatever brings you here this time of the night?' the Captain asked with a nervous laugh.

She did not answer at once. She gathered the collar of her coat up close around her neck. When at last she spoke, her voice had a wooden tone, as if shock had deadened the vibrations. 'I think you had better go up to your wife's room,' she said.

This announcement, together with the strangeness of her appearance, startled the Captain greatly. But even stronger than his inward tumult was the thought that he must not lose his composure. In a flash a number of conflicting assumptions came to the Captain's mind. Her words could mean only one thing — that Morris Langdon was in Leonora's room. But surely not, for they would hardly be so willy-nilly as that! And if so what a position it would put him in! The Captain's smile was sugary and controlled. He did not reveal in any way his feelings of anger, doubt, and intense annoyance.

'Come, my dear,' he said in a motherly voice, 'you shouldn't be roaming around like this. I'll take you home.'

Alison gave the Captain a long piercing look. She seemed to be fitting together some mental puzzle. After a time she said slowly: 'You don't mean to sit there and tell me you know this and do nothing about it?'

Stubbornly the Captain retained his poise. 'I'll take you home,' he said. 'You're not yourself and you don't know what you're talking about.'

He got up hurriedly and took Alison by the arm. The feel of her frail, brittle elbow beneath the cloth of her coat repelled him. He hurried her down the steps and across the lawn. The front door of her house was open, but the Captain gave the doorbell a long ring. After a few moments Anacleto came into the hall, and before the Captain could make his departure he also saw Morris come out of his room at the top of the stairs. With mixed feelings of confusion and relief, he went back home, leaving Alison to explain herself as she chose.

The next morning Captain Penderton was not greatly surprised to learn that Alison Langdon had altogether lost her mind. By noon the whole post knew of this. (Her condition was referred to as a 'nervous breakdown,' but no one was misled by this.) When the Captain and Leonora went over to offer their services, they found the Major standing outside the closed door of his wife's room, holding a towel over his arm. He had been standing there patiently almost all the day. His light-colored eyes were wide with surprise and he kept twisting and mashing the flap of his ear. When he came down to see the Pendertons, he shook hands with them in a strangely formal fashion and blushed painfully.

With the exception of the doctor, Major Langdon kept the details of this tragedy a secret in his own shocked heart. Alison did not tear up the sheets or foam at the mouth as he had imagined the insane to do. On coming into the house in her nightgown at one o'clock in the morning, she had simply said that not only did Leonora deceive her husband—but that she deceived the Major as well, and with an enlisted man. Then Alison said that, furthermore, she herself was going to get a divorce, and she added that as she had no money she would appreciate it if he, the Major, would lend her the sum of five hundred dollars at four per cent interest with Anacleto and Lieutenant Weincheck as guarantors. In answer to his startled questions, she said that she and Anacleto were going into some business together or would buy a prawn boat. Anacleto had hauled her trunk into the room and all night he was busy packing under her supervision. They stopped off now and then to drink hot tea and study a map to decide where they would go. Sometime before dawn they settled on Moultrieville, South Carolina.

Major Langdon was greatly shaken. He stood in the corner of Alison's room for a long time and watched them pack. He dared not open his mouth. After a long time, when all that she had said had soaked into his mind and he was forced to acknowledge to himself that she was crazy, he took her nail scissors and the fire tongs out of the room. Then he went downstairs and sat at the kitchen table with a bottle of whiskey. He cried and sucked the salty tears from his wet mustache. Not only did he grieve for Alison's sake, but he felt ashamed, as though this were a reflection on his own respectability. The more he drank the more his misfortune seemed to him incomprehensible. Once he rolled his eyes up toward the ceiling and called out in the silent kitchen with a questioning roar of supplication:

'God? O God — ?'

Again he banged his head on the table until a knot came out on his forehead. By six-thirty in the morning he had finished more than a quart of whiskey. He took a shower, dressed, and telephoned Alison's doctor, who was a Colonel in the medical corps and the Major's own friend. Later another doctor was called in and they struck matches in front of Alison's nose and asked her various questions. It was during this examination that the Major had picked up the towel from the rack in her bathroom and put it over his arm. It gave him the look of being prepared for any emergency and was somehow a comfort to him. Before leaving, the Colonel talked for a long while, using the word 'psychology' many times, and the Major nodded dumbly at the end of every sentence. The doctor finished by advising that she be sent to a sanatorium as soon as possible.

'But look here,' the Major said helplessly. 'No strait-jacket or any place like that. You understand — where she can play the phonograph — comfortable. You know what I mean.'

Within two days a place in Virginia had been chosen. Due to hurry the institution had been selected more because of the price (it was astonishingly expensive) than for the therapeutic reputation. Alison only listened bitterly when the plans were told to her. Anacleto, of course, was going also. A few days later the three of them left on the train.

This establishment in Virginia catered to patients who were both physically and mentally ill. And the diseases that attack the body and the brain simultaneously are of a special kind. There were a number of old gentlemen who floundered about in a state of total confusion and had to keep a close watch on their unwieldy legs. There were a few lady morphinists and any number of rich young liquor-heads. But the place had a pretty terrace where tea was served in the afternoon, the gardens were well kept, and the rooms furnished luxuriously; the Major was satisfied and rather proud that he could afford it.

Alison, however, made no comment just at first. Indeed she did not speak at all to her husband until they sat down to dinner that night. As an exception, on the evening of her arrival she was to dine downstairs, but beginning with the next morning she was to rest in bed until the condition of her heart improved. At their table there were candles and hothouse roses. The service and the table linen were of the best quality.

Alison, however, seemed not to observe these niceties. On sitting down to the table she took in the room with one long, wandering gaze. Her eyes, dark and shrewd as always, examined the occupants at all the other tables. Then finally she spoke quietly and with bitter relish:

'My God, what a choice crew!'

Major Langdon was never to forget that dinner, for it was the last time he was with his wife. He left very early the next morning and stopped off to spend the night in Pinehurst where he had an old polo friend. Then, when he returned to the post a telegram was waiting for him. On the second night of her stay there Alison had had a heart attack and died.

This autumn Captain Penderton was thirty-five years old. Despite his comparative youth he was soon to wear the maple leaves of a Major; and in the army, where promotion is largely contingent on seniority, this premature advancement was a marked tribute to his ability. The Captain had worked hard and his mind was brilliant from a military point of view — it was the opinion of many officers, including the Captain himself, that he would one day be a high ranking General. Nevertheless, Captain Penderton showed the strain of his long efforts. This autumn, especially during the past few weeks, he seemed to have aged disproportionately. There were bruise-like circles beneath his eyes and his complexion was of a yellow, mottled color. His teeth had begun to trouble him considerably. The dentist told him that two of the lower molars would have to be extracted and some bridgework put in, but the Captain kept deferring this operation, as he felt he did not have the time to spare. The Captain's face was habitually tense and a tic had developed in the muscles of his left eye. This spasmodic twitching of the eyelid gave to his drawn face a strangely paralyzed expression.

He was in a constant state of repressed agitation. His preoccupation with the soldier grew in him like a disease. As in cancer, when the cells unaccountably rebel and begin the insidious self-multiplication that will ultimately destroy the body, so in his mind did the thoughts of the soldier grow out of all proportion to their normal sphere. Sometimes with dismay he made a wondering résumé of the steps that had brought about this condition — beginning with the carelessly spilt coffee on a new pair of trousers, and continuing with the clearing of the woods, the encounter after the ride on Firebird, and the brief meetings on the streets of the post. How his annoyance could have grown to hate, and the hate to this diseased obsession, the Captain could not logically understand.

A peculiar reverie had taken hold of him. As he always had been keenly ambitious, he had often amused himself by anticipating his promotions far in advance. Thus, when he was still a young West-Pointer the name and the title 'Colonel Weldon Penderton' had to him a familiar and pleasing sound. And during the past summer of this year he had imagined himself as a Corps Area Commander of great brilliance and power. Sometimes he had even whispered the words 'Major General Penderton' aloud to himself — and it seemed to him he should have been born to the title, so well did the sound of it fit with his name. But now during the past weeks this idle dream had strangely reversed itself. One night —

or rather it was one-thirty in the morning — he had sat at his desk in a trauma of fatigue. Suddenly in the silent room three words had come unbidden to his tongue: 'Private Weldon Penderton.' And these words, with the associations they engendered, aroused in the Captain a perverse feeling of relief and satisfaction. Instead of dreaming of honor and rank, he now experienced a subtle pleasure in imagining himself as an enlisted man. In these phantasies he saw himself as a youth, a twin almost of the soldier whom he hated — with a young, easy body that even the cheap uniform of a common soldier could not make ungraceful, with thick glossy hair and round eyes unshadowed by study and strain. The image of Private Williams wove itself through all these day-dreams. And the background of all this was the barracks: the hubbub of young male voices, the genial loafing in the sun, the irresponsible shenanigans of camaraderie.

Captain Penderton had formed the habit of walking each afternoon before the quadrangle where Private Williams was quartered. Usually he saw the soldier sitting alone on the same bench. Walking on the sidewalk the Captain would pass within two yards of the soldier, and at his approach Private Williams would get up reluctantly and give a lazy salute. The days were growing short, and at this time in the late afternoon a hint of darkness was already in the air. For a brief period after sunset there was in the atmosphere a misty lavender glow.

The Captain on passing always looked full into the soldier's face and slowed his footsteps. He knew that the soldier must now realize that these afternoon walks were made on his account. It even occurred to the Captain to wonder why the soldier did not evade him and go elsewhere at this time. The fact that the soldier clung to his habit gave to these daily contacts a flavor of assignation that filled the Captain with excitement. After he had passed the soldier he had to suppress a craving to turn around, and as he walked away he felt his heart swell with a wild, nostalgic sadness which he could not control.

At the Captain's house there were a few changes. Major Langdon had attached himself to the Pendertons like a third member of the family, and this state of affairs was agreeable both to the Captain and Leonora. The Major was left quite stunned and helpless by the death of his wife. Even physically there was a difference in him. His jovial poise had deserted him, and when the three of them were sitting before the fire in the evening, he seemed to want to get himself into the most hobbledehoy and uncomfortable positions possible. He would twist his legs around each other like a contortionist or hike up one heavy shoulder while he mashed his ear. His thoughts and his words now centered entirely on Alison and the part of his life that had now come so abruptly to an end. He was inclined to make doleful platitudes concerning God, the soul, suffering, and death — subjects the mention of which would hitherto have made his tongue grow thick and awkward with embarrassment. Leonora looked after him, fed him excellent dinners, and listened to any mournful observations he might have to make. 'If only Anacleto would come back,' he said often.

For Anacleto had left the sanatorium the morning after Alison had died and no one had heard of him since. He had repacked the luggage and put all of her things in order. Then he had simply disappeared. To replace him Leonora had hired for the Major one of Susie's brothers who could cook. For years the Major had longed for an ordinary colored boy who would maybe steal his liquor and leave dust under the rug, but who at any rate, by God, would not fiddle around with the piano and jabber in French. Susie's brother was a good boy; he played on a comb wrapped in toilet paper, got drunk, and cooked good cornbread. But at the same time the Major did not feel the satisfaction he had anticipated. He missed Anacleto in many ways and felt concerning him the most uncomfortable remorse.

'You know I used to devil Anacleto by describing what I would do to him if I could get him into the service. You don't suppose the little rascal really believed me, do you? I was mostly kidding him — but in a way it always seemed to me that if he would enlist it would be the best thing in the world for him.'

The Captain was weary of the talk about Alison and Anacleto. It was a pity the nasty little Filipino hadn't been carried off by a heart attack also. The Captain was tired of almost everything around the house these days. The plain, heavy Southern meals that Leonora and Morris enjoyed were especially distasteful to him. The kitchen was filthy and Susie too slovenly for words. The Captain was a connoisseur of good food and a neat amateur chef. He appreciated the subtle cookery of New Orleans, and the delicate, balanced harmony of French food. Often in the old days he used to go into the kitchen when he was in the house alone and prepare for his own enjoyment some luscious tidbit. His favorite dish was fillet of beef à la Béarnaise. However, the Captain was a perfectionist and a crank; if the tournedos were too well done, or if the sauce got hot and curdled even the slightest bit—he would take it all out to the back yard, dig a hole, and bury it. But now he had lost all appetite for food. This afternoon Leonora had gone to the movies and he sent Susie away. He had thought that he would like to cook something special. But in the midst of preparing a rissole he had suddenly lost all interest, left everything as it was, and walked out of the house.

'I can imagine Anacleto on K.P.,' Leonora said.

'Alison always thought I brought up the subject just to be cruel,' said the Major. 'But that wasn't so. Anacleto wouldn't have been happy in the army, no, but it might have made a man of him. Would have knocked all the nonsense out of him anyway. But what I mean is that in a way it always seemed to me terrible for a grown man twenty-three years old to be dancing around to music and messing with water-colors. In the army they would have run him ragged and he would have been miserable, but even that seems to me better than the other.'

'You mean,' Captain Penderton said, 'that any fulfilment obtained at the expense of normalcy is wrong, and should not be allowed to bring happiness. In short, it is better, because it is morally honorable, for the square peg to keep scraping about the round hole rather than to discover and use the unorthodox square that would fit it?'

'Why, you put it exactly right,' the Major said. 'Don't you agree with me?'

'No,' said the Captain, after a short pause. With gruesome vividness the Captain suddenly looked into his soul and saw himself. For once he did not see himself as others saw him; there came to him a distorted doll-like image, mean of countenance and grotesque in form. The Captain dwelt on this vision without compassion. He accepted it with neither alteration nor excuse. 'I don't agree,' he repeated absently.

Major Langdon thought over this unexpected reply, but did not continue the conversation. He always found it difficult to follow up any one line of thought beyond the first, bare exposition. With a headshake he returned to his own bewildering affairs. 'Once I waked up just before daylight.' he said. 'I saw the lamp was on in her room and I went in. And there I found Anacleto sitting on the edge of the bed and they were both of them looking down and fooling with something. And what was it they were doing?' The Major pressed his blunt fingers against his eyeballs and shook his head again. 'Oh yes. They were dropping little things into a bowl of water. Some sort of Japanese mess Anacleto had bought at the ten-cent store — these little particles open like flowers in the water. And they were just sitting there at four o'clock in the morning trifling with that. It made me suddenly irritable, and when I stumbled over Alison's slippers by the side of the bed, I lost my temper and kicked them across the room. Alison was disgusted with me, cold as ice for days. And Anacleto put salt in the sugar bowl before he brought me my coffee. It was sad. Those nights she must have suffered.'

'They giveth it and then they taketh it away,' said Leonora, whose intentions were better than her command of Scripture.

Leonora herself had altered a little during the past weeks. She was approaching the phase of her full maturity. In this short time her body seemed to have lost some of its youthful muscularity. Her face was broader, and her expression in repose was one of lazy tenderness. She looked like a woman who has had several wellborn babies and who hopefully expects another in about eight months. Her complexion was still of a delicate, healthy texture, and although she was gradually putting on weight there was as yet no sign of flabbiness. She had been dismayed by the death of her lover's wife. The sight of the dead body in the coffin had so fascinated her that for several days after the funeral she had spoken in an awed whisper, even when ordering groceries at the Post Exchange. She treated the Major with a sort of vacant sweetness and repeated any happy ancedotes concerning Alison that she could remember.

'By the way,' said the Captain suddenly, 'I can't stop wondering about that night — when she came over here. What did she say to you in your room, Leonora?'

'I told you I didn't even know she came. She didn't wake me up.'

But on this subject Captain Penderton was still unsatisfied. The more he remembered the scene in his study, the stranger and more compelling it became to him. He did not doubt that Leonora told the truth, for whenever she lied it was instantly plain to everyone. But what had Alison meant and why on coming back home had he not gone upstairs to see? He felt he knew the answer somewhere in the shadowy unconscious of his mind. But the more he thought about this matter, the sharper was his uneasiness.

'I remember one time when I was certainly surprised,' said Leonora, holding her pink, school-girlish hands out to the fire. 'It was when we all drove up to North Carolina, the afternoon after we ate those good partridges at the house of that friend of yours, Morris. Alison and Anacleto and I were walking along this country road when a little boy came along leading this plow horse — close kin to a mule, he was. But Alison liked the old plug's face and suddenly decided she wanted to ride him. So she made friends with the little Tarheel and then climbed up on a fence post and slipped on — no saddle and wearing a dress. Think of it! I guess the horse hadn't been ridden for years and soon as she got on him he just lay down and started to roll her. And I thought to myself that that was the end of Alison Langdon and shut my eyes. But do you know she had got that horse up in a minute and was trotting around the field as though nothing at all had happened. You never could have done it, Weldon. And Anacleto was running up and down like a drunk jay-bird. Lord, what a good time—I never was so surprised!'

Captain Penderton yawned, not because he was sleepy, but because Leonora's reference to his horsemanship had piqued him and he wanted to be discourteous. There had been some bitter scenes between the Captain and Leonora over Firebird. After the frenzied, runaway ride the horse had never been altogether the same, and Leonora blamed her husband vehemently. The events of the past two weeks, however, had served to deflect the course of their feud and the Captain was confident that soon she would forget.

Major Langdon closed this particular evening's conversation with one of his favorite aphorisms: 'Only two things matter to me now—to be a good animal and to serve my country. A healthy body and patriotism.'

At this time Captain Penderton's house was not an ideal place for a person undergoing an acute psychic crisis. Formerly the Captain would have found the laments of Morris Langdon ridiculous. But now there was the atmosphere of death in the house. To him it seemed that not only had Alison died, but that in some mysterious way the lives of all three of them had come to a close. The old fear that Leonora might divorce him and go away with Morris Langdon did not trouble him any more. Any inclination he had once had toward the Major seemed now a mere velleity compared to his feelings for the soldier.

The house itself irritated the Captain exceedingly these days. Their quarters were furnished in haphazard fashion. In the sitting-room there was the conventional sofa covered with flower-patterned chintz, a couple of easy-chairs, a rug of garish red, and an antique secretary. The room had an air of flossiness that the Captain abhorred. The lace curtains looked cheap and rather dingy, and on the mantelpiece there was a heterogeneous collection of ornaments and gewgaws—a procession of sham-ivory elephants, a pair of beautiful wrought-iron candlesticks, a painted statuette of a pickaninny grinning over a red slice of watermelon, and a blue glass Mexican bowl into which Leonora had dumped old visiting cards. All of the furniture was slightly rickety from too much moving, and the feminine, cluttered impression made by the room as a whole so exasperated the Captain that he stayed out of it as much as possible. With deep secret longing he thought of the barracks, seeing in his mind the neat cots placed in a row, the bare floors, and stark curtainless windows. Against one of the walls of this imaginary room, ascetic and austere, there was for some reason an ancient carved chest with brass bindings.

Captain Penderton on his long walks during the late afternoon was in a state of sharpened sensitivity close to delirium. He felt himself adrift, cut off from all human influence, and he carried with him the brooding image of the young soldier much as a witch would hug to her bosom some cunning charm. He experienced during this time a peculiar vulnerability. Although he felt himself isolated from all other persons, the things which he saw on his walks took on an abnormal importance in his eyes. Everything with which he came in contact, even the most common-place objects, seemed to have some mysterious bearing on his own destiny. If, for instance, he chanced to notice a sparrow in the gutter, he could stand for minutes, completely absorbed in this ordinary sight. For the time being he had lost the primitive faculty that instinctively classifies the various sensory impressions according to their relative values. One afternoon he saw a transport truck run into an automobile. But this bloody accident impressed him no more vividly than the sight, a few minutes later, of a scrap of newspaper fluttering in the wind.

For a long time now he had ceased to attribute his feelings for Private Williams to hate. Also he no longer tried to find justification for the emotion that had so taken possession of him. He thought of the soldier in terms neither of love nor hate; he was conscious only of the irresistible yearning to break down the barrier between them. When from a distance he saw the soldier resting before the barracks, he wanted to shout to him, or to strike him with his fist, to make him respond in some way to violence. It was almost two years now since he had first seen the soldier. More than a month had gone by since he had been sent on special fatigue to clear the woods. And in all this time they had hardly spoken to each other more than a few dozen words.

On the afternoon of the twelfth of November, Captain Penderton went out as usual. He had had a trying day. That morning in the classroom, while standing before the blackboard in the process of illustrating a tactical problem, he had had an unexplainable attack of amnesia. In the middle of a sentence his mind went blank. Not only did he totally forget every word of the remainder of his lecture, even the faces of the student officers in the room seemed unfamiliar to him. In his mind he could see Private Williams very clearly — that was all. For some moments he stood dumbly with the chalk still in his hand. Then he found presence of mind to dismiss the class. Fortunately the lecture was almost ended when his lapse had occurred.

The Captain walked very stiffly along one of the sidewalks leading toward the quadrangle. The weather on this afternoon was extraordinary. There were dour storm clouds in the sky, but down near the horizon the heavens were still clear and the sun shone with gentle radiance. The Captain swung his arms as though they would not bend at the elbow and kept his eyes on the bottoms of his army slacks and his highly polished narrow shoes. He looked up just as he reached the bench where Private Williams sat, and after staring at him for a few seconds he went up to him. Sluggishly the soldier rose to attention.

'Private Williams,' the Captain said.

The soldier waited, but Captain Penderton did not continue. He had meant to reprimand the soldier for a violation of the regulations concerning the uniform. As he approached, it had seemed to him that Private Williams had buttoned his coat improperly. At first glance the soldier always looked as though he were only in partial uniform, or had neglected some necessary part of his attire. But when they were face to face, Captain Penderton saw that there was nothing for him to criticize. The impression of civilian carelessness was due to the very body of the soldier himself and to no particular infringement of army rules. Again the Captain stood mute and suffocated before the young man. In his heart there coursed a wild tirade of curses, words of love, supplications, and abuse. But in the end he turned away, still silent.

The rain that had been threatening held off until Captain Penderton was almost home. This was not a slow, drizzling winter rain — it came down with the roaring vehemence of a summer thunderstorm. The Captain was within twenty yards of his house when the first drops fell on him. With a short sprint he could have easily reached shelter. But his dragging footsteps did not quicken, even when the icy, pouring torrent soaked into him. When he opened his front door he was bright-eyed and shivering.

Private Williams went into the barracks when he scented in the atmosphere the coming rain. He sat in the day-room until supper-time and then, amid the rowdy exuberance of the mess hall, he ate a copious, leisurely meal. Afterward he took from his locker a sack of mixed penny candies. While still chewing a marshmallow, he paid a visit to the latrine and there he picked a fight. At the time of his entrance all of the commodes except one were in use, and there was a soldier ahead of him in the act of unbuttoning his trousers. But just as the man started to sit down, Private Williams gave him a rough push and tried to oust him from his place. A little crowd gathered about the fight which followed. From the first Private Williams had the best of it, as he was both quick and strong. While fighting, his face expressed neither effort nor anger; his features still were impassive and only the sweat on his forehead, the look of blindness in his eyes, showed the results of his struggle. Private Williams had his opponent in a helpless condition and the fight was already won when all at once he himself suddenly gave up. He seemed completely to lose interest in the fight and did not even bother to defend himself. He was soundly beaten and his head was banged viciously against the cement floor. When it was over, he stood up groggily and left the latrine without even using the commode after all.

This was not the first fight that Private Williams had provoked.

During the past two weeks he had stayed in the barracks every night, and stirred up much trouble. This was a new side of his personality that his barrack mates had not suspected. For hours he would sit in torpid silence and then all at once he would perpetrate some inexcusable offense. He no longer walked in the woods in his spare time, and at night he slept badly, disturbing the room with nightmare mutters. No one, however, gave any thought to his oddities. There was much behavior in the barracks far queerer than this. One old Corporal wrote a letter every night to Shirley Temple making it a sort of diary of all that he had done during the day, and mailing it before breakfast the next morning. Another man, who had ten years' service behind him, jumped out of a three-story window because a friend would not lend him fifty cents for beer. A cook in the same battery was haunted by the fixed idea that he had cancer of the tongue, an illusion that no medical denials could dispel. He brooded before a mirror with his tongue out so far that he could see the taste-buds, and he starved himself to the point of emaciation.

After the fight Private Williams went to the sleeping room and lay down on his cot. He put the sack of candy beneath his pillow and stared up at the ceiling. Outside the rain had slackened and it was now night. A number of lazy reveries colored the mind of Private Williams. He thought of the Captain, but he only saw a series of mental pictures that had no meaning. To this young Southern soldier the officers were in the same vague category as negroes — they had a place in his life, but he did not look on them as being human. He accepted the Captain as fatalistically as though he were the weather or some natural phenomenon. The Captain's behavior might seem unexpected, but he did not identify it with himself. And it did not occur to him to question it, any more than he would question a thunderstorm or the fading of a flower.

He had not been near the quarters of Captain Penderton since the night the lamp had been switched on and he saw the dark woman looking at him from the doorway. At that time a great fright had come in him — but this terror had been more physical than mental, more unconscious than understood. After he had heard the front door shut, he had looked out cautiously and seen the way clear. Once safe again in the woods he had run desperately, silently, although he did not realize exactly what it was he feared.

But the memory of the Captain's wife had not left him. He dreamed of The Lady every night. Once, soon after his enlistment, he had got ptomaine poisoning and had been sent into hospital. The thought of the bad sickness in women had made him shudder beneath the cover whenever the nurses came near him, and he had lain for hours in misery rather than ask of them some service. But he had touched The Lady and he was afraid of this sickness no more. Every day he groomed and saddled her horse and watched her ride away. In the early morning there was a wintry bitterness in the air and the Captain's wife was rosy and high-spirited. She always had a joke or a friendly word for Private Williams, but he never looked at her directly or answered her pleasantries.

He never thought of her in connection with the stables or the open air. To him she was always in the room where he had watched her in the night with such absorption. His memory of these times was wholly sensual. There was the thick rug beneath his feet, the silk spread, the faint scent of perfume. There was the soft luxurious warmth of woman-flesh, the quiet darkness—the alien sweetness in his heart and the tense power in his body as he crouched there near to her. Once having known this he could not let it go; in him was engendered a dark, drugged craving as certain of fulfillment as death.

The rain stopped at midnight. Long ago the lights in the barracks had been turned off. Private Williams had not undressed himself, and when the rain was over he put on his tennis shoes and went outside. On his way to the Captain's quarters he took his usual route, skirting the woods surrounding the post. But tonight there was no moon and the soldier was walking much faster than usual. Once he lost himself, and when at last he reached the Captain's house he had an accident. In the darkness he stumbled into what seemed to him at first to be a deep pit. In order to get his bearings he struck a few matches and saw that he had fallen into a recently dug hole. The house was dark, and the soldier, who was now scratched, muddy, and breathless, waited a few moments before going inside. In all he had come six times before, and this was the seventh and would be the last.

Captain Penderton was standing at the back window of his bedroom. He had taken three capsules, but still he could not sleep. He was slightly drunk with brandy, and a little drugged—but that was all. The Captain, who was keenly sensitive to luxury and a finicky dresser, wore only the coarsest sleeping garments. He had on now a wrapper of rough black wool that might have been bought for a recently widowed matron of a jail. His pajamas were of some unbleached material as stiff as canvas. He was barefooted, although the floor was now cold.

The Captain was listening to the sough of the wind in the pine trees when he saw out in the night a tiny flicker of flame. The light was blown out by the wind in only a moment, but during that instant the Captain had seen a face. And that face, brightened by the flame and set in darkness, made the Captain stop his breath. He watched and could vaguely make out the figure that crossed the lawn. The Captain clutched the front of his wrapper and pressed his hand against his breast. He closed his eyes and waited.

At first no sound came to him. Then he could feel rather than hear the cautious footsteps on the stairs. The Captain's door was ajar and through the crack he saw a dark silhouette. He whispered something, but his voice was so sibilant and low that it sounded like the wind outside.

Captain Penderton waited. With his eyes closed again, he stood there for moments of anguished suspense. Then he went out into the hall and saw outlined against the pale gray window of his wife's room the one for whom he sought. Afterward the Captain was to tell himself that in this one instant he knew everything. Actually, in a moment when a great but unknown shock is expected, the mind instinctively prepares itself by abandoning momentarily the faculty of surprise. In that vulnerable instant a kaleidoscope of half-guessed possibilities project themselves, and when the disaster has defined itself there is the feeling of having understood beforehand in some supernatural way. The Captain took his pistol from the drawer of his bed-table, crossed the hall, and switched on the light in his wife's room. As he did this, certain dormant fragments of memory — a shadow at the window, a sound in the night — came to him. He said to himself that he knew all. But what it was he knew he could not have expressed. He was only certain that this was the end.

The soldier did not have time to rise from his squatting position. He blinked at the light and there was no fear in his face; his expression was one of dazed annoyance, as if he had been inexcusably disturbed. The Captain was a good marksman, and although he shot twice only one raw hole was left in the center of the soldier's chest.

The reports from the pistol aroused Leonora and she sat up in bed. As yet she was still only half-awake, and she stared about her as though witnessing some scene in a play, some tragedy that was gruesome but not necessary to believe. Almost immediately Major Langdon knocked on the back door and then hurried up the stairs wearing slippers and a dressing-gown. The Captain had slumped against the wall. In his queer, coarse wrapper he resembled a broken and dissipated monk. Even in death the body of the soldier still had the look of warm, animal comfort. His grave face was unchanged, and his sun-browned hands lay palms upward on the carpet as though in sleep.

THE END

The Member of the Wedding

For Elizabeth Ames

PART ONE

IT HAPPENED that green and crazy summer when Frankie was twelve years old. This was the summer when for a long time she had not been a member. She belonged to no club and was a member of nothing in the world. Frankie had become an unjoined person who hung around in doorways, and she was afraid. In June the trees were bright dizzy green, but later the leaves darkened, and the town turned black and shrunken under the glare of the sun. At first Frankie walked around doing one thing and another. The sidewalks of the town were gray in the early morning and at night, but the noon sun put a glaze on them, so that the cement burned and glittered like glass. The sidewalks finally became too hot for Frankie's feet, and also she got herself in trouble. She was in so much secret trouble that she thought it was better to stay at home — and at home there was only Berenice Sadie Brown and John Henry West. The three of them sat at the kitchen table, saying the same things over and over, so that by August the words began to rhyme with each other and sound strange. The world seemed to die each afternoon and nothing moved any longer. At last the summer was like a green sick dream, or like a silent crazy jungle under glass. And then, on the last Friday of August, all this was changed: it was so sudden that Frankie puzzled the whole blank afternoon, and still she did not understand.

'It is so very queer,' she said. 'The way it all just happened.'

'Happened? Happened?' said Berenice.

John Henry listened and watched them quietly.

'I have never been so puzzled.'

'But puzzled about what?'

'The whole thing,' Frankie said.

And Berenice remarked: 'I believe the sun has fried your brains.'

'Me too,' John Henry whispered.

Frankie herself almost admitted maybe so. It was four o'clock in the afternoon and the kitchen was square and gray and quiet. Frankie sat at the table with her eyes half closed, and she thought about a wedding. She saw a silent church, a strange snow slanting down against the colored windows. The groom in this wedding was her brother, and there was a brightness where his face should be. The bride was there in a long white train, and the bride also was faceless. There was something about this wedding that gave Frankie a feeling she could not name.

'Look here at me,' said Berenice. 'You jealous?'

'Jealous?'

'Jealous because your brother going to be married?'

'No,' said Frankie. 'I just never saw any two people like them. When they walked in the house today it was so queer.'

'You jealous,' said Berenice. 'Go and behold yourself in the mirror. I can see from the color in your eye.'

There was a watery kitchen mirror hanging above the sink. Frankie looked, but her eyes were gray as they always were. This summer she was grown so tall that she was almost a big freak, and her shoulders were narrow, her legs too long. She wore a pair of blue track shorts, a B.V.D. undervest, and she was barefooted. Her hair had been cut like a boy's, but it had not been cut for a long time and was now not even parted. The reflection in the glass was warped and crooked, but Frankie knew well what she looked like; she drew up her left shoulder and turned her head aside.

'Oh,' she said. 'They were the two prettiest people I ever saw. I just can't understand how it happened.'

'But what, Foolish?' said Berenice. 'Your brother come home with the girl he means to marry and took dinner today with you and your Daddy. They intend to marry at her home in Winter Hill this coming Sunday. You and your Daddy are going to the wedding. And that is the A and the Z of the matter. So whatever ails you?'

'I don't know,' said Frankie. 'I bet they have a good time every minute of the day.'

'Less us have a good time,' John Henry said.

'Us have a good time?' Frankie asked. 'Us?'

The three of them sat at the table again and Berenice dealt the cards for three-handed bridge. Berenice had been the cook since Frankie could remember. She was very black and broad-shouldered and short. She always said that she was thirty-five years old, but she had been saying that at least three years. Her hair was parted, plaited, and greased close to the skull, and she had a flat and quiet face. There was only one thing wrong about Berenice — her left eye was bright blue glass. It stared out fixed and wild from her quiet, colored face, and why she had wanted a blue eye nobody human would ever know. Her right eye was dark and sad. Berenice dealt slowly, licking her thumb when the sweaty cards stuck together. John Henry watched each card as it was being dealt. His chest was white and wet and naked, and he wore around his neck a tiny lead donkey tied by a string. He was blood kin to Frankie, first cousin, and all summer he would eat dinner and spend the day with her, or eat supper and spend the night; and she could not make him go home. He was small to be six years old, but he had the largest knees that Frankie had ever seen, and on one of them there was always a scab or a bandage where he had fallen down and skinned himself. John Henry had a little screwed white face and he wore tiny gold-rimmed glasses. He watched all of the cards very carefully, because he was in debt; he owed Berenice more than five million dollars.

'I bid one heart,' said Berenice.

'A spade,' said Frankie.

'I want to bid spades,' said John Henry. 'That's what I was going to bid.'

'Well, that's your tough luck. I bid them first.'

'Oh, you fool jackass!' he said. 'It's not fair!'

'Hush quarreling,' said Berenice. 'To tell the truth, I don't think either one of you got such a grand hand to fight over the bid about. I bid two hearts.'

'I don't give a durn about it,' Frankie said. 'It is immaterial with me.'

As a matter of fact this was so: she played bridge that afternoon like John Henry, just putting down any card that suddenly occurred to her. They sat together in the kitchen, and the kitchen was a sad and ugly room. John Henry had covered the walls with queer, child drawings, as far up as his arm would reach. This gave the kitchen a crazy look, like that of a room in the crazy-house. And now the old kitchen made Frankie sick. The name for what had happened to her Frankie did not know, but she could feel her squeezed heart beating against the table edge.

'The world is certainy a small place,' she said.

'What makes you say that?"

'I mean sudden,' said Frankie. 'The world is certainy a sudden place.'

'Well, I don't know,' said Berenice. 'Sometimes sudden and sometimes slow.'

Frankie's eyes were half closed, and to her own ears her voice sounded ragged, far away:

'To me it is sudden.'

For only yesterday Frankie had never thought seriously about a wedding. She knew that her only brother, Jarvis, was to be married. He had become engaged to a girl in Winter Hill just before he went to Alaska. Jarvis was a corporal in the army and he had spent almost two years in Alaska. Frankie had not seen her brother for a long, long time, and his face had become masked and changing, like a face seen under water. But Alaska! Frankie had dreamed of it constantly, and especially this summer it was very real. She saw the snow and frozen sea and ice glaciers. Esquimau igloos and polar bears and the beautiful Northern lights. When Jarvis had first gone to Alaska, she had sent him a box of homemade fudge, packing it carefully and wrapping each piece separately in waxed paper. It had thrilled her to think that her fudge would be eaten in Alaska, and she had a vision of her brother passing it around to furry Esquimaux. Three months later, a thank-you letter had come from Jarvis with a five-dollar bill enclosed. For a while she mailed candy almost every week, sometimes divinity instead of fudge, but Jarvis did not send her another bill, except at Christmas time. Sometimes his short letters to her father disturbed her a little. For instance, this summer he mentioned once that he had been in swimming and that the mosquitoes were something fierce. This letter jarred upon her dream, but after a few days of bewilderment, she returned to her frozen seas and snow. When Jarvis had come back from Alaska, he had gone straight to Winter Hill. The bride was named Janice Evans and the plans for the wedding were like this: her brother had wired that he and the bride were coming this Friday to spend the day, then on the following Sunday there was to be the wedding at Winter Hill. Frankie and her father were going to the wedding, traveling nearly a hundred miles to Winter Hill, and Frankie had already packed a suitcase. She looked forward to the time her brother and the bride should come, but she did not picture them to herself, and did not think about the wedding. So on the day before the visit she only commented to Berenice:

'I think it's a curious coincidence that Jarvis would get to go to Alaska and that the very bride he picked to marry would come from a place called Winter Hill. Winter Hill,' she repeated slowly, her eyes closed, and the name blended with dreams of Alaska and cold snow. 'I wish tomorrow was Sunday instead of Friday. I wish I had already left town.'

'Sunday will come,' said Berenice.

'I doubt it,' said Frankie. 'I've been ready to leave this town so long. I wish I didn't have to come back here after the wedding. I wish I was going somewhere for good. I wish I had a hundred dollars and could just light out and never see this town again.'

'It seems to me you wish for a lot of things,' said Berenice.

'I wish I was somebody else except me.'

So the afternoon before it happened was like the other August afternoons. Frankie had hung around the kitchen, then toward dark she had gone out into the yard. The scuppernong arbor behind the house was purple and dark in the twilight. She walked slowly. John Henry West was sitting beneath the August arbor in a wicker chair, his legs crossed and his hands in his pockets.

'What are you doing?' she asked.

'I'm thinking.'

'About what?'

He did not answer.

Frankie was too tall this summer to walk beneath the arbor as she had always done before. Other twelve-year-old people could still walk around inside, give shows, and have a good time. Even small grown ladies could walk underneath the arbor. And already Frankie was too big; this year she had to hang around and pick from the edges like the grown people. She stared into the tangle of dark vines, and there was the smell of crushed scuppernongs and dust. Standing beside the arbor, with dark coming on, Frankie was afraid. She did not know what caused this fear, but she was afraid.

'I tell you what,' she said. 'Suppose you eat supper and spend the night with me.'

John Henry took his dollar watch from his pocket and looked at it as though the time would decide whether or not he would come, but it was too dark under the arbor for him to read the numbers.

'Go on home and tell Aunt Pet. I'll meet you in the kitchen.'

'All right.'

She was afraid. The evening sky was pale and empty and the light from the kitchen window made a yellow square reflection in the darkening yard. She remembered that when she was a little girl she believed that three ghosts were living in the coal house, and one of the ghosts wore a silver ring.

She ran up the back steps and said: 'I just now invited John Henry to eat supper and spend the night with me.'

Berenice was kneading a lump of biscuit dough, and she dropped it on the flour-dusted table. 'I thought you were sick and tired of him.'

'I am sick and tired of him,' said Frankie. 'But it seemed to me he looked scared.'

'Scared of what?'

Frankie shook her head. 'Maybe I mean lonesome,' she said finally.

'Well, I'll save him a scrap of dough.'

After the darkening yard the kitchen was hot and bright and queer. The walls of the kitchen bothered Frankie — the queer drawings of Christmas trees, airplanes, freak soldiers, flowers. John Henry had started the first pictures one long afternoon in June, and having already ruined the wall, he went on and drew whenever he wished. Sometimes Frankie had drawn also. At first her father had been furious about the walls, but later he said for them to draw all the pictures out of their systems, and he would have the kitchen painted in the fall. But as the summer lasted, and would not end, the walls had begun to bother Frankie. That evening the kitchen looked strange to her, and she was afraid.

She stood in the doorway and said: 'I just thought I might as well invite him.'

So at dark John Henry came to the back door with a little week-end bag. He was dressed in his white recital suit and had put on shoes and socks. There was a dagger buckled to his belt. John Henry had seen snow. Although he was only six years old, he had gone to Birmingham last winter, and there he had seen snow. Frankie had never seen snow.

'I'll take the week-end bag,' said Frankie. 'You can start right in making a biscuit man.'

'O.K.'

John Henry did not play with the dough; he worked on the biscuit man as though it were a very serious business. Now and then he stopped off, settled his glasses with his little hand, and studied what he had done. He was like a tiny watchmaker, and he drew up a chair and knelt on it so that he could get directly over the work. When Berenice gave him some raisins, he did not stick them all around as any other human child would do; he used only two for the eyes; but immediately he realized they were too large — so he divided one raisin carefully and put in eyes, two specks for the nose, and a little grinning raisin mouth. When he had finished, he wiped his hands on the seat of his shorts, and there was a little biscuit man with separate fingers, a hat on, and even walking stick. John Henry had worked so hard that the dough was now gray and wet. But it was a perfect little biscuit man, and, as a matter of fact, it reminded Frankie of John Henry himself.

'I better entertain you now,' she said.

They ate supper at the kitchen table with Berenice, since her father had telephoned that he was working late at his jewelry store. When Berenice brought the biscuit man from the oven, they saw that it looked exactly like any biscuit man ever made by a child — it had swelled so that all the work of John Henry had been cooked out, the fingers were run together, and the walking stick resembled a sort of tail. But John Henry just looked at it through his glasses, wiped it with his napkin, and buttered the left foot.

It was a dark, hot August night. The radio in the dining

room was playing a mixture of many stations: a war voice crossed with the gabble of an advertiser, and underneath there was the sleazy music of a sweet band. The radio had stayed on all the summer long, so finally it was a sound that as a rule they did not notice. Sometimes, when the noise became so loud that they could not hear their own ears, Frankie would turn it down a little. Otherwise, music and voices came and went and crossed and twisted with each other, and by August they did not listen any more.

'What do you want to do?' asked Frankie. 'Would you like for me to read to you out of Hans Brinker or would you rather do something else?'

'I rather do something else,' he said.

'What?'

'Less play out.'

'I don't want to,' Frankie said.

'There's a big crowd going to play out tonight.'

'You got ears,' Frankie said. 'You heard me.'

John Henry stood with his big knees locked, then finally he said: 'I think I better go home.'

'Why, you haven't spent the night! You can't eat supper and just go on off like that.'

'I know it,' he said quietly. Along with the radio they could hear the voices of the children playing in the night. 'But less go out, Frankie. They sound like they having a mighty good time.'

'No they're not,' she said. 'Just a lot of ugly silly children. Running and hollering and running and hollering. Nothing to it. We'll go upstairs and unpack your week-end bag.'

Frankie's room was an elevated sleeping porch which had been built onto the house, with a stairway leading up from the kitchen. The room was furnished with an iron bed, a bureau, and a desk. Also Frankie had a motor which could be turned on and off; the motor could sharpen knives, and, if they were long enough, it could be used for filing down your fingernails. Against the wall was the suitcase packed and ready for the trip to Winter Hill. On the desk there was a very old typewriter, and Frankie sat down before it, trying to think of any letters she could write: but there was nobody for her to write to, as every possible letter had already been answered, and answered even several times. So she covered the typewriter with a raincoat and pushed it aside.

'Honestly,' John Henry said, 'don't you think I better go home?'

'No,' she answered, without looking around at him. 'You sit there in the corner and play with the motor.'

Before Frankie there were now two objects — a lavender seashell and a glass globe with snow inside that could be shaken into a snowstorm. When she held the seashell to her ear, she could hear the warm wash of the Gulf of Mexico, and think of a green palm island far away. And she could hold the snow globe to her narrowed eyes and watch the whirling white flakes fall until they blinded her. She dreamed of Alaska. She walked up a cold white hill and looked on a snowy wasteland far below. She watched the sun make colors in the ice, and heard dream voices, saw dream things. And everywhere there was the cold white gentle snow.

'Look,' John Henry said, and he was staring out of the window. 'I think those big girls are having a party in their clubhouse.'

'Hush!' Frankie screamed suddenly. 'Don't mention those crooks to me.'

There was in the neighborhood a clubhouse, and Frankie was not a member. The members of the club were girls who were thirteen and fourteen and even fifteen years old. They had parties with boys on Saturday night. Frankie knew all of the club members, and until this summer she had been like a younger member of their crowd, but now they had this club and she was not a member. They had said she was too young and mean. On Saturday night she could hear the terrible music and see from far away their light. Sometimes she went around to the alley behind the clubhouse and stood near a honeysuckle fence. She stood in the alley and watched and listened. They were very long, those parties.

'Maybe they will change their mind and invite you,' John Henry said.

'The son-of-a-bitches.'

Frankie sniffled and wiped her nose in the crook of her arm. She sat down on the edge of the bed, her shoulders slumped and her elbows resting on her knees. 'I think they have been spreading it all over town that I smell bad,' she said. 'When I had those boils and that black bitter smelling ointment, old Helen Fletcher asked what was that funny smell I had. Oh, I could shoot every one of them with a pistol.'

She heard John Henry walking up to the bed, and then she felt his hand patting her neck with tiny little pats. 'I don't think you smell so bad,' he said. 'You smell sweet.'

'The son-of-a-bitches,' she said again. 'And there was something else. They were talking nasty lies about married people. When I think of Aunt Pet and Uncle Ustace. And my own father! The nasty lies! I don't know what kind of fool they take me for.'

'I can smell you the minute you walk in the house without even looking to see if it is you. Like a hundred flowers.'

'I don't care,' she said. 'I just don't care.'

'Like a thousand flowers,' said John Henry, and still he was patting his sticky hand on the back of her bent neck.

Frankie sat up, licked the tears from around her mouth, and wiped off her face with her shirttail. She sat still, her nose widened, smelling herself. Then she went to her suitcase and took out a bottle of Sweet Serenade. She rubbed some on the top of her head and poured some more down inside the neck of her shirt.

'Want some on you?'

John Henry was squatting beside the open suitcase and he gave a little shiver when she poured the perfume over him. He wanted to meddle in her traveling suitcase and look carefully at everything she owned. But Frankie only wanted him to get a general impression, and not count and know just what she had and what she did not have. So she strapped the suitcase and pushed it back against the wall.

'Boy!' she said. 'I bet I use more perfume than anybody in this town.'

The house was quiet except for the low rumble of the radio in the dining room downstairs. Long ago her father had come home and Berenice had closed the back door and gone away. There was no longer the sound of children's voices in the summer night.

'I guess we ought to have a good time,' said Frankie.

But there was nothing to do. John Henry stood, his knees locked and his hands clasped behind his back, in the middle of the room. There were moths at the window — pale green moths and yellow moths that fluttered and spread their wings against the screen.

'Those beautiful butterflies,' he said. 'They are trying to get in.'

Frankie watched the soft moths tremble and press against the window screen. The moths came every evening when the lamp on her desk was lighted. They came from out of the August night and fluttered and clung against the screen.

'To me it is the irony of fate,' she said. 'The way they come here. Those moths could fly anywhere. Yet they keep hanging around the windows of this house.'

John Henry touched the gold rim of his glasses to settle them on his nose and Frankie studied his flat little freckled face.

'Take off those glasses,' she said suddenly.

John Henry took them off and blew on them. She looked through the glasses and the room was loose and crooked. Then she pushed back her chair and stared at John Henry. There were two damp white circles around his eyes.

'I bet you don't need those glasses,' she said. She put her hand down on the typewriter. 'What is this?'

'The typewriter,' he said.

Frankie picked up the shell. 'And this?'

'The shell from the Bay.'

'What is that little thing crawling there on the floor?'

'Where?' he asked, looking around him.

'That little thing crawling along near your feet.'

'Oh,' he said. He squatted down. 'Why, it's an ant. I wonder how it got up here.'

Frankie tilted back in her chair and crossed her bare feet on her desk. 'If I were you I'd just throw those glasses away,' she said. 'You can see good as anybody.'

John Henry did not answer.

'They don't look becoming.'

She handed the folded glasses to John Henry and he wiped them with his pink flannel glasses rag. He put them back on and did not answer.

'O.K.' she said. 'Suit yourself. I was only telling you for your own good.'

They went to bed. They undressed with their backs turned to each other and then Frankie switched off the motor and the light. John Henry knelt down to say his prayers and he prayed for a long time, not saying the words aloud. Then he lay down beside her.

'Good night,' she said.

'Good night.'

Frankie stared up into the dark. 'You know it is still hard for me to realize that the world turns around at the rate of about a thousand miles an hour.'

'I know it,' he said.

'And to understand why it is that when you jump up in the air you don't come down in Fairview or Selma or somewhere fifty miles away.'

John Henry turned over and made a sleepy sound.

'Or Winter Hill,' she said. 'I wish I was starting for Winter Hill right now.'

Already John Henry was asleep. She heard him breathe in the darkness, and now she had what she had wanted so many nights that summer; there was somebody sleeping in the bed with her. She lay in the dark and listened to him breathe, then after a while she raised herself on her elbow. He lay freckled and small in the moonlight, his chest white and naked, and one foot hanging from the edge of the bed. Carefully she put her hand on his stomach and moved closer; it felt as though a little clock was ticking inside him and he smelled of sweat and Sweet Serenade. He smelled like a sour little rose. Frankie leaned down and licked him behind the ear. Then she breathed deeply, settled herself with her chin on his sharp damp shoulder, and closed her eyes: for now, with somebody sleeping in the dark with her, she was not so much afraid.

The sun woke them early the next morning, the white August sun. Frankie could not make John Henry go home. He saw the ham Berenice was cooking, and that the special company dinner was going to be good. Frankie's father read the paper in the living room, then went downtown to wind the watches at his jewelry store.

'If that brother of mine don't bring me a present from Alaska, I will be seriously mad,' said Frankie.

'Me too,' agreed John Henry.

And what were they doing that August morning when her brother and the bride came home? They were sitting in the arbor shade and talking about Christmas. The glare was hard and bright, the sun-drunk bluejays screamed and murdered among themselves. They talked, and their voices tired down into a little tune and they said the same things over and over. They just drowsed in the dark shade of the arbor, and Frankie was a person who had never thought about a wedding. That was the way they were that August morning when her brother and the bride walked in the house.

'Oh, Jesus!' Frankie said. The cards on the table were greasy and the late sun slanted across the yard. 'The world is certainy a sudden place.'

'Well, stop commenting about it,' said Berenice. 'You don't have your mind on the game.'

Frankie, however, had some of her mind on the game. She played the queen of spades, which were trumps, and

John Henry threw off a little two of diamonds. She looked at him. He was staring at the back of her hand as though what he wanted and needed was angled eyesight that could cut around corners and read people's cards.

'You got a spade,' said Frankie.

John Henry put his donkey necklace in his mouth and looked away.

'Cheater,' she said.

'Go on and play your spade,' said Berenice.

Then he argued: 'It was hid behind the other card.'

'Cheater.'

But still he would not play. He sat there sad and holding up the game.

'Make haste,' said Berenice.

'I can't,' he said finally. 'It's a jack. The only spade I got is a jack. I don't want to play my jack down under Frankie's queen. I'm not going to do it either.'

Frankie threw her cards down on the table. 'See!' she said to Berenice. 'He don't even follow the first beginning laws! He is a child! It is hopeless! Hopeless! Hopeless!'

'Maybe so,' said Berenice.

'Oh,' Frankie said, 'I am sick unto death.'

She sat with her bare feet on the rungs of the chair, her eyes closed, and her chest against the table edge. The red greasy cards were messed together on the table, and the sight of them made Frankie sick. They had played cards after dinner every single afternoon; if you would eat those old cards, they would taste like a combination of all the dinners of that August, together with a sweaty-handed nasty taste. Frankie swept the cards from the table. The wedding was bright and beautiful as snow and the heart in her was mashed. She got up from the table.

'It is a known truth that gray-eyed people are jealous.'

'I told you I wasn't jealous,' Frankie said, and she was walking fast around the room. 'I couldn't be jealous of one of them without being jealous of them both. I sociate the two of them together.'

'Well, I were jealous when my foster brother married,' said Berenice. 'I admit that when John married Clorina I sent a warning I would tear the ears off her head. But you see I didn't. Clorina got ears like anybody else. And now I love her.'

'J A,' said Frankie. 'Janice and Jarvis. Isn't that the strangest thing?'

'What?'

'J A,' she said. 'Both their names begin with J A.'

'And? What about it?'

Frankie walked round and round the kitchen table. 'If only my name was Jane,' she said. 'Jane or Jasmine.'

'I don't follow your frame of mind,' said Berenice.

'Jarvis and Janice and Jasmine. See?'

'No,' said Berenice. 'By the way, I heard this morning on the radio that the French people are chasing the Germans out of Paris.'

'Paris,' Frankie repeated in a hollow tone. 'I wonder if it is against the law to change your name. Or to add to it.'

'Naturally. It is against the law.'

'Well, I don't care,' she said. 'F. Jasmine Addams.'

On the staircase leading to her room there was a doll, and John Henry brought it to the table and sat rocking it in his arms. 'You serious when you gave me this,' he said. He pulled up the doll's dress and fingered the real panties and body-waist. 'I will name her Belle.'

Frankie stared at the doll for a minute. 'I don't know

what went on in Jarvis's mind when he brought me that doll. Imagine bringing me a doll! And Janice tried to explain that she had pictured me as a little girl. I had counted on Jarvis bringing me something from Alaska.'

'Your face when you unwrapped the package was a study,' said Berenice.

It was a large doll with red hair and china eyes that opened and closed, and yellow eyelashes. John Henry held her in a lying-down position, so that the eyes were shut, and he was now trying to open them by pulling up the eyelashes.

'Don't do that! It makes me nervous. In fact, take that doll somewhere out of my sight.'

John Henry took it to the back porch where he could pick it up when he went home.

'Her name is Lily Belle,' he said.

The clock ticked very slowly on the shelf above the stove, and it was only quarter to six. The glare outside the window was still hard and yellow and bright. In the back yard the shade beneath the arbor was black and solid. Nothing moved. From somewhere far away came the sound of whistling, and it was a grieving August song that did not end. The minutes were very long.

Frankie went again to the kitchen mirror and stared at her own face. 'The big mistake I made was to get this close crew-cut. For the wedding I ought to have long bright yellow hair. Don't you think so?'

She stood before the mirror and she was afraid. It was the summer of fear, for Frankie, and there was one fear that could be figured in arithmetic with paper and a pencil at the table. This August she was twelve and five-sixths years old. She was five feet five and three quarter inches tall, and she wore a number seven shoe. In the past year she had grown four inches, or at least that was what she judged. Already the hateful little summer children hollered to her: 'Is it cold up there?' And the comments of grown people made Frankie shrivel on her heels. If she reached her height on her eighteenth birthday, she had five and one-sixth growing years ahead of her. Therefore, according to mathematics and unless she could somehow stop herself, she would grow to be over nine feet tall. And what would be a lady who is over nine feet high? She would be a Freak.

In the early autumn of every year the Chattahoochee Exposition came to town. For a whole October week the fair went on down at the fair grounds. There was the Ferris Wheel, the Flying Jinney, the Palace of Mirrors — and there, too, was the House of the Freaks. The House of the Freaks was a long pavilion which was lined on the inside with a row of booths. It cost a quarter to go into the general tent, and you could look at each Freak in his booth. Then there were special private exhibitions farther back in the tent which cost a dime apiece. Frankie had seen all of the members of the Freak House last October:

The Giant
The Fat Lady
The Midget
The Wild Nigger
The Pin Head
The Alligator Boy
The Half-Man Half-Woman

The Giant was more than eight feet high, with huge loose hands and a hang-jaw face. The Fat Lady sat in a chair, and the fat on her was like loose-powdered dough which she kept slapping and working with her hands — next was the squeezed Midget who minced around in little trick evening clothes. The Wild Nigger came from a savage island. He squatted in his booth among the dusty bones and palm leaves and he ate raw living rats. The fair gave a free admission to his show to all who brought rats of the right size, and so children carried them down in strong sacks and shoe boxes. The Wild Nigger knocked the rat's head over his squatted knee and ripped off the fur and crunched and gobbled and flashed his greedy Wild Nigger eyes. Some said that he was not a genuine Wild Nigger, but a crazy colored man from Selma. Anyway, Frankie did not like to watch him very long. She pushed through the crowd to the Pin Head booth, where John Henry had stood all afternoon. The little Pin Head skipped and giggled and sassed around, with a shrunken head no larger than an orange, which was shaved except for one lock tied with a pink bow at the top. The last booth was always very crowded, for it was the booth of the Half-Man Half-Woman, a morphidite and a miracle of science. This Freak was divided completely in half — the left side was a man and the right side a woman. The costume on the left was a leopard skin and on the right side a brassiere and a spangled skirt. Half the face was dark-bearded and the other half bright glazed with paint. Both eyes were strange. Frankie had wandered around the tent and looked at every booth. She was afraid of all the Freaks, for it seemed to her that they had looked at her in a secret way and tried to connect their eyes with hers, as though to say: we know you. She was afraid of their long Freak eyes. And all the year she had remembered them, until this day.

'I doubt if they ever get married or go to a wedding,' she said. 'Those Freaks.'

'What freaks you talking about?' asked Berenice.

'At the fair,' said Frankie. 'The ones we saw there last October.'

'Oh, those folks.'

'I wonder if they make a big salary,' she said.

And Berenice answered: 'How would I know?'

John Henry held out an imaginary skirt and, touching his finger to the top of his big head, he skipped and danced like the Pin Head around the kitchen table.

Then he said: 'She was the cutest little girl I ever saw. I never saw anything so cute in my whole life. Did you, Frankie?'

'No,' she said. 'I didn't think she was cute.'

'Me and you both,' said Berenice.

'Shoo!' John Henry argued. 'She was, too.'

'If you want my candy opinion,' said Berenice, 'that whole crowd of folks down yonder at the fair just give me the creeps. Ever last one of them.'

Frankie watched Berenice through the mirror, and finally she asked in a slow voice. 'Do *I* give you the creeps?'

'You?' asked Berenice.

'Do you think I will grow into a Freak?' Frankie whispered.

'You?' said Berenice again. 'Why, certainy not, I trust Jesus.'

Frankie felt better. She looked sidewise at herself in the mirror. The clock ticked six slow times, and then she said: 'Well, do you think I will be pretty?'

'Maybe. If you file down them horns a inch or two.'

Frankie stood with her weight resting on her left leg, and

she slowly shuffled the ball of her right foot on the floor. She felt a splinter go beneath the skin. 'Seriously,' she said.

'I think when you fill out you will do very well. If you behave.'

'But by Sunday,' Frankie said. 'I want to do something to improve myself before the wedding.'

'Get clean for a change. Scrub your elbows and fix yourself nice. You will do very well.'

Frankie looked for a last time at herself in the mirror, and then she turned away. She thought about her brother and the bride, and there was a tightness in her that would not break.

'I don't know what to do. I just wish I would die.'

'Well, die then!' said Berenice.

And: 'Die,' John Henry echoed in a whisper.

The world stopped.

'Go home,' said Frankie to John Henry.

He stood with his big knees locked, his dirty little hand on the edge of the white table, and he did not move.

'You heard me,' Frankie said. She made a terrible face at him and grabbed the frying pan that hung above the stove. She chased him three times around the table, then up through the front hall and out of the door. She locked the front door and called again: 'Go home.'

'Now what makes you act like that?' asked Berenice. 'You are too mean to live.'

Frankie opened the door to the stairway that led up to her room, and sat down on one of the lower steps. The kitchen was silent and crazy and sad.

'I know it,' she said. 'I intend to sit still by myself and think over everything for a while.'

This was the summer when Frankie was sick and tired of being Frankie. She hated herself, and had become a loafer and a big no-good who hung around the summer kitchen: dirty and greedy and mean and sad. Besides being too mean to live, she was a criminal. If the Law knew about her, she could be tried in the courthouse and locked up in the jail. Yet Frankie had not always been a criminal and a big no-good. Until the April of that year, and all the years of her life before, she had been like other people. She belonged to a club and was in the seventh grade at school. She worked for her father on Saturday morning and went to the show every Saturday afternoon. She was not the kind of person ever to think of being afraid. At night she slept in the bed with her father, but not because she was scared of the dark.

Then the spring of that year had been a long queer season. Things began to change and Frankie did not understand this change. After the plain gray winter the March winds banged on the windowpanes, and clouds were shirred and white on the blue sky. April that year came sudden and still, and the green of the trees was a wild bright green. The pale wistarias bloomed all over town, and silently the blossoms shattered. There was something about the green trees and the flowers of April that made Frankie sad. She did not know why she was sad, but because of this peculiar sadness, she began to realize she ought to leave the town. She read the war news and thought about the world and packed her suitcase to go away; but she did not know where she should go.

It was the year when Frankie thought about the world. And she did not see it as a round school globe, with the countries neat and different-colored. She thought of the world as huge and cracked and loose and turning a thousand miles an hour. The geography book at school was out of date; the countries of the world had changed. Frankie read the war news in the paper, but there were so many foreign places, and the war was happening so fast, that sometimes she did not understand. It was the summer when Patton was chasing the Germans across France. And they were fighting, too, in Russia and Saipan. She saw the battles, and the soldiers. But there were too many different battles, and she could not see in her mind the millions and millions of soldiers all at once. She saw one Russian soldier, dark and frozen with a frozen gun, in Russian snow. The single Japs with slanted eyes on a jungle island gliding among green vines. Europe and the people hung in trees and the battleships on the blue oceans. Four-motor planes and burning cities and a soldier in a steel war helmet, laughing. Sometimes these pictures of the war, the world, whirled in her mind and she was dizzy. A long time ago she had predicted that it would take two months to win the whole war, but now she did not know. She wanted to be a boy and go to the war as a Marine. She thought about flying aeroplanes and winning gold medals for bravery. But she could not join the war, and this made her sometimes feel restless and blue. She decided to donate blood to the Red Cross; she wanted to donate a quart a week and her blood would be in the veins of Australians and Fighting French and Chinese, all over the whole world, and it would be as though she were close kin to all of these people. She could hear the army doctors saying that the blood of Frankie Addams was the reddest and the strongest blood that they had ever known. And she could picture ahead, in the years after the war, meeting the soldiers who had her blood, and they would say that they owed their life to her; and they would not call her Frankie — they would call her Addams. But this plan for donating her blood to the war did not come true. The Red Cross would not take her blood. She was too young. Frankie felt mad with the Red Cross, and left out of everything. The war and the world were too fast and big and strange. To think about the world for very long made her afraid. She was not afraid of Germans or bombs or Japanese. She was afraid because in the war they would not include her, and because the world seemed somehow separate from herself.

So she knew she ought to leave the town and go to some place far away. For the late spring, that year, was lazy and too sweet. The long afternoons flowered and lasted and the green sweetness sickened her. The town began to hurt Frankie. Sad and terrible happenings had never made Frankie cry, but this season many things made Frankie suddenly wish to cry. Very early in the morning she would sometimes go out into the yard and stand for a long time looking at the sunrise sky. And it was as though a question came into her heart, and the sky did not answer. Things she had never noticed much before began to hurt her: home lights watched from the evening sidewalks, an unknown voice from an alley. She would stare at the lights and listen to the voice, and something inside her stiffened and waited. But the lights would darken, the voice fall silent, and though she waited, that was all. She was afraid of these things that made her suddenly wonder who she was, and what she was going to be in the world, and why she was standing at that minute, seeing a light, or listening, or staring up into the sky: alone. She was afraid, and there was a queer tightness in her chest.

One night in April, when she and her father were going to

bed, he looked at her and said, all of a sudden: 'Who is this great big long-legged twelve-year-old blunderbuss who still wants to sleep with her old Papa.' And she was too big to sleep with her father any more. She had to sleep in her upstairs room alone. She began to have a grudge against her father and they looked at each other in a slant-eyed way. She did not like to stay at home.

She went around town, and the things she saw and heard seemed to be left somehow unfinished, and there was the tightness in her that would not break. She would hurry to do something, but what she did was always wrong. She would call her best friend, Evelyn Owen, who owned a football suit and a Spanish shawl, and one would dress in the football suit and the other in the Spanish shawl and they would go down to the ten-cent store together. But that was a wrong thing and not what Frankie wanted. Or after the pale spring twilights, with the smell of dust and flowers sweet and bitter in the air, evenings of lighted windows and the long drawn calls at supper time, when the chimney swifts had gathered and whirled above the town and flown off somewhere to their home together, leaving the sky empty and wide; after the long twilights of this season, when Frankie had walked around the sidewalks of the town, a jazz sadness quivered her nerves and her heart stiffened and almost stopped.

Because she could not break this tightness gathering within her, she would hurry to do something. She would go home and put the coal scuttle on her head, like a crazy person's hat, and walk around the kitchen table. She would do anything that suddenly occurred to her — but whatever she did was always wrong, and not at all what she had wanted. Then, having done these wrong and silly things, she would stand, sickened and empty, in the kitchen door and say:

'I just wish I could tear down this whole town.'

'Well, tear it down, then. But quit hanging around here with that gloomy face. Do something.'

And finally the troubles started.

She did things and she got herself in trouble. She broke the law. And having once become a criminal, she broke the law again, and then again. She took the pistol from her father's bureau drawer and carried it all over town and shot up the cartridges in a vacant lot. She changed into a robber and stole a three-way knife from the Sears and Roebuck Store. One Saturday afternoon in May she committed a secret and unknown sin. In the MacKeans' garage, with Barney MacKean, they committed a queer sin, and how bad it was she did not know. The sin made a shriveling sickness in her stomach, and she dreaded the eyes of everyone. She hated Barney and wanted to kill him. Sometimes alone in the bed at night she planned to shoot him with the pistol or throw a knife between his eyes.

Her best friend, Evelyn Owen, moved away to Florida, and Frankie did not play with anybody any more. The long and flowering spring was over and the summer in the town was ugly and lonesome and very hot. Every day she wanted more and more to leave the town: to light out for South America or Hollywood or New York City. But although she packed her suitcase many times, she could never decide to which of these places she ought to go, or how she would get there by herself.

So she stayed home and hung around the kitchen, and the summer did not end. By dog days she was five feet five and three-quarter inches tall, a great big greedy loafer who was too mean to live. She was afraid, but not as she had been before. There was only the fear of Barney, her father, and the Law. But even these fears were finally gone; after a long time the sin in the MacKeans' garage became far from her and was remembered only in her dreams. And she would not think of her father or the Law. She stuck close in the kitchen with John Henry and Berenice. She did not think about the war, the world. Nothing hurt her any longer; she did not care. She never stood alone in the back yard in order to stare up at the sky. She paid no attention to sounds and summer voices, and did not walk the streets of town at night. She would not let things make her sad and she would not care. She ate and wrote shows and practiced throwing knives against the side of the garage and played bridge at the kitchen table. Each day was like the day before, except that it was longer, and nothing hurt her any more.

So that Sunday when it happened, when her brother and the bride came to the house, Frankie knew that everything was changed; but why this was so, and what would happen to her next, she did not know. And though she tried to talk with Berenice, Berenice did not know either.

'It gives me this kind of a pain,' she said, 'to think about them.'

'Well, don't,' said Berenice. 'You done nothing but think and carry on about them all this afternoon.'

Frankie sat on the bottom step of the stairs to her room, staring into the kitchen. But although it gave her a kind of a pain, she had to think about the wedding. She remembered the way her brother and the bride had looked when she walked into the living room, that morning at eleven o'clock. There had been in the house a sudden silence, for

Jarvis had turned off the radio when they came in; after the long summer, when the radio had gone on day and night, so that no one heard it any more, the curious silence had startled Frankie. She stood in the doorway, coming from the hall, and the first sight of her brother and the bride had shocked her heart. Together they made in her this feeling that she could not name. But it was like the feelings of the spring, only more sudden and more sharp. There was the same tightness and in the same queer way she was afraid. Frankie thought until her mind was dizzy and her foot had gone to sleep.

Then she asked Berenice: 'How old were you when you married your first husband?'

While Frankie was thinking, Berenice had changed into her Sunday clothes, and now she sat reading a magazine. She was waiting for the people who were due to meet her at six o'clock, Honey and T. T. Williams; the three of them were going to eat supper at the New Metropolitan Tea Room and sashay together around the town. As Berenice read, she moved her lips to shape each word. Her dark eye looked up as Frankie spoke, but, since Berenice did not raise her head, the blue glass eye seemed to go on reading the magazine. This two-sighted expression bothered Frankie.

'I were thirteen years old,' said Berenice.

'What made you get married so young for?'

'Because I wanted to,' said Berenice. 'I were thirteen years old and I haven't growed a inch since.'

Berenice was very short, and Frankie looked hard at her and asked: 'Does marrying really stop your growth?'

'It certainy do,' said Berenice.

'I didn't know that,' Frankie said.

Berenice had been married four different times. Her

first husband was Ludie Freeman, a brickmason, and the favorite and best one of the four; he gave Berenice her fox fur, and once they had gone to Cincinnati and seen snow. Berenice and Ludie Freeman had seen a whole winter of Northern snow. They loved each other and were married for nine years, until the November he was sick and died. The other three husbands were all bad, each one worse than the one before, and it made Frankie blue just to hear about them. The first was a sorry old liquor-drinker. The next went crazy on Berenice: he did crazy things, had eating dreams in the night and swallowed a corner of the sheet; and what with one thing and another he distracted Berenice so much that finally she had to quit him. The last husband was terrible. He gouged out Berenice's eye and stole her furniture away from her. She had to call the Law on him.

'Did you marry with a veil every time?' asked Frankie.

'Two times with a veil,' said Berenice.

Frankie could not keep still. She walked around the kitchen, although there was a splinter in her right foot and she was limping, her thumbs hooked in the belt of her shorts and her undershirt clinging and wet.

Finally she opened the drawer of the kitchen table and selected a long sharp butcher knife. Then she sat down and rested the ankle of her sore foot on her left knee. The sole of her foot was long and narrow, pitted with ragged whitish scars, as every summer Frankie stepped on many nails; Frankie had the toughest feet in town. She could slice off waxy yellow rinds from the bottoms of her feet, and it did not hurt her very much, although it would hurt other people. But she did not chisel for the splinter immediately — she just sat there, her ankle on her knee and the knife in her right hand, looking across the table at Berenice.

'Tell me,' she said. 'Tell me exactly how it was.'

'You know!' said Berenice. 'You seen them.'

'But tell me,' Frankie said.

'I will discuss it for the last time,' said Berenice. 'Your brother and the bride come late this morning and you and John Henry hurried in from the back yard to see them. Then next thing I realize you busted back through the kitchen and run up to your room. You came down with your organdie dress on and lipstick a inch thick from one ear to the next. Then you all just sat around up in the living room. It was hot. Jarvis had brought Mr. Addams a bottle of whiskey and they had liquor drinks and you and John Henry had lemonade. Then after dinner your brother and the bride took the three-o'clock train back to Winter Hill. The wedding will be this coming Sunday. And that is all. Now, is you satisfied?'

'I am so disappointed they couldn't stay longer — at least spend the night. After Jarvis being away so long. But I guess they want to be together as long as they can. Jarvis said he had some army papers to fill out at Winter Hill.' She took a deep breath. 'I wonder where they will go after the wedding.'

'On their honeymoon. Your brother will have a few days' leave.'

'I wonder where that honeymoon will be.'

'Well, I'm sure I don't know.'

'Tell me,' Frankie said again. 'Exactly what did they look like?'

'Look like?' said Berenice. 'Why, they looked natural. Your brother is a good-looking blond white boy. And the girl is kind of brunette and small and pretty. They make a nice white couple. You seen them, Foolish.'

Frankie closed her eyes, and, though she did not see them as a picture, she could feel them leaving her. She could feel the two of them together on the train, riding and riding away from her. They were them, and leaving her, and she was her, and sitting left all by herself there at the kitchen table. But a part of her was with them, and she could feel this part of her own self going away, and farther away; farther and farther, so that a drawn-out sickness came in her, going away and farther away, so that the kitchen Frankie was an old hull left there at the table.

'It is so queer,' she said.

She bent over the sole of her foot, and there was something wet, like tears or sweat drops on her face; she sniffled and began to cut for the splinter.

'Don't that hurt you none?' asked Berenice.

Frankie shook her head and did not answer. Then after a moment she said: 'Have you ever seen any people that afterward you remembered more like a feeling than a picture?'

'How you mean?'

'I mean this,' said Frankie slowly. 'I saw them O.K. Janice had on a green dress and green high-heel dainty shoes. Her hair was done up in a knot. Dark hair and a little piece of it was loose. Jarvis sat by her on the sofa. He had on his brown uniform and he was sunburned and very clean. They were the two prettiest people I ever saw. Yet it was like I couldn't see all of them I wanted to see. My brains couldn't gather together quick enough and take it all in. And then they were gone. You see what I mean?'

'You hurting yourself,' said Berenice. 'What you need is a needle.'

'I don't care anything about my old feet,' Frankie said.

It was only half-past six, and the minutes of the afternoon were like bright mirrors. From outside there was no longer the sound of whistling and in the kitchen nothing moved. Frankie sat facing the door that opened onto the back porch. There was a square cat-hole cut in a corner of the back door, and near-by a saucer of lavender sour milk. In the beginning of dog days Frankie's cat had gone away. And the season of dog days is like this: it is the time at the end of the summer when as a rule nothing can happen — but if a change does come about, that change remains until dog days are over. Things that are done are not undone and a mistake once made is not corrected.

That August Berenice scratched a mosquito bite under her right arm and it became a sore: that sore would never heal until dog days were over. Two little families of August gnats picked out the corners of John Henry's eyes to settle down in, and though he often shook himself and blinked, those gnats were there to stay. Then Charles disappeared. Frankie did not see him leave the house and walk away, but on the fourteenth of August, when she called him to his supper, he did not come, and he was gone. She looked for him everywhere and sent John Henry wailing out his name through all the streets of town. But it was the season of dog days and Charles did not come back again. Every afternoon Frankie said exactly the same words to Berenice, and the answers of Berenice were always the same. So that now the words were like an ugly little tune they sang by heart.

'If only I just knew where he has gone.'

'Quit worrying yourself about that old alley cat. I done told you he ain't coming back.'

'Charles is not alley. He is almost pure Persian.'

'Persian as I is,' Berenice would say. 'You seen the last of that old tom cat. He gone off to hunt a friend.'

'To hunt a friend?'

'Why, certainy. He roamed off to find himself a lady-friend.'

'You really think so?'

'Naturally.'

'Well, why don't he bring his friend home with him. He ought to know I would be only too glad to have a whole family of cats.'

'You seen the last of that old alley cat.'

'If only I just knew where he is gone.'

And so each gloomy afternoon their voices sawed against each other, saying the same words, which finally reminded Frankie of a raggedy rhyme said by two crazies. She would end by telling Berenice: 'It looks to me like everything has just walked off and left me.' And she would put her head down on the table and feel afraid.

But this afternoon Frankie suddenly changed all this. An idea came to her, and she put down the knife and got up from the table.

'I know what I ought to do,' she suddenly said. 'Listen.'

'I can hear.'

'I ought to notify the police force. They will find Charles.'

'I wouldn't do that,' said Berenice.

Frankie went to the hall telephone and explained to the Law about her cat. 'He is almost pure Persian,' she said. 'But with short hair. A very lovely color of gray and with a little white spot on his throat. He answers to the name of *Charles*, but if he don't answer to that, he might come if you call *Charlina*. My name is Miss F. Jasmine Addams and the address is 124 Grove Street.'

Berenice was giggling when she came back, a soft high giggle. 'Whew! They going to send around here and tie you up and drag you off to Milledgeville. Them fat blue police chasing tomcats around alleys and hollering: *Oh Charles, Oh come here, Charlina!* Sweet Jesus!'

'Aw, shut up,' Frankie said.

Berenice was sitting at the table; she had stopped giggling and her dark eye roved in a teasing way as she sloshed coffee into a white china saucer to cool.

'At the same time,' she said, 'I can't see how it is such a wise idea to trifle around with the Law. No matter for what reason.'

'I'm not trifling with the Law.'

'You just now set there and spelled them out your name and your house number. Where they can lay hold of you if ever they take the notion.'

'Well, let them!' said Frankie angrily. 'I don't care! I don't care!' And suddenly she did not care if anybody knew she was a criminal or not. 'Let them come get me for all I care.'

'I was just teasing you,' said Berenice. 'The trouble with you is that you don't have no sense of humor any more.'

'Maybe I'd be better off in jail.'

Frankie walked around the table and she could feel them going away. The train was traveling to the North. Mile after mile they went away, farther and farther away from the town, and as they traveled to the North, a coolness came into the air and dark was falling like the evening dark of wintertime. The train was winding up into the hills, the whistle wailing in a winter tone, and mile after mile they went away. They passed among themselves a box of bought store candy, with chocolates set in dainty, pleated shells, and watched the winter miles pass by the window. Now they had gone a long, long way from town and soon would be in Winter Hill.

'Sit down,' said Berenice. 'You make me nervous.'

Suddenly Frankie began to laugh. She wiped her face with the back of her hand and went back to the table. 'Did you hear what Jarvis said?'

'What?'

Frankie laughed and laughed.

'They were talking about whether to vote for C. P. MacDonald. And Jarvis said: *Why, I wouldn't vote for that scoundrel if he was running to be the dog-catcher*. I never heard anything so witty in my life.'

Berenice did not laugh. Her dark eye glanced down in a corner, quickly saw the joke, and then looked back at Frankie. Berenice wore her pink crepe dress and her hat with the pink plume was on the table. The blue glass eye made the sweat on her dark face look bluish also. Berenice was stroking the hat plume with her hand.

'And you know what Janice remarked?' asked Frankie. 'When Papa mentioned about how much I've grown, she said she didn't think I looked so terribly big. She said she got the major portion of her growth before she was thirteen. She did, Berenice!'

'O.K.! All right.'

'She said she thought I was a lovely size and would probably not grow any taller. She said all fashion models and movie stars ——'

'She did not,' said Berenice. 'I heard her. She only remarked that you probably had already got your growth. But she didn't go on and on like that. To hear you tell it, anybody would think she took her text on the subject.'

'She said ——'

'This is a serious fault with you, Frankie. Somebody just makes a loose remark and then you cozen it in your mind until nobody would recognize it. Your Aunt Pet happened to mention to Clorina that you had sweet manners and Clorina passed it on to you. For what it was worth. Then next thing I know you are going all around and bragging how Mrs. West thought you had the finest manners in town and ought to go to Hollywood, and I don't know what all you didn't say. You keep building on to any little compliment you hear about yourself. Or, if it is a bad thing, you do the same. You cozen and change things too much in your own mind. And that is a serious fault.'

'Quit preaching at me,' Frankie said.

'I ain't preaching. It is the solemn truth.'

'I admit it a little,' said Frankie finally. She closed her eyes and the kitchen was very quiet. She could feel the beating of her heart, and when she spoke her voice was a whisper. 'What I need to know is this. Do you think I made a good impression?'

'Impression? Impression?'

'Yes,' said Frankie, her eyes still closed.

'Well, how would I know?' said Berenice.

'I mean how did I act? What did I do?'

'Why, you didn't do anything.'

'Nothing?' asked Frankie.

'No. You just watched the pair of them like they was ghosts. Then, when they talked about the wedding, them ears of yours stiffened out the size of cabbage leaves ——'

Frankie raised her hand to her left ear. 'They didn't,' she said bitterly. Then after a while she added. 'Some day you going to look down and find that big fat tongue of yours pulled out by the roots and laying there before you on the table. Then how do you think you will feel?'

'Quit talking so rude,' said Berenice.

Frankie scowled down at the splinter in her foot. She finished cutting it out with the knife and said, 'That would have hurt anybody else but me.' Then she was walking round and round the room again. 'I am so scared I didn't make a good impression.'

'What of it?' said Berenice. 'I wish Honey and T. T. would come on. You make me nervous.'

Frankie drew up her left shoulder and bit her lower lip. Then suddenly she sat down and banged her forehead on the table.

'Come on,' said Berenice. 'Don't act like that.'

But Frankie sat stiff, her face in the crook of her elbow and her fists clenched tight. Her voice had a ragged and strangled sound. 'They were so pretty,' she was saying. 'They must have such a good time. And they went away and left me.'

'Sit up,' said Berenice. 'Behave yourself.'

'They came and went away,' she said. 'They went away and left me with this feeling.'

'Hooee!' said Berenice finally. 'I bet I know something.'

The kitchen was silent and she tapped four times with her heel: one, two, three — *bang!* Her live eye was dark and teasing and she tapped with her heel, then took up the beating with a dark jazz voice that was like a song.

Frankie got a crush!
Frankie got a crush!
Frankie got a crush!
On the *Wedd*-ing!

'Quit,' said Frankie.

Frankie got a crush!
Frankie got a crush!

Berenice went on and on, and her voice was jazzed like the heart that beats in your head when you have fever. Frankie was dizzy, and she picked up the knife from the kitchen table.

'You better quit!'

Berenice stopped very suddenly. The kitchen was suddenly shrunken and quiet.

'You lay down that knife.'

'Make me.'

She steadied the end of the handle against her palm and bent the blade slowly. The knife was limber, sharp, and long.

'Lay it down, DEVIL!'

But Frankie stood up and took careful aim. Her eyes were narrowed and the feel of the knife made her hands stop trembling.

'Just throw it!' said Berenice. 'You just!'

All the house was very quiet. The empty house seemed to be waiting. And then there was the knife whistle in the air and the sound the blade made when it struck. The knife hit the middle of the stairway door and shivered there. She watched the knife until it did not shiver any longer.

'I am the best knife-thrower in this town,' she said.

Berenice, who stood behind her, did not speak.

'If they would have a contest I would win.'

Frankie pulled the knife from the door and laid it on the kitchen table. Then she spat on her palm and rubbed her hands together.

Berenice said finally: 'Frances Addams, you going to do that once too often.'

'I never miss outside of a few inches.'

'You know what your father said about knife-throwing in this house.'

'I warned you to quit picking with me.'

'You are not fit to live in a house,' said Berenice.

'I won't be living in this one much longer. I'm going to run away from home.'

'And a good riddance to a big old bad rubbage,' said Berenice.

'You wait and see. I'm leaving town.'

'And where you think you are going?'

Frankie looked at all the corners of the room, and then said, 'I don't know.'

'I do,' said Berenice. 'You going crazy. That's where you going.'

'No,' said Frankie. She stood very still, looking around the queerly pictured wall, and then she closed her eyes. 'I'm going to Winter Hill. I'm going to the wedding. And I swear to Jesus by my two eyes I'm never coming back here any more.'

She had not been sure that she would throw the knife until it struck and shivered on the stairway door. And she had not known that she would say these words until already they were spoken. The swear was like the sudden knife;

she felt it strike in her and tremble. Then when the words were quiet, she said again:

'After the wedding I'm not coming back.'

Berenice pushed back the damp bangs of Frankie's hair and finally she asked: 'Sugar? You serious?'

'Of course!' said Frankie. 'Do you think I would stand here and swear that swear and tell a story? Sometimes, Berenice, I think it takes you longer to realize a fact than it does anybody who ever lived.'

'But,' said Berenice, 'you say you don't know where you're going. You going, but you don't know where. That don't make no sense to me.'

Frankie stood looking up and down the four walls of the room. She thought of the world, and it was fast and loose and turning, faster and looser and bigger than ever it had been before. The pictures of the War sprang out and clashed together in her mind. She saw bright flowered islands and a land by a northern sea with the gray waves on the shore. Bombed eyes and the shuffle of soldiers' feet. Tanks and a plane, wing broken, burning and downward-falling in a desert sky. The world was cracked by the loud battles and turning a thousand miles a minute. The names of places spun in Frankie's mind: China, Peachville, New Zealand, Paris, Cincinnati, Rome. She thought of the huge and turning world until her legs began to tremble and there was sweat on the palms of her hands. But still she did not know where she should go. Finally she stopped looking around the four kitchen walls and said to Berenice:

'I feel just exactly like somebody has peeled all the skin off me. I wish I had some cold good chocolate ice cream.'

Berenice had her hands on Frankie's shoulders and was

shaking her head and staring with the live eye narrowed into Frankie's face.

'But every word I told you was the solemn truth,' she said. 'I'm not coming back here after the wedding.'

There was a sound, and when they turned they saw that Honey and T. T. Williams were standing in the doorway. Honey, though he was her foster brother, did not resemble Berenice — and it was almost as though he came from some foreign country, like Cuba or Mexico. He was light-skinned, almost lavender in color, with quiet narrow eyes like oil, and a limber body. Behind the two of them stood T. T. Williams, and he was very big and black; he was gray-haired, older even than Berenice, and he wore a church suit with a red badge in the buttonhole. T. T. Williams was a beau of Berenice, a well-off colored man who owned a colored restaurant. Honey was a sick, loose person. The army would not include him, and he had shoveled in a gravel pit until he broke one of his insides and could not do heavy work any more. They stood, the three of them, dark and grouped together in the door.

'What you all creep up like that for?' asked Berenice. 'I didn't even hear you.'

'You and Frankie too busy discussing something,' said T. T.

'I am ready to go,' said Berenice. 'I been ready. But do you wish a small little quickie before we start?'

T. T. Williams looked at Frankie and shuffled his feet. He was very proper, and he liked to please everybody, and he always wanted to do the right thing.

'Frankie ain't no tattle-tale,' said Berenice. 'Is you?'

Frankie would not even answer such a question. Honey wore a dark red rayon slack suit and she said: 'That sure is a cute suit you got on, Honey. Where did you get it?'

Honey could talk like a white school-teacher; his lavender lips could move as quick and light as butterflies. But he only answered with a colored word, a dark sound from the throat that can mean anything. 'Ahhnnh,' he said.

The glasses were before them on the table, and the hair-straightening bottle that held gin, but they did not drink. Berenice said something about Paris and Frankie had the extra feeling that they were waiting for her to leave. She stood in the door and looked at them. She did not want to go away.

'You wish water in yours, T. T.?' asked Berenice.

They were together around the table and Frankie stood extra in the door alone. 'So long, you all,' she said.

''Bye, Sugar,' said Berenice. 'You forget all that foolishness we was discussing. And if Mr. Addams don't come home by dark, you go on over to the Wests. Go play with John Henry.'

'Since when have I been scared of the dark?' said Frankie. 'So long.'

'So long,' they said.

She closed the door, but behind her she could hear their voices. With her head against the kitchen door she could hear the murmuring dark sounds that rose and fell in a gentle way. Ayee — ayee. And then Honey spoke above the idle wash of voices and he asked: 'What was it between you and Frankie when we come in the house?' She waited, her ear pressed close against the door, to hear what Berenice would say. And finally the words were: 'Just foolishness. Frankie was carrying on with foolishness.' She listened until at last she heard them go away.

The empty house was darkening. She and her father

were alone at night, as Berenice went to her own home directly after supper. Once they had rented the front bedroom. It was the year after her grandmother died, when Frankie was nine. They rented the front bedroom to Mr. and Mrs. Marlowe. The only thing Frankie remembered about them was the remark said at the last, that they were common people. Yet for the season they were there, Frankie was fascinated by Mr. and Mrs. Marlowe and the front room. She loved to go in when they were away and carefully, lightly meddle with their things — with Mrs. Marlowe's atomizer which skeeted perfume, the gray-pink powder puff, the wooden shoe-trees of Mr. Marlowe. They left mysteriously after an afternoon that Frankie did not understand. It was a summer Sunday and the hall door of the Marlowes' room was open. She could see only a portion of the room, part of the dresser and only the footpiece of the bed with Mrs. Marlowe's corset on it. But there was a sound in the quiet room she could not place, and when she stepped over the threshold she was startled by a sight that, after a single glance, sent her running to the kitchen, crying: Mr. Marlowe is having a fit! Berenice had hurried through the hall, but when she looked into the front room, she merely bunched her lips and banged the door. And evidently told her father, for that evening he said the Marlowes would have to leave. Frankie had tried to question Berenice and find out what was the matter. But Berenice had only said that they were common people and added that with a certain party in the house they ought at least to know enough to shut a door. Though Frankie knew she was the certain party, still she did not understand. What kind of a fit was it? she asked. But Berenice would only answer: Baby, just a common fit. And Frankie knew from the voice's tones that there was more to it than she was told. Later she only remembered the Marlowes as common people, and being common they owned common things — so that long after she had ceased to think about the Marlowes or fits, remembering merely the name and the fact that once they had rented the front bedroom, she associated common people with gray-pink powder puffs and perfume atomizers. The front bedroom had not been rented since.

Frankie went to the hall hatrack and put on one of her father's hats. She looked at her dark ugly mug in the mirror. The conversation about the wedding had somehow been wrong. The questions she had asked that afternoon had all been the wrong questions, and Berenice had answered her with jokes. She could not name the feeling in her, and she stood there until dark shadows made her think of ghosts.

Frankie went out to the street before the house and looked up into the sky. She stood staring with her fist on her hip and her mouth open. The sky was lavender and slowly darkening. She heard in the neighborhood the sound of evening voices and noticed the light fresh smell of watered grass. This was the time of the early evening when, since the kitchen was too hot, she would go for a little while outdoors. She practiced knife-throwing, or sat before the cold-drink store in the front yard. Or she would go around to the back yard, and there the arbor was cool and dark. She wrote shows, although she had outgrown all of her costumes, and was too big to act in them beneath the arbor; this summer she had written very cold shows — shows about Esquimaux and frozen explorers. Then when night had come she would go again back in the house.

But this evening Frankie did not have her mind on knives or cold-drink stores or shows. Nor did she want to stand there staring up into the sky; for her heart asked the old questions, and in the old way of the spring she was afraid.

She felt she needed to think about something ugly and plain, so she turned from the evening sky and stared at her own house. Frankie lived in the ugliest house in town, but now she knew that she would not be living there much longer. The house was empty, dark. Frankie turned and walked to the end of the block, and around the corner, and down the sidewalk to the Wests'. John Henry was leaning against the banisters of his front porch, with a lighted window behind him, so that he looked like a little black paper doll on a piece of yellow paper.

'Hey,' she said. 'I wonder when that Papa of mine is coming home from town.'

John Henry did not answer.

'I don't want to go back in that dark old ugly house all by myself.'

She stood on the sidewalk, looking at John Henry, and the smart political remark came back to her. She hooked her thumb in the pockets of her pants and asked: 'If you were going to vote in an election, who would you vote for?'

John Henry's voice was bright and high in the summer night. 'I don't know,' he said.

'For instance, would you cast your vote for C. P. MacDonald to be mayor of this town?'

John Henry did not answer.

'Would you?'

But she could not get him to talk. There were times when John Henry would not answer anything you said to him. So she had to remark without an argument behind her, and all by herself like that it did not sound so very smart: 'Why, I wouldn't vote for him if he was running to be dog-catcher.'

The darkening town was very quiet. For a long time now her brother and the bride had been at Winter Hill. They had left the town a hundred miles behind them, and now were in a city far away. They were them and in Winter Hill, together, while she was her and in the same old town all by herself. The long hundred miles did not make her sadder and make her feel more far away than the knowing that they were them and both together and she was only her and parted from them, by herself. And as she sickened with this feeling a thought and explanation suddenly came to her, so that she knew and almost said aloud: *They are the we of me.* Yesterday, and all the twelve years of her life, she had only been Frankie. She was an *I* person who had to walk around and do things by herself. All other people had a *we* to claim, all other except her. When Berenice said *we*, she meant Honey and Big Mama, her lodge, or her church. The *we* of her father was the store. All members of clubs have a *we* to belong to and talk about. The soldiers in the army can say *we*, and even the criminals on chain-gangs. But the old Frankie had had no *we* to claim, unless it would be the terrible summer *we* of her and John Henry and Berenice — and that was the last *we* in the world she wanted. Now all this was suddenly over with and changed. There was her brother and the bride, and it was as though when first she saw them something she had known inside of her: *They are the we of me.* And that was why it made her feel so queer, for them to be away in Winter Hill while she was left all by herself; the hull of the old Frankie left there in the town alone.

'Why are you all bent over like that?' John Henry called.

'I think I have a kind of pain,' said Frankie. 'I must have ate something.'

John Henry was still standing on the banisters, holding to the post.

'Listen,' she said finally. 'Suppose you come on over and eat supper and spend the night with me.'

'I can't,' he answered.

'Why?'

John Henry walked across the banisters, holding out his arms for balance, so that he was like a little blackbird against the yellow window light. He did not answer until he safely reached the other post.

'Just because.'

'Because why?'

He did not say anything, and so she added: 'I thought maybe me and you could put up my Indian tepee and sleep out in the back yard. And have a good time.'

Still John Henry did not speak.

'We're blood first cousins. I entertain you all the time. I've given you so many presents.'

Quietly, lightly, John Henry walked back across the banisters and then stood looking out at her with his arm around the post again.

'Sure enough,' she called. 'Why can't you come?'

At last he said. 'Because, Frankie, I don't want to.'

'Fool jackass!' she screamed. 'I only asked you because I thought you looked so ugly and so lonesome.'

Lightly John Henry jumped down from the banisters. And his voice as he called back to her was a clear child's voice.

'Why, I'm not a bit lonesome.'

Frankie rubbed the wet palms of her hands along the sides of her shorts and said in her mind: Now turn around and take yourself on home. But in spite of this order, she was somehow unable to turn around and go. It was not yet night. Houses along the street were dark, lights showed in windows. Darkness had gathered in the thick-leaved trees and shapes in the distance were ragged and gray. But the night was not yet in the sky.

'I think something is wrong,' she said. 'It is too quiet. I have a peculiar warning in my bones. I bet you a hundred dollars it's going to storm.'

John Henry watched her from behind the banister.

'A terrible terrible dog day storm. Or maybe even a cyclone.'

Frankie stood waiting for the night. And just at that moment a horn began to play. Somewhere in the town, not far away, a horn began a blues tune. The tune was grieving and low. It was the sad horn of some colored boy, but who he was she did not know. Frankie stood stiff, her head bent and her eyes closed, listening. There was something about the tune that brought back to her all of the spring: flowers, the eyes of strangers, rain.

The tune was low and dark and sad. Then all at once, as Frankie listened, the horn danced into a wild jazz spangle that zigzagged upward with sassy nigger trickiness. At the end of the jazz spangle the music rattled thin and far away. Then the tune returned to the first blues song, and it was like the telling of that long season of trouble. She stood there on the dark sidewalk and the drawn tightness of her heart made her knees lock and her throat feel stiffened. Then, without warning, the thing happened that at first Frankie could not believe. Just at the time when the tune should be laid, the music finished, the horn broke off. All of a sudden the horn stopped playing. For a moment Frankie could not take it in, she felt so lost.

She whispered finally to John Henry West: 'He has stopped to bang the spit out of his horn. In a second he will finish.'

But the music did not come again. The tune was left broken, unfinished. And the drawn tightness she could no longer stand. She felt she must do something wild and sudden that never had been done before. She hit herself on the head with her fist, but that did not help any at all. And she began to talk aloud, although at first she paid no attention to her own words and did not know in advance what she would say.

'I told Berenice that I was leaving town for good and she did not believe me. Sometimes I honestly think she is the biggest fool that ever drew breath.' She complained aloud, and her voice was fringed and sharp like the edge of a saw. She talked and did not know from one word to the next what she would say. She listened to her own voice, but the words she heard did not make much sense. 'You try to impress something on a big fool like that and it's just like talking to a block of cement. I kept on telling and telling and telling her. I told her I had to leave this town for good because it is inevitable.'

She was not talking to John Henry. She did not see him any more. He had moved from the lighted window; but he was still listening from the porch, and after a little while he asked her:

'Where?'

Frankie did not answer. She was suddenly very still and quiet. For a new feeling had come to her. The sudden feeling was that she knew deep in her where she would go. She knew, and in another minute the name of the place would come to her. Frankie bit the knuckles of her fist and waited: but she did not hunt for the name of the place and did not think about the turning world. She saw in her mind her brother and the bride, and the heart in her was squeezed so hard that Frankie almost felt it break.

John Henry was asking in his high child voice: 'You want me to eat supper and sleep in the tepee with you?'

She answered: 'No.'

'You just a little while ago invited me!'

But she could not argue with John Henry West or answer anything he said. For it was just at that moment that Frankie understood. She knew who she was and how she was going into the world. Her squeezed heart suddenly opened and divided. Her heart divided like two wings. And when she spoke her voice was sure.

'I know where I'm going,' she said.

He asked her: 'Where?'

'I'm going to Winter Hill,' she said. 'I'm going to the wedding.'

She waited, to give him a chance to say: 'I already knew that, anyhow.' Then finally she spoke the sudden truth aloud.

'I'm going with them. After the wedding at Winter Hill, I'm going off with the two of them to whatever place that they will ever go. I'm going with them.'

He did not answer.

'I love the two of them so much. We'll go to every place together. It's like I've known it all my life, that I belong to be with them. I love the two of them so much.'

And having said this, she did not need to wonder and

puzzle any more. She opened her eyes, and it was night. The lavender sky had at last grown dark and there was slanted starlight and twisted shade. Her heart had divided like two wings and she had never seen a night so beautiful.

Frankie stood looking into the sky. For when the old question came to her — the who she was and what she would be in the world, and why she was standing there that minute — when the old question came to her, she did not feel hurt and unanswered. At last she knew just who she was and understood where she was going. She loved her brother and the bride and she was a member of the wedding. The three of them would go into the world and they would always be together. And finally, after the scared spring and the crazy summer, she was no more afraid.

PART TWO

1

THE DAY before the wedding was not like any day that F. Jasmine had ever known. It was the Saturday she went into the town, and suddenly, after the closed blank summer, the town opened before her and in a new way she belonged. Because of the wedding, F. Jasmine felt connected with all she saw, and it was as a sudden member that on this Saturday she went around the town. She walked the streets entitled as a queen and mingled everywhere. It was the day when, from the beginning, the world seemed no longer separate from herself and when all at once she felt included. Therefore, many things began to happen — nothing that came about surprised F. Jasmine and, until the last at least, all was natural in a magic way.

At the country house of an uncle of John Henry, Uncle Charles, she had seen old blindered mules going round and round in the same circle, grinding juice from the sugar cane for syrup. In the sameness of her tracks that summer, the old Frankie had somehow resembled that country mule; in town she browsed around the counters of the ten-cent store, or sat on the front row of the Palace show, or hung around her father's store, or stood on street corners watching soldiers. Now this morning was altogether different. She went into places she had never dreamed of entering until that day. For one thing, F. Jasmine went to a hotel — it was not the finest hotel in the town, or even the next to the finest, but nevertheless it was a hotel and F. Jasmine was there. Furthermore, she was there with a soldier, and that, too, was an unforeseen event, as she had never in her life laid eyes on him until that day. Only yesterday, if the old Frankie had glimpsed a box-like vision of this scene, as a view seen through a wizard's periscope, she would have bunched her mouth with unbelief. But it was a morning when many things occurred, and a curious fact about this day was a twisted sense of the astonishing; the unexpected did not make her wonder, and only the long known, the familiar, struck her with a strange surprise.

The day began when she waked up at dawn, and it was as though her brother and the bride had, in the night, slept on the bottom of her heart, so that the first instant she recognized the wedding. Next, and immediately, she thought about the town. Now that she was leaving home she felt in a curious way as though on this last day the town called to her and was now waiting. The windows of her room were cool dawn-blue. The old cock at the MacKeans' was crowing. Quickly she got up and turned on the bed-lamp and the motor.

It was the old Frankie of yesterday who had been puzzled, but F. Jasmine did not wonder any more; already she felt familiar with the wedding for a long, long time. The black dividing night has something to do with this. In the twelve years before, whenever a sudden change had come about there was a certain doubt during the time when it was happening; but after sleeping through a night, and on the very next day, the change did not seem so sudden after all. Two summers past, when she had traveled with the Wests to Port Saint Peter on the bay, the first sea evening with the scalloped gray ocean and empty sand was to her like a foreign place, and she had gone around with slanted eyes and put her hands on things in doubt. But after the first night, as soon as she awoke next day, it was as though she had known Port Saint Peter all her life. Now it was likewise with the wedding. No longer questioning, she turned to other things.

She sat at her desk wearing only the blue-and-white striped trousers of her pajamas which were rolled up above the knees, vibrating her right foot on the ball of her bare foot, and considering all that she must do on this last day. Some of these things she could name to herself, but there were other things that could not be counted on her fingers or made into a list with words. To start with, she decided to make herself some visiting cards with *Miss F. Jasmine Addams, Esq.*, engraved with squinted letters on a tiny card. So she put on her green visor eyeshade, cut up some cardboard, and fitted ink pens behind both ears. But her mind was restless and zigzagged to other things, and soon she began to get ready for town. She dressed carefully that morning in her most grown and best, the pink organdie, and put on lipstick and Sweet Serenade. Her father, a very early riser, was stirring in the kitchen when she went downstairs.

'Good morning, Papa.'

Her father was Royal Quincy Addams and he owned a jewelry store just off the main street of the town. He answered her with a kind of grunt, for he was a grown person who liked to drink three cups of coffee before he started conversation for the day; he deserved a little peace and quiet before he put his nose down to the grindstone. F. Jasmine had heard him bungling about his room when once she waked up to drink water in the night, and his face was pale as cheese this morning, his eyes had a pink and ragged look. It was a morning when he despised a saucer because his cup would rattle against it and not fit, so he put his cup down on the table or stove top until brown circles were left all over everywhere and flies settled in quiet rings. There was some sugar spilt on the floor, and each time his step made a gritty sound his face shivered. This morning he wore a pair of saggy-kneed gray trousers and a blue shirt unfastened at the collar and with the tie loose. Since June she had had this secret grudge against him that almost she did not admit — since the night he had asked who was the great big blunderbuss who still wanted to sleep with her old Papa — but now she had this grudge no longer. All of a sudden it seemed to F. Jasmine that she saw her father for the first time, and she did not see him only as he was at that one minute, but pictures of the old days swirled in her mind and crossed each other. Remembrance, changing and fast, made F. Jasmine stop very still and stand with her head cocked, watching him both in the actual room and from somewhere inside her. But there were things that must be said, and when she spoke her voice was not unnatural.

'Papa, I think I ought to tell you now. I'm not coming back here after the wedding.'

He had ears to hear with, loose large ears with lavender rims, but he did not listen. He was a widowman, for her mother had died the very day that she was born — and, as a widowman, set in his ways. Sometimes, especially in the early morning, he did not listen to things she said or new suggestions. So she sharpened her voice and chiseled the words into his head.

'I have to buy a wedding dress and some wedding shoes and a pair of pink, sheer stockings.'

He heard and, after a consideration, gave her a permission nod. The grits boiled slowly with blue gluey bubbles, and as she set the table, she watched him and remembered. There were the winter mornings with frost flowers on the windowpanes and the roaring stove and the look of his brown crusty hand as he leaned over her shoulder to help with a hard part of the last-minute arithmetic that she was working at the table, his voice explaining. Blue long spring evenings, she saw also, and her father on the dark front porch with his feet propped on the banisters, drinking the frosted bottles of beer he had sent her to bring home from Finny's Place. She saw him bent over the workbench down at the store, dipping a tiny spring in gasoline, or whistling and peering with his round jeweler's glass into a watch. Remembrances came sudden and swirled, each colored with its own season, and for the first time she looked back on all the twelve years of her life and thought of them from a distance as a whole.

'Papa,' she said, 'I will write you letters.'

Now he walked the dawn-stale kitchen like a person who has lost something, but has forgotten what it is that he has lost. Watching him, the old grudge was forgotten, and she felt sorry. He would miss her in the house all by himself when she was gone. He would be lonesome. She wanted to speak some sorry words and love her father, but just at that moment he cleared his throat in the special way he used when he was going to lay down the law to her and said:

'Will you please tell me what has become of the monkey-wrench and screw-driver that were in my tool chest on the back porch?'

'The monkey-wrench and screw-driver ——' F. Jasmine

stood with her shoulders hunched, her left foot drawn up to the calf of the right leg. 'I borrowed them, Papa.'

'Where are they now?'

F. Jasmine considered. 'Over at the Wests'.'

'Now pay attention and listen to me,' her father said, holding the spoon that had been stirring the grits, and shaking it to mark the words. 'If you don't have the sense and judgment to leave things alone ——' He stared at her in a long and threatening way, and finished: 'You'll have to be taught. From now on you walk the chalkline. Or you'll have to be taught.' He sniffed suddenly. 'Is that toast burning?'

It was still early in the morning when F. Jasmine left the house that day. The soft gray of the dawn had lightened and the sky was the wet pale blue of a watercolor sky just painted and not yet dried. There was a freshness in the bright air and cool dew on the burnt brown grass. From a back yard down the street, F. Jasmine could hear children's voices. She heard the calling voices of the neighborhood children who were trying to dig a swimming pool. They were all sizes and ages, members of nothing, and in the summers before, the old Frankie had been like leader or president of the swimming-pool diggers in that part of town — but now that she was twelve years old, she knew in advance that, though they would work and dig in various yards, not doubting to the very last the cool clear swimming pool of water, it would all end in a big wide ditch of shallow mud.

Now, as F. Jasmine crossed her yard, she saw in her mind's eye the swarming children and heard from down the street their chanting cries — and this morning, for the first time in her life, she heard a sweetness in these sounds, and she was touched. And, strange to say, her own home yard which she had hated touched her a little too; she felt she had not seen it for a long time. There, under the elm tree was her old cold-drink store, a light packing case that could be dragged around according to the shade, with a sign reading, DEW DROP INN. It was the time of morning when, the lemonade in a bucket underneath the store, she used to settle herself with her bare feet on the counter and the Mexican hat tilted down over her face — her eyes closed, smelling the strong smell of sun-warmed straw, waiting. And sometimes there would be customers, and she would send John Henry to the A. & P. to buy some candy, but other times the Tempter Satan got the best of her and she drank up all the stock instead. But now this morning the store looked very small and staggered, and she knew that she would never run it any more. F. Jasmine thought of the whole idea as something over and done with that had happened long ago. A sudden plan came to her: after tomorrow, when she was with Janice and Jarvis, in the far place where they would be, she would look back on the old days and — But this was a plan F. Jasmine did not finish, for, as the names lingered in her mind, the gladness of the wedding rose up inside her and, although the day was an August day, she shivered.

The main street, too, seemed to F. Jasmine like a street returned to after many years, although she had walked up and down it only Wednesday. There were the same brick stores, about four blocks of them, the big white bank, and in the distance the many-windowed cotton mill. The wide street was divided by a narrow aisle of grass on either side of which the cars drove slowly in a browsing way. The glittering gray sidewalks and passing people, the striped awning over the stores, all was the same — yet, as she walked the street that morning, she felt free as a traveler who had never seen the town before.

And that was not all; she had no sooner walked down the left side of the main street and up again on the right sidewalk, when she realized a further happening. It had to do with various people, some known to her and others strangers, she met and passed along the street. An old colored man, stiff and proud on his rattling wagon seat, drove a sad blindered mule down toward the Saturday market. F. Jasmine looked at him, he looked at her, and to the outward appearance that was all. But in that glance, F. Jasmine felt between his eyes and her own eyes a new unnamable connection, as though they were known to each other — and there even came an instant vision of his home field and country roads and quiet dark pine trees as the wagon rattled past her on the paved town street. And she wanted him to know her, too — about the wedding.

Now the same thing happened again and again on those four blocks: with a lady going into MacDougal's store, with a small man waiting for the bus before the big First National Bank, with a friend of her father's called Tut Ryan. It was a feeling impossible to explain in words — and later when she tried to tell of it at home Berenice raised up her eyebrows and dragged the word in a mocking way: Connection? Connection? But nevertheless it was there, this feeling — a connection close as answers to calls. Furthermore, on the sidewalk before the First National Bank she found a dime and any other day that would have been a grand surprise, but now this morning she only paused to shine the dime on her dress front and put it in her pink pocketbook. Under the fresh blue early sky the feeling as she walked along was one of newly risen lightness, power, entitlement.

It was in a place called the Blue Moon that she first told about the wedding, and she came to the Blue Moon in a roundabout way, as it was not on the main street, but on the street called Front Avenue which bordered the river. She was in this neighborhood because she had heard the organ of the monkey and the monkey-man and had set out immediately to find them. She had not seen the monkey and the monkey-man through the whole summer and it seemed a sign to her that she should run across them on this last day in town. She had not seen them for so long that sometimes she thought the pair of them might even be dead. They did not go around the streets in wintertime, for the cold wind made them sick; they went South in October to Florida and came back to the town in warm late spring.

They, the monkey and the monkey-man, wandered to other towns also — but the old Frankie would come across them on various shaded streets through all the summers she could remember, except this one. He was a darling little monkey, and the monkey-man was nice also; the old Frankie had always loved them, and now she was dying to tell her plans and let them know about the wedding. So, when she first heard the broken-sounding, faint organ, she went at once in search of it, and the music seemed to come from near the river on Front Avenue. So she turned from the main street and hurried down the side street, but just before she reached Front Avenue the organ stopped, and when she gazed up and down the avenue she could not see the monkey or the monkey-man and all was silent and they were nowhere in sight. They had stopped, maybe, in a doorway or a shop — so F. Jasmine walked slowly with a watchful air.

Front Avenue was a street that had always drawn her, although it had the sorriest, smallest stores in town. On the left side of the street there were warehouses, and in between were glimpses of brown river and green trees. On the right side there was a place with a sign reading Prophylactic Military, the business of which had often puzzled her, then other various places: a smelly fish shop with the shocked eyes of a single fish staring from some crushed ice in the window, a pawnshop, a second-hand clothing store with out-of-style garments hanging from the narrow entrance and a row of broken shoes lined up on the sidewalk outside. Then finally there was the place called the Blue Moon. The street itself was cobbled with brick and angry-looking in the glare, and along the gutter she passed some eggshells and rotten lemon peels. It was not a fine street, but nevertheless the old Frankie had liked to come here now and then at certain times.

The street was quiet in the mornings and on the week-day afternoons. But toward evening, or on holidays, the street would fill with the soldiers who came from the camp nine miles away. They seemed to prefer Front Avenue to almost any other street, and sometimes the pavement resembled a flowing river of brown soldiers. They came to town on holidays and went around in glad, loud gangs together, or walked the sidewalks with grown girls. And the old Frankie had always watched them with a jealous heart; they came from all over the whole country and were soon going all over the world. They went around in gangs together, those lasting twilights of the summertime — while the old Frankie dressed in her khaki shorts and Mexican hat, watched from a distance by herself. Noises and weathers of distant places seemed to hover about them in the air.

She imagined the many cities that these soldiers came from, and thought of the countries where they would go — while she was stuck there in the town forever. And stealing jealousy sickened her heart. But now this morning her heart was occupied with one intention: to tell of the wedding and her plans. So, after walking down the burning pavement, hunting for the monkey and the monkey-man, she came to the Blue Moon and it occurred to her that maybe they were there.

The Blue Moon was a place at the end of Front Avenue, and often the old Frankie had stood out on the sidewalk with her palms and nose pressed flat against the screen door, watching all that went on there. Customers, most of them soldiers, sat at the boothed tables, or stood at the counter having drinks, or crowded around the juke-box. Here sometimes there were sudden commotions. Late one afternoon when she passed the Blue Moon, she heard wild angry voices and a sound like a bottle being thrown, and as she stood there a policeman came out on the sidewalk pushing and jerking a torn-looking man with wobbly legs. The man was crying, shouting; there was blood on his ripped shirt and dirty tears dripped down his face. It was an April afternoon of rainbow showers, and by and by the Black Maria screamed down the street, and the poor, arrested criminal was thrown into the prisoners' cage and carried off down to the jail. The old Frankie knew the Blue Moon well, although she had never been inside. There was no written law to keep her out, no lock and chain on the screen door. But she had known in an unworded way that it was a forbidden place to children. The Blue Moon was a place for holiday soldiers and the grown and free. The old Frankie had known she had no valid right to enter there, so she had only hung around the edges and never once had she gone inside. But now this morning before the wedding all of this was changed. The old laws she had known before meant nothing to F. Jasmine, and without a second thought she left the street and went inside.

There in the Blue Moon was the red-headed soldier who was to weave in such an unexpected way through all that day before the wedding. F. Jasmine, however, did not notice him at first; she looked for the monkey-man, but he was not there. Aside from the soldier the only other person in the room was the Blue Moon owner, a Portuguese, who stood behind the counter. This was the person F. Jasmine picked to be the first to hear about the wedding, and he was chosen simply because he was the one most likely and near.

After the fresh brightness of the street, the Blue Moon seemed dark. Blue neon lights burned over the dim mirror behind the counter, tinting the faces in the place pale green, and an electric fan turned slowly so that the room was scalloped with warm stale waves of breeze. At that early morning hour the place was very quiet. There were booth tables across the room, all empty. At the back of the Blue Moon a lighted wooden stairway led up to the second floor. The place smelled of dead beer and morning coffee. F. Jasmine ordered coffee from the owner behind the counter, and after he had brought it to her, he sat down on a stool across from her. He was a sad, pale man with a very flat face. He wore a long white apron and, hunched on the stool with his feet on the rungs, he was reading a romance magazine. The telling of the wedding gathered inside her, and when it was so ready she could no longer resist, she hunted in her mind a good opening remark — something grown and offhand, to start between them the conversation. She said in a voice that trembled a little: 'It certainly has been an unseasonable summer, hasn't it?'

The Portuguese at first did not seem to hear her and went on reading the romance magazine. So she repeated her remark, and when his eyes were turned to hers and his attention caught, she went on in a higher voice: 'Tomorrow this brother of mine and his bride are marrying at Winter Hill.' She went straight to the story, as a circus dog breaks through the paper hoop, and as she talked, her voice became clearer, more definite, and sure. She told her plans in a way that made them sound completely settled, and not in the least open to question. The Portuguese listened with his head cocked to one side, his dark eyes ringed with ash-gray circles, and now and then he wiped his damp veined dead-white hands on his stained apron. She told about the wedding and her plans and he did not dispute with her or doubt.

It is far easier, it came to her as she remembered Berenice, to convince strangers of the coming to pass of dearest wants than those in your own home kitchen. The thrill of speaking certain words — Jarvis and Janice, wedding and Winter Hill — was such that F. Jasmine, when she had finished, wanted to start all over again. The Portuguese took form behind his ear a cigarette which he tapped on the counter but did not light. In the unnatural neon glow his face looked startled, and when she had finished he did not speak. With the telling of the wedding still sounding inside her, as the last chord of a guitar murmurs a long time after the strings are struck, F. Jasmine turned toward the entrance and the framed blazing street beyond the door: dark people passed along the sidewalk and footsteps echoed in the Blue Moon.

'It gives me a funny feeling,' she said. 'After living in this town all my whole life, to know that after tomorrow I'll never be back here any more.'

It was then she noticed him for the first time, the soldier who at the very end would twist so strangely that last, long day. Later, on thinking back, she tried to recall some warning hint of future craziness — but at the time he looked to her like any other soldier standing at a counter drinking beer. He was not tall, nor short, nor fat, nor thin — except for the red hair there was nothing at all unusual about him. He was one of the thousands of soldiers who came to the town from the camp near-by. But as she looked into this soldier's eyes, in the dim light of the Blue Moon, she realized that she gazed at him in a new way.

That morning, for the first time, F. Jasmine was not jealous. He might have come from New York or California — but she did not envy him. He might be on his way to England or India — she was not jealous. In the restless spring and crazy summer, she had watched the soldiers with a sickened heart, for they were the ones who came and went, while she was stuck there in the town forever. But now, on this day before the wedding, all this was changed; her eyes as she looked into the soldier's eyes were clear of jealousy and want. Not only did she feel that unexplainable connection she was to feel between herself and other total strangers of that day, there was another sense of recognition: it seemed to F. Jasmine they exchanged the special look of friendly, free travelers who meet for a moment at some stop along the way. The look was long. And with the lifting of the jealous weight, F. Jasmine felt at peace. It was quiet in the Blue

Moon, and the telling of the wedding seemed still to murmur in the room. After this long gaze of fellow travelers, it was the soldier who finally turned his face away.

'Yes,' said F. Jasmine, after a moment and to no one in particular, 'it gives me a mighty funny feeling. In a way it's like I ought to do all the things I would have done if I was staying in the town forever. Instead of this one day. So I guess I better get a move on. Adios.' She spoke the last word to the Portuguese, and at the same time her hand reached automatically to lift the Mexican hat she had worn all summer until that day, but, finding nothing, the gesture withered and her hand felt shamed. Quickly she scratched her head, and with a last glance at the soldier, left the Blue Moon.

It was the morning different from all other mornings she had ever known because of several reasons. First, of course, there was the telling of the wedding. Once, and a long time ago, the old Frankie had liked to go around the town playing a game. She had walked all around — through the north side of town with the grass-lawned houses and the sad mills section and colored Sugarville — wearing her Mexican hat and the high-laced boots and a cowboy rope tied round her waist, she had gone around pretending to be Mexican. Me no speak English — Adios Buenos Noches — abla pokie peekie poo, she had jabbered in mock Mexican. Sometimes a little crowd of children gathered and the old Frankie would swell up with pride and trickery — but when the game was over, and she was home, there would come over her a cheated discontent. Now this morning reminded her of those old days of the Mexican game. She went to the same places, and the people, mostly strangers to her, were the same. But this morning she was not trying to trick people and pretend; far from it, she wanted only to be recognized for her true self. It was a need so strong, this want to be known and recognized, that F. Jasmine forgot the wild hard glare and choking dust and miles (it must have been at least five miles) of wandering all over town.

A second fact about that day was the forgotten music that sprang suddenly into her mind — snatches of orchestra minuets, march tunes and waltzes, and the jazz horn of Honey Brown — so that her feet in the patent-leather shoes stepped always according to a tune. A last difference about that morning was the way her world seemed layered in three different parts, all the twelve years of the old Frankie, the present day itself, and the future ahead when the J A three of them would be together in all the many distant places.

As she walked along, it seemed as though the ghost of the old Frankie, dirty and hungry-eyed, trudged silently along not far from her, and the thought of the future, after the wedding, was constant as the very sky. That day alone seemed equally important as both the long past and the bright future — as a hinge is important to a swinging door. And since it was the day when past and future mingled, F. Jasmine did not wonder that it was strange and long. So these were the main reasons why F. Jasmine felt, in an unworded way, that this was a morning different from all mornings she had ever known. And of all these facts and feelings the strongest of all was the need to be known for her true self and recognized.

Along the shaded sidewalks on the north side of the town, near the main street, she passed a row of lace-curtained boarding houses with empty chairs behind the banisters until she came upon a lady sweeping her front porch. To this lady, after the opening remark about the weather, F. Jasmine told her plans and, as with the Portuguese in the Blue Moon café and all the other people she was to meet that day, the telling of the wedding had an end and a beginning, a shape like a song.

First, just at the moment she commenced, a sudden hush came in her heart; then, as the names were named and the plan unfolded, there was a wild rising lightness and at the end content. The lady meanwhile leaned on the broom, listening. Behind her there was a dark open hall, with a bare stairway, and to the left a table for letters, and from this dark hall came the strong hot smell of cooking turnip greens. The strong waves of smell and the dark hall seemed to mingle with F. Jasmine's joy, and when she looked into the lady's eyes, she loved her, though she did not even know her name.

The lady neither argued nor accused. She did not say anything. Until at the very end, just as F. Jasmine turned to go, she said: 'Well, I declare.' But already F. Jasmine, a quick gay band tune marching her feet, was hurrying on her way again.

In a neighborhood of shaded summer lawns she turned down a side street and met some men mending the road. The sharp smell of melted tar and hot gravel and the loud tractor filled the air with noisy excitement. It was the tractor-man F. Jasmine chose to hear her plans — running beside him, her head thrown back to watch his sunburned face, she had to cup her hands around her mouth to make her voice heard. Even so it was uncertain if he understood, for when she stopped, he laughed and yelled back to her something she could not quite catch. Here, among the racket and excitement, was the place F. Jasmine saw the ghost of the old Frankie plainest of all — hovering close to the commotion, chewing a great big lump of tar, hanging around at noon to watch the lunch-pails being opened. There was a fine big motorcycle parked near the street-menders, and before going on F. Jasmine looked at it admiringly, then spat on the broad leather seat and shined it carefully with her fist. She was in a very nice neighborhood near the edge of town, a place of new brick houses with flower-bordered sidewalks and cars parked in paved driveways; but the finer the neighborhood, the fewer people are about, so F. Jasmine turned back toward the center of the town. The sun burned like an iron lid on her head and her slip was stuck wet to her chest, and even the organdie dress was wet and clinging in spots also. The march tune had softened to a dreaming song on a violin that slowed her footsteps to a wander. To this kind of music she crossed to the opposite side of the town, beyond the main street and the mill, to the gray crooked streets of the mill section, where, among the choking dust and sad gray rotten shacks, there were more listeners to tell about the wedding.

(From time to time, as she went around, a little conversation buzzed on the bottom of her mind. It was the voice of Berenice when later she would know about this morning. And you just roamed around, the voice said, taking up with total strangers! I never heard of such a thing in all my life! So the Berenice voice sounded, heard but unnoticed like the buzzing of a fly.)

From the sad alleys and crooked streets of the mill section she crossed the unseen line dividing Sugarville from the white people's town. Here were the same two-room shacks and rotted privies, as in the mill section, but round thick chinaberry trees cast solid shade and often cool ferns grew in pots upon the porches. This was a part of town well known to her, and as she walked along she found herself remembering these familiar lanes in long-past times and other weathers — the ice-pale mornings in the wintertime when even the orange fires under the black iron pots of wash-women seemed to be shivering, the windy autumn nights.

Meanwhile, the glare was dizzy bright and she met and talked to many people, some known to her by sight and name, some strangers. The plans about the wedding stiffened and fixed with each new telling and finally came unchangeable. By eleven-thirty she was very tired, and even the tunes dragged with exhaustion; the need to be recognized for her true self was for the time being satisfied. So she went back to the place from which she started — to the main street where the glittering sidewalks were baked and half-deserted in the white glare.

Always she went by her father's store whenever she came to town. Her father's store was on the same block as the Blue Moon, but two doors from the main street and in a much better location. It was a narrow store with precious jewels in velvet boxes placed in the window. Beyond the window was her father's workbench, and when you walked along the sidewalk you could see her father working there, his head bent over the tiny watches, and his big brown hands hovered as carefully as butterflies. You could see her father like a public person in the town, well known to all by sight and name. But her father was not proud and did not even look up at those who stopped and gazed at him. This morning, however, he was not at his bench, but behind the counter rolling down his shirt-sleeves as though making ready to put on his coat and go outside.

The long glass showcase was bright with jewels and watches and silverware and the store smelled of watch-fixing kerosene. Her father wiped the sweat from his long upper lip with his forefinger and rubbed his nose in a troubled way.

'Where in the world have you been all morning? Berenice has called here twice trying to locate you.'

'I've been all over the whole town,' she said.

But he did not listen. 'I'm going around to your Aunt Pet's,' he said. 'She's had a sad piece of news today.'

'What sad piece of news?' F. Jasmine asked.

'Uncle Charles is dead.'

Uncle Charles was the great-uncle of John Henry West, but though she and John Henry were first cousins, Uncle Charles was not blood kin to her. He lived twenty-one miles out on the Renfroe Road in a shaded wooden country house surrounded by red cotton fields. An old, old man, he had been sick a long time; it was said he had one foot in the grave — and he always wore bedroom slippers. Now he was dead. But that had nothing to do with the wedding, and so F. Jasmine only said: 'Poor Uncle Charles. That certainy is a pity.'

Her father went back behind the gray sour velvet curtain that divided the store into two parts, the larger public part in front and behind a small dusty private part. Behind the curtain was the water cooler, some shelves of boxes, and the big iron safe where diamond rings were locked away from robbers in the night. F. Jasmine heard her Papa moving around back there, and she settled herself carefully at the workbench before the front window. A watch, already taken apart, was laid out on the green blotter.

There was a strong streak of watchmaker's blood in her

and always the old Frankie had loved to sit at her father's bench. She would put on her father's glasses with the jeweler's loupe attached and, scowling busily, dip them in gasoline. She worked with the lathe, too. Sometimes a little crowd of sidewalk lazies would collect to watch her from the street and she would imagine how they said: 'Frankie Addams works for her father and makes fifteen dollars a week. She fixes the hardest watches in the store and goes to the Woodmen of the World Club with her father. Look at her. She is a credit to the family and a big credit to the whole town.' So she would imagine these conversations, as she scowled with a busy expression at a watch. But now today she looked down at the watch spread out on the blotter, and did not put on the jeweler's loupe. There was something more she ought to say about the death of Uncle Charles.

When her father returned to the front of the store, she said: 'At one time Uncle Charles was one of the leading citizens. It will be a loss to the whole county.'

The words did not seem to impress her father. 'You had better go on home. Berenice has been phoning to locate you.'

'Well, remember you said I could get a wedding dress. And stockings and shoes.'

'Charge them at MacDougal's.'

'I don't see why we always have to trade at MacDougal's just because it's a local store,' she grumbled as she went out of the door. 'Where I am going there will be stores a hundred times bigger than MacDougal's.'

The clock in the tower of the First Baptist Church clanged twelve, the mill whistle wailed. There was a drowsing quietness about the street, and even the very cars, parked slantwise with their noses toward the center aisle of grass, were like exhausted cars that have all gone to sleep. The few people out at the noon hour kept close beneath the blunt shade of the awnings. The sun took the color from the sky and the brick stores seemed shrunken, dark, beneath the glare — one building had an overhanging cornice at the top which, from a distance, gave it the queer look of a brick building that has begun to melt. In this noon quietness, she heard again the organ of the monkey-man, the sound that always magnetized her footsteps so that she automatically went toward it. This time she would find them and tell them good-bye.

As F. Jasmine hurried down the street, she saw the two of them in her mind's eye — and wondered if they would remember her. The old Frankie had always loved the monkey and the monkey-man. They resembled each other — they both had an anxious, questioning expression, as though they wondered every minute if what they did was wrong. The monkey, in fact, was nearly always wrong; after he danced to the organ tune, he was supposed to take off his darling little cap and pass it around to the audience, but likely as not he would get mixed up and bow and reach out his cap to the monkey-man, and not the audience. And the monkey-man would plead with him, and finally begin to chatter and fuss. When he would make as if to slap the monkey, the monkey would cringe down and chatter also — and they would look at each other with the same scared exasperation, their wrinkled faces very sad. After watching them a long time, the old Frankie, fascinated, began to take on the same expression as she followed them around. And now F. Jasmine was eager to see them.

She could hear the broken-sounding organ plainly,

although they were not on the main street, but up farther and probably just around the corner of the next block. So F. Jasmine hurried toward them. As she neared the corner, she heard other sounds that puzzled her curiosity so that she listened and stopped. Above the music of the organ there was the sound of a man's voice quarreling and the excited higher fussing of the monkey-man. She could hear the monkey chattering also. Then suddenly the organ stopped and the two different voices were loud and mad. F. Jasmine had reached the corner, and it was the corner by the Sears and Roebuck store; she passed the store slowly, then turned and faced a curious sight.

It was a narrow street that went downhill toward Front Avenue, blinding bright in the wild glare. There on the sidewalk was the monkey, the monkey-man, and a soldier holding out a whole fistful of dollar bills — it looked at the first glance like a hundred dollars. The soldier looked angry, and the monkey-man was pale and excited also. Their voices were quarreling and F. Jasmine gathered that the soldier was trying to buy the monkey. The monkey himself was crouched and shivering down on the sidewalk close to the brick wall of the Sears and Roebuck store. In spite of the hot day, he had on his little red coat with silver buttons and his little face, scared and desperate, had the look of someone who is just about to sneeze. Shivering and pitiful, he kept bowing at nobody and offering his cap into the air. He knew the furious voices were about him and he felt blamed.

F. Jasmine was standing near-by, trying to take in the commotion, listening and still. Then suddenly the soldier grabbed at the monkey's chain, but the monkey screamed, and before she knew what it was all about, the monkey had skittered up her leg and body and was huddled on her shoulder with his little monkey hands around her head. It happened in a flash, and she was so shocked she could not move. The voices stopped and, except for the monkey's jibbered scream, the street was silent. The soldier stood slack-jawed, surprised, still holding out the handful of dollar bills.

The monkey-man was the first to recover; he spoke to the monkey in a gentle voice, and in another second the monkey sprang from off her shoulder and landed on the organ which the monkey-man was carrying on his back. The two of them went away. They quickly hurried around the corner and at the last second, just as they turned, they both looked back with the same expression — reproaching and sly. F. Jasmine leaned against the brick wall, and she still felt the monkey on her shoulder and smelt his dusty, sour smell; she shivered. The soldier muttered until the pair of them were out of sight, and F. Jasmine noticed then that he was red-haired and the same soldier who had been in the Blue Moon. He stuffed the bills in his side pocket.

'He certainy is a darling monkey,' F. Jasmine said. 'But it gave me a mighty funny feeling to have him run up me like that.'

The soldier seemed to realize her for the first time. The look on his face changed slowly, and the angry expression went away. He was looking at F. Jasmine from the top of her head, down the organdie best dress, and to the black pumps she was wearing.

'I guess you must have wanted the monkey a whole lot,' she said. 'I've always wanted a monkey, too.'

'What?' he asked. Then he remarked in a muffled voice, as if his tongue were made of felt or a very thick piece of blotting paper, 'Which way are we going?' the soldier said. 'Are you going my way or am I going yours?'

F. Jasmine had not expected this. The soldier was joining with her like a traveler who meets another traveler in a tourist town. For a second, it occurred to her that she had heard this remark before, perhaps in a picture show — that furthermore it was a set remark requiring a set answer. Not knowing the ready-made reply, she answered carefully.

'Which way are you going?'

'Hook on,' he said, sticking out his elbow.

They walked down the side street, on their shrunken noontime shadows. The soldier was the only person during that day who spoke first to F. Jasmine and invited her to join with him. But, when she began to tell about the wedding, something seemed lacking. Perhaps it was because she had already told her plans to so many people all over town that now she could rest satisfied. Or perhaps it was because she felt the soldier was not really listening. He looked at the pink organdie dress from the corner of his eye, and there was a half-smile on his mouth. F. Jasmine could not match her steps to his, although she tried, for his legs seemed loosely fastened to his body so that he walked in a rambling way.

'What state do you come from, if I may ask?' she said politely.

In that second that passed before his answer there was time for her skimming mind to picture Hollywood, New York, and Maine. The soldier answered: 'Arkansas.'

Now of all the forty-eight states in the Union, Arkansas was one of the very few that had never especially appealed to her — but her imagination, balked, immediately turned the opposite way so that she asked:

'Do you have any idea where you will be going?'

'Just banging around,' the soldier said. 'I'm out loose on a three-day pass.'

He had mistaken the meaning of her question, for she had asked it to him as a soldier liable to be sent to any foreign country in the world, but, before she could explain what she had meant, he said:

'There's a kind of hotel around the corner I'm staying at.' Then, still looking at the pleated collar of her dress, he added: 'It seems like I've seen you somewhere before. Do you ever go dancing at the Idle Hour?'

They walked down Front Avenue, and now the street was beginning to have the air of Saturday afternoon. A lady was drying her yellow hair in the window of the second floor above the fish store, and she called down to two soldiers who passed along the street. A street preacher, a known town character, was preaching on a corner to a group of warehouse colored boys and scraggly children. But F. Jasmine did not have her mind on what was going on around her. The soldier's mention of dancing and the Idle Hour touched like a story-tale wand upon her mind. She realized for the first time that she was walking with a soldier, with one of the groups of loud, glad gangs that roamed around the streets together or walked with the grown girls. They danced at the Idle Hour and had a good time, while the old Frankie was asleep. And she had never danced with anybody, excepting Evelyn Owen, and had never put foot in the Idle Hour.

And now F. Jasmine walked with a soldier who in his mind included her in such unknown pleasures. But she was not altogether proud. There was an uneasy doubt that she could not quite place or name. The noon air was thick and sticky as hot syrup, and there was the stifling smell of the dye-rooms from the cotton mill. She heard the organ-grinder sounding faintly from the main street.

The soldier stopped: 'This is the hotel,' he said.

They were before the Blue Moon and F. Jasmine was surprised to hear it spoken of as a hotel, as she had thought it was only a café. When the soldier held the screen door open for her, she noticed that he swayed a little. Her eyes saw blinding red, then black, after the glare, and it took them a minute to get used to the blue light. She followed the soldier to one of the booths on the right.

'Care for a beer,' he said, not in an asking voice, but as though he took her reply for granted.

F. Jasmine did not enjoy the taste of beer; once or twice she had sneaked swallows from her father's glass and it was sour. But the soldier had not left her any choice. 'I would be delighted,' she said. 'Thank you.'

Never had she been in a hotel, although she had often thought about them and written about them in her shows. Her father had stayed in hotels several times, and once, from Montgomery, he had brought her two little tiny cakes of hotel soap which she had saved. She looked around the Blue Moon with new curiosity. All of a sudden she felt very proper. On seating herself at the booth table, she carefully smoothed down her dress, as she did when at a party or in church, so as not to sit the pleats out of the skirt. She sat up straight and on her face there was a proper expression. But the Blue Moon still seemed to her more like a kind of café than a real hotel. She did not see the sad, pale Portuguese, and a laughing fat lady with a golden tooth poured beer for the soldier at the counter. The stairway at the back led probably to the hotel rooms upstairs, and the steps were lighted by a blue neon bulb and covered with a runner of linoleum. A sassy chorus on the radio was singing an advertisement: Denteen Chewing Gum! Denteen Chewing Gum! Denteen! The beery air reminded her of a room where a rat has died behind a wall. The soldier walked back to the booth, carrying two glasses of the beer; he licked some foam that had spilled over his hand and wiped the hand on his trousers seat. When he was settled in the booth, F. Jasmine said, in a voice that was absolutely new to her — a high voice spoken through the nose, dainty and dignified:

'Don't you think it is mighty exciting? Here we are sitting here at this table and in a month from now there's no telling where on earth we'll be. Maybe tomorrow the army will send you to Alaska like they sent my brother. Or to France or Africa or Burma. And I don't have any idea where I will be. I'd like for us to go to Alaska for a while, and then go somewhere else. They say that Paris has been liberated. In my opinion the war will be over next month.'

The soldier raised his glass, and threw back his head to gulp the beer. F. Jasmine took a few swallows also, although it tasted nasty to her. Today she did not see the world as loose and cracked and turning a thousand miles an hour, so that the spinning views of war and distant lands made her mind dizzy. The world had never been so close to her. Sitting across from the soldier at that booth in the Blue Moon, she suddenly saw the three of them — herself, her brother, and the bride — walking beneath a cold Alaskan sky, along the sea where green ice waves lay frozen and folded on the shore; they climbed a sunny glacier shot through with pale cold colors and a rope tied the three of them together, and friends from another glacier called in

Alaskan their J A names. She saw them next in Africa, where, with a crowd of sheeted Arabs, they galloped on camels in the sandy wind. Burma was jungle-dark, and she had seen pictures in *Life* magazine. Because of the wedding, these distant lands, the world, seemed altogether possible and near: as close to Winter Hill as Winter Hill was to the town. It was the actual present, in fact, that seemed to F. Jasmine a little bit unreal.

'Yes, it's mighty exciting,' she said again.

The soldier, his beer finished, wiped his wet mouth with the back of his freckled hand. His face, although not fat, seemed swollen, and it was glossy in the neon light. He had a thousand little freckles, and the only thing that seemed to her pretty was his bright, red curly hair. His eyes were blue, set close together, and the whites were raw. He was staring at her with a peculiar expression, not as one traveler gazes at another, but as a person who shares a secret scheme. For several minutes he did not talk. Then, when at last he spoke, the words did not make sense to her and she did not understand. It seemed to her the soldier said:

'Who is a cute dish?'

There were no dishes on the table and she had the uneasy feeling he had begun to talk a kind of double-talk. She tried to turn the conversation.

'I told you my brother is a Member of the Armed Forces.'

But the soldier did not seem to listen. 'I could of sworn I'd run into you some place before.'

The doubt in F. Jasmine deepened. She realized now that the soldier thought she was much older than she was, but her pleasure in this was somehow uncertain. To make conversation she remarked:

'Some people are not partial to red hair. But to me it's

my favorite color.' She added, remembering her brother and the bride. 'Except dark brown and yellow. I always think it's a pity for the Lord to waste curly hair on boys. When so many girls are going around with hair as straight as pokers.'

The soldier leaned over the booth table and, still staring at her, he began to walk his fingers, the second and third fingers of both hands, across the table toward her. The fingers were dirty, with rinds of black beneath the nails. F. Jasmine had the sense that something strange was going to happen, when just at that moment there was a sudden racket and commotion and three or four soldiers shoved each other into the hotel. There was a babble of voices and the screen door banged. The soldier's fingers stopped walking across the table and, when he glanced at the other soldiers, the peculiar expression was scattered from his eyes.

'That certainy is a darling little monkey,' she said.

'What monkey?'

The doubt deepened to the feeling that something was wrong. 'Why, the monkey you tried to buy a few minutes ago. What's the matter with you?'

Something was wrong and the soldier put his fists up to his head. His body limpened and he leaned back in the seat of the booth, as though collapsed. 'Oh, that monkey!' he said in his slurred voice. 'The walk in the sun after all those beers. I was slamming around all night.' He sighed, and his hands were open loose upon the table. 'I guess maybe I'm just about beat.'

For the first time F. Jasmine began to wonder what she was doing there and if she ought not to take herself on home. The other soldiers had crowded around a table near the stairway, and the lady with the golden tooth was busy behind the counter. F. Jasmine had finished her beer and a lace of creamy foam lined the inside of the empty glass. The hot, close smell in the hotel suddenly made her feel a little queer.

'I have to go home now. Thank you for treating me.'

She got up from the booth, but the soldier reached out toward her and caught a piece of her dress. 'Hey!' he said. 'Don't just walk off like that. Let's fix up something for this evening. How bout a date for nine o'clock?'

'A date?' F. Jasmine felt as though her head was big and loose. The beer made her legs feel peculiar, too, almost as though she had four legs to manage instead of two. On any other day than this it would have seemed almost impossible that anyone, much less a soldier, would have invited her to a date. The very word, *date*, was a grown word used by older girls. But here again there was a blight upon her pleasure. If he knew she was not yet thirteen, he would never have invited her, or probably never joined with her at all. There was a troubled sense, a light uneasiness. 'I don't know —'

'Sure,' he urged. 'Suppose we link up here at nine o'clock. We can go to the Idle Hour or something. That suit you all right? Here at nine o'clock.'

'O.K.' she said finally. 'I will be delighted.'

Again she was on the burning sidewalks, where passing walkers looked dark and shrunken in the angry glare. It took her a little while to come back to the wedding feeling of that morning, for the half-hour in the hotel had slightly distracted her frame of mind. But it did not take her very long, and by the time she reached the main street, the wedding feeling was recovered. She met a little girl, two grades below her at the school, and stopped her on the street to tell her her plans. She told her also that a soldier had invited her to have a date, and now she told it in a bragging tone. The girl went with her to buy the wedding clothes, which took an hour and meant the trying-on of more than a dozen beautiful dresses.

But the main thing that brought back the wedding frame of mind was an accident that occurred on the way home. It was a mysterious trick of sight and the imagination. She was walking home when all at once there was a shock in her as though a thrown knife struck and shivered in her chest. F. Jasmine stopped dead in her tracks, one foot still raised, and at first she could not take it in just what had happened. There was something sideways and behind her that had flashed across the very corner edge of her left eye; she had half-seen something, a dark double shape, in the alley she had just that moment passed. And because of this half-seen object, the quick flash in the corner of her eye, there had sprung up in her the sudden picture of her brother and the bride. Ragged and bright as lightning she saw the two of them as they had been when, for a moment, they stood together before the living-room mantelpiece, his arm around her shoulders. So strong was this picture that F. Jasmine felt suddenly that Jarvis and Janice were there behind her in the alley, and she had caught a glimpse of them — although she knew, and well enough, that they were in Winter Hill, almost a hundred miles away.

F. Jasmine lowered her raised foot to the pavement and slowly turned to look around. The alley lay between two grocery stores: a narrow alley, dark in the glare. She did not look at it directly, for somehow it was as though she was almost afraid. Her eyes stole slowly down the brick wall and she glimpsed again the dark double shapes. And what was there? F. Jasmine was stunned. There in the alley were only two colored boys, one taller than the other and with his arm resting on the shorter boy's shoulder. That was all — but something about the angle or the way they stood, or the pose of their shapes, had reflected the sudden picture of her brother and the bride that had so shocked her. And with this vision of them plain and exact the morning ended, and she was home by two o'clock.

2

The afternoon was like the center of the cake that Berenice had baked last Monday, a cake which failed. The old Frankie had been glad the cake had failed, not out of spite, but because she loved these fallen cakes the best. She enjoyed the damp, gummy richness near the center, and did not understand why grown people thought such cakes a failure. It was a loaf cake, that last Monday, with the edges risen light and high and the middle moist and altogether fallen — after the bright, high morning the afternoon was dense and solid as the center of that cake. And because it was the last of all the afternoons, F. Jasmine found an unfamiliar sweetness in the known old kitchen ways and tones. At two o'clock, when she came in, Berenice was pressing clothes. John Henry sat at the table blowing soap-bubbles with a spool, and he gave her a long, green, secret look.

'Where in the world have you been?' asked Berenice.

'We know something you don't know,' John Henry said. 'Do you know what?'

'What?'

'Berenice and me are going to the wedding.'

F. Jasmine was taking off her organdie dress, and his words startled her.

'Uncle Charles is dead.'

'I heard that, but ——'

'Yes,' said Berenice. 'The poor old soul passed on this morning. They're taking the body to the family graveyard in Opelika. And John Henry is to stay with us for several days.'

Now that she knew the death of Uncle Charles would in a sense affect the wedding, she made room for it in her thoughts. While Berenice finished pressing clothes, F. Jasmine sat in her petticoat on the stairs leading up to her room; she closed her eyes. Uncle Charles lived in a shady wooden house out in the country, and he was too old to eat corn on the cob. In June of this summer he took sick, and ever since he had been critical. He lay in the bed, shrunken and brown and very old. He complained that the pictures were hung crooked on the wall, and they took down all the framed pictures — it was not that. He complained that his bed was placed in a wrong corner, and so they moved the bed — it was not that. Then his voice failed, and when he tried to talk, it was as though his throat had filled with glue, and they could not understand the words. One Sunday the Wests had gone out to see him and taken Frankie with them; she had tiptoed to the open door of the back bedroom. He looked like an old man carved in brown wood and covered with a sheet. Only his eyes had moved, and they were like blue jelly, and she had felt they might come out from the sockets and roll like blue wet jelly down his stiff face. She had stood in the doorway staring at him — then tiptoed away, afraid. They finally made out that he complained the sun shone the wrong way through the window, but that was not the thing that hurt him so. And it was death.

F. Jasmine opened her eyes and stretched herself.

'It is a terrible thing to be dead!' she said.

'Well,' said Berenice. 'The old man suffered a lot and he had lived up his span. The Lord appointed the time for him.'

'I know. But at the same time it seems mighty queer that he would have to die the very day before the wedding. And why on earth do you and John Henry have to go tagging to the wedding? Seems to me like you would just stay home.'

'Frankie Addams,' said Berenice, and she suddenly put her arms akimbo, 'you are the most selfish human being that ever breathed. We all been cooped up in this kitchen and ——'

'Don't call me Frankie!' she said. 'I don't wish to have to remind you any more.'

It was the time of early afternoon when in the old days a sweet band would be playing. Now with the radio turned off, the kitchen was solemn and silent and there were sounds from far away. A colored voice called from the sidewalk, calling the names of vegetables in a dark slurred tone, a long unwinding hollering in which there were no words. Somewhere, near in the neighborhood, there was the sound of a hammer and each stroke left a round echo.

'You would be mighty surprised if you knew whereall I've been today. I was all over this whole town. I saw the monkey and the monkey-man. There was this soldier who was trying to buy the monkey and holding a hundred dollars in his hand. Have you ever seen anybody try to buy a monkey on the street?'

'No. Was he drunk?'

'Drunk?' F. Jasmine said.

'Oh,' said John Henry. 'The monkey and the monkey-man!'

Berenice's question had disturbed F. Jasmine, and she took a minute to consider. 'I don't think he was drunk. People don't get drunk in broad daylight.' She had meant to tell Berenice about the soldier, but now she hesitated. 'All the same there was something ——' Her voice trailed at the end, and she watched a rainbow soapbubble floating in silence across the room. Here in the kitchen, barefooted and wearing only her petticoat, it was hard to realize and judge the soldier. About the promise for that evening she felt double-minded. The indecision bothered her, and so she changed the subject. 'I hope you washed and ironed everything good of mine today. I have to take them to Winter Hill.'

'What for?' said Berenice. 'You only going to be there just one day.'

'You heard me,' F. Jasmine said. 'I told you I wasn't coming back here after the wedding.'

'Fool's hill. You have a whole lot less of sense than I was giving you credit for. What makes you think they want to take you along with them? Two is company and three is a crowd. And that is the main thing about a wedding. Two is company and three is a crowd.'

F. Jasmine always found it hard to argue with a known saying. She loved to use them in her shows and in her conversation, but they were very hard to argue with, and so she said:

'You wait and see.'

'Remember back to the time of the flood? Remember Noah and the ark?'

'And what has that got to do with it?' she asked.

'Remember the way he admitted them creatures.'

'Oh, hush up your big old mouth,' she said.

'Two by two,' said Berenice. 'He admitted them creatures two by two.'

The argument that afternoon was, from the beginning to the end, about the wedding. Berenice refused to follow F. Jasmine's frame of mind. From the first it was as though she tried to catch F. Jasmine by the collar, like the Law catches a no-good in the wrong, and jerk her back where she had started — back to the sad and crazy summer that now seemed to F. Jasmine like a time remembered from long ago. But F. Jasmine was stubborn and not to be caught. Berenice had flaws to find in all of her ideas, and from the first word to the last she did her terrible, level best to try and deny the wedding. But F. Jasmine would not let it be denied.

'Look,' F. Jasmine said, and she picked up the pink organdie dress that she had just taken off. 'Remember when I bought this dress the collar had teeny little pleats. But you have been ironing the collar like it was supposed to be ruffled. Now we got to set those little pleats like they ought to be.'

'And who is going to do it?' said Berenice. She picked up the dress and judged the collar. 'I got more to do with my time and trouble.'

'Well, it's got to be done,' F. Jasmine argued. 'It's the way the collar is supposed to be. And besides, I might be wearing it out somewhere this evening.'

'And where, pray tell me?' said Berenice. 'Answer the question I asked when you came in. Where in the world have you been all morning?'

It was exactly as F. Jasmine had known it would be — the way Berenice refused to understand. And, since it was more a matter of feelings than of words or facts, she found it difficult to explain. When she spoke of connections, Berenice gave her a long, uncomprehending stare — and, when she went on to the Blue Moon and the many people, the broad, flat nose of Berenice widened and she shook her head. F. Jasmine did not mention the soldier; although she was on the verge of speaking of him several times, something warned her not to.

When she had finished, Berenice said:

'Frankie, I honestly believe you have turned crazy on us. Walking around all over town and telling total strangers this big tale. You know in your soul this mania of yours is pure foolishness.'

'You wait and see,' F. Jasmine said. 'They will take me.'

'And if they don't?'

F. Jasmine picked up the shoe box with the silver slippers and the wrapped box with the wedding dress. 'These are my wedding clothes. I'll show them to you later.'

'And if they don't?'

F. Jasmine had already started up the stairs, but she stopped and turned back toward the kitchen. The room was silent.

'If they don't, I will kill myself,' she said. 'But they will.'

'Kill yourself how?' asked Berenice.

'I will shoot myself in the side of the head with a pistol.'

'Which pistol?'

'The pistol that Papa keeps under his handkerchiefs

along with Mother's picture in the right-hand bureau drawer.'

Berenice did not answer for a minute and her face was a puzzle. 'You heard what Mr. Addams told you about playing with that pistol. Go on upstairs now. Dinner will be ready in a little while.'

It was a late dinner, this last meal that the three of them would ever eat together at the kitchen table. On Saturdays they were not regular about the times of meals, and they began the dinner at four o'clock, when already the August sun was slanting long and stale across the yard. It was the time of afternoon when the bars of sunlight crossed the back yard like the bars of a bright strange jail. The two fig trees were green and flat, the arbor sun-crossed and casting solid shade. The sun in the afternoon did not slant through the back windows of the house, so that the kitchen was gray. The three of them began their dinner at four o'clock, and the dinner lasted until twilight. There was hopping-john cooked with the ham bone, and as they ate they began to talk of love. It was a subject F. Jasmine had never talked about in all her life. In the first place, she had never believed in love and had never put any of it in her shows. But this afternoon when Berenice began this conversation, F. Jasmine did not stop up both her ears, but as she quietly ate the peas and rice and pot-liquor she listened.

'I have heard of many a queer thing,' said Berenice. 'I have knew mens to fall in love with girls so ugly that you wonder if their eyes is straight. I have seen some of the most peculiar weddings anybody could conjecture. Once I knew a boy with his whole face burned off so that ——'

'Who?' asked John Henry.

Berenice swallowed a piece of cornbread and wiped her

mouth with the back of her hand. 'I have knew womens to love veritable Satans and thank Jesus when they put their split hooves over the threshold. I have knew boys to take it into their heads to fall in love with other boys. You know Lily Mae Jenkins?'

F. Jasmine thought a minute, and then answered: 'I'm not sure.'

'Well, you either know him or you don't know him. He prisses around with a pink satin blouse and one arm akimbo. Now this Lily Mae fell in love with a man name Juney Jones. A man, mind you. And Lily Mae turned into a girl. He changed his nature and his sex and turned into a girl.'

'Honest?' F. Jasmine asked. 'Did he really?'

'He did,' said Berenice. 'To all intents and purposes.'

F. Jasmine scratched behind her ear and said: 'It's funny I can't think who you are talking about. I used to think I knew so many people.'

'Well, you don't need to know Lily Mae Jenkins. You can live without knowing him.'

'Anyway, I don't believe you,' F. Jasmine said.

'Well, I ain't arguring with you,' said Berenice. 'What was it we was speaking about?'

'About peculiar things.'

'Oh, yes.'

They stopped off a few minutes to get on with the dinner. F. Jasmine ate with her elbows on the table and her bare heels hooked on the rungs of the chair. She and Berenice sat opposite each other, and John Henry faced the window. Now hopping-john was F. Jasmine's very favorite food. She had always warned them to wave a plate of rice and peas before her nose when she was in her coffin, to make certain there was no mistake; for if a breath of life was left in her, she would sit up and eat, but if she smelled the hopping-john, and did not stir, then they could just nail down the coffin and be certain she was truly dead. Now Berenice had chosen for her death-test a piece of fried fresh-water trout, and for John Henry it was divinity fudge. But though F. Jasmine loved the hopping-john the very best, the others also liked it well enough, and all three of them enjoyed the dinner that day: the ham knuckle, the hopping-john, corn-bread, hot baked sweet potatoes, and the buttermilk. And as they ate, they carried on the conversation.

'Yes, as I was just now telling you,' said Berenice. 'I have seen many a peculiar thing in my day. But one thing I never knew and never heard tell about. No siree, I never did.'

Berenice stopped talking and sat there shaking her head, waiting for them to question her. But F. Jasmine would not speak. And it was John Henry who raised his curious face from his plate and asked: 'What, Berenice?'

'No,' said Berenice. 'I never before in all my days heard of anybody falling in love with a wedding. I have knew many peculiar things, but I never heard of that before.'

F. Jasmine grumbled something.

'So I have been thinking it over and have come to a conclusion.'

'How?' John Henry suddenly asked. 'How did that boy change into a girl?'

Berenice glanced at him and straightened the napkin tied around his neck. 'It was just one of them things, Candy Lamb. I don't know.'

'Don't listen at her,' F. Jasmine said.

'So I have been thinking it over in my mind and come to this conclusion. What you ought to begin thinking about is a beau.'

'What?' F. Jasmine asked.

'You heard me,' said Berenice. 'A beau. A nice little white boy beau.'

F. Jasmine put down her fork and sat with her head turned to one side. 'I don't want any beau. What would I do with one?'

'Do, Foolish?' asked Berenice. 'Why, make him treat you to the picture show. For one thing.'

F. Jasmine pulled the bangs of her hair down over her forehead and slid her feet across the rung of the chair.

'Now you belong to change from being so rough and greedy and big,' said Berenice. 'You ought to fix yourself up nice in your dresses. And speak sweetly and act sly.'

F. Jasmine said in a low voice: 'I'm not rough and greedy any more. I already changed that way.'

'Well, excellent,' said Berenice. 'Now catch you a beau.'

F. Jasmine wanted to tell Berenice about the soldier, the hotel, and the invitation for the evening date. But something checked her, and she hinted around the edges of the subject: 'What kind of a beau? Do you mean something like ——' F. Jasmine paused, for at home in the kitchen that last afternoon, the soldier seemed unreal.

'Now that I cannot advise,' said Berenice. 'You got to decide for yourself.'

'Something like a soldier who would maybe take me dancing at the Idle Hour?' She did not look at Berenice.

'Who is talking about soldiers and dancing? I'm talking about a nice little white boy beau your own age. How about that little old Barney?'

'Barney MacKean?'

'Why, certainy. He would do very well to begin with.

You could make out with him until somebody else comes along. He would do.'

'That mean nasty Barney!' The garage had been dark, with thin needling sunlight coming through the cracks of the closed door, and with the smell of dust. But she did not let herself remember the unknown sin that he had showed her, that later made her want to throw a knife between his eyes. Instead, she shook herself hard and began mashing peas and rice together on her plate. 'You are the biggest crazy in this town.'

'The crazy calls the sane the crazy.'

So they began to eat again, all except John Henry. F. Jasmine was busy slicing open cornbread and spreading it with butter and mashing her hopping-john and drinking milk. Berenice ate more slowly, peeling off bits of ham from the knuckle in a dainty way. John Henry looked from one of them to the other, and after listening to their talk he had stopped eating to think for a little while. Then after a minute he asked:

'How many of them did you catch? Them beaus.'

'How many?' said Berenice. 'Lamb, how many hairs is in these plaits? You talking to Berenice Sadie Brown.'

So Berenice was started, and her voice went on and on. And when she had begun this way, on a long and serious subject, the words flowed one into the other and her voice began to sing. In the gray of the kitchen on summer afternoons the tone of her voice was golden and quiet, and you could listen to the color and the singing of her voice and not follow the words. F. Jasmine let the long tones linger and spin inside her ears, but her mind did not stamp the voice with sense or sentences. She sat there listening at the table, and now and then she thought of a fact that all her life had seemed to her most curious: Berenice always spoke of herself as though she was somebody very beautiful. Almost on this one subject, Berenice was really not in her right mind. F. Jasmine listened to the voice and stared at Berenice across the table: the dark face with the wild blue eye, the eleven greased plaits that fitted her head like a skull-cap, the wide flat nose that quivered as she spoke. And whatever else Berenice might be, she was not beautiful. It seemed to her she ought to give Berenice advice. So she said at the next pause:

'I think you ought to quit worrying about beaus and be content with T. T. I bet you are forty years old. It is time for you to settle down.'

Berenice bunched up her lips and stared at F. Jasmine with the dark live eye. 'Wisemouth,' she said. 'How do you know so much? I got as much right as anybody else to continue to have a good time so long as I can. And as far as that goes, I'm not so old as some peoples would try and make out. I can still ministrate. And I got many a long year ahead of me before I resign myself to a corner.'

'Well, I didn't mean go into a corner,' F. Jasmine said.

'I heard what you meant,' said Berenice.

John Henry had been watching and listening, and there was a little crust of pot-liquor around his mouth. A big blue lazy fly was hovering around him and trying to light on his sticky face, so that from time to time John Henry waved his hand to shoo the fly away.

'Did they all treat you to the picture show?' he asked. 'All those beaus.'

'To the show, or to one thing or another,' she answered.

'You mean you never pay your own way?' John Henry asked.

'That's what I'm telling you,' said Berenice. 'Not when I go out with a beau. Now if I was to go somewhere with a crowd of womens, I would have to pay my way. But I'm not the kind of person to go around with crowds of womens.'

'When you all took the trip to Fairview ——' F. Jasmine said — for one Sunday that last spring there had been a colored pilot who took up colored people in his aeroplane. 'Who paid the way?'

'Now let me see,' said Berenice. 'Honey and Clorina took care of their expense, except I loaned Honey one dollar and forty cents. Cape Clyde paid his own way. And T. T. paid for himself and for me.'

'Then T. T. treated you to the aeroplane ride?'

'That's what I'm telling you. He paid the bus tickets to and from Fairview and the aeroplane ride and the refreshments. The complete trip. Why, naturally he paid the way. How else do you think I could afford to fly around in an aeroplane? Me making six dollars a week.'

'I didn't realize that,' F. Jasmine admitted finally. 'I wonder where T. T. got all of his money.'

'Earned it,' said Berenice. 'John Henry, wipe off your mouth.'

So they rested at the table, for the way they ate their meals, this summer, was in rounds: they would eat awhile and then let the food have a chance to spread out and settle inside their stomachs, and a little later they would start in again. F. Jasmine crossed her knife and fork on her empty plate, and began to question Berenice about a matter that had bothered her.

'Tell me. Is it just us who call this hopping-john? Or is it known by that name through all the country. It seems a strange name somehow.'

'Well, I have heard it called various things,' said Berenice.

'What?'

'Well, I have heard it called peas and rice. Or rice and peas and pot-liquor. Or hopping-john. You can vary and take your pick.'

'But I'm not talking about this town,' F. Jasmine said. I mean in other places. I mean through all the world. I wonder what the French call it.'

'Oh,' said Berenice. 'Well, you ask me a question I cannot answer.'

'Merci a la parlez,' F. Jasmine said.

They sat at the table and did not speak. F. Jasmine was tilted back in her chair, her head turned toward the window and the sun-crossed empty yard. The town was silent and the kitchen was silent except for the clock. F. Jasmine could not feel the world go round, and nothing moved.

'Now a funny thing has happened to me,' F. Jasmine began. 'I don't hardly know how to tell just what I mean. It was one of those strange things you can't exactly explain.'

'What, Frankie?' John Henry asked.

F. Jasmine turned from the window, but before she could speak again there was the sound. In the silence of the kitchen they heard the tone shaft quietly across the room, then again the same note was repeated. A piano scale slanted across the August afternoon. A chord was struck. Then in a dreaming way a chain of chords climbed slowly upward like a flight of castle stairs: but just at the end, when the eighth chord should have sounded and the scale made complete, there was a stop. This next to the last chord was repeated. The seventh chord, which seems to echo all of the unfinished scale, struck and insisted again and again. And finally there was a silence. F. Jasmine and John Henry and Berenice looked at each other. Somewhere in the neighborhood an August piano was being tuned.

'Jesus!' said Berenice. 'I seriously believe this will be the last straw.'

John Henry shivered. 'Me too,' he said.

F. Jasmine sat perfectly still before the table crowded with plates and dinner dishes. The gray of the kitchen was a stale gray and the room was too flat and too square. After the silence another note was sounded, and then repeated an octave higher. F. Jasmine raised her eyes each time the tone climbed higher, as though she watched the note move from one part of the kitchen to another; at the highest point her eyes had reached a ceiling corner, then, when a long scale slid downward, her head turned slowly as her eyes crossed from the ceiling corner to the floor corner at the opposite side of the room. The bottom bass note was struck six times, and F. Jasmine was left staring at an old pair of bedroom slippers and an empty beer bottle which were in that corner of the room. Finally she shut her eyes, and shook herself, and got up from the table.

'It makes me sad,' F. Jasmine said. 'And jittery too.' She began to walk around the room. 'They tell me that when they want to punish them over in Milledgeville, they tie them up and make them listen to piano-tuning.' She walked three times around the table. 'There's something I want to ask you. Suppose you ran into somebody who seemed to you terribly peculiar, but you didn't know the reason why.'

'In what ways peculiar?'

F. Jasmine thought of the soldier, but she could not further explain. 'Say you might meet somebody you think he almost might be a *drunk*, but you're not sure about anything. And he wanted you to join with him and go to a big party or dance. What would you do?'

'Well, on the face of it, I don't know. It would depend on how I feel. I might go with him to the big party and meet up with somebody that suited me better.' The live eye of Berenice suddenly narrowed, and she looked hard at F. Jasmine. 'But why do you ask that?'

The quietness in the room stretched out until F. Jasmine could hear the drip-drop from the faucet of the sink. She was trying to frame away to tell Berenice about the soldier. Then all at once the telephone rang. F. Jasmine jumped up and, turning over her empty milk glass, dashed to the hall — but John Henry, who was nearer, reached the telephone first. He knelt on the telephone chair and smiled into the mouthpiece before he said hello. Then he kept on saying hello until F. Jasmine took the receiver from him and repeated the hellos at least two dozen times before she finally hung up.

'Anything like that makes me so mad,' she said when they had gone back to the kitchen. 'Or when the express truck stops before the door and the man peers at our number and then takes the box somewhere else. I look on those things as a kind of sign.' She raked her fingers through her crew-cut blond hair. 'You know I'm really going to get my fortune told before I leave home in the morning. It's something I've been meaning to do for a long time.'

Berenice said: 'Changing the subject, when are you going to show me the new dress? I'm anxious to see what you selected.'

So F. Jasmine went up to get the dress. Her room was what was known as a hotbox; the heat from the rest of the house rose up to her room and stayed there. In the afternoon the air seemed to make a buzzing sound, so it was a good idea to keep the motor running. F. Jasmine turned on the motor and opened the closet door. Until this day before the wedding she had always kept her six costumes hung in a row on coat-hangers, and she just threw her ordinary clothes up on the shelf or kicked them into a corner. But when she had come home this afternoon, she had changed this: the costumes were thrown up on the shelf and the wedding dress hung alone in the closet on a coat-hanger. The silver slippers were placed carefully on the floor beneath the dress with the toes pointed north, toward Winter Hill. For some reason F. Jasmine tiptoed around the room as she began to dress.

'Shut your eyes!' she called. 'Don't watch me coming down the stairs. Don't open your eyes until I tell you.'

It was as though the four walls of the kitchen watched her, and the skillet hanging on the wall was a watching round black eye. The piano-tuning was for a minute silent. Berenice sat with her head bowed, as though she was in church. And John Henry had his head bowed also, but he was peeking. F. Jasmine stood at the foot of the stairs and placed her left hand on her hip.

'Oh, how pretty!' John Henry said.

Berenice raised her head, and when she saw F. Jasmine her face was a study. The dark eye looked from the silver hair ribbon to the soles of the silver slippers. She said nothing.

'Now tell me your honest opinion,' F. Jasmine said.

But Berenice looked at the orange satin evening dress and shook her head and did not comment. At first she shook her head with short little turns, but the longer she stared, the longer these shakes became, until at the last shake F. Jasmine heard her neck crack.

'What's the matter?' F. Jasmine asked.

'I thought you was going to get a pink dress.'

'But when I got in the store I changed my mind. What is wrong with this dress? Don't you like it, Berenice?'

'No,' said Berenice. 'It don't do.'

'What do you mean? It don't do.'

'Exactly that. It just don't do.'

F. Jasmine turned to look in the mirror, and she still thought the dress was beautiful. But Berenice had a sour and stubborn look on her face, an expression like that of an old long-eared mule, and F. Jasmine could not understand.

'But I don't see what you mean,' she complained. 'What is wrong?'

Berenice folded her arms over her chest and said: 'Well, if you don't see it I can't explain it to you. Look there at your head, to begin with.'

F. Jasmine looked at her head in the mirror.

'You had all your hair shaved off like a convict, and now you tie a silver ribbon around this head without any hair. It just looks peculiar.'

'Oh, but I'm washing my hair tonight and going to try to curl it,' F. Jasmine said.

'And look at them elbows,' Berenice continued. 'Here you got on this grown woman's evening dress. Orange satin. And that brown crust on your elbows. The two things just don't mix.'

F. Jasmine hunched her shoulders and covered her rusty elbows with her hands.

Berenice gave her head another quick wide shake, then bunched her lips in judgment. 'Take it back down to the store.'

'But I can't!' said F. Jasmine. 'It's bargain basement. They don't take back.'

Berenice always had two mottoes. One was the known saying that you can't make a silk purse out of a sow's ear. And the other was the motto that you have to cut your suit according to the cloth, and make the best of what you have. So F. Jasmine was not certain if it was the last of these mottoes that made Berenice change her mind, or if she really began to improve her feelings about the dress. Anyway, Berenice stared for several seconds with her head to one side, and finally said:

'Come here. We'll make it fit better at the waist and see what we can do.'

'I think you're just not accustomed to seeing anybody dressed up,' F. Jasmine said.

'I'm not accustomed to human Christmas trees in August.'

So Berenice took off the sash and patted and pulled the dress in various places. F. Jasmine stood stiff like a hatrack and let her work with the dress. John Henry had got up from his chair and was watching, with the napkin still tied around his neck.

'Frankie's dress looks like a Christmas tree,' he said.

'Two-faced Judas!' F. Jasmine said. 'You just now said it was pretty. Old double-faced Judas!'

The piano tuned. Whose piano it was F. Jasmine did not know, but the sound of the tuning was solemn and insistent in the kitchen, and it came from somewhere not so far away. The piano-tuner would sometimes fling out a rattling little tune, and then he would go back to one note. And repeat. And bang the same note in a solemn and crazy way. And repeat. And bang. The name of the piano-tuner in the town was Mr. Schwarzenbaum. The sound was enough to shiver the gizzards of musicians and make all listeners feel queer.

'It almost makes me wonder if he does that just to torment us,' F. Jasmine said.

But Berenice said no: 'They tune pianos the same way in Cincinnati and the world over. It is just the way they do it. Less turn on the radio in the dining room and drown him out.'

F. Jasmine shook her head. 'No,' she said. 'I can't explain why. But I don't want to have that radio turned on again. It reminds me too much of this summer.'

'Step back a little now,' said Berenice.

She had pinned the waist higher and done one thing and another to the dress. F. Jasmine looked in the mirror over the sink. She could only see herself from the chest up, so after admiring this top part of herself, she stood on a chair and looked at the middle section. Then she began to clear away a corner of the table so she could climb up and see in the mirror the silver shoes, but Berenice prevented her.

'Don't you honestly think it is pretty?' F. Jasmine said. 'I think so. Seriously, Berenice. Give me your candy opinion.'

But Berenice rared up and spoke in an accusing voice: 'I never knew somebody so unreasonable! You ask me my candy opinion, and I give it to you. Then you ask me again, and I give it to you. But what you want is not my honest opinion, but my good opinion on something I know is wrong. Now what kind of way is that to act?'

'All right,' F. Jasmine said. 'I only want to look good.'

'Well, you look very well,' said Berenice. 'Pretty is as pretty does. You look well enough for anybody's wedding.

Excepting your own. And then, pray Jesus, we will be in a position to do better. What I have to do now is get John Henry a fresh suit and figure about the outfit I'm going to wear myself.'

'Uncle Charles is dead,' John Henry said. 'And we are going to the wedding.'

'Yes, Baby,' said Berenice. And from the sudden dreaming quietness of her, F. Jasmine felt that Berenice was carried back to all the other dead people she knew. The dead were walking in her heart, and she was remembering back to Ludie Freeman and the long-gone time of Cincinnati and the snow.

F. Jasmine thought back to the other seven dead people she knew. Her mother had died the very day that she was born, so she could not count her. There was a picture of her mother in the right-hand drawer of her father's bureau: and the face looked timid and sorry, shut up with the cold folded handkerchiefs in the drawer. Then there was her grandmother who had died when Frankie was nine years old, and F. Jasmine remembered her very well — but with crooked little pictures that were sunken far back in her mind. A soldier from that town called William Boyd had been killed that year in Italy, and she had known him both by sight and name. Mrs. Selway, two blocks away, had died; and F. Jasmine had watched the funeral from the sidewalk, but she was not invited. The solemn grown men stood around out on the front porch and it had rained, there was a gray silk ribbon on the door. She knew Lon Baker, and he was dead also. Lon Baker was a colored boy and he was murdered in the alley out behind her father's store. On an April afternoon his throat was slashed with a razor blade, and all the alley people disappeared in back doorways, and later it was said his cut throat opened like a crazy shivering mouth that spoke ghost words into the April sun. Lon Baker was dead and Frankie knew him. She knew, but only in a chancing kind of way, Mr. Pitkin at Brawer's Shoe Shop, Miss Birdie Grimes, and a man who had climbed poles for the telephone company: all dead.

'Do you think very frequently about Ludie?' F. Jasmine asked.

'You know I do,' said Berenice. 'I think about the years when me and Ludie was together, and about all the bad times I seen since. Ludie would never have let me be lonesome so that I took up with all kinds of no-good men. Me and Ludie,' she said. 'Ludie and me.'

F. Jasmine sat vibrating her leg and thinking of Ludie and Cincinnati. Of all the dead people out of the world, Ludie Freeman was the one F. Jasmine knew the best, although she had never laid eyes on him, and was not even born when he had died. She knew Ludie and the city of Cincinnati, and the winter when Ludie and Berenice had gone together to the North and seen the snow. A thousand times they had talked of all these things, and it was a conversation that Berenice talked slowly, making each sentence like a song. And the old Frankie used to ask and question about Cincinnati. What exactly they would eat in Cincinnati and how wide would be the Cincinnati streets? And in a chanting kind of voice they talked about the Cincinnati fish, the parlor in the Cincinnati house on Myrtle Street, the Cincinnati picture shows. And Ludie Freeman was a brickmason, making a grand and a regular salary, and he was the man of all her husbands that Berenice had loved.

'Sometimes I almost wish I had never knew Ludie at all,' said Berenice. 'It spoils you too much. It leaves you too lonesome afterward. When you walk home in the evening on the way from work, it makes a little lonesome quinch come in you. And you take up with too many sorry men to try to get over the feeling.'

'I know it,' F. Jasmine said. 'But T. T. Williams is not sorry.'

'I wasn't referring to T. T. He and me is just good friends.'

'Don't you think you will marry him?' F. Jasmine asked.

'Well, T. T. is a fine upstanding colored gentleman,' said Berenice. 'You never hear tell of T. T. raring around like a lot of other mens. If I was to marry T. T., I could get out of this kitchen and stand behind the cash register at the restaurant and pat my foot. Furthermore, I respect T. T. sincerely. He has walked in a state of grace all of his life.'

'Well, when are you going to marry him?' she asked. 'He is crazy about you.'

Berenice said: 'I ain't going to marry him.'

'But you just now was saying —' said F. Jasmine.

'I was saying how sincerely I respect T. T. and sincerely regard him.'

'Well, then —?' F. Jasmine said.

'I respect and regard him highly,' said Berenice. Her dark eye was quiet and sober and her flat nose widened as she spoke. 'But he don't make me shiver none.'

After a moment F. Jasmine said: 'To think about the wedding makes me shiver.'

'Well, it's a pity,' said Berenice.

'It makes me shiver, too, to think about how many dead people I already know. Seven in all,' she said. 'And now Uncle Charles.'

F. Jasmine put her fingers in her ears and closed her eyes,

but it was not death. She could feel the heat from the stove and smell the dinner. She could feel a rumble in her stomach and the beating of her heart. And the dead feel nothing, hear nothing, see nothing: only black.

'It would be terrible to be dead,' she said, and in the wedding dress she began to walk around the room.

There was a rubber ball on the shelf, and she threw it against the hall door and caught it on the rebound.

'Put that down,' said Berenice. 'Go take off the dress before you dirty it. Go do something. Go turn on the radio.'

'I told you I don't want that radio on.'

And she was walking around the room, and Berenice had said to go do something, but she did not know what to do. She walked in the wedding dress, with her hand on her hip. The silver slippers had squeezed her feet so that the toes felt swollen and mashed like ten big sore cauliflowers.

'But I advise you to keep the radio on when you come back,' F. Jasmine said suddenly. 'Some day very likely you will hear us speaking over the radio.'

'What's that?'

'I say very likely we might be asked to speak over the radio some day.'

'Speak about what, pray tell me,' said Berenice.

'I don't know exactly what about,' F. Jasmine said. 'But probably some eye-witness account about something. We will be asked to speak.'

'I don't follow you,' said Berenice. 'What are we going to eye-witness? And who will ask us to speak?'

F. Jasmine whirled around and, putting both fists on her hips, she set herself in a staring position. 'Did you think I meant you and John Henry and me? Why, I have never heard of anything so funny in my whole life.'

John Henry's voice was high and excited. 'What, Frankie? Who is speaking on the radio?'

'When I said *we*, you thought I meant you and me and John Henry West. To speak over the world radio. I have never heard of anything so funny since I was born.'

John Henry had climbed up to kneel on the seat of his chair and the blue veins showed in his forehead and you could see the strained chords of his neck. 'Who?' he hollered. 'What?'

'Ha ha ha!' she said, and then she burst out laughing; she went banging around the room and hitting things with her fist. 'Ho ho ho!'

And John Henry wailed and F. Jasmine banged around the kitchen in the wedding dress and Berenice got up from the table and raised her right hand for peace. Then suddenly they all stopped at once. F. Jasmine stood absolutely still before the window, and John Henry hurried to the window also and watched on tiptoe with his hands to the sill. Berenice turned her head to see what had happened. And at that moment the piano was quiet.

'Oh!' F. Jasmine whispered.

Four girls were crossing the back yard. They were girls of fourteen and fifteen years old, and they were the club members. First came Helen Fletcher, and then the others walking slowly in single file. They had cut across from the O'Neils' back yard and were passing slowly before the arbor. The long gold sun slanted down on them and made their skin look golden also, and they were dressed in clean, fresh dresses. When they had passed the arbor, their single shadows stretched out long and gangling across the yard. Soon they would be gone. F. Jasmine stood motionless. In the old days that summer she would have waited in the hope that they might call her and tell her she had been elected to the club — and only at the very last, when it was plain that they were only passing, she would have shouted in angry loudness that they were not to cut across her yard. But now she watched them quietly, without jealousy. At the last there came an urge to call out to them about the wedding, but before the words could be formed and spoken, the club of girls was gone. There was only the arbor and the spinning sun.

'Now I wonder —' F. Jasmine said finally. But Berenice cut her short:

'Nothing, Curiosity,' she said. 'Curiosity, nothing.'

When they began the second round of that last dinner, it was past five o'clock, and nearing twilight. It was the time of afternoon when in the old days, sitting with the red cards at the table, they would sometimes begin to criticize the Creator. They would judge the work of God, and mention the ways how they would improve the world. And Holy Lord God John Henry's voice would rise up happy and high and strange, and his world was a mixture of delicious and freak, and he did not think in global terms: the sudden long arm that could stretch from here to California, chocolate dirt and rains of lemonade, the extra eye seeing a thousand miles, a hinged tail that could be let down as a kind of prop to sit on when you wished to rest, the candy flowers.

But the world of the Holy Lord God Berenice Sadie Brown was a different world, and it was round and just and reasonable. First, there would be no separate colored people in the world, but all human beings would be light brown color with blue eyes and black hair. There would be no colored people and no white people to make the colored people feel cheap and sorry all through their lives. No colored people, but all human men and ladies and children as one loving family on the earth. And when Berenice spoke of this first principle her voice was a strong deep song that soared and sang in beautiful dark tones leaving an echo in the corners of the room that trembled for a long time until silence.

No war, said Berenice. No stiff corpses hanging from the Europe trees and no Jews murdered anywhere. No war, and the young boys leaving home in army suits, and no wild cruel Germans and Japanese. No war in the whole world, but peace in all countries everywhere. Also, no starving. To begin with, the real Lord God had made free air and free rain and free dirt for the benefit of all. There would be free food for every human mouth, free meals and two pounds of fatback a week, and after that each able-bodied person would work for whatever else he wished to eat or own. No killed Jews and no hurt colored people. No war and no hunger in the world. And, finally, Ludie Freeman would be alive.

The world of Berenice was a round world, and the old Frankie would listen to the strong deep singing voice, and she would agree with Berenice. But the old Frankie's world was the best of the three worlds. She agreed with Berenice about the main laws of her creation, but she added many things: an aeroplane and a motorcycle to each person, a world club with certificates and badges, and a better law of gravity. She did not completely agree with Berenice about the war; and sometimes she said she would have one War Island in the world where those who wanted to could go, and fight or donate blood, and she might go for a while as a WAC in the Air Corps.

She also changed the seasons, leaving out summer altogether, and adding much snow. She planned it so that people could instantly change back and forth from boys to girls, whichever way they felt like and wanted. But Berenice would argue with her about this, insisting that the law of human sex was exactly right just as it was and could in no way be improved. And then John Henry West would very likely add his two cents' worth about this time, and think that people ought to be half boy and half girl, and when the old Frankie threatened to take him to the Fair and sell him to the Freak Pavilion, he would only close his eyes and smile.

So the three of them would sit there at the kitchen table and criticize the Creator and the work of God. Sometimes their voices crossed and the three worlds twisted. The Holy Lord God John Henry West. The Holy Lord God Berenice Sadie Brown. The Holy Lord God Frankie Addams. The Worlds at the end of the long stale afternoons.

But this was a different day. They were not loafing or playing cards, but still eating dinner. F. Jasmine had taken off the wedding dress and was barefooted and comfortable in her petticoat once more. The brown gravy of the peas had stiffened, the food was neither hot nor cold, and the butter had melted. They started in on second helpings, passing the dishes back and forth among themselves, and they did not talk of the ordinary subjects that usually they thought about this time of the afternoon. Instead, there began a strange conversation, and it came about in this way:

'Frankie,' said Berenice, 'Awhile back you started to say something. And we veered off from the subject. It was about something unnatural, I think.'

'Oh, yes,' F. Jasmine said. 'I was going to tell you about something peculiar that happened to me today that I don't hardly realize. Now I don't exactly know how to explain just what I mean.'

F. Jasmine broke open a sweet potato and tilted back in her chair. She began to try to tell Berenice what had happened when she had been walking home and suddenly seen something from the tail of her eye, and when she turned to look, it was the two colored boys back at the end of the alley. As she talked, F. Jasmine stopped now and then to pull her lower lip and study just for the right words to tell of a feeling that she had never heard named before. Occasionally she glanced at Berenice, to see if she was following her, and a remarkable look was breaking on Berenice's face: the glass blue eye was bright and astonished, as always, and at first her dark eye was astonished also; then a queer and conniving look changed her expression, and from time to time she turned her head with short little jerks, as though to listen from different earpoints and make sure that what she heard was true.

Before F. Jasmine finished, Berenice had pushed back her plate and reached into her bosom for her cigarettes. She smoked home-rolled cigarettes, but she carried them in a Chesterfield package, so that from the outward appearance she was smoking store Chesterfields. She twisted off a ragged fringe of loose tobacco and raised back her head when she held the match, so that the flame would not go up her nose. A blue layer of smoke hung over the three of them at the table. Berenice held the cigarette between her thumb and forefinger; her hand had been drawn and stiffened by a winter rheumatism so that the last two fingers could not be straightened out. She sat listening and smoking, and when

F. Jasmine had finished, there was a long pause, then Berenice leaned forward and asked suddenly:

'Listen at me! Can you see through them bones in my forehead? Have you, Frankie Addams, been reading my mind?'

F. Jasmine did not know what to answer.

'This is one of the queerest things I ever heard of,' Berenice went on. 'I cannot get over it.'

'What I mean —' F. Jasmine started again.

'I know what you mean,' said Berenice. 'Right here in this very corner of the eye.' She pointed to the red-webbed outside corner of the dark eye. 'You suddenly catch something there. And this cold shiver run all the way down you. And you whirl around. And then you stand facing Jesus knows what. But not Ludie and not who you want. And for a minute you feel like you been dropped down a well.'

'Yes,' F. Jasmine said. 'That is it.'

'Well, this is mighty remarkable,' said Berenice. 'This is a thing been happening to me all my life. Yet just now is the first time I ever heard it put into words.'

F. Jasmine covered her nose and her mouth with her hand, so that it would not be noticed that she was pleased about being so remarkable, and her eyes were closed in a modest way.

'Yes, that is the way when you are in love,' said Berenice. 'Invariably. A thing known and not spoken.'

So that was how the queer conversation began at quarter to six on the last afternoon. It was the first time ever they had talked about love, with F. Jasmine included in the conversation as a person who understood and had worth-while opinions. The old Frankie had laughed at love, maintained it was a big fake, and did not believe in it. She never put any of it in her shows, and never went to love shows at the Palace. The old Frankie had always gone to the Saturday matinee, when the shows were crook shows, war shows, or cowboy shows. And who was it who had caused the confusion at the Palace that last May, when the movie had run an old show on Saturday called *Camille*? The old Frankie. She had been in her seat on the second row and she stamped and put two fingers in her mouth and began to whistle. And the other half-fare people in the first three rows began to whistle and stamp also, and the longer the love picture lasted, the louder they became. So that finally the manager came down with a flashlight and rooted the whole crowd of them out of their seats and marched them up the aisle and left them standing on the sidewalk: done out of their dimes, and disgusted.

The old Frankie had never admitted love. Yet here F. Jasmine was sitting at the table with her knees crossed, and now and then she patted her bare foot on the floor in an accustomed way, and nodded at what Berenice was saying. Furthermore, when she reached out quietly toward the Chesterfield package beside the saucer of melted butter, Berenice did not slap her hand away, and F. Jasmine took herself a cigarette. She and Berenice were two grown people smoking at the dinner table. And John Henry West had his big child head hunched close to his shoulder, watching and listening to all that went on.

'Now I will tell you a story,' said Berenice. 'And it is to be a warning to you. You hear me, John Henry? You hear me, Frankie?'

'Yes,' John Henry whispered. He pointed with his gray little forefinger. 'Frankie is smoking.'

Berenice sat up straight, her shoulders square, and her

dark twisted hands folded before her on the table. She raised her chin and drew in her breath in the way of a singer who is beginning a song. The piano tuned and insisted, but when Berenice began to speak, her dark gold voice rang in the kitchen and they did not listen to the piano notes. But to start this warning Berenice began with the old same story that they had heard many times before. The story of her and Ludie Freeman. A long time ago.

'Now I am here to tell you I was happy. There was no human woman in all the world more happy than I was in them days,' she said. 'And that includes everybody. You listening to me, John Henry? It includes all queens and millionaires and first ladies of the land. And I mean it includes people of all color. You hear me, Frankie? No human woman in all the world was happier than Berenice Sadie Brown.'

She had started with the old story of Ludie. And it began an afternoon in late October almost twenty years ago. The story started at the place where first they met each other, in front of Camp Campbell's Filling Station outside of the city limits of the town. It was the time of the year when the leaves were turning and the countryside was smoky and autumn gray and gold. And the story went on from that first meeting to the wedding at the Welcome Ascension Church in Sugarville. And then on through the years with the two of them together. The house with the brick front steps and the glass windows on the corner of Barrow Street. The Christmas of the fox fur, and the June of the fish fry thrown for twenty-eight invited relatives and guests. The years with Berenice cooking dinner and sewing Ludie's suits and shirts on the machine and the two of them always having a good time. And the nine months they lived up North, in the city of Cincinnati, where there was snow. Then Sugarville again, and days merging one into another, and the weeks, the months, the years together. And the pair of them always had a good time, yet it was not so much the happenings she mentioned as the way she told about these happenings that made F. Jasmine understand.

Berenice spoke in an unwinding kind of voice, and she had said that she was happier than a queen. As she told the story, it seemed to F. Jasmine that Berenice resembled a strange queen, if a queen can be colored and sitting at a kitchen table. She unwound the story of her and Ludie like a colored queen unwinding a bolt of cloth of gold — and at the end, when the story was over, her expression was always the same: the dark eye staring straight ahead, her flat nose widened and trembling, her mouth finished and sad and quiet. As a rule, when the story was over, they would sit for a moment and then suddenly get busy doing something in a hurry: start a hand of cards, or make milkshakes, or just stir around the kitchen with no particular purpose. But this afternoon they did not move or speak for a long time after Berenice had finished, until finally F. Jasmine asked:

'What exactly did Ludie die of?'

'It was something similar to pneumonia,' said Berenice. 'November the year 1931.'

'The very year and the very month I was born,' F. Jasmine said.

'The coldest November I ever seen. Every morning there was frost and puddles were crusted with ice. The sunshine was pale yellow like it is in wintertime. Sounds carried far away, and I remember a hound dog that used to howl toward sundown. I kept a fire in the hearth going day and night, and in the evening when I walk around the room there was this shaking shadow following alongside of me on the wall. And everything I seen come to me as a kind of sign.'

'I think it is a kind of sign I was born the same year and the same month he died,' F. Jasmine said. 'Only the dates are different.'

'And then it was a Thursday toward six o'clock in the afternoon. About this time of day. Only November. I remember I went to the passage and opened the front door. We were living that year at 233 Prince Street. Dark was coming on, the old hound was howling far away. And I go back in the room and lay down on Ludie's bed. I lay myself down over Ludie with my arms spread out and my face on his face. And I pray that the Lord would contage my strenth to him. And I ask the Lord let it be anybody, but not let it be Ludie. And I lay there and pray for a long time. Until night.'

'How?' John Henry asked. It was a question that did not mean anything, but he repeated it in a higher, wailing voice: 'How, Berenice?'

'That night he died,' she said. She spoke in a sharp tone, as though they had disputed with her. 'I tell you he died. Ludie! Ludie Freeman! Ludie Maxwell Freeman died!'

She was finished, and they sat there at the table. Nobody moved. John Henry stared at Berenice, and the fly that had been hovering above him lighted on the left rim of his glasses; the fly walked slowly across the left lens, and over the nosepiece, and across the right lens. It was only when the fly had flown away that John Henry blinked and waved his hand.

'One thing,' F. Jasmine said finally. 'There is Uncle

Charles laying there dead right now. Yet somehow I can't cry. I know I ought to feel sad. Yet I feel sadder about Ludie than I do about Uncle Charles. Although I never laid eyes on Ludie. And I knew Uncle Charles all my life and he was blood kin to blood kin of mine. Maybe it's because I was born so soon after Ludie died.'

'Maybe so,' said Berenice.

It seemed to F. Jasmine that they might just sit there the rest of the afternoon, without moving or speaking, when suddenly she remembered something.

'You were starting out to tell a different story,' she said. 'It was some kind of warning.'

Berenice looked puzzled for a moment, then she jerked her head up and said: 'Oh, yes! I was going to tell you how this thing we was talking about applies to me. And what happened with them other husbands. Now you perk your ears.'

But the story of the other three husbands was an old story also. As Berenice began to talk, F. Jasmine went to the refrigerator and brought back to the table some sweetened condensed milk to pour on crackers as a dessert. At first she did not listen very carefully.

'It was the April of the following year that I went one Sunday to the Forks Falls Church. And you ask what I was doing out there and I tell you. I was visiting that Jackson branch of my foster cousins who live out there and we had gone to their church. So there I was praying in this church where the congregation was strangers to me. I had my forehead down on the top of the pew in front of me, and my eyes were open — not gazing around in secret, mind you, but just open. When suddenly this shiver run all the way through me. I had caught sight of something from the corner of my eye. And I looked slowly to the left. And guess what I seen there? There on the pew, just six inches from my eye, was this *thumb*.'

'What thumb?' F. Jasmine asked.

'Now I'm telling you,' said Berenice. 'To understand this, you have to know that there was only one little portion of Ludie Freeman which was not pretty. Every other part about him was handsome and pretty as anyone would ever wish. All except his right thumb, which had been mashed in a hinge. This one thumb had a mashed chewed appearance that was not pretty. You understand?'

'You mean you suddenly saw Ludie's thumb when you were praying?'

'I mean I seen *this* thumb. And as I kneel there a shiver run from my head to my heels. I just kneel there staring at this thumb, and before I looked any further, to find out whose thumb it might be, I begun to pray in earnest. I prayed out loud: Lord, manifest! Lord, manifest!'

'And did He?' F. Jasmine asked. 'Manifest?'

Berenice turned aside and made a sound like spitting. 'Manifest, my foot!' she said. 'You know who that thumb belonged to?'

'Who?'

'Why Jamie Beale,' said Berenice. 'That big old no-good Jamie Beale. It was the first time I ever laid eyes on him.'

'Is that why you married him?' F. Jasmine asked, for Jamie Beale was the name of the sorry old liquor-drinker, who was the second husband. 'Because he had a mashed thumb like Ludie's?'

'Jesus knows,' said Berenice. 'I don't. I felt drawn to him on account of the thumb. And then one thing led to another. First thing I knew I had married him.'

'Well, I think that was silly,' F. Jasmine said. 'To marry him just because of that thumb.'

'Me too,' said Berenice. 'I'm not trying to dispute with you. I'm just telling you what happened. And the very same thing occurred in the case of Henry Johnson.'

Henry Johnson was the third husband, the one who had gone crazy on Berenice. He was all right for three weeks after they had married, but then he went crazy, and he behaved in such a crazy way that finally she had to quit him.

'You mean to sit there and tell me Henry Johnson had one of those mashed thumbs too?'

'No,' said Berenice. 'It was not the thumb that time. It was the coat.'

F. Jasmine and John Henry looked at each other, for what she was saying did not seem to make much sense. But Berenice's dark eye was sober and certain, and she nodded to them in a definite way.

'To understand this, you have to know what happened after Ludie died. He had a policy due to pay off two hundred and fifty dollars. I won't go into the whole business, but what happened was that I was cheated by them policy people out of fifty dollars. And in two days I had to scour around and raise the fifty dollars to make out for the funeral. Because I couldn't let Ludie be put away cheap. I pawned everything I could lay hands on. And I sold my coat and Ludie's coat. To that second-hand clothing store on Front Avenue.'

'Oh!' F. Jasmine said. 'Then you mean Henry Johnson bought Ludie's coat and you married him because of it.'

'Not exactly,' said Berenice. 'I was walking down that street alongside of the City Hall one evening when I suddenly seen this shape before me. Now the shape of this boy ahead of me was so similar to Ludie through the shoulders and the back of the head that I almost dropped dead there on the sidewalk. I followed and run behind him. It was Henry Johnson, and that was the first time I ever saw him also, since he lived in the country and didn't come much into town. But he had chanced to buy Ludie's coat and he was built on the same shape as Ludie. And from the back view it looked like he was Ludie's ghost or Ludie's twin. But how I married him I don't exactly know, for to begin with it was clear that he did not have his share of sense. But you let a boy hang around and you get fond of him. Anyway, that's how I married Henry Johnson.'

'People certainy do curious things.'

'You telling me,' said Berenice. She glanced at F. Jasmine, who was pouring a slow ribbon of condensed milk over a soda cracker, to finish her dinner with a sweet sandwich.

'I swear, Frankie! I believe you got a tate worm. I am perfectly serious. Your father looks over them big grocery bills and he naturally suspicions that I carry things off.'

'You do,' F. Jasmine said. 'Sometimes.'

'He reads over them grocery bills and he complains to me, Berenice, what in the name of holy creation did we do with six cans of condensed milk and forty-leven dozen eggs and eight boxes of marshmallows in one week. And I have to admit to him: Frankie eat them. I have to say to him: Mr. Addams, you think you feeding something human back here in your kitchen. That's what you think. I have to say to him: Yes, you imagine it is something human.'

'After today I'm not going to be greedy any more,' F. Jasmine said. 'But I don't understand the point of what you was telling. I don't see how that about Jamie Beale and Henry Johnson applies to me.'

'It applies to everybody and it is a warning.'

'But how?'

'Why, don't you see what I was doing?' asked Berenice. 'I loved Ludie and he was the first man I loved. Therefore, I had to go and copy myself forever afterward. What I did was to marry off little pieces of Ludie whenever I come across them. It was just my misfortune they all turned out to be the wrong pieces. My intention was to repeat me and Ludie. Now don't you see?'

'I see what you're driving at,' F. Jasmine said. 'But I don't see how it is a warning applied to me.'

'Then do I have to tell you?' asked Berenice.

F. Jasmine did not nod or answer, for she felt that Berenice had laid a trap for her, and was going to make remarks she did not want to hear. Berenice stopped to light herself another cigarette and two blue slow scrolls of smoke came from her nostrils and lazed above the dirty dishes on the table. Mr. Schwarzenbaum was playing an arpeggio. F. Jasmine waited and it seemed a long time.

'You and that wedding at Winter Hill,' Berenice said finally. 'That is what I am warning about. I can see right through them two gray eyes of yours like they was glass. And what I see is the saddest piece of foolishness I ever knew.'

'Gray eyes is glass,' John Henry whispered.

But F. Jasmine would not let herself be seen through and outstared; she hardened and tensed her eyes and did not look away from Berenice.

'I see what you have in your mind. Don't think I don't. You see something unheard of at Winter Hill tomorrow, and you right in the center. You think you going to march down the center of the aisle right in between your brother and the bride. You think you going to break into that wedding, and then Jesus knows what else.'

'No,' F. Jasmine said. 'I don't see myself walking down the center of the aisle between them.'

'I see through them eyes,' said Berenice. 'Don't argue with me.'

John Henry said again, but softer: 'Gray eyes is glass.'

'But what I'm warning is this,' said Berenice. 'If you start out falling in love with some unheard-of thing like that, what is going to happen to you? If you take a mania like this, it won't be the last time and of that you can be sure. So what will become of you? Will you be trying to break into weddings the rest of your days? And what kind of life would that be?'

'It makes me sick to listen at people who don't have any sense,' F. Jasmine said, and she put her two fingers in her ears, but she did not push in the fingers very tight and she could still hear Berenice.

'You just laying yourself this fancy trap to catch yourself in trouble,' Berenice went on. 'And you know it. You been through the B section of the seventh grade and you are already twelve years old.'

F. Jasmine did not speak of the wedding, but her argument passed over it, and she said: 'They will take me. You wait and see.'

'And when they don't?'

'I told you,' F. Jasmine said. 'I will shoot myself with Papa's pistol. But they will take me. And we're never coming back to this part of the country again.'

'Well, I been trying to reason seriously,' said Berenice. 'But I see it is no use. You determined to suffer.'

'Who said I was going to suffer?' F. Jasmine said.

'I know you,' said Berenice. 'You will suffer.'

'You are just jealous,' F. Jasmine said. 'You are just trying to deprive me of all the pleasure of leaving town. And kill the joy of it.'

'I am just trying to head this off,' said Berenice. 'But I see it is no use.'

John Henry whispered for the last time: 'Gray eyes is glass.'

It was past six o'clock, and the slow old afternoon began slowly to die. F. Jasmine took her fingers from her ears and breathed a long tired sigh. When she had sighed, John Henry sighed also, and Berenice concluded with the longest sigh of all. Mr. Schwarzenbaum had played a ragged little waltz; but the piano was not yet tuned to suit him, and he began to harp and insist on another note. Again he played the scale up until the seventh note, and again he stuck there and did not finish. F. Jasmine was no longer watching the music with her eyes; but John Henry was watching, and when the piano stuck on the last note F. Jasmine could see him harden his behind and sit there stiff in the chair, his eyes raised, waiting.

'It is that last note,' F. Jasmine said. 'If you start with A and go on up to G, there is a curious thing that seems to make the difference between G and A all the difference in the world. Twice as much difference as between any other two notes in the scale. Yet they are side by side there on the piano just as close together as the other notes. Do ray mee fa sol la tee. Tee. Tee. Tee. It could drive you wild.'

John Henry was grinning with his snaggle teeth and giggling softly. 'Tee-tee,' he said, and he pulled at Berenice's sleeve. 'Did you hear what Frankie said? Tee-tee.'

'Shut your trap,' F. Jasmine said. 'Quit always being so evil-minded.' She got up from the table, but she did not know where to go. 'You didn't say anything about Willis Rhodes. Did he have a mashed thumb or a coat or something?'

'Lord!' said Berenice, and her voice was so sudden and shocked that F. Jasmine turned and went back to the table. 'Now that is a story would make the hair rise on your head. You mean to say I never told you about what happened with me and Willis Rhodes?'

'No,' F. Jasmine said. Willis Rhodes was the last and the worst of the four husbands, and he was so terrible that Berenice had had to call the Law on him. 'What?'

'Well, imagine this!' said Berenice. 'Imagine a cold bitter January night. And me laying all by myself in the big parlor bed. Alone in the house, because everybody else had gone for the Saturday night to Forks Falls. Me, mind you, who hates to sleep in a empty old bed all by myself and is nervous in a house alone. Past twelve o'clock on this cold bitter January night. Can you remember wintertime, John Henry?'

John Henry nodded.

'Now imagine this!' said Berenice again. She had begun stacking the dishes so that three dirty plates were piled before her on the table. Her dark eye circled around the table, roping in F. Jasmine and John Henry as her audience. F. Jasmine leaned forward, her mouth open and her hands holding the table edge. John Henry shivered down in his chair and he watched Berenice through his glasses without batting his eyes. Berenice had started in a low and creepy voice, then suddenly she stopped and sat there looking at the two of them.

'So what?' F. Jasmine urged, leaning closer across the table. 'What happened?'

But Berenice did not speak. She looked from one of them to the other, and shook her head slowly. Then when she spoke again her voice was completely changed, and she said: 'Why, I wish you would look yonder. I wish you would look.'

F. Jasmine glanced quickly behind her, but there was only the stove, the wall, the empty stair.

'What?' she asked. 'What happened?'

'I wish you would look,' Berenice repeated. 'Them two little pitchers and them four big ears.' She got up suddenly from the table. 'Come on, less wash the dishes. Then we going to make some cup cakes to take tomorrow on the trip.'

There was nothing F. Jasmine could do to show Berenice how she felt. After a long time, when the table before her was already cleared and Berenice stood washing dishes at the sink, she only said:

'If it's anything I mortally despise it's a person who starts out to tell something and works up people's interest and then stops.'

'I admit it,' said Berenice. 'And I am sorry. But it was just one of them things I suddenly realize I couldn't tell you and John Henry.'

John Henry was skipping and scuttling back and forth across the kitchen, from the stairway to the back porch door. 'Cup cakes!' he sang. 'Cup cakes! Cup cakes!'

'You could have sent him out of the room,' F. Jasmine said. 'And told me. But don't think I care. I don't care a particle what happened. I just wish Willis Rhodes had come in about that time and slit your throat.'

'That is a ugly way to talk,' said Berenice. 'Especially

since I got a surprise for you. Go out on the back porch and look in the wicker basket covered with a newspaper.'

F. Jasmine got up, but grudgingly, and she walked in a crippled way to the back porch. Then she stood in the doorway holding the pink organdie dress. Contrary to all that Berenice had maintained, the collar was pleated with tiny little pleats, as it was meant to be. She must have done it before dinner when F. Jasmine was upstairs.

'Well, this is mighty nice of you,' she said. 'I appreciate it.'

She would have liked for her expression to be split into two parts, so that one eye stared at Berenice in an accusing way, and the other eye thanked her with a grateful look. But the human face does not divide like this, and the two expressions canceled out each other.

'Cheer up,' said Berenice. 'Who can tell what will happen? You might dress up in that fresh pink dress tomorrow and meet the cutest little white boy in Winter Hill you ever seen. It's just on such trips as these that you run into beaus.'

'But that's not what I'm talking about,' F. Jasmine said. Then, after a while, still leaning against the doorway, she added: 'Somehow we got off on the wrong kind of conversation.'

The twilight was white, and it lasted for a long while. Time in August could be divided into four parts: morning, afternoon, twilight, and dark. At twilight the sky became a curious blue-green which soon faded to white. The air was soft gray, and the arbor and trees were slowly darkening. It was the hour when sparrows gathered and whirled above the rooftops of the town, and when in the darkened elms along the street there was the August sound of the cicadas.

Noises at twilight had a blurred sound, and they lingered: the slam of a screen door down the street, voices of children, the whir of a lawnmower from a yard somewhere. F. Jasmine brought in the evening newspaper, and dark was coming in the kitchen. The corners in the room at first were dark, then the drawings on the wall faded. The three of them watched the dark come on in silence.

'The army is now in Paris.'

'That's good.'

They were quiet awhile and then F. Jasmine said: 'I have a lot of things to do. I ought to start out now.'

But although she stood ready in the doorway, she did not go. On this last evening, the last time with the three of them together in the kitchen, she felt there was some final thing she ought to say or do before she went away. For many months she had been ready to leave this kitchen, never to return again; but now that the time had come, she stood there with her head and shoulder leaning against the door jamb, somehow unready. It was the darkening hour when the remarks they made had a sad and beautiful sound, although there would be nothing sad or beautiful about the meanings of the words.

F. Jasmine said quietly: 'I intend to take two baths tonight. One long soaking bath and scrub with a brush. I'm going to try to scrape this brown crust off my elbows. Then let out the dirty water and take a second bath.'

'That's a good idea,' said Berenice. 'I will be glad to see you clean.'

'I will take another bath,' John Henry said. His voice was thin and sad; she could not see him in the darkening room, since he stood in the corner by the stove. At seven Berenice had bathed him and dressed him in his shorts again. She heard him shuffle carefully across the room, for after the bath he had put on Berenice's hat and was trying to walk in Berenice's high-heeled shoes. Again he asked a question which by itself meant nothing. 'Why?' he asked.

'Why what, Baby?' said Berenice.

He did not answer, and it was F. Jasmine who finally said: 'Why is it against the law to change your name?'

Berenice sat in a chair against the pale white light of the window. She held the newspaper open before her, and her head was twisted down and to one side as she strained to see what was printed there. When F. Jasmine spoke, she folded the paper and put it away on the table.

'You can figure that out,' she said. 'Just because. Think of the confusion.'

'I don't see why,' F. Jasmine said.

'What is that on your neck?' said Berenice. 'I thought it was a head you carried on that neck. Just think. Suppose I would suddenly up and call myself Mrs. Eleanor Roosevelt. And you would begin naming yourself Joe Louis. And John Henry would try to pass off as Henry Ford. Now what kind of confusion do you think that would cause?'

'Don't talk childish,' F. Jasmine said. 'That is not the kind of changing I mean. I mean from a name that doesn't suit you to a name you prefer. Like I changed from Frankie to F. Jasmine.'

'But still it would be a confusion,' Berenice insisted. 'Suppose we all suddenly change to entirely different names. Nobody would ever know who anybody was talking about. The whole world would go crazy.'

'I don't see ——'

'Because things accumulate around your name,' said Berenice. 'You have a name and one thing after another happens to you, and you behave in various ways and do things, so that soon the name begins to have a meaning. Things have accumulated around the name. If it is bad and you have a bad reputation, then you just can't jump out of your name and escape like that. And if it is good and you have a good reputation, then you should be content and satisfied.'

'But what had accumulated around my old name?' F. Jasmine asked. Then, when Berenice did not reply at once, F. Jasmine answered her own question. 'Nothing! See? My name just didn't mean anything.'

'Well, that's not exactly so,' said Berenice. 'People think of Frankie Addams and it brings to the mind that Frankie is finished with the B section of the seventh grade. And Frankie found the golden egg at the Baptist Easter Hunt. And Frankie lives on Grove Street and——'

'But those things are nothing,' F. Jasmine said. 'See? They're not worth while. Nothing ever happened to me.'

'But it will,' said Berenice. 'Things will happen.'

'What?' F. Jasmine asked.

Berenice sighed and reached for the Chesterfield package inside her bosom. 'You pin me down like that and I can't tell you truthfully. If I could I would be a wizard. I wouldn't be sitting here in this kitchen right now, but making a fine living on Wall Street as a wizard. All I can say is that things will happen. Just what, I don't know.'

'By the way,' F. Jasmine said after a while. 'I thought I would go around to your house and see Big Mama. I don't believe in those fortunes, or anything like that, but I thought I might as well.'

'Suit yourself. However, I don't think it is necessary.'

'I suppose I ought to leave now,' F. Jasmine said.

But still she waited in the darkening door and did not go away. The sounds of the summer twilight crossed within the silence of the kitchen. Mr. Schwarzenbaum had finished tuning the piano, and for the past quarter of an hour he had been playing little pieces. He played music memorized by note, and he was a nervous spry old man who reminded F. Jasmine of a silver spider. His music was spry and stiff also, and he played faint jerking waltzes and nervous lullabies. Farther down the block a solemn radio announced something they could not hear. In the O'Neils' back yard, next door, children were calling and swatting a ball. The sounds of evening canceled out each other, and they were faded in the darkening twilight air. The kitchen itself was very quiet.

'Listen,' F. Jasmine said. 'What I've been trying to say is this. Doesn't it strike you as strange that I am I, and you are you? I am F. Jasmine Addams. And you are Berenice Sadie Brown. And we can look at each other, and touch each other, and stay together year in and year out in the same room. Yet always I am I, and you are you. And I can't ever be anything else but me, and you can't ever be anything else but you. Have you ever thought of that? And does it seem to you strange?'

Berenice had been rocking slightly in the chair. She was not sitting in a rocking chair, but she had been tilting back in the straight chair, then letting the front legs hit the floor with little taps, her dark stiff hand held to the table edge for balance. She stopped rocking herself when F. Jasmine spoke. And finally she said: 'I have thought of it occasionally.'

It was the hour when the shapes in the kitchen darkened and voices bloomed. They spoke softly and their voices bloomed like flowers — if sounds can be like flowers and voices bloom. F. Jasmine stood with her hands clasped behind her head, facing the darkening room. She had the feeling that unknown words were in her throat, and she was ready to speak them. Strange words were flowering in her throat and now was the time for her to name them.

'This,' she said. 'I see a green tree. And to me it is green. And you would call the tree green also. And we would agree on this. But is the color you see as green the same color I see as green? Or say we both call a color black. But how do we know that what you see as black is the same color I see as black?'

Berenice said after a moment: 'Those things we just cannot prove.'

F. Jasmine scraped her head against the door, and put her hand up to her throat. Her voice shattered and died. 'That's not what I meant to say, anyway.'

The smoke of Berenice's cigarette lay bitter and warm and stagnant in the room. John Henry shuffled in the high-heeled shoes from the stove to the table and back again. A rat rattled behind the wall.

'This is what I mean,' F. Jasmine said. 'You are walking down a street and you meet somebody. Anybody. And you look at each other. And you are you. And he is him. Yet when you look at each other, the eyes make a connection. Then you go off one way. And he goes off another way. You go off into different parts of town, and maybe you never see each other again. Not in your whole life. Do you see what I mean?'

'Not exactly,' said Berenice.

'I'm talking about this town,' F. Jasmine said in a higher voice. 'There are all these people here I don't even know by sight or name. And we pass alongside each other and don't have any connection. And they don't know me and I don't know them. And now I'm leaving town and there are all these people I will never know.'

'But who do you want to know?' asked Berenice.

F. Jasmine answered: 'Everybody. In the world. Everybody in the world.'

'Why, I wish you would listen to that,' said Berenice. 'How about people like Willis Rhodes? How about them Germans? Them Japanese?'

F. Jasmine knocked her head against the door jamb and looked up at the dark ceiling. Her voice broke, and again she said: 'That's not what I mean. That's not what I'm talking about.'

'Well, what *is* you talking about?' asked Berenice.

F. Jasmine shook her head, almost as though she did not know. Her heart was dark and silent, and from her heart the unknown words flowered and bloomed and she waited to name them. From next door there was the evening sound of childrens' baseball and the long call: Batteruup! Batteruup! Then the hollow pock of a ball and the clatter of a thrown bat and running footsteps and wild voices. The window was a rectangle of pale clear light and a child ran across the yard and under the dark arbor after the ball. The child was quick as a shadow and F. Jasmine did not see his face — his white shirttails flapped loose behind him like queer wings. Beyond the window the twilight was lasting and pale and still.

'Less play out, Frankie,' John Henry whispered. 'They sound like they having a mighty good time.'

'No,' F. Jasmine said. 'You go.'

Berenice stirred in her chair and said: 'I suppose we could turn on the light.'

But they did not turn on the light. F. Jasmine felt the unsaid words stick in her throat and a choked sickness made her groan and knock her head against the door jamb. Finally she said again in a high ragged voice:

'This:'

Berenice waited, and when she did not speak again, she asked: 'What on earth is wrong with you?'

F. Jasmine could not speak the unknown words, so after a minute she knocked her head a last time on the door and then began to walk around the kitchen table. She walked in a stiff-legged delicate way, as she felt sick, and did not wish to joggle the different foods that she had eaten and mix them up inside her stomach. She began to talk in a high fast voice, but they were the wrong words, and not what she had meant to say.

'Boyoman! Manoboy!' she said. 'When we leave Winter Hill we're going to more places than you ever thought about or even knew existed. Just where we will go first I don't know, and it don't matter. Because after we go to that place we're going on to another. We mean to keep moving, the three of us. Here today and gone tomorrow. Alaska, China, Iceland, South America. Traveling on trains. Letting her rip on motorcycles. Flying around all over the world in aeroplanes. Here today and gone tomorrow. All over the world. It's the damn truth. Boyoman!'

F. Jasmine jerked open the drawer of the table and fumbled inside for the butcher knife. She did not need the butcher knife, but she wanted something to grasp in her hand and wave about as she hurried around the table.

'And talking of things happening,' she said. 'Things will happen so fast we won't hardly have time to realize them. Captain Jarvis Addams sinks twelve Jap battleships and decorated by the President. Miss F. Jasmine Addams breaks all records. Mrs. Janice Addams elected Miss United Nations in beauty contest. One thing after another happening so fast we don't hardly notice them.'

'Hold still, Fool,' said Berenice. 'And lay down that knife.'

'And we will meet them. Everybody. We will just walk up to people and know them right away. We will be walking down a dark road and see a lighted house and knock on the door and strangers will rush to meet us and say: Come in! Come in! We will know decorated aviators and New York people and movie stars. We will have thousands of friends, thousands and thousands and thousands of friends. We will belong to so many clubs that we can't even keep track of all of them. We will be members of the whole world. Boyoman! Manoboy!'

Berenice had a very strong long right arm, and when F. Jasmine passed her the next time as she was running around the table, this arm reached out and snatched her by the petticoat so quickly that she was caught up with a jerk that made her bones crack and her teeth rattle.

'*Is* you gone raving wild?' she asked. The long arm pulled F. Jasmine closer and wrapped around her waist. 'You sweating like a mule. Lean down and let me feel your forehead. Is you got a fever?'

F. Jasmine pulled one of Berenice's plaits and pretended she was going to saw it off with the knife.

'You trembling,' said Berenice. 'I truly believe you took a fever walking around in that sun today. Baby, you sure you ain't sick?'

'Sick?' asked F. Jasmine. 'Who, me?'

'Set here in my lap,' said Berenice. 'And rest a minute.'

F. Jasmine put the knife on the table and settled down on Berenice's lap. She leaned back and put her face against Berenice's neck; her face was sweaty and Berenice's neck was sweaty also, and they both smelled salty and sour and sharp. Her right leg was flung across Berenice's knee, and it was trembling — but when she steadied her toes on the floor, her leg did not tremble any more. John Henry shuffled toward them in the high-heeled shoes and crowded up jealous and close to Berenice. He put his arm around Berenice's head and held on to her ear. Then after a moment he tried to push F. Jasmine out of her lap, and he pinched F. Jasmine with a mean and tiny little pinch.

'Leave Frankie alone,' said Berenice. 'She ain't bothered you.'

He made a fretting sound: 'I'm sick.'

'Now no, you ain't. Be quiet and don't grudge your cousin a little bit of love.'

'Old mean bossy Frankie,' he complained in a high sad voice.

'What she doing so mean right now? She just laying here wore out.'

F. Jasmine rolled her head and rested her face against Berenice's shoulder. She could feel Berenice's soft big ninnas against her back, and her soft wide stomach, her warm solid legs. She had been breathing very fast, but after a minute her breath slowed down so that she breathed in time with Berenice; the two of them were close together as one body, and Berenice's stiffened hands were clasped around F. Jasmine's chest. Their backs were to the window, and before them the kitchen was now almost dark. It was Berenice who finally sighed and started the conclusion of that last queer conversation.

'I think I have a vague idea what you were driving at,' she said. 'We all of us somehow caught. We born this way or that way and we don't know why. But we caught anyhow. I born Berenice. You born Frankie. John Henry born John Henry. And maybe we wants to widen and bust free. But no matter what we do we still caught. Me is me and you is you and he is he. We each one of us somehow caught all by ourself. Is that what you was trying to say?'

'I don't know,' F. Jasmine said. 'But I don't want to be caught.'

'Me neither,' said Berenice. 'Don't none of us. I'm caught worse than you is.'

F. Jasmine understood why she had said this, and it was John Henry who asked in his child voice: 'Why?'

'Because I am black,' said Berenice. 'Because I am colored. Everybody is caught one way or another. But they done drawn completely extra bounds around all colored people. They done squeezed us off in one corner by ourself. So we caught that firstway I was telling you, as all human beings is caught. And we caught as colored people also. Sometimes a boy like Honey feel like he just can't breathe no more. He feel like he got to break something or break himself. Sometimes it just about more than we can stand.'

'I know it,' F. Jasmine said. 'I wish Honey could do something.'

'He just feels desperate like.'

'Yes,' F. Jasmine said. 'Sometimes I feel like I want to break something, too. I feel like I wish I could just tear down the whole town.'

'So I have heard you mention,' said Berenice. 'But that won't help none. The point is that we all caught. And we try in one way or another to widen ourself free. For instance, me and Ludie. When I was with Ludie, I didn't feel so caught. But then Ludie died. We go around trying one thing or another, but we caught anyhow.'

The conversation made F. Jasmine almost afraid. She lay there close to Berenice and they were breathing very slowly. She could not see John Henry, but she could feel him; he had climbed up on the back rungs of the chair and was hugging Berenice's head. He was holding her ears, for in a moment Berenice said: 'Candy, don't wrench my ears like that. Me and Frankie ain't going to float up through the ceiling and leave you.'

Water dropped slowly in the kitchen sink and the rat was knocking behind the wall.

'I believe I realize what you were saying,' F. Jasmine said. 'Yet at the same time you almost might use the word loose instead of caught. Although they are two opposite words. I mean you walk around and you see all the people. And to me they look loose.'

'Wild, you mean?'

'Oh, no!' she said. 'I mean you don't see what joins them up together. You don't know where they all came from, or where they're going to. For instance, what made anybody ever come to this town in the first place? Where did all these people come from and what are they going to do? Think of all those soldiers.'

'They were born,' said Berenice. 'And they going to die.'

F. Jasmine's voice was thin and high. 'I know,' she said. 'But what is it all about? People loose and at the same time caught. Caught and loose. All these people and you don't know what joins them up. There's bound to be some sort of reason and connection. Yet somehow I can't seem to name it. I don't know.'

'If you did you would be God,' said Berenice. 'Didn't you know that?'

'Maybe so.'

'We just know so much. Then beyond that we don't know no more.'

'But I wish I did.' Her back was cramped and she stirred and stretched herself on Berenice's lap, her long legs sprawling out beneath the kitchen table. 'Anyway, after we leave Winter Hill I won't have to worry about things any more.'

'You don't have to now. Nobody requires you to solve the riddles of the world.' Berenice took a deep meaning breath and said: 'Frankie, you got the sharpest set of human bones I ever felt.'

This was a strong hint for F. Jasmine to stand up. She would turn on the light, then take one of the cup cakes from the stove, and go out to finish her business in the town. But for a moment longer she lay there with her face pressed close to Berenice's shoulder. The sounds of the summer evening were mingled and long-drawn.

'I never did say just what I was talking about,' she said finally. 'But there's this. I wonder if you have ever thought about this. Here we are — right now. This very minute. Now. But while we're talking right now, this minute is passing. And it will never come again. Never in all the world. When it is gone it is gone. No power on earth could bring it back again. It is gone. Have you ever thought about that?'

Berenice did not answer, and the kitchen was now dark. The three of them sat silent, close together, and they could feel and hear each other's breaths. Then suddenly it started, though why and how they did not know; the three of them began to cry. They started at exactly the same moment, in the way that often on these summer evenings they would suddenly start a song. Often in the dark, that August, they would all at once begin to sing a Christmas carol, or a song like the Slitbelly Blues. Sometimes they knew in advance that they would sing, and they would agree on the tune among themselves.

Or again, they would disagree and start off on three different songs at once, until at last the tunes began to merge and they sang a special music that the three of them made up together. John Henry sang in a high wailing voice, and no matter what he named his tune, it sounded always just the same: one high trembling note that hung like a musical ceiling over the rest of the song. Berenice's voice was dark and definite and deep, and she rapped the offbeats with her heel. The old Frankie sang up and down the middle space between John Henry and Berenice, so that their three voices were joined, and the parts of the song were woven together.

Often they would sing like this and their tunes were sweet and queer in the August kitchen after it was dark. But never before had they suddenly begun to cry; and though their reasons were three different reasons, yet they started at the same instant as though they had agreed together. John Henry was crying because he was jealous, though later he tried to say he cried because of the rat behind the wall. Berenice was crying because of their talk about colored people, or because of Ludie, or perhaps because F. Jasmine's bones were really sharp. F. Jasmine did not know why she cried, but the reason she named was the crew-cut and the fact that her elbows were so rusty. They cried in the dark for about a minute. Then they stopped as suddenly as they had begun. The unaccustomed sound had quieted the rat behind the wall.

'Get up from there,' said Berenice. They stood around the kitchen table and F. Jasmine turned on the light. Berenice scratched her head and sniffled a little. 'We certainy is a gloomy crowd. Now I wonder what started that.'

The light was sudden and sharp after the darkness. F. Jasmine ran the faucet of the sink and put her head beneath the stream of water. And Berenice wiped off her face with a dishrag and patted her plaits before the mirror. John Henry stood like a little old woman dwarf, wearing the pink hat with the plume, and the high-heel shoes. The walls of the kitchen were crazy drawn and very bright. The three of them blinked at each other in the light as though they were three strangers or three ghosts. Then the front door opened and F. Jasmine heard her father trudging slowly down the hall. Already the moths were at the window, flattening their wings against the screen, and the final kitchen afternoon was over at last.

3

Early that evening F. Jasmine passed before the jail; she was on her way to Sugarville to have her fortune told and, though the jail was not directly on the way, she had wanted to have one final look at it before she left the town forever. For the jail had scared and haunted her that spring and summer. It was an old brick jail, three stories high, and surrounded by a cyclone fence topped with barbed wire. Inside were thieves, robbers, and murderers. The criminals were caged in stone cells with iron bars before the windows, and though they might beat on the stone walls or wrench at the iron bars, they could never get out. They wore striped jail clothes and ate cold peas with cockroaches cooked in them and cold cornbread.

F. Jasmine knew some people who had been locked up in jail, all of them colored — a boy called Cape, and a friend of Berenice who was accused by the white lady she worked for of stealing a sweater and a pair of shoes. When you were arrested, the Black Maria screamed to your house and a crowd of policemen burst in the door to haul you off down to the jail. After she took the three-bladed knife from the Sears and Roebuck Store, the jail had drawn the old Frankie — and sometimes on those late spring afternoons she would come to the street across from the jail, a place known as Jail-Widow's Walk, and stare for a long time. Often some criminals would be hanging to the bars; it seemed to her that their eyes, like the long eyes of the Freaks at the fair, had called to her as though to say: We know you. Occasionally, on Saturday afternoon, there would be wild yells and singing and hollering from the big cell known as the Bull Pen. But now this evening the jail was quiet — but from a lighted cell there was one criminal, or rather the outline of his head and his two fists around the bars. The brick jail was gloomy dark, although the yard and some cells were lighted.

'What are you locked up for?' John Henry called. He stood at a little distance from F. Jasmine and he was wearing the jonquil dress, as F. Jasmine had given him all the costumes. She had not wished to take him with her; but he had pleased and pleaded, and finally followed at a distance, anyway. When the criminal did not answer, he called again in a thin, high voice. 'Are you going to be hung?'

'Hush up!' F. Jasmine said. The jail did not frighten her this evening, for this time tomorrow she would be far away. She gave the jail a last glance and then walked on. 'How would you like for somebody to holler something like that to you if you were in jail?'

It was past eight o'clock when she reached Sugarville. The evening was dusty and lavender. Doors of the crowded houses on either side were open, and from some parlors there was the quavered flutter of oil lamps, lighting up the front-room beds and decorated mantelpieces. Voices sounded slurred and from a distance came the jazz of a piano and horn. Children played in alleyways, leaving whorled footsteps in the dust. The people were dressed for Saturday night, and on a corner she passed a group of jesting colored boys and girls in shining evening dresses. There was a party air about the street that reminded her that she, also, could go that very evening to a date at the Blue Moon. She spoke to people on the street and felt again the unexplainable connection between her eyes and other eyes. Mixed with the bitter dust, and smells of privies and suppertime, the smell of a clematis vine threaded the evening air. The house where Berenice lived was on the corner of Chinaberry Street — a two-room house with a tiny front yard bordered by shards and bottle-caps. A bench on the front porch held pots of cool, dark ferns. The door was only partly open and F. Jasmine could see the gold-gray flutters of the lamplight inside.

'You stay out here,' she said to John Henry.

There was the murmuring of a strong, cracked voice behind the door, and when F. Jasmine knocked, the voice was quiet a second and then asked:

'Who that? Who is it?'

'Me,' she said, for if she answered her true name, Big Mama would not recognize it. 'Frankie.'

The room was close, although the wooden shutter stood open, and there was the smell of sickness and fish. The crowded parlor was neat. One bed stood against the right wall, and on the opposite side of the room were a sewing machine and a pump organ. Over the hearth hung a photograph of Ludie Freeman; the mantelpiece was decorated with fancy calendars, fair prizes, souvenirs. Big Mama lay in the bed against the wall next to the door, so that in the daytime she could look out through the front window onto the ferny porch and street outside. She was an old colored woman, shriveled and with bones like broomsticks; on the left side of her face and neck the skin was the color of tallow, so that part of her face was almost white and the rest copper-colored. The old Frankie used to think that Big Mama was slowly turning to a white person, but Berenice had said it was a skin disease that sometimes happened to colored people. Big Mama had done fancy washing and fluted curtains until the year the misery had stiffened her back so that she took to bed. But she had not lost any faculties; instead, she suddenly found second-sight. The old Frankie had always thought she was uncanny, and when she was a little girl Big Mama was connected in her mind with the three ghosts who lived inside the coalhouse. And even now, a child no longer, she still had an eerie feeling about Big Mama. She was lying on three feather pillows, the covers of which were bordered with crochet, and over her bony legs there was a many-colored quilt. The parlor table with the lamp was pulled up close beside the bed so that she could reach the objects on it: a dream-book, a white saucer, a workbasket, a jellyglass of water, a Bible, and other things. Big Mama had been talking to herself before F. Jasmine came in, as she had the constant habit of telling herself just who she was and what she was doing and what she intended to do as she lay there in the bed. There were three mirrors on the walls which reflected the wavelike light from the lamp that fluttered gold-gray in the room and cast giant shadows; the lampwick needed trimming. Someone was walking in the back room.

'I came to get my fortune told,' F. Jasmine said.

While Big Mama talked to herself when alone, she could be very silent at other times. She stared at F. Jasmine for several seconds before she answered: 'Very well. Draw up that stool before the organ.'

F. Jasmine brought the stool close to the bed, and leaning forward, stretched out her palm. But Big Mama did not take her palm. She examined F. Jasmine's face, then spat the wad of snuff into a chamberpot which she pulled from underneath the bed, and finally put on her glasses. She waited so long that it occurred to F. Jasmine that she was trying to read her mind, and this made her uneasy. The walking in the back room stopped and there was no sound in the house.

'Cast back your mind and remember,' she said finally. 'Tell me the revelation of your last dream.'

F. Jasmine tried to cast back her mind, but she did not dream often. Then finally she remembered a dream she had had that summer: 'I dreamed there was a door,' she said. 'I was just looking at it and while I watched, it began slowly to open. And it made me feel funny and I woke up.'

'Was there a hand in the dream?'

F. Jasmine thought. 'I don't think so.'

'Was there a cockroach on that door?'

'Why — I don't think so.'

'It signifies as follows.' Big Mama slowly closed and opened her eyes. 'There going be a change in your life.'

Next she took F. Jasmine's palm and studied it for quite a while. 'I see here where you going to marry a boy with blue eyes and light hair. You will live to be your threescore and ten, but you must act careful about water. I see here a red-clay ditch and a bale of cotton.'

F. Jasmine thought to herself that there was nothing to it, only a pure waste of money and time. 'What does that signify?'

But suddenly the old woman raised her head and the cords of her neck stiffened as she called: 'You, Satan!'

She was looking at the wall between the parlor and the kitchen, and F. Jasmine turned to look over her shoulder also.

'Yessum,' a voice replied from the back room, and it sounded like Honey.

'How many times is I got to tell you to take them big feets off the kitchen table!'

'Yessum.' Honey said again. His voice was meek as Moses, and F. Jasmine could hear him put his feet down on the floor.

'Your nose is going to grow into that book, Honey Brown. Put it down and finish up your supper.'

F. Jasmine shivered. Had Big Mama looked clear through the wall and seen Honey reading with his feet up on the table? Could those eyes pierce through a pure plank wall? It seemed as though it would behoove her to listen carefully to every word.

'I see here a sum of money. A sum of money. And I see a wedding.'

F. Jasmine's outstretched hand trembled a little. 'That!' she said. 'Tell me about that!'

'The wedding or the money?'

'The wedding.'

The lamplight made an enormous shadow of them on the bare boards of the wall. 'It's the wedding of a near relation. And I foresee a trip ahead.'

'A trip?' she asked. 'What kind of a trip? A long trip?'

Big Mama's hands were crooked, spotted with freckly pale blots, and the palms were like melted pink birthday candles. 'A short trip,' she said.

'But how —?' F. Jasmine began.

'I see a going and a coming back. A departure and a return.'

There was nothing to it, for surely Berenice had told her about the trip to Winter Hill and the wedding. But if she could see straight through a wall — 'Are you sure?'

'Well —' This time the old cracked voice was not so certain. 'I see a departure and a return, but it may not be for *now*. I can't guarantee. For at the same time I see roads, trains, and a sum of money.'

'Oh!' F. Jasmine said.

There was the sound of footsteps, and Honey Camden Brown stood on the threshold between the kitchen and the parlor. He wore tonight a yellow shirt with a bow tie, for he was usually a natty dresser — but his dark eyes were sad, and his long face still as stone. F. Jasmine knew what Big Mama had said about Honey Brown. She said he was a boy God had not finished. The Creator had withdrawn His hand from him too soon. God had not finished him, and so he had to go around doing one thing and then another to finish himself up. When she had first heard this remark, the old Frankie did not understand the hidden meaning. Such a remark put her in mind of a peculiar half-boy — one arm, one leg, half a face — a half-person hopping in the gloomy summer sun around the corners of the town. But later she understood it a little better. Honey played the horn, and had been first in his studies at the colored high school. He ordered a French book from Atlanta and learned himself some French. At the same time he would suddenly run hog-wild all over Sugarville and tear around for several days, until his friends would bring him home more dead than living. His lips could move as light as butterflies and he could talk as well as any human she had ever heard — but other times he would answer with a colored jumble that even his own family could not follow. The Creator, Big Mama said, had withdrawn His hand from him too soon, so that he was left eternally unsatisfied. Now he stood there leaning against the door jamb, bony and limp, and although the sweat showed on his face he somehow looked cold.

'Do you wish anything before I go?' he asked.

There was something about Honey that evening that struck F. Jasmine; it was as though, on looking into his sad, still eyes, she felt she had something to say to him. His skin in the lamplight was the color of dark wistaria and the lips were quiet and blue.

'Did Berenice tell you about the wedding?' F. Jasmine asked. But, for once, it was not about the wedding that she felt she had to speak.

'Aaannh,' he answered.

'There's nothing I wish now. T. T. is due here in a minute to visit with me for a while and meet up with Berenice. Where you off to, boy?'

'I'm going over to Forks Falls.'

'Well, Mr. Up and Sudden, when you done decide that?'

Honey stood leaning against the door jamb, stubborn and quiet.

'Why can't you act like everybody else?' Big Mama said.

'I'll just stay over through Sunday and come back Monday morning.'

The feeling that she had something to say to Honey Brown still troubled F. Jasmine. She said to Big Mama: 'You were telling me about the wedding.'

'Yes.' She was not looking at F. Jasmine's palm, but at the organdie dress and the silk hose and the new silver slippers. 'I told you you would marry a light-haired boy with blue eyes. Later on.'

'But that's not what I'm talking about. I mean the other wedding. And the trip and what you saw about the roads and trains.'

'Exactly,' said Big Mama, but F. Jasmine had the feeling she was no longer paying much mind to her, although she looked again at her palm. 'I foresee a trip with a departure and a return and later a sum of money, roads and trains. Your lucky number is six, although thirteen is sometimes lucky for you too.'

F. Jasmine wanted to protest and argue, but how could you argue with a fortune-teller? She wanted at least to understand the fortune better, for the trip with the return did not fit in with the foreseeing of roads and trains.

But as she was about to question further, there were footsteps on the front porch, a door knock, and T. T. came into the parlor. He was very proper, scraping his feet, and bringing Big Mama a carton of ice cream. Berenice had said he did not make her shiver, and it was true he was nobody's pretty man; his stomach was like a watermelon underneath his vest and there were rolls of fat on the back of his neck. He brought in with him the stir of company that she had always loved and envied about this two-room house. Always it had seemed to the old Frankie, when she could come here hunting Berenice, that there would be many people in the room — the family, various cousins, friends. In the wintertime they would sit by the hearth around the draughty, shivering fire and talk with woven voices. On clear autumn nights they were always the first to have sugar cane and Berenice would hack the joints of the slick, purple cane and they would throw the chewed, twisted pieces, marked with their teethprints, on a newspaper spread upon the floor. The lamplight gave the room a special look, a special smell.

Now, with the coming of T. T., there was the old sense of company and commotion. The fortune was evidently over, and F. Jasmine put a dime in the white china saucer on the parlor table — for, although there was no fixed price, the future-anxious folks who came to Big Mama usually paid what they felt due.

'I declare I never did see anybody grow like you do, Frankie,' Big Mama remarked. 'What you ought to do is tie a brickbat to your head.' F. Jasmine shriveled on her heels, her knees bent slightly, and her shoulders hunched. 'That's a sweet dress you got on. And them silver shoes! And silk stockings! You look like a regular grown girl.'

F. Jasmine and Honey left the house at the same time, and she was still fretted by the feeling that she had something to say to him. John Henry, who had been waiting in the lane, rushed toward them, but Honey did not pick him up and swing him around as he sometimes did. There was a cold sadness about Honey this evening. The moonlight was white.

'What are you going to do in Forks Falls?'

'Just mess around.'

'Do you put any faith in those fortunes?' When Honey did not answer, she went on: 'You remember when she hollered back to you to take your feet off the table. Gave me a shock. How did she know your feet were on the table?'

'The mirror,' Honey said. 'She has a mirror by the door so she can see what goes on in the kitchen.'

'Oh,' she said. 'I never have believed in fortunes.'

John Henry was holding Honey's hand and looking up into his face. 'What are horsepowers?'

F. Jasmine felt the power of the wedding; it was as though, on this last evening, she ought to order and advise. There was something she ought to tell Honey, a warning or some wise advice. And as she fumbled in her mind, an idea came to her. It was so new, so unexpected, that she stopped walking and stood absolutely still.

'I know what you ought to do. You ought to go to Cuba or Mexico.'

Honey had walked on a few steps farther, but when she spoke he stopped also. John Henry was midway between them, and as he looked from one to the other, his face in the white moonlight had a mysterious expression.

'Sure enough. I'm perfectly serious. It don't do you any good to mess around between Fork Falls and this town. I've seen a whole lot of pictures of Cubans and Mexicans. They have a good time.' She paused. 'This is what I'm trying to discuss. I don't think you will ever be happy in this town. I think you ought to go to Cuba. You are so light-skinned and you even have a kind of Cuban expression. You could go there and change into a Cuban. You could learn to speak the foreign language and none of those Cubans would ever know you are a colored boy. Don't you see what I mean?'

Honey was still as a dark statue, and as silent.

'What?' John Henry asked again. 'What do they look like — them horsepowers?'

With a jerk Honey turned and went on down the lane. 'It is fantastic.'

'No, it is not!' Pleased that Honey had used the word fantastic to her, she said it quietly to herself before she went on to insist. 'It's not a particle fantastic. You mark my words. It's the best thing you can do.'

But Honey only laughed and turned off at the next alley. 'So long.'

The streets in the middle of the town reminded F. Jasmine of a carnival fair. There was the same air of holiday freedom; and, as in the early morning, she felt herself a part of everything, included and gay. On a Main Street corner a man was selling mechanical mice, and an armless beggar, with a tin cup in his lap, sat cross-legged on the sidewalk, watching. She had never seen Front Avenue at night before, for in the evening she was supposed to play in the neighborhood close to home. The warehouses across the street were black, but the square mill at the far end of the avenue was lighted in all its many windows and there was a faint mill humming and the smell of dyeing vats. Most of the businesses were open, and the neon signs made a mingling of varied lights that gave to the avenue a watery look. There were soldiers on corners, and other soldiers strolling along with grown date girls. The sounds were slurred late-summer sounds — footsteps, laughter, and above the shuffled noises, the voices of someone calling from an upper story down into the summer street. The buildings smelled of sunbaked brick and the sidewalk was warm beneath the soles of her new silver shoes. F. Jasmine stopped on the corner across from the Blue Moon. It seemed a long time since that morning when she had joined up with the soldier; the long kitchen afternoon had come between, and the soldier had somehow faded. The date, that afternoon, had seemed so very far away. And now that it was almost nine o'clock, she hesitated. She had the unexplainable feeling that there was a mistake.

'Where are we going?' John Henry asked. 'I think it's high time we went home.'

His voice startled her, as she had almost forgotten him. He stood there with his knees locked, big-eyed and drabbled in the old tarletan costume. 'I have business in town. You go home.' He stared up at her and took the bubble gum he had been chewing from his mouth — he tried to park the gum behind his ear, but sweat had made his ear too slippery, so finally he put the gum back in his mouth again. 'You know the way home as well as I do. So do what I tell you.' For a wonder, John Henry minded her; but, as she watched him going away from her down the crowded street, she felt a hollow sorriness — he looked so babyish and pitiful in the costume.

The change from the street to the inside of the Blue Moon was like the change that comes on leaving the open fairway and entering a booth. Blue lights and moving faces, noise. The counter and tables were crowded with soldiers, and men, and bright-faced ladies. The soldier she had promised to meet was playing the slot machine in a far corner, putting in nickel after nickel, but winning none.

'Oh, it's you,' he said when he noticed her standing at his elbow. For a second his eyes had the blank look of eyes that are peering back into the brain to recollect — but only for a second. 'I was scared you had stood me up.' After putting in a final nickel, he banged the slot machine with his fist. 'Let's find a place.'

They sat at a table between the counter and the slot machine, and, although by the clock the time was not long, it seemed to F. Jasmine endless. Not that the soldier was not nice to her. He was nice, but their two conversations would not join together, and underneath there was a layer of queerness she could not place and understand. The soldier had washed, and his swollen face, his ears and hands, were clean; his red hair was darkened from wetting and ridged with a comb. He said he had slept that afternoon. He was gay and his talk was sassy. But although she liked gay people and sassy talk, she could not think of any answers. It was again as though the soldier talked a kind of double-talk that, try as she would, she could not follow — yet it was not so much the actual remarks as the tone underneath she failed to understand.

The soldier brought two drinks to the table; after a swallow F. Jasmine suspected there was liquor in them and, although a child no longer, she was shocked. It was a sin and against the law for people under eighteen to drink real liquor, and she pushed the glass away. The soldier was both nice and gay, but after he had had two other drinks she wondered if he could be drunk. To make conversation she remarked that her brother had been swimming in Alaska, but this did not seem to impress him very much. Nor would he talk about the war, nor foreign countries and the world. To his joking remarks she could never find replies that fitted, although she tried. Like a nightmare pupil in a recital who has to play a duet to a piece she does not know, F. Jasmine did her best to catch the tune and follow. But soon she broke down and grinned until her mouth felt wooden. The blue lights in the crowded room, the smoke and noisy commotion, confused her also.

'You're a funny kind of girl,' the soldier said finally.

'Patton,' she said. 'I bet he will win the war in two weeks.'

The soldier was quiet now and his face had a heavy look. His eyes gazed at her with the same strange expression she had noticed that day at noon, a look she had never seen on anyone before and could not place. After a while he said, and his voice was softened, blurred:

'What did you say your name is, Beautiful?'

F. Jasmine did not know whether or not to like the way he called her, and she spoke her name in a proper voice.

'Well, Jasmine, how bout going on upstairs?' His tone was asking, but when she did not answer at once, he stood up from the table. 'I've got a room here.'

'Why, I thought we were going to the Idle Hour. Or dancing or something.'

'What's the rush?' he said. 'The band don't hardly tune up until eleven o'clock.'

F. Jasmine did not want to go upstairs, but she did not know how to refuse. It was like going into a fair booth, or fair ride, that once having entered you cannot leave until the exhibition or the ride is finished. Now it was the same with this soldier, this date. She could not leave until it ended. The soldier was waiting at the foot of the stairs and, unable to refuse, she followed after him. They went up two flights, and then along a narrow hall that smelled of wee-wee and linoleum. But every footstep F. Jasmine took, she felt somehow was wrong.

'This sure is a funny hotel,' she said.

It was the silence in the hotel room that warned and frightened her, a silence she noticed as soon as the door was closed. In the light of the bare electric bulb that hung down from the ceiling, the room looked hard and very ugly. The flaked iron bed had been slept in and a suitcase of jumbled soldier's clothes lay open in the middle of the floor. On the light oak bureau there was a glass pitcher full of water and a half-eaten package of cinnamon rolls covered with blue-white icing and fat flies. The screenless window was open and the sleazy voile curtains had been tied at the top in a knot together to let in air. There was a lavatory in the corner and, cupping his hands, the soldier dashed cold water to his face — the soap was only a bar of ordinary soap, already used, and over the lavatory a sign read: STRICTLY WASHING. Although the soldier's footsteps sounded, and the water made a trickling noise, the sense of silence somehow remained.

F. Jasmine went to the window which overlooked a narrow alley and a brick wall; a rickety fire-escape led to the ground and light shafted from the two lower stories. Outside there was the August evening sounds of voices and a radio, and in the room there were sounds also — so how could the silence be explained? The soldier sat on the bed, and now she was seeing him altogether as a single person, not as a member of the loud free gangs who for a season roamed the streets of town and then went out into the world together. In the silent room he seemed to her unjoined and ugly. She could not see him any more in Burma, Africa, or Iceland, or even for that matter in Arkansas. She saw him only as he sat there in the room. His light blue eyes, set close together, were staring at her with the peculiar look — with a filmed softness, like eyes that have been washed with milk.

The silence in the room was like that silence in the kitchen when, on a drowsy afternoon, the ticking of the clock would stop — and there would steal over her a mysterious uneasiness that lasted until she realized what was wrong. A few times before she had known such silence — once in the Sears and Roebuck store the moment before she suddenly became a thief, and again that April afternoon in the MacKeans' garage. It was the forewarning hush that comes before an unknown trouble, a silence caused, not by lack of sounds, but by a waiting, a suspense. The soldier did not take those strange eyes from her and she was scared.

'Come on, Jasmine,' he said, in an unnatural voice, broken and low, as he reached out his hand, palm upward, toward her. 'Let's quit this stalling.'

The next minute was like a minute in the fair Crazy-House, or real Milledgeville. Already F. Jasmine had started for the door, for she could no longer stand the silence. But as she passed the soldier, he grasped her skirt and, limpened by fright, she was pulled down beside him on the bed. The next minute happened, but it was too crazy to be realized. She felt his arms around her and smelled his sweaty shirt. He was not rough, but it was crazier than if he had been rough — and in a second she was paralyzed by horror. She could not push away, but she bit down with all her might upon what must have been the crazy soldier's tongue — so that he screamed out and she was free. Then he was coming toward her with an amazed pained face, and her hand reached the glass pitcher and brought it down upon his head. He swayed a second, then slowly his legs began to crumple, and slowly he sank sprawling to the floor. The sound was hollow like the hammer on a coconut, and with it the silence was broken at last. He lay there still, with the amazed expression on his freckled face that was now pale, and a froth of blood showed on his mouth. But his head was not broken, or even cracked, and whether he was dead or not she did not know.

The silence was over, and it was like those kitchen times when, after the first uncanny moments, she realized the reason for her uneasiness and knew that the ticking of the clock had stopped — but now there was no clock to shake and hold for a minute to her ear before she wound it, feeling relieved. There slanted across her mind twisted remembrances of a common fit in the front room, basement remarks, and nasty Barney; but she did not let these separate glimpses fall together, and the word she repeated was 'crazy.' There was water on the walls which had been slung out from the pitcher and the soldier had a broken look in the strewn room. F. Jasmine told herself: Get out! And after first starting toward the door, she turned and climbed out on the fire-escape and quickly reached the alley ground.

She ran like a chased person fleeing from the crazy-house at Milledgeville, looking neither to the right nor left, and when she reached the corner of her own home block, she was glad to see John Henry West. He was out looking for bats around the street light, and the familiar sight of him calmed her a little.

'Uncle Royal has been calling you,' he said. 'What makes you shake like that for, Frankie?'

'I just now brained a crazy man,' she told him when she could get her breath. 'I brained him and I don't know if he is dead. He was a crazy man.'

John Henry stared without surprise. 'How did he act like?' And when she did not answer all at once, he went on: 'Did he crawl on the ground and moan and slobber?' For that was what the old Frankie had done one day to try to fool Berenice and create some excitement. Berenice had not been fooled. 'Did he?'

'No,' F. Jasmine said. 'He—' But as she looked into those cold, child eyes she knew that she could not explain. John Henry would not understand, and his green eyes gave her a funny feeling. Sometimes his mind was like the pictures he drew with crayons on tablet paper. The other day he had drawn such a one and showed it to her. It was a picture of a telephone man on a telephone pole. The telephone man was leaning against his safety belt, and the picture was complete down to his climbing shoes. It was a careful picture, but after she had looked at it uneasiness had lingered in her mind. She looked at the picture again until she realized what was wrong. The telephone man was drawn in side-view profile, yet this profile had two eyes — one eye just above the nose bridge and another drawn just below. And it was no hurried mistake; both eyes had careful lashes, pupils, and lids. Those two eyes drawn in a side-view face gave her a funny feeling. But reason with John Henry, argue with him? You might as well argue with cement. What did he do it? Why? Because it was a telephone man. What? Because he was climbing the pole. It was impossible to understand his point of view. And he did not understand her either.

'Forget what I just now told you,' she said. But after saying it, she realized that was the worst remark she could have said, for he would be sure not to forget. So she took him by the shoulders and shook him slightly. 'Swear you won't tell. Swear this: If I tell I hope God will sew up my mouth and sew down my eyes and cut off my ears with the scissors.'

But John Henry would not swear; he only hunched his big head down near his shoulders and answered, very quietly: 'Shoo.'

She tried again. 'If you tell anybody I might be put in jail and we couldn't go to the wedding.'

'I ain't going to tell,' John Henry said. Sometimes he could be trusted, and other times not. 'I'm not a tattletale.'

Once inside the house, F. Jasmine locked the front door before she went into the living room. Her father was reading the evening paper, in his sock feet, on the sofa. F. Jasmine was glad to have her father between her and the front door. She was afraid of the Black Maria and listened anxiously.

'I wish we were going to the wedding right this minute,' she said. 'I think that would be the best thing to do.'

She went back to the icebox and ate six tablespoons of sweetened condensed milk, and the disgust in her mouth began to go away. The waiting made her feel restless. She gathered up the library books, and stacked them on the living-room table. On one of them, a book from the grown sections which she had not read, she wrote in the front with pencil: *If you want to read something that will shock you, turn to page 66.* On page 66 she wrote: *Electricity. Ha! Ha!* By and by her anxiousness was eased; close to her father she felt less afraid.

'These books belong to go back to the library.'

Her father, who was forty-one, looked at the clock: 'It's time for everybody under forty-one to get to bed. Quick, march, and without any argument. We have to be up at five o'clock.'

F. Jasmine stood in the doorway, unable to leave. 'Papa,' she said, after a minute, 'if somebody hits somebody with a glass pitcher and he falls out cold, do you think he is dead?'

She had to repeat the question, feeling a bitter grudge against him because he did not take her seriously, so that her questions must be asked twice.

'Why, come to think about it, I never hit anybody with a pitcher,' he said. 'Did you?'

F. Jasmine knew he asked this as a joke, so she only said as she went away: 'I'll never be so glad to get to any place in all my life as Winter Hill tomorrow. I will be so thankful when the wedding is over and we have gone away. I will be so thankful.'

Upstairs she and John Henry undressed, and after the motor and the light were off, they lay down on the bed together — although she said she could not sleep a wink. But nevertheless she closed her eyes, and when she opened them again a voice was calling and the room was early gray.

PART THREE

SHE SAID: 'Farewell, old ugly house,' as, wearing a dotted Swiss dress and carrying the suitcase, she passed through the hall at quarter to six. The wedding dress was in the suitcase, ready to be put on when she reached Winter Hill. At that still hour the sky was the dim silver of a mirror, and beneath it the gray town looked, not like a real town, but like an exact reflection of itself, and to this unreal town she also said farewell. The bus left the station at ten past six — and she sat proud, like an accustomed traveler, apart from her father, John Henry, and Berenice. But after a while a serious doubt came in her, which even the answers of the bus-driver could not quite satisfy. They were supposed to be traveling north, but it seemed to her rather that the bus was going south instead. The sky turned burning pale and the day blazed. They passed the fields of windless corn that had a blue look in the glare, red-furrowed cotton land, stretches of black pine woods. And mile by mile the countryside became more southern. The towns they passed — New City, Leeville, Cheehaw — each town seemed smaller than the one before, until at nine o'clock they reached the ugliest place of all, where they changed busses, called Flowering Branch. Despite its name there were no flowers and no branch — only a solitary country store, with a sad old shredded circus poster on the clapboard wall and a chinaberry tree beneath which stood an empty wagon and a sleeping mule. There they waited for the bus to Sweet Well, and, still doubting anxiously, Frances did not despise the box of lunch that had so shamed her at the first, because it made them look like family people who do not travel very much. The bus left at ten o'clock, and they were in Sweet Well by eleven. The next hours were unexplainable. The wedding was like a dream, for all that came about occurred in a world beyond her power; from the moment when, sedate and proper, she shook hands with the grown people until the time, the wrecked wedding over, when she watched the car with the two of them driving away from her, and, flinging herself down in the sizzling dust, she cried out for the last time: 'Take me! Take me!' — from the beginning to the end the wedding was unmanaged as a nightmare. By mid-afternoon it was all finished and the return bus left at four o'clock.

'The show is over and the monkey's dead,' John Henry quoted, as he settled himself in the next to the last bus seat beside her father. 'Now we go home and go to bed.'

Frances wanted the whole world to die. She sat on the back seat, between the window and Berenice, and, though she was no longer sobbing, the tears were like two little brooks, and also her nose ran water. Her shoulders were hunched over her swollen heart and she no longer wore the wedding dress. She was sitting next to Berenice, back with the colored people, and when she thought of it she used the mean word she had never used before, nigger — for now she hated everyone and wanted only to spite and shame. For John Henry West the wedding had only been a great big show, and he had enjoyed her misery at the end as he had enjoyed the angel cake. She mortally despised him, dressed in his best white suit, now stained with strawberry ice cream. Berenice she hated also, for to her it had only meant a pleasure trip to Winter Hill. Her father, who had said that he would attend to her when they got home, she would like to kill. She was against every single person, even strangers in the crowded bus, though she only saw them blurred by tears — and she wished the bus would fall in a river or run into a train. Herself she hated the worst of all, and she wanted the whole world to die.

'Cheer up,' said Berenice. 'Wipe your face and blow your nose and things will look better by and by.'

Berenice had a blue party handkerchief, to match her blue best dress and blue kid shoes — and this she offered to Frances, although it was made of fine georgette and not, of course, due to be blown on. She would not notice it. In the seat between them there were three wet handkerchiefs of her father's, and Berenice began to dry the tears with one, but Frances did not move or budge.

'They put old Frankie out of the wedding.' John Henry's big head bobbed over the back of his seat, smiling and snaggled-toothed. Her father cleared his throat and said: 'That's sufficient, John Henry. Leave Frankie alone.' And Berenice added: 'Sit down in that seat now and behave.'

The bus rode for a long time, and now direction made no difference to her; she did not care. From the beginning the wedding had been queer like the card games in the kitchen the first week last June. In those bridge games they played and played for many days, but nobody ever drew a good hand, the cards were all sorry, and no high bids made — until finally Berenice suspicioned, saying: 'Less us get busy and count these old cards.' And they got busy and counted the old cards, and it turned out the jacks and the queens were missing. John Henry at last admitted that he had cut out the jacks and then the queens to keep them company and, after hiding the clipped scraps in the stove, had secretly taken the pictures home. So the fault of the card game was discovered. But how could the failure of the wedding be explained?

The wedding was all wrong, although she could not point out single faults. The house was a neat brick house out near the limits of the small, baked town, and when she first put foot inside, it was as though her eyeballs had been slightly stirred; there were mixed impressions of pink roses, the smell of floor wax, mints and nuts in silver trays. Everybody was lovely to her. Mrs. Williams wore a lace dress, and she asked F. Jasmine two times what grade she was in at school. But she asked, also, if she would like to play out on the swing before the wedding, in the tone grown people use when speaking to a child. Mr. Williams was nice to her, too. He was a sallow man with folds in his cheeks and the skin beneath his eyes was the grain and color of an old apple core. Mr. Williams also asked her what grade she was in at school; in fact, that was the main question asked her at the wedding.

She wanted to speak to her brother and the bride, to talk to them and tell them of her plans, the three of them alone together. But they were never once alone; Jarvis was out checking the car someone was lending for the honeymoon, while Janice dressed in the front bedroom among a crowd of beautiful grown girls. She wandered from one to the other of them, unable to explain. And once Janice put her arms around her, and said she was so glad to have a little sister — and when Janice kissed her, F. Jasmine felt an aching in her throat and could not speak. Jarvis, when she went to find him in the yard, lifted her up in a rough-house way and said: Frankie the lankie the alaga fankie, the tee-legged toe-legged bow-legged Frankie. And he gave her a dollar.

She stood in the corner of the bride's room, wanting to say: I love the two of you so much and you are the we of me. Please take me with you from the wedding, for we belong to be together. Or even if she could have said: May I trouble you to step into the next room, as I have something to reveal to you and Jarvis? And get the three of them in a room alone together and somehow manage to explain. If only she had written it down on the typewriter in advance, so that she could hand it to them and they would read! But this she had not thought to do, and her tongue was heavy in her mouth and dumb. She could only speak in a voice that shook a little — to ask where was the veil?

'I can feel in the atmosphere a storm is brewing,' said Berenice. 'These two crooked joints can always tell.'

There was no veil except a little veil that came down from the wedding hat, and nobody was wearing fancy clothes. The bride was wearing a daytime suit. The only mercy of it was that she had not worn her wedding dress on the bus, as she had first intended, and found it out in time. She stood in a corner of the bride's room until the piano played the first notes of the wedding march. They were all lovely to her at Winter Hill, except that they called her Frankie and treated her too young. It was so unlike what she had expected, and, as in those June card games, there was, from first to last, the sense of something terribly gone wrong.

'Perk up,' said Berenice. 'I'm planning a big surprise for you. I'm just sitting here planning. Don't you want to know what it is?'

Frances did not answer even by a glance. The wedding was like a dream outside her power, or like a show unmanaged by her in which she was supposed to have no part. The living room was crowded with Winter Hill company, and the bride and her brother stood before the mantelpiece at the end of the room. And seeing them again together was more like singing feeling than a picture that her dizzied eyes could truly see. She watched them with her heart, but all the time she was only thinking: I have not told them and they don't know. And knowing this was heavy as a swallowed stone. And afterward, during the kissing of the bride, refreshments served in the dining room, the stir and party bustle — she hovered close to the two of them, but words would not come. They are not going to take me, she was thinking, and this was the one thought she could not bear.

When Mr. Williams brought their bags, she hastened after with her own suitcase. The rest was like some nightmare show in which a wild girl in the audience breaks onto the stage to take upon herself an unplanned part that was never written or meant to be. You are the we of me, her heart was saying, but she could only say aloud: 'Take me!' And they pleaded and begged with her, but she was already in the car. At the last she clung to the steering wheel until her father and somebody else had hauled and dragged her from the car, and even then she could only cry in the dust of the empty road: 'Take me! Take me!' But there was only the wedding company to hear, for the bride and her brother had driven away.

Berenice said: 'School will begin now in only three more weeks. And you'll go into the A section of the seventh grade and meet a lot of nice new children and make another bosom friend like that Evelyn Owen you were so wild about.'

The kind tone Frances could not stand. 'I never meant to go with them!' she said. 'It was all just a joke. They said they were going to invite me to a visit when they get settled, but I wouldn't go. Not for a million dollars.'

'We know all about that,' said Berenice. 'Now listen to my surprise I've planned. Soon as you get settled in school and have a chance to make these friends, I think it would be a good idea to have a party. A lovely bridge party in the living room, with potato salad and those little olive sandwiches your Aunt Pet had for a club meeting you were so carried away about — the round-shaped kind with the tiny round hole in the middle and the olive showing. A lovely bridge party with delicious refreshments. How would you like that?'

The baby promises rasped her nerves. Her cheap heart hurt, and she pressed her crossed arms over it and rocked a little. 'It was a framed game. The cards were stacked. It was a frame-up all around.'

'We can have that bridge party going on in the living room. And out in the back yard we can have another party at the same time. A costume party with hot dogs. One party dainty and the other one rough. With prizes for the highest bridge score and the funniest costume. How does that strike you?'

Frances refused to look at Berenice or answer.

'You could call up the society editor of the *Evening Journal* and have the party written up in the paper. And that would make the fourth time your name has been published in the paper.'

It would, but a thing like that no longer mattered to her. Once, when her bike ran into an automobile, the paper had called her Fankie Addams. *Fankie!* But now she did not care.

'Don't be so blue,' said Berenice. 'This is not doomsday.'

'Frankie, don't cry,' John Henry said. 'We will go home and put up the tepee and have a good time.'

She could not stop crying and the sobbing had a strangled sound. 'Oh, hush up your mouth!'

'Listen to me. Tell me what you would like and I'll try to do it if it's in my power.'

'All I would like,' said Frances, after a minute, 'all I wish in the world, is for no human being ever to speak to me so long as I live.'

And Berenice said, finally: 'Well. Then bawl, then, Misery.'

They did not talk the rest of the way back to the town. Her father slept with a handkerchief over his nose and eyes, snoring a little. John Henry West lay in her father's lap and slept also. The other passengers were drowsy quiet and the bus rocked like a cradle and made a softly roaring sound. Outside the afternoon shimmered and now and then there was a buzzard lazily balanced against the blazing pale sky. They passed red empty crossroads with deep red gulches on either side, and rotten gray shacks set in the lonesome cotton fields. Only the dark pine trees looked cool — and the low blue hills when seen from miles away. Frances watched from the window with a stiff sick face and for four hours did not say a word. They were entering the town, and a change came. The sky lowered and turned a purple-gray against which the trees were a poison green. There was a jellied stillness in the air and then the mutter of the first thunder. A wind came through the treetops with a sound like rushing water, forewarning storm.

'I told you so,' said Berenice, and she was not speaking of the wedding. 'I could feel the misery in these joints. After a good storm we will all feel much better.'

The rain did not come, and there was only a feeling of expectation in the air. The wind was hot. Frances smiled a little at Berenice's words, but it was a scorning smile that hurt.

'You think it's all over,' she said, 'but that only shows how little you know.'

They thought it was finished, but she would show them. The wedding had not included her, but she would still go into the world. Where she was going she did not know; however, she was leaving town that night. If she could not go in the way she had planned, safe with her brother and the bride, she would go, anyway. Even if she had to commit every crime. For the first time since the night before she thought about the soldier — but only in a glancing way, for her mind was busy with hasty plans. There was a train that passed through the town at two o'clock, and she would take it; the train went north in a general way, probably to Chicago or New York. If the train went to Chicago, she would go on to Hollywood and write shows or get a job as a movie starlet — or, if worse came to worse, even act in comedies. If the train went to New York, she would dress like a boy and give a false name and a false age and join the Marines. Meanwhile, she had to wait until her father was asleep, and she could still hear him moving in the kitchen. She sat at the typewriter and wrote a letter.

Dear Father:

This is a farewell letter until I write you from a diferent place. I told you I was going to leave town because it is inevitable. I cannot stand this existance any longer because my life has become a burden. I am taking the pistol because who can tell when it might come in handy and I will send back the money to you at the very first opportunaty. Tell Berenice not to worry. The whole thing is a irony of fate and it is inevitable. Later I will write. Please Papa do not try to capture me.

Sincerely yours,

Frances Addams

The green-and-white moths were nervous at the window screen and the night outside was queer. The hot wind had stopped and the air was so still that it seemed solid and there was a weight against you when you moved. The thunder grumbled low occasionally. Frances sat motionless before the typewriter, wearing the dotted Swiss dress, and the strapped suitcase was beside the door. After a while the light in the kitchen was turned off and her father called from the foot of the stairs: 'Good night, Picklepriss. Good night, John Henry.'

Frances waited a long time. John Henry was sleeping across the foot of the bed, still dressed and with his shoes on, and his mouth was open and one ear of his glasses frame had come loose. After waiting as long as she could stand it, she took the suitcase and tiptoed very quietly down the stairs. It was dark down there, dark in her father's room, dark through the house. She stood on the threshold of her father's room and he was snoring softly. The hardest time was the few minutes she stood there, listening.

The rest was easy. Her father was a widow-man, set in

his ways, and at night he folded his pants over a straight chair and left his wallet, watch, and glasses on the right-hand side of the bureau. She moved very quietly in the darkness and laid hand on the wallet almost immediately. She was careful opening the bureau drawer, stopping to listen each time there was a scraping sound. The pistol felt heavy and cool in her hot hand. It was easy except for the loudness of beating heart and for an accident that happened just as she crept from the room. She stumbled over a waste-paper basket and the snoring stopped. Her father stirred, muttered. She held her breath — then finally, after a minute, the snoring went on again.

She put the letter on the table and tiptoed to the back porch. But there was one thing she had not counted on — John Henry began to call.

'Frankie!' The high child voice seemed to carry through all the rooms of the night house. 'Where are you?'

'Hush,' she whispered. 'Go back to sleep.'

She had left the light on in her room, and he stood in the stairway door and looked down into the dark kitchen. 'What are you doing down there in the dark?'

'Hush!' she said again in a loud whisper. 'I'll be there by the time you get to sleep.'

She waited a few minutes after John Henry had gone, then groped to the back door, unlocked it, and stepped outside. But, though she was very quiet, he must have heard her. 'Wait, Frankie!' he wailed. 'I'm coming.'

The child wailing had waked her father, and she knew it before she reached the corner of the house. The night was dark and heavy, and as she ran, she heard her father calling her. Behind the corner of the house she looked and saw the kitchen light go on; the bulb swung back and forth, making a swinging gold reflection on the arbor and the dark yard. He will read the letter now, she thought, and chase and try to capture me. But after she had run a few blocks, the suitcase bumping against her legs and sometimes nearly tripping her, she remembered that her father would have to put on pants and a shirt — for he would not chase her through the streets dressed only in pajama bottoms. She stopped for a second to look behind. No one was there. At the first street light she put down the suitcase and, taking the wallet from the front pocket of her dress, opened it with shaking hands. Inside there was three dollars and fifteen cents. She would have to hop a box car, or something.

All at once, alone there in the night-empty street, she realized she did not know how. It is easy to talk about hopping a freight train, but how did bums and people really do it? She was three blocks from the station and she walked toward it slowly. The station was closed and she went round it and stared at the platform, long and empty under the pale lights, with the Chiclet machines against the station wall and scraps of chewing-gum paper and candy wrappings on the platform. The train tracks gleamed silver and exact and some freight cars were off on a siding in the distance, but they were not hooked to any engine. The train would not come until two o'clock, and would she be able to hop a car, as she had read about, and get away? There was a red lantern a little way down the tracks, and against this colored light she saw a railroad man come walking slowly. She could not hang around like that until two o'clock — but as she left the station, one shoulder dragged down by the weight of the bag, she did not know where she should go.

The streets were lonesome and idle with Sunday night. The red-and-green neon lights in the signboards mixed with the street lights to make a pale hot haze above the town, but the sky was starless, black. A man in a tilted hat took out his cigarette and turned to stare at her as she passed by. She could not wander around the town like this, for by this time her father would be chasing her. In the alley behind Finny's Place she sat down on the suitcase, and only then she realized that the pistol was still in her left hand. She had been going around with the pistol held right in her hand, and she felt that she had lost her mind. She had said that she would shoot herself if the bride and her brother would not take her. She pointed the pistol at the side of her head and held it there a minute or two. If she squeezed down on the trigger she would be dead — and deadness was blackness, nothing but pure terrible blackness that went on and on and never ended until the end of all the world. When she lowered the pistol, she told herself that at the last minute she had changed her mind. The pistol she put in her suitcase.

The alley was black and smelled of garbage cans, and it was in this alley where Lon Baker had his throat slashed that spring afternoon so that his neck was like a bloody mouth that gibbered in the sun. It was here Lon Baker had been killed. And had she killed the soldier, when she brained his head with the water pitcher? She was scared in the dark alley and her mind felt splintered. If only there was someone with her! If only she could hunt down Honey Brown and they could go away together! But Honey had gone to Forks Falls and would not be back until tomorrow. Or if she could find the monkey and the monkey-man and join with them to run away! There was a scuttling noise, and she jerked with terror. A cat had leaped up on a garbage can, and in the darkness she could see its outline against the light at the end of the alley. She whispered: 'Charles!' and then, 'Charlina.' But it was not her Persian cat, and when she stumbled toward the can it sprang away.

She could stand the black sour alley no longer and, carrying the suitcase toward the light at the end, she stood close to the sidewalk, but still inside the shadow of a wall. If there was only somebody to tell her what to do and where to go and how to get there! The fortune of Big Mama had turned out true — about the sort of trip and a departure and a return, and even the cotton bales, for the bus had passed a truck of them on the way back from Winter Hill. And there was the sum of money in her father's wallet, so that already she had lived up all the fortune Big Mama had foreseen. Should she go down to the house in Sugarville and say that she had used up the whole future, and what was she now to do?

Beyond the shadow of the alley the gloomy street was like a street that waited, with the winking neon Coco-Cola sign on the next corner, and a lady walking back and forth beneath a street light as though expecting someone. A car, a long closed car that maybe was a Packard, came slowly down the street, and the way it cruised close to the curb reminded her of a gangster's car, so that she shrank back closer to the wall. Then, on the opposite sidewalk, two people passed, and a feeling like a sudden flame sprang up inside her, and for less than a second it seemed that her brother and the bride had come for her and were now *there*. But the feeling blew out instantly and she was just watching a stranger couple passing down the street. There was a hollow in her chest, but at the bottom of this emptiness a heavy weight pressed down and bruised her stomach, so that she felt sick. She told herself she ought to get busy and pick up her feet and go away. But she still stood there, her eyes closed, and her head against the warm brick wall.

When she left the alley, it was a long time after midnight and she had reached the point where any sudden idea seemed a good idea. She had seized on first one notion and then another. To hitch-hike to Forks Falls and track down Honey, or to wire Evelyn Owen to meet her in Atlanta, or even to go back to the house and get John Henry, so that at least there would be somebody with her and she would not have to go into the world alone. But there was some objection to each of these ideas.

Then, all at once, from the tangle of turning impossibilities, she thought of the soldier; and this time the thought was not a glancing one — it lingered, stuck, and did not go away. She wondered if she ought to go to the Blue Moon and find if she had killed the soldier, before she left the town forever. The idea, once seized on, seemed to her good, and she started for Front Avenue. If she had not killed the soldier, then when she found him what could she say? How the next thought occurred to her she did not know, but suddenly it seemed she might as well ask the soldier to marry with her, and then the two of them could go away. Before he had gone crazy, he had been a little nice. And because it was a new and sudden idea, it also seemed reasonable. She remembered a part of the fortune she had forgotten, that she would marry a light-haired person with blue eyes, and the fact that the soldier had light red hair and blue eyes were like a proof that this was the right thing to do.

She hurried faster. The night before was like a time that had happened so long ago that the soldier was unraveled in her memory. But she recalled the silence in the hotel room; and all at once a fit in a front room, the silence, the nasty talk behind the garage — these separate recollections fell together in the darkness of her mind, as shafting searchlights meet in the night sky upon an aeroplane, so that in a flash there came in her an understanding. There was a feeling of cold surprise; she stopped a minute, then went on toward the Blue Moon. The stores were dark and closed, the pawnshop window locked with criss-crossed steel against night robbers, and the only lights were those from the open wooden stairs of buildings and the greenish splash of brightness from the Blue Moon. There was a sound of quarreling voices from an upper story, and the footsteps of two men, far down the street, walking away. She was no longer thinking of the soldier; the discovery of the moment before had scattered him from her mind. There was only knowing that she must find somebody, anybody, that she could join with to go away. For now she admitted she was too scared to go into the world alone.

She did not leave the town that night, for the Law caught her in the Blue Moon. Officer Wylie was there when she walked in, although she did not see him until she was settled at the window table with the suitcase on the floor beside her. The juke-box sounded a sleazy blues and the Portuguese owner stood with his eyes closed, playing up and down the wooden counter in time to the sad juke tune. There were only a few people in a corner booth and the blue light gave the place a look of being underseas. She did not see the Law until he was standing beside the table, and when she looked up at him, her startled heart quivered a little and then stopped still.

'You're Royal Addams's daughter,' the Law said, and her head admitted with a nod. 'I'll phone in to headquarters to say you're found. Just stay right here.'

The Law went back to the telephone booth. He was calling the Black Maria to haul her off down to the jail, but she did not care. Very likely she had killed that soldier, and they had been following clues and hunting her all over town. Or the Law maybe had found out about the three-way knife she had stolen from the Sears and Roebuck Store. It was not plain just what she was captured for, and the crimes of the long spring and summer merged together as one guilt which she had lost the power to understand. It was as though the things that she had done, the sins committed, had all been done by someone else — a stranger a long time ago. She sat very still, her legs wrapped tight around each other, and her hands clasped in her lap. The Law was a long time at the telephone, and, staring straight ahead of her, she watched two people leave a booth and, leaning close against each other, start to dance. A soldier banged the screen door and walked through the café, and only the distant stranger in her recognized him; when he had climbed up the stairs, she only thought slowly and with no feeling that a curly red head such as that one was like cement. Then her mind went back to thoughts of jail and cold peas and cold cornbread and iron-barred cells. The Law came back from the telephone and sat down across from her and said:

'How did you happen to come in here?'

The Law was big in his blue policeman's suit and, once arrested, it was a bad policy to lie or trifle. He had a heavy face, with a squatty forehead and unmatched ears — one ear was larger than the other one, and had a torn look. When he questioned her, he did not look into her face, but at some point just above her head.

'What am I doing in here?' she repeated. For all at once

she had forgotten, and she told the truth when she said finally, 'I don't know.'

The voice of the Law seemed to come from a distance like a question asked through a long corridor. 'Where were you headed for?'

The world was now so far away that Frances could no longer think of it. She did not see the earth as in the old days, cracked and loose and turning a thousand miles an hour; the earth was enormous and still and flat. Between herself and all the places there was a space like an enormous canyon she could not hope to bridge or cross. The plans for the movies or the Marines were only child plans that would never work, and she was careful when she answered. She named the littlest, ugliest place she knew, for to run away there could not be considered so very wrong.

'Flowering Branch.'

'Your father phoned headquarters you had left a letter that you were running away. We located him at the bus station and he'll be here in a minute to take you home.'

It was her father who had sicked the Law on her, and she would not be carried to the jail. In a way she was sorry. It was better to be in a jail where you could bang the walls than in a jail you could not see. The world was too far away, and there was no way any more that she could be included. She was back to the fear of the summertime, the old feelings that the world was separate from herself — and the failed wedding had quickened the fear to terror. There had been a time, only yesterday, when she felt that every person that she saw was somehow connected with herself and there was between the two of them an instant recognition. Frances watched the Portuguese who still played a mock piano on the counter to the juke-box tune. He swayed as he played and his fingers skittered up and down the counter, so that a man at the far end protected his glass with his hand. When the tune was over, the Portuguese folded his arms upon his chest; Frances narrowed and tensed her eyes to will him to look at her. He had been the first person she had told the day before about the wedding, but as he gave an owner's look around the place, his glance passed by her in a casual way and there was in those eyes no feeling of connection. She turned to the others in the room, and it was the same with all of them and they were strangers. In the blue light she felt queer as a person drowning. At last she was staring at the Law and finally he looked into her eyes. He looked at her with eyes as china as a doll's, and in them there was only the reflection of her own lost face.

The screen door slammed and the Law said: 'Here's your Daddy come to take you home.'

Frances was never once to speak about the wedding. Weathers had turned and it was in another season. There were the changes and Frances was now thirteen. She was in the kitchen with Berenice on the day before they moved, the last afternoon that Berenice would be with them; for when it had been decided that she and her father would share with Aunt Pet and Uncle Ustace a house out in the new suburb of town, Berenice had given quit notice and said that she might as well marry T. T. It was the end of an afternoon in late November, and in the east the sky was the color of a winter geranium.

Frances had come back to the kitchen, for the other rooms were hollow since the van had taken the furniture away. There were only the two beds in the downstairs bedrooms and the kitchen furniture, and they were to be moved tomorrow. It was the first time in a long while that Frances had spent an afternoon back in the kitchen, alone with Berenice. It was not the same kitchen of the summer that now seemed so long ago. The pencil pictures had disappeared beneath a coat of calcimine, and new linoleum covered the splintery floor. Even the table had been moved, pushed back against the wall, since now there was nobody to take meals with Berenice.

The kitchen, done over and almost modern, had nothing that would bring to mind John Henry West. But nevertheless there were times when Frances felt his presence there, solemn and hovering and ghost-gray. And at those times there would come a hush — a hush quivered by voiceless words. A similar hush would come, also, when Honey was mentioned or brought to mind, for Honey was out on the road now with a sentence of eight years. Now the hush came that late November afternoon as Frances was making the sandwiches, cutting them into fancy shapes and taking great pains — for Mary Littlejohn was coming at five o'clock. Frances glanced at Berenice, who was sitting idle in a chair, wearing an old raveled sweater, her limp arms hanging at her sides. In her lap there was the thin little pinched fox fur that Ludie had given her many years ago. The fur was sticky and the sharp little face foxwise and sad. The fire from the red stove brushed the room with flickers of light and changing shadows.

'I am just mad about Michelangelo,' she said.

Mary was coming at five o'clock to take dinner, spend the night, and ride in the van to the new house tomorrow. Mary collected pictures of great masters and pasted them in an art book. They read poets like Tennyson together; and

Mary was going to be a great painter and Frances a great poet — or else the foremost authority on radar. Mr. Littlejohn had been connected with a tractor company and before the war the Littlejohns had lived abroad. When Frances was sixteen and Mary eighteen, they were going around the world together. Frances placed the sandwiches on a plate, along with eight chocolates and some salted nuts; this was to be a midnight feast, to be eaten in the bed at twelve o'clock.

'I told you we're going to travel around the world together.'

'Mary Littlejohn,' said Berenice, in a tinged voice. 'Mary Littlejohn.'

Berenice could not appreciate Michelangelo or poetry, let alone Mary Littlejohn. There had at first been words between them on the subject. Berenice had spoken of Mary as being lumpy and marshmallow-white, and Frances had defended fiercely. Mary had long braids that she could very nearly sit on, braids of a woven mixture of corn-yellow and brown, fastened at the ends with rubber bands and, on occasions, ribbons. She had brown eyes with yellow eyelashes, and her dimpled hands tapered at the fingers to little pink blobs of flesh, as Mary bit her nails. The Littlejohns were Catholics, and even on this point Berenice was all of a sudden narrowminded, saying that Roman Catholics worshiped Graven Images and wanted the Pope to rule the world. But for Frances this difference was a final touch of strangeness, silent terror, that completed the wonder of her love.

'There's no use our discussing a certain party. You could not possibly ever understand her. It's just not in you.' She had said that once before to Berenice, and from the sudden faded stillness in her eye she knew that the words had hurt. And now she repeated them, angered because of the tinged way Berenice had said the name, but once the words were spoken she was sorry. 'Anyhow, I consider it the greatest honor of my existence that Mary has picked me out to be her one most intimate friend. Me! Of all people!'

'Have I ever said anything against her?' said Berenice. 'All I said was it makes me nervous to watch her just sitting there sucking them pigtails.'

'Braids!'

A flock of strong-winged arrowed geese flew over the yard, and Frances went to the window. There had been frost that morning, silvering the brown grass and the roofs of neighbors' houses, and even the thinned leaves of the rusty arbor. When she turned back to the kitchen, the hush was in the room again. Berenice sat hunched with her elbow on her knee, and her forehead resting in her hand, staring with one mottled eye at the coal scuttle.

The changes had come about at the same time, during the middle of October. Frances had met Mary at a raffle two weeks before. It was the time when countless white and yellow butterflies danced among the last fall flowers; the time, too, of the Fair. First, it was Honey. Made crazy one night by a marihuana cigarette, by something called smoke or snow, he broke into the drugstore of the white man who had been selling them to him, desperate for more. He was locked in the jail, awaiting trial, and Berenice rushed back and forth, canvassing money, seeing a lawyer, and trying to get admission to the jail. She came in on the third day, worn out, and with the red curdled glare already in the eye. A headache, she said she had, and John Henry West put his head down on the table and said he had a headache, also. But nobody paid any mind to him, thinking he copied Berenice. 'Run along,' she said, 'for I don't have the patience to fool with you.' Those were the last words spoken to him in the kitchen, and later Berenice recalled them as judgment on her from the Lord. John Henry had meningitis and after ten days he was dead. Until it was all over, Frances had never believed for a serious minute that he could die. It was the time of golden weather and Shasta daisies and the butterflies. The air was chilled, and day after day the sky was a clear green-blue, but filled with light, the color of a shallow wave.

Frances was never allowed to visit John Henry, but Berenice helped the trained nurse every day. She would come in toward dark, and the things that she said in her cracked voice seemed to make John Henry West unreal. 'I don't see why he has to suffer so,' Berenice would say: and the word *suffer* was one she could not associate with John Henry, a word she shrank from as before an unknown hollow darkness of the heart.

It was the time of the Fair and a big banner arched the main street and for six days and nights the Fair went on down at the fairground. Frances went twice, both times with Mary, and they rode on nearly everything, but did not enter the Freak Pavilion, as Mrs. Littlejohn said it was morbid to gaze at Freaks. Frances bought John Henry a walking stick and sent him the rug she had won at Lotto. But Berenice remarked that he was beyond all this, and the words were eerie and unreal. As the bright days followed one upon the other, the words of Berenice became so terrible that she would listen in a spell of horror, but a part of her could not believe. John Henry had been screaming for three days and his eyeballs were walled up in a corner, stuck and blind. He lay there finally with his head drawn back in a buckled way, and he had lost the strength to scream. He died the Tuesday after the Fair was gone, a golden morning of the most butterflies, the clearest sky.

Meanwhile Berenice had got a lawyer and had seen Honey at the jail. 'I don't know what I've done,' she kept saying. 'Honey in this fix and now John Henry.' Still, there was some part of Frances that did not even yet believe. But on the day he was to be taken to the family graveyard in Opelika, the same place where they had buried Uncle Charles, she saw the coffin, and then she knew. He came to her once or twice in nightmare dreams, like an escaped child dummy from the window of a department store, the wax legs moving stiffly only at joints, and the wax face wizened and faintly painted, coming toward her until terror snatched her awake. But the dreams came only once or twice, and the daytime now was filled with radar, school, and Mary Littlejohn. She remembered John Henry more as he used to be, and it was seldom now that she felt his presence — solemn, hovering, and ghost-gray. Only occasionally at twilight time or when the special hush would come into the room.

'I was by the store about school and Papa had a letter from Jarvis. He is in Luxembourg,' said Frances. 'Luxembourg. Don't you think that's a lovely name?'

Berenice roused herself. 'Well, Baby — it brings to my mind soapy water. But it's a kind of pretty name.'

'There is a basement in the new house. And a laundry room.' She added, after a minute, 'We will most likely pass through Luxembourg when we go around the world together.'

Frances turned back to the window. It was almost five

o'clock and the geranium glow had faded from the sky. The last pale colors were crushed and cold on the horizon. Dark, when it came, would come on quickly, as it does in wintertime. 'I am simply mad about ——' But the sentence was left unfinished for the hush was shattered when, with an instant shock of happiness, she heard the ringing of the bell.

THE END

